A Lifetime of Yankee Octobers

Sal Maiorana

Sleeping Bear Press

Sleeping Bear Press
310 North Main Street
P.O. Box 20
Chelsea, MI 48118
www.sleepingbearpress.com

Printed and bound in Canada

10 9 8 7 6 5 4 3 2 1

Library of Congress Cataloging-in-Publication Data

Maiorana, Salvatore.
     A lifetime of Yankee Octobers / by Sal Maiorana.
          p. cm.
     ISBN: 1-58536-039-2
     1. New York Yankees (Baseball team)—Fiction. 2. New York
(N.Y.)—Fiction. 3. Baseball teams—Fiction. 4. Baseball
fans—Fiction. I. Title
     PS3613.A3456 L54 2002
     813'.6—dc21   2002002229

This book is primarily a work of fiction. Although the story is set in the context of actual historical events and figures, the principal character in this story is a product of the author's imagination. Any similarity to any actual person is purely coincidental.

Dedication

To Christine, Taylor, Holden, and Caroline: You are to families what the Yankees are to baseball—the best. You have provided love, support, and understanding every step of the way.

Preface

As THE NEW YORK YANKEES' chartered jet began its climb out of the hot Arizona desert and rose into a sky once thought to be so peaceful and friendly, Joe Torre glanced at me across the aisle of the first-class cabin and said with a warm yet somber smile, "It wasn't supposed to end this way, was it Joe?"

I reflected for a moment understanding full well the scope of his question, and as I stared blankly at the gray seatback in front of me, the bitter taste of the Yankees' heartbreaking Game Seven loss to the Arizona Diamondbacks in the 2001 World Series still rolling around my palate, the unforgettable events of the previous two months flashed vividly through my 85-year-old mind.

I thought of those two airplanes crashing into the 110-story twin towers of the World Trade Center, and the resulting fire and thick black smoke that billowed from those buildings, buildings that to me did not extend skyward so much as they seemed to descend from the heavens like the arms of God, the ultimate symbols of American pride and power and prosperity.

I thought of the incomprehensible sight of the two structures collapsing into a horrifying and murderous pile of rubble, thousands of my fellow New Yorkers buried in an open-air grave of concrete and metal and debris.

I thought of the other two planes that were hijacked on the history-altering morning of September 11, 2001, one of which smashed into the Pentagon in Washington, D.C. killing a couple hundred more people, and the other that never completed its ghastly mission because heroic Americans on board foiled the evil terrorists and crashed the converted weapon of mass destruction into a rural wooded field in western Pennsylvania.

I thought about what the final moments of the lives of the passengers on those planes must have been like, and I tried to imagine the terror the people in the upper stories of the towers must have experienced as they looked out their windows and saw death staring at them in the form of a runaway airplane.

I thought of the hundreds of New York City firemen, police officers, and emergency medical service personnel who lost their lives when they ignored the danger and bravely ran into the towers to try to rescue their fellow citizens before the buildings fell down on top of them.

I thought of the thousands of children whose mothers or fathers never came home that day, and will never come home again.

I thought of my grandson, Robert, who thankfully did come home because he ignored the announcement, made in the south tower after the north tower had been struck by the first plane, that everything was all right. He vacated his 34th floor office and was standing on the Brooklyn Bridge along with thousands of others, talking on his cell phone to his mother, my daughter Katherine, when the south tower, his tower, crumbled.

I thought of the makeshift morgue that was set up at Shea Stadium, the candlelight vigils that were held throughout the city in the days after the attack, and the helpless faces of the victims' relatives as they passed out fliers with pictures of their missing loved ones, hoping and praying that someone had seen them alive.

I thought about my visit to Ground Zero a month earlier and how I was struck by the acrid smell wafting through the air, so uniquely pungent that it flared my nostrils and burned my eyes and made me wonder if this is what it was like for the men and women who fought this country's wars in Europe and Korea and Vietnam and the Persian Gulf.

Lastly, I thought about the Yankees, Torre's Yankees, my beloved Yankees, and how this fabulous group of baseball players took it upon themselves to help ease the pain of a badly wounded, grief-stricken city. Baseball is such a meaningless part of our society when weighed against the tragedy that befell my city and our country. But there was no doubt in my mind that by coming within two outs of winning the World Series, the Yankees lifted the spirits of all New Yorkers, helped them cope with the harsh reality that our lives had been changed forever, and provided a constant reminder to the rest of the world that New Yorkers—and all Americans—have pounding inside their chests the heart of a champion.

I recalled the words of our great mayor, Rudy Giuliani, who said just before the start of the Series, "The Yankees typify what we all feel in this city—that New York is on the rebound. We'll be back stronger and more determined than ever. We needed the Yankees. They helped show the rest of the world that our spirit is not only unaffected, it's as strong and vibrant as ever."

It was then that I gazed back at Torre, who for nearly 45 years has been like a second son to me, and replied, "No, Joe, that's not how it was supposed to end."

Three hours earlier, Torre's wonderful ball club, which had won three World Series in a row and four of the last five, entered the bottom of the ninth inning at Bank One Ballpark in Phoenix with a 2-1 lead. Despite being outplayed throughout the Series, the indomitable Yankees had managed to split the first six games with the Diamondbacks, and thanks to rookie Alfonso Soriano's clutch solo home run in the eighth inning of Game Seven, they were on the verge of winning yet another championship. Perhaps this would be their most improbable World Series triumph; certainly it would be a World Series victory that would have dwarfed in importance any of the other 26 titles the Yankees had won in their unprecedented history.

Who the hell am I to make a statement like that? Just an ordinary Joe, last name Kimmerle, no one of particular significance, but a man who knows a thing or two about the Yankees thanks to an eight-decade association with the team which has enabled me to personally witness every one of those 26 championships.

I was seven years old when my father and I, using tickets provided to us by our friend, the great Babe Ruth, attended the first World Series games ever played in Yankee Stadium, the year they won their first championship in 1923.

Four years later I was in my first year as an assistant batboy for the 1927 team—led by Ruth and Lou Gehrig and considered by most baseball experts to be the greatest team in history—when it won the franchise's second crown. It was in my 10th year of Yankee employment, then as clubhouse assistant in 1936, when Joe DiMaggio made his major league debut and kick-started the Yankees' four-year reign of supremacy in the late 1930s.

Starting in 1937, and spanning the next 45 years, I covered the Yankees as a sportswriter, first for the *Bronx Home News* and later the *New York Post*. During that privileged period when I was afforded a front-row press box vantage point, a locker-room pass, and a seat on the team train or plane, the Yankees won the Series 17 times as the torch of excellence passed from Gehrig to DiMaggio to Mickey Mantle to Reggie Jackson.

And now, during the past six years when I have served as a "special consultant" to Torre—whom I have known since the mid-1950s when he was a chubby Brooklyn teenager playing third base on the same sand-lot team as my nephew Sammy—the Yankees have tacked on four more titles to the most impressive resume in professional sports.

This could have been the fifth of the Torre era, the fourth in succession, and No. 27 overall. But this is not Hollywood. This is real life, a life that for many of us in the aftermath of September 11 has never been more real. In life we cannot script the outcome, and the Diamondbacks reminded us of that. They acted like the Yankees in the bottom of the ninth inning, scoring two runs off Mariano Rivera, the greatest postseason relief pitcher baseball has ever known, and they won Game Seven, 3-2.

Arizona won, the Yankees lost. No, it wasn't supposed to end like that. But as our plane seared its way through the half-moonlit night en route to New York, I shook my head in amazement as I replayed in my mind how the Yankees even managed to get into position to have their champion hearts ripped from their chests.

They began the play-offs against an Oakland team that many baseball observers considered the best in either league at the end of the regular season. The Athletics closed the year winning 29 of their last 33 games, and they didn't stop winning once their divisional series began at Yankee Stadium. They won the first two games without breaking a sweat, and now the next two games were scheduled for Oakland-Alameda County Coliseum where they were riding a 17-game winning streak. It was an impossible position for anyone else but the Yankees. Mike Mussina, backed by a Jorge Posada home run and a dynamic fielding play by Derek Jeter, won a tense Game Three, 1-0, and then the Yankee bats finally awoke in Game Four during a 9-2 victory which forced a fifth and deciding game back in New York. When the Yankees captured the finale, 5-3, they became the first team in major league history to win a five-game series after losing the first two at home, and Torre characterized the comeback victory by saying, "For a non-World Series, this is right at the top." I was sitting in my usual seat in owner George Steinbrenner's private box that night, and I remember thinking to myself, "Something is going on here. Something special is in the air."

Next up were the Seattle Mariners who had won 116 games during the regular season, tying the all-time major league record and breaking the American League mark of 114 set in 1998 by the Yankees. The Mariners never had a chance. New York won the first two games in Seattle behind the pitching of Andy Pettitte, Mussina, and Rivera, and for the next three nights Yankee Stadium was electric in anticipation of the team's 38th American League pennant. After a major hiccup in Game Three when they lost 14-3, the Yankees bounced back to win the next two, Game Four decided by Soriano's game-winning two-run homer, and Game Five a take-that, exclamation point 12-3 rout. "We recognize there's a certain responsibility when you're wearing the 'NY' on your cap," said Torre. "I think what makes this special is that this city needed something."

Now it was off to the desert to play a franchise that was only four years old. In fact, since the Diamondbacks began playing in 1998, they had never known another baseball champion than the Yankees, but they showed no respect for the champs in winning the first two games. In its 9-1 and 4-0 victories, Arizona received dominating pitching performances from its two aces, Curt Schilling and Randy Johnson, and with those two scheduled to pitch three more games, the Yankees seemed to have little chance. Well, the Yankees had heard that before.

After making it through the tightest security check I had ever been subjected to, I sat in Steinbrenner's box watching President George W. Bush throw out the first ball before Game Three, then enjoyed one of the thrills of my life as I sat with Mr. Bush for the first three innings of what became a 2-1 Yankee victory. Steinbrenner garnered much of Mr. Bush's attention, but I did speak to the Commander in Chief, remarking at one point that he'd thrown a "nice pitch, excellent location." Chuckling, he said he'd learned a thing or two when he was part-owner of the Texas Rangers a few years earlier.

That night I looked at the American flag waving in the cool autumn breeze high above the stadium's center field façade, and it occurred to me again that this Yankee team might be one of destiny. That flag had been recovered in the rubble of the World Trade Center three days after the attack, and it was transported in its tattered and torn state, missing 12 stars, to the stadium especially for the Series.

The next two nights, that flag presided over two of the most inconceivable and exciting moments Yankee Stadium has ever played host to. With two outs in the bottom of the ninth and the Yankees trailing Game Four by 3-1, Tino Martinez hit a monstrous game-tying two-run homer off Arizona reliever Byung-Hyun Kim. An inning later, with Kim still on the mound, Jeter hit a game-winning solo shot into the short porch in right field, evening the Series at two games apiece. And then it happened again in Game Five, the first Series game ever played in November. This time it was Scott Brosius hitting a two-run, game-tying homer with two outs in the bottom of the ninth off Kim to force extra innings, where Soriano eventually delivered a game-winning RBI single in the 12th to give the Yankees a three-games-to-two lead. "Last night was a night dreams are made of," said Yankee pitcher Mike Stanton, "but tonight, wow, you don't even dream that."

Back to Phoenix we went and Arizona unloaded its pent-up frustration in Game Six and embarrassed the Yankees, 15-2, setting the stage for a winner-take-all seventh game. For seven innings Roger Clemens dueled Schilling to a 1-1 draw, and when Soriano took the tiring Schilling deep in the eighth, Torre pumped his fist, the Yankees leaped for joy, and amidst the silence in the Diamondbacks' new-age, state-of-the-art stadium, I clasped my hands together and prayed it would be enough to win the game.

It wasn't.

Rivera got into a jam in the ninth, and when Luis Gonzalez fisted a bases-loaded broken-bat blooper just over the dirt cutout of the infield behind second base, the Diamondbacks won the game, and the championship.

Exuding a touch of class, Schilling said of the Yankees, "They are the epitome of what this sport is, and that's why this is so special. We are honored to have been a part of such an amazing Series. That's an unbelievable baseball team over there. The city of New York should be very proud of that team."

We are.

We have been for nearly 80 years.

Acknowledgments

I WISH TO THANK A NUMBER OF PEOPLE who provided either their support, their proofreading skills, or their willingness to be a sounding board: Christine Maiorana, Sam and Joan Maiorana, Scott Pitoniak, Steve Bradley, Jim Mandelaro, and Jim Bohannon.

Many thanks to the team at Sleeping Bear Press including publicist Kolleen O'Meara, copyeditor Vivian Collier, and most notably, my editor, Adam Rifenberick. It was Adam I originally made contact with at Sleeping Bear, and his enthusiasm about the project played a major role in bringing what you are about to read to fruition. Adam was a shining light, a beacon of hope and inspiration throughout a lengthy and tedious writing and editing process. As true-blue Yankee fans, he and I strove for the perfect manuscript, and in my mind and my heart, I think we succeeded.

Prologue

I CAN TRACE MY LOVE AFFAIR WITH BASEBALL and the Yankees back to the days when I would spend hours looking out my bedroom window, watching in awe as venerable Yankee Stadium came into existence.

Day by day in the summer of 1922, workers from the White Construction Company of New York City labored at a feverish pace because Yankee owner Colonel Jacob Ruppert had ambitiously targeted Opening Day 1923 as the afternoon he wanted his team to play its first game in the sparkling new ballpark.

With such a tight deadline to meet, not a day went by when I didn't notice structural progress being made. It was a fascinating experience to see this baseball shrine—a place that would ultimately become the center of my universe—rise before me in a massive confluence of wood and concrete and steel and glory. When ground was initially broken on May 5, 1922, my father said they'd never get it built in time. "How in the hell are they going to build a baseball park that size in 11 months?" he asked my mother one night as we sat around the dinner table. "It can't be done." Mom didn't have an answer.

Having just celebrated my sixth birthday, I was not burdened with skepticism and my expectations were much greater. "But look, Dad," I would say, pulling him over to the window to point out the latest development in the construction. "Look how much they did today." He'd smile at me, then halfheartedly appease me by agreeing that the workers would indeed meet the deadline, though I sensed he still didn't believe it.

When the gates opened on April 18, 1923—the day I celebrated in unforgettable fashion my seventh birthday—and the Yankees beat the Boston Red Sox, 4-1, I looked at my dad who was sitting next to me along the first-base line right behind the Yankees dugout, and I realized this was the first time he'd ever been wrong about anything. As far as I can recall, it was the only thing he was ever wrong about.

I grew up in what, at the time, was an amenity-filled sixth-floor apartment on the corner of East 162nd Street and River Avenue, one block away from where the new stadium was being erected in the west Bronx. Our borough was one of the more progressive areas of New York City in the early twentieth century, as most apartment buildings and tenement houses were equipped with private bathrooms, central heat, and hot water. We even had a refrigerator.

My father was a shoemaker of Italian and German descent, educated only through the 10th grade, but a wise and able-bodied man who was well-respected in our tight-knit community. People used to say Jack Kimmerle was a magician, so impressed were they by the way he crafted and repaired leather shoes and boots and handbags, and his clientele was consistent and plentiful.

Dad had a simple daily routine. He would leave the apartment by 6:30 A.M. and his first stop would be Mr. Alongi's newsstand, where he would buy a pack of cigarettes and a copy of the *Bronx Home News*— our borough's popular daily newspaper for which I would later work. Dad and Mr. Alongi would exchange pleasantries, then Dad would continue walking down River Avenue to Calumeta's Café where hot coffee, a fresh doughnut, and lively morning chitchat with other neighborhood businessmen awaited him.

Mr. Sansieri, who owned the hardware store next door to Dad's shop, was an interesting character, a heavyset, dark-skinned Italian whose favorite words were the ones that, if spoken by me, would have guaranteed me a mouthful of soap. He was a hard-boiled Republican who never stopped extolling the virtues of his political party, and he did so in a voluble, accented manner, his hands flying in more directions than a frightened flock of birds. When Herbert Hoover was elected president in 1928, Mr. Sansieri predicted that the Roaring Twenties were going to become the "Thriving Thirties." Mr. Sansieri was wrong. Ten months into Hoover's term the stock market crashed, the country plunged into the Great Depression, and by the time Hoover left office in 1933 one out of every four American wage earners was out of work.

Mr. Calumeta was his favorite foil, a dyed-in-the-wool Democrat who happily balanced the discussion by offering rebuttals for everything that flowed from Mr. Sansieri's mouth. Usually Dad just sat there and chuckled to himself as the two men argued. Neither a Republican, nor a Democrat, Dad had his own opinions on the news of the day and he preferred to keep them to himself. Sometimes Mr. Sansieri made sense, other times it was Mr. Calumeta. But no matter who was right and who was wrong, the morning bull sessions always ended with all of the men advising each other to "Have a good day."

By 7 A.M. Dad's shop—which was located on the east side of the street—was open, and customers filed in and out regularly until Dad closed his doors at 6 P.M. and retraced his steps back up River to our apartment. He put in long hours, but the result was a thriving business that provided my mother, my sister, and me with a comfortable post-World War I lifestyle.

Dad's shop stood directly across from what became the stadium's right-center field bleacher seats. Hovering over the street and blotting out the sun was the elevated portion of the subway line that only a few blocks south submerged beneath the Harlem River on its way into upper Manhattan.

The four-block section of River Avenue within the parameters of the ballpark between East 161st and East 158th streets was a bustling business district that included Dad's shop, Calumeta's, Mr. Sansieri's hardware store, a grocery store, a produce market, a bank, a candy store, a restaurant, a couple of pubs, and other specialty shops. I always found it odd that—until the stadium was built—there was nothing on the other side of the street. It was just a 10-acre plot of scrubby, undeveloped land previously owned by the estate of William Waldorf Astor.

The story goes that the land was originally granted by the British to a man named John Lion Gardiner prior to the Revolutionary War. During the late nineteenth century it had been home to a lumberyard, but for as long as I could remember, it was just a dirty, trash-strewn, abandoned blight on the neighborhood. Colonel Ruppert finally solved the dilemma in 1921 by purchasing the property at a cost of $675,000 for the purpose of providing his soon-to-be homeless team a place to play. The coexistence between the Giants and the Yankees at the Polo Grounds had become so abrasive that the Giants told the Yankees they were no longer welcome once the 1922 season ended. This is why the stadium had to be built so quickly. Given that the total cost of the construction came to $2.5 million, it turned out to be quite a prosperous real estate deal for the colonel.

I was born in 1916 and given the name Joseph Samuel Kimmerle. Dad was there for my birth, and my mother told me years later that when the nurse came out to announce me, it was the first time Dad had ever cried. My sister Carmela had come along three years earlier, and he loved her with all his heart, but he longed to have a son, and my arrival was his proudest moment.

But a year later, with the United States having been dragged into the raging great war in Europe, Dad was called into military service and for nearly two years my mother Florence was left to raise Carmela and me. She took odd jobs wherever she could find them and Mrs. Grabowski—an elderly neighbor from down the hall—would watch us kids. This was the life I knew.

It was peculiar when Dad returned from the war. Mom always kept pictures of him visible throughout the apartment, and she continually read his letters to us, but I was too young to have known him when he left. He was a mystery to me, and when this veritable stranger suddenly thrust himself into my life, I didn't know what to make of him. However, when I saw my mother crying uncontrollable tears of joy when he stepped off the train at Grand Central Station, I guess I figured this was somebody who was going to have a positive influence on me. Sure enough, it wasn't long before I realized that having a dad was pretty special.

There were many days before I started my schooling that he would take me to the shop with him and I would play in the back room where he did all of his work. It was his way of supplementing the time we'd lost during his military absence. Mr. DiRenzio would man the front counter and greet customers, and Dad would make or repair shoes and handbags out of sight from the patronage. Most of the people were folks from the neighborhood, and whenever I was in the store the women would always ask to see "little Joey." So Mr. DiRenzio would come fetch me and to my great dismay they'd pinch my puffy cheeks and rub my mop of brown hair.

When I completed the first year of my elementary school education, I spent an inordinate amount of time between neighborhood stickball games in the summer of 1922 at Dad's shop. I loved being with Dad, but I must admit I had an ulterior motive: I wanted to keep tabs on what was going on over at the stadium. I would start out in the shop, but inevitably I'd sneak across the street and find little cubbyholes where I could watch the workers.

The original plans designed by the Osborne Engineering Company of Cleveland—the architectural firm that was owned by Ruppert's former Yankee co-owner, Cap Huston—called for a completely enclosed stadium, described in a Yankee press release as "impenetrable to all human eyes, save those of aviators." They didn't go through with that elaborate and costly contrivance, but they did set new standards for stadium construction. Among the innovations were a three-tiered grandstand that extended from foul pole to foul pole around the diamond, so high it seemed to scrape against the passing clouds; a 16-foot-deep copper facade that adorned much of the third deck and gave the place an unmatched air of dignity; and a gigantic electric scoreboard that displayed the inning-by-inning score of the game, both teams' lineups, and scores from out-of-town games—ballpark luxuries heretofore unheard-of.

More than 20,000 cubic yards of concrete and 2,300 tons of steel, fastened together by more than a million brass screws, were used to erect the structure. Almost a million feet of Pacific Coast fir—transported through the Panama Canal which had just opened in 1914—were transformed into endless rows of bleachers, and 16,000 square feet of rich green sod was laid on the field. The colonel expected grand, and he got it.

Baseball was Dad's passion and it became mine as well. From the time Dad came back from the war and introduced me to the game, he would plant me on his lap and share stories about the old Highlanders—New York's original American League team that later changed its nickname when *New York Press* sports editor Jim Price began calling them the Yankees because it was easier to fit that moniker into narrow headlines.

He would tell me about spitballing pitcher Jack Chesbro who in 1904 won a never-to-be-broken major league record 41 games, and he spun yarns about Wee Willie Keeler, Prince Hal Chase, Hippo Vaughn, Birdie Cree, Wid Conroy, Al Orth, Russ Ford, and manager Clark Griffith. The team played its home games at Hilltop Park over in the Washington Heights section of Manhattan between 165th and 168th streets. Compared to the extravagance of Yankee Stadium, Hilltop wasn't much more than a quaint 16,000-seat sandlot but Dad remembered its charms, such as the huge Bull Durham sign that was shaped like a bull and stood 540 feet from home plate in center field, the views of the Hudson River and the New Jersey Palisades, and the spectators who brought their own seats and watched the games from the outfield perimeter.

When fire destroyed the stands at the Polo Grounds in 1911, the Giants were invited by the Highlanders to play home games at Hilltop, and when the Polo Grounds were rebuilt, the Giants returned the favor and allowed the Highlanders to use their facility. Hilltop Park was razed and became Columbia Presbyterian Church, prompting a New York scribe to write "All they did was swap one church for another."

Dad made only occasional trips up to Hilltop, but when the High-landers moved into the nearby Polo Grounds—situated just across the Harlem River, a short subway ride from our home—he was able to attend more games.

One of his fondest Polo Grounds recollections was watching the newly-renamed Yankees defeat the Red Sox, 4-3 in a 13-inning thriller. Boston's starting pitcher was none other than Babe Ruth, who later became one of my father's best friends. That day—May 6, 1915—Dad saw Ruth hit the first of his 714 major league home runs, a towering shot into the second deck in right field off Yankee starter Jack Warhop. This was Ruth's first appearance in New York City, and he was brilliant. At the plate he went 3-for-5, and on the mound he pitched all 13 innings. Though he was saddled with the loss, he gave up only two earned runs, and according to a *New York Times* account of the game which Dad had saved in a scrapbook, Ruth's performance "was of high order, and it was only after the hardest kind of effort that the Yankees were able to break through his service."

Dad took me on the subway over to Coogans Bluff for my first major-league game in 1920, Ruth's inaugural year with the Yankees. I had just turned four and could not read, but Dad made sure he clipped the game story from the *Times* and inserted it into that same scrapbook for safekeeping. I still have that scrapbook, and the story from that June 13 game describes an 11-8 Yankee victory over Ty Cobb and the Detroit Tigers. Ruth was the starting pitcher and he lasted five innings to get the win, and he also crashed two home runs, the second a 460-foot howitzer that carried into the distant right-center field bleachers. Estimates at the time pegged it as the longest home run ever hit in the big leagues. To me it looked like the ball had flown halfway to California, and when I close my eyes more than 80 years later I can still see its flight path.

From that moment on, I was hooked. The Yankees became ingrained in my soul, and for more than eight decades my world has revolved around the team either as a fan, batboy, clubhouse assistant, newspaper beat reporter and columnist, official scorer, and now, in my role as special consultant to manager Joe Torre.

Through all those years, one aspect of life as a Yankee follower has remained fascinatingly constant: watching the team play in October. It is the goal of every Major League Baseball team, but none have done it with the amazing frequency and success of the Yankees.

October in New York has always meant the World Series, and to me, as well as I'm sure, millions of Yankee fans through the decades, there isn't a more extraordinary time of the year. That's the way it used to be, that's the way it is today, and it will never change.

I can't say that I've played in a World Series, but I can remember every World Series game the Yankees have played. Come along now and let me take you on a journey through *A Lifetime of Yankee Octobers.*

There are indelible moments that mark all of our lives, and walking into the massive Polo Grounds to witness my first Yankees game was my first. I experienced a genuine explosion of my senses seeing the brilliant green grass, smelling the peanuts roasting and popcorn popping at the concession stand, and listening to the crack of the bat and the shrieks of thousands upon thousands of spectators when the Yankees made good.

At the time I couldn't have imagined any day being better than that one, but as I reflect on my blessed life, I can count four other occasions that topped it: the day I married my wife Marie, the days our children Phillip and Katherine were born, and my seventh birthday—the same day in 1923 when Yankee Stadium opened.

I don't know why I was so spellbound that chilly April afternoon because I had watched the stadium being built for much of the previous year and knew what to expect, but for some reason it was overwhelming when I actually walked in and saw the finished product. In those first moments spent gawking at the palatial new home of the Yankees, I somehow sensed this was a place where I would be spending an awful lot of time. What I didn't realize was how the stadium and its primary tenant would become such permanent fixtures in my life.

By early 1923 the nation had come out of its postwar recession and America was on its way to enjoying what became known as the "Roaring Twenties"—a decade during which our country became a worldwide symbol for prosperity and frivolity. In New York City, Manhattan had become grossly overpopulated, and so a migration started to the surrounding boroughs, such as the Bronx. First- and second-generation working immigrants began advancing into the middle class sector, no longer trapped in their ethnic ghettos. These people—Italians, Irish, Jews, Germans—sought a better quality of life that included larger living spaces and improved public schools, and they found refuge in places like the Grand Concourse in the Bronx, Jackson Heights in Queens, Eastern Parkway in Brooklyn, and Rockaway out on Long Island. The Grand Concourse—which I called home for more than 10 years and where my two children were born during the mid-1940s—was once called "the Park Avenue of the middle class." It was a broad, tree-lined boulevard that stretched nearly five miles, and the residents who occupied the spacious art deco-style five- and six-story apartment *buildings were doctors, dentists, lawyers, manufacturers, tradesmen, engineers, and teachers.*

Good times were upon us, and nowhere was that more evident than across the street from the River Avenue apartment of my youth where this luxurious new baseball shrine now stood.

Even though my parents had agreed to let me skip school—a pretty neat birthday present in itself—to attend the opening game, my eagerness to get to the ballpark was too much to bear and I was awake at the crack of dawn. The morning dragged on, and every time I glanced at the clock on the kitchen wall it seemed as if it hadn't moved at all. I wandered down to Dad's shop at noon, and even though the first pitch wouldn't be thrown until 3 P.M., I managed to talk Dad into leaving work early, reasoning that it would give us time to take a tour of the facility before the start of the game. It didn't take much prodding because in his subtle way Dad was just as excited as I was. Mr. DiRenzio didn't have to explain Dad's absence to the customers very often that day because just about all the Bronx was either in the stadium or trying to find a way to get in.

We walked through the shiny silver turnstiles at Gate 6, which was almost directly across the street from Dad's shop, and after having our tickets torn in half, we showed our stubs—which I still have, thanks to Dad putting them in that trusty scrapbook—to an usher, who pointed us in the right direction. As we made our way through the crowded concourse my heart began racing, and after what seemed like an eternity we finally reached the entranceway to our section. As we walked down the narrow tunnel I couldn't see anything except a wall of overcoats worn by the men towering above me, but as they reached the end and began turning left or right to go to their seats, all of a sudden there was a burst of light and when I looked up, there it was in all its glorious splendor—Yankee Stadium.

Rows and rows of bleachers piled three levels high; the dirt infield skillfully carved into the lush green grass that somehow seemed to stretch out to center field further than what I remembered from the Polo Grounds; the players milling about, some playing catch, others playing pepper, and still others gazing around just as I was, awed by the sights and sounds and smells. Renowned conductor John Philip Sousa was leading the Seventh Regiment Band in brassy song, while baseball Commissioner Kenesaw Mountain Landis and New York Governor Alfred E. Smith—who would throw out the first ball—were situated in a front-row field box, shaking hands with patrons and posing for the phalanx of photographers whose flashbulbs lit up the cloudy, dreary day like a fireworks display. Dad and I looked at each other, but neither of us could say a word, rendered speechless as we were by the beauty of it all. The place was so big it looked like a city, and while reports numbering the crowd to be in excess of 74,000 were grossly inaccurate, given that capacity was just over 60,000, it looked like a million people to me.

Babe Ruth was asked what he thought of the new stadium and he said, "Some ball yard!" then promised to do his best to commemorate Opening Day properly with a home run. Naturally, he came through. In the bottom of the third inning with two runners aboard he turned on a Howard Ehmke fastball and sent a missile into the right-field bleachers, christening what would later be called "The House That Ruth Built." I can still hear the roar of the crowd as the ball soared through the air before plummeting into a sea of humanity, instantly transforming itself into a very valuable souvenir.

I can remember jumping up and down and slapping Dad's arm with glee when our friend, the great Bambino, doffed his cap upon touching home plate and then, just before he disappeared into the dugout along the third-base line, he spied the two of us sitting in the seats he had provided and shot us that classic Ruth wink.

Dad and I probably attended five or six other games in the summer of 1923, a few times as Ruth's guest, and for me each trip brought more excitement than the last. One time Ruth even escorted Dad and me into the clubhouse to meet some of the other players, but I was too shy to say anything. I just stuck out my tiny little hand and locked my focus on the floor beneath me when Waite Hoyt or Wally Pipp or Joe Dugan—all, like Ruth, heroes to me—said hello.

When the regular season ended and the Yankees had captured their third consecutive American League pennant, Ruth's generosity reached an unprecedented level when he bestowed on us tickets to each of the three World Series games that were played at the stadium that fall. What a thrill it was to watch the Yankees battle the hated Giants, though that first game was quite a heartbreak when Casey Stengel—the Giants center fielder and future manager of the Yankees—hit a ninth-inning inside-the-park home run to win it for John McGraw's troops. But in the end the Yankees won the Series in six games, the clincher coming over at the Polo Grounds with Dad and me huddled around the radio in the back room of the shop, listening to what was just the second World Series ever broadcast over the airwaves.

Nobody could have known that the Yankees would repeat this feat 25 more times in my lifetime. All I knew then was that my team had won the World Series, and there was no sweeter feeling for a seven-year-old to experience.

– Chapter 1 –

1923

THE ROAD TO THAT 1923 World Series championship actually began just after the Yankees had been humbled by the New York Giants in the 1922 Fall Classic.

In November a dinner was held at the Elks Club in Manhattan, arranged by Babe Ruth's publicity manager, Christy Walsh, for the sole purpose of cleansing Ruth's tattered image following what had been for him a truly awful 1922 season. It had been a year during which the game's greatest hero acted anything like a hero as he argued with umpires, threatened bodily harm to booing fans, fought with teammates, and drank himself into frequent oblivion. His actions resulted in his being suspended on three separate occasions, but more importantly, Ruth suffered a loss of respect and reverence.

Ruth had joined the Yankees in 1920, acquired from the Boston Red Sox in a landmark deal that at once set in motion the Yankees' journey to nearly a century of dominance and cursed the Red Sox, possibly forevermore. That first year in New York, Ruth's major league record 54 home runs were more than every team in baseball except the Philadelphia Phillies, and he single-handedly rescued the game from the doldrums of the 1919 Black Sox fiasco.

"Babe Ruth found baseball lying in the gutter as a result of the Chicago White Sox World Series scandal in 1919," Waite Hoyt said. "He reached down with his bat and lifted it to the status of America's national pastime."

In 1921 Ruth guided the Yankees to their first American League pennant, hitting 59 home runs, but with Ruth sitting out the final three games due to an abscess on his elbow, the Yankees lost in their inaugural World Series appearance to their Polo Grounds landlord, the Giants.

Over the next calendar year, things only deteriorated for Ruth.

Following the 1919 and 1920 seasons, Ruth had earned sizable fees playing in postseason barnstorming tours, and he lined up another trip which would start after the 1921 World Series. There was one glaring problem. A baseball rule at the time prohibited players on the World Series teams from going on tour. The reasoning behind the edict—established by the team owners in 1912—was to ensure prime interest and focus on the World Series.

Ruth ignored the rule, figuring the worst thing baseball commissioner Kenesaw Mountain Landis would do was fine him the amount of his World Series check. Ruth did the math and surmised that he could easily make that back—and then some—on the tour. Landis stood firm and warned Ruth that if he didn't cancel the tour, he would have to deal with "a lot of consequences." Ruth's Yankee teammates, Wally Schang and Carl Mays, feared the repercussions and backed out, but Ruth, Bob Meusel, and Bill Piercy decided to play anyway. It would prove to be a costly decision.

In an unprecedented disciplinary action, Landis suspended the three players for the first six weeks of the 1922 season, plus withheld their World Series checks, though they eventually received that money. Landis charged them with "mutinous defiance intended by the players to present this question: Which is bigger—baseball or any individual in baseball?" So began one of the most tumultuous years in team history, rivaled perhaps only by the Reggie Jackson-Billy Martin Bronx Zoo period in the late 1970s.

Ruth's suspension rocked the team, and then when he returned to action in late May his batting stroke was way off and his average dipped to .093 at one point. Though Ruth's average eventually began to rise, so too did his temper. The normally fun-loving slugger, unaccustomed to failure and the booing that came with it, became unusually surly. Not only did he fight with umpires and fans, he even slugged it out with teammate Wally Pipp one day.

Incredibly, the Yankees kept winning through all the madness and they eventually clinched their second straight American League pennant during the final week of the season. However, Ruth—who despite missing 44 games due to his series of suspensions still managed to bat .315 with 35 homers—hit an embarrassing .118 with no homers in the Series against the Giants, and the Yankees bowed out in four straight.

Ruth was in desperate need of what today is called "spin control," so Walsh invited to the Elks Club a large contingent of Ruth's friends and associates, potential business and endorsement partners, and most importantly, the baseball writers of New York who had robustly criticized Ruth for his demeanor during the season and his flameout in the Series. Walsh envisioned a public relations coup where Ruth would apologize for his many transgressions and the guests would fawn over the great man and pledge their undying love and forgiveness.

Babe had personally invited my father to the dinner, and though I was only six years old at the time, I vividly remember Dad telling Mom the next morning at breakfast about what had happened that night. Jimmy Walker, a New York state senator who would soon become the mayor of Gotham, wasn't ready to forgive Ruth for his boorish behavior and he shocked the gathering with a blistering speech that drove a dagger into Ruth's heart.

"Babe Ruth is not only a great athlete, but also a great fool," Walker said. "His employer, Colonel Jacob Ruppert, makes millions of gallons of beer and Ruth is of the opinion that he can drink it faster than the colonel and his brewmasters can make it."

Turning toward Ruth, Walker said, "Well, you can't! You are making a bigger salary than anyone ever received as a ballplayer, but the bigger the salary, the bigger the fool you have become."

My dad, sitting at a table with other Bronx merchants, was stunned by the verbal attack, and he expected a titanic reply from the Babe. Instead, when the initial surprise and anger over this character assassination wore off, Ruth's eyes began to moisten as he realized Walker was right. Walker closed his remarks by saying, "If we did not love you, Babe, and if I myself did not love you sincerely, I would not tell you these things. Will you or not, for the kids of America, solemnly promise to mend your ways? Will you not give back to those kids their great idol?"

When it was his turn to speak, an emotional Ruth promised an end to his shenanigans and he vowed unbowed professionalism when the 1923 season—the Yankees' first at newly-erected Yankee Stadium—began. The crowd stood as one and cheered loudly as Ruth waved back, wiping tears away as he returned to his seat on the dais.

Years later, while attending the Babe's funeral, I spoke to his adopted daughter from his first marriage, Dorothy Ruth Pirone, and she fondly recalled that evening, saying, "When I think of turning points in his career, that night belongs at the top." I know my father felt the same way.

*   *   *

Ruth had befriended my father early in the 1921 season when the team was still playing second fiddle to the Giants over in the Polo Grounds and was two years away from moving to our Bronx neighborhood. One day Ruth happened to be strolling down River Avenue when he came upon Dad's shop and walked in. Ruth looked around at the impressive array of footwear, inquired of Mr. DiRenzio if he was "the fella who runs this place" and when told that no, Jack Kimmerle was the proprietor, Ruth asked to speak to him.

Dad walked out and his eyes practically leaped out of their sockets when he saw to whom he was about to talk. Ruth had cut the leather on his left baseball shoe and he asked Dad if he could make the repair. Naturally Dad jumped at the chance to help the Babe, and early the next morning, before the Yankees were to play at the Polo Grounds, back came the Babe with his tattered shoe in hand.

Dad invited Ruth to the back room where he did his work—a place no other customer was allowed—and as he nervously made the necessary restoration, he bombarded the Babe with questions about the Yankees, all of which Ruth gladly answered. It was Dad's opinion that the day the Yankees acquired Ruth from the Red Sox following the 1919 season the team's fortunes would surely change, and he shared that theory with Ruth. Ruth smiled, but remembering that his 54 home runs in 1920 weren't enough to deliver to the Yankees their first pennant, he said "Well, mister, we couldn't beat Cleveland last year, but I hope you're right." During Ruth's 15 years with the team the Yankees won seven pennants and four World Series, so I guess Dad was right.

So impressed was Ruth with Dad's work, he spread the word around the Yankee clubhouse and soon Dad had a star-studded group of customers seeking his expertise, not only with baseball spikes but personal belongings. Ultimately, Dad's proximity to Yankee Stadium turned his shop into "the shoe store where the pros go." Not only were the Yankees regulars through the years, so, too, were their wives, and even visiting players stopped by if they had particular needs.

When the Yankees took up residence in the Bronx, Ruth routinely stopped by the shop—probably two or three times a week during the season—and Dad gradually became a trusted and valued member of Ruth's inner circle, a circle that was for the most part filled with phonies looking to capitalize on Ruth's celebrity for their own benefit.

Ruth took a liking to my father because once Dad stopped acting like an admittedly starstruck boob, Ruth realized he was a genuine person, someone Ruth could talk to on a man-to-man rather than hero-to-fan level. When Ruth would visit the shop, it was an opportunity to discuss the events of the day or share an unpretentious laugh in an environment that served as a safe haven from the hectic world he lived in. Everywhere he went he was mobbed by adoring fans, and when he was out in public, he loved being the center of attention. Expected it, actually. He was a bombastic showman who sought the limelight the way a fish seeks water. But few people saw the side of Ruth that my father saw, the reflective man who talked openly about his childhood on the mean streets of Baltimore where he grew up in his father's saloon, learning how to cheat and steal while other boys were learning to read and write. He often recalled his days at St. Mary's, a reform school that indeed reformed him. Before being sent to St. Mary's, Ruth had about as much use for school as he did a two-out, bases-empty single, but his enrollment there probably spared him a criminal life. It also introduced him to the game of baseball, and the rest, as they say, is history.

Although the hero's halo always shone above Ruth, with Dad he was a pretty regular guy, and I saw that on the numerous occasions when Ruth was a guest at our modest apartment for dinner. Ruth always insisted on carving the roast or chicken, and to my mother's astonishment, he was quite accomplished in this task. Having filmed a few movies, he enjoyed talking about Hollywood, and he lauded the acting of George Bancroft and Janet Gaynor. And like my parents, his favorite radio program was *The Lone Ranger*.

Ruth loved children more than he loved baseball, and nowhere was he more comfortable than when he was surrounded by us kids. Whenever he came over, he'd go outside before and after the meal to talk to my friends, many of whom I never knew were my friends. He'd always bring a few baseballs with him to pass out, and then he'd play catch with us and give us tips on how to hit home runs. Invariably, I was the most popular kid in the neighborhood, at least for the next week or so after a Babe visit.

Ruth never had a son of his own, so in a way every little boy was his son, but there were countless times when he told me he considered me to be the one son he never had. Babe Ruth told me that. Babe Ruth.

He was a special man. A man I came to love.

It was Ruth who had provided us with our tickets to Opening Day, it was he who paved the way for my becoming one of the Yankee batboys in 1927, and his was a friendship my dad and I cherished until cancer took him from us in the summer of 1948.

* * *

While Walker's sobering words weren't part of the original agenda, they turned that Elks Club dinner into a rousing success because they galled Ruth into mending his ways. Rather than boozing and gallivanting around New York City that winter, Ruth and his wife Helen purchased a farmhouse in Sudbury, Massachusetts, and there Ruth spent the off-season getting into shape and rededicating himself to baseball. When he reported to spring training weighing a fit 215 pounds, it was apparent he and the Yankees were in for a magical 1923 season.

New York's starting lineup was virtually the same as it had been in 1922 when it won 94 times and edged the St. Louis Browns by one game in the final standings. There was Pipp at first, Aaron Ward at second, Everett Scott playing short, and Joe Dugan manning third. The outfield was comprised of Ruth in right, Meusel in left, and Whitey Witt in center, with Schang behind the plate.

The pitching staff returned mostly intact with Mays, Hoyt, Sad Sam Jones, Bullet Joe Bush, and Bob Shawkey, and there was a key addition in the form of Herb Pennock, pilfered from the Red Sox in exchange for three nominal players and cash. This assemblage was determined to put 1922 behind them, and they were helped by the fact that they were moving into their luxurious new home in the Bronx.

By winning 21 of 27 games in May the Yankees opened an eight-game lead, and with Ruth enjoying one of the greatest seasons in baseball history, they never looked back. Ruth finished with a .393 average, second only to Detroit's Harry Heilmann who batted .403, and Ruth led the league in homers (41), RBI (131), runs scored (151), total bases (399), walks (170), on-base percentage (.545), and slugging percentage (.764).

Esteemed sportswriter Hugh Fullerton, whom I came to know during my days with the *Home News* and the *Post*, wrote in the *Chicago Tribune* of Ruth: "The big boy is sincere and earnest, is hustling, fighting, playing for his team instead of for his individual record, and the result is that his record, save for those ballyhoo home runs, is better than ever and he is the greatest ballplayer of all."

When the regular season was finished, the Yankees were an astounding 16 games clear of second-place Detroit. There was only one thing left to do: beat the Giants in the World Series.

– *1923 World Series* –

I know it is hard for me—as I'm sure it is for any true Yankee fan—
to imagine Casey Stengel as anything other than the stumpy little old
man wearing a baggy pinstriped uniform and speaking a form of fractured English that was inaudible to virtually everyone except his players
and his wife Edna.

The visions of Stengel resonate even today, four decades after he
last managed the Yankees. Stengel leaning against that post in front of
the visitors' dugout at Ebbets Field during the five World Series clashes
between his Yankees and the Dodgers; or sitting in the Yankee Stadium
dugout with his face drooping into his chest, watching his team win
another pennant; or hobbling out to the mound to replace a tiring
pitcher; or wrapping his arm around Mickey Mantle or Billy Martin or
Whitey Ford and imparting on the kids a bit of priceless Stengelese; or
standing behind a lectern on the off-season banquet circuit, staring out
at a crowd he had just transformed into a howling mob with some whim-
sical one-liner.

But while his baseball life reached unprecedented heights during
his 12-year tenure as the Yankee skipper from 1949–1960, his life in baseball had existed long before he took up his historic residence in the
Bronx. In fact, it was Stengel who almost single-handedly kept the Yankees from winning their first world championship in 1923. As a 33-year-
old outfielder for the New York Giants, Stengel hit a pair of home runs
that beat the Yankees in the first and third games of that World Series.
Had it not been for a lackluster performance by the rest of John
McGraw's club, the Yankees would have one less title to call their own.

This was the third year in a row the World Series was an all-New
York affair, and McGraw's Giants had defeated Miller Huggins's Yankees in the first two meetings in 1921 and 1922. But with the Yankees
having been so dominant in the American League and the Giants having worked hard to outdistance Cincinnati by a scant four games in the
National League, it appeared the tide was about to turn in the Yankees'
favor.

The Giants were led by Bob Meusel's brother, Irish, plus Frankie
Frisch and George Kelly, all of whom had driven in more than 100 runs
during the season. Seven of their eight starting-position players had batted at least .290, and their pitching was well-balanced with Art Nehf,
Rosy Ryan, Hugh McQuillan, Jack Bentley, and Jack Scott. Stengel was
second on the team with a .339 average in 75 games and he led New York

in slugging average at .505, but if you had polled the Yankees as to which Giant player they feared most, Stengel wouldn't have received a vote. This was a very good Giant team, but the Yankees were confident they could be conquered.

In the first Series game ever played at Yankee Stadium, McGraw tapped Mule Watson as his starting pitcher while Huggins went with Waite Hoyt, but neither pitcher survived three innings. The Yankees jumped to an early 3-0 lead, fell behind when the Giants put together a four-run rally in the third, then tied the score in the seventh on Joe Dugan's RBI triple, and so it was left for Stengel to become the unsuspecting hero.

With two outs in the ninth, Stengel worked the count full, and then Bush went by the book and attacked Stengel's weakness, throwing a fastball to the outside corner. Stengel reached out with a mighty left-handed swing, connected solidly, and the ball rocketed out to the deepest part of the new stadium, left center. Both Whitey Witt and Bob Meusel gave chase as Stengel rambled around the bases, arms flailing, knees buckling, a piece of his shoe flying off, which made his awkward running style even more hilarious.

All 55,307 fans—including Dad and me, thanks to the generosity of Ruth—were on their feet watching breathlessly as this unforgettable play unfolded. Witt tracked the ball down, flipped it to the strong-armed Meusel, and he fired home to catcher Wally Schang. The ball arrived a split second after Stengel stumbled across the plate with the winning run.

It was truly unbelievable, and all a seven-year-old could do in a moment like that was cry, so I did.

When Rosy Ryan mowed the Yankees down in order in the ninth the Giants were up one game. "It's the same thing, we draw first blood, now watch us," said McGraw. "The team pulled through victorious in one of the best games I think I've ever seen. I guess the team showed itself superior as a machine to the satisfaction of everybody."

Huggins, who had grown tired of losing to McGraw—this was his 10th loss in 13 Series games to date—found solace in the fact that his troops had managed 12 hits in the game. "We showed today that we could hit the Giants pitchers," he said. "It is not in the cards for us to have the breaks go against us in every game as they did today and we'll come back all right."

The teams moved across the Harlem River to play Game Two in the Polo Grounds and Ruth stole the show by launching two home runs, joining Pat Dougherty of the 1903 Boston Red Sox in accomplishing that feat. Ruth's performance backed the superb pitching of Herb Pennock who went the distance, scattering nine hits in the Yankees' 4-2 victory.

"Say, if I had met that ball in the ninth square, I would have knocked that ball into the bleachers and made a fine day finer," Ruth said of his deep fly to center that almost left the park but landed in Stengel's mitt. "I wonder what McGraw's system will be from now on. Just let him tell his pitchers to throw 'em to me and watch the Babe. I'll show them that last year was an accident." Ruth, of course, was referring to his abysmal showing during the Giants' Series sweep of the Yankees in 1922.

McGraw conceded defeat by saying, "I want to give a lot of credit to Pennock for his fine performance. We have no excuses to offer. It was a game of hitting and we were out-hit. It was a game of pitching and we were out-pitched. They were due to win one and we'll see if we can't make that one the only one."

*   *   *

Pennock was the last in the parade of former Boston players who had been dealt to the Yankees for next to nothing by frugal Red Sox owner Harry Frazee.

Between 1919 and 1923 the Red Sox literally served as New York's farm club, as half the Yankees' 1923 roster was comprised of players acquired from Boston, including stars such as Ruth, Hoyt, Dugan, Schang, Carl Mays, Bob Shawkey, Everett Scott, Sad Sam Jones, Bullet Joe Bush, and George Pipgras. While Ruth was certainly the most important figure, Pennock became what Huggins called "the greatest left-hander in the history of baseball," a statement that, along with his 241 career victories, helped gain Pennock induction into the Hall of Fame.

Pennock, then just a teenager, was pitching for a semipro team in Atlantic City in 1911 and was a teammate of Connie Mack's son, Earl. Earl Mack was a catcher, and after helping Pennock throw a no-hitter, the younger Mack called his father, and less than a year later Pennock was pitching for the Philadelphia Athletics. But success in the major leagues came slowly, and after 10 nondescript years with Philadelphia and Boston Frazee figured that at age 29 Pennock was over the hill. That proved to be another ill-fated decision by Frazee.

Huggins had gone to Yankee general manager Ed Barrow following the 1922 season and said, "We can win the whole thing if we could only pick up a strong left-handed pitcher." Barrow, who had managed Pennock in Boston, knew he was the man Huggins needed. Over the next 11 years he would win 162 regular-season games for the Yankees, plus go 5-0 with three saves in World Series play.

Pennock was a master technician on the mound, always looking for ways to improve himself, and much of the time his work wasn't physical, it was mental. "If you were to cut that bird's head open," Huggins said, "the weakness of every batter in the league would fall out."

I remember in my first year as the team's assistant batboy in 1927, I was in the clubhouse one day telling Pennock about my pitching prowess during a recent stickball game on the street. I told him that I dreamed of becoming a major league pitcher some day, and he shared with me one of his baseball philosophies that helped him become the pitcher he was. "The first commandment is observation," Pennock explained to me. "Look around, notice the little quirks in the batter and notice your own quirks. Your doctor never stops learning. The great pitcher imitates him."

And Pennock preached practice.

"When I was struggling I pitched in games, in batting practice, before games, in morning games, and during the off-season," he said. "When I couldn't get anyone to catch me I'd throw against a stone wall or against a barn door. It wasn't always fun, but I kept on plugging away because it meant so much to me."

I'm pretty sure I ran home that night after the game and threw my rubber ball against the side of our apartment building until dark, or at least until Mr. Ferguson—a crotchety old man who lived on the first floor and was always telling us kids to go play somewhere else—came out and yelled at me to stop.

Pennock used to regale me with stories of his youth. He grew up in Kennett Square, Pennsylvania, a well-to-do suburb of Philadelphia. He had gone to fine prep schools and was well-educated, a trait that ballplayers in those days rarely possessed. He told me of the fox hunts he used to conduct on his family's spacious land, and of his breeding of silver foxes, all of which fascinated me because his was a life I was so unfamiliar with. He was a unique man amid the crusty world of roaring '20s baseball, and he was one of the first players to make me feel welcome in the Yankee clubhouse when I began working for the team.

* * *

Prior to Game Three back at Yankee Stadium, Huggins boldly predicted that his starter, Jones, would run through the Giants' batting order without incident. "I will pitch Sam Jones and he will win, I don't care who faces him," said Huggins. There was one hitch. Stengel wasn't finished tanning himself in the spotlight, as he emerged the hero again. Jones was nearly as dominant as Huggins had promised, but he made one mistake, a poorly spotted change-up that Stengel ripped for a solo home run in the seventh. It was the lone score of the day as Nehf quieted the Yankee bats with a six-hitter and the Giants regained the Series lead with a 1-0 victory.

"That makes two games for Stengel and one game for the Yankees," Stengel quipped afterward.

It also meant the end of Stengel's Cinderella story, and the end of the Giants' reign atop the baseball world as the Yankees went on to win the final three games by scores of 8-4, 8-1, and 6-4.

After losing the fourth and fifth games, the Giants' last hope was Nehf in Game Six, the one man Huggins felt could at least slow the Yankees. And for seven innings, the left-hander did just that. After Ruth homered in the first inning, Nehf settled down and the Giants built a 4-1 lead by pecking away at Pennock, and it appeared a seventh game would be necessary.

As soon as school let out I raced over to Dad's shop to sit with him in the workroom and listen to the game on the radio. Like Huggins, Dad had been worried about Nehf, too, and he tried to cushion the blow of a potential Yankee loss for me by saying, "Joey, if they don't win today, that means we get to go to the game tomorrow and watch them win it in person." That perked up my spirits, but what happened a few minutes later did the trick a little better. The ever-dangerous Yankees exploded for five runs in the eighth, Bob Meusel's two-out, two-run go-ahead single the clutch hit, to put themselves in position to win their first world championship.

Jones, who hadn't pitched since his Game Three duel with Nehf, strode confidently to the mound with the intention of putting the Giants away and wrapping up the Series. With two outs and one on, McGraw looked into his dugout and signaled for Stengel to pinch-hit. I was biting my nails thinking about the success Stengel had already enjoyed in the Series. Who was this guy, anyway?

I needn't have worried. Stengel fouled out meekly to Dugan behind third base to end the threat. In the ninth Jones didn't permit a ball to leave the infield, the Giants went down 1-2-3, and Dad and I rejoiced.

"Nehf is one of the finest, gamest, and most able pitchers the game has known," said McGraw. "It was not his fault that he faltered there. The Yankees played great ball this year. They have won a great victory."

It was just the beginning.

When I became a sportswriter and began working for the Bronx Home News *in the mid-1930s, I promised myself that I would never write a story on any subject until I was positive I had the facts straight. No matter how important or inconsequential the topic, it was a creed I lived by because I never forgot an incident that occurred during my childhood when a reporter for a Canadian wire service penned a special bulletin dated April 8, 1925 proclaiming Babe Ruth had died.*

His egregious error set off a nationwide panic, and nowhere was the fear more prevalent than in the back room of Dad's shop, where he put aside his work and set up a lengthy vigil in front of the radio listening to hourly updates on what exactly had happened to the Babe.

As it turned out, Ruth collapsed on a train platform in Asheville, North Carolina while the Yankees were traveling through the South on their way back from spring training to start the regular season. He was rushed to a local hotel and treated for a high fever and flu symptoms, then was transported back to the train station so he could return to New York for further medical care. When he and Yankee scout Paul Krichell missed a connection, the Canadian wire service reporter, waiting for the train in Washington, carelessly assumed Ruth must have died and ran with the story. By the time Ruth reached New York, the city was in an uproar demanding news and a mob estimated at nearly 25,000 gathered at Penn Station. Ruth was secretly transported to St. Vincent's Hospital, where hours later it was finally announced to the frenzied press that Ruth was alive, the victim of a severe case of the flu.

Ultimately, it was discovered that he was also suffering from an intestinal abscess which was surgically removed, and he remained in the hospital nearly three weeks, not only alive, but his usual larger-than-life self.

The Yankees, who had seen their string of three straight pennants ended in 1924 by the Washington Senators, got off to a slow start in 1925 without their star player, and despite a fine rookie season by a strapping young first baseman and Columbia graduate named Lou Gehrig, they sank to seventh place in the standings, lowest since 1913.

However, Ruth returned with a vengeance in 1926, leading the league in home runs, RBI, runs, walks, and slugging percentage and the Yankees surged back to the top and won the pennant, though they were defeated in a classic seven-game World Series by St. Louis.

Throughout these years, Dad's relationship with Ruth strengthened and it would not be a stretch to say that my father was the Babe's most trusted friend. Ruth continued to visit Dad's shop, he was a frequent dinner guest at our apartment, often bringing along a woman named Claire Hodgson whom he would marry shortly after his estranged first wife, Helen, died in 1929, and I remained his favorite little boy — the so-called son he never had.

I thought I was the luckiest kid in the world. Never mind the tickets Ruth would give Dad and me, enabling us to attend so many more games than Dad could have ever afforded to take me to. Never mind the visits to the clubhouse, nor the dinners at our apartment. I — little Joey Kimmerle — could say without hesitation that Babe Ruth, icon to millions, was my personal friend.

But just in case there was any doubt, in 1927, it was officially confirmed that I was indeed the luckiest kid in the world as I became a member of the Yankee family. Thanks to Ruth talking me up to manager Miller Huggins and general manager Ed Barrow, I became the Yankees' assistant batboy, thus allowing me to spend the summer of my 11th year working side by side with the men who comprised what many people consider to be the greatest ball club of all time.

With Eddie Bennett entrenched as the team's regular batboy and mascot, I became his helper as well as a general team go-fer from 1927 through 1932. Later I became the assistant clubhouse boy from 1933 to 1936, and during the time of my employment with the team I witnessed, up close and personal, the Yankees' World Series triumphs in 1927, 1928, 1932, and 1936.

What an experience it was to be in the clubhouse for those 10 years associating with men like Ruth, Huggins, Gehrig, Bill Dickey, Tony Lazzeri, Joe Dugan, Mark Koenig, Bob Meusel, Earle Combs, Herb Pennock, Joe McCarthy, Joe DiMaggio, and all the rest. You name it, and I did it for the Yankees. I cleaned their shoes, collected their dirty uniforms and laundered them, ran errands, opened and sorted their fan mail, and, on Ruth's orders, snuck up behind his teammates' backs and peaked at their cards during poker and bridge games and relayed the information back to the Babe in our secret code. Of course, I would have run through a wall for Ruth, had he asked.

The young man who previously held my position was named William Bendix. He, too, had been a favorite of the Babe and Bendix catered to Ruth's every need. But one day Bendix brought Ruth a half dozen or so hot dogs and a couple quarts of soda for a pregame lunch. Ruth devoured the food, then fell deathly ill and had to be rushed to a hospital. When Barrow learned that Bendix had provided the food, he fired him, even though Bendix had acted on Ruth's orders. Ironi-

cally, Bendix became an actor and he played the part of Ruth in the forgettable Babe Ruth Story. *My first day on the job, Bennett relayed the tale about Bendix and he barked at me, "Don't go gettin' any of these ballplayers sick!"*

Eddie was a New York legend himself. As a small child he fell out of his baby carriage and sustained a spinal injury that resulted in the development of a hunchback which in turn stunted his growth at about 4 1/2 feet. He had been hired by the Chicago White Sox at the age of 15 to serve as batboy in 1919, the year they won the American League pennant and then threw the World Series, allowing Cincinnati to win baseball's most tainted and controversial championship. The following year Eddie returned to his native Brooklyn to work for the Dodgers and they, too, won a pennant and lost in the World Series. Even though Eddie was 0-for-2 in the Series, Colonel Ruppert must have considered him some kind of good luck charm and he pried Eddie away from the Dodgers in time for the Yankees' 1921 season. The Yankees proceeded to win three straight pennants, and after Eddie's losing streak in the Series reached four in a row when the Giants beat the Yankees in 1921 and 1922, the hex was finally broken when the Yankees whipped the Giants in 1923.

Ruth adored Eddie. Every time Babe kneeled in the on-deck circle, Eddie knelt right next to him, and Eddie was always the first person to shake Ruth's hand after one of his home runs. Ruth and Eddie used to entertain the fans who came to the ballpark early by playing catch. They would start out with a normal toss back and forth, but then Ruth would purposely throw the ball just above Eddie's limited reach, and he'd hobble to the backstop to pick up the ball. After returning it to Ruth, Babe would throw it over Eddie's head again, and the folks got a nice chuckle out of that. Sometimes I would substitute for Eddie if he was busy with something else, but I don't think it was quite as funny because while we were about the same height, Eddie was an adult and I was a little kid.

Eddie served as the team's batboy until the middle of the 1933 season when he was run over by a taxicab and suffered a broken leg. That year I had been promoted to assistant clubhouse boy under Pete Sheehy, but I inherited Eddie's duties during his absence. Sadly, Eddie never returned to the team. Always a heavy drinker, he was found dead in his apartment on West 84th Street a few years later. The cause of death was ruled acute alcoholism.

– Chapter 2 –

1927

I CAME HOME FROM SCHOOL one wintry February afternoon, soaked and shivering from a wet snow that was falling in the Bronx, and my mother was waiting for me at the kitchen table. My first thought was "Oh no, what did I do now?" I was a typically adventurous child, never averse to getting myself into trouble, but for the life of me, I couldn't think of anything I'd done in the past couple of days that would have riled Mom.

"Your father wanted me to send you over to the shop as soon as you got home from school, so put your things away and run down there," Mom told me, her voice showing no sign of discontent. I obeyed, and as I was running down River Avenue through the blanket of snow, I tried to think if I'd done anything that would have upset Dad, and perhaps Mom didn't know about it, but I came up blank. I'd actually been pretty good lately. So what could be so urgent that Dad was sending for me as soon as I got home from school?

I burst into the shop, said hello to Mr. DiRenzio who was busy with a customer, took off my galoshes and overcoat, then strolled into the back room where Dad was stitching together a shoe. "Joey!" Dad said with a wide-eyed smile.

"Hi Dad, you wanted to see me?" I asked with a tinge of trepidation.

"Joey, you're not going to believe who called me this morning on the telephone," Dad said with excitement. Before I could venture a guess, Dad said, "Ed Barrow, the general manager of the Yankees. He said the team would like to hire you to be their assistant batboy this season. You're gonna get to go to every home game they play!"

Dad was right. I didn't believe it, and for a moment my head began to spin and my eyes glazed over. It was no accident that Ed Barrow called my father and requested my services. This was the work of Ruth, our good friend. I had remarked the year before to Ruth on one of our post-game visits with him in the clubhouse that I sure thought Eddie Bennett had a great job as the batboy of the Yankees. Ruth apparently remembered that I'd said that, and just before the team left for spring training, he asked Barrow to consider hiring me to be a helper for Bennett, whose health was always a source of concern. Barrow had seen Dad and me around the ballpark, he knew who I was and he knew I lived just a block away from the stadium. He agreed to Ruth's request, and when the team returned from St. Petersburg, Florida, in April to start the season, I was fitted with a Yankee pinstripe uniform, the finest garment a young New York City boy could ever dream of wearing.

The team—as well as this particular young fan—was still reeling from the heartbreaking loss in the 1926 Series to the Cardinals which featured one of the all-time classic World Series moments. Rookie second baseman Tony Lazzeri, who'd driven in 114 runs during the regular season, came to the plate in the bottom of the seventh inning with two outs, the bases loaded, and the Yankees trailing 3-2 in Game Seven at the stadium. Before Lazzeri could dig in, Cardinals player-manager Rogers Hornsby was forced to lift his pitcher, Jesse Haines, because he had developed a blister on his throwing hand, and Hornsby signaled for 39-year-old veteran Grover Cleveland Alexander.

The day before, Lazzeri had gone 0-for-4 against Alexander and the Cardinals won the game, 10-2, tying the Series at three apiece. Having thrown two complete-game victories, Alexander figured his work was done for the Series and legend has it that he went out after the game, had far too many cocktails, and was in no shape to pitch. All of it was bunk as it was later confirmed by sources in the know that Alexander had not imbibed the night before and was perfectly fine.

Alexander worked the count to 1-1, then made a mistake that nearly cost his team the Series. He threw a belt-high fastball over the plate and Lazzeri crushed it deep to left field. Dad and I leaped from our seats along with 38,000 others, thinking Lazzeri had just put the Yankees ahead, but the ball hooked foul at the last instant. "Less than a foot made the difference between a hero and a bum," Alexander said.

After breathing a sigh of relief, Alexander threw a nasty curve that Lazzeri swung at and missed, ending the threat. Alexander proceeded to pitch two more scoreless innings and Dad and I sat there in moribund silence as the Cardinals celebrated their championship in our stadium.

"I gave him the signals on those pitches, but it didn't make any difference what the signal was," said Cardinals catcher Bob O'Farrell. "His excellent control was his greatest asset. Lazzeri would have had to have been Houdini to get good wood on that last pitch."

*   *   *

I have always felt it was unfair that nearly every reference to Lazzeri—and I am guilty as well in this compilation—includes the recounting of that historic confrontation with Alexander because it overshadows the marvelous career Lazzeri enjoyed.

Lazzeri played 12 seasons for the Yankees, but he never really entered the spotlight, which was a good thing because he was not the friendliest of men and he despised talking to the sportswriters. "Interviewing that guy is like mining coal with a nail file and a pair of scissors," one of them once said. Lazzeri was perfectly content letting Ruth, Lou Gehrig, Earle Combs, Bob Meusel, Bill Dickey, Lefty Gomez, Red Ruffing, and Joe DiMaggio hog the headlines while day after day, he trotted out to second base and performed with great skill.

When Lazzeri broke in with the Yankees in 1926 Miller Huggins said, "Tony is a great natural player, make no mistake about that. This is his first year in the majors, but he's no flash in the pan. He should improve."

Ruth and Gehrig carried the 1927 club, but Lazzeri was a vital cog in the machine as he hit 18 homers (which incredibly was third-best in the American League behind Ruth's 60 and Gehrig's 47), drove in 102 runs and batted .309. Longtime American League umpire Tom Connolly once remarked that "When things get tough out there, the others don't look to Ruth or any of the veterans. They look to (Lazzeri), and he never fails them."

Barrow also had tremendous respect for the man nicknamed "Poosh 'Em Up." Superscout Paul Krichell had spotted Lazzeri in the Pacific Coast League, but despite his terrific statistics, he warned Barrow that Lazzeri suffered from epileptic fits. Barrow's response: "As long as he doesn't take fits between 3 and 6 in the afternoon, that's good enough for me."

Many years later, I called Barrow for a comment after we learned that Lazzeri had suffered an epileptic seizure at his home in San Francisco, had fallen down the stairs and died at the age of 42. Barrow said Lazzeri "was one of the greatest ballplayers I have ever known."

"Here was the man who really made the 1926 club, and all people ever said about him was that Alexander struck him out," Huggins said in reference to that unfortunate at-bat. "Anyone can strike out, but ballplayers like Lazzeri come along once in a generation."

*   *   *

The 1927 Yankees—who in my mind were the greatest team in the history of baseball for seven decades until the 1998 Yankees surpassed them—were a work in progress as far back as 1925. That year Gehrig took over for Wally Pipp at first base and didn't miss another game for 14 years, and Earle Combs replaced Whitey Witt in center field. The middle of the infield was solidified in 1926 when Lazzeri and shortstop Mark Koenig joined the team, and before the 1927 season began, pitchers Dutch Ruether, George Pipgras (a Yankee in 1923–1924 who had spent the previous two years honing his skills in the minors) and Wilcy Moore (a 30-year-old career minor leaguer) were signed. That threesome joined forces with an already excellent trio of starters—Waite Hoyt, Herb Pennock, and Urban Shocker—to give the Yankees unmatched pitching. With Ruth, Joe Dugan, and Bob Meusel already in place, it wasn't even fair.

When the team came north to start the season, it was a determined bunch looking to wash away the bitter taste of losing the final two games of the 1926 Series on its home turf. On April 12, in front of what was believed to be the largest Opening Day crowd to that point in baseball history (73,206 at the newly expanded stadium), the Yankees whipped the Athletics, 8-3, as Hoyt outpitched Lefty Grove. That victory put the Yankees in first place, and that's where they stayed for 174 consecutive days, wire-to-wire leaders, a feat matched since then only by the 1984 Detroit Tigers, 1997 Baltimore Orioles, and 2001 Seattle Mariners.

That day I made my debut in Yankee pinstripes, sitting next to the visiting dugout and collecting any foul balls that were hit into the screen behind home plate. It was also my duty to replenish the umpire's supply of balls, and to collect the visitors' bats after each at-bat. From his seat on the first-base side behind the Yankees dugout—again courtesy of the Babe—my dad was beaming and I think he watched me more than the game.

I was perfectly capable of dressing myself, but that morning Dad had insisted on assisting, and I understood why. I was standing in front of my bedroom window staring at the tranquil stadium four hours before the first pitch was scheduled to be thrown when Dad came in. "How about we get you into your uniform?" Dad said, and I nodded my head in excited anticipation. He took my Yankee uniform out of the box, carefully laid it on my bed, and the two of us just stared at it for a minute before beginning the process of draping it over my 95-pound body. Handling each piece as if it were delicate china, we started by stretching the navy blue socks over my white sanitaries. Then I stepped into the white pants with the thin blue pinstripes, and before I buckled the belt, I slipped into the button-down white shirt with the same blue pinstripes. I buttoned the shirt, Dad helped me tuck it into the pants, and after I fastened the belt, Dad covered my head with the famous Yankee cap adorned with the interlocking 'NY' on the front. Dad stepped back to gaze up and down at the finished product, and as he hitched up my pants and straightened my cap, I could feel the bursts of satisfaction and pride he was feeling.

Ruth didn't hit his first home run of this momentous season until April 15, and that was the only one he hit in the first 10 days. He had just four at the end of April and while the Yankees were in first place, they weren't as yet dominant. But Ruth cracked 12 homers in May and the team—backed by solid pitching and Ruth's fellow members of Murderer's Row—Gehrig, Lazzeri, and Meusel—started to pull away from the Senators and Athletics.

During the months of June and July the Yankees won 45 of 58 games, and on July 4 it became plainly clear that no one in the American League was going to compete with them. In front of a massive holiday gathering at the stadium, the Yankees drubbed the Senators in a doubleheader, 12-1 and 21-1, prompting Washington first baseman Joe Judge to say, "Those fellows not only beat you, they tear your heart out. I wish the season was over."

It was, except for the dramatic home run race between Ruth and Gehrig. Ruth was grabbing most of the attention, but Gehrig was doing just as much mashing and on September 5, both players had 44 homers. Over the next two days, Ruth walloped five in three games against the Red Sox, and he finished with 17 in September. Gehrig would hit just three more.

The historic 60th came on September 30, the next-to-last day of the season, when Ruth golfed at a screwball thrown by Washington's Tom Zachary and sent it down the right-field line. There were barely 10,000 fans in attendance because the game meant nothing and everyone was eagerly awaiting the start of the Series, but I was there, and it was a thrill to watch that ball clear the fence. Sure, Ruth had once hit 59 homers in a season and now he had increased the record by just one. But that one made it 60, and as we learned through the years, 60 was a monumental figure.

When I would play stickball or baseball in the streets and sandlots of the Bronx, I would mimic Ruth's swing. The day he hit the 60th, I happened to ask him before the game how he came to swing the way he did and he said, "I copied my swing after Joe Jackson's. Joe aimed his right shoulder square at the pitcher with his feet about 20 inches apart. But I close my stance to about eight inches or less. I find I pivot better. Once my swing starts, though, I can't change it or pull up. It's all or nothing at all." True to form for Ruth, who went through his entire life with an "all or nothing" attitude.

The Yankees won 110 of 154 games, finished 19 lengths in front of the Athletics, and as Hoyt said, "The '27 Yankees were an exceptional team because they met every demand. When we were challenged, when we had to win, we all stuck together and played with a fury and determination that could only come from team spirit. We felt we were superior people and I do believe we left a heritage that became a Yankee tradition."

– *1927 World Series* –

Though I was only 11 years old, I was astute enough to know on the eve of the 1927 Series that the Pittsburgh Pirates had no chance against the Yankees.

I didn't travel to road games during the regular season, but the team took me along each year it played in the Series. When I boarded the Pullman bound for Pittsburgh on the afternoon of October 3, 1927, it was the first time I would be leaving the boundaries of New York City and I was flushed with anxiety. To me, Pittsburgh might as well have been Paris, the same place Charles Lindbergh had flown to from Long Island earlier that year, completing the historic first solo, nonstop flight across the Atlantic in the *Spirit of St. Louis.*

The day before Game One, after the Pirates completed their workout some of them took seats up in the stands at Forbes Field to watch the Yankees take batting practice. I was back by the dugout, lining up the bats for each player as he stepped into the cage, and at one point I looked up into the stands and could see the awe in the Pirates' faces as the men who made up Murderers Row—Babe Ruth, Lou Gehrig, Tony

Lazzeri, and Bob Meusel—sent baseballs flying over the fences in all directions.

It was reported in some publications that the Pirates were psyched out by this display, and for years, star outfielder Lloyd Waner didn't know what the writers were talking about, and for good reason. Somehow it came out that Lloyd and his brother Paul were among the Pirate players sitting in the stands, and Paul is alleged to have leaned over and said to Lloyd, "Gee, they're big, aren't they."

"I don't know how that got started," Lloyd said many years later. "I never even saw the Yankees work out that day. I was leaving the ballpark just as they were coming out on to the field. I know some of our players stayed, but I never heard anybody talk about what they saw."

I can vouch for him that neither he nor his brother were there when the Yankees put on their long ball show. However, shortstop Glenn Wright did witness the exhibition, and it was he who admitted aloud— to me—that he'd "never seen anything like this."

"Do they do this all the time?" Wright said about halfway through the workout. I just smiled and said, "Yes sir," and right then, I knew the Yankees would win.

Quite frankly, it wouldn't have mattered if the Pirates were in the stands or not. They'd enjoyed a nice season in the National League, winning 94 games to outleg St. Louis by a scant game and a half. And although Paul Waner, Lloyd Waner, and Pie Traynor formed a productive trio, they were no match for the Yankees, and whether they were psyched out or not wasn't the issue. The Pirates just couldn't compete with the Yankees, and everyone—including this 11-year-old—knew it.

Before the Series, a reporter foolishly told Ruth the Yankees were in for a tough fight because the Pirates "have seven good starting pitchers." Ruth answered him by saying, "What good are seven starting pitchers in a four-game series?" That comment didn't get quite as much attention as his alleged called shot in 1932 against the Chicago Cubs, but again, Ruth nailed it as the Yankees indeed dispatched the Pirates in four quick games by a combined score of 23-10.

Miller Huggins pointed out before the Series began that the Pirates had a few more hits than the Yankees during the season, but that the Yankees had scored many more runs "and it is runs that win ballgames," Huggins said. "I have studied the Pittsburgh team and although they have a bunch of good hitters, they are not generally a slugging team. Against us, the Pirates will face a team that has power from the first to the last man up."

That power was not evident in Game One. The Yankees managed just six hits against Pirate pitchers Ray Kremer and John Miljus—none of them home runs—and the game was decided by Pittsburgh's shoddy fielding.

With Ruth on first after a single in the top of the first, Gehrig came up with two outs and looped a sinking fly ball to right. Paul Waner charged in and tried to make a shoestring catch and failed. The ball skipped past him and Ruth scored from first as Gehrig chugged into third for a triple.

With the score 1-1 in the third, the Yankees surged ahead with three runs, again aided by Pittsburgh misplays. The Pirates pulled within 5-4 in the eighth, but Huggins pulled starter Waite Hoyt and called for Wilcy Moore, and the sinker-balling righty preserved New York's victory by getting the last four outs.

* * *

One day in 1926 Ed Barrow was flipping through an issue of *The Sporting News* and he noticed that a pitcher for Greenville, South Carolina, in the South Atlantic League had a record of 20-1. He dispatched scout Bob Gilks to inquire about this fellow named Wilcy Moore, and Gilks reported back, saying, "He can't pitch, and anyway, he says he's 30 but he must be 40."

Still, Barrow was intrigued and he said, "Anyone who can win that many games is worth what they're asking for him." The price was $3,500, which the Yankees paid.

Moore, who was 29 years old though he looked much older, wound up 30-4 that season for the Spinners, and his success was due in large part to the development of a devastating sinker. Moore had been hit by a batted ball earlier in his career and suffered a broken forearm. He resorted to a sidearm delivery to alleviate pain in his wrist caused by the injury, and the result was a sinking action on his fastball that proved nearly unhittable in the bush leagues.

In 1927, it was unhittable to American League hitters as well. "Wilcy was a character," Barrow once told me. "He was a big, raw-boned, heavy-handed farmer with a bald head from Hollis, Oklahoma who threw a heavy ball that sank as it got close to the plate. It was the perfect equipment for a relief pitcher coming in with men on base."

At first glance, Huggins wasn't convinced Moore could help the Yankees. "I figure it's more sensible to take a pessimistic view because of his age," he said. "He's one of those old youngsters. He is breaking into the majors at 30 — that's old for a pitcher."

It didn't take long for Huggins to come around. He used Moore as a part-time starter, part-time reliever, and Moore pitched 213 innings despite starting just 12 games. With so many innings, he was eligible for the league's ERA title, which he won with a 2.26 mark.

"I don't know where Moore was when all the scouts were gumshoeing around those parts," Ruth said, "because he was just about the best pitcher in our league in 1927."

*　*　*

Another pitcher who became a surprising producer was George Pipgras, a man who'd spent the previous three years in the minor leagues learning how to pitch. During Game One of the Series, Pipgras was sitting on the bench when Huggins leaned over and asked him if he could pitch the next game. Urban Shocker was the scheduled starter, but Huggins was playing a hunch. "He told me to get a good night's rest," Pipgras said. "A good night's rest! I'll tell you what I did, I went back to the hotel and began studying that Pirate lineup until my eyes started to hurt."

Pipgras's studying paid off. Lloyd Waner led off the bottom of the first inning with a triple and he scored moments later when Clyde Barnhart hit a sacrifice fly. Thereafter the Pirates managed just six hits and one run and when the Yankees put up a pair of three spots in the third and eighth innings, Pipgras was the winner by a 6-2 count.

"George has speed to burn and a real hop on his fastball," said Bob Shawkey, who at this point in his career was serving as a player/pitching coach for Huggins. "He has a great curve, too, when he needs to use it, but today he just had to stand up there and throw it past 'em."

As I was collecting the Yankees' uniforms after the game, Ruth was holding court in front of his locker with the writers. As he tossed me his socks, he said, "Looks like a breeze, just a breeze. Two more games and the Series will be over."

Rogers Hornsby, who joined the Giants prior to the start of the 1927 season and missed out on another Series appearance when the Pirates edged his new club by two games, had predicted that Pittsburgh would give the Yankees all kinds of trouble if Huggins decided to pitch his left-handed starters, Pennock and Dutch Ruether.

"I believe that Huggins will make a mistake if he starts either of his southpaws against the Pirates because they murder this kind of pitching," Hornsby said.

Hoyt, Moore, and Pipgras were righties and they'd had no problem with the Pirate batting order. In Game Three Huggins ignored Hornsby's advice and started the wily 13-year veteran, Pennock. All Pennock did was throw a perfect game for 7 1/3 innings before Traynor broke it up with a single. By then Ruth had hit a three-run homer during a six-run seventh inning that gave Pennock an 8-0 lead, and the Pirates wound up "murdering" him to the tune of three hits during an 8-1 loss that dropped Pittsburgh into an insurmountable three games to none hole.

Pennock, who'd broken into the major leagues with the Athletics in 1912 and had learned his deadly screwball from Chief Bender, baffled the Pirates. It was thought that he wouldn't pitch in the Series because he'd been hit by a ball in batting practice the day the Yankees psyched out the Pirates with their pyrotechnic display. Further, Pennock could never sleep on train rides, and he'd been awake all night when the teams traveled from Pittsburgh to New York. Imagine if he'd been totally healthy and rested.

"The way the gang played today was marvelous," Pennock said afterward. "No pitcher ever got better support. I'm mighty grateful. I had good control, the ball just went where I wanted it to, and I had good luck."

With a chance to wrap it up, Moore took the ball in Game Four, and it was appropriate that the most unlikely of Yankee heroes in 1927 was the winning pitcher in the season's final game. And how Moore became the winner was equally as unlikely as the power-packing Yankees brought an end to the Series not with a home run by Ruth or Gehrig, but with Earle Combs sprinting across home plate after a wild pitch by Miljus. How's that for anticlimactic?

"I felt that wild pitch coming, and I was sorry," Huggins said. "Miljus was trying so hard that something was bound to slip. An infield error would have been a better ending."

Ruth's two-run homer gave New York a 3-1 lead in the fifth, but when the Yankees came to bat in the bottom of the ninth, the score was tied at 3-3. They quickly loaded the bases with none out, then Miljus heroically struck out Gehrig and Meusel and it looked like the Pirates might extend the game. Instead, with Lazzeri at the plate, Miljus threw one past catcher Johnny Gooch to give the Yankees a 4-3 victory and the world championship that cemented the 1927 team's place in history.

"Just putting on a Yankee uniform gave me a little confidence," said Mark Koenig, who hit .500 in the Series. "We won 26 out of 27 games at one point. I don't think it entered any of our minds that we were the best ever. We just went on winning."

Baseball careers aren't supposed to end when you're 12 years old. Mine did.

From the time I turned seven I played for one or two sandlot teams during the summer, and when I wasn't playing on a diamond, I was playing the uniquely New York game of stickball in the street with my neighborhood friends. I couldn't get enough of baseball or any variation of the game, and I envisioned myself becoming a major league ballplayer. So did my father.

Thanks to nightly catches with my dad in front of our apartment building, I became rather proficient at baseball. Dad taught me the basics, and whenever I was at Yankee Stadium spectating or working, he implored me to watch how the players did things—how they caught the ball and set themselves to throw, or how they stood at the plate and swung the bat. When I'd come home, Dad would help me practice what I had just seen at the game. He used to tell me I had what it took to play professional baseball, as long as I kept working at it.

We weren't wealthy by any means, but Dad always made sure I had the finest baseball glove and bat he could afford. With all the attention my father gave me, I was usually one of the best players on whatever team I was on. I could hit pretty well, but my forte was fielding and pitching. I had a strong arm that made me a natural pitcher, and when it wasn't my turn to pitch, I played shortstop.

One year, probably when I was nine or 10, one of my teams won our divisional championship and we advanced to play in an age-group tournament that included other championship-winning teams from the Bronx. We won that tournament when I pitched a two-hit shutout in the final game and we moved on to play a citywide tournament where teams from all over New York were competing. We ended up losing to a squad from Queens, but at that age we didn't much care. Of course we wanted to win, but the fun of baseball wasn't in the winning of the game so much as the playing of the game.

As I got older and stronger my baseball skills improved, but my activity decreased because I started working for the Yankees and I was forced to miss some of my games when they conflicted with a Yankee home game. It was a tough choice for an 11-year-old to make, but as much as I loved to play, nothing was more exciting than working for the Yankees and watching Major League Baseball games from my chair right there on the field. It wasn't like my choice was playing baseball or bagging groceries. Every kid my age would have gladly traded positions with me and skipped a few games to be a Yankee batboy.

I think in some way my dad thought that working for the Yankees would give me a better chance of playing for them some day, so he never objected to my missing a game. Dad's rationalizations were a bit far-fetched. My own were predicated on the youthful innocence of thinking that I'd have my whole life to play baseball, especially if my dream of playing in the majors came true. As for working for the Yankees, how long could that last? It was a once-in-a-lifetime thrill to be able to do what I was doing and I figured I should ride that opportunity for all it was worth.

So I missed my share of games in the summer of 1927, and I missed another batch of games in the summer of 1928. It did not deter my development as a ballplayer, and what it really did was make me hunger to play even harder and better when I was able to suit up.

How could I have known that when the summer of 1928 came to an end when my American Legion team lost in the semifinals of a city tournament that I would never again be able to play organized baseball? How could I have known that a few months later on a wintry January day I would fall down the steps in front of St. Jerome's grammar school, break my leg, and ultimately contract a bone disease called osteomyelitis that would forever alter the course of my life?

– Chapter 3 –

1928

EVERY AFTERNOON AT FIVE O'CLOCK, fans at Yankee Stadium could hear a shrill whistle blowing from a nearby factory, the signal that another long workday for its laborers was complete. It also served as a warning to visiting teams that it was just about time for another Yankee victory to be wrapped up.

In the days when stadiums were not equipped with lights and baseball games were played in the afternoon, the Yankees were usually putting the finishing touches on a game-winning rally right around the time that whistle blew, and it became known—thanks to Earle Combs—as "Five O'Clock Lightning."

"The team struck so often in the late innings," observed Frank Graham of the *New York Sun,* "it caught on, spread through the league and seeped into the consciousness of opposing pitchers. They began to dread the approach of five o'clock and the eighth inning."

During 1928 five o'clock was a happy hour for the first half of the season as the Yankees won 53 of their first 70 games and by July 1 they led the American League by a whopping 13 1/2 games. But five o'clock became a very nerve-wracking time from mid-July on when injuries riddled the roster, and the red-hot Athletics turned a second straight pennant walkover for New York into a heated race.

In the 15 years before I was born, Connie Mack's Philadelphia Athletics had been one of baseball's strongest teams, winning six pennants and three World Series. Now, after a downfall aided greatly by the Yankees' rise to prominence in the 1920s, Mack was rebuilding his franchise with the emergence of Mickey Cochrane, Al Simmons, and newcomer

Jimmie Foxx, the acquisition of legendary Ty Cobb from Detroit, and the indomitable pitching of Lefty Grove.

In July, the Mackmen went 25-8 and began to inch closer to the Yankees, who at various times were without the services of Combs, Bob Meusel, Benny Bengough, Tony Lazzeri, and Herb Pennock. Throughout August and the first week of September, Philadelphia continued to put the pressure on until finally, on September 8, the Athletics swept a doubleheader in Boston and overtook New York by half a game.

As fate would have it, Philadelphia was scheduled to come to Yankee Stadium the next day for a doubleheader, the start of a four-game series that would most likely decide the pennant.

It was odd, but personally, I was much more nervous the morning of that doubleheader than I had been for any of the four World Series games from the previous fall. I guess it was so obvious to me that the Yankees were going to blow the Pirates away that I never bothered to worry. But now, my beloved Yankees were clearly in some trouble and the red-hot Athletics had momentum on their side and appeared capable of winning the pennant.

I was fortunate that this huge twin bill was being played on a Sunday afternoon. Summer vacation had come to a close, school was starting the next day, and had the games been scheduled for midweek I would have missed most of the first game. Instead, as soon as Father Edwards made the sign of the cross to finish mass, I was the first one out the old oak doors, and after a six-block jog down River Avenue, I was in the Yankee clubhouse by mid-morning, helping get things organized for the players who began arriving soon thereafter.

As I watched these men file in, it hit me that I had no reason to worry. They were loose, smiling, joking, just like they always were. In a few hours they would be playing in the two biggest games of the season, but it might as well have been a Sunday afternoon in May. These were the Yankees, supremely confident in their skills and their ability to win the pressure-packed games.

What a scene it was at the stadium that day. On Saturday Babe Ruth's three-run homer gave the Yankees a 6-3 victory over Washington, but word came from Boston that the Athletics had won twice and were now in first place as they boarded a train bound for the Bronx.

When I left the ballpark to go home that night at about 6 o'clock, three men were already in line at the box office, making sure they would have first crack at the unreserved seats which were going on sale the next morning. By the time my family finished dinner, I looked out my bedroom window and saw hundreds congregating on the sidewalk, prepared for an all-night vigil. When I returned the next morning after church, it was estimated that 20,000 were lingering outside the gates.

Normally when the Yankees took batting practice, the grandstands were spottily occupied, but on this day there had to be 50,000 already in the stadium because the turnstiles began rolling 90 minutes earlier than usual to handle the overflow crowd. As I looked out beyond the bleachers to our apartment building, there were people leaning out windows, hanging off fire escapes, and they were 10 deep on the roof. It was a similar scene on the neighboring rooftops and the Bronx police chief, John O'Brien, told my father the next day over coffee at Calumeta's Café that he estimated about 5,000 people watched the two games from those distant vantage points.

As the stadium continued to fill beyond its capacity, I remember the distinct smell of gasoline fumes permeating the air as there had never been more automobiles around the stadium. But the pungent air was also energized and the sounds of bat meeting ball and ball plunging into mitt indicated that this was no ordinary day. Remember, this was a time when baseball ruled the sporting scene in America, and baseball didn't get any better than this—two teams engaged in a fierce fight for the pennant, meeting head-to-head twice on a warm, mostly cloudless, late season afternoon in the Bronx. I get goose bumps today just thinking of it.

In the first game, the Yankees' George Pipgras—he in the midst of his greatest season—squared off with Philadelphia's Jack Quinn. A pitchers' duel developed, with neither in a spot of trouble until the Yankees broke through in the sixth with four hits and a walk resulting in three runs.

Pipgras allowed a Jimmy Dykes double in the seventh, but Dykes advanced no further, and then in the Athletics' eighth, a single and two walks loaded the bases with two out, setting the stage for Pipgras's dramatic strikeout of Jimmie Foxx, the overflow crowd erupting as Foxx swung and missed at the last pitch. Clearly fired up, the Yankees tacked on two more runs in the bottom of the inning for a 5-0 final.

New York was back in first place, however precariously, and now it was time to choke the life out of the Athletics. In the first inning of the nightcap, Combs led off with a triple against Philadelphia starter Rube Walberg and he scored moments later on Mark Koenig's grounder to short.

Unsung Fred Heimach drew the start for the Yankees, one of only nine he would make in 1928, and he permitted one hit through four innings. Singles by Dykes and Joe Boley created a stir in the fifth as they wound up at second and third with two outs before Heimach slipped one past Mule Haas on a 3-2 count to end the threat and the masses rose to salute the Yankee left-hander.

Undaunted, the Athletics battled back as Al Simmons ripped a two-run homer to right in the sixth, then increased their lead to 3-1 in the seventh when Simmons knocked Heimach out by delivering a RBI single after a Lazzeri error had kept the rally alive. Knowing a split would do the team no good, Ruth bounded into the dugout after Wilcy Moore struck out Foxx to end the seventh and profanely instructed his team-mates to "get this bum," referring to Walberg.

Though not a Hall of Famer, Walberg was not at all a bum, as 155 career victories would attest. Nonetheless, the Yankees did indeed get him in their half of the seventh, scoring twice to tie it at 3-3. Waite Hoyt, on in relief of Moore, set the Athletics down peacefully in the eighth, and then it was time for five o'clock lightning, though because this was the second game of the day, it was closer to six o'clock. Koenig led off with a single, Gehrig laced Eddie Rommel's next pitch to right-center for a double, and Ruth was walked intentionally, bringing Meusel to the plate with the bases loaded and nobody out. Throughout the at-bat the stadium was rocking as the fans seemed to sense something big was about to happen. Rommel worked the count full, then laid the payoff pitch right down the middle and the mighty Meusel—so often overlooked in the wake of Ruth and Gehrig—deposited it into the left-field stands for a grand slam which touched off a riotous celebration.

Ruth greeted Meusel at home with a massive bear hug, and the delirious fans hurled hundreds of straw hats, felts, and fedoras onto the field, most of which Eddie Bennett and I were responsible for picking up. I wasn't always a fan of cleaning my bedroom, but I sure didn't mind picking up this mess at the stadium. There was bedlam all around as the Yankees were now ahead 7-3, and for all intents and purposes, the game, and the pennant race, were over.

For Meusel, it was a well-deserved moment in the sun. He had broken in with the Yankees in 1920, Ruth's first year with the club, and despite outstanding numbers, Meusel languished in Ruth's lengthy shadow his entire career. Meusel was a superb player, surely capable of being the primary star if he had played on most any other team. He was blessed with a rocket for a throwing arm and a sweet batting stroke that produced 156 homers, 1,067 RBI and a .309 career average.

I never felt particularly close to Bob, though. He was a very private person, distant almost. He rarely spoke to the writers and when he did, he offered little in the way of color. In fact, his aloofness was often mis-interpreted by his own teammates, and Miller Huggins even said one time, "His attitude is just plain indifference." But Meusel didn't need to be boisterous to make his point because his consistent performance spoke volumes.

In the field, opposing base runners feared taking the extra base against him. "Meusel could hit a dime at 100 yards and flatten it against a wall," Joe Dugan once said. And Casey Stengel, who played against Meusel in two World Series, said, "I never saw a better thrower. He had lightning on the ball."

As he skipped into the clubhouse after Hoyt dispatched Philadel-phia in order in the ninth to complete the sweep, Meusel did his best to share some insight into how he became the hero of the day. "I hit a curve ball and it was about as fast as he could throw," Meusel said with a wide smile. It wasn't much, but it would have to do.

Naturally, Ruth rescued the scribes who were in need of a juicy quote and as they crowded around his locker he bellowed, "The same old A's, the same old A's. We broke their hearts today. And we gave that greatest crowd in baseball history some real baseball."

Of New York's 15th win over the Athletics in 20 meetings to date, Huggins said: "We ought to play them every day. Things would be easier then. They were two great games to win, but beyond that I won't say a word. The season isn't over yet."

Oh, but it was. The Yankees never trailed in the race again and they clinched the pennant two weeks later.

Ruth had another monster season. After hitting 60 home runs the year before, his 54 seemed almost unacceptable until you realized that the second-place home run hitter in the league was Gehrig at 27. Ruth alone outhomered seven major-league teams, and Ruth and Gehrig com-bined outhomered 10 teams.

The Yankees won nine fewer games than in 1927, and they were pushed to the limit by the Athletics, but while they weren't as good as they had been in '27, they were still pretty damned good, as the Cardi-nals found out.

– *1928 World Series* –

One of the funniest sights I've ever witnessed was Miller Huggins, on the morning after the Yankees won their second straight World Se-ries in a clean four-game sweep over the Cardinals, stumbling around a

Pullman car topless and toothless, his eyes glazed over from a night of uncharacteristic hard drinking.

"Have you seen my teeth?" he asked me as well as a few others in the traveling party. Seems he had misplaced his false teeth sometime during the victory celebration and hadn't been able to locate them.

Unlike many of his players, Huggins was not a drinking man. A bad digestive tract made it difficult for him to process booze, and he knew it, so he stayed clear of liquor. But no one—that is anyone who wasn't underaged like me—stayed clear of the spirits that were flowing freely on the train ride back from St. Louis. Because I was 12 years old I was afforded a sober view of the madness, and it is my opinion that no team has ever celebrated a world championship quite like this bunch of Yankees in 1928.

"When you win two straight World Series without the loss of a game, it calls for something special," Babe Ruth once wrote in one of the books chronicling his life.

Coming off their boundless success in 1927, there was a certain amount of pressure on the Yankees in 1928. With a lineup that was virtually unchanged, they were supposed to run roughshod over the American League and devour anyone the National League would throw at them in the Series. However, the last three months of the regular season had been difficult and their struggle with the Athletics took a lot out of the team. It was somewhat surprising that they handled St. Louis so easily in the Series, but their desire to gain revenge from the 1926 Series loss served as a tremendous motivation and they seemed to forget their pain and struggles from the season long enough to embarrass the Cardinals.

So when it was through, and the Yankees were able to take their place among the all-time great teams by winning a second straight championship, every ounce of pressure that had built up came screaming out during the overnight ride back to New York.

"By midnight we were as crazy as a bunch of wild Indians," said Ruth, long before the term "political correctness" was born.

The Yankees drank, and they ate, and they drank some more. Then they drank a little more and finally, they drank a lot more. During the course of the night the players formed a single-file line and paraded throughout the entire train demanding male passengers relinquish their shirts or pajama tops and soon the majority of the men on board were topless. When they arrived at the berth of Colonel Ruppert, they found his door locked, so Ruth and Lou Gehrig began pounding until the colonel said, "Go away Ruth!" Ruth's reply was, "This is no night for sleeping," and on the count of three, he and Gehrig slammed their shoulders into the door, broke it off the hinges and tumbled into the room. Ruth left with Ruppert's lavender-colored pajama top and Ruppert asking him "Is this normal?"

Every time the train pulled into a station, be it in Indiana, Illinois, Ohio, or New York, crowds that had been notified by telegraph that the Yankees were coming would gather in the hope that they would catch a glimpse of Ruth. He never disappointed as he would step onto the platform and raise his beer and bask in the cheers.

The next morning, bodies were strewn everywhere, reeking of beer and whiskey and cigar smoke. The colonel came out to survey the damage that he would have to pay for, saw that I had awakened, and asked me if I'd seen his pajama top. When I said no, he enlisted my help in finding it, and after a few minutes, we located it tucked under Waite Hoyt's head as he lay sound asleep on the floor.

* * *

Hoyt was a notorious partier and was often a companion of Ruth's on his many drinking binges. Though he had changed his ways ever so slightly after a disastrous 1925 season during which he saw his record drop to 11-14, Hoyt was an able and ready participant in the train ride shenanigans.

And he deserved to go on a bender because he was one of the prime reasons why the Yankees were celebrating another world championship. He pitched two complete game victories including the clincher earlier in the day, a 7-3 triumph at Sportsman's Park.

Hoyt uttered one of the all-time great quotes when he recalled his Yankee career by saying, "In the daytime you sat in the dugout and talked about women, in the nighttime you went out with women and talked about baseball. Small wonder—it's great to be young and a Yankee."

I can tell you it was great that Hoyt was a Yankee.

He had been a high school phenom in Brooklyn and by the time he was 15, he had thrown three no-hitters and was pitching batting practice for John McGraw's Giants at the Polo Grounds. Always brazen, Hoyt asked for compensation and McGraw responded by signing him to a contract which made him one of the youngest pros in history.

He bounced around the minor leagues for a few years, then made his major league debut in 1918 and struck out two of the three batters he faced, yet McGraw was not impressed and he traded him to Rochester.

Hoyt, tired of toiling in the minors, refused to report and signed with a semipro team in Baltimore before eventually joining the Boston Red Sox, where he pitched adequately for two seasons. Fortunately for Hoyt he was in Boston during the period when Red Sox owner Harry Frazee was in the practice of selling or trading his best players to the Yankees, and in the decade following Hoyt's swap of red socks for Yankee pinstripes, he became New York's most reliable pitcher.

"He had a good arm, meaning speed and stuff, a smart head which meant control and pitching know-how, and he had guts," scout Paul Krichell once said of Hoyt.

Upon retirement Hoyt became a baseball broadcaster for the Cincinnati Reds and was nearly as accomplished in that field, drawing praise from former Giants play-by-play man Russ Hodges who said, "Waite Hoyt is authoritative. When he makes a statement there is no doubt as to its accuracy. When Hoyt says it's so, the Cincinnati public goes by what he says."

*   *   *

Figuratively what Hoyt said to the Cardinals in 1928 is "Here's my best, and you're not going to touch it."

The Yankees were a battered team entering the Series as Pennock was sidelined by a sore arm, Earle Combs was out with a broken finger, Tony Lazzeri was bothered by a bad arm, Dugan was slowed by a wrist injury, and Ruth had a sprained ankle. None of this mattered because Hoyt was brilliant in Games One and Four, and Ruth and Gehrig were a tag-team wrecking crew combining for seven homers and 13 RBI in the four games.

In Game One, Hoyt handcuffed the Cardinals on three hits, one a Jim Bottomley home run in the seventh. "Waite Hoyt pitched a marvelous game, there was nothing we could do about it," said Cardinals manager Bill McKechnie. "He was just in there and right, and that's all there was to it. Bill Sherdel pitched a great game, too, and his own brand of hurling would have won nine out of ten."

Perhaps, but this was the one he didn't win. In the first inning Ruth and Gehrig hit back-to-back doubles for one run, Ruth doubled in the fourth and scored in front of Bob Meusel's two-run homer, and Gehrig's RBI single in the eighth wrapped up a 4-1 victory.

"Looks like the cripples did pretty well," Ruth said afterward, poking fun at the pundits who said the Yankees, in their banged-up state, would struggle against the Cardinals. "We'll do it some more. Four games is enough to win this Series."

McKechnie disagreed, saying, "Don't think this Series is on the chutes, though. The Yanks won the first game of the 1926 Series, too, but the Cardinals won the championship. Pete Alexander will be in there tomorrow and it will be another story."

Oh, it was a different story all right. Unlike 1926 when Alexander beat the Yankees twice, then saved the seventh game in dramatic fashion, the now 41-year-old star was battered by a New York team hell-bent on paying him back.

In the clubhouse before the game the Yankees were clearly enlivened by the prospect of facing Alexander. They had grown quite tired of hearing about his heroic performance against them in 1926, and they had targeted this as the day they would get even. Ruth called me over because he needed his shoes buffed, and he told me, "Joey, the old guy's gonna be outta there quick." His confidence was legendary, but what made Ruth the rarest of athletes is that he could back up that confidence just about every time.

Within three innings Alexander was in the showers as the Yankees scored eight times on their way to an easy 9-3 victory and a two-game lead. "Just wasn't going today," Alexander said. "But I still don't understand it. Two years ago that same gang got four hits off me. I pitched them exactly the same balls in the same places and they knocked me out of the box."

The carnage began early, just as Ruth predicted, when Gehrig cracked a three-run homer in the first inning. "That ball Gehrig hit into the right-field stands was exactly the kind of a pitch he couldn't touch the year we beat them for the championship," said Alexander. "I threw him a screwball low on the outside corner. It went exactly where I wanted it to go; I couldn't have asked for anything better, and he hit it into the bleachers."

The Cardinals tied it in the second against George Pipgras, but the Yankees blew it open with a run in the bottom of the second and four more in the third.

"It's a cinch," Ruth reiterated.

The Cardinals were hoping a return to Sportsman's Park would spark them, but Tom Zachary—the same guy who had yielded Ruth's 60th home run a year earlier— pitched New York's third straight complete game, scattering nine hits during a 7-3 triumph. New York fell behind 2-0 on Jim Bottomley's two-run triple, but Gehrig hit a solo homer in the second and a two-run inside-the-park homer in the fourth. After the Cardinals pulled even in the fifth, the Yankees broke away with three runs in the sixth.

With a sweep in sight, Huggins gave the ball to his ace, Hoyt, and though he wasn't as sharp as he'd been in the opener, he didn't need to be. He gave up 11 hits and was trailing 2-1 after six, but Ruth—who had already homered in the fourth inning and would do so again in the eighth—launched one over the right-field pavilion to tie the game in the seventh, providing this Series with its most memorable moment.

McKechnie had tapped Sherdel to oppose Hoyt again, and the little lefty was battling gamely. With one out in the seventh he threw two slow balls past Ruth, who never lifted the bat off his shoulder. After the second strike was returned to him by catcher Earl Smith, Sherdel fired in a fastball that caught Ruth by surprise and was thought to be strike three. However, umpire Charley Pfirman ruled that Sherdel had quick-pitched Ruth, a tactic that was legal in the National League during the regular season, but had been banned for the Series on a suggestion made by St. Louis' own Frankie Frisch.

As soon as Sherdel threw the ball, Ruth complained, and the umpire did not hesitate in ruling it an illegal pitch. The Cardinals erupted in anger as McKechnie and Frisch rushed in to confront Pfirman, but they lost their argument and Ruth stepped back into the box as he exchanged obscenities with Sherdel. Sitting in the dugout, I could hear Ruth telling Sherdel to "Throw it over and I'll knock it out of the park." Once again, Ruth being Ruth, Sherdel threw it over and Babe knocked it out of the park for a game-tying home run. Frazzled by that turn of events, two pitches later Sherdel was watching another home run—this one by Gehrig—sailing over the pavilion in right that put the Yankees ahead for good.

The last out was a Frisch fly ball that drifted into foul territory in left field where temporary box seating had been erected. Ruth had switched positions with Meusel because he was uncomfortable glaring into the right-field sun, so it was left for him to make the catch. He waded in amongst the spectators and despite having programs swung at him, he reached above their heads and arms and plucked the ball out of the air, then trotted off the field laughing and holding the ball aloft for all to see.

"Say, wasn't that a pip?" he said of the catch.

Ruth hit a Series record .625 while Gehrig weighed in with an average of .545. They combined for 16 of the Yankees' 37 hits, 41 of their 71 total bases, scored 14 of the 27 runs, and had 13 of the 25 RBI.

They were truly a dynamic 1-2 punch, the best there's ever been in baseball in my opinion. And as we whisked home from St. Louis later that evening on that wild party train, I would have bet this Yankee outfit was going to just keep winning World Series championships until the day Ruth and/or Gehrig decided to quit playing.

Fortunately, I was never a bettor.

The euphoria over the back-to-back World Series titles wore off rather quickly for me, and for the rest of the Yankees. Quite simply, 1929 was not a good year, and the Yankees' failure to secure a fourth straight pennant and third straight world championship was the least of the woes. First, there was my broken leg. A week later, the Babe's first wife, Helen, died in a fire at their Massachusetts home. And in September, about a month before the stock market crashed and plunged the country into the Great Depression, Miller Huggins died of a blood disorder at the age of 50.

Huggins hadn't been feeling well in the weeks before his death, and I even remarked to my father that "Mr. Huggins looks like he's sick." Everyone noticed the red spot under his eye, and I was in the training room one day when Pete Sheehy—who in 1927 had begun what became a 60-year career as the Yankees clubhouse man—told Huggins he should go to see a doctor. Huggins, who admittedly had been feeling rundown, replied, "Me, who took the spikes of Frank Chance and Fred Clarke, see a doctor just because of a little blotch on my face?" He never went. A couple weeks later, he died.

My recollections of Huggins were that he was a modest man which explained one of his famous quotes—"Great players make great managers." He had his rhubarbs with old Cap Huston who wanted him fired after the 1922 Series loss to the Giants, but he was Jacob Ruppert's man and the Colonel stuck by him. And Huggins always battled with Ruth, once suspending and fining him in 1925. But in my mind what he should best be remembered for is that he inherited a mediocre Yankee team in 1918 and turned it into a winner, charting a course for more than three-quarters of a century of excellence. As Joe McCarthy said of Huggins, "This is the man who cut the Yankee pennant pattern."

Connie Mack had rebuilt his Philadelphia Athletics into an awesome powerhouse and they won three consecutive pennants from 1929 to 1931. The closest the Yankees came to challenging was in 1931 when they finished 13 1/2 games back. That was the year McCarthy came to New York and it wasn't long after McCarthy's managerial term began—which by the way is the longest in team history at 15 1/2 years—that we all knew the Yankees were going to become regular participants in the Series.

No less than Mack once dubbed McCarthy "the greatest manager of all" and Marse Joe's winning percentage of .627 with eight American League pennants and seven World Series championships in New York would certainly back up that bold proclamation.

Ruth wasn't enamored originally with the choice of McCarthy, mainly because he wanted to become player/manager of the club, but was twice denied by Ruppert. Babe was in Dad's shop one day after the McCarthy hiring was announced, and he told my father that McCarthy was "a weak-hitting busher." McCarthy had toiled in the minor leagues for 15 years and never made it to the majors, and Ruth remembered pitching against him in the International League. Ruth and a few other Yankees were also leery of McCarthy because he had cut his managerial teeth in the rival National League with the Cubs. Furthermore, while he inherited a last-place team in 1926 and won the National League pennant by 1929, he hadn't won the big one because Chicago lost to the Athletics in the World Series.

The Yankees went 94-59 in McCarthy's first year and he quickly gained the respect of the players, even, to a degree, Ruth. There was nothing the team could do about the Athletics who won 107 times that season, but in 1932 the roles were reversed as the Yankees won 107, the Athletics 94. The Yankees were back in the Series, and as fate would have it, they were opposite McCarthy's old Cubs, who won the National League.

– Chapter 4 –

1932

I KNEW IT WAS SLIPPERY, and more than 70 years later it still upsets me that I wasn't more careful on that cold January day in 1929. The cement steps in front of St. Jerome's grammar school were always slick whenever snow was falling and as I began my descent that day after school was dismissed, I did so cautiously. As it turned out, I was not cautious enough because I still lost my footing and plummeted down to the sidewalk. About halfway through my tumble my left leg got caught under my body and I screamed in agony as my tibia snapped and protruded through my skin. After initially mocking me as they watched me fall, my friends quickly realized it was no laughing matter and ran for help. Little did I know as I lay there crying that my dreams of pursuing a baseball career were shattered as badly as my leg.

I was transported by ambulance to Bronx Hospital, and for the next nine days I had to lie in an uncomfortable bed with my casted leg elevated, a throbbing pain my constant companion. There were no television or handheld video games in those days, so I spent the time sleeping, reading, or talking to my roommates or my mother, who spent just about every moment she could at my side. It was not the most memorable of experiences, until, of course, the Yankees came to the rescue one afternoon when Babe Ruth, Lou Gehrig, and Waite Hoyt visited me.

Dad and I had forged a lasting relationship with Ruth, but during my first two years as a Yankee batboy I had become close to many of the other players as well. There's a fellowship that exists inside a big-league clubhouse, and it extends beyond the players to everyone who works for the team, even the little guys like me. Most of the players were twice my age, but that didn't prevent them from including me in their conversations, their disagreements, their pranks. No one could ever replace my father, a man whose love and support and guidance influenced my entire life, but being part of the Yankee family was like having 25 big brothers.

I assumed that brotherhood was confined to the baseball season, though. Once the season ended, the players went their separate ways and I never expected to be in contact with anyone except our good friend, the Babe, until the following spring. So you can imagine my surprise that day when Ruth, Gehrig, and Hoyt—three of the greatest major league ballplayers of their era—took the time during their off-season to visit me at the Bronx Hospital. Needless to say I got plenty of mileage out of that story with my friends.

They spent a half-hour in the room I was sharing with three other boys who were in varying degrees of illness or pain. They awed us with their presence, made us laugh with their hijinks, thrilled us with the baseballs they signed and presented to us, and when they said good-bye they toured the rest of the children's ward and brought unbridled smiles to countless other young faces.

It wasn't long after their departure before word got around that I was a Yankee batboy, and over the last three days of my stay, my room became a veritable tourist attraction as children of all ages flocked in, begging me to tell them stories about the Yankees.

The last full day I was there, I received another famous visitor, this time the manager of the Yankees, Miller Huggins. His was a quieter appearance, creating almost no commotion, but it meant just as much to me. Huggins was a caring man and when he'd heard that I was laid up, he said he just wanted to come down and see how I was doing. He stayed more than an hour, and we talked mostly about the upcoming 1929 season. When he left, he said, "I'll see ya in April."

Actually, he didn't see much of me in April, or for most of the season. My leg was slow to heal and the pain was so great that on many days I couldn't walk. If you can't walk, it's awfully tough to serve as a batboy, so while I was only able to work occasionally, Eddie Bennett flew solo for much of that year.

Not being with the team full-time was terrible for me. On the days I was able to get around, being in that clubhouse was like being in heaven. The other days, the ones where I had to sit at home while a block away a ballgame was being played, I was miserable.

I had a stretch in early September when I was feeling well enough to work and as I was picking up laundry following a game, I happened to notice Huggins in his cramped office struggling to get out of his chair. He looked dizzy and weak, and when he finally made it to his feet, he deduced that sitting was a better option. He then put his head down on his desk and stayed in that position for about five minutes. I opted not to bother him, but I did relay what I saw to Doc Painter, the team's trainer.

The next day Huggins was getting a rubdown from Painter when Pete Sheehy told him he should see a doctor, but Huggins just shrugged him off and no one really gave the manager's health another thought. We figured if he said he was all right, then he was all right.

About 10 days later, I was the one seeing the doctor as my leg swelled to grotesque proportions and I was rushed to the hospital. We had assumed the pain I had been feeling the previous few months was just the natural healing process, but tests revealed that osteomyelitis had settled in and I was transferred over to St. Vincent's Hospital where they were better prepared to treat the condition.

I spent another week in a hospital bed, dealing not only with the pain in my leg, but with the realization that I probably would never be able to play organized baseball again. It was during that week when Huggins was admitted to St. Vincent's in serious condition suffering from erysipelas, a strep infection of the skin that dissolves red blood corpuscles. Despite three blood transfusions, Huggins died a few days later, two floors above my room.

Two days before his death, Ed Barrow learned that I, too, was in the hospital and he came down to my room to say hello. He asked permission from the nurses to let me visit Huggins, thinking maybe "the little guy" could cheer up the manager, and they obliged, so Barrow pushed me in a wheelchair down the hall, loaded me onto the elevator and brought me up to Huggins's room.

I had never experienced death in my family, but when I saw Huggins that day, I knew death was imminent. He looked terrible, and my own pain disintegrated as I looked at this frail little man losing his battle with mortality. He managed a smile, asked me how I was doing, and then sort of turned his head, too tired to say anything more. As Barrow returned me to my room, he insisted I'd been a great help in boosting Huggins's spirits, but I didn't believe him. I was deeply saddened, but not at all surprised, when news came that Huggins had passed.

Art Fletcher, who had been Huggins's assistant coach since 1927, managed the last 11 games of 1929, then Bob Shawkey was named manager for the 1930 season. Shawkey had retired as a player following a season in the minors in 1928 and had served as Huggins's pitching coach during 1929. Though Ruth campaigned heavily to become Huggins's successor, Colonel Ruppert literally laughed in his face, saying he couldn't take care of himself let alone an entire ballclub.

Ruth was deeply angered and he held out briefly before spring training in 1930, then changed his outlook and enjoyed a terrific season with 49 homers and 153 RBI, but the Athletics were again superior and the Yankees finished 16 games back in third place. Because Shawkey had been a teammate of many of these Yankees, Ruppert surmised that his easygoing style just wasn't going to work with this club. He fired Shawkey, who never managed in the big leagues thereafter, and shunning Ruth again, chose Joe McCarthy as his new skipper.

* * *

After the rollicking years under Huggins, working for McCarthy took a little getting used to. He was a no-nonsense guy and his rules were to be followed to the letter. The players had to wear jackets and ties on the road, and if they weren't in the hotel dining room for breakfast by 8:30 A.M. there was hell to pay. He would always arrive first, sipping his coffee and reading a newspaper, and he would watch each player come in. He knew if they'd been out late the night before just by looking at them, and when they were called on it, none of the players had the nerve to lie because they figured he'd find out anyway.

In the clubhouse, there was no need for me to help Ruth cheat at cards because McCarthy had the card table removed. He also banned shaving in the clubhouse because he expected the Yankees—like bankers or shop owners—to arrive at work already clean-shaven. "This is a clubhouse, not a club room," he said.

Pete Sheehy's orders were clear. Things were to be neat and orderly in the clubhouse, and the players' uniforms were to be washed every night, no excuses. He wanted the Yankees dressed in clean, crisp uniforms for every game. As for Eddie Bennett and me, the bats had better be lined up properly on the rack, the balls in bags, and the equipment cleaned or we were out on the street.

Discipline was one of the keys to McCarthy's success. His rationale was disciplined ballplayers did not make the types of mistakes that could lose games, and that discipline had to start off the field. "I think a lot of the Yankees' success in those days was due to McCarthy's leadership," Lefty Gomez once said. "He was a tough guy, but he really knew the game. He was always trying to be perfect in everything, on and off the field."

One incident that sticks out in my mind occurred sometime around 1943, I believe. I had gone out to dinner one night in Boston with one of my sportswriting buddies, Dick Young, and we were returning to the Copley Plaza Hotel. A group of players were sitting and chatting on the marble staircase when McCarthy came into the lobby. He walked over and said, "Are these the world champion Yankees sitting on the steps?" Without saying a word, they all got up and sat in chairs. The man was always in control.

He was also a master psychologist. He consistently brought out the best in his players because he knew their strengths and weaknesses, and he knew just when to get on a player or back off.

Earle Combs once told me a story from his minor league days when McCarthy was his manager in Louisville. Combs had never played center field, but McCarthy thought his excellent speed would be ideal for the position. In his first game he made three errors and he figured his career was over. "McCarthy came over after the game and said, 'Look, if I didn't think you belonged in center field, I wouldn't put you there, and I'm going to keep you there,'" Combs recalled. Combs went on to become a Hall of Fame player for the Yankees and he said of that conversation he had with McCarthy, "I think I can say that from that minute on I was a ballplayer."

Ruth was diametrically opposed to McCarthy's hiring, and McCarthy knew it. But he also knew that Ruth was a superstar, the toast of New York, the toast of the country, and he could not afford to get into a popularity contest with him. "He was an institution in himself," McCarthy said of Ruth many years after he retired from baseball. "I tried to treat him accordingly. It would have been silly to curb him in any way." So McCarthy largely ignored Ruth's eccentricities, he rarely spoke to Ruth once a game was over, and he built solid relationships with Gehrig and Bill Dickey, the other leaders of the team.

There was rough sledding for a while in 1931 as Ruth had managed to convince some of the players that McCarthy was a bum. But gradually the Yankees came to realize that McCarthy was an astute manager who could lead this team back to the top of the baseball world, and that's exactly what he did.

* * *

The 1932 club was still led by the nucleus of Ruth, Gehrig, Tony
Lazzeri, and Combs, but some important fortifications were also in place.
Dickey was now a mainstay behind the plate, well on his way to becoming one of the greatest catchers in history; Frank Crosetti debuted at
shortstop; future Hall of Famer Joe Sewell was in his second season at
third base after 11 standout years with Cleveland; and the pitching staff
was led by 24-game winner Gomez and Red Ruffing and aided by Johnny
Allen, George Pipgras, and the ageless Herb Pennock.

The Yankees won seven of their first 10 games even though Ruth
missed some time in the first week due to a respiratory problem, and by
June 3, when Gehrig became the first player in the twentieth century to
hit four home runs in one game during a 20-13 pasting of the Athletics,
it was clear that the tables were turned again and New York was superior to Philadelphia.

They had to play most of July without Dickey after the mild-mannered catcher lost his cool and broke the jaw of Washington's Carl
Reynolds during a fight following a rough play at the plate. Dickey drew a
30-day suspension and a $1,000 fine, yet with Dickey simmering on the
sidelines, the Yankees' lead swelled to nine games by the middle of the
month, and the only race the Athletics were going to win was the individual home run title. For the first time since 1922, a player who was not a
Yankee won the American League home run crown as Jimmie Foxx belted
58 for Philadelphia. Ruth had won eight of the previous nine (he tied in
1931 with Gehrig) and Bob Meusel had won the 1925 title, the year Ruth
missed the first portion of the season because of a stomach ailment.

Late in the season Ruth was diagnosed with appendicitis and he sat
out a few games, but it was not an emergency situation, and he returned
a week before the season ended to hone his batting stroke in time for
the Series against McCarthy's old team, the Cubs.

– 1932 *World Series* –

It is one of the most famous moments in World Series history, and it
certainly is the most disputed famous moment in World Series history.
So, did Babe Ruth really call his shot on the afternoon of October 1 during Game Three at Wrigley Field against the Cubs? I was sitting in my
customary spot next to the Yankee dugout, and he called his shot all
right, but he did it privately to me, and no one else.

This Series was a bitter grudge match for two reasons. First,
McCarthy was returning to Chicago where he'd been fired, and revenge

was on his mind. Cubs owner William Wrigley wasn't satisfied with the 1929 pennant McCarthy had won because the Cubs went on to lose the Series to the Athletics. So late in 1930, when it was apparent the Cubs weren't going to repeat in the National League, Wrigley fired McCarthy in favor of Rogers Hornsby because, as Wrigley said, he wanted "somebody who can get me a world championship." In his pre-Series meeting with his Yankees, McCarthy told them to "kill" the Cubs.

Second, the Yankees were perturbed at the Cubs for voting their former teammate, Mark Koenig, a mere half-share of the Series prize money. Koenig had left the Yankees following the 1930 season, played a year and a half in Detroit, then joined the Cubs in August 1932 and proceeded to play a key role in their surge to the pennant. He'd been a popular player in the Yankee clubhouse and still had many friends on the team, so when the Yankees found out the Cubs were slighting him monetarily, they verbally accosted the Cubs, Ruth leading the way.

"Hi Mark, who are those cheapskate nickel-nursing sons-a-bitches you're with," he said during the workout before Game One. Other Yankees joined the act, the Cubs counter-cussed, and the war of words was vicious during the first two games in New York, both of which the Yankees won. It then grew to outlandish heights during Game Three, prompting baseball commissioner Kenesaw Mountain Landis to warn both teams that if the foul language did not cease during Game Four, there would be heavy fines.

Having worked for the ballclub for six years now, I thought I had heard it all, but I was wrong. This was mean-spirited, and the fans got involved as well, throwing fruit at the Yankees during both games that were played in Chicago. When I got back to New York and shared some of the stories with my family, my mother was none too thrilled that her son had been "exposed to that kind of foul behavior."

"I'd never known there was so many cuss words in the language or so many ways of stringing them together," said Joe Sewell. Cubs' second baseman Billy Herman agreed, saying, "What were jokes in the first game became personal insults by the third game. By the middle of that third game things were really hot."

Ruth had already hit a three-run homer in the first inning of Game Three off Charlie Root, but the Cubs had rallied to tie it at 4-4 in the fourth and they and their fans were really chirping when the Yankees came to bat in the fifth.

As he stood in the on-deck circle while Sewell was leading off the inning, Ruth, tired of the venomous bench jockeying, turned around and said to me, "Joey, I'm sick of this shit. I'm gonna go up there and show 'em where I'm gonna knock the goddamn ball out of the park." I said something like, "Ok, Babe, go get 'em." I was 16 years old now, not the naïve kid I'd been when I first put on the Yankee pinstripes in 1927. I really didn't think he'd have the audacity to stand in the batter's box and point to where he was going to hit a home run, and, contrary to six decades of debate, he didn't.

This is what happened. After Sewell grounded out, the fans roared their disapproval as Ruth stepped up to the plate. He just listened to the noise, smiled, and stared out at Root. Root's first pitch was a called strike and the Cubs' bench really tore into Ruth, so Ruth responded by holding up one finger as if to say "that's one." Root threw two balls, then came in with another strike and Ruth—who hadn't yet swung—held up two fingers and yelled to Root, "Throw it in there and I'll knock it down your goddamn throat." He also muttered to Cubs catcher Gabby Hartnett, "It only takes one to hit."

This is where the confusion starts. On a recent home movie that has been unearthed, you can see Ruth raising his arm, and everyone who claimed he called his shot said he was pointing to the center-field bleachers in that moment. He wasn't. He was motioning at the Cubs bench, mockingly dismissing their taunting.

Root then delivered his fifth pitch and Ruth swung with all his might and launched a home run exactly where everyone thought he had pointed, and thus was born the myth. I almost fell out of my chair because only I knew that he had predicted he was going to "hit the goddamn ball out of the ballpark." After he touched home plate to complete what turned out to be his 15th and final World Series home run trot, on the way back to the dugout he winked at me and said, "I told you, kid."

Sewell, who'd only been a teammate of Ruth's for two years, was astonished by the display. "He rubbed his hands, looking square into the dugout, and what was coming out of there was just turning the air blue," Sewell recalled. "The ball was just above Ruth's knee, a good pitch, a strike. Babe uncoiled one of those beautiful swings. I can still see that ball going out of Wrigley Field. He called it. He probably couldn't have done it again in a thousand years, but he did it that time."

Well, he really didn't, but Sewell—like so many other players, writers and fans—was caught up in the moment, and you couldn't blame him or anyone else.

"Naturally the writers made something that wasn't," Frank Crosetti said to me years later when he was a Yankee coach, I was on the beat covering the team, and the subject of the called shot came up in a casual conversation. "And (Ruth's) reaction was 'If the writers want to think I pointed, let them, I don't care.'"

Besides, as the Cubs' Herman correctly pointed out, "If he'd pointed, do you think Root would've thrown him a strike to hit? I'll tell you what he would've done. Ruth would've been sitting in the dirt, maybe rubbing himself where it hurt."

Prior to the first game, Chicago player/manager Charlie Grimm boldly said, "We're going to win. We expect a real battle, but whether it's five, six, or seven games, I feel that we'll win."

It was a ridiculous statement, and the Yankees proved that with a Series-opening 12-6 rout. The Cubs scored two in the first inning aided by a Ruth error, and their pitcher, Guy Bush, retired the first nine New York batters in order. But in the fourth, Ruth hit a RBI single and trotted home on Gehrig's two-run homer for a 3-2 lead, and then the Yankees erupted for five runs in the sixth and it was over.

"Today's game wasn't any classic, but if you win it's all right," said McCarthy. "Our boys delivered when they had to."

After the press left, I went into McCarthy's office to collect his uniform and as I was walking out, Colonel Ruppert peeked his head in and said, "Make it four straight." McCarthy winked and said, "We'll sure try."

Grimm promised that his club would be better prepared for the second game and the Cubs were, but it didn't matter because Lefty Gomez pitched a neat complete game and Ben Chapman came through with a go-ahead two-run single in the third to lift the Yankees to a 5-2 victory. "One of the greatest pitchers I ever saw," said Grimm, who managed two of Chicago's nine hits off Gomez. "He bests Lefty Grove with me. Today he was as fast as Grove and what control. There's no other answer to that one. Too much Gomez."

We packed up the clubhouse quickly because our train was leaving 90 minutes after the last out was recorded. All the way out to Chicago the mood was light because the Yankees fully expected to make short work of the Cubs. What they didn't expect was the greeting they received upon arriving in the Windy City the next morning. Word of the nasty tone set in the first two games had been widely reported in the Chicago newspapers, and a huge throng of fans came to the LaSalle Street train station to "welcome" the Yankees. A police escort was needed for the team to get through the mob.

There were hundreds more Cubs fans at the Edgewater Beach Hotel waiting for the Yankees, too, and more vituperation was spewed, not to mention saliva. Fans actually spit at the players, and Ruth's second wife, Claire, caught a healthy dose of it, infuriating the Babe. I was a little scared, and I made sure I stayed as far away from the Ruths as possible. Once we were safely into the lobby, everything calmed down and the players found refuge in their rooms for a few hours before they had to go over to Wrigley Field for their workout.

When the practice session was over, McCarthy held a team meeting. He told the players, "Take it in stride boys. We're out here for a couple of ball games, maybe three. Don't get excited. Just imagine you're down on the South side getting ready for a series with the White Sox. There isn't any pressure. All we've got to do is go out and play our regular everyday game."

With that, the players cheered, and when they returned the next day for Game Three, they were focused on the task at hand. It was a warm, sunny and windy day in Chicago and after Gomez ate breakfast at the Edgewater he walked outside and felt the stiff breeze. When he learned it would be gusting out toward right field at the ballpark, he came back into the restaurant and exaggerated, "The wind's blowing 60 miles an hour . . . Babe and Lou ought to hit a dozen."

They didn't hit a dozen, but they hit four during the 7-5 victory.

In the top of the first, Combs reached base when shortstop Billy Jurges fielded his game-starting grounder and threw it into the Yankee dugout. Sewell walked, and Ruth sauntered up to the plate with a cacophony of catcalls ringing in his ears. All was quiet, though, when he pounded a 2-0 pitch from Root into the right-field seats for a three-run homer.

Gehrig homered in the third inning to give New York a 4-1 lead before the Cubs lit up George Pipgras for two runs in the third and one in the fourth to tie the score. The fateful fifth inning began with Sewell's groundout, then Ruth delivered his prodigious home run. "As I hit the ball, every muscle in my system, every sense I had, told me that I had never hit a better one, that as long as I lived nothing would ever feel as good as this," Ruth said.

On his home run trot, Ruth had words with Grimm as he passed first, Herman at second, and Jurges at short, and then he clasped his hands over his head like a winning prize fighter as he rounded third and trotted home where Gehrig wore a wide grin as he shook Babe's hand. After Ruth winked at me, he shot a glance over to the man sitting just behind the dugout who'd thrown out the ceremonial first pitch, Franklin

D. Roosevelt, the governor of New York who in a few weeks would be elected President of the United States.

Perhaps stunned by Ruth's homer, Root grooved his next pitch and Gehrig launched his own cannon shot into the right-field stands for a 6-4 Yankee lead, and when Pipgras relaxed and blanked the Cubs over the next four innings, the Yankees were one victory away from the championship.

"Get your bags packed tomorrow morning fellas, I think we'll be leaving right after the game," said a confident McCarthy in the jubilant clubhouse afterward.

McCarthy was right, and he had his revenge when the Yankees completed the rout with a 13-6 thrashing. "I am the happiest man in the world," McCarthy said when it was over. "I figured we could do it, we simply had too much power for them. I'm proud of the Yankees, proud of them as players and as men."

The Cubs didn't go quietly as they knocked out Yankee starter Johnny Allen in the first inning with a four-run uprising, but the Yankees chipped away and the game was even at 5-5 through six innings. New York then scored four runs in the seventh and four more in the ninth to put an exclamation point on its 12th consecutive Series game victory, a record that stood until 2000, when another group of Yankees broke it.

"Those guys were just too good for us," said Hartnett.

That was usually the case in those days.

My promotion to Pete Sheehy's assistant in 1933 meant a slight raise in pay for me, and my family needed it. The Great Depression had by now gripped the nation, and we were certainly affected, as Dad's business had declined. We were fortunate in that people still needed shoes, and at least in the West Bronx, Dad's was the place they went, but money was tight, so to help out, I worked two jobs.

During baseball season I concentrated on my duties with the Yankees, but in the off-season I spent my days after school working as a delivery boy for Lunetta's Market, peddling my bicycle regardless of weather and the pain in my leg to bring people—mostly older folks—their groceries. I even hooked on at the stadium as a vendor in the fall, hawking peanuts during Saturday afternoon college football games including the annual battle between Notre Dame and Army, and on Sundays when the New York Giants played their National Football League games.

My mother called on her sewing skills, dormant since Dad was away during the war, to take occasional seamstress jobs, and my sister Carmela continued to live at home after she graduated from high school and shared the paycheck she received for working as an accountant's secretary.

We were lucky. My father never had to stand in the One-Cent Restaurant line that snaked its way up West 43rd Street. He never stood in the breadline at the Municipal Lodging House in Manhattan where one day it was reported that more than 10,000 desperate men and women passed through. He was not one of the four million people unemployed nationally by the spring of 1930, nor was he one of the 15 million who were jobless at the Depression's peak in 1935. We never took up residence in any of the Hoovervilles that popped up, the name given to the little shantytowns where the unemployed lived, a mocking reference to President Herbert Hoover, who shouldered much of the blame for the economy's collapse.

When the stock market crashed in October 1929, wiping out vast fortunes as well as middle class prosperity, the American dream became a nightmare, and New York Senator Robert Wagner proclaimed, "We are in a life-and-death struggle with the forces of social and economic dissolution."

But the Kimmerles survived because we were a hard-working, loving, and sharing family. There were always clothes on our backs, shoes on our feet, food on the table, and a roof over our heads.

Though I proposed to my parents on numerous occasions my willingness to help out financially by quitting school, they wouldn't hear of it. Full-time factory work was available, and I could have hooked on with one of the crews building the fabulous Triborough Bridge that towered over the East River, connecting the lower Bronx with upper Queens and upper Manhattan. But it was my parents' belief that education was vital, and no matter how difficult times were, I was going to complete my schooling.

As I progressed from grade to grade, I began to take an interest in creative writing. I always enjoyed English class and I spent much of my free time reading the classic books of the day such as William Faulkner's As I Lay Dying, *John Dos Passos's* The 42nd Parallel, *and F. Scott Fitzgerald's* Tender Is the Night, *but I was most fascinated by the sportswriters who covered the Yankees. Some of the giants of the business wrote for the many New York newspapers, men like Grantland Rice, Damon Runyon, Fred Lieb, Heywood Broun, Tom Meany, Dan Daniel, John Drebinger, Frank Graham, and Sid Mercer. I devoured their prose on a daily basis because all of the papers were delivered to the clubhouse so the players could keep tabs on their critics.*

Knowing that my damaged leg would prevent me from being an athlete, I thought writing about athletes would be a neat way to earn a wage, and I turned to none other than the legendary Rice to gauge my proclivity for the profession. During the 1933 season I started to write my own stories about Yankee games in my journal. I would watch from the dugout and in between performing my duties, I would make mental notes of things that happened during the game and then when I went home at night, I would put together an account.

One time I summoned the courage to go up to Mr. Rice and present him with one of my stories and asked if he would read it if he had the time. He agreed, and the next day he returned to the clubhouse and sought me out. He told me he thought I had a future in his business if I cleaned up a few style points which he happily shared with me. Imagine being 17 years old and getting writing tips from Grantland Rice! A charmed life I've led, indeed.

Rice and his cronies, many of whom became my future colleagues, had taken to calling Joe McCarthy "Second Place Joe" by 1936 as the Yankees had finished runner-up in the American League three years in succession following the 1932 championship. But the arrival of a kid named Joe DiMaggio virtually guaranteed the end of that frustrating spat.

DiMaggio came to the Yankees as a phenom who had torn up the Pacific Coast League while playing for the San Francisco Seals. Bill Essick was the Yankees' West Coast scout, and after watching DiMaggio play, he told general manager Ed Barrow, "This boy isn't 20 yet and he's the best I've ever seen." The Yankees *traded five players and $25,000 for the rights to sign DiMaggio, and Barrow later called it one of the best deals he ever made.*

I felt a certain kinship with DiMaggio. Heading into my 10th year as a Yankee employee, he was the first player who was fairly close to my age because I turned 20 just before the 21-year-old DiMaggio made his Yankee debut. I found myself gravitating toward him in the locker room, and even though he was a very private man away from baseball, early in his career before his stardom strangled him he was comfortable inside the clubhouse, his domain, and we always had lively discussions. There were many nights in that 1936 season when I would accompany DiMaggio to some restaurant—usually Toots Shor's place on West 51st Street, which was a quick subway ride into midtown Manhattan—for dinner and drinks and most times DiMaggio would pick up my tab. Of course picking up the tab became passé for DiMaggio in years to come because everywhere he went, he was usually comped, but I gladly accepted his kindness that first season.

I was now out of high school two years and working the night shift on the copydesk of the Bronx Home News, *our borough's daily newspaper. My interest in writing had continued to blossom, and knowing that my future was not as an assistant clubhouse boy, I began to explore ways to gain employment as a writer for the* Home News.

Upon graduation I started on the dock, loading the bundles of newspapers onto the delivery trucks, figuring I'd at least get my foot in the door at the company, plus the hours fit nicely during the baseball season. After about six months I moved indoors to the newsroom, where I worked as a copyboy running typewritten pages from the news desk to the typesetters, and occasionally, I was asked to write short stories about neighborhood happenings or rewrite press releases.

There wasn't a lot of turnover at the Home News *in normal times, let alone the Depression years when jobs were sacred, so full-time writing positions rarely opened, but I remained patient, continued to hone my writing skills, and held on to the belief that soon I would be given an opportunity.*

In the late summer of 1936 my big break occurred. Arthur Nevers, who had been covering the Yankees for 12 years, decided to take an editorial position with Life *magazine. During my time as a copyboy, sports editor Ray Reynolds occasionally used me to cover a big high school baseball or football game, and I had impressed him with my hustle and knowledge of sports. With Nevers scheduled to work through the Yankees season, Reynolds had about two months to interview candidates to fill the void on the sports staff and he brought in young, aspiring writers from all over New York City.*

My interview went smoothly. Reynolds had seen me do work at the paper, and I was a born and bred Bronx boy, so even though he conducted a somewhat extensive search, I always felt I had the inside track. However, when Reynolds finally offered me the job a month after the Yankees polished off the Giants in the World Series, I was stunned to find out which job he was offering.

There were eight other sportswriters on the staff, and I fully expected that he would promote one of them to the Yankees beat and plug me into a less visible position such as high schools or sports rewrite. Instead, knowing of my 10-year association with the team and of my terrific connections inside the clubhouse, Reynolds informed me that effective January 1, 1937, I would be the Home News' *Yankees beat reporter.*

I don't think my feet touched the pavement on the way home that day. I burst through the door and was so excited I could barely get the words out, but once I shared the news with my family, my dad told me he'd never been prouder of me. "Journalism is a noble profession," he said. A profession I was proud to perform for the next 45 years.

– Chapter 5 –

1936

On the afternoon of September 24, 1934, neither I, nor anyone else in the Yankee organization, had any idea that we were seeing Babe Ruth in Yankee pinstripes for the final time at the stadium. It was a lost season because the Yankees were to finish in second place seven games behind Detroit, and in a game against the Red Sox, Ruth drew a walk and was replaced by pinch-runner Myril Hoag. As he trotted back to the dugout, the small crowd gave him a cheer, but it was nothing special because we all assumed the Babe would be back for his 16th season with the club in 1935.

Ruth was clearly slowing down as he hit 34 homers in 1933 and just 22 in 1934, and he had hinted that he was going to retire as a player, but only if he could have Joe McCarthy's job as manager of the Yankees. It was a never-ending irritation for him that he couldn't convince Colonel Ruppert and Ed Barrow to make him manager.

Ruppert was perfectly happy with McCarthy, so he told Barrow to offer Ruth the managerial job at Newark, the Yankees' top farm team, with the promise that if he succeeded there, Ruth would be considered for the top job in New York. Ruth made a crack that his managing at Newark would be like the brewing tycoon Ruppert running a soda fountain. That sealed Ruth's fate in New York. The colonel got wind that new Boston Braves owner Emil Fuchs wanted to hire Ruth to be a player/ assistant manager/vice-president, and after discussing the matter with Ruth, it was decided that Ruth would be released by the Yankees to allow him to pursue the job in Boston.

Just before the final agreement was signed, Ruth went on a pheasant hunt—one of his favorite past times—and he invited my father to

go along. Dad was not a sportsman, but he went for the hell of it because Ruth had asked him to go. It was then that Ruth informed my
father of what was about to take place, and Dad came home that night
in a depressed state, even though he'd somehow bagged a bird. He broke
the news to me, and then we talked well past midnight about the blas-
phemy of Ruth wearing any other uniform. It's silly to think back on
that night when neither of us could imagine the Yankees moving on without Ruth and how we thought Yankee Stadium would never be the same.
Of course we missed Ruth terribly, but as it turned out, the Yankees did
just fine without him.

On February 26, 1935, Ruth officially became an ex-Yankee, and a
glorious era in New York sports history was complete.

Just in time for another one to begin.

A year later, I was standing in the middle of the clubhouse one morning a couple of weeks before the start of the 1936 season when I first
met Joe DiMaggio. He had been sent north by the club two weeks before the end of spring training because he had suffered a badly burned
foot while receiving treatment under a diathermy lamp.

DiMaggio could not play, so rather than have him traveling around
with the club on the annual end-of-spring barnstorming tour, McCarthy
sent him back to New York so he could get the necessary medical care
and rest he needed. Pete Sheehy called me from St. Petersburg to tell
me that Yankee scout Paul Krichell would be gathering DiMaggio at
Penn Station, then transporting him to the stadium, and he asked me to
meet them in the clubhouse and help get the rookie situated.

I had heard all about DiMaggio. I knew he'd been a superstar in the
Pacific Coast League with San Francisco, knew he was a fabulous hitter
who at the age of 19 had authored an incredible 61-game hitting streak
for the Seals and a year later batted .398 for the same club. I read all the
columns touting him as the next great Yankee and I'd heard Sheehy, a
man not prone to hyperbole, gush about him. Sheehy had told me a
couple weeks earlier, "Joe, wait 'til you see this kid hit. It's unbelievable.
He makes solid contact every time he hits the ball, line drives all over
the place."

Dan Daniel agreed with Sheehy because he wrote in one of his columns in the *World Telegram*, "Here is the replacement for Babe Ruth."

Despite being armed with all this information, I was a little skeptical, only because Ruth had been my hero, was still my friend, and in my
eyes, no one could ever replace him.

Well, DiMaggio did not become the next Babe Ruth. But he became the first Joe DiMaggio, and there's never been another since.

When DiMaggio and Krichell walked in, I went right over and politely introduced myself. DiMaggio shook my hand, said it was a pleasure to meet me, then asked where his locker was. I pointed him in the right direction, and when he was about halfway across the room, he turned to look back at me, his large Italian nose presenting an awkward profile, and asked if I could get him a half cup of coffee, please.

"He don't say much," Sheehy had warned me, "but he'll ask you for a lot of coffee. He loves coffee, and he wants it a half cup at a time so it stays hot."

As DiMaggio unpacked his bag and organized his new Yankee locker, Krichell and I made small talk in another corner of the room. I asked how the team had looked in Florida and he said, "We're good, and I'm guessing Detroit's not going to win the flag again this year." After a few minutes, I told Krichell if he wanted to leave, I could escort DiMaggio the few blocks over to the Concourse Plaza Hotel where he was staying, and Krichell agreed.

When DiMaggio was ready to leave, he said, "Do you mind if I take a peak at the stadium?" So DiMaggio followed me up the ramp leading to the field that would become his stage for the next 16 years (minus the three years he spent in the service), the place where he would carve his legend and thrill millions of spectators. As he stood there, I could see the reverence in his eyes as he looked around at the massive three-tiered grandstand, the lush green field, and the huge scoreboard in right-center field. As I looked at him, I couldn't help but think that DiMaggio was going to fit right in with this club, with this stadium, with this town.

He once said, "I want to thank the good Lord for making me a Yankee." Throughout his career, I can't count the number of times I said, "Thank you Lord for making him a Yankee."

When we left the stadium and began the trek over to the Plaza, there was very little conversation as DiMaggio studied his new Bronx neighborhood closely. He nodded to passersby in the street, people who had no idea who he was, but soon would. He asked me where he could get a good Italian meal and I provided a couple of suggestions, and then he asked me where he could get a couple pairs of shoes made. Well, I knew exactly the right place for that.

"Joe, my father is a shoemaker and his shop is right across the street from the stadium," I said. "If you want, I can take you over there tomorrow and you can look around and see if there's anything you'd like."

"That sounds like a swell idea, Joe," he replied. "I have to go see the doctor in the morning, so how about lunch time—would that be good for you?"

The next day I took him over to Dad's shop, and he was genuinely impressed by my father's craftsmanship. Dad measured DiMaggio's feet, showed him a few styles, and when DiMaggio picked what he wanted, Dad promised he'd have them ready in a couple days. As we were leaving, I took it upon myself to invite DiMaggio to dinner at my parents' house that evening. I knew he had no plans because he didn't know a soul in town and the team was still more than a week away from arriving. He had nowhere to go but back to his lonely room at the Plaza and I figured he might like an evening of company. He gladly agreed, and from that day forward I counted DiMaggio as my friend.

When I reflect on my newspapering career, I always point to the 1936 season as a monumental year, even though I wasn't even working the Yankee beat yet. I forged a trusting friendship with DiMaggio that year, so when I began to cover the team for the *Home News* in 1937, I never had the problems talking to Joe that so many of the other writers—even the big-name veterans—had during his first few years. He trusted me and he knew that what he told me in confidence would never make it into newsprint, yet he also knew that when he made a bad play or went into a slump—not that it happened very often—it was my job to write about that.

I know some of my colleagues resented me because I had risen so quickly to this important beat and I hadn't even reached my 21st birthday. And there was jealousy regarding the relationships I had with DiMaggio and the other players. But once I began to prove that I wasn't merely a mouthpiece for the team, that I could cover the team objectively and break news through my own hard work and diligence, I earned their respect.

DiMaggio's arrival signaled the end of the Yankees' pennant drought and set the table for the next Yankee dynasty. Since winning the 1932 World Series, the Yankees had finished second three years in a row. During that time the team said good-bye to Ruth, Earle Combs, Joe Sewell, Herb Pennock, George Pipgras, and Johnny Allen. But McCarthy had begun to reload in 1935 when Red Rolfe took over at third base and George Selkirk inherited the dubious role of replacing Ruth in right field. Then DiMaggio came aboard in 1936 and when the Yankees won 10 of their first 15 games—before DiMaggio even stepped on the field—it was clear they were the class of the league. Eddie Brannick, the traveling secretary of the New York Giants, was asked to assess the team his club would eventually face in the World Series and he called them "Window Breakers," the inference being that with all their long balls the Yankees could smash windows—not to mention records—everywhere they went.

DiMaggio made his major league debut on May 3, and everyone present that afternoon—players, media, and fans—knew we were looking at a young man destined to become one of the all-time greats. He grounded to third in his first at-bat, singled his next time up against St. Louis Browns right-hander Jack Knott, and later added another single and a triple as the Yankees went on to a 14-5 victory. He hit his first home run a week later, and that same day the Yankees moved into first place for good.

They won 20 of 28 games in May, and by the end of June they were 9 1/2 games ahead, and while Gehrig was having a monster season—he would ultimately be named MVP of the league—and Bill Dickey and Red Ruffing were nearly as superb, most of the attention was focused on DiMaggio. He had an unmistakable star quality to him, and though he was actually quite unwilling to cooperate with the press, mainly because of his shyness, the writers did not hold this against him. Most recognized that it was his nature to be cautious around strangers, so rather than rap him for his apprehension they emphasized his on-field brilliance which helped to accelerate his stardom.

Everyone's eyes were on DiMaggio during that summer of '36, including those of my sister, Carmela. She had taken a shine to DiMaggio that first evening he'd eaten dinner at our house, and the next day she asked me to ask DiMaggio if he'd like to see a movie or go out to dinner sometime. He agreed, and by the middle of the season, my sister was dating New York's most eligible bachelor.

It was a short-lived romance because DiMaggio wasn't ready to settle down with one gal, but with typical DiMaggio class he let my sister down easily and Carmela never spoke a cross word about him. DiMaggio was actually worried that his reluctance to get involved with Carmela was going to harm his friendship with me, but one night while having dinner with him at the place that would become his favorite hangout, Toots Shor's restaurant in Manhattan, I assured him that would never be the case. Even after he married Dorothy Arnold, and later when he married Marilyn Monroe, he would make it a point to ask me how Carmela was doing, and when I would relay that query to her, she would melt.

By winning 21 of 29 games in August, the Yankees made a mockery of the pennant chase and in their 138th game, on September 9, they

clinched the flag earlier than any team in major league history. It was
one of the great team performances of all-time, on par, in my book, with
the accomplishments in 1927, 1961, and 1998, and according to Ruffing,
DiMaggio was the key.

"I played a lot of years so I can't say what our best ballclub was, but
I know we were better after DiMaggio joined us than before," he said.
"There's no question about that. It was just nice to turn around and watch
him out there in center field. You saw him standing out there and you
knew you had a pretty damn good chance to win the baseball game."

– 1936 World Series –

There was an awful lot going on in the world in 1936. In America,
the economy continued to stagger and citizens from all corners of our
country were suffering; devastation reigned in Spain with the outbreak
of the Spanish Civil War; in the Soviet Union Joseph Stalin began his
"great purge" which would see more than eight million people killed and
another 10 million imprisoned over the next four years; and in Germany,
Adolf Hitler's supposedly superior Aryan race was embarrassed by a
young African-American track athlete named Jesse Owens who won four
gold medals in the Berlin Summer Olympics. But for one autumn week
in New York, none of this seemed to matter because the Yankees and
Giants were squaring off in the World Series.

As we would also experience later when the Yankees and Dodgers
became frequent World Series opponents in the 1940s and 1950s, and
when the Yankees and New York Mets battled in 2000, it was remarkable how insular the city could be when two New York teams were meeting to decide baseball's championship.

In the old days, my days, baseball was to New York what Times
Square is to New Year's Eve. When the Yankees played the Giants or
Dodgers in the World Series, the entire city went to the games. Maybe
not with a ticket in hand to Yankee Stadium, the Polo Grounds, or Ebbets
Field, but the masses were there in spirit thanks to that most prized of
possessions—the radio. Just as there was tremendous cheering at the
ballparks, it was nearly as boisterous on the streets, in the restaurants,
in the office buildings, in the apartment houses, in the courtyards, and
in the subways.

For those two or three hours when the games were being played, it
was almost as if the city came to a standstill. Nobody wanted to work,
nobody wanted to play, nobody wanted to talk, nobody wanted to

breathe. All people wanted to do was press their ear to a radio and live and die with each word that emanated from the golden throat of announcers Red Barber and Mel Allen.

In front of the *New York Times* building a big scoreboard—called a Play-O-Graph—was erected, and with the game blaring over a loudspeaker, a man would update the score each half inning, giving the assembled crowd a visual aid. Street vendors would sell their hot dogs and for no extra charge provide play-by-play commentary to their customers. Any restaurant or bar that expected business was tuned in to the broadcasts, and patrons would resonate with the ebb and flow of the game. Housewives airing their laundry on the lines that stretched between tenements would share their thoughts on why Joe McCarthy called for a sacrifice, why Red Ruffing threw the curve ball, or why Lou Gehrig swung at a 3-0 pitch. On the busiest streets of midtown Manhattan, crowds would gather in the biggest department stores or tiniest specialty shops to catch an update. And it wasn't much different in Gramercy, Greenwich Village, Soho, the theater district, Murray Hill, Queens, Staten Island, Long Island, Harlem, or anywhere in the Bronx or Brooklyn.

Like the glamorous Broadway shows, the dynamic night clubs, the rich ethnicity of the neighborhoods, and the towering skyscrapers that were now springing up on the Manhattan skyline, baseball was a vibrant part of New York's culture, its soul, its identity. Everyone loved baseball, everyone followed baseball, so when baseball's ultimate event was an all-New York affair, its grip on the city's emotions and passions was unbreakable.

By 1936, New Yorkers had waited 13 years for a subway series, and when it came to pass the city just about exploded. New Yorkers felt good about themselves that week. They forgot about the Depression and allowed themselves to smile. It was only baseball, but it was such a therapeutic balm for a wounded city amidst a wounded country. When the Series was over they would return to the reality of their lives, but oh, at least for a few days, how those unemployment lines would sing with lively conversation and playful banter. It was only baseball, but it was an important part of our lives.

* * *

The Yankees had long ago supplanted the Giants as the consistently strongest ballclub in New York City, but their superiority did not alter the rooting interests of much of the region. While the Bronx-based

Yankees and the Brooklyn-based Dodgers had sizable pockets of fans outside their home boroughs, the Giants were still the preferred team in New York. Their lineage dated back to 1883, and though the Dodgers were nearly as old, their sad record of no world championships cast them in the roll of the ugly stepchild next to the Giants' 13 pennants and six championships.

The legendary John McGraw endured just three losing seasons in his 30 years as Giants manager, but one of those came in 1932 and it was too much for him to bear, so he bowed out and turned the reins of the team over to his brilliant first baseman, Bill Terry. In 1933, Terry's first full year as player-manager, he guided the Giants to the World Series title, then followed up with National League pennants in 1934 and now 1936.

In '36, the key to New York's success had been the pitching of Carl Hubbell who won 26 games, including 16 in a row to end the season. It was apparent the Yankees were the better team, but in a seven-game series the Giants' faithful reasoned that Hubbell might be able to pitch three times and that could be enough to deliver the championship to the lords of the Polo Grounds.

Jake Powell thought otherwise. The Yankees left-fielder shrugged off Hubbell's season-long dominance on the eve of the Series opener, saying, "Who's afraid of Hubbell? He's been striking out those National League bushers and getting a reputation. I'll hit him like I own him. He's only human and I'll be in there swinging."

Powell backed up his acid-tongued comments by rapping out three hits in the rainy, chilly first game at the Polo Grounds, but his teammates chipped in with just four other safeties and Hubbell cruised to a 6-1 victory over Red Ruffing. The defeat snapped the Yankees' record 12-game World Series winning streak that encompassed the sweeps of Pittsburgh (1927), Cincinnati (1928), and Chicago (1932), and served as a cold slap in the face.

When the game was over, the Yankees were a grim bunch. Hubbell had frustrated them with his masterful screwball, and Powell was swearing a blue streak when he entered the clubhouse, appalled that the rest of the Yankees couldn't hit Hubbell. Lou Gehrig, as usual the voice of reason, told the volatile Powell, "It's one game, there's a long way to go."

The Yankees entered the eighth inning trailing 2-1 but put runners on first and third with nobody out and Joe DiMaggio, Gehrig, and Bill Dickey coming to the plate. On Hubbell's first pitch to DiMaggio, the rookie lashed a line drive right at second baseman Burgess Whitehead, who speared the ball and threw to first to easily double up Red Rolfe while Frank Crosetti remained parked at third, and when Dickey grounded out to end the inning, the Yankees still trailed.

Seemingly let down by his team's inability to tie the game, Red Ruffing was roughed up in the bottom half for a four-run game-clinching spurt. "I'll say this," Joe McCarthy said following the game. "That double play that DiMaggio hit into was the break of the game, but those things happen and they even up usually."

The miserable weather that plagued the opener continued into the next day and forced postponement of Game Two for 24 hours. It was well worth the wait for the Yankees as the Window Breakers busted up the Polo Grounds almost as effectively as the wrecking ball a few decades later. The Yankees hung a convincing 18-4 defeat on their cross-river rivals. President Roosevelt threw out the first ball, and that was about the only ball the Yankees didn't hit as they rapped out 17 hits to set a Series scoring record.

Tony Lazzeri and Dickey each drove in five runs, four for Lazzeri coming on one swing in the third when he keyed a seven-run uprising with a grand slam. Every Yankee had at least one hit and one run scored, while benefiting from this show of strength was Lefty Gomez, who pitched nine effortless innings to get the win, yielding only six hits.

"Those guys just shellacked us," Terry said. "Toughest team I've ever faced. It was sort of sad to keep the boys in there taking it, but I was in there taking it with 'em and if I could stand it, they ought to."

*   *   *

That night, I had dinner with DiMaggio and Rolfe at Lindy's—the original joint on Broadway between 49th and 50th streets where famed sportswriter Damon Runyon hung out—and this was the first time I'd ever been out socially with the red-headed Yankee third baseman. Rolfe had always intrigued me, mainly because he wasn't a typical ballplayer in that he had a deep love for reading and writing. He was an Ivy Leaguer, earning a degree in English while playing shortstop at Dartmouth. Late in his Yankee career he admitted to me that ghostwriting a newspaper column—which Ed Barrow ordered him to stop doing because he was revealing too much "inside dope"—had always been a dream of his because he had originally wanted to become a sportswriter before baseball intervened.

Rolfe made his Yankee debut in 1931 as a pinch runner in one game, then was farmed out to Albany and Newark for the next two seasons, finally making it to New York part-time in 1934, and for good in 1935.

Rolfe was a master at hitting behind the runner to move him into scoring position, and he was adept at finding an opponent's weakness. Never a fast runner, he legged out an inordinate amount of doubles and triples because he studied the way outfielders fielded his hits. For instance, Wally Moses of the Athletics always used to drop to one knee to scoop up the ball, so Rolfe would often take the extra base against him. "When I hit toward Moses or a fielder who backed up, I never stopped running around first and I slid safely into second easily," Rolfe said.

Moses' manager, the great Connie Mack, saw all of the great Yankees of this era, and Rolfe was one of the ones he respected the most. "He's the greatest team player in the game," Mack said. "Half the time when you're playing the Yankees you don't know he's in the park. He'll go 0-for-3 in a tight game, maybe, and then when it means the ballgame he'll drag a bunt and beat it out or stick a single through the infield or work your pitcher for a walk. Whatever it takes to beat you, he'll do it. If a manager had nine Rolfes, he could stay away from the park and go fishing until the World Series."

Barrow recognized Rolfe's ability, too. "He never did anything much wrong," the general manager once said. "He never got into any spectacular kind of trouble. And so there aren't any stories to tell about him."

As a player, Rolfe always kept a little black book handy, not for the phone numbers of women he would meet, but for taking notes on every pitcher he faced. This was a quality McCarthy said was going to make Rolfe a fine manager, a profession he took up after his playing career ended prematurely in 1942 due to an intestinal problem.

"Red Rolfe has personality, he has color, and I don't just mean his hair," McCarthy said. "He asks plenty of questions and writes down the answers. He also has a lot of other information in his little black book. He writes down what every pitcher throws in the clutch so the batter can be set in the pinch."

When we were sitting there at dinner, Rolfe told me, "I always hoped when I was a kid that I might play big-league baseball some day, but not even in the heights of my imagination did I ever think it would come true. Babe Ruth was a god to me. The next thing I knew, I was his teammate."

I sort of knew the feeling.

*   *   *

Back at Yankee Stadium for Game Three, the Giants' Freddy Fitzsimmons baffled the Yankees with his knuckleball and allowed only four hits, but one was a home run by Gehrig in the second inning and another was Frank Crosetti's game-winning RBI single that Fitzsimmons stopped, but couldn't gain control of as the ball bounded behind the pitcher's mound. Powell raced in from third base on that play to provide the Yankees with a 2-1 victory in front of 64,842 fans, the largest crowd to have ever witnessed a Series game.

"You wouldn't mind if a ball was hit good, but to have been beaten like that is tough to take," Fitzsimmons said of Crosetti's hit. "I can't do anything right enough. That ball looked like a cinch to me. I've gone over much farther to get those nasty hoppers, but today the ball was a half inch too far."

The Yankees' joy was curtailed by the fact that now they had to face the impregnable Hubbell the next day, and another Series record crowd came out, fully intending to help their Yankees in any way possible. The Yankees didn't need much help, though, as they figured out Hubbell's screwball and rapped him for eight hits and four runs during a 5-2 victory.

Gehrig crashed a two-run homer in the third to make it 4-0, and starter Monte Pearson had all the run support he would need. Before the game, Pearson was feeling terrible. He was complaining of back pain, his shoulder was sore, and he was suffering from dizzy spells. I looked at him and figured there was no way he was going to pitch. Gomez peeked in to the trainer's room and asked him "How do you feel, Mont?" and Pearson replied, "Worse than I look." Well, a little tape and some iron tonic and Pearson was fine because he gave up just seven hits and two runs while striking out seven.

"Nothing to this guy," Powell said to me after the game, referring to Hubbell, still unimpressed.

Hal Schumacher, who had been the starter in Game Two before being routed inside three innings, obliterated that nightmarish day and rescued the Giants in Game Five. He pitched all 10 innings and extended the Series with a hard-earned 5-4 victory.

After blowing a 3-0 lead, Schumacher blanked the Yankees over the final four innings, escaping trouble in the ninth by retiring Gehrig on a grounder with runners dancing off first and second. "Who wouldn't be worried?" Schumacher said of facing the Iron Horse in that situation. "But I didn't have time to think about that. All I had to do was get him out. We had to get those fellows out a lot of times to stay in the game."

Inspired by their gutty pitcher, the Giants produced the winning run in the 10th as Jo-Jo Moore opened with a double and later scored on Bill Terry's fly to center.

"They've got to win two, we've only got to win one," was McCarthy's response afterward.

And the Yankees got that one the next day over at the Polo Grounds. The Giants made it tough for eight innings as they trailed only 6-5, but a seven-run explosion in the ninth blew it open for the Yankees.

"They've got everything, including pitching," said Terry. "Who told me they didn't have a good pitching staff? I'll say they were pretty good."

The day after the 1936 Series ended I was back in the Yankee Stadium club-house with Pete Sheehy, performing our annual end-of-the-season cleanup. The players were all there, reliving the exciting events of the previous few days while emptying their lockers for the winter, and after they'd made a mess, Pete and I would tidy it up. McCarthy demanded a neat locker room, and Sheehy and I never failed him.

As I shook hands and bid each player a fond off-season, I continually used the refrain "See you next year." Of course, I wasn't quite sure that was true. Though my interview for the vacant sportswriting position at the Bronx Home News wasn't taking place for another two days, newsroom scuttlebutt had me firmly in the driver's seat as long as I didn't bomb. If I were to get the job it would mean the end of my tenure as a Yankee employee. Nighttime copydesk hours enabled me to continue working for the Yankees because the team always played day games. As a writer, I would no longer have the flexibility to perform the two jobs because a journalist's hours change daily due to the unpredictable nature of news.

McCarthy sensed my days as a clubhouse attendant were over. He called me into his office after most of the players had departed and said to me, "Joe, I just want you to know that I've enjoyed having you work in our clubhouse. I think you're going to do a fine job working for that newspaper; you're a hell of a young man and we're going to miss you."

I told him I hadn't had my interview yet and I didn't know what my future held, but he said, "They'd be foolish not to hire you, and I wouldn't be surprised if you're right back here writing about us pretty soon."

Maybe McCarthy knew something I didn't.

A month later sports editor Ray Reynolds informed me the job was mine, and my first reaction was genuine excitement, followed by a tinge of sadness because it hit me that my days in the Yankee clubhouse—at least for now—were indeed over. That unpleasant thought barely crept into my consciousness before Reynolds confirmed McCarthy's hunch by telling me he was putting me on the Yankees beat.

"Joe, I like the work you've done for the paper, I think your writing has really improved, and you know all the players so well," Reynolds said. "I think you'll be able to get information that the fellas we already have on staff wouldn't *be privy to. It's a big responsibility, and I'll be watching you closely, but I want you to cover the Yankees for us."*

A big responsibility? As far as I was concerned, it was the most important job at the newspaper, and it was mine!

It was a night for celebration so I phoned a girl I had been dating casually, a pretty brown-eyed blonde named Margaret Castle, and we went to the Pennsylvania Hotel in Manhattan for dinner and dancing to the jazz ensemble of Benny Goodman. About halfway through our meal, Red Ruffing and his wife, Pauline, came in along with Red Rolfe and his wife, Isabella. They were seated at a table adjacent to ours, and after dinner, we all spent the night dancing and drinking and laughing, Margaret no doubt impressed by the company that I kept.

While the women were off on an excursion to the ladies' room, Ruffing, Rolfe, and I bellied up to the bar where Ruffing bought a round of whiskey. He held his glass aloft in a congratulatory toast, wished me well in my new role as a "snoop," and with Goodman wailing away on his clarinet in the background, we clinked our glasses together before gunning down the harsh golden liquor. "So I guess nothing is sacred anymore," Ruffing said, referring to the conversations we used to have together after the reporters had left the clubhouse. "Red," I said to him, "I'm going to do the best I can to scoop everyone for stories, but I promise you that if you ever tell me something off the record, it'll never see newsprint under my byline." At that we shook hands, smiled, and returned our attention to the King of Swing as the brass section picked up the rhythm and the women spun like tops on the dance floor in front of us.

The next morning I walked over to the stadium to inform Ed Barrow that I would have to resign my position with the team. The gruff Yankee general manager thanked me for 10 "excellent" years of service and told me he'd look forward to seeing me in St. Petersburg for the start of spring training in late February.

Spring training. I hadn't even thought of that perk. Six weeks in sunny Florida, away from the horror of a Bronx winter. My sister, Carmela, was quite jealous of her younger brother, while my mother was worried that I wouldn't be able to take care of myself. The only times I had ever been away from home were the occasions when I traveled to the road World Series games with the Yankees, and those trips lasted only a few days. At this time I was still living at my parents' apartment at East 162nd and River, only because it was convenient to the stadium as well as the Home News office and it allowed me to save a little cash. For me to be going so far away for so long, well, my mother was having a tough time with that one.

I was 20 years old and I now had my dream job, but what I didn't have was a driver's license. Without one, Reynolds told me, my dream job was nonexistent.

He made it clear that being able to drive was a prerequisite because when news was breaking, you couldn't always rely on a taxi or the subway. My mother and father never had an automobile because they didn't need one. Everything in our Bronx neighborhood was within walking distance, and if not, we would just hop on the subway to reach our destination. Reynolds knew of my driving status when he hired me, so he set a deadline of mid-February for me to attain my driving privileges.

I obtained a permit, then enrolled in a training course that lasted six weeks and concluded with a road test, which I failed. I was crushed when I received the news, and all Reynolds did was shrug his shoulders and warn me that the clock was ticking. He was holding firm on his demand, so I had to quickly re-schedule another exam. Talk about pressure. The day I climbed into that DeSoto, I'm sure the feeling I had in my stomach was similar to what a major league pitcher must feel when he takes the mound to start a World Series game. Thankfully I overcame my nerves, drove the car and performed the necessary tasks flawlessly, and one week before I was to leave for Florida I received my license in the mail.

Dad and I spent the next two days searching for a suitable used car, neither of us armed with an ounce of information because we'd never owned one. When we settled on a dark blue 1932 Packard, it required a $500 payment, thus wiping out my savings account.

– Chapter 6 –

1937

IT TOOK ME ALMOST FOUR DAYS to get to St. Petersburg as I drove through New Jersey, Pennsylvania, Delaware, Maryland, Virginia, North and South Carolina and Georgia before reaching the Florida state line. I'd been as far west as St. Louis, but I'd never been south of Pittsburgh, and as I drove through some of the small rural southern towns, I was appalled by what I saw. I thought New York City had poverty, but when I saw people living in straw shacks with no running water or indoor plumbing, it hit me that I was living in a big world filled with depravity and it made me thank God for what I had. President Roosevelt's New Deal had started to make a dent in the Great Depression up north, but it sure wasn't doing much good for these folks in the south.

When I arrived in St. Pete I checked into a low-budget hotel, feeling guilty after what I'd just seen, but also afraid of spending the newspaper's money. The place had a bed, a toilet, sink and tub, a small desk to work at and a telephone, plus it was reasonably close to the Yankees' training facility. In other words, it was perfect, at least until I realized that every one of my colleagues from the other papers were staying at swank places. "Kid," John Drebinger of the *Times* said to me one day, "if they're willing to pay, then you oughta be willing to spend."

With only a few minor league catchers and pitchers having reported this early, my first visit to camp left me in search of someone recognizable, and Bill Dickey fit that bill. Now here was a man who could have waited to come to St. Pete with the rest of the veterans, but because he was a catcher, he felt obligated to come in with these unknowns because, as he told me, "Someone's got to catch these fellas."

I'd known him his entire Yankee career, and he truly was the consummate and classy professional, a man whose intelligence on a baseball field was matched only by his sheer talent.

Though I had written some minor off-season news stories about the team in the previous two months, I decided a feature story on Dickey would be the ideal way to "officially" begin my career as the Yankee beat writer, so I approached him for an interview and he gladly agreed. This is the story, as it appeared, in the February 28, 1937 edition of the *Bronx Home News:*

By Joe Kimmerle
Bronx Home News

ST. PETERSBURG, Fla.—The moment Bill Dickey realized he wasn't going to be the next Babe Ruth, he set his sights on a more attainable goal—becoming the greatest catcher baseball has ever known.

The defensive skills were always there, even when he was plying his craft in the minor leagues, and after watching Dickey play for his hometown team in Little Rock, Ark., Yankee scout Johnny Nee sent a wire to general manager Ed Barrow declaring "If this boy doesn't make it, I'll quit scouting."

Former Yankee manager Miller Huggins knew Dickey possessed a wealth of talent, too, and he said so in the spring of 1928. "We have bought a young man who is destined to become one of the greatest catchers in the game. I'm not kidding you. I have a hunch about this kid because every other club is trying to make a deal for him."

But when Dickey finally got his chance the following year, he tried to copy the home run swings of sluggers Ruth and Lou Gehrig, and it resulted in his hitting what he called "the highest pop flies you ever saw."

"Miller Huggins straightened me out," Dickey explained while taking a break from spring workouts in St. Petersburg. "He said, 'Young man, choke up on the bat and stop unbuttoning your shirt on every pitch. That way you'll be around longer.'"

This is the ninth year Dickey has been around the Yankees, and his is a career matched perhaps only by Detroit's Mickey Cochrane in the annals of big-league receiving.

Once Dickey altered his left-handed batting stroke and began swinging the way he always had, line drives were seen sailing all over Yankee

Stadium. As he prepares for the 1937 season, Dickey counts only one year when he did not bat over .300, that in 1935, and he enters this campaign basking in the glory of his wondrous .362 average of 1936, the highest ever for a man who caught at least 100 games in one season.

Dickey's batting exploits are indeed impressive, but it is his work behind the plate and his ability to lead that draws rave reviews from the Yankee pitching staff as well as players and managers from around the American League.

Waite Hoyt, who was Dickey's teammate and battery mate in 1929 and 1930, remembers the way Dickey made an instant impression on him, and many of the other veteran players, when he took over as the starting catcher in 1929.

"He was a young kid, but in his quiet way he took right over," said Hoyt, who is still kicking around the big leagues, ready to begin his fifth season with the National League Pirates in Pittsburgh. "He was a no-nonsense guy and you did what he said or he wanted to know why."

Like his good friend and bridge partner, Gehrig, Dickey commands respect in the Yankee clubhouse, but he need not ask for it. It comes naturally. Players young and old look up to him because he brings a calming influence to the ballclub.

If a teammate makes a mistake, he'll let him know, but he'll also tell him what the correct play would have been. He is like a second manager, and unlike the gruff Joe McCarthy, Dickey has a Southern kindness to him that soothes the criticism like lemonade quenches a thirst on a hot summer day.

Dickey is tall and lanky for a catcher, but he has never been fleet afoot, so catching always seemed to be his natural position as he was growing up in Little Rock. "I guess I was always too slow to play anywhere else," he said. "But I love it back of the bat. To be a good catcher, you have to want to be a catcher. When I was a boy everyone wanted to be a pitcher. Then a few years later when Babe Ruth was breaking records, everyone wanted to be a slugger. The emphasis is still on hitting. Catching is a hard, disagreeable job, but it gives an opportunity to heavy men who are slow runners. If I had my choice to make over again, I'd still be a catcher."

Catching is an art, and Dickey reeled off his list of the finer points of the position:

"A catcher must want to catch," he began. "He must make up his mind that it isn't the terrible job it is painted. A backstop must learn not to get discouraged. Getting banged up, being knocked over are all in a day's work. He must devote all his spare time to mastering the trick of catching low balls. Anybody can catch a high ball, but to take low pitching right, that's the real trademark.

"He has to impress it on himself that throwing is the softest part of his work and must come automatically. He must get the ball away fast and smoothly, which I never found that difficult. And the catcher must make the pitcher glad that he has that particular catcher working with him. He must build up his pitcher's confidence and that means studying the hitters."

No catcher has ever put together that full arsenal of attitude and skills quite like the Yankee backstop, and one could venture a guess that no one ever will.

When his career was complete, Dickey's batting average was a sparkling .313 with 202 home runs and 1,209 RBI, all with the Yankees. Dan Daniel summed up Dickey's value to the team best when he wrote "Dickey isn't just a catcher. He's a ball club. He isn't just a player. He's an influence."

One of the few nonpitchers in the Hall of Fame who never led the league in a single offensive category, Dickey nonetheless hit .300 or better 11 times, and in 6,300 at-bats he struck out only 289 times. His record of catching at least 100 games in 13 straight seasons stood until Cincinnati's Johnny Bench tied it four decades later.

The great Cleveland pitcher Bob Feller, recognizing what a brilliant handler of pitchers Dickey was, once said, "If I had Dickey catching me, I believe I could win 35 games." Wartime Yankee pitcher Ernie Bonham agreed when he said, "I never shake off Dickey. I just let him pitch my game."

As I wrote on that February day in 1937, it would have been my guess at that time that no catcher would ever match Dickey, and I stand by that. In my estimation, no one ever has.

* * *

That first spring in St. Petersburg was certainly strange. I was still a popular figure in the clubhouse because of my 10-year association with the ballclub, but there was no mistaking the fact that I was now an outsider, no longer an employee of the Yankees. I knew all of the players, most of them intimately, and our relationships remained intact, but the line was distinct, and the rules were different.

Where once I would talk about girls over half cups of coffee with Joe DiMaggio, or fetch Lou Gehrig the newspaper and a pouch of tobacco for his pipe, or adjust the straps on Dickey's shin guards and chest protector, now my dealings with the players were professional, not personal. While it was tough for me, I quickly noticed that these men, most of them grizzled veterans, did not have a problem making this adjustment. I was a reporter, and no matter how much they may have liked me, they fully recognized the power of the pen, a power I now possessed. Ballplayers—even when I broke into the business during a time when reporters didn't dare pry into off-field issues—considered the press a nuisance, a necessary evil. Remember, our job is to report the news, and it was news if DiMaggio hit a game-winning home run, just like it was news if he popped up with the bases loaded to end a game. It was news if Red Ruffing won five starts in a row, just as it was news if Ruffing lost five starts in a row. Human nature being what it is, ballplayers cooperate with reporters in the good times, and avoid us like the plague in bad times. It has always been that way.

I wielded my new power in May of 1937 when I wrote my first significant story. Roy Johnson, a reserve outfielder, made a crack to me—on the record—that ultimately cost him his job. The Yankees had just lost two in a row to Detroit and McCarthy was in a foul mood. After he verbally lashed his troops behind closed doors, the press was ushered in and I chose to interview Johnson. He stood in front of his locker and said to me, "What does McCarthy want? Does he expect us to win every day?"

The next morning McCarthy read my story which included that quote, called me into his office before the game and asked, "Joe, is that what he said? You didn't misunderstand him, did you?" I assured him I printed what Johnson said, and after dismissing me, he went up to Barrow's office and told him to dump Johnson. Barrow agreed, and the man he recalled from the top farm club in Newark to replace Johnson was Tommy Henrich, who would go on to become one of the greatest Yankees of all. I often joked with Henrich that if I hadn't written that story about Johnson, he'd still be bushing it with the Bears.

The 1937 season was very similar to 1936 in that the Yankees barely broke a sweat on their way to winning the American League pennant by 13 games over Detroit. It began rather slowly as the Yankees were in and out of first place most of the first month, and part of the problem was Dickey's apathetic start at the plate.

In early June the Yankees and White Sox were tied for the lead, but then Dickey got hot and the Yankees began to seize control. New York won its first five games after the All-Star break, and any thoughts about a race developing were crushed in early August. The White Sox had gone on a winning streak and when they visited Yankee Stadium for a five-game series they were within shouting distance, just five games out of first. Their deficit promptly doubled as they lost all five games, and New York was never threatened again, clinching the pennant on September 23.

DiMaggio produced one of the greatest seasons in Yankee history as he led the league in home runs (46) and runs scored (151), while driving in 167 runs and batting .346. Had he not played half his games in Yankee Stadium, a graveyard for right-handed power hitters, DiMaggio might have challenged Ruth's record of 60 homers in a season. Gehrig enjoyed his final great season batting .351 with 37 homers, 159 RBI, and a league-high 127 walks, while on the mound Lefty Gomez and Red Ruffing each reached the 20-win plateau.

For the second year in a row, New York was aglow in another Subway Series as Bill Terry's Giants survived a tough National League pennant chase to outlast the Chicago Cubs by three games. Once again, the world outside New York City ceased to exist for one glorious baseball week.

– *1937 World Series* –

It was a few minutes after the first World Series game I covered as a sportswriter had ended, and my fellow scribes and I were standing in the victorious Yankee clubhouse talking to that day's winning pitcher, Lefty Gomez.

Gomez had just hurled a complete game six-hitter, allowing a solitary run as the Yankees rolled to an 8-1 victory at Yankee Stadium over Carl Hubbell to get a one-game jump on the Giants. He had pitched beautifully, matching Hubbell out for out through the first five innings until the Yankee bats came alive in the sixth, producing an explosive seven-run rally that blew the game open and made the rest of his afternoon easy.

Gomez's legendary fastball was jumping past the Giant batters, his control was pinpoint, and he offered further proof that Joe McCarthy was right on when he said one time of Gomez, "If there's one game I have to win, I wouldn't be afraid to give the ball to Gomez."

But rather than regale us with how he managed to retire all those Giants, all Gomez wanted to talk about was that sixth inning offensive orgy. "Any of you guys know if two walks in an inning is a World Series record?" he asked the assembled press corps. As a matter of fact, it was.

Gomez was a notoriously poor hitter, but on this day he stood his ground and drew a pair of walks during the decisive sixth inning that helped set the table for the big boomers in the order. And later on in the eighth inning, he lined a shot into the gap that would have gone for a double had not right fielder Jimmy Ripple made a fine running catch. "Imagine that," he said between gulps of beer. "Me hitting a double in a World Series game and then getting robbed of it. Nuts."

Nuts was an appropriate description of Gomez, the all-time funniest Yankee. If not for his golden left arm, Gomez would have killed in the nightclubs, had he so chosen. Gomez made a career out of blowing pitches past the opposition, then blowing smoke in the Yankee clubhouse, keeping the atmosphere loose and light with his antics and one-liners.

I remember on the train ride out to St. Louis for the start of the 1942 World Series, I was sitting at a table with a couple of other writers along with Joe DiMaggio and Gomez. Gomez's arm had been giving him trouble and he was no longer part of McCarthy's rotation in what would turn out to be his last year with the club. McCarthy walked by us, stopped for a moment to say hello, then continued on. One of the fellas said, "Smart manager, isn't he Lefty?" Gomez replied, "Must be, he hasn't asked me to pitch in over a month."

That was the essence of Gomez, always quick with a line, always the guy to lift the spirits of everyone he came in contact with. A sampling of his wit:

Gomez was asked one time if he ever talked to the ball on the mound and he said, "Sure, lots of times." What did you say? "Go foul, go foul."

Upon his induction into the Baseball Hall of Fame in 1972, Gomez opined that "it's only fair, I helped a lot of hitters get in."

After his career ended, he was asked what the key to his success was: "Clean living, a fast outfield, and (relief pitcher) Johnny Murphy."

Of his allegorical nightlife, Gomez said, "I've never had a bad night in my life, but I've had a few bad mornings."

He rarely had many bad afternoons. You could easily see right through his self-deprecating humor because Gomez possessed startling talent and the ability to pitch his best when games meant the most. He poked fun at himself, but he also owned a career World Series record of 6-0.

"On a ballclub that approached its baseball in a business-like manner such as the Yankees, Lefty was just the touch of comic relief we needed," said his best friend on the team and longtime roommate and drinking partner, DiMaggio. But whenever DiMaggio talked of Gomez's satirical nature, he never failed to add that "Gomez was first and foremost a great pitcher. His kidding was strictly a sideline. If he had been a clown, he wouldn't have lasted with McCarthy, who had no use for comedians."

I interviewed DiMaggio for a story I was doing on Gomez sometime around 1940. Gomez used to drive DiMaggio to the ballpark, and Joe told me that he and Gomez would often go over the opposing team's lineup together on those rides and that Gomez always had a keen analysis of how to pitch to certain hitters or where to play them in the field. He was an artist on the mound, and much of his success had to do with his ability to figure out the weakness of the batters he faced.

The one hitter Gomez never figured out was slugger Jimmie Foxx. "His hair has muscles," Gomez used to say. One afternoon Gomez peered in, looking for the signs from Bill Dickey, and he shook everything off. Dickey called time, trotted out to the mound and asked Gomez what he wanted to throw. "Nothing. Let's wait a while, maybe he'll get a phone call."

Foxx was the exception. Gomez won 189 games as a Yankee. Only Red Ruffing and Whitey Ford won more.

*   *   *

In the opener, Gomez allowed just one single through four innings before the Giants scored their lone run in the fifth. That run meant nothing a short while later when the Yankees scored a touchdown and kicked the extra point, and it all started when Gomez walked to lead off. Frank Crosetti followed with a single, and Gomez moved to second. So unaccustomed to being on base, Gomez nearly cost the Yankees an out when he wandered too far while taking his lead. Catcher Gus Mancuso gunned the ball to shortstop Dick Bartell, but Bartell dropped the throw and Gomez made it back safely.

Red Rolfe singled to load the bases, then DiMaggio drove a single to left-center scoring two runs. Lou Gehrig was walked intentionally to reload the bases, and Dickey beat out an infield hit that chased Rolfe home with the third run. Myril Hoag's grounder forced DiMaggio at the plate, but George Selkirk delivered a two-run single which made the score 5-1 and ended Hubbell's day.

Harry Gumbert relieved, and should have been out of the inning when Tony Lazzeri hit a ground ball to second baseman Burgess Whitehead. Instead, Whitehead fumbled it, everyone was safe and Hoag scored. Dick Coffman relieved and promptly walked Gomez and Rolfe to force in the last run.

"The Yanks are a tough ball club," Giants manager Bill Terry said, echoing his comments from the previous year. "When they get started, they're hard to stop."

Hubbell, who had handcuffed the Yankees in the 1936 Series opener, said, "I had some stuff, but it just wasn't enough. Say, that Gomez is a right good pitcher, isn't he?"

The same could be said for the Yankees' Game Two starter, Ruffing. And unlike Gomez, Ruffing was an excellent batsman, and he was his own best friend as the Yankees pounded out their second straight 8-1 blowout.

Ruffing, who had held out at the start of the 1937 season demanding an extra $1,000 be added to his contract due to his skill at the plate, proved it was money he truly deserved as he banged out a pair of hits that drove in three runs. As for his true specialty, he yielded a first-inning run, then blanked the Giants the rest of the way, scattering seven hits and three walks while striking out eight.

"I don't know which gave me my greatest thrill, pitching or hitting," Ruffing said afterward. "You know, I'm proud of both."

Up two games to none, the Yankees began to smell victory, and George Selkirk seemed prophetic when he said, "If Monte has his stuff he'll handle 'em as easy as Gomez and Ruffing."

Pearson had his stuff in Game Three, and while he didn't have it as easy as Gomez and Ruffing thanks to a late Giant threat, he pitched comfortably almost all day during a 5-1 victory that left the Yankees one win away from a clean sweep.

The Yankees chipped away at Giants starter Hal Schumacher as they loaded the bases in the second to score one run, tacked on two more in the third, another in the fourth, and one more in the fifth for a 5-0 lead, casting a pall over the Polo Grounds. To this point, Pearson had retired all 12 batters he had faced, but the Giants broke up his perfect game in the fifth and his shutout in the seventh. No matter. They didn't score again.

"Say, for a bunch of reputed sluggers, we're hitting the ball like a lot of old washwomen," said Selkirk. "What's going to happen to those Giants if we really find the range tomorrow? Imagine any team holding the great Yankees to one home run in three games."

It was true. The Bronx Bombers, as they had become known by now, had gone deep only once—Lazzeri in the eighth inning of the first game.

"It's all over but the counting [of Series money] now," was a popular refrain in the Yankee clubhouse, but the counting was delayed by a day when the Giants triumphed, 7-3, behind Hubbell and a six-run second-inning eruption off Bump Hadley.

Hubbell's catcher, Mancuso, was amazed by the crafty left-hander's performance. "Ever see anyone like him?" Mancuso asked. "With only two days rest he comes back to pitch one of the greatest games of his career."

Unfortunately for the Giants, Hubbell couldn't pitch the next day. Cliff Melton gave it a valiant effort, but the Yankees did just enough damage to produce four runs, and that was all Gomez needed. In what served as a perfect conclusion for this one-sided competition, it was the light-hitting Gomez who drove in what proved to be the winning run with a single in the fifth inning.

When Babe Ruth was with the Yankees and he and Gomez were roommates, they had a standing wager every year. Ruth would put up $250 to Gomez's $50 that Gomez would not collect 10 base hits in a season. Gomez made out on that deal because he failed four times, but turned the trick once.

Ruth would have been proud of his pal on this day. Hoag and DiMaggio hit solo home runs in the second and third innings, respectively, to stake Gomez to a 2-0 lead, but the Giants tied the game in their half of the third.

In the fifth, Lazzeri—playing his final game as a member of the Yankees—tripled to deep center, and Gomez followed with a liner that went off Whitehead's glove at second base to give the Yankees a 3-2 lead. Rolfe walked, and with two outs, Gehrig slashed a double to center that scored Gomez.

The Giants could work only five more singles and no runs off Gomez, and fittingly, Gomez recorded the last putout when Jo-Jo Moore grounded to Gehrig who flipped to Gomez covering the bag, wrapping up the Yankees' sixth world championship.

On the afternoon of April 30, 1938 Joe DiMaggio stepped to the plate at Griffith Stadium in Washington, D.C. and something happened that he'd never experienced before.

He was booed.

As I sat up in the press box listening to the discountenance, it struck me that this was not just the normal wrath you would expect a visiting ballplayer to endure. This was virulent booing that clearly rattled the proud and sensitive DiMaggio.

Almost overnight DiMaggio had become an American hero, his first two seasons in Yankee pinstripes straight out of a storybook, and baseball fans everywhere—except in the seven other American League cities—were enamored with his Italian good looks, pleasant manners, and supreme skill.

Little boys dreamed of being Joe DiMaggio, and grown men were awed by the sight of DiMaggio drifting back effortlessly to haul in a long fly at Yankee Stadium or taking a mighty rip at a fastball and sending it screaming into the faraway bleacher seats.

But now he stood in the batter's box with a puppy dog look on his face, obviously stunned by the vile treatment he was receiving, and he knew it was his own fault. DiMaggio stripped himself of his innocence when he decided to hold out prior to the start of the 1938 season, seeking a raise in pay from the $15,000 he had made in 1937 to $40,000, a preposterous figure in those days for a 23-year-old third-year ballplayer.

For a country full of people still trying to fight through the Depression, a country where nearly eight million were still out of work, DiMaggio's perplexing stance and unwillingness to come to spring training to play baseball struck an angry chord with the populace.

"Who the hell does he think he is?" was a common refrain, and the same people asking that question answered it by calling him a greedy and selfish young man.

If DiMaggio thought his treatment in Washington was crude, he received an even greater shock when the hometown Yankee fans—patrons who worshipped the ground he walked on the previous two years—showered him with taunts and insults a few days later when he made his first appearance at the stadium.

"I deserved it," he said to me a couple months after his play in the field had silenced the critics and won back his legion of fans. Given the fact that my salary was about $3,000 in 1938, and I was in the middle of the wage scale in comparison to millions of other American men, I agreed with him. He did deserve it.

DiMaggio had come to New York in mid-January to accept a player of the year award from the New York chapter of the Baseball Writers Association of America, of which I was a new member. I spoke to DiMaggio that night, and he seemed perfectly content with his life, reveling in his second straight involvement in a World Series championship. He asked about my sister, Carmela, and my parents, and he told me to tell my father he'd be in to the shop in April to get a few new pairs of shoes. Because he had permitted me to enter his inner circle, the people he trusted the most, I inquired—off the record of course—about his contract status. He told me he was meeting with Colonel Ruppert and Ed Barrow later in the week, and that he did not expect any problems to arise. That night, I did not know what DiMaggio had in store for the men who ran the Yankees.

The meeting was held at Ruppert Brewery on the upper east side of Manhattan. I was there, as were about 10 other reporters, waiting outside Ruppert's office for word on what DiMaggio had signed for. When the doors opened, DiMaggio exited with a brisk stride, wearing a look of frustration on his face, and he stormed right past the press as if we weren't even there. I knew DiMaggio was staying at the Hotel Commodore where the dinner had been held, so I drove over there, phoned his room, and he agreed to allow me to come up.

"I think I'm worth $40,000 to the ballclub, Joe," DiMaggio said to me as he lounged on the sofa in his room, puffing on a Camel cigarette and recounting what happened behind the closed doors of Ruppert's office. "They're offering $25,000, and I said forget it. Then Barrow said, 'Young man, do you know how long Lou Gehrig has been with this club? Well I'll tell you, 13 years. And do you know he's never been paid more than $40,000. What do you have to say to that?' So I said, 'Mr. Barrow, Gehrig is grossly underpaid.'"

I had to laugh at that one. I could just see Barrow's enormous eyebrows furrowing together in a scowl. I admitted to DiMaggio that I thought his demand was a bit excessive, and he politely replied, "Well, Joe, that's your opinion, and I happen to disagree with it."

I asked him what his next move was going to be and he said he was taking the train back to San Francisco and he was going to stay there until the Yankees met his demand. Again, I expressed my concern by saying, "Gee, Joe, do you think they're really going to break down?"

"I want $40,000, that's what I think I'm worth, and if they don't want to pay it, then I'll stay home."

DiMaggio made me promise not to divulge his salary demand in print, and I gave him my word. That's the way it always was with DiMaggio. Anything he said or did that didn't pertain to what happened on the field that day was not for public consumption, and I played that game for many years with him. We all did. Every writer in New York City played by DiMaggio's rules because if you didn't, you were an outcast and Joe wouldn't give you the time of day. And if DiMaggio did not deem you worthy of his time, the rest of the Yankees followed suit and that made doing your job a bit tedious.

I didn't say a word about DiMaggio's salary, and Ruppert had promised Joe the same, but the next day the Colonel revealed the team's offer anyway. "I suppose there'll be no end of wild guessing among you fellows," Ruppert told the writers. "So I might as well tell. It's $25,000 and I think that is a very fair salary. I don't intend to go any higher."

Ruppert knew once the figure was out there, public sentiment would be on his side, and he was right. The fans seethed over DiMaggio's outlandish demand, and their anger built steadily during spring training when DiMaggio stuck to his guns and refused to leave San Francisco. When the team broke camp at St. Petersburg to begin its annual barnstorming tour up the Eastern seaboard, Ruppert said, "Twenty-five thousand and not a button more. I have forgotten all about him. Presidents go into eclipse. Kings have their thrones moved from under them. Great ballplayers pass on. If DiMaggio isn't out there, we have Myril Hoag for center field."

– Chapter 7 –

1938

WHEN SPRING TRAINING OPENED in late February down in St. Petersburg, Joe DiMaggio was 3,000 miles away, and his holdout was the hot topic. Almost every day Joe McCarthy was asked where the negotiations stood, and McCarthy's pat response was, "I don't get involved in player contracts, that's up to Ed Barrow and Colonel Ruppert."

The DiMaggio story dominated the newspapers, and because I was one of the few writers that DiMaggio would agree to talk to concerning the subject, I was ahead of the curve most days in reporting the latest news.

However, the DiMaggio saga did not deter me from sizing up the latest Yankee club, and in my estimation, the biggest story of spring training was the arrival of Joe Gordon to play second base. We all knew the DiMaggio situation was going to play itself out. There was no way DiMaggio was going to skip the season, so sooner or later, he'd be back with the team. But the departure of longtime star Tony Lazzeri, who was released by the Yankees and was now a member of the Chicago Cubs, left a void on the infield, and Gordon was primed to fill it.

The year before, Oscar Vitt, who was the manager of the Yankees top farm team in Newark, was at the stadium one day talking with McCarthy in the presence of some of us writers. Vitt was raving about Gordon and he told McCarthy he would be "the greatest second baseman you ever saw." Grantland Rice scoffed at Vitt and said, "Take it easy Oscar, I've seen some pretty good second basemen." Vitt replied, "So have I. I've seen Lajoie, Collins, Evers, Hornsby, Frisch, Lazzeri, and Gehringer. I don't say this kid is better than them, all I'm saying is that someday he will be. He's better than anybody in the big leagues right now with the exception of Gehringer and he'll catch him next year." Rice was still skeptical, but not after watching Gordon play his first year in pinstripes.

Gordon had hit .280 with 26 home runs at Newark in 1937, and after making the transition from shortstop to second base, he played the field flawlessly. During the spring, you could see Gordon's ability shining through. He moved so gracefully around the bag turning double plays, and his great range allowed him to get to so many hard-hit balls that would normally have been base hits. At the plate he flashed some of his power, but he did the little things so well such as hitting behind runners to move them up, or slapping outside pitches into right field for singles rather than swinging for the fences.

McCarthy loved that unselfish nature, that willingness to do whatever it took to win the game. One day a few years into Gordon's career I was standing around the batting cage with McCarthy watching Gordon take his swings, and McCarthy said to me, "I'll take Gordon's kind of baseball and I'll show you why. 'Hey Joe, what are you hitting now?'" the manager asked Gordon. "I don't know," Gordon said. Then McCarthy asked him "What's your fielding average?" Gordon said, "How the hell would I know?" McCarthy looked at me with a smile and said, "See what I mean. All he does is try to beat you."

Lazzeri had been a popular player in the Bronx, but I surmised that the stadium crowds would grow to love Gordon pretty quickly. Respect didn't come right away, though. The first time Gordon showed up at Yankee Stadium he was refused entrance by one of the security guards. "I never heard of no Joe Gordon," the guy said. Gordon answered curtly, "You will."

No one expected Gordon to match his minor-league numbers in his rookie year with the Yankees, but he came damn close with 25 homers, 97 RBI, and a .255 average while playing the slickest second base in the league. Over the next six seasons he proved Vitt correct as he was the league's preeminent second baseman, and in 1942 he won the league's MVP award, outpolling Boston's Ted Williams, who had won the triple crown.

When Gordon died of a heart attack in 1978, I talked to Phil Rizzuto about him, and Phil told me, "Joe was the most acrobatic fielder I ever played with. The plays he could make off balance, throwing in midair or off one foot or lying down. Unbelievable."

Bob Feller, who was Gordon's teammate in Cleveland after Gordon was traded there following the 1946 season for pitcher Allie Reynolds, said, "Joe Gordon was as good a second baseman as anyone I ever played with or saw, including Charlie Gehringer."

*   *   *

As the spring progressed, it became apparent that Gordon was going to be fine at second, and everywhere else this Yankee team was just as strong as it had been the previous year. But there was that one missing element: DiMaggio.

In the final week of spring training I spoke to a number of players about the DiMaggio situation and though none would lend their names for the record, the general consensus was they were angry with DiMaggio because he wasn't thinking of the team. "He just wants to get rich quick," said one veteran player.

I thought DiMaggio was going to crack and come east to join the team for the start of the regular season, but he stubbornly held his course, and the Yankees opened at Fenway Park without him and lost 8-4. I called him that night to get his reaction and he said rather coldly, "That's too bad, but I'm sure it's going to happen again this season."

I had seen the wire photos of DiMaggio cooking spaghetti in the San Francisco restaurant that bore his name. This was the life he had worked so hard to avoid and though he remained diligent in his stance, I could sense this silly holdout wasn't going to last much longer. If nothing else, I know the negative publicity it was generating was killing him. All Joe ever wanted was to be rich and to be worshipped. By sitting home in San Francisco, he was neither.

After a doubleheader split with the Red Sox the next day, Barrow received a telegram from DiMaggio stating his intention to accept the $25,000 and report to the team. DiMaggio had lost, as we all knew he would. He had no recourse. Because baseball contracts contained a reserve clause that bound a player to his team, DiMaggio couldn't peddle his services to the highest bidder the way today's players can. It was either play for the Yankees or don't play, and DiMaggio couldn't fathom not playing, even if it meant his pride absorbing a titanic dent.

DiMaggio was supposed to arrive at Penn Station on a Saturday morning, so I and a dozen other members of the New York press corps went to greet him. But there was no DiMaggio. Anticipating a horde of reporters and photographers waiting for him, he got off the train in Newark and was picked up by fight manager Joe Gould, who had become his good friend. Eventually we caught up to DiMaggio while he was having breakfast at Jimmy Braddock's in Manhattan, and he said, "This year I'm going to have such a good season that there won't be any room for argument next year."

He was a man of his word. Putting his troubles behind him, and rising above the incessant booing he heard in every town, DiMaggio enjoyed another wonderful season on the field. He batted .324 with 32 homers and 140 RBI, and though the Yankees had a tougher time winning their third consecutive American League pennant, it wasn't that strenuous as they were 9 1/2 games clear of Boston at the end.

Nothing could stop this Yankee dynasty, because it was bigger than just one player. Sure, the Yankees would have missed DiMaggio if he had really chosen to sit the season out, but it's unlikely the pennant race would have been altered.

For the 13th straight season Gehrig surpassed the century mark in runs scored (115) and runs driven in (114), and he again did not miss a game, stretching his consecutive games played streak to 2,122. Though it was obvious he was losing a step, we assumed it was just advancing age catching up to the 35-year-old Iron Horse.

Gordon was a rock at second. Bill Dickey joined DiMaggio and Gehrig in the 100 RBI club with 115, and remained the best defensive catcher in the game. And Tommy Henrich, who played about a third of the 1937 season, became a regular fixture in right field in 1938 and flashed some power with 22 homers and 91 RBI.

On the mound, the Yankee staff led the American League in ERA (3.91) for the fifth straight season as Red Ruffing and Lefty Gomez continued to be the most dominant 1-2 pitching punch in baseball. Monte Pearson and Spud Chandler proved to be reliable members of the rotation, Pearson twirling a no-hitter in August, the first in Yankee Stadium history. And when the starters faltered, ace reliever Johnny Murphy put out their fires.

Although the victory total dipped to 99, Joe McCarthy said this was the best Yankee team he had ever managed, and his rival, Connie Mack of the Athletics, agreed that this was the finest team he had ever competed against, including the 1927 Yankees. Never was this more apparent than during the month of August. Because of poor early-season weather, the Yankees were faced with a grueling schedule that called for their playing 36 games in 31 August days. Many teams would have crumbled, but the Yankees won 28 times, setting a record for most victories in one month. Instead of cutting their deficit in the standings, the Red Sox actually lost ground, and after the hard work of August, the Yankees coasted home in September.

— 1938 *World Series* —

One week before the start of the World Series, the Yankees were in a relaxed state, playing out the end of the schedule without an ounce of pressure as they had long ago wrapped up another American League pennant. Who they were going to play in the fall classic was still an issue yet to be decided. The Cubs and Pirates were locked in a furious duel, and as fate would have it, they were lined up face-to-face for a three-game series at Wrigley Field that would ultimately decide the National League champion.

Chicago took the opener for its eighth win in a row, and the next day, with the score tied at 5-5 and darkness enveloping the Windy City, player/manager Gabby Hartnett slammed Mace Brown's two-strike pitch for a game-winning bottom-of-the-ninth home run, vaulting the Cubs into first place. It became known as the Homer in the Gloamin' and when the Cubs finally clinched the pennant, Hartnett's home run took on a life of its own. To this day, it is considered one of baseball's greatest moments.

Hartnett's euphoria didn't last long, though. There was no gloamin' during the Yankees systematic four-game sweep of the Cubs, but there was plenty of gloatin' for Yankee manager Joe McCarthy. The man who Cubs owner William Wrigley had fired back in 1930 now owned two Series victories over the Cubs without the loss of a single game.

As was the case in 1932, the Cubs were no match for the Yankees. They had expended too much energy in the final month of the season trying to catch Pittsburgh, and after winning 21 of 25 games to qualify for the Series, they were simply incapable of giving Hartnett any more. Anything less than 100% was never good enough to beat the Yankees.

With Red Ruffing hurling complete game gems to open and close the Series and light-hitting shortstop Frank Crosetti driving in six runs, the Yankees rolled to their seventh world championship, which also happened to be their third in a row, an unprecedented feat. "The National League should feel very happy," said Washington Senators manager and future Yankee skipper Bucky Harris. "All its pennant winner has to do is face those Yanks in one series a year. How about us in the American League who have to see 'em around all year?"

As Cubs first baseman Rip Collins surmised when it was over, "We came, we saw, and now we go home. Thank God none of us was hurt."

At the conclusion of the fourth and final game, Ruffing bounded joyfully off the mound, his teammates clapping him on the back as a Yankee Stadium throng roared its approval. I couldn't imagine the glee he felt, considering the way his life, and his baseball career, had begun.

*   *   *

Ruffing was 15 years old when his father told him to quit school and come to work with him in the coal mines of Nokomis, Illinois. While underground, Ruffing caught his left foot between two mining cars, and the result was the loss of four toes.

He had been playing the outfield for the company baseball team which his father managed, but the injury sidelined him for a year and there were many days when he thought he'd never play baseball again. But he did return, as a pitcher, despite playing with constant pain. "The foot bothered me the rest of my career and I had to land on the side of my left foot in my follow-through," he said.

Ruffing caught the eye of the manager of the local semipro team, and after a brief stint, he signed his first pro contract with Danville of the 3-I League in 1923. By 1924 he was pitching for the Boston Red Sox, though not very impressively. In his first three full major league seasons he walked more batters than he struck out, and he was a perpetual loser thanks to the lousy Boston teams that played behind him.

Ruffing was enduring a typically horrific season in 1929 as Boston was in the midst of finishing last in the American League for the fifth year in a row. Ruffing had lost a league-worst 25 games in 1928 and he would lead the league in that dubious category again in 1929 with 22. Remarkably, his batting average exceeded his winning percentage in both those years, which prompted Red Sox manager Bill Carrigan to experiment with Ruffing in the outfield. Alas, Ruffing's fielding couldn't match his hitting, and he went back to pitching full-time, seemingly doomed to a lifetime of losing.

Yankees manager Miller Huggins saw something in Ruffing that his gloomy statistics overshadowed: He had a strong arm and a bulldog mentality on the mound. On one of the few days I was able to perform my batboy duties in 1929, I was standing on the field behind the batting cage prior to a Yankees-Red Sox game and overheard Huggins tell Ruffing

"I never talk to players from other clubs, but in this case I think I should open my mouth. You never will be more than a fair outfielder, but you could be a great pitcher. I mean, a real pitcher. Now the Yanks need pitchers and I'm going after you. Keep pitching, don't let them kill you in the outfield."

Huggins died a few months later, but he had told Bob Shawkey about Ruffing, and when Shawkey was managing the club in 1930, the Yankees acquired Ruffing in exchange for Cedric Durst and $50,000 cash. Once again, the Yankees had fleeced the Red Sox.

"The Red Sox of my time weren't even a good double-A team," Ruffing said. "I wasn't a better pitcher (once he came to New York). The year I lost 25 for the Sox, I would have won 25 with the Yankees behind me."

When Ruffing joined the Yankees his major league record stood at 39-96. By the time he retired in 1946, after nearly 16 years in New York, his mark was 273-225. He remains the club's all-time leader in innings pitched and complete games, and among Yankee right-handers, Ruffing is No. 1 in games, starts, wins, and strikeouts. During the Yankees' run to four straight championships in the late 1930s, Ruffing topped 20 victories each year, and his lifetime Series record was a sparkling 7-2.

Equally as impressive was his skill as a batter. A career .269 hitter, he drove in more runs than any modern pitcher in major league history (273), he batted .300 in eight seasons (six with the Yankees) and his 36 lifetime homers rank third among pitchers behind only Wes Ferrell and Bob Lemon.

A few years after he retired he came to the stadium for a function and I sat down and talked to him about his hitting prowess. "When I started out, I was like most pitchers at the plate, scared. I'd jump back from a tight pitch and hit with a foot in the bucket. Then one day it happened. I got hit by a pitched ball and I was amazed; it didn't hurt me at all. From that day on I dug in at the plate and became a hitter."

I felt guilty every time I saw Ruffing after World War II. Here I was stateside because of my childhood case of osteomyelitis, which by the time the war began really didn't affect my life anymore, and over in Europe was Ruffing. At the age of 38, a husband and father of two children, a man with four toes missing on his left foot, Ruffing was drafted into the Army in 1942. He never fought in combat, but still, he was part of the war effort for two years. I really admired him for that, as well as the way he appreciated the game.

"Money isn't everything in baseball, though it helps," he told me. "Baseball is a great game, it's been marvelous to me and I never will be able to repay the debt. It took me out of the coal mines. Baseball put me on the lift, out of the shafts and into the sunshine, into a grand game among grand guys, into a way of life that's remarkable. That's the good old USA for you."

*   *   *

Ruffing dominated Game One at Wrigley Field, though we weren't able to talk to him about it because McCarthy barred all of the writers from the clubhouse after the game. We thought this strange, considering that his team had won, and we complained to him long and hard about it the next day but none of our whining meant a thing to McCarthy. It was his clubhouse, and he decided to close it, end of story.

The Yankees led 2-1 in the sixth when Tommy Henrich, like Joe Gordon playing in his first Series game, lined a double to left and scored on Bill Dickey's RBI single. With that two-run cushion, Ruffing was home free. He allowed nine hits, but didn't walk a batter, struck out five, and benefited from a couple of superb plays in the field by shortstop Frank Crosetti. The Cubs had base runners in each of the last four innings, including Hartnett who tripled with two out in the seventh, but couldn't score another run.

"What the hell," Hartnett said. "Those guys [the Yankees] better look better tomorrow than they did today or they had better look out. They were just lucky, that's all. We'll battle them silly tomorrow. They're more scared than we are."

The massive press corps would have loved to hear McCarthy's response to that one. Instead, he urged his team to do its talking on the field the next day.

In Game Two Lefty Gomez opposed the longtime great, Dizzy Dean, and the two future Hall of Famers struggled early before settling into a classic duel. The Cubs took a 3-2 lead into the eighth before Crosetti, whose nine homers during the season were the fewest of any Yankee regular, jacked a go-ahead two-run blast to left, and Joe DiMaggio's two-run homer in the ninth finished off a 6-3 Yankee victory.

Dean, who had begun to tire, was pushed to the limit by Crosetti and was forced to throw 10 pitches during the at-bat. "I threw myself out," Dean would say afterward. "I had them beat until Crosetti hit his homer. The Yankees were the luckiest ball club in the last two days that I ever saw. I can understand how the Yankees won the American League pennant. They're lucky."

On the train ride back to New York, McCarthy held court with some of the reporters, including me, and while he praised Dean for a gutsy performance, he did not hesitate to add, "I think ol' Diz was getting just a little bit cocky along about the eighth inning."

Two games up and going home, the Yankees were in a playful mood during that trip. As we pulled into Fort Wayne, Indiana, a photographer, grossly overweight, panting breathlessly and obviously assigned to get a shot of the world-famous Yankees passing through town, asked Gomez where the ballplayers were. Gomez, sensing a priceless moment, pointed in the direction of batboy Timmy Sullivan and said, "There's DiMaggio." Taking his cue, the photographer got all set to shoot pictures of Sullivan before he realized he was being duped, and the entire club car erupted in laughter.

A little later, Crosetti came in, crawling on his hands and knees, lit a match, and set one of the waiter's shoes on fire, a classic hotfoot that had the young man dancing like a chorus girl. More laughter from these giddy Yankees, and no one was laughing harder than the usually crusty Crosetti.

*   *   *

Besides the hijinks, the other thing I remember about that trip was my spending an inordinate amount of time shooting the breeze and drinking beers with Crosetti, the dean of Yankee service. We were both there the day Ruth hit his alleged "called shot" in the 1932 Series, and we were both there the day Mickey Mantle hit the last of his 536 home runs in 1968. Crosetti spent 37 years as a player or coach for the Yankees, the longest on-field tenure of anyone in the organization's history.

For the most part Crosetti was a serious man, at the ballpark and away from it, and though we shared a long association and we were relatively close in age (he was six years older than I), we were never particularly chummy, even when I was working for the team. I didn't understand why Crosetti always seemed to be in a grouchy mood, but Phil Rizzuto, who replaced the Crow as the team's regular shortstop in 1941 and was very close to him, clued me in when Crosetti left the team prior to the 1969 season to join the expansion Seattle Pilots as a coach. "People who didn't know him thought he was an ogre, that he was a miserable, mean old man," said the Scooter, who had a polar opposite personality. "He wasn't. It was just that there was no fooling around, which is the way it should be."

Crosetti was a light hitter, as his .245 career average indicates, but he found other ways to get on base. During his career he drew 792 walks and eight times he led the American League in being hit by pitches, though he rarely got hurt doing it. His secret was to wear a uniform top that was a bit baggy, and when pitches were close, he would craftily move his body into the ball so it would graze his shirt. Umpires always assumed the pitch hit him, and he'd trot happily—at least for him—down to first base.

Rogers Hornsby once said, "Crosetti is the sparkplug of the Yankees. Without him they wouldn't have a chance. He is a great player and he's about the only one on that club who does any hollering."

Crow was a chatterbox on the field, and his was a distinctive voice. "When he was playing and hollering he had a whistle that you could hear all over the ballpark," said Rizzuto. "His voice was shrill, which was great because you could hear him (if you were) the cutoff man."

* * *

Crosetti's stellar defensive play had been a key to the Game One victory, and his home run had won Game Two. That was the thing about the Yankees in those years. They won all the time, and it seemed like there was a different hero every day. So whose turn would it be in Game Three? Monte Pearson and Gordon.

Pearson improved his Series record to 3-0 with a smooth five-hitter while Gordon delivered a solo home run and a two-run single during a 5-2 victory that put the Yankees in complete command.

Clay Bryant had held the Yankees hitless for 4 2/3 innings and was leading 1-0 when he tried to slip a two-strike change-up past Gordon, only to see the ball sail into the lower left-field seats. In the sixth Gordon roped a bases-loaded single that sent DiMaggio and Lou Gehrig scurrying home for a 4-1 lead which Pearson had little trouble protecting.

It was now hopeless for the Cubs, and with Ruffing going the distance the next day, it soon was over. Ruffing's RBI single and Crosetti's two-run triple made it 3-0 in the second, and Henrich's home run in the sixth made it 4-1 before Chicago stirred in the eighth when Ken O'Dea hit a two-run homer. Just as the Cubs were feeling their oats and entertaining thoughts of living to see another day, the Yankees went for the jugular in the bottom half, scoring four runs while two were out, the key hit a two-run bloop double by Crosetti.

In the clubhouse there was madness all around him, but the stoic one, Lou Gehrig, sat in front of his locker dragging on a cigarette, sipping a beer, smiling, taking it all in. This was the sixth time he'd won a World Series, and while it was still exciting, it was old hat, too.

Gehrig looked tired to me that day. In fact, he'd looked tired most of the year. Though he had scored and driven in 100 runs each for the 13th straight year, the Iron Horse had not been the same player in 1938. His 114 RBI were his fewest since 1926, his .295 batting average his lowest since 1925, and he'd been lethargic in the field and on the base paths. In the Series, he managed four singles in 14 at-bats and this was the first time in his postseason career that he'd failed to drive in a run.

I sat down next to him, shook his hand in congratulations, and after some brief small talk, without prompting from me, he talked about his future. "I think I'll do fine," Gehrig said, referring to the 1939 season. "This was just a bad year for me."

With that he stood up and joined his teammates in singing "The Sidewalks of New York." This was not the time to think about 1939. It was time to celebrate 1938.

The first time I cried as an adult was also the first time many of the people present at Yankee Stadium on the afternoon of July 4, 1939 cried as adults. That day I stood in the press box gazing down at one of my heroes, Lou Gehrig—a man who two weeks earlier had been handed a veritable death certificate—as he delivered one of the most famous orations in American history.

"Fans, for the past two weeks you have been reading about a bad break I got, yet today I consider myself the luckiest man on the face of the earth. I have been in ballparks for 17 years and I have never received anything but kindness and encouragement from you fans. Look at these grand men. Which of you wouldn't consider it the highlight of his career just to associate with them for even one day? Sure, I'm lucky. Who wouldn't consider it an honor to have known Jacob Ruppert? Also, the builder of baseball's greatest empire, Ed Barrow? To have spent six years with that wonderful little fellow, Miller Huggins? Then to have spent the next nine years with that outstanding leader, that smart student of psychology, the best manager in baseball today, Joe McCarthy? Sure, I'm lucky. When the New York Giants, a team you would give your right arm to beat, and vice-versa, sends you a gift, that's something. When everybody down to the groundskeepers and those boys in white coats remember you with trophies, that's something. When you have a father and mother who work all their lives so that you can have an education and build your body, it's a blessing. When you have a wife who has been a tower of strength and shown more courage than you dreamed existed, that's the finest I know. So in closing I say that I might have had a bad break, but I have an awful lot to live for. Thank you."

My God, the courage of this man.

It was a scene that was burned into my memory forever.

An eerie silence enveloped the stadium as Gehrig spoke in a halted manner, allowing for the echoes to catch up to him. When he finished his speech there was a brief pause for reflection, almost as if the magnitude of the moment had to sink in before a tremendous, heartfelt ovation rained down on Gehrig. And as the crowd roared its thank you, Babe Ruth, always sensing the moment, came up to Gehrig and wrapped him in a hug, even though he and Lou hadn't spoken to each other for about five years, their silence a product of a rather silly feud.

All around me were writers, typically hard-boiled men not prone to empathy, dabbing their eyes with handkerchiefs. On the field were the ballplayers *who formed a semicircle around Gehrig, members of the current Yankee club and a collection of his former teammates, some of the greatest names in baseball history, trying to hide their sadness by bowing their heads. Most poignant to me were the looks on the faces of the children in the jam-packed stands, unaware of what was happening, unable to understand why tears were flowing down the cheeks of their fathers and mothers.*

Under a brilliant blue sky, in the grandest arena in America, a place where he had brought smiles to the faces of millions of fans and where he was now bringing such deep sorrow, Gehrig stood in the epicenter of this emotional earthquake and never flinched. Though his body was being ravaged by amyotrophic lateral sclerosis, an insidious disease of the central nervous system that causes muscular atrophy and, ultimately, paralysis and death, Gehrig hovered over the microphone erected at home plate and displayed the same strength and reliability that allowed him to man first base for more than 14 years without missing a single game.

His legs never buckled, his hands never shook, his speech was never slurred. On that unforgettable day, ALS, later to be referred to as Lou Gehrig's Disease, could not defeat Gehrig.

– Chapter 8 –

1939

IT WAS A SUN-SPLASHED FEBRUARY Florida morning, and as a gentle breeze blew across the Yankees' spring training practice field, Lou Gehrig closed his eyes and let the warm air wash over him. He had arrived in St. Petersburg determined to prove that his 1938 decline was just an aberration, that he could still wield a mighty bat and play first base with the skill and grace he had displayed during 14 glorious seasons in New York. Gehrig had felt tired at the end of 1938, so he'd taken it easy during the off-season, resting his weary body more than he ever had, and he came to Florida convinced that 1939 would be a bounce-back season for him. Sadly, it would not be, though it had nothing to do with deteriorating baseball skills.

On this day he grabbed a couple bats, swished them back and forth to loosen his muscles, and when he felt sufficiently limber, he stepped into the batting cage to take his cuts, a knot of reporters fixated on him. The first pitch came coasting in, grooved right down the middle, not more than 60 miles an hour, high school speed. Gehrig swung and missed. Here came the next offering, same spot, same speed. Gehrig swung and missed. I remember looking down at the ground, this exhibition almost too painful to watch. On and on it went. Nineteen pitches were thrown and not once did Gehrig put his bat on the ball.

He finally held up his hand instructing the pitcher to stop throwing, and he walked dejectedly out of the cage, the gentle smile transformed into a confused grimace. He had no explanation for his struggles. No one did. It pained me to write that day in the *Home News* that it looked as if the end was near for the great Gehrig. Of course, I only meant the end of his baseball career.

It didn't get much better for Gehrig as the spring progressed. His timing was terribly off, he appeared unsteady in the field, and there were days when it looked like he was catching the ball only to protect himself from getting hit by it. I was in the clubhouse on two occasions when Gehrig collapsed to the floor. One time he was trying to put on his pants and tumbled over, and when Pete Sheehy and Joe DiMaggio offered to help him up, he embarrassingly said, "Please, I can get up." Another time he climbed on top of a bench to look out the window, lost his balance and fell backward, landing hard on his rear end. He lay there for a moment, a puzzled look on his face as he wondered what was going on.

In the first 10 exhibition games Gehrig hit an abysmal .100, and when a writer from the Orlando newspaper asked him what was wrong, Gehrig uncharacteristically slammed his glove into his locker and shouted, "Why in hell don't you leave me alone?"

By the time the spring schedule was complete Gehrig's average stood at .215, and among his 26 hits were 24 singles and two home runs that were both hit over a short right-field fence in Norfolk, Virginia, when the team was barnstorming its way back up north. He had driven home a respectable 21 runs, but had also committed eight errors in the field.

"I don't know" is all Joe McCarthy would say when asked what he thought was wrong with Gehrig. But McCarthy made one thing very clear. Gehrig was his starting first baseman until Gehrig told him he wasn't.

On May 2, Gehrig told him he wasn't.

In the first eight games of the regular season, Gehrig went hitless in five, and his batting average stood at .143. John Kieran wrote in the *New York Times* that Gehrig "looked like a man trying to lift heavy trunks into a truck."

I had known Gehrig for 13 years and regarded him as one of the classiest human beings I'd ever encountered. He was a quiet leader, but he was an engaging personality once you got to know him. I considered him a good friend, even though he was 13 years older than me, so one day in the second week of the season I went up to him at his locker, put away my notebook, and asked off the record, man-to-man, if everything was all right. He shrugged me off, but when I prodded him further, he told me in confidence, "Joe, I just don't have any energy. I can't put my finger on it, but my body feels limp and I don't seem to have any strength."

He went 0-for-4 the next day, April 30, and the Yankees lost at home to the Washington Senators. It was the last game he would ever play. A routine fielding chance that Gehrig was barely able to make served as his final indignation. A ball was chopped between the mound and first base and pitcher Johnny Murphy fielded it, then had to wait for Gehrig to get to the bag and the batter nearly beat it out for a hit. Murphy sympathetically told Gehrig he'd made a nice play, and that's when Gehrig knew he was through.

After the game Gehrig told me of the exchange he had with Murphy, and when I asked him on that Sunday afternoon if he was considering taking a rest, thus bringing to an end his remarkable consecutive games played streak which stood at 2,130, he admitted he was. This is no big deal in this day and age. Today's players take more days off than government employees, but remember, Gehrig hadn't missed a game in nearly 14 years, a record I still can't believe did not stand forever.

Finding the words difficult to type on my Remington portable, I broke the story in the next day's *Home News* that Gehrig was contemplating sitting down. Even for a readership that knew he was slumping terribly, it still came as a shock to think that someone named Babe Dahlgren might be playing first base for the Yankees Tuesday in Detroit.

The team traveled to Detroit that Monday, and the next morning Gehrig huddled with McCarthy in the manager's room at the team hotel and asked to be taken out of the lineup "for the good of the team." McCarthy balked at first, but he knew it was best for the Yankees, and more importantly, best for Gehrig.

Gehrig presented the Yankees lineup card to umpire Stephen Basil, and just before the first pitch was thrown, an announcement was made informing the sparse crowd at Briggs Stadium that Gehrig would not be playing. The Detroit fans paid tribute to Gehrig by standing and applauding for nearly two minutes.

With Dahlgren hitting a home run and a double, the Yankees steamrolled the Tigers, 22-2, but the result mattered little. Afterward, all conversation focused on Gehrig. The press is allowed to talk to the players on the field before games, but we are not allowed in the clubhouse until after the game, so I asked DiMaggio what the mood was like in there when McCarthy announced that Gehrig would not play. He compared it to that of standing in a funeral parlor for a wake.

"It would not be fair to the boys, to Joe, or to the baseball public for me to try going on," Gehrig said glumly to the reporters gathered around him. "Maybe a rest will do me some good. Maybe it won't. Who knows? Who can tell? I'm just hoping."

McCarthy, clearly upset by what had transpired, said, "Lou just told me he felt it would be best for the club if he took himself out of the lineup. I asked him if he really felt that way. He told me he was serious. He feels blue. He is dejected."

Six weeks later, the world shared in that dejection when Dr. Harold Harbein of the Mayo Clinic in Rochester, Minnesota, released a statement that solved the mystery of Gehrig's physical malady. After a week of examinations at the renowned medical facility, Gehrig was found to be suffering from amyotrophic lateral sclerosis. Though a timetable was not put on his imminent death, research indicated that he would likely be gone within two years, no more than three.

Many of us knew Gehrig had to be sick because as DiMaggio said one day, "Ballplayers like Gehrig don't collapse overnight." But no one ever considered this grave prognosis.

The July 4 Gehrig Appreciation Day was an opportunity for his teammates, the press and the fans to pay homage to his great career, but it also served as a reminder of how fragile life is. Here was a marvelously gifted athlete, one of the greatest baseball players ever, and only a few months removed from playing in a World Series, he could barely tie his own shoes.

Gehrig remained with the club throughout the year, even when the team was on the road. He brought the lineup card out to home plate before every game, then sat on the bench lending his teammates moral support. It was definitely the best thing for his spirits to stay with the team, but he told me on a number of occasions that it was difficult to sit there and not play, even though he knew he physically couldn't.

The Yankees had gotten off to a solid start despite the distraction and were in first place for good by May 11. But after the emotional July 4 doubleheader split with the Senators, the Yankees lost five games in a row at home to the Red Sox, part of a six-game losing streak that suddenly tightened the standings. Their response to that was an eight-game winning streak which helped to offset Boston's 23-10 record in July. It put the Yankees back in control, and we in the press began referring to the rest of the American League as the Seven Dwarfs.

By the time the season was over—a season in which home games of all three New York City baseball teams were broadcast on the radio for the first time, and a season in which the Yankees played the first night game of their history against Philadelphia at Shibe Park—the pennant race was a joke. The Yankees won 106 games, were 17 games ahead of second-place Boston, and an unheard of 64 1/2 games better than the lowly St. Louis Browns.

The World's Fair was hosted by New York City in 1939, and more than 33 million people attended. *Gone with the Wind* and *The Wizard of Oz* debuted on the silver screen, John Steinbeck published *The Grapes of Wrath*, and Irving Berlin composed "God Bless America." But once again, there was no better entertainment than the Yankees.

– *1939 World Series* –

I asked Monte Pearson one day for his reaction to the claim made by some of my fellow New York baseball writers that he was a hypochondriac and he said, "I didn't even know what the word meant until I looked it up in the dictionary." When he looked it up, I'm surprised he didn't find his picture illustrating the definition.

Pearson was a hypochondriac. This I know because his first year with the team was also my last as a clubhouse attendant, and I heard him whine about every little ache and pain he incurred. If the team trainer, Doc Painter, had been paid per rubdown, Pearson would have enabled old Doc to retire at an early age.

One time during that 1936 season Pearson disappeared for about three days and no one knew where he was. Ed Barrow told me to hail a taxi and go over to Pearson's apartment to see if he was there, and when I knocked on the door, here came Pearson.

"Hey, Joe, what're you doing here?" he asked me.

"Well, Monte, Mr. Barrow hasn't heard from you in a few days and he wanted me to see if you were OK."

It turned out that Pearson had been feeling the effects of the flu and Barrow had told him to go home and wait for a doctor to arrive. For three days no one showed up, but rather than call Barrow, Pearson just stayed in bed.

When I told Barrow that Pearson was indeed at home, waiting for a doctor to come check him out, Barrow slammed his fist down, dismissed me, then ordered a physician to go check on Pearson. I wasn't sure who Barrow was more upset with—the doctor or Pearson.

Another time that year, Joe McCarthy, who often doubted Pearson when the pitcher would complain about a sore arm, consulted a physician regarding Pearson's wing. After inspecting Pearson the doctor told McCarthy "This man has no more right to be pitching than I have. He has the worst looking arm I've ever examined. It's full of bone chips and calcium deposits and most of the time it hurts like hell. But there are days when he won't have a twinge. Those are the days he can help you."

Four of those days happened to come in World Series play.

The Yankee front office didn't always appreciate Pearson's chronic ailments, real or perceived, but they recognized that he was one of the most important cogs during the team's run to four straight World Series championships from 1936 to 1939. Pearson won 56 games during that period and each year he seemed to save his best for the postseason, as he won a game in all four Series including 1939 when he carried a no-hitter into the eighth inning of Game Two against Cincinnati.

Pearson made it to the majors in 1932 with Cleveland, was demoted to the minors, then returned for good in 1933 when newfound control of his curveball helped him lead the American League in ERA. His manager, Hall of Fame pitcher Walter Johnson, claimed Pearson had more natural ability than any other pitcher he had ever seen, but a slump in 1935 convinced the Indians to give up on him and Pearson was dealt to the Yankees along with Steve Sundra in exchange for Johnny Allen.

Colonel Ruppert admitted later that Sundra was the pitcher he and Barrow really wanted because they had received a glowing report on him from one of their scouts. They figured Allen was a better pitcher than Pearson, but Sundra would tilt the scales in New York's favor. Sundra wound up being a serviceable player for the Yankees, but he never approached Pearson's productiveness.

*   *   *

Everyone in attendance on an overcast but pleasantly warm afternoon in the Bronx expected to see the best pitching of the 1939 Series in the opener as Red Ruffing, a 21-game winner, opposed Cincinnati's 25-game winner Paul Derringer. No one left disappointed as Ruffing and Derringer were brilliant and the Yankees squeezed out a 2-1 victory when Charlie Keller tripled to the gap in right-center and scored the winning run on Bill Dickey's single over second in the bottom of the ninth inning.

"My arm hurt plenty right at the start, but I figured I'd keep throwing 'em and either come out with a bad arm or as a winner," Ruffing said.

The Reds took a 1-0 lead in the fourth when Ival Goodman walked on four pitches, stole second, and came around to score on Frank McCormick's single past Red Rolfe into left field, but the Yankees tied it in the fifth when third-base coach Art Fletcher made a heads-up decision. Joe Gordon lined a one-out single to left and Babe Dahlgren followed with a double down the line in left. Gordon was steaming into third thinking Fletcher would hold him, but Fletcher gave him the green light when he saw the relay throw from Wally Berger sailing into Lonnie Frey at second base. Frey wheeled and fired home, but Gordon slid under catcher Ernie Lombardi's tag for the tying run.

"If you ask me," McCarthy said, "I'd say the outstanding play was Fletcher sending Gordon in on Dahlgren's double. That was smart. Art saw that Berger's throw was going to second base and he kept Joe going around third at top speed."

Neither team could scratch anything else off these two pitchers until the last of the ninth. Rolfe grounded out to first, but then Keller hit Derringer's next offering high and deep to right-center. Goodman raced over from center and Harry Craft gave chase from right, and just when it looked like the two men might collide, each pulled up and the ball glanced off Goodman's glove and rolled to the wall as Keller lumbered into third. Joe DiMaggio was intentionally walked as Reds manager Bill McKechnie opted to pitch to Dickey, but Dickey ruined that strategy by singling to win the game.

The Reds may have felt like they cheated themselves out of that first game, but there was nothing they could do about Pearson in Game Two. McKechnie trotted out the other half of his dynamic pitching duo, Bucky Walters, who wound up being voted the National League's most valuable player. McKechnie knew he had to win at least one game in New York, and Walters seemed like his best bet. On any other day, he may have been.

"I didn't know I had a no-hitter," said Pearson. "I just knew they didn't have many hits, but all I was trying to do was get those fellas out."

It didn't appear to me that Pearson had anything special working for him in this game. He started off rather routinely and the Reds hit a couple balls hard, most notably a drive into left-center off Lombardi's bat that George Selkirk made a nice running catch on to save an extra base hit. But as the game wore on, I began to notice that Pearson's curve was biting a little harder, and he was keeping the Reds off balance with a nifty change-up.

Walters managed to get through the first two innings without any damage, but the Yankees got to him in the third for three runs, and Dahlgren's solo homer in the fourth made it 4-0 and the only issue left to decide was whether Pearson could complete his march to immortality.

Through seven innings, only one Cincinnati batter had reached base, Bill Werber on a walk in the fourth, and he was quickly erased by a double play. When McCormick lined to Selkirk in left to open the eighth, Pearson had faced the minimum 22 batters and was five outs away from the no-hitter. But I succinctly remember that I had a bad feeling about Pearson facing Lombardi. Ernie had hit a solid rope back in the second, and it just seemed like he had a groove on Pearson. Sure enough, after taking a ball outside, Lombardi wheeled on a fastball and lined it solidly for a history-ruining single.

My heart sank because I was excited about chronicling the first no-hitter in World Series play. I would be teased by another near no-hitter eight years later by Bill Bevens, but I finally got to write that story in 1956 when Don Larsen pitched his perfect game.

Pearson settled for a two-hit 4-0 shutout that put the Yankees up two games to none. In the clubhouse Pearson was all smiles, and when he was asked how he felt, rather than recite one of his oft-heard mantras, Pearson said, "I felt pretty good out there, and I feel a lot better now."

*   *   *

On the train ride out to Cincinnati I sat for a long time with Mel Allen, who in 1939 was teaming with Arch McDonald to describe Yankee games to radio listeners for the first time on a regular basis. The management of all three New York City-based teams were the last in the major leagues to allow their regular-season games to be heard on the radio. For years they resisted the trend, arguing that in a competitive market they couldn't afford to give their product away for free. They needed big gates to pay the bills, and the Yankees, Giants, and Dodgers feared that radio would detract from their live audience. Once they relented, Allen joined the Yankees, and we became fast friends.

Allen had enrolled at the University of Alabama as a 15-year-old in 1928, and he went on to earn a law degree there by the time he was 24. But while Allen had a fervent mind, he also had a golden voice, and rather than put that degree to use, he fell in love with the radio. At the time it may have seemed like a poor career choice, but it certainly turned out all right.

His first taste of radio came while he was still at Alabama as he became the voice of the Crimson Tide when he was 20 years old, broadcasting the school's football games for the CBS affiliate in Birmingham. Ted Husing, who was a CBS sportscaster, heard Allen's work and suggested he audition for CBS, which he did, and Allen passed the test. However, he stayed in school to complete his law degree and it wasn't until 1937 when he went to New York to take a $45-a-week job for the network.

He was the national voice of the 1938 World Series between the Yankees and Cubs, and when Larry MacPhail—then with the Dodgers, six years away from becoming partial owner of the Yankees—broke the New York radio ban by allowing Brooklyn's games to be broadcast, the Yankees hired Allen and McDonald to do their home games live. For the road games, they sat in a studio and recreated the action using a sports ticker and sound effects.

McDonald stayed in New York just for the 1939 season, then returned to Washington where he had worked previously as the Senators broadcaster. That cleared the way for Allen to become a New York baseball institution, just like Dodgers play-by-play man Red Barber, who in 1954 joined Allen in the Yankees booth to create the greatest announcing tandem in sports history.

All of my fellow writers were older than me when I started in the business, but Allen was only three years my senior so our bond was natural. With his catch phrases "How about that?" and "Going, going, gone" it's safe to say that Mel became just a bit more famous than me, but what I liked about Mel was that fame never changed him.

The Yankees were absent from the airwaves in 1943 and 1944 because of the war, and Allen went off to serve in the army, but when he returned in 1946, the team made a pioneer move. With Allen at the microphone, the Yankees became the first club in the major leagues to nix studio recreations and broadcast all of their games live. Allen had been the national voice of the World Series and we'd traveled together on a few occasions when the Yankees were Series participants, but once he hit the road with the team full-time, he became one of my primary dinner and drinking companions.

Allen remained with the club until 1964 before being unceremoniously fired by the new ownership. That was a sad day, and it coincided with the beginning of the end of the Yankee empire. Allen didn't miss much in New York as the team went into steep decline, and by the time it pulled out of its nosedive by winning the World Series in 1977, Allen had become the voice of the syndicated Major League Baseball show *This Week In Baseball,* where he furthered his legend for a new generation of baseball fans.

* * *

When we arrived in Cincinnati, we were fortunate that our hotel accommodations at The Netherland Plaza had already been taken care of because the city was booked solid as World Series hysteria had arrived. More than 5,000 people, undeterred by their team's predicament, greeted the Reds at Union Terminal when they arrived. The players, those who didn't duck out, were then whisked to waiting cars for a parade through downtown attended by about 30,000 horn-blowing, pennant-waving fans.

Not since 1919 had the Reds played in the Series, and the fine citizens of Cincinnati weren't going to let a two-game deficit spoil their fun. Of course the mood changed drastically the next day when the Yankees made it three games to none with a 7-3 victory.

In sweltering heat that made it feel like July rather than October, the Yankee bats boomed as Keller swatted a pair of home runs and DiMaggio and Dickey had one each, all off Reds rookie starter Gene Thompson.

"There's nothing much to say," said McCarthy. "Keller, DiMaggio, and Dickey did all the talking today. They were kind of noisy, too, weren't they?"

And so was Bump Hadley, who replaced Lefty Gomez at the start of the second inning when Lefty—who allowed three hits and a run in the first—had to retire with an injury to his side. Hadley pitched eight unexpected innings and while the Reds touched him for seven hits and three walks, he yielded only two runs, none over the final seven innings.

Keller's first homer was a two-run shot in the first, and after Cincinnati rallied to take a 3-2 lead in the second, Keller drew a two-out walk in the third and trotted home when DiMaggio unleashed a long home run to dead center to reestablish the Yankee lead. And then in the fifth, Keller hit his second two-run homer and Dickey tacked on a solo shot to make it 7-3.

In the clubhouse I saw road secretary Mark Roth holding a handful of train tickets with a departure date for the next day, so confident was he that the Yankees would finish off the sweep. But McCarthy said to him, "Better wait until tomorrow" to start passing them out.

And that's what Roth did when the Yankees closed it out with a dramatic 7-4 victory in 10 innings. The game was scoreless through six innings as Derringer for the Reds and Oral Hildebrand and Sundra for the Yankees pitched very well. Derringer blinked first as Keller and Dickey both hit solo homers in the seventh to give the Yankees a 2-0 lead, but the Reds stormed back with three unearned runs in their half to take the lead.

When Lombardi hit a RBI single in the eighth for a 4-2 lead it looked like Cincinnati would get to host another game at Crosley Field. Instead, with Walters on in relief in the ninth, Keller and DiMaggio opened with singles and both scored to tie the game.

After Johnny Murphy set the Reds down in the ninth, the Yankees took advantage of shoddy fielding by the Reds and manufactured one of the wildest plays in Series history. Frank Crosetti led off with a walk and was sacrifice-bunted to second by Red Rolfe. Keller reached first when shortstop Billy Myers misplayed his grounder, then DiMaggio hit what appeared to be a routine single into right field. Here's where it got interesting. Crosetti trotted home with the go-ahead run, and then Keller made a sprint for the plate when Goodman booted the ball. Goodman threw home in an attempt to nail Keller, but Keller beat it by knocking the ball out of Lombardi's glove and injuring the big catcher at the same time. DiMaggio, who had never stopped running, saw the ball lying unattended near the prone Lombardi and he took off for home. With a classic fadeaway slide, DiMaggio just beat the recovering Lombardi's tag, and the Yankees had three runs on one single. Ballgame. Championship; the Yankees' record fourth in a row.

"You just can't explain that 10th inning," said a downhearted McKechnie. "There is just nothing to explain it. It's just one of those things."

In between the celebratory choruses of *Roll Out the Barrel* which he was leading in the clubhouse afterward, Art Fletcher said of DiMaggio's heads-up base-running, "I told him nothing but watch the ball, and boy did he watch it. He gave us one of the greatest pieces of sliding I've ever seen. Lombardi found out you can't sit down with those Yankees on the base paths."

As the players carried on in glee, Gehrig sat in a corner of the clubhouse, smiling that easy smile. He was happy for his teammates, but he was also cognizant of the fact that as of today, he was no longer their teammate. Gehrig's playing career ended that day in Detroit back in May, but he had remained with the team all season. At the conclusion of the Series, though, it was over.

I stood next to him for a couple of minutes, watching the revelry, and I didn't quite know what to say to him. He broke the uncomfortable silence by saying, "That was one heck of a finish, eh Joe?" I replied,

"Sure was Lou, it sure was." As we talked he began to take off his Yankee uniform for the final time, and a wave of sadness washed over me as I watched him struggle to unbutton his jersey. His hands were trembling out of his control, and I considered offering to help him, but I thought wiser of it.

As the train transported us back to New York, the Yankees continued to celebrate throughout the night, and at one point they formed a line and paraded joyously through the cars, a tradition that had been carried over from Babe Ruth's days. However, when they reached the car where McCarthy and Dickey were sitting, McCarthy barked, "Cut that kid stuff out, I thought I was managing professionals."

The players quieted down and retreated like a bunch of school children after a reprimand by the principal. McCarthy was just as happy about the championship as the players, but the cessation of Gehrig's tenure as a Yankee, as the Iron Horse, had finally struck him. McCarthy loved Gehrig like he loved no other player, and as the night rolled by his window, he stared out into the darkness knowing that his good friend was dying, and his team would never be quite the same again.

Most people remember the year 1941 for two particular events: Joe DiMaggio's incredible 56-game hitting streak during the spring and early summer, and the Japanese attack on Pearl Harbor in December which catapulted America into World War II. I remember it as the year I fell in love.

I had known of Marie Giordano since high school. She attended Mount Mercy, an all-girls Catholic school about five Bronx blocks from my high school, Dewitt Clinton. When our schools would mingle for dances, I would see her from across the gym floor, always dressed perfectly in her chiffon dresses, her brunette hair resting comfortably on her shoulders, her green eyes glistening.

Like me, she was raised in a predominantly Italian household, but she was one of six children, and her father—who owned a bakery on Jerome Avenue near the corner of East 167th—worked long hours to support his family. I never quite had the gumption to ask Marie out on a date when we were in school, and when I would see her out in social situations, I would say hello and talk casually, mostly about the Yankees because she knew I worked for the team and she admitted to being a fan. Most of the time she was in the company of her girlfriends, but occasionally she'd be with a male companion, though she never seemed to be too serious with any of them.

I had had girlfriends growing up, and I dated off and on after I graduated from Dewitt Clinton, but I really didn't have time to maintain a relationship with anyone, what with working two jobs. However, I would have definitely squeezed Marie into my life if I'd had the chance, and when that chance arose on a sunny summer afternoon during the year of DiMaggio and Pearl Harbor, I pounced on it.

The Yankees were scheduled to conclude a weekend series with the St. Louis Browns at the stadium, but a water main burst overnight and by the time anyone realized it the next morning the infield was flooded and the game had to be postponed. I wrote a short story for the Home News *explaining what had happened, and then I had the rest of the day off because there was no ballgame. My parents, my sister, and her boyfriend had planned to attend a church picnic at Crotona Park, about a mile north of our home in the wedge between Prospect Avenue and Tremont Avenue. It was an annual affair sponsored by a number of the Catholic churches in the Bronx, and something I always missed because for me, Sundays in the summer were spent at a ballpark—either Yankee Stadium or some other American League locale.*

When I told my mother of the cancellation she invited me to walk the two blocks from my Third Avenue apartment over to the park to join the picnic and, in what proved to be a fortuitous decision, I accepted. Thanks be to God, Marie was at the picnic, minus a male escort, and on that day, I took the first step toward a lifetime of personal happiness. My sister knew I had an interest in Marie, and when Carmela noticed that Marie was standing alone, she elbowed me in the ribs and implored me to go over and talk to her. I summoned the courage to do so, and was relieved to see that Marie seemed happy I had. We had an effortless conversation on a variety of topics, even extending beyond baseball and the Yankees. I learned that since high school she had worked an assortment of jobs and was presently employed as a salesperson in a department store on Fifth Avenue and was living in an apartment near the upper tip of Manhattan on West 145th, about 10 blocks from the Polo Grounds. We spent most of the day together, leaving our families to fend for themselves, and when dusk settled and it was time to leave, I asked if she would like to have dinner some night and she happily agreed.

Our first official date was dinner a week later at Toots Shor's restaurant following an 8-4 Yankee win over the Red Sox during which DiMaggio extended his hitting streak to 45 games, breaking the major league record of 44 set by Wee Willie Keeler. DiMaggio also chose Toots' place—his regular hangout—to celebrate his achievement, and he even stopped by our table to say hello, which gave Marie one of the great thrills of her 25-year life. I'd be lying if I said I didn't feel like a big shot that night.

– Chapter 9 –

1941

ON THE EVENING OF DECEMBER 29, 1940, I sat in the living room of my parents' home digesting a wonderful Sunday meal and listening to President Roosevelt—during one of his "Fireside Chats"—deliver the most shocking and frightening speech I had ever heard.

"Never before since Jamestown and Plymouth Rock has our American civilization been in such danger," said Roosevelt, adding that if Adolf Hitler and his Nazi German troops captured Britain, "All of us in the United States will be living at the point of a gun."

As my mother, my sister, and I sat there grim-faced as Roosevelt's voice crackled over the radio, my father lounged in his chair and said, "I told you so."

Sixteen months earlier in the late summer of 1939 when Dad read in the *New York Times* that Germany and the Soviet Union had entered into a nonaggression pact, he called me on the phone and said, "Joe, do you know what this means?" To be honest, I really didn't, so he enlightened me.

"If Russia and Germany are in cahoots, that bastard Hitler is going to run right through Poland and there's going to be a war," Dad told me. A week later, Hitler stormed Poland, and just as Dad predicted, Great Britain and France declared war on Germany.

Until Roosevelt's chilling dissertation on that December 1940 evening, my father was among a slim minority of Americans who considered Hitler a threat to our way of life. Like the outbreak of the Spanish Civil War in 1936, the fighting overseas did not seem to have anything to do with us and we went about our lives paying only mild attention to the conflict.

Throughout 1939 and 1940, Hitler's Nazi troops plowed through Europe on a murderous pillage, overtaking countries such as Denmark, Norway, Belgium, the Netherlands, Luxembourg, and France, yet we in the United States regarded news of the war as secondary even to baseball. It seems foolish to admit it now, but the Yankees failing to win their fifth consecutive American League pennant in 1940 seemed more newsworthy to me at the time.

That changed when Roosevelt scared the hell out of us during the Christmas/New Year's holiday, and then on May 27, 1941 he did it again, informing us via another nationwide broadcast that the U.S. was now under a state of national emergency. The President said our armed forces were being deployed to various strategic military positions, that U.S. naval ships were already patrolling the North Atlantic, and that if provoked he was ready to go to war against the Axis powers: Germany, Italy, and Japan.

The threat of war was imminent, and the country—barely 20 years removed from the first World War when more than 53,000 Americans died on European battlefields—was nervous. But life, and baseball, went on.

* * *

As Roosevelt sat in the Oval Office delivering that second address, I was a few miles away in the nation's capital sitting in the press box at Griffith Stadium watching Joe DiMaggio go 4-for-5, score three runs and drive in three more to lead the Yankees to a 10-8 victory over the Senators, extending his modest hitting streak to 12 games.

For the first time since the streak began on May 15 against the White Sox at Yankee Stadium, I made mention of it in my game story for the *Home News*. For the next two months, I don't think I wrote a story that did not include prose concerning the streak which ultimately topped out at a mind-boggling 56 consecutive games, a record feat that Boston's Ted Williams—who that season became the last man to hit over .400—called "the greatest batting achievement of all."

Coming off a hugely disappointing 1940 season, the Yankees jumped out of the gate quickly in 1941 and were back in their customary position atop the standings for the first couple of weeks. However, DiMaggio went into a batting slump and he dragged the entire team down with him. During one stretch the Yankees lost 11 of 16 games and by submerging below the .500 mark, they fell to fifth place.

Incredibly, it was an observation by DiMaggio's wife, Dorothy Arnold, that snapped him out of his early-season doldrums. From her seat at the stadium, Dorothy noticed that when Joe finished his swing, the number on his jersey was in a different position than it was when he was going good. DiMaggio had developed a hitch in his swing, but once he made the alteration, away he went.

Cleveland was red-hot early in the year as it put together separate winning streaks of 11 and 7 games, and the day DiMaggio ignited his streak, the Indians led New York by 5 1/2 games. By the time the streak was stopped by the Indians on July 17, the Yankees were in first place by six games.

During the streak DiMaggio went 91-for-223 (.408), scored 56 runs, had 16 doubles, four triples, 15 home runs, and 55 RBI while striking out just seven times, and the Yankees posted a record of 41-13 (there were two ties that didn't count in the standings, but the statistics counted).

"He gave the most consistent performance under pressure I have ever seen," said Bill Dickey.

And he took our minds off the mounting pressures of what now seemed like our unavoidable entrance into the war.

It was an unforgettable summer for me as I chronicled this historic baseball drama from day to day, fell in love with my future wife, and, unaware at the time that my medical condition would prevent me from joining the Army, nervously anticipated a call from Uncle Sam instructing me to go fight the Nazis.

A few years ago I was reading Robert Creamer's wonderful book, *Baseball in '41*, and in his eloquent style Creamer wrote that the streak transcended the Yankees and their fans, transcended New York, and transcended baseball.

I think what he meant was DiMaggio's performance brought together a nation that, hearing of Hitler's advances, knew deep down it was about to be called into battle and was searching for a way to shove the bad news emanating from Europe out of its consciousness. There was a fascinating anecdote in the book which, to me, summed up what DiMaggio's streak meant to baseball and to America, and also served to define the prewar purity of the country.

Creamer recalled a story told to him by his one-time colleague at *Sports Illustrated*, Andy Crichton. Crichton, his brother, and a couple of pals piled into an old jalopy and set out on a cross-country trip that summer, a veritable last fling before the inevitability of the war. There were many stops along the way, but one in particular—at a cafe in a sleepy farming town in Montana—provided the New York City boys an eye-opening experience. There they learned that people in Montana weren't much different than their neighbors back home. These folks knew about baseball, knew who DiMaggio was, and they knew he was in the midst of compiling one of the greatest records in the history of sports.

Remember, there was no ESPN back then. In fact, there wasn't even television. Radio reports were, at best, sketchy, and the closest Major League Baseball team to Montana was in St. Louis, about 1,000 miles to the east. But Montana had newspapers, and the proprietor of the cafe had one on his counter. Every man who came in asked him, "Did he get one yesterday?" On the day Crichton and company were there—and every day for more than two months—the reply was, "Yep."

The country was spellbound by what Roosevelt was telling us, and DiMaggio was the perfect diversion. It was magical. DiMaggio commanded the daily attention of sports fans like no athlete ever had, and in the six decades since, it is my opinion that only Roger Maris in 1961 has done the same. DiMaggio's record remains unbroken, and even in an era when we have seen Cal Ripken demolish what was once thought to be the most unassailable of records—Lou Gehrig's consecutive games played streak—baseball experts and purists still contend that DiMaggio's mark will never fall.

"You can talk all you want about (Rogers) Hornsby's .424 average and Hack Wilson's 190 RBIs, but when DiMaggio hit in those 56 straight games, he put a line in the record book and it's the one that will never be changed," said Williams, who despite batting .406 in 1941—including .412 during the period of DiMaggio's streak—lost the MVP vote to DiMaggio that year.

About halfway through the streak, when it became apparent something special was transpiring, I started keeping a journal. I leafed through the *Home News* archive to recount the first portion of the streak, and then I kept a day-by-day account of what DiMaggio did. Its corners are now bent and the pages have yellowed, but its binding has held up through nearly 60 years, and that journal is a keepsake that I cherish. These were a few of the entries I made:

May 15—Announced crowd was 9,040 on the day the streak began. Joe had a RBI single but the Yankees lost to the White Sox, 13-1.

May 24—Joe hit a shot to center that his brother, Dom, misplayed, and rather than scoring it a triple, Dan Daniel (serving as official scorer) gave Dom a three-base error. In the seventh inning Joe hit a two-out, two-run single off Earl Johnson to give the Yankees a 7-6 victory. Hitting streak at 10.

June 3—When we got to Detroit last night, news came that Lou Gehrig died yesterday. Joe McCarthy and Bill Dickey took the first train back to New York while the team stayed. Joe had a single, but the Tigers won, 4-2. Streak at 20.

June 8—Yankees swept a doubleheader at Sportsman's Park in St. Louis. Joe was 2-for-4 in both games. Streak at 24, one game better than his personal best of 23 set in 1940.

June 17—Joe stretched his streak to 29 to break the Yankee record shared by Roger Peckinpaugh and Earle Combs. He had one hit, and it was dubious. It looked like [White Sox shortstop] Luke Appling booted his grounder, but Dan Daniel scored it a hit. White Sox won the game, 8-7.

June 24—Joe was hitless until the eighth before he singled off Bob Muncrief. We heard that Browns manager Luke Sewell asked Muncrief why he didn't walk DiMaggio to end the streak and Muncrief said, "That wouldn't have been fair, to him or to me. Hell, he's the greatest ballplayer I've ever seen."

June 26—Very interesting day. First of all, Marius Russo had a no-hitter into the seventh before losing it, but it seemed like no one knew. "They care only for one thing, to see Joe get a hit," Russo said after the game. Elden Auker is always tough on Joe, and Joe was 0-for-3 and scheduled to bat fourth in the eighth inning. Yankees were leading the Browns 3-1 so it was likely they wouldn't have to bat in the ninth, so a 1-2-3 inning might have meant the end of the streak. Johnny Sturm popped out, then Red Rolfe walked. Tommy Henrich was up next, but he trotted from the on-deck circle to the dugout and conferred with McCarthy. We found out later that he asked McCarthy if he could bunt. Henrich explained to us that by bunting, he would avoid a potential inning-ending double play, thus ensuring Joe one more crack. "I knew that if Joe got a chance to hit, Auker was a class guy who would never walk him," said Henrich. "McCarthy never hesitated. You don't bunt with one out in the eighth inning and your team ahead by two runs, but he gave his blessing immediately." Henrich sacrificed successfully, and up came Joe. On the first pitch he lined a RBI double over third base. Streak at 38.

June 29—Joe tied George Sisler's modern-day major league record 41-game streak in the first game of a doubleheader against the Senators, then broke it in the second game. But in between games, both Yankee wins, his bat—a 36-ounce, 36-inch Louisville Slugger with an ink mark on the bottom of the knob—was stolen. He was 0-for-3 using one of Henrich's bats before he singled in the seventh.

July 2—Joe set the all-time hitting streak record as he broke Wee Willie Keeler's 44-game streak in 1897. Joe hit a three-run homer after his brother Dom had robbed him of a hit in his previous at-bat. After the game I took Marie Giordano out to dinner at Toots Shor's and Joe and Dom stopped by to say hello. "It was a great catch," Joe said of the grab Dom made. "It was one of the best Dom ever made, but at that moment the only thing on my mind was the temptation to withdraw the dinner invitation." Joe admitted that in the past week the pressure had really gotten intense as he was shooting for Keeler's record. I asked him about an incident a few days earlier when he was called out on strikes and he turned around and said something to the umpire, something he rarely did. Joe said he never said anything because before he could, the umpire blurted out, "Honest to God, Joe, it was right down the middle." You don't hear that too often, but that's how much respect Joe has.

July 6—Streak now at 48 as Joe went 6-for-9 during a sweep against Philadelphia. A plaque honoring Lou Gehrig was unveiled in center field next to the one for Miller Huggins.

My last entry came on the evening of July 17 when the largest crowd to witness a night baseball game to that point, 67,468, jammed into Cleveland's Municipal Stadium to watch their Indians halt DiMaggio.

In the first inning DiMaggio hit a vicious grounder down the third-base line and Ken Keltner backhanded it beautifully and threw across the diamond, nipping DiMaggio by a stride. "When they take 'em away from you like that, there's nothing a fellow can do about it," DiMaggio said that night.

DiMaggio walked in the fourth, then Keltner robbed him of a hit again in the seventh with another tough backhanded stab. DiMaggio's final at-bat came in the eighth after New York scored twice for a 4-1 lead. The bases were loaded with one out and Jim Bagby was on in relief of starter Al Smith. With the crowd rooting for DiMaggio to keep his streak alive, Bagby fell behind 2-1, then threw a fastball on the inside portion of the plate. DiMaggio took a mighty cut and the ball exploded up the middle, "As hard as I ever hit a ground ball in my life," DiMaggio said. However, shortstop Lou Boudreau moved to his left, speared the ball despite a bad hop, tossed to second baseman Ray Mack for one out, and Mack relayed to first to complete a double play.

The next day DiMaggio singled and doubled off Bob Feller and he was off and running on what became a 16-game hitting streak during which time the Yankees continued to pull away from Cleveland. During the course of the two streaks, the Yankees won 55 games—including 14 in a row during one stretch—and this led to them wrapping up the American League pennant on September 4, breaking their own record for earliest clinching.

At season's end the Yankees were 17 games ahead of second-place Boston while Cleveland fell 26 games in arrears. DiMaggio hit .357, had a .643 slugging average, 193 hits, 43 doubles, 11 triples, 30 home runs, and a league-leading 125 RBI. He struck out just 13 times in 541 at-bats.

After a one-year hiatus, the Yankees were back in the World Series and it seemed like things were back to normal in the world of baseball. Well, almost. Fantasy finally became reality for Brooklyn as their Dodgers won the National League pennant for the first time since 1920, and New York prepared for another provincial World Series, the first of seven meetings between the Yankees and Dodgers over the next 16 years.

– *1941 World Series* –

In October 1941, if you had asked 100 people on the streets of New York City what or where Pearl Harbor was, my guess is that maybe five might have known that it was the home base of the U.S. Pacific Fleet and was located on the island of Oahu, Hawaii. Within two months every American would come to know exactly where Pearl Harbor was, but at the start of the 1941 World Series, Pearl Harbor's existence was as mysterious to us as the World Series was to fans of the Brooklyn Dodgers.

Brooklyn had never won the Series and had only played in it three times, the last being 21 years earlier. The Yankees were playing in it for the fifth time in six years. So it was easy to understand why more than 10,000 Bum-lovers flocked to Grand Central Terminal to welcome home their heroes after they had clinched the National League pennant in Boston. There were bands, there were balloons, and there was banter, most of that centering around how the Dodgers were going to deal the arrogant Yankees a dose of comeuppance.

A few days later when the regular season ended and the Dodgers had finished with exactly 100 victories, the streets and sidewalks of Brooklyn were lined by nearly one million people as the borough feted its team with a parade that stretched from Grand Army Plaza off Prospect Avenue to Borough Hall in downtown Brooklyn.

The Dodgers smiled and waved from slow-moving cars as banners flapped from buildings and storms of confetti floated down from the skies. It was a glorious day to be a Brooklynite. There was only one small problem: The World Series had yet to begin.

And six days later when it was over, the streets of Brooklyn were once again quiet, the Dodgers cooked in five games, and the only sound decipherable was that of the residents muttering, "Wait 'til next year."

Dodgers manager Leo Durocher made a strange tactical move in the opener at Yankee Stadium, choosing 38-year-old Curt Davis to pitch instead of his well-rested pair of 22-game winners, Kirby Higbe and Whit Wyatt. While Davis didn't pitch poorly, he didn't pitch well enough to win as the Yankees came away with a 3-2 victory.

Joe Gordon homered in the second inning, and Bill Dickey followed a Charlie Keller walk in the fourth with a two-out RBI double to stake the Yankees to a 2-0 lead, and when Red Ruffing escaped a couple of late-inning jams, New York was one game up.

Wyatt was Durocher's choice in Game Two, and it was a wise one. He scattered nine hits in a complete-game 3-2 victory that evened the Series at a game apiece and kick-started the burgeoning Yankee-Dodger hostilities.

These teams shared a city, but until this year, the only times they had shared a ball field were during harmless exhibition games. Emotions were running high in the opener when Pee Wee Reese slid hard into Phil Rizzuto trying to break up a double play and Johnny Sturm had retaliated against Dodgers second baseman Billy Herman. They nearly boiled over in Game Two.

Mickey Owen went out of his way to upend Rizzuto on a double play ball, and though Rizzuto completed the fifth-inning twin-killing, he was furious with Owen. "He tried to spike me, and he had no reason, the play was over," fumed the diminutive Rizzuto in the clubhouse afterward. Owen replied, "That's too bad, I feel so, so sorry for him. Sure

I gave him the business, but nobody's sweet and gentle with me either. That's baseball. I wasn't trying to spike him, I was trying to break up a double play. They don't ask permission to come into me at home plate, they come in hard, and why shouldn't they?"

Baseball commissioner Kenesaw Mountain Landis had warned the two teams before the Series about excessive bench jockeying, but the Yankees ignored the edict after Owen's play and taunted the Dodgers the rest of the game. "They called Mickey some nice names," said Dressen, the Dodgers third-base coach. "The voice I heard loudest was Art Fletcher's."

The Yankees were ahead 2-0 when Brooklyn tied it in the fiery fifth, Owen's single driving in the second run. The Dodgers manufactured the winning run in the sixth when Dixie Walker reached on Gordon's error and later scored on Dolph Camilli's RBI single, ending the Yankees 10-game World Series winning streak that dated back to 1937.

They had waited a long time to play a World Series game at Ebbets Field, so one more day didn't matter. The third game was postponed until Saturday due to rain, and it certainly was well worth the wait. Bill Grieve umpired behind the plate that day, and I saw him a few months later and he told me it was the best-pitched game he'd ever called.

Freddie Fitzsimmons, whom the Yankees had beaten twice in the 1936 Series when he pitched for the Giants, handcuffed the Bombers for seven innings, allowing just four hits, three walks, and no runs. Marius Russo was just as effective for New York, matching Fitzsimmons zero for zero on the scoreboard.

The duel came to an end, though, when Russo knocked his counterpart out of the game by lashing a line drive off Fitzsimmons's left knee. The ball caromed into the air and was caught by Reese for the third out of the seventh inning, but the 40-year-old Fitzsimmons limped into the dugout, unable to continue.

Hugh Casey entered in the top of the eighth and the Yankees immediately went to work, scoring twice as Red Rolfe, Tommy Henrich, Joe DiMaggio, and Keller singled in succession. Brooklyn tallied once on Russo in the bottom half, but he worked a perfect ninth to complete the 2-1 victory.

Durocher was frustrated by the turn of events, saying, "If Fitz had been able to stay in there, we'd have won the game, 1-0. But that's baseball."

Sure it was a bad break for the Dodgers, losing Fitzsimmons the way they did. But that piece of bad luck was nothing compared to what happened to Brooklyn the next day. In one of the most famous incidents in

World Series history, Owen dropped what would have been a game-ending third strike pitch from Casey, setting the stage for a four-run New York rally that turned an apparent 4-3 Series-tying Dodgers triumph into a gut-wrenching 7-4 defeat.

"Is that the most famous strikeout in baseball history?" Henrich asked me one time. "It could well be."

I can still remember the drastic change in the atmosphere at the ballpark after Henrich reached first safely and the Yankees turned the base paths into a merry-go-round as they stole the victory. The Dodger fans exploded with joy and many had run onto the field to celebrate when Henrich swung and missed for the apparent third out, only to be chased off the field so the game could resume. A few minutes later it was so quiet you could hear toilets flushing in the concourse.

After the game Rizzuto told me that when Henrich swung and missed, he was already into the runway that led back to the clubhouse thinking that the game was over, but he came scurrying back out when he heard his teammates scream as the ball bounded away from Owen.

This is how I reported that day's events in the *Home News:*

By Joe Kimmerle
Bronx Home News

In the moment it took for Tommy Henrich to realize that he had just swung and missed at one of the wickedest curve balls he'd ever seen, a thought popped into his head.

"If I'm having as much trouble with this pitch, maybe Mickey is, too," Henrich recounted in the deliriously happy Yankee clubhouse after the Bronx Bombers pulled off a comeback for the ages yesterday afternoon in the bedeviled borough of Brooklyn.

In a finish that will certainly be remembered years from now as one of the most improbable in World Series history, the Yankees orchestrated a startling rally in the top of the ninth inning, ignited by Dodgers catcher Mickey Owen, who misplayed what should have been a game-ending third strike to Henrich.

Ever wary of an opportunity, the Yankees took advantage of the calamitous error and proceeded to score four runs to defeat the Dodgers, 7-4, thus grabbing a commanding three games to one lead in this all-New York Fall Classic.

"Well, they say everything happens in Brooklyn," said the normally un-emotional Joe DiMaggio, who was genuinely tickled by the remarkable way in which the Yankees won the game. "They'll never come back from this."

DiMaggio could be right. The Dodgers had this fourth game won, they had this exciting Series tied at two games each, and for proof, there was home-plate umpire Larry Goetz raising his arm as he bellowed "strike three" after Henrich had waved helplessly at Hugh Casey's 3-and-2, two-out offering.

But as Brooklynites ran onto the field in glee celebrating their apparent victory, the ball was dribbling back toward the Dodgers' dugout because Owen could not handle the hard-breaking pitch. As soon as Henrich swung through, he looked behind him, saw that Owen had botched the catch, and sprinted to first base, making it easily to the bag to give the Yankees new life.

"When I got there, [Dodger first baseman] Dolph Camilli didn't say a word," Henrich said.

How could he? Like the rest of the Dodgers, like the 33,813 disbelieving patrons in the Ebbets Field stands, Camilli knew the Dodgers had just made a potentially ruinous error against a team known for breaking down doors when they are opened just a crack.

And sure enough, here came the Yankees. DiMaggio ripped Casey's next pitch into left field for a single. Then Charlie Keller—after swinging and missing twice, leaving the Yankees for the second time just one strike shy of defeat—lashed a double off the screen in right. Henrich scored the tying run with ease and DiMaggio, running hard from the moment of contact, hustled all the way around to slide in with the go-ahead tally.

Unnerved and pitching amidst stunned silence, Casey walked Bill Dickey, then was tagged for another two-run double, this time by Joe Gordon, to add insult to injury.

"It was all my fault," a red-eyed Owen lamented in the locker room. "It was a great breaking curve that I should have had. But I guess the ball hit the side of my glove. It got away from me and by the time I got hold of it, I couldn't have thrown anybody out at first."

Lefty Gomez, ever the comedian, announced that, "It was just the way we planned it. We've been working on that play for months, on the quiet you understand, and we didn't have it perfected until today."

As laughter filled the room, Gordon chimed in "The game's never over 'til the last man's out, hey." But therein lies the misery for the Dodgers. They had the last man out.

"I tell you, there are angels flying around those Yankees," Dodgers left-fielder Jimmy Wasdell said.

Dodgers manager Leo Durocher has been under fire all week because he had decided not to use fireballing right-hander Kirby Higbe until this fourth game. Higbe won 22 games during the regular season, tied for the National League lead with his teammate, Whit Wyatt, yet Durocher played a hunch and started Curt Davis in the opener and he lost.

The Lip came back with Wyatt in Game Two, then used Fred Fitzsimmons in Game Three, meaning if the Series were to go the distance, Higbe would only be able to start once, in this fourth game. Now, with Higbe having been inactive for more than a week, he wasn't sharp and the Yankees knocked him out of the box inside four innings as they took a 3-0 lead.

Keller drove a RBI single to right in the first, and New York added two runs in the fourth on light-hitting first baseman Johnny Sturm's two-out, bases-loaded single to left. Durocher rescued Higbe at that point.

Brooklyn rallied in its half of the fourth as Yankees starter Atley Donald walked Owen and Pete Coscarart with two outs, then was tagged for a two-run pinch-hit double by Wasdell. In the fifth, the Dodgers took the lead on Pete Reiser's two-run homer, which finished Donald.

Casey—the goat of Game Three when he ambled into a scoreless fray in the eighth in relief of the injured Fitzsimmons and was roughed up for four hits and two runs as the Yankees won, 2-1—had entered this game with two outs and the bases loaded in the top of the fifth and induced Gordon to fly out.

He handcuffed the Yankees for the next three innings, then retired Sturm and Red Rolfe without pause to start the ninth before his luck ran out.

"With the count 3-and-2 on Henrich, I figured I'd throw him a curve and put everything I had on the pitch," said Casey. "The ball really had a great break on it, but it didn't hit the dirt."

Clearly shell-shocked, the Dodgers were no match for Johnny Murphy in the ninth and went down 1-2-3. "Boy, was that great, or was it great?" Henrich said. "What a finish. What a game. Never been anything like this, never will be again, I'll bet."

As the fans filed quietly out of the ballpark, a banner hanging from the upper deck was left to flap in the breeze. It read, "We've waited 21 years, Don't Fail Us Now."

But the Dodgers had failed, and now it seems as if the wait will continue for the championship-starved fans of Brooklyn.

———————————————

When Sturm calmly fielded Reiser's game-ending grounder and tossed it to Murphy covering the bag, the Yankees skipped off the field pounding each other on their backs while the Dodgers sat watching from their dugout motionless, pulse-less. The overflow crowd didn't seem to have the energy to get up and walk out of the somber ballpark. Up in the press box we all got a chuckle when Louis Effrat of the *Times* said there should be an asterisk in the box score of the game with a line that reads "three out when winning run scored."

Generations of ballplayers, regardless of the sport, have said that the toughest game to win in any championship series is always the last one. That wasn't the case in this World Series. After Owen's bobble, the Dodgers were dead, and they played that way the next day. They managed four meek hits off Ernie Bonham on an amazingly hot October day, and in 89-degree heat the Yankees completed a clean sweep of the three games in Brooklyn and closed out the Series with a 3-1 victory.

As I was walking down from the press box to the clubhouse, I heard one Brooklyn fan call the result "an American Tragedy." Well, it was certainly a Brooklyn tragedy, but in all honesty, the Dodgers just weren't good enough, nor lucky enough, to compete with the Yankees.

The Yankees scored twice in the second off Wyatt, who contributed a damaging wild pitch, and after Brooklyn pulled within 2-1, Henrich swatted a solo homer in the fifth to complete the scoring.

Fittingly, it was 1941's shining star, DiMaggio, who caught the ball that represented the final out. DiMaggio did not have a great go of it against the Dodgers, hitting just .263 with one RBI. But after the season he'd had, did it really matter? No one remembers that he batted .263 in the World Series that year. But no one will ever forget that he hit safely in 56 consecutive games, forever stamping his legacy on the game.

"When I was a kid, I had two separate fastballs I threw to Joe," Hall of Famer Bob Feller told me a few years ago when I saw him at a card show in New Jersey. "One had this big hop and rose up and in on him. The other jumped away from him. He hit them both."

He hit everybody, and everything, especially in 1941.

Marie and I spent as much time as possible together during the summer and fall of 1941, but with the Yankees on their way to another World Series appearance and Marie busy with her own life, it was difficult to coordinate our schedules. Still, there were many evenings spent on the town, our favorite place being Billy Rose's Diamond Horseshoe in the Hotel Paramount off Broadway. There, for a one-dollar cover charge, you could watch a floor show, have dinner and then dance the rest of the evening away without even needing to dab perspiration from your brow because Billy Rose's was air-conditioned, a real rarity in those days.

By Christmas I was unabashedly in love, and I was hoping and praying that Marie felt the same way. During the holidays I talked to my father about Marie and our possible future together, and he gave me one piece of advice that I have never forgotten: "Follow your heart." So that's what I did.

On Valentine's Day 1942, after receiving permission from Mr. Giordano, I asked Marie to marry me. That was one of the most nerve-wracking days of my life, and the hours leading up to our dinner at Billy Rose's turned my stomach upside down. But when I pulled that ring out of my pocket and gleefully proposed, the most wonderful sensation flowed through my body as her smiling face glistened and her tear ducts burst open. As the Glenn Miller Band played Moonlight Serenade in the background, Marie did me the honor of agreeing to become my partner for life.

Throughout the spring and summer of 1942, Marie eagerly planned for our wedding while I prepared for another October of excitement in the Bronx. The Yankees were once again the dominant team in the American League, winning 103 games to leave Joe Cronin's revitalized Red Sox in the dust. For the first time in his career Joe DiMaggio played an entire season without injury and did not miss a game, but his average plummeted to a career-low .305, and then he suffered his first World Series defeat as Billy Southworth's Cardinals rolled past the Yankees in five games.

That was quite a season for the Cardinals. They trailed the Dodgers by 10 1/2 games in early August, but won 43 of their final 51 games to finish with 106 victories, two more than Brooklyn. It was typical of the Dodgers' luck to win 104 games and finish second.

In the opener of the Series at Sportsman's Park, Red Ruffing no-hit the Cardinals for 7 2/3 innings as the Yankees built a 7-0 lead before the roof caved in on Ruffing and he allowed four runs in the ninth. Though New York held on for the victory, the Cardinals were stoked with confidence, and they shocked the Yankees by winning the next four games, dealing New York its first World Series setback since 1926.

When the Series ended, I only had about two weeks to fulfill my end of the wedding planning, but I pulled it off, and Marie and I were married on Saturday, October 24, 1942.

I was very fortunate—though not particularly proud of the reason—that I was able to marry Marie that day. By all rights, I should have been fighting for my country in World War II, but I was rejected by the draft board due to my childhood case of osteomyelitis, the same condition that labeled Mickey Mantle 4-F and prevented him from going to Korea a decade later.

Osteomyelitis is caused by various infections that inflame bone or bone marrow, causing softening and erosion of the long bones, often with the formation of pus-filled abscesses which eventually spread over the entire bone. Mantle's case was touched off by a kick to the shin he received while playing high school football. Mine came from my broken leg in the winter of 1929. Osteomyelitis kept me from playing competitive sports in high school, an experience I sorely missed. There were many times when I would develop fevers or feel numbing pain in my leg, and I suffered for years until the miracle drug penicillin was discovered in the early 1940s. As soon as I started taking doses, my osteomyelitis literally disappeared and by the time Marie and I were married, I was virtually pain-free, but my preexisting condition was enough to keep me at home during the war. Because Dad had fought in the first world war, I naturally felt an obligation to serve when our nation entered the second war, but Dad knew the horrors of combat and he was genuinely happy that his only son would not have to risk his life.

When Mantle came up to the Yankees in 1951 shortly after the hullabaloo over his 4-F status, I shared my tale with him, and it was an instant icebreaker for us. Our common disability served as a bond and we had about as good a relationship as a sportswriter and an athlete could have. Mickey was very wary of the press throughout his career, but I would have to say that of the hundreds and hundreds of Yankees I have known, Mantle was the player I was closest to because he allowed himself to trust me.

– Chapter 10 –

1943

PRESIDENT ROOSEVELT CALLED IT "A date which will live in infamy." He was not referring to the fact that December 7, 1941 had been proclaimed by the New York football Giants as Tuffy Leemans Day.

Weeks earlier the Giants had decided to honor Leemans—the star offensive and defensive back who had been one of New York's most celebrated players since joining the team in 1936—prior to the regular-season finale against the crosstown rival Brooklyn Dodgers.

A record Polo Grounds crowd of 55,051 turned out to cheer Leemans, who was showered with gifts. There were $1,500 in defense bonds presented by former Postmaster General Jim Farley, a silver tray inscribed by his teammates, a trophy given to him by the Giants' captain, Mel Hein, and a gold watch from his old college coach at George Washington University. Upon shy acceptance of this largess, Leemans delivered a sincere 10-minute thank-you speech.

I know all this because I was at the Polo Grounds that day, consigned by my sports editor at the *Bronx Home News*, Ray Reynolds, to do a sidebar on Leemans. Once the baseball season was over, I served as a general assignment reporter until spring training, so I would often cover college or pro football games, the occasional New York Rangers hockey game, and sometimes important high school events. Leemans was my assignment this day, a day that until September 11, 2001, was unlike any other in the history of our country.

At almost the precise moment the Giants and Dodgers kicked off their game, which Brooklyn would win with surprising ease, 21-7, Japanese war planes hovered over the island of Oahu, Hawaii, in preparation for a sneak attack on the United States naval base at Pearl Harbor.

Over the next 90 minutes—with the attack coming in segmented waves—Japanese bombs killed 2,403 Americans, wounded 1,778 others, and destroyed eight ships and 140 fighter planes. And during those 90 minutes, almost all of America was oblivious to what was going on.

As I sat in the press box, I remember thinking something was amiss when I heard over the stadium's public address system late in the first half that a Colonel was being paged by Washington. A few minutes later one of the workers in the press box tore an urgent story off the news ticker that said the Japanese had bombed Pearl Harbor, and about five minutes after that, an ominous announcement was made. "All Navy men in the audience are ordered to report to their posts immediately. All Army men are to report to their posts tomorrow morning. This is important."

And suddenly, Tuffy Leemans wasn't so important.

Nothing was.

The next day Roosevelt addressed the nation and told us, "There is no blinking at the fact that our people, our territory, and our interests are in grave danger. With confidence in our armed forces, with the unbounding determination of our people, we will gain the inevitable triumph, so help us God."

We declared war on Japan, and later the entire Axis, and our lives changed over the course of the next four years.

As for baseball, it went on, just as it had during the first war, just as it had during the Great Depression. "I honestly feel it would be best for the country to keep baseball going," Roosevelt said on January 15, 1942 in response to a letter from baseball commissioner Kenesaw Mountain Landis. "These players are a definite recreational asset to their fellow citizens, and that, in my judgement, is thoroughly worthwhile."

So they played games, and when I found out that the armed forces would not take me, I covered the games.

During the 1942 season baseball was largely unaffected by the war, because most of the teams remained intact, that meant the Yankees were once again the class of the American League. The only regular called into the military that year was first baseman Johnny Sturm, so McCarthy plugged in Buddy Hassett and he batted a respectable .284.

Though DiMaggio fell far short of duplicating his remarkable 1941 season, he still led the Yankees with 114 RBI, but the Cardinals were too much for New York in the Series and when mass military defections began in 1943, it seemed unlikely the Yankees could regain the championship.

Then again, these were the Yankees, and their manager was Joe McCarthy.

DiMaggio, Hassett, George Selkirk, Phil Rizzuto, Tommy Henrich, and Red Ruffing were all called into service while Red Rolfe decided to retire, leaving McCarthy to fend off the challenges of Washington and Cleveland using players such as Nick Etten, Billy Johnson, Bud Metheny, and Johnny Lindell. The only veteran position players were Charlie Keller, Joe Gordon, and Bill Dickey, plus Frank Crosetti, who regained his starting role at shortstop with the departure of Rizzuto.

*   *   *

With DiMaggio and Henrich gone Keller was left all alone in the outfield, and he was also the lone remaining big bopper in the lineup. But for a man who had played in the shadow of those and other Yankee players since joining the club in 1939, this was Keller's moment to shine before he, too, would leave for military duty in 1944.

Keller was born and raised on a farm in Middleton, Maryland, and his days as a youth began at 4 A.M. milking the cows. He was a strong man, powerfully built, and he had thick dark eyebrows and hairy forearms, prompting the nickname "King Kong," which he despised. Lefty Gomez used to say, "He wasn't scouted, he was trapped," and only the comical Gomez could get away with that.

Keller attended the University of Maryland on a baseball scholarship and also played basketball, soccer, and he even tried football. In the summers he played semipro baseball and when the lefty-swinger hit .466 with 25 homers for Kinston, North Carolina in 1936, Ed Barrow called super-scout Paul Krichell one night in Buffalo and told him to drop everything and go to Kinston and "don't come back without Keller."

Krichell corralled Keller, and after two high-average years at Newark that included an International League batting title, Keller earned a promotion to the Yankees in 1939.

Keller was a line-drive hitter who could knock the ball out of any park in any direction, but when he arrived at Yankee Stadium, the vast left-center power alley proved troublesome and some of his line shots became long singles or outs. He hit only 11 homers as a rookie, and though he batted an impressive .334, McCarthy preferred home runs. He instructed Keller to change his swing so he could pull the ball and take advantage of the short porch in right field. His home run totals improved, but he never topped .300 again in a full season.

Henrich told me years later he always thought McCarthy made a mistake with Keller, that he should have left him alone and let him slash line drives to all fields.

Still, opponents feared Keller.

Red Sox manager Joe Cronin once said, "Keller is the Yankees' second Gehrig. He's a small edition of Lou in build, in bearing down on a pitcher, the way he hits and the distance he gets on a long ball. Can Keller hit them as far as Ted Williams? I'd say so. I've seen Keller hit balls as far as Gehrig did."

Keller was always a quiet man, and it seems like every time I saw him on a train or during moments of downtime in the clubhouse, he was reading a Zane Grey novel. And though he usually didn't participate in the excessive clubhouse roasting, I remember one time when he cracked everyone up. Yogi Berra, who like Keller wasn't one of the best-looking men in America, was getting teased about his appearance and Keller chimed in with, "I'm gonna have a picture taken of me and Yogi. Then I'm going to take it home and tell my wife anytime she thinks I'm not so good-looking that she should take a look at you."

Keller's career declined after 1943. He joined the Merchant Marines and missed all of 1944 and most of 1945. After an excellent 1946 season, he slipped a disk in his back in 1947 and was never the same player. He toiled in New York for three more years, then was released and signed with Detroit where he spent three uninspiring seasons. The Tigers let him go late in 1952, New York re-signed him, and he finished the season with the Yankees, which enabled him to retire as a member of the team.

Sometime in the late 1960s Marie and I drove down to Florida for our annual winter vacation and I stopped off to visit Keller at his horse farm—which he called "Yankeeland"—near Frederick, Maryland. Keller had become a successful horse breeder, and he admitted his life was much more fulfilling than it had been when he was playing.

"I detested baseball, especially after my back operation in 1947," he said. "I couldn't do anything after that. Night ball ruined it for me. It used to be a pleasure to play a ballgame at 2 o'clock in the afternoon. I've got nothing against baseball, it gave me all that I've got today and I enjoyed actually playing the game. It's just that the life of a ballplayer isn't normal. It was always too much bouncing around and living in hotel rooms and going too long on the road without seeing your family. There isn't a ballplayer alive who will tell you it's normal."

As someone who traveled with the team and spent just as many days away from my family as the ballplayers, I had to agree with him.

*   *   *

As a team the Yankees hit only 100 home runs in 1943, Keller supplying 31. McCarthy had a lineup full of holes backed up by a thin bench, so he put the pressure on his pitching staff to carry the club. It responded with a Herculean effort led by Spud Chandler, who enjoyed one of the greatest seasons in Yankee hurling history with a 20-4 mark and a team-record 1.64 ERA on his way to winning the American League's MVP award.

During the second half of the season the Yankees won nine series in succession, and also swept 14 doubleheaders to set a league record and turn the pennant race into another exercise in futility for the teams chasing them. But the National League race was even more one-sided as the defending champion Cardinals finished 18 games ahead of Cincinnati. By all indications St. Louis was the favored team heading into the rematch of the 1942 Series with the Yankees. It wasn't often that the Yankees were considered underdogs, and based on what happened in the Series, they clearly reveled in that status.

– *1943 World Series* –

What I remember most about the 1943 season were vast rows of empty seats at ballparks all around baseball. I would buy Marie 50-cent bleacher tickets at Yankee Stadium and tell her to come around to the box seats by about the second or third inning because they were routinely empty. From my perch in the press box above home plate I could always pick her out, my allies being her beauty and the lack of traffic.

President Roosevelt had told baseball to keep playing, but the game just didn't mean much, even to the most ardent of rooters, many of whom were more concerned about their loved ones or their neighbors fighting the good fight on the other side of the world. In the 21-year history of Yankee Stadium, attendance had never been lower.

Then again, there wasn't much to cheer. Both pennant races were uneventful bores, and with so many of the star players in the service, every team's roster was badly diluted. Quite naturally the quality of play was poor, and while the uniforms remained the same, the game was as unrecognizable as the names in the box scores.

Baseball's only saving grace in 1943 was the World Series because—well, it was the World Series—but also because the matchup was a juicy one. Even with Joe DiMaggio, Red Ruffing, Tommy Henrich, and Phil

Rizzuto missing from the Yankees and Enos Slaughter, Creepy Crespi, Terry Moore, and Johnny Beazley unavailable to the Cardinals, there was a palpable tension to the Series, mostly from the Yankees side because they felt they had a score to settle with the Cardinals, their conquerors from 1942. So for one week in October, baseball regained some of its luster, and the Yankees regained their rightful place in the baseball world.

There would be no sneaking into the box seats for Marie during the Series. With wartime travel restrictions in effect, baseball commissioner Kenesaw Mountain Landis instituted a special setup for the Series whereby the first three games would be contested at Yankee Stadium and the remaining games at Sportsman's Park in St. Louis. All three in New York drew massive crowds and the final count was more than 207,000, or nearly one-third the number of people who had passed through the turnstiles the previous 5 1/2 months. When the scene shifted to St. Louis, nary a seat was unoccupied and what fans in both ballparks saw were five interesting and exciting games, two of which were won by the man who was voted the American League's most valuable player in 1943—Spud Chandler.

Chandler won the opener by 4-2 and the clincher by 2-0, going the distance in each, even though he admitted of his unusual 10-hit shutout in Game Five, "I didn't have my best stuff, but I guess I was just lucky. I had what I call just average pitching, my control was a little shaky, but I still managed to get them all out."

*   *   *

Actually, it wasn't such a great mystery. Chandler was a superb pitcher and is probably one of the least appreciated players in Yankee history. During his 11 years with the team, he cobbled together a record of 109-43, a winning percentage of .717 that is the highest for any pitcher in major league history with at least 100 victories.

Chandler's rookie season with the Yankees was 1937, also my first year as a beat writer covering the team. The first time I talked to him, sometime in the middle of that initial spring, I found him to be quite engaging, and he shared one anecdote during our conversation that I recounted in my story. Chandler was a Georgian who attended the University of Georgia, where he played baseball and football and ran track. The football Bulldogs came north for a game against New York University at Yankee Stadium, and the day before the game, Chandler stood on the pitcher's mound with a football in his right hand and declared to a few of his teammates, "Right here is where I'm going to be."

Baseball was Chandler's best sport and he had been scouted by the Cardinals and Cubs, though he spurned offers from both clubs in the hope that the Yankees would sign him, which they did in 1932. "I guess it was that Yankee magic that got me, they were always the No. 1 club in my mind," he said. "I received a much greater offer to go with the Cubs than I did with the Yankees, but there you are, that Yankee magic."

His major league debut was delayed because he didn't have an out pitch, so despite a decent fastball, he was batted around pretty good in the minors. Plus there was no room for him on the Yankee roster. When he arrived for the 1937 season, he saw Lefty Gomez, Red Ruffing, Bump Hadley, and Monte Pearson already cemented in the rotation and wondered if he was doomed to a sixth year in the bushes. Instead, he made the Yankees.

In his first game at Yankee Stadium with a baseball in his hand, he pitched a four-hitter, but lost a heartbreaking 1-0 decision to the White Sox. He went on to win seven of 11 decisions before hurting his arm, prompting a demotion to Newark where he finished the year with the Little World Series champion Bears.

Chandler returned to New York in 1938 and had an excellent 14-5 record, and after missing most of 1939 with a broken leg, he established himself as a key member of the staff starting in 1940, right around the time he began to develop a slider that was murder on right-handed batters. "I came up with that extra pitch, a slider, and that turned everything around for me," he said to me a few years after he had retired and was working as a Yankee scout.

He lost World Series starts in 1941 and 1942, but in 1943, Chandler was almost unhittable. The one thing I remember most about Chandler is that he was such a serious player on the day of a game. Milton Gross, who was a columnist for the *New York Post,* wrote a freelance cover story for the *Saturday Evening Post* that carried the headline "The Yankees' Angry Ace."

"I used to have this reputation for keying myself up before a game to the point where I was so angry people couldn't talk to me," Chandler explained to me. "They said I used to sit in the clubhouse and scowl and glower, and that not until I was full of rancor was I ready to go out and pitch."

As he told me this story, I couldn't contain a grin and a chuckle because there were many times when I would be on the field gathering pregame notes and Chandler would walk by and not say a word to any of the writers, nor his teammates.

"Well, it just wasn't true," he said. "I was just so determined to win that it might have looked that way. But I never got what you would call mad or disgruntled or overbearing. My father-in-law read [Gross's story] and began wondering what kind of monster his daughter was married to."

*　　*　　*

The Cardinals were probably wondering what kind of monster was on the mound in the first game.

"Spud Chandler pitched a great game all the way, I thought," said Joe McCarthy in reference to Chandler stifling the Cardinals on seven hits.

He started out a little shaky when the Cardinals scored once in the second and could have had another had not Yankee right fielder Tuck Stainback gunned down Danny Litwhiler at the plate for the third out.

St. Louis' Max Lanier mowed the Yankees down for three innings without much effort, but in the fourth, his own error led to a pair of unearned runs, the second coming on a lengthy Joe Gordon home run for a 2-1 Yankee lead.

After the Cardinals pulled even in the fifth, Frank Crosetti scored from second base on a Lanier wild pitch in the sixth, Bill Dickey made it 4-2 with a bloop RBI single, and Chandler made the lead hold up.

Cardinals manager Billy Southworth was nonplussed by the defeat. "There's nothing to feel badly about," he said. "Lanier had great stuff and we've seen as good pitching as Chandler showed us. I know we can play better ball than we did today and can hit Spud's kind of pitching."

The Cardinals certainly hit Ernie Bonham's kind of pitching in Game Two as Marty Marion and Ray Sanders both whacked home runs to support the courageous pitching performance of Mort Cooper, lifting the Cardinals to an emotional 4-3 Series-tying victory.

Just hours before the start of the game, the Cooper brothers, Mort and Walker, were informed that their father Robert had died of a heart attack at the age of 58 back at the family home in Independence, Missouri. Before the team took infield practice, the brothers met the press and Mort said, "My brother and I are going to stay on and play today. We are doing this because we both feel Dad would want it."

Their dad would have been proud. By the time the Yankees notched their first hit—a bunt single by Crosetti in the fourth—the Cardinals were already ahead 4-0. The Yankees clawed back into contention and with two runs in the ninth pulled within 4-3, but fittingly, Mort Cooper induced Gordon to pop up in foul ground where Walker Cooper made the putout to end the game.

The Cardinals had done the same thing in the 1942 Series, losing the opener before winning the second game to get even. St. Louis then went on to win the next three to win the championship, and when it took a 2-1 lead into the eighth inning of Game Three, a record Series crowd of 69,990 began to wonder if history was about to repeat itself. Litwhiler's two-run fourth-inning single seemed more than enough as rookie Al Brazile was baffling the Yankees on two hits through seven innings.

But as was so often the case then, as it is now, the Yankees found a way to win. They erupted for five runs, the highlight a bases-loaded triple by Billy Johnson that sent them into a 4-2 lead on their way to a 6-2 victory.

The Cardinals were their own worst enemy in the fateful eighth. Johnny Lindell led off with a single to center which Harry Walker misplayed, allowing Lindell to reach second. Snuffy Stirnweiss, pinch-hitting for Hank Borowy who pitched well and was deserving of the victory, bunted toward first base. Sanders scooped the dribbler and fired to third in an effort to nail Lindell, but Lindell crashed into Whitey Kurowski and the ball fell to the ground for a second error, so both runners were safe. Stirnweiss tagged and went to second on a fly ball, and Crosetti was walked intentionally to load the bases. Up came Johnson, and the wide-eyed rookie ripped one through the left-center gap and as the ball rolled all the way to the wall, three runs scored and that was the ballgame.

Lindell flashed a chipped tooth in the clubhouse courtesy of his collision with Kurowski, who suffered a jammed neck on the play. Lindell's play was borderline dirty, but he explained that when he saw Sanders throwing to third, "I hit the dirt quick and hard." On this point the Cardinals were half in agreement. Lindell certainly came in hard.

"It's a good thing Lindell wasn't playing in the infield," Cardinals coach Buzzy Wares said, implying that there would have been retribution. I asked Southworth if he thought Lindell's play was cheap and whether he thought Lindell tried to spike Kurowski. Southworth replied, "He didn't come in low."

McCarthy was later asked for a reaction and he spat, "Well, it's not a pink tea, you know."

After the game both teams, officials, and members of the press boarded various trains for the journey out to the Midwest for the concluding games of the Series. The Cardinals were fully confident that a return to familiar surroundings at Sportsman's Park would alter their luck, and on the off day Southworth said, "If we play our regular game we'll surely win the next one."

St. Louis' problem in the first three games was its unsteady play in the field as the Cardinals committed eight errors that led to five unearned Yankee runs. Once they returned home their bats went to sleep, and when they scored only two runs combined in the fourth and fifth games, the Cardinals lost both and the Series came to an abrupt end.

McCarthy raised a few eyebrows when he tabbed Marius Russo to start the fourth game. Russo had struggled in the regular season, mainly due to a lame arm, but he checked the Cardinals on seven hits and the only run he allowed during New York's 2-1 victory was unearned. "That was as well-pitched a game as I ever want to look at," said Dickey, who had seen his share in 15 years.

"Russo should have had a shutout," lamented Crosetti, whose error in the seventh set up the only Cardinal run. "I spoiled it for him."

The Yankees went ahead in the fourth when Gordon doubled to left-center with two outs and scored on Dickey's single up the middle, and that lead held up until the seventh when the Cardinals put together a two-out rally keyed by Crosetti's muff of a pop fly.

Having pinch-hit for Lanier in the seventh, Southworth brought in Harry Brecheen to pitch the eighth, and Russo, who had already walked and doubled in the game, doubled again. Stainback promptly sacrificed him to third from where he scored on Crosetti's fly ball, and when Russo escaped jams in the eighth and ninth innings, the Yankees were up three games to one.

So confident were the Yankees that they were going to win the fifth game, Pete Sheehy was told to pack the bags before the game so that the team could make the first available train back to New York. As dusk was settling over St. Louis, the Yankees were on that train thanks to a 2-0 victory delivered by Chandler's shutout and Dickey's game-winning two-run homer in the sixth.

It was a jubilant, song-filled Yankee clubhouse we entered that afternoon. The boys, led by third-base coach Art Fletcher, sang, "East side,

West side, all around the town," then broke into their theme song during the 1941 run to the championship, "Beer Barrel Polka." Finally, it was "Pistol Packin' Mama," which they had adopted a few weeks earlier as their victory song for 1943.

McCarthy waddled over to Chandler, put his arm around the Georgian and said, "Oh my boy, you pitched two wonderful games, just like I thought you would."

Champions again, and now it seemed like the loss in 1942 hadn't even occurred. It was as if the Yankees had merely loaned the championship to the Cardinals, and now they had come to take back what was theirs.

On the train ride back home, McCarthy sat down with me and I asked if this championship—given the depleted state of his roster— meant more to him than any of the previous six. "It was just another pennant and another championship," he said matter-of-factly.

Unfortunately for Joe, this was his last pennant and last championship.

As the war raged on in Europe, major league teams suffered further roster losses, and finally, the trend caught up to the mighty Yankees in 1944. Bill Dickey, Charlie Keller, Joe Gordon, Billy Johnson, Roy Weatherly, and Marius Russo were among those who left for the service following the 1943 championship, and not even a manager as wise as Joe McCarthy could win with the talent that remained.

Baseball was so out of whack the unthinkable occurred in 1944. The St. Louis Browns—one of the sorriest franchises in history—won the World Series, beating the crosstown rival Cardinals in the first and last all-St. Louis Fall Classic.

The Yankees finished third in the American League, six games out, then slipped to fourth in 1945, but while that was a down year in the standings, it was not a year to be overlooked. In late January, Dan Topping, Del Webb, and Larry MacPhail purchased the Yankees from the heirs of Colonel Ruppert for $2.8 million, and a new course was charted for Yankee success that would see the team dominate baseball for the better part of another two decades.

We in the media received a press release describing Topping—who was still in the military—as a "millionaire sportsman, heir to a fortune, a café society headline maker." Webb, just out of the service, had made his money in contracting work, mainly in the Southwest in places such as Phoenix and Las Vegas. They were the money men. Then there was MacPhail, a baseball man, and a pioneer if there ever was one.

He began his career as general manager of the Cincinnati Reds in 1933 and during his five-year stint he introduced night baseball to the major leagues on the evening of May 24, 1935 as his Reds hosted the Phillies at Crosley Field. He took over the sagging operation of the Dodgers in 1938, and while in Brooklyn he lit Ebbets Field, broke the New York City radio ban by airing Dodgers home games with Red Barber at the microphone, and in 1939 he was largely responsible for the first television broadcast of a baseball game as the Dodgers hosted the Reds.

In 1942, at the age of 52, he left the Dodgers to enlist in the Army, became a high-ranking officer, and when he returned stateside he set out to purchase the Yankees. Topping and Webb allowed MacPhail to serve as general manager because Ed Barrow was pushed upstairs into a nonfunctional role as chairman of *the board. MacPhail was, in effect, in charge of the operation and though he stayed with the Yankees only three years, it was a remarkable tenure that helped revitalize the franchise.*

Because of MacPhail's decision to broadcast Dodger games over the radio, the Yankees had been forced to follow suit starting in 1939. The Yankees had remained a day-games-only team, but once MacPhail took up residence in the Bronx, lights were installed atop Yankee Stadium in 1946, and crowds increased dramatically at night because more businessmen could attend games without skipping work. During MacPhail's three seasons, approximately 5.3 million fans passed through the turnstiles at 161st and River and the team made more money in those three years than any other team had made in 10.

Under MacPhail the Yankees became the first club to travel regularly via airplane. And despite the fact that only about 500 New York City homes were equipped with televisions in 1946, he sold baseball's first commercial television rights, procuring $75,000 from the DuMont company.

I found Larry to be quite engaging when he was in a good mood. He was bright, energetic, and creative, and he was often very generous. But he could also be an outrageous ogre, especially when he had a few drinks in him. One day, he and Red Patterson, who was then working for the Herald Tribune, *actually got into a fistfight, yet MacPhail ultimately hired Patterson to be the publicity man for the Yankees when he took over the club. For all the good he did for the Yankees, there were no tears shed following the 1947 season when he announced he was selling his interest in the team.*

While the Yankees were struggling to regain their form on the field in the mid-1940s, this was a period of tremendous accomplishment and wonderment for Marie and me. Both our children, Phillip and Katherine were born, and we moved into a lovely apartment in the Grand Concourse section of the Bronx, considered at the time to be the most desirable place in the borough to live. Phillip came along first in July of 1944, and Katherine entered our lives in May of 1946, and as I stated earlier, those were two of the greatest thrills I've ever experienced. We also were relieved to learn that both of Marie's brothers, Arnold and John, had survived the war and would be coming home, though John had had his left leg amputated after stepping on a land mine in France.

Things were good in the Kimmerle hearth, and they got even better on the evening of May 23, 1946. After a splendid couple days off from the beat spent at Bronx Hospital with Marie and newborn Katherine, I rejoined the Yankees at the start of a road trip through Cleveland and Detroit, and I stumbled onto a huge story, one of the biggest I broke in my career—McCarthy's decision to quit as manager.

The Yankees had just lost to Cleveland on a ninth-inning home run and McCarthy was furious. He put on quite a show in the clubhouse, swearing a blue streak in front of all the writers, and I honestly thought he was going to keel over from a stroke. On the plane ride up to Detroit, McCarthy went over to where pitcher Joe Page was sitting. The big lefty clearly possessed talent. McCarthy knew this, but the kid was having a lousy year and he didn't seem to care, and McCarthy had lost his patience. The two engaged in a heated shouting match that was impossible to ignore. Everyone—players, coaches, and the writers—sat there in silence as McCarthy and Page went at it.

When we landed in Detroit we all checked in at the hotel and I assumed I was in for a quiet night. Instead, as I was standing in the gift shop leafing through the latest issue of Life magazine, I noticed McCarthy heading out the lobby door. Just for the hell of it I decided to follow him, and to this day I still don't know what prompted me to do it. He walked about two blocks, then dove into a little downtown tavern. McCarthy was a notorious drinker, the beverage of his choice always White Horse Scotch because he said it was the best. Usually he did his imbibing in private, but on this occasion he was there in a public establishment for all to see, "riding the White Horse" as the players would say whenever he was on a bender.

Like some private detective, I waited outside about 15 minutes to see what McCarthy might do, and when I realized he was locked in at his bar stool, I went into the place and acted like I was just bumping into him. "Hiya, Joe," I said to him. Startled that anyone in Detroit knew him, he turned around and I could see he had started drinking in his hotel room because he was already glassy-eyed. "Well hello there young Joe," he said hazily. "Why don't you pull up a stool and have a belt with me."

I ordered a vodka on the rocks and started idly chitchatting with the obviously disturbed manager. Not 10 minutes after I'd sat down, he dropped my jaw by saying, "Joe, I've had it with this shit. I'm quitting tomorrow." I couldn't believe what he'd just said and I asked him to repeat it, which he did. He further explained that he was frustrated with the ballclub, but more importantly, he hated dealing with the new ownership of the team, particularly MacPhail, whom he never got along with.

Joe DiMaggio, back with the club now that the war had ended, made a comment to me during spring training a couple months earlier that he had noticed the manager's drinking was becoming more prevalent and it was starting to affect how he ran the team. I thought about what DiMaggio had said as I was talking to McCarthy, and all of this began to make some sense to me.

After asking McCarthy if what he had just told me was "for the record," he said, "Aw Joe, what the hell, it doesn't matter because I'm not changin' my mind. I'm goin' home tomorrow, and I ain't comin' back." I pulled out my notebook—a good reporter is never without his notebook—and talked to McCarthy for probably 15 more minutes trying to get additional details concerning his decision. When I had all I needed, I thanked him for 15 1/2 wonderful years and wished him well in his next endeavor. He said if anyone deserved to get this "scoop" it was me because I'd been part of the team when he first arrived back in 1931.

I ran back to the hotel, phoned the night editor at the Home News, *and was informed that I had about 45 minutes before deadline. I hauled out my new Underwood and banged out the story, then hustled over to the Western Union station to wire it back to the office.*

With a banner headline screaming "McCARTHY TO QUIT" and my byline underneath, this story was the hottest news in New York City the next day and was certainly a proud moment for me. Barrow, who was back in New York, called me that morning at the hotel in shock and anger, wondering how I could print such a lie. McCarthy hadn't told anyone but me of his intentions; no one knew. That day McCarthy boarded a plane and flew to his off-season home outside Buffalo, then called Barrow to announce he was retiring, bringing to a close the greatest managerial term in team history.

Bill Dickey, also back from the war and playing his final season, assumed the manager's position, and when he quit in September, Johnny Neun finished out the year as the Yankees wound up in third place, 17 games behind the Red Sox.

After the Cardinals edged Boston in a spine-tingling seven-game World Series, the stage was set for one of the most dramatic years baseball had ever encountered.

– *Chapter 11* –

1947

SOMETIME IN THE MID-1980s I picked up a baseball magazine and was reading a story about Vince Coleman, a base-stealing sparkplug who at the time was playing for the St. Louis Cardinals. During the course of the writer's interview he asked Coleman, who is black, what he knew about the legendary exploits of Jackie Robinson.

"I don't know nothing about no Jackie Robinson," Coleman said of the man who in 1947 broke baseball's color barrier and thus became one of the most important figures not only in American sports, but in American society.

Boy, that really fried me and it struck me that Coleman's ignorance was a sad commentary on the modern-day athlete's inability and/or unwillingness to acknowledge that the world doesn't always revolve solely around their own private universe. For Coleman not to know anything about Jackie Robinson was a degradation to Robinson nearly as intolerable as the blatant racism the man endured from players, coaches, and fans alike, people who hated him not because he was a Brooklyn Dodger, not because he could beat their team with his supreme baseball skills, but because the color of his skin happened to be black.

A few months later I ran into Joe Black, a former Dodger teammate of Robinson's who also happens to be black, and I asked him if he'd seen the article. He hadn't, and when I relayed Coleman's comment, he was as upset as I was and he told me, "I think every black player is a direct descendant of Jackie Robinson. For a black kid not to know Jackie Robinson and what he did is very disturbing to me. Jackie was a major influence in the lives of many blacks in this country, on and off the ball field. Not know Jackie Robinson? That's almost like not knowing your family."

I've certainly had the privilege of witnessing more baseball history than a man could ever dream of during eight decades of following the Yankees. But on the afternoon of April 15, 1947, as I was watching former President Herbert Hoover throw out the first ball on Opening Day at Yankee Stadium, officially starting Bucky Harris's two-year managerial reign with the Yankees, I missed a remarkable event taking place at Brooklyn's Ebbets Field.

Robinson trotted out to play first base against the Boston Braves, and in becoming the first black man to play in a regular-season Major League Baseball game, he began to blaze a trail that continues to burn unfinished today. While African-Americans now hold the majority of roster spots on baseball, basketball, and football teams thanks largely to Robinson's courage, determination, and sacrifice, there is a glaring deficit in the number of coaching, front office, and ownership positions, which remain dominated by whites. Robinson's passion for baseball was matched only by his desire to advance the cause of equal opportunity for the black man, and if he hadn't died prematurely in 1972 of heart failure at the age of 53, perhaps the scales wouldn't still—in the twenty-first century—be drooping so heavily to one side.

Because I only covered Dodger games when they were playing the Yankees in the World Series or in the annual preseason exhibitions, I never really got to know Robinson, but I knew much about him, and learned more through reading some of the books that have been penned about his life.

He was born January 31, 1919 in Cairo, Georgia, in the farmhouse of a sharecropper, the fifth child of Jerry and Mallie Robinson. His father left with another woman two months later and Jackie never saw or heard from his father again. His mother moved the family to Pasadena, California, and he attended Pasadena Junior College and later went to UCLA, where he became the first athlete in the school's history to attain varsity letters in four sports (baseball, football, basketball, and track) in one year.

He did not graduate from UCLA because he felt no amount of education would help a black man get a productive job, although upon leaving school he worked briefly for the National Youth Administration as an assistant athletic director. When America entered the war he found himself out of work because the government closed down the NYA programs, so he accepted an offer to go to Hawaii to play semipro football. Robinson left the island at the end of the season on December 5, 1941, two days before the Japanese bombed Pearl Harbor.

Soon thereafter he was drafted into the service, but after encountering numerous racial difficulties he was granted a separation from service on medical grounds in November 1944. A few months later his professional baseball career began to take shape when he signed a contract with a Negro league team called the Kansas City Monarchs. By this time Brooklyn Dodgers owner Branch Rickey was already working on a plan—which he had held in abeyance for a number of years—to integrate Major League Baseball. He had his scouts scouring the country looking for the perfect black ballplayer to participate in what was called the "noble experiment."

The primary requirement was simple: The candidate had to be a superb player, someone who was so good that the other players would be forced to respect his ability and accept him as an equal, and the fans would come to cheer for because he could help their Dodgers win the World Series. But Rickey's prototype also had to exude character and mental toughness. He had to be strong enough to put up with the certain racism he would face and be able to turn the other cheek and not respond to the hateful slurs. Rickey also wanted him to be stable in his personal life, with a steady girlfriend or a wife, so people wouldn't get the impression that a black man was out carousing with white women.

Just writing that paragraph is bothersome, but these were the times we lived in.

Robinson was analyzed by the Dodgers' three top scouts—George Sisler, Clyde Sukeforth, and Wid Matthews—and after Rickey read the glowing reports pertaining to his playing skills, he went to Los Angeles himself to gather personal background information on the potential candidate. Rickey first met with Robinson in August 1945, at the Dodgers' office at 215 Montague Street in Brooklyn. Rickey peppered Robinson with questions, and acted out ugly racist scenarios Robinson might encounter in an effort to gauge whether Robinson could handle himself. He came away impressed.

Robinson asked Rickey if he was "looking for a Negro who is afraid to fight back?" and Rickey replied, "I'm looking for a ballplayer with guts enough not to fight back."

Robinson knew he was the man for the job, and at that point, the deal was consummated, although the official announcement of the signing didn't occur until October 1945. Robinson would earn a $3,500 bonus and $600 a month in salary playing for the Montreal Royals, Brooklyn's top farm club.

Robinson went to Sanford, Florida, for spring training with the Royals in 1946, made the club, and wound up winning the International League batting title with a .349 average, proving a black man could play on a white professional team.

Before the historic 1947 season, blacks had not been allowed to play in the major leagues, mainly because baseball commissioner Kenesaw Mountain Landis refused to permit any clubs to sign players from the Negro leagues. However, Landis died in 1944, and A.B. "Happy" Chandler became commissioner in 1945. Chandler had been a state senator and governor of Kentucky; he had seen black men go to war and fight for America, and his understanding of the black man's repression was far more sympathetic than Landis's had been. When Rickey proposed bringing Robinson up to the Brooklyn club in 1947, a secret vote was held among the owners of the 16 major league clubs. The vote went 15-1 against Rickey, but a few days later, at Rickey's behest, Chandler overturned it.

Some Dodger players wanted no part of Robinson as a teammate and a petition was formulated asking for Robinson's banishment from the team. Manager Leo Durocher's response was, "Well boys, you know what you can do with that petition? You can wipe your ass with it. If this fellow is good enough to play on this ballclub—and from what I've seen and heard, he is—he's going to play on this ballclub. And here's something else to think about. He's only the first. Only the first, boys. There's many more coming right behind him and they have talent and they're coming to play."

The petition died, and on April 9, 1947, Rickey made history. The Dodgers were blindsided that day by commissioner Chandler as he suspended Durocher for the season for "conduct detrimental to baseball" stemming from Durocher's involvement in a dispute with Larry MacPhail and the Yankees. Rickey, trying to circumvent the negative publicity, chose this same day to announce that he was signing Robinson to a major league contract. Less than a week later, Robinson took the field against the Braves, and baseball was changed for the better.

*   *   *

It was compelling day-by-day drama in Brooklyn, and while things weren't quite as theatrical over in the Bronx, they were not boring.

First, there was the arrival of Harris into the managerial hot seat. Harris had pieced together a successful playing career with Washington from 1919 to 1931, but his claim to fame occurred in 1924 when, at the youthful age of 27, he player-managed the Senators to their only World Series title. Harris continued on as a manager and more than 20 years later, after stops in Detroit, Boston, and Philadelphia, MacPhail gave him the glamour job in baseball.

After the turmoil of 1946, the Yankees were in desperate need of stability and leadership and Harris provided that. The players loved him because he was a players' manager and while he demanded performance on the field, he did not pester them off the field. Likewise, Harris did not want to be bothered off the field. Always a very private man, he didn't even give out his phone number to the players or the front office, let alone to the media. George Weiss, the czar of the Yankee farm system for 15 years, would become general manager of the club in 1948 and he clashed often with Harris. Weiss called him "the four-hour manager" because once the game was done, so, too, was Harris's day. This is what led to Harris's ouster following 1948, but in 1947 Harris was just the right straw to stir the Yankees' drink.

It was a vastly different Yankee club because MacPhail revamped the lineup through trades and the farm system. He dealt—at the urging of Weiss—second baseman Joe Gordon to Cleveland for pitcher Allie Reynolds. Gordon played well for the Indians, but Reynolds became a star during eight seasons with the Bombers. George McQuinn was signed as a free agent following his release by the Athletics and he replaced Nick Etten at first base. Snuffy Stirnweiss moved from third to second, Billy Johnson, back from the military, reclaimed his third base job, and Phil Rizzuto was a holdover at short. In the outfield were Joe DiMaggio, Tommy Henrich, and Johnny Lindell, and behind the plate, the retirement of Bill Dickey left young Aaron Robinson to share the receiving duties with a rookie named Yogi Berra.

The everyday lineup was reliable, but Harris encountered great difficulty with the pitching staff. Reynolds was a horse, but injuries forced Harris to use a vast array of starters including Spud Chandler and rookie Spec Shea. They were both felled by late-season arm woes, so Vic Raschi was recalled from the minors, Bobo Newsom was acquired from Washington in a July trade, and Karl Drews, Butch Wensloff, Randy Gumpert, and Don Johnson all made a handful of starts. Thankfully, Joe Page, the same Joe Page who used to drive Joe McCarthy crazy, finally blossomed. He became the closer after longtime ace reliever Johnny Murphy was released before the season, and he excelled, winning 14 games and saving a league-best 17.

My excitement over the start of a new baseball season was tempered in the very first week when my father informed me that Babe Ruth had been diagnosed with throat cancer. The news buckled me. How could my hero, the large, hulking man who could swat home runs farther than anyone, possibly be riddled by cancer?

I still kept in contact with Ruth, talking to him about a half dozen times a year, so I knew he hadn't been feeling well recently, but never did I suspect he was dying. Ruth's condition had not yet been made public, and my father swore me to secrecy. He knew as a journalist it was my job to report the news, but he implored me to sit on this one. He need not have worried. I would never have made that news public, nor would any of the other writers and broadcasters on the beat. It was a different time, and players' personal lives and private matters were not for public consumption. No one hesitated to rip a player for having a bad game, but once these men stepped off the field, they were no longer fodder for our slings and arrows. To a certain degree we protected the players by not divulging their indiscretions, unlike today's media that feeds on controversy and feels the need to reveal every secret, good or bad, a man may have.

Without mentioning the word cancer, the Yankees hastily organized a tribute, and the rest of the teams in the major leagues followed suit. April 27, 1947 was proclaimed Babe Ruth Day, and a crowd of more than 60,000 came to Yankee Stadium where Ruth appeared in his familiar camel's hair overcoat and cap, looking so fragile and ill that it brought tears to my eyes. Via a special radio hookup, Ruth's short speech was broadcast to every other stadium, and when it was done, he received a rousing standing ovation from his adoring fans.

Almost as if they were numbed by the sadness surrounding Ruth, the Yankees stumbled out of the gate and were 9-10 in the middle of May. MacPhail was growing impatient with the team, and he fined a number of players—including DiMaggio—for silly things such as failing to pose for promotional pictures or skipping banquets. Harris did not panic, though. He knew the team was solid and soon enough the tide would turn.

In late May the turn began. The Yankees swept a four-game series from the Red Sox, and by mid-June they were in first place and were never headed again, thanks to a magnificent 19-game winning streak that ran from late June to mid-July. The official clinching of the team's 15th American League pennant came appropriately enough on September 15, and the Yankees didn't even have to work that day. They were rained out, but the Red Sox lost, mathematically ending the race.

MacPhail was ecstatic, and his glee only grew when the Dodgers won the National League, providing Larry with a chance to beat his rival, Rickey, in the World Series.

– *1947 World Series* –

Rickety old Ebbets Field was rocking, its denizens cheering wildly for their beloved Dodgers, and as Yankees pitcher Bill Bevens trotted out to the mound to begin his warm-up throws in the bottom of the ninth inning, I leaned over to Frank Graham and mumbled, "The Yankees are gonna lose this game."

The venerable Graham, at the time the lead columnist for the *Journal-American* after a long tenure at the *Sun*, shot me a quizzical glance, but I was undeterred in my despondency. It was just one of those feelings that comes over you, when you know something bad is going to happen, and by gosh, it happens.

We were sitting up in the press box watching history unfold before our eyes as Bevens, a hard-throwing right-hander who had endured a dispiriting season losing 13 of 20 decisions for a pennant-winning team, was three outs away from hurling the first no-hitter in World Series play. No one in 44 previous World Series had come this close, but for some reason, I sensed that Bevens was going to etch his name into baseball lore for the wrong reason.

The Yankees had won two of the first three games, they led in this fourth game by a 2-1 score, and they had just blown a golden opportunity in the top of the ninth to break open what was a tight and tense conflict.

Hank Behrman, the third Brooklyn pitcher on this fabulously sunny afternoon, had worked himself into a sticky situation. The Yankees loaded the bases with one out, and Tommy Henrich—one of the great clutch hitters of his era—was due to step into the batter's box.

Dodgers manager Burt Shotton lifted Behrman, and as if he was reading from a Hollywood script, he brought in Hugh Casey, the same Casey who in the 1941 Series had thrown the third strike pitch that Mickey Owen failed to catch, opening the door for a magnificent Yankee rally and victory. That day, the man at the plate was Henrich, the scene was Ebbets Field, it was Game Four, the Yankees were holding a 2-1 advantage in games, and they were batting in the top of the ninth. The circumstances were eerily similar, but what happened in the next instant couldn't have been more in contrast.

On Casey's first pitch, a change-up screwball, Henrich tapped a grounder right back to the mound. Casey fired to catcher Bruce Edwards, who stomped on the plate and relayed to Jackie Robinson at first to double up Henrich and end the inning. The crowd exploded in relieved merriment as their Dodgers were still alive, and at that moment, a feeling of doom for the Yankees infiltrated my soul. I guess I just felt the Yankees had let the Dodgers hang around too long, and it was due to catch up to them.

Though he hadn't allowed a hit, Bevens wasn't really pitching that well. He issued eight walks in the first eight innings, and thanks to some sparkling fielding behind him he had continually wriggled out of trouble. His only hiccup came in the fifth when he walked Spider Jorgensen and Hal Gregg, and Jorgensen eventually scored on Pee Wee Reese's fielder's choice grounder. Bevens's velocity was barely passable, his location was obviously suspect, yet as he completed his warm-up before the ninth, immortality was within his grasp.

"I wasn't even thinking of the no-hitter," Bevens said afterward. "I knew it was riding, but never mind about that. I'm trying to win."

In a matter of 15 breathless and heartbreaking seconds, he lost the no-hitter, he lost the game, and I earned from Graham a grudging, "Nice call, kid."

Edwards led off the Brooklyn ninth by hitting a fly ball to left field that for a second seemed deep enough to leave the park, but Johnny Lindell went back and hauled it in just in front of the wall for the first out. Bevens's day-long bugaboo, the base on balls, reared its ugly head as he issued a free pass to Carl Furillo, but he regained control when Jorgensen fouled out meekly to George McQuinn at first base, leaving him one out away from becoming one of the most unsuspecting heroes in Series history.

Shotton sent Al Gionfriddo in to pinch-run for Furillo, and with Casey scheduled to bat, he looked down his bench and pointed to the only left-handed batter he had left, Pete Reiser, who had sprained his ankle the day before and was thought to be unavailable for duty. With Reiser at the plate, Shotton shocked everyone by flashing the steal sign to Gionfriddo, and when Gionfriddo slipped on his takeoff, it looked as if he was going to be a dead duck and the game would end. Though Yogi Berra's throw was a bit high, it looked to me and many others that Gionfriddo was out, but umpire Babe Pinelli saw it differently and called him safe. After logging the stolen base on my scorecard, I looked over at Graham, but didn't say a word.

With first base open and a 3-1 count on Reiser, Yankee manager Bucky Harris told Bevens to throw ball four. While that took the bat out of the dangerous Reiser's hands, and it set up a force play at every base, it also put the winning run on for Brooklyn.

"I knew it was against baseball tradition to put the winning run on base," Harris said. "But this was an exceptional case. Who would you rather pitch to— Reiser or Eddie Stanky?"

Harris knew Shotton had already used all his left-handed pinch-hitters, so he assumed Shotton would stick with the next scheduled batter, Stanky, a right-handed slap hitter who Harris felt Bevens could handle. He assumed wrong. Like Harris, Shotton thought Bevens would handle Stanky, so he sent aging veteran Cookie Lavagetto up to hit for Stanky, and he also inserted Eddie Miksis as a pinch-runner for Reiser.

"It surprised me," Gionfriddo said of Shotton's decision to hit for Stanky. "Eddie can get on base. I don't give a darn who's pitching, in a tight spot Eddie would get on."

Lavagetto had batted just 67 times all season and averaged .261. He was 34 years old and playing in what would be his final year in the big leagues. It just didn't seem to be a smart move, and Graham looked at me and said, "Game over, Yankees win." Graham was of the popular opinion that Lavagetto had no chance of producing the winning hit and that Shotton should have stuck with Stanky, if for no other reason than he had played all day and had already seen Bevens during four previous at-bats.

I must admit when I saw Lavagetto stride to the plate, I wavered ever so slightly on my prediction. But I learned a lesson that day: Trust your gut instinct.

Bevens blew his first pitch past Lavagetto, but his second was on the outside corner of the plate and Lavagetto met it squarely, sending the ball careening toward the wall in right field. The crowd rose in unison and let out a primal scream as Henrich drifted back trying to find the ball amid the glaring sun and white-shirted background. Once he located it, he realized he had no chance of catching it so he stopped running in order to position himself to play the carom off the wall.

"I didn't want it flying back past me toward the infield," he explained. However, Henrich didn't plan for the crazy bounce the ball took, causing him to misplay it. By the time he picked the ball up and threw to McQuinn in the cutoff position, Gionfriddo was across home plate with the tying run and Miksis was about to slide in with the winning run. McQuinn made the throw to Berra, but it was woefully late and just like that the Dodgers had tied the Series at two games apiece with an improbable 3-2 victory.

"One pitch and I was the hero and he was the goat. That's sure baseball," Lavagetto said.

As soon as the ball was hit, Bevens knew it was trouble. "I ran to back up the plate," he said. "After Miksis slid across almost on Gionfriddo's heels, I saw [umpire] Larry Goetz move up to dust off the plate. He was so wrapped up in the game he didn't know it was over. But I did."

So did all of Brooklyn. Fans poured onto the field in celebration, and I can remember hearing car horns blaring a symphony outside the ballpark on Bedford Avenue as fans listened to Red Barber's call on the radio.

The Yankees clubhouse door remained locked for 20 minutes after the game, and when the press was finally allowed in, most of my colleagues sought out Bevens. I walked over to Henrich instead.

"If I had seen the ball throughout its flight I could have headed straight for the right-field foul line parallel to the wall and adjusted enough to catch it or field it on one bounce and get some steam on my throw," Henrich said.

Henrich was depressed. He really felt he had let Bevens and the entire team down, but the truth was he couldn't have caught the ball because it hit too high on the wall. The best he could have done was prevent Miksis from scoring, but even a perfect play might not have cut down Miksis, who was running at the crack of the bat.

After I finished talking to Henrich, I joined the crowd around Bevens. He was an unemotional man, prompting someone to say of him, "If Bill nods to you, he's practically boisterous." True to his nature, in the aftermath of this bitter disappointment Bevens was the picture of calm and cool. "Those base on balls certainly kill you," he said evenly. "I felt strong, I never got tired, but my control was off. I walked 10 and, to me, a walk is as bad as a base hit. You don't deserve to win when you walk that many."

Harris was prepared for the onslaught of second-guessing concerning his decision to walk Reiser. "I'd do it again tomorrow if I had to," he argued. "The count is 3-1 and Reiser is a long-ball hitter. After Gionfriddo steals, a single drives him home and the winning run is on first anyhow. I'm not going to give Reiser a chance to whack one over the fence. The second guess is always the best one, and I only get one."

Ironically, Henrich had Joe Page hitting fungoes off the wall out in right for 15 minutes in the pregame drills so he could get used to the caroms, but it didn't matter. This game was meant to be won by the Dodgers, and like I said, for reasons I can't explain, I just I knew it.

* * *

The good news for the Yankees is that it was just one game, and the Series was far from over.

New York had gotten off to a wonderful start, winning the first two games at the stadium by counts of 5-3 and 10-5.

The opener, played on a crisp, breezy day, drew a new World Series record crowd of 73,365 and was decided by one furious flurry as the Yankees scored all of their runs in the fifth inning after Brooklyn starter Ralph Branca had set down the first 12 Yankees he had faced.

Joe Page came out of the bullpen in relief of Spec Shea and pitched the last four innings, allowing four hits and two runs. As for Jackie Robinson, playing in his first World Series game and his first meaningful game against the Yankees, he went 0-for-2 with a walk and a stolen base, but he was caught in a rundown in the first inning which short-circuited a Dodger rally. Of Berra, Robinson said, "I wish he were catching in the National League. I'd steal 60 bases on him."

Perhaps spurred by Robinson's acid tongue, the Yankee bats, mostly silent in the first game, woke with a vengeance for Game Two as they made 15 hits in a runaway victory. "Jackie Robinson thought the Yankees didn't show those Dodgers anything yesterday? Ask him what he saw today," Page said. "I'd guess we showed them something, didn't we?"

Brooklyn starter Vic Lombardi was routed inside five innings as he gave up nine hits and five runs, and Gregg and Behrman were equally ineffective in relief stints. Behrman summed up the day best when he turned to a group of us writers seeking answers and belched, "No comment."

The Yankees broke a 2-2 tie in the fourth when Billy Johnson led off with a triple and came home on Phil Rizzuto's bloop double. In the fifth, Henrich homered to right-center, and a four-run burst in the seventh off Behrman ended all suspense on another frosty afternoon. "Tomorrow we'll be at home and it'll be different," said Shotton.

He was right.

The Dodgers pummeled Bobo Newsom for six runs in the second inning of Game Three at Ebbets Field, and though the Yankees fought back all day, they came up one run short and lost, 9-8. The teams combined for 26 hits off eight pitchers with Joe DiMaggio and Berra homering. Berra's clout was of particular renown as it was the first by a pinch-hitter in World Series history, a solo shot in the seventh that pulled New York within 9-8.

The game's crucial play occurred in the eighth. Henrich walked, Lindell singled, and then DiMaggio hit a slow roller toward second. Stanky scooted in to field the ball, swept a tag at Lindell for one out and threw on to Robinson to complete a double play. Lindell went ballistic, claiming Stanky never touched him.

"You've never seen me kick that way on a play in your life," he said to me after the game. "I never kick when the play is right, but the umpire missed that play completely. I know Stanky never touched me."

Stanky's reply? "I tagged him."

Henrich went to third on the play, but he was stranded when McQuinn grounded to first, and Casey retired the Yankees without incident in the ninth.

When the Dodgers pulled out Game Four they were stoked with confidence and Shea was thrust into a difficult situation. The rookie responded with one of the great pitching performances in Yankee history, limiting the Dodgers to four hits during a complete game gem that sucked the fervor out of Flatbush and put the Yankees back in the lead at three games to two.

It had been a white-knuckler of a game with Shea pitching out of trouble in the sixth, seventh, and ninth innings to hold on for the 2-1 victory, and afterward, he was beside himself with joy. I had talked to him briefly before the game and he said he was determined to silence the Dodgers after their miraculous win the day before. "Joe, I just want to win it for Bev because he didn't deserve to lose that game," Shea said to me.

"I told you I'd do it," he yelled to me in the locker room afterward. "I told you I'd get even and I did. I wanted to square what they did to Bev yesterday. That hurt me almost as much as it hurt him."

Ironically, the last batter to face Shea was Lavagetto. Shotton sent him up to pinch-hit with two outs and the tying run on second, but Shea whistled a 3-2 fastball past him to end the game. "He never saw it," said Shea. "Boy, that revenge was sweet."

After most of the press had cleared out of the locker room, I noticed DiMaggio and Henrich chuckling in front of DiMaggio's locker so I wandered over to inquire about their animated conversation. Henrich looked at me and said, "You know what the great DiMaggio said to me just before Lavagetto was up? 'Say a prayer.' Imagine the great DiMaggio asking for divine intervention on a baseball field."

The Yankees were one victory away from their 11th world championship, and ace Allie Reynolds was due to pitch the potential clincher, but these Dodgers were nothing if not scrappy. With another Series record crowd of 74,085 wedged into every seat and standing area available at Yankee Stadium, the Dodgers showed remarkable resolve in pulling out an 8-6 victory. They routed Reynolds for four runs inside three innings, then held on for dear life as the Yankees mounted another charge that fell just short in a game that ranks as one of the most exciting I've ever seen.

Harris and Shotton combined to use 38 players in a battle that lasted a then-record three hours, 19 minutes, and by the time it was over, my brain was as scrambled as my scorecard. This game provided a deluge of dramatic moments, none more electrifying than Gionfriddo's spectacular catch of DiMaggio's deep fly to left-center in the sixth inning, the famous one where DiMaggio kicked the dirt with his spikes as he neared second base, the only real flash of emotion I could ever remember him displaying on a ball field.

The Yankees were trailing 8-5 at the time and they had runners on first and second with two out when DiMaggio flushed a Joe Hatten fastball. Had the game been at Ebbets Field the ball might have cleared the roof, but at Yankee Stadium left-center was death valley for right-handed power hitters. Gionfriddo, a tiny 5-foot-6 sparkplug of a player who had just replaced Miksis, angled over from left field in a dead sprint and thrust his gloved hand out just before the ball reached the gate in front of the visiting bullpen. Somehow the ball found the glove as Gionfriddo hit the fence, and what should have been a game-tying homer or at least a two-run triple became the third out as the huge crowd screamed in disbelief.

DiMaggio never said a word about the play after the game, but the following spring we were having dinner down in St. Petersburg and I asked him about it and he said, "That was one of the greatest catches I've ever seen, and don't it figure the little bastard caught it on me."

Reynolds was sent to the showers after Brooklyn took a quick 4-0 lead, but before he had finished drying himself, the game was tied as New York lit up Lombardi for four runs in the bottom of the third on the strength of six hits, a wild pitch, and an error. And the Yankees took the Chief off the hook with a run in the fourth on Berra's controversial two-out RBI single which the Dodgers argued long and hard was foul, but to no avail.

The Dodgers came back with four runs in the sixth against Page to take an 8-5 lead as Lavagetto contributed a game-tying sacrifice fly and Pee Wee Reese a two-run single. After DiMaggio was robbed, the Yankees threatened again in the seventh as they loaded the bases with two outs, only to have Snuffy Stirnweiss fly to center. Then in the ninth the Yankees scored once, but Casey worked out of a bases-loaded jam by getting Stirnweiss to ground out to end the game.

And so it came down to Game Seven, and there is nothing like a Game Seven. It's the ultimate finality: you either win or lose, there is no tomorrow. Although they had played in the Series 14 times, the Yankees had been stretched to a seventh game only once, and they had lost it in 1926 to the Cardinals. It looked for a while like the Yankees weren't going to win this one, either.

Given that Shea had already won two games, Harris was banking on the rookie being able to put together one more solid outing. But Shea had nothing, and when the Brooks grabbed a quick 2-0 lead in the second inning, Harris wasted no time getting him out of there and inserting Bevens.

The Yankees retrieved one of those runs in the bottom of the second when Rizzuto stroked a RBI single, and after Bevens worked two uneventful innings, New York gained the lead for good in the fourth.

Billy Johnson walked and after two were out, Rizzuto singled him to second. Even though Bevens seemed to be finding his groove Harris decided to pinch-hit for him in this spot, and Bobby Brown came through with a clutch double that scored Johnson and chased Rizzuto to third. Shotton lifted Gregg in favor of Behrman, and he quickly walked Stirnweiss on four pitches to load the bases, and Henrich took his next pitch to right field for the go-ahead RBI single.

On came Page, about a week removed from his superb effort in Game One, and one day removed from his flogging in Game Six. What was Harris going to get from his star reliever in this situation? Only one of his best performances of the year. Page retired the first 13 batters he faced until Miksis singled in the ninth, but by then the Yankees had annexed a 5-2 lead. With Miksis on first, Page worked to Bruce Edwards and induced him to hit into a Series-ending double play, Rizzuto to Stirnweiss to McQuinn.

"I'm just about the happiest guy in the world," said Page. "This makes up for everything, particularly that cuffing they gave me yesterday. They had their fun then, I had mine today."

On the Brooklyn side, the Bums were rightfully subdued. They had given it a tremendous effort, and after the way they won the fourth game and then the sixth game, it sure looked like the gods were on their side and they would, at long last, bring a championship home to Brooklyn.

Shotton admitted his team "lost to the better club this time." He then added, "I'll tell you this. We'll beat the Yankees during the next 10 years a whale of a lot more times than they will beat us."

The Yankees hadn't even reached the clubhouse to begin celebrating their 1947 World Series championship when Larry MacPhail, watching the final game of the thrilling Series against the Dodgers from up in the Yankee Stadium press box, announced to the media that he was retiring from baseball. We all thought he was kidding. He wasn't.

No one knew at the time, but shortly before the Series began, MacPhail had approached co-owners Dan Topping and Del Webb with an interesting proposal. He wanted to pool all their shares in the team together, then sell half to a group of bankers who would in turn conduct a public sale. Topping and Webb declined, but offered to buy out MacPhail's one-third stake in the team, and MacPhail decided netting about $1 million for three years' work was a pretty good deal and he accepted. Thus, as soon as Game Seven ended, MacPhail upstaged the victory festivities by saying, "That's it, that does it, that's my retirement" as tears dripped down his face.

When he entered the clubhouse, he hugged everybody in sight, and the players weren't quite sure what to make of the spectacle. He then put his arm around George Weiss and barked at me, "I want you to put this in your story, Joe. I built the losing team out there (meaning the Dodgers), but here's the guy who built the winners."

It was an odd concession from the egotistical MacPhail, but it was a properly aimed plaudit for Weiss, a man who had played such a vital role in developing the Yankees' farm system which was the root of the team's success.

With MacPhail's retirement, Weiss was promoted to general manager, and by the time his reign was complete in 1960, the Yankees would win seven more championships, all with Casey Stengel managing the team.

But first, there was the 1948 season, a year when the Yankees put up a gallant fight to defend their title, but lost in a down-to-the-final-weekend pennant race to Boston and Cleveland, who tied for first before the Indians won the one-game play-off to earn the World Series berth.

It was essentially the same team as the 1947 edition except that pitchers Spud Chandler and Bill Bevens had retired and were replaced by Eddie Lopat who had come over from the White Sox, and Vic Raschi, who was ready for full-time duty in the rotation. The Yankees were good, but they weren't quite good enough, and it opened the door for Weiss to get rid of manager Bucky Harris. Weiss never appreciated Harris's laid-back style and even if the Yankees had won the pennant, Weiss wasn't going to rehire Harris. A third-place finish was all the ammunition he needed.

Harris's dismissal brought the inimitable Casey Stengel back into our lives. The same Stengel who made me cry at the first World Series game I attended back in 1923, the same Stengel who had failed miserably as a major league manager with the Braves and Dodgers and most recently had been toiling in the minor leagues, became the new manager of the proud Yankees.

Weiss really had no firm reason to hire Stengel, and he admitted to me years later that he was merely playing a hunch. Like most of Weiss's hunches, it sure paid off.

Ordinarily, not winning the pennant would have irked Yankee fans, but in 1948, melancholy hung in the air and forgiveness came easy. As in 1941 when Lou Gehrig died, the entire baseball world came to a standstill on August 16, 1948 when word was received that Babe Ruth had died of throat cancer. We all knew it was coming, but still, when one of the world's most beloved characters and most recognized celebrities passes away, the news knocks you for a loop. His death seemed to cast a pall over New York, and when the Yankees failed to make the World Series, it just didn't seem to matter as much.

As soon as I heard the news, I went over to my parents' house and shared a hug and a cry with my grieving father. The Babe's second wife, Claire, knowing her husband's grave condition, had asked my father months earlier if he would serve as a pallbearer at the funeral, and Dad had proudly agreed.

In what was certainly one of the most memorable events in the long history of Yankee Stadium, Babe's casket was brought to the main entrance where more than 100,000 people flocked to pay their final respects. This was a man who was a hero to millions, but for 27 years was not only my hero, but my friend. My eyes puddled as I took my final glance at the Babe and tucked in his suit jacket pocket a clipping of a feature story I had written about him years after he had left the Yankees. I had always felt it was one of the finest pieces I'd ever crafted, and I thought he'd like to take it along with him on his next journey.

An estimated 7,000 people attended the funeral at St. Patrick's Cathedral and tears flowed freely. It was a somber day, but my dad said the mood was lightened somewhat by a wisecrack Waite Hoyt made. Like my dad, Hoyt was serving as a pallbearer along with Joe Dugan, Connie Mack, Whitey Witt, and sportswriter Fred Lieb, the man who long ago dubbed Yankee Stadium "The House That Ruth Built." As they were carrying Ruth's casket on that muggy, rainy day, Dugan said, "I'd give a hundred bucks for an ice-cold beer," and without missing a beat, Hoyt replied, "So would the Babe."

There was another funeral I attended in 1948, though this one did not elicit the far-reaching sorrow of Ruth's. Declining advertising revenue and subscriptions plus heavy competition from so many other dailies in New York City brought the demise of the Bronx Home News, the only newspaper I had ever worked for.

For 11 years I poured my heart and soul into the paper and I was not alone in this endeavor. All of us at the Home News were hardworking folks who took pride in our borough, and that pride manifested itself every morning in our newspaper. In the end, none of that mattered. The newspaper industry, just like any other business, is all about turning a profit, and the Home News—which at its peak in 1939 had a circulation of more than 110,000—had fallen into irreversible debt during the war years. The owners of the New York Post bought us out in May 1945, realized the operation was unsalvageable, and finally folded us for good in February of 1948.

The termination of the Home News thrust a couple hundred people—many of whom I considered close friends—into unemployment. I happened to be very fortunate in that within two weeks, the Post hired me to help with the baseball coverage, and I wound up sharing the Yankees beat with Arch Murray, Milton Gross, and the estimable columnist Jimmy Cannon. With a wife and two children under the age of four to provide for, it was unquestionably a character-building two weeks for me.

"Oh, thank God" was Marie's reaction when I came home and told her the Post had hired me. Of course, two days later I was on my way down to St. Petersburg for spring training, leaving her alone to care for the kids for five weeks. That was always a difficult time for Marie, more so because she missed me, but this was one road trip she didn't mind my taking.

– Chapter 12 –

1949

I HAPPENED TO BE STANDING NEXT TO Joe DiMaggio in spring training one day in 1949 as he and *New York Times* sports columnist Arthur Daley were talking about the team's new manager, Casey Stengel. Daley asked DiMaggio what he thought of Stengel and DiMaggio answered, "I've never seen such a bewildered guy in my life. He doesn't seem to know what it's all about. That's the impression I have and the rest of the fellows feel the same way."

Oh how that lummox named Stengel changed Joe D's attitude. How he changed everyone's attitude. Ten pennants and seven World Series titles in 12 years will do that.

He was born Charles Dillon Stengel in Kansas City, Missouri, in 1890. His young pals called him Dutch, and it is uncertain how he got the nickname Casey. Stengel himself wasn't positive. One theory was that when he first reached the majors as a player with Brooklyn in 1912 a teammate asked where he was from and when he replied "Kansas City" the Dodgers immediately took to calling him "KC," which then became Casey. Stengel used to offer this explanation: "Just when, where, and how I got the Casey business I ain't so sure. In them days everybody was reciting that famous poem 'Casey at the Bat,' so maybe I got the handle from that. Could be I struck out too often."

Before he became Casey Stengel, Dutch Stengel played baseball, football, basketball, and ran track at Kansas City Central High and he helped lead his teams to Missouri state championships in both baseball and basketball. Equally as impressive as his play was his ability to keep his teammates laughing, and he was quite unanimously the most popular boy in school, a friend to all.

In the spring of 1910 Stengel joined the minor league baseball team in Kansas City, the Blues, but his intention was not to one day make it to the major leagues. Instead, he wanted to earn enough money to put himself through dental school. As he would say years later, "I'm just glad I had baseball knuckles and couldn't become a dentist."

It took him just over two years—after stops in four minor league towns—to make it to Brooklyn as the Dodgers' center fielder. He batted .316 during a late-season call-up, earning him a starting position for the next five years in Flatbush. He helped the Dodgers win the National League pennant in 1916, but his .364 average in the World Series wasn't enough during Brooklyn's loss to the Babe Ruth-led Boston Red Sox.

Despite his productivity and popularity, baseball was a business even then, and in January 1918 Stengel was surprisingly traded to Pittsburgh. Stengel was bitter and he considered not reporting to the Pirates, but he eventually relented and that led to one of the great moments in baseball lore. In his return to Brooklyn in June, Stengel was greeted with a cacophony of boos which shocked him because he had been a fan favorite. Unbowed by the reception, he took the cold greeting good-naturedly, and then provided an unforgettable response. When he strode to the plate for his first at-bat, boos ringing in his ears, Stengel smiled, doffed his cap and when he did, out flew a tiny sparrow which he had commandeered down by the bullpen. The fans gasped, then roared their approval and stopped booing him. At least for the time being.

Stengel's playing career began a downward spiral from that moment on. He bounced around the National League from the Pirates to the Philadelphia Phillies to the New York Giants to the Boston Braves before finally retiring early in the 1925 season, when he was asked by Braves president Emil Fuchs to go manage and serve as president of Boston's new Class C farm club in Worcester, Massachusetts. Stengel reluctantly accepted the job, and just to prove that he wasn't done as a player, he played in 100 games for Worcester and hit .320.

Stengel eventually concentrated solely on managing, and after a successful stint at Triple-A Toledo, he returned to the major leagues as a coach with the Dodgers, ultimately taking over as manager in 1934, thus beginning what essentially became a 15-year apprenticeship for the Yankees job.

The Dodgers were horrible under Stengel, and one time he allegedly told his barber, "Don't cut my throat friend, I'm saving that for myself." After finishing in the second division three years in a row, Stengel was fired, and he summed up his managerial term there by saying, "Brooklyn, that borough of churches and bad ball clubs, many of which I had."

The same could be said about his woeful Braves clubs. He took over as skipper in Boston in 1938 and never bettered fifth place in six years. Fired again and with no other major league offers on his plate, Stengel took a step backward and spent five years in triple-A at Milwaukee, Kansas City, and Oakland and Bill Veeck, who owned the Milwaukee club at the time, labeled him "a chronic loser."

However, when Yankees general manager George Weiss, who had hired Stengel to manage the Yankees' farm club in Kansas City a few years earlier, fired Bucky Harris, he did so with the intention of offering the enviable Yankee job to Stengel. Weiss knew Stengel would be the type of manager who, first of all, would have a listed phone number and would be at his beck and call. More importantly, Stengel was the type of man who would work with the young kids, teach them the game.

Dave Egan, a columnist for one of the Boston papers, wrote on the day Stengel was hired, "Well, sirs and ladies, the Yankees have now been mathematically eliminated from the 1949 pennant race. They eliminated themselves when they engaged perfesser Casey Stengel to mismanage them for the next two years, and you may be sure the perfesser will oblige to the best of his unique ability."

At Stengel's introductory press conference I remember looking around at the other writers in the room, all of whom were gazing at him with varying degrees of curiosity. We had grudgingly grown accustomed to the gruffness of Joe McCarthy, who never liked talking to the writers and was usually quite uncooperative. Harris had been a little better, but he never seemed to have time to sit down and talk baseball. We could tell right away that Stengel was going to be different.

"The Yankees represent an investment of millions of dollars. They don't hand out jobs like this just because they like your company, I got the job because the people here think I can produce for them," Stengel said. "I know I can make people laugh, and some of you think I'm a damn fool."

Actually, most everyone thought he was a fool. Though his luminous quotes could fill my notebook, I must admit it was difficult at first to look at him in a serious manner, given his cartoon-like appearance and ignominious managerial record. No one in the baseball world could believe the Yankees had hired him, and DiMaggio wasn't the only Yankee player who doubted Stengel's competence.

"We thought we got us a clown," Lopat said. "I think a lot of us thought of him as an interim manager. But it was a treat for him to be with us after all the donkey clubs he'd been with. He was something."

*   *   *

And Stengel's first season at the helm sure was something.

One of Stengel's favorite sayings was, "If you give me the horses, I can win you a pennant." That first season, Stengel had the horses, but they played like mules all during the spring and Stengel was heard to say, "This was the greatest club in baseball?"

The Yankees made minor alterations to the roster as rookie Jerry Coleman took over at second base and teamed with shortstop Phil Rizzuto to form the league's most effective double play combination. Bobby Brown joined Billy Johnson in a platoon at third base, while first base was a season-long problem as seven players played the position including Tommy Henrich, rookie Joe Collins and old veteran Johnny Mize, who was obtained from the Giants in August.

With DiMaggio limited to a half season due to injuries and illness, and Henrich playing much of the time at first base, men like Hank Bauer, Gene Woodling, Johnny Lindell, and Cliff Mapes patrolled the outfield.

Yogi Berra, tutored expertly by coach Bill Dickey, improved immensely as a defensive catcher, and he handled a pitching staff anchored by Vic Raschi, Eddie Lopat, Allie Reynolds, and Tommy Byrne, a foursome that combined for 68 of the team's 97 victories. And when they couldn't close the deal, reliever Joe Page was used 60 times by Stengel and he won 13 games and saved 27.

After a disastrous spring which included three straight losses to the Dodgers in the annual Mayors' Cup games, veteran Charlie Keller—coming off a serious back injury that would soon end his career—stood up at a team meeting before the start of the regular season and told his teammates, "If we don't start bearing down, we're going to be an embarrassment to the New York Yankees."

The Yankees paid heed and began to play like the Yankees, but then the injury bug took hold and the team couldn't shake it all year. No Yankee team had ever experienced the onslaught of ailments that this one did and Stengel rarely knew from day to day who would be available for duty. He was forced into unrelenting position switching and platooning, yet the Yankees consistently won, and all of it proved one thing to the fans, the media, and the Yankees themselves: Stengel could manage, something Weiss knew all along.

I was up in the press box before one game sometime around June when the Yankees were about eight games in front of the pack in the American League and everything Stengel was doing was turning out right. I was talking to Weiss about Stengel, and I admitted to him that I was shocked by Stengel's proficiency. Though Weiss was normally guarded in conversations with the writers, he was never unwilling to laud his skipper, and he did so on this occasion.

"I've been in this game a long time and I've never known a man who could talk baseball all night the way Casey can," Weiss told me. "He is a dedicated baseball man. You can ask him anything about any move he makes in a game and he'll always have an answer. He isn't a clown, he's a great baseball man."

Most impressive about the Yankees' awakening after the Keller speech was that they built their early lead without DiMaggio, who sat out the first 2 1/2 months because of foot surgery.

After having a bone spur removed from his left heel in 1947, DiMaggio had played the entire 1948 schedule with a bone spur in his right heel. Despite constant pain, he missed only one game and turned in one of his greatest seasons with a .320 average and league-leading totals of 39 homers and 155 RBI. That November he had the spur removed and spent the next six weeks on crutches, but it was thought that he would be fine for spring training and he could pick up right where he left off on the field.

However, DiMaggio's heel began to bother him as soon as he arrived in St. Petersburg and he couldn't do anything. The team sent him to John Hopkins in Baltimore, where DiMaggio was told the pain would eventually go away. It didn't. Never mind the stress his foot was under on the ball field running and sliding and pivoting, it hurt for him to walk, period. After his trip to Baltimore, it was decided that his street shoes should be altered to alleviate pain, so he flew to New York and went right over to Dad's shop where he always bought his shoes. On the outside of DiMaggio's right shoe, my father nailed a leather arch support between the ball of his foot and the heel. It helped slightly, but DiMaggio was still in discomfort, and it was decided he would need another operation.

His career was clearly in jeopardy and John Drebinger even wrote in the *Times*, "It is a pretty solid conviction that DiMaggio will never again be the DiMaggio of old." To an extent, Drebinger was right, but a lesser

DiMaggio was still a wondrous player. He made a dramatic return in late June, and by swatting four homers and driving in nine runs during a three-game Fenway Park sweep of the Red Sox, he wrote another chapter to his precipitous legend.

With DiMaggio back in form, it looked as if the Yankees would roll to the pennant, but the injuries never stopped coming and eventually they took their toll. The Yankees sputtered late in the summer and the Red Sox—now managed by Joe McCarthy, which to me was as strange as Babe Ruth once wearing the Red Sox uniform—got hot. On the next-to-last weekend of the regular season, Boston swept three from New York at Fenway to take over first place, knocking the Yankees off the top rung for the first time all year. With two games left to play, Boston led by a game, and fittingly, those last two games were in New York against the Yankees.

Before the first game was played the Yankees honored DiMaggio with a lavish gift-giving display, and nearly 70,000 fans came to pay homage to the great man. DiMaggio, clearly uncomfortable amidst this fete, made an eloquent speech at the end and he uttered the line that soon became legendary—"I want to thank the good Lord for making me a Yankee."

The Red Sox even presented DiMaggio with a silver tray, but once the party was over the Boston players set out to prevent DiMaggio from receiving the one thing he truly wanted—another pennant. Boston jumped to a 4-0 lead before DiMaggio ignited New York in the fourth as he sliced a double to right and scored on Bauer's single. By the fifth the game was tied and it stayed that way until the eighth when Lindell roped one into the left-field stands for the game-winning homer.

And so it came down to the final day and Stengel exuded confidence in the Yankee clubhouse beforehand. "I think we've got 'em, I can feel it in my bones."

That Sunday afternoon was a glorious day in the rich history of New York City baseball. The Yankees pulled out a hard-fought 5-3 victory over Boston behind Raschi to win the American League, and in Philadelphia, the Dodgers—clinging to a one-game lead on St. Louis in the National League—defeated the Phillies, 9-7, in 10 innings to set up another all-New York World Series.

The Red Sox made it interesting by scoring three runs in the ninth, but Raschi induced Birdie Tebbetts to foul out to Henrich behind first base to end the game. Bill Dickey was so excited he leaped out of the dugout, banged his head on the roof, and nearly knocked himself out. It was yet another injury, but nothing could stop what DiMaggio called "The fightingest team I've ever been on."

– 1949 *World Series* –

Yankees broadcaster Mel Allen started calling Tommy Henrich "Old Reliable" sometime during Tommy's last few years with the club, and there couldn't have been a more apt nickname for a ballplayer. "Old Reliable" was the train that ran from Cincinnati to Allen's home state of Alabama, and it was always on time, just as Henrich was always in the right place at the right time doing whatever it took for the Yankees to win.

Henrich was the definition of clutch during his Yankee career, and he reached new heights during the 1949 season at a time when the injury-ravaged Yankees needed him most.

My colleague at the *Post*, Milton Gross, sat down one day and catalogued all the key hits Henrich had collected during the first half of the season when Joe DiMaggio was out of the lineup, and when he finished, we couldn't believe the extensiveness of the list.

Casey Stengel knew how valuable Henrich was to the team that year, and ol' Casey used to pamper Henrich like an infant. He told Henrich to drive carefully, avoid drafts so he wouldn't get a stiff neck or catch a cold, and "under no circumstances are you to eat fish because them bones could be murder. Sit quietly in the clubhouse until the game begins. I can't let anything happen to you."

Despite Stengel's precautions, Henrich still suffered injuries to both knees, his toe, his ribs, and his thumb during the year. After playing through those nuisances, he finally went down for what many of us thought would be the rest of the season when he crashed into the right-field wall at Chicago's Comiskey Park in late August. Henrich fractured two vertebrae in his back and when he returned to New York he was admitted to St. Luke's Hospital and fitted for a plaster cast.

I was one of the reporters who wrote that the 36-year-old warrior was done for the year, and upon his release from the hospital he made it a point to politely inform me that I was wrong.

Was I ever. Henrich made it back into the lineup well before the final weekend showdown with Boston, and when the Series got underway at Yankee Stadium, Henrich won the first game against the Dodgers with a dramatic bottom-of-the-ninth home run to break up a scoreless pitching duel between Allie Reynolds and Brooklyn's Don Newcombe.

DiMaggio used to tell me, "Tommy Henrich is the steadiest ballplayer I've ever seen." High praise from a man who had every right to lay claim to that title, but Henrich indeed was one of the most "reliable" Yankees of them all.

Henrich made it to New York in 1937, and after a quick trip back to Triple-A Newark, he returned for good in 1938 and began carving out his niche in Yankee lore. His was not as expansive as Babe Ruth or Lou Gehrig or DiMaggio, but by the time he retired following the 1950 season, Henrich had left an indelible mark on the franchise.

Henrich was making $22.50 per week as a typist when he took a pay cut to $80 per month to sign his first minor-league contract with the Indians organization in 1933. After three years of being jockeyed around the minors despite outstanding batting averages, Henrich became embroiled in a controversy when the Indians sold his contract to the minor league Milwaukee Brewers. Not knowing which team he was on, and feeling his career was being shunted by the Indians, Henrich brazenly enlisted the help of baseball commissioner Kenesaw Mountain Landis to settle the dispute. After weeks of meetings, Landis determined the Indians had wronged Henrich, and he ruled Henrich to be a free agent— the first in baseball history—meaning any team could sign him. Eight pursued the nifty outfielder, but there was only one team he wanted to play for—the Yankees.

Henrich had grown up a Yankee fan and Ruth worshipper in football-crazed Massillon, Ohio, and as luck would have it, Yankee scout Johnny Nee had been following Henrich's progress that spring before the Landis ruling and he liked what he saw. He met with Henrich, and that was it. The St. Louis Browns had offered more money, but as Henrich told his father, "Suppose I sign with the Browns and find I'm good enough to play major-league ball. Then I'm stuck with the Browns, one of the worst teams in baseball. If I sign with the Yanks and find I can make it as a major-leaguer, I'm sitting pretty with the best team in baseball. I'm willing to take that chance." Shrewd man, that Henrich.

On his first visit to New York he checked into the New Yorker Hotel and was greeted by a bellboy who said, "So you're Henrich. The papers say you're going to break into the lineup right away. Hey, wait 'til you see DiMaggio and Selkirk and Hoag. You ever seen those guys play?" Without hesitation, Henrich replied, "You ever see Henrich play?"

Henrich exuded class. His mannerisms were professional in every way, he was such a marvelous team player, and later in his career, he became a leader who was respected nearly as much as DiMaggio.

"He didn't care what it took to win," Billy Johnson said years later in an interview. "He was a leader on the Yankees in the years after the war. He was an intense player who would tell young players 'If you don't want to hustle with this club, there's no use playing. Everybody has to go all out, everybody has to play together or we won't win.' Tommy didn't joke around too much, he was all business."

Henrich wasn't the most gifted player, but he worked hard and paid attention to detail. He once told me, "Catching a fly ball is a pleasure, but knowing what to do with it after you catch it is a business." He appreciated the intricacies of the game, and he appreciated the opportunity to play the game, knowing his special skill as a ballplayer saved him from a life as a common laborer.

Henrich was a frequent companion of mine on the many train rides we shared to and from American League cities. We were about the same age, he three years older, so many of our interests were the same and we passed many hours conversing about topics other than baseball. He enjoyed going to the picture shows at the Rialto or the Paramount, and our tastes in music were similar, as we both had a fondness for Glenn Miller and his orchestra.

Marie and I would occasionally see Henrich and his wife, Eileen, taking in the floor shows at Billy Rose's Diamond Horseshoe, and after bumping into the Henrichs so often there, our wives began to get friendly. In 1949, one of the greatest years in the history of live theatre, Marie and I attended three new plays with the Henrichs—*A Streetcar Named Desire, South Pacific,* and *Death of a Salesman*—a lineup every bit as impressive as DiMaggio-Henrich-Berra.

Long after he retired, Henrich and I stayed in touch. He coached with the Yankees for a while and later with the Giants and Tigers before taking a job as president of a brewing company. Last I knew, he was sunning himself down in Arizona, and I'm sure that Yankee pride and tradition which he represented and lived for is still oozing out of his pores.

*   *   *

I know it was coursing through his veins at the end of the opening game of the Series as he was dancing around the bases after having hit the game-winning home run.

Reynolds and Newcombe had been overpowering. Reynolds completed nine innings of work, having yielded just two hits and only one runner touched third base. Newcombe, a 17-game winner in his rookie

big-league season, had pitched five-hit ball through eight. He had surpassed Reynolds in strikeouts by an 11-9 margin, and while Allie had
walked four, Newcombe hadn't issued a free pass.

One of the Yankee hits was a double by Jerry Coleman in the eighth,
and with one out, Stengel was confronted with a tricky decision.
Reynolds was due up, he was pitching wonderfully, and he had two of
the hits off Newcombe, but the situation seemed ripe for a pinch-hitter. Instead, Stengel allowed Reynolds to bat and he was called out on
strikes, then Phil Rizzuto flied to center to end the threat, and it looked
as if the teams might play all afternoon.

Reynolds justified Stengel's confidence by mowing down the Dodgers in order again in the ninth, and Newcombe lumbered out to the
mound intent on doing the same, but he would have to wade his way
through Henrich, Yogi Berra, and DiMaggio. He never got past Henrich.

On a 2-0 pitch, Newcombe tried to throw a hard curve past Henrich
and it cost him the game because Henrich smashed it over the right-
field fence.

"His curve usually doesn't break a whole lot," Henrich said. "It was a
fast curve and that was to my advantage because I didn't have to adjust
as much to the difference in speed between that pitch and a fastball. As
I was running down the first-base line I was watching Furillo who was
running to his left toward the foul line. He lifted his head to follow the
flight of the ball and as soon as he did that I said to myself 'the game is
over.' I knew I had a home run and we had won the game."

Joe Page didn't even bother looking. Stationed out in the bullpen,
the Yankee reliever hopped the gate and was on the field jumping up
and down before Henrich reached first because "I knew as soon as I
heard the crack of the bat where that ball was going."

It was the first World Series victory for Stengel, and he milked it for
all it was worth. I remember the clubhouse being nearly empty, but
Stengel was still fully dressed, still fully beside himself with excitement.
There had only been one other 1-0 World Series game decided by a home
run, and Stengel had hit it in Game Three of the 1923 Series against the
Yankees. "How that Henrich hit it, what a blast, the touch of a master,"
Stengel bellowed.

Stengel wasn't quite as illuminated the next day when Preacher Roe
did to the Yankees exactly what Reynolds had done to the Dodgers—he
pitched a 1-0 shutout to even the Series at one game apiece.

Vic Raschi was the hard-luck loser, the only run coming in the second inning when Jackie Robinson led off with a double and scored on a

single by Gil Hodges. "Roe pitched a good game, he never lost control of the ball," observed Stengel. "The pitching has been good on both sides, ours was all right today, too. Raschi pitched a good game, good enough to win if we got him some runs."

The scene shifted to Ebbets Field for the next three games, and, as it turned out, the last three games of the Series. New York pulled off a clean sweep, and once again the Bronx celebrated while Brooklyn mourned.

Game Three provided the final vestige of drama. The teams were locked in a 1-1 struggle as Brooklyn's Ralph Branca allowed a mere two hits through eight innings and the combination of Tommy Byrne and Page had given the Dodgers only five hits. At last, both teams awoke from their offensive slumbers, and the Yankees found one more run than Brooklyn in a wild ninth inning. In the top half Berra walked with one out, and after DiMaggio fouled out, the Yankees went to work as Bobby Brown singled and Gene Woodling walked to fill the bases. Stengel sent Johnny Mize up to pinch-hit for Cliff Mapes and Big John—who began his professional career in 1930 and was at long last playing in his first World Series—came through with a two-run single off the right-field fence. Branca left in favor of Jack Banta, who allowed Coleman's RBI single before striking out Page amidst silence at the little bandbox in Flatbush.

Soon the place was rocking again as Luis Olmo and Roy Campanella hit solo homers off Page to close the gap to 4-3. "Those Brooklyn hitters can make life interesting for you," said Page.

Page, who had blown some games early in the season before hitting stride, appeared fidgety on the mound and he was clearly wilting, but Stengel had relied on him all year to close games, and Page didn't let him down. Bruce Edwards pinch-hit for Banta and looked at a called third strike to end the game.

"Say, that big guy came through, didn't he?" Stengel said of Mize. "And I was satisfied with that man Page. I wasn't too worried. We were three runs ahead when they started hitting those homers, and we were still in front when Page finished 'em."

Brooklyn manager Burt Shotton came back in Game Four with Newcombe on just two days' rest, and it turned out to be a bad decision. "The Yankees looked for everything fast and low from me and they were a fastball-hitting, low-ball hitting club," said Newcombe. New York lit him up for three runs in the fourth inning—the key hit Mapes's two-run double—before Shotton rescued him. Joe Hatten took over and he was strafed in the fifth when Brown hit a three-run triple that inflated the Yankee lead to 6-0.

Brooklyn exploded for seven hits in the sixth to chase Eddie Lopat off the mound, but all were singles and they produced only four runs. Stengel turned to Reynolds to douse the flame, which he did, and the Brooks were never heard from again. For the second day in a row Ebbets Field emptied quickly and quietly as Reynolds retired all 10 batters he faced to secure the 6-4 victory.

"Reynolds was my pitcher for tomorrow, but when I saw how things were going I had to get Allie in there," said Stengel. "What a pitcher he is. I don't believe in saving pitchers in such a spot. I want today's game today. Let tomorrow take care of itself."

The Yankees didn't need Reynolds in the finale. Raschi went back to work on just two days' rest and while he wasn't very sharp, it didn't matter because the Yankees routed Rex Barney and five other Brooklyn hurlers during a 10-6 clinching victory.

Barney was brutally bad, allowing three hits and six walks in less than three innings as the Dodgers fell behind, 5-0. DiMaggio's home run in the fourth offset Reese's RBI single in the third to make it 6-1, and the Yankees ran away for good with three in the sixth off Carl Erskine, the key blow Brown's RBI triple on which he also scored when Robinson threw the relay over Campanella's head at the plate.

Robinson was at a loss to explain what had happened to the Dodgers, again. "They beat us, I don't know what you can say about that. They really knocked us down and stepped on us. But I still don't see how a team like ours could have been licked by a team like that. I'm not knocking the Yankees, but I still think we had the better team before the Series started."

Yet once again, when the Series was over, it was the Yankees who were hoisting the hardware.

The last time I had sat in the stands at Yankee Stadium I was 10 years old and watching the Yankees lose Game Seven of the 1926 World Series to the St. Louis Cardinals. In the intervening 24 years I was either working for the club and stationed on the field or in the dugout, or I was covering the team from my perch in the press box. But on June 20, 1950 I broke my streak and mingled with the masses. That was the day I took my son, Phillip, to his first Yankees game. I'm not sure who was more excited, Phillip or me.

Through the first five years of his life Phillip really hadn't shown an interest in baseball or any other sport, and that was my fault. Even though my professional life was dominated by baseball and the Yankees, I tried to keep work out of the house. When I was a kid, baseball was all I heard about from the time I was old enough to comprehend. My dad loved the game, he made sure I loved it, too, and I did. I was four years old when I saw my first game in person, and I've never forgotten it. I was hooked the moment I peered out at the vast Polo Grounds that day back in 1920, and baseball was all I ever thought about. As I look back on my life, I wouldn't have wanted it any other way.

However, just because I loved baseball, it didn't mean that my children had to love baseball, and I guess my thinking at the time was that I didn't want to force my interests onto Phillip and Katherine. I wanted my children to decide what they liked, so I didn't talk about the Yankees around the dinner table. My position was that if either of the kids ever asked me questions about baseball or the Yankees, I would be more than happy to fill their heads with tales from the ballpark. Marie did not disagree with my approach. She enjoyed baseball, but she would have been perfectly content if Phillip never followed or played the game. Like most mothers, she didn't want him dreaming of being a ballplayer, she wanted him to dream of becoming a doctor.

My hectic schedule certainly didn't enhance Phillip's chances of getting interested in baseball. When the factory whistles blew at five o'clock, scores of fathers went home to their families and they'd play catch with their sons on the streets or the sandlots before or after dinner. At five o'clock I was usually in some major league clubhouse doing interviews or I was back up in the press box writing my story for the day.

I bought Phillip his first baseball glove for his fourth birthday, but he'd hardly used it. It was still stiff as cardboard and there was no one to blame but myself. I was so wrapped up in my life and my job that I just didn't make the time I should have, and this angered my father to no end. Dad finally grabbed hold of me one day early in the 1950 season and he said, "Don't you think it's about time you bring Phillip to a game?"

Dad had wanted to take his grandson for a couple of years, but knowing how special it was for him when he brought me to my first game, he wasn't about to rob me of that unique bonding experience. But now Dad was getting impatient. In lamely defending myself, I pointed out that it was a little tougher for me because the Yankees were my job. I went to every game because I had to. For me to take Phillip, I would have to take a day off, and in 1950, as a husband and father of two trying to make ends meet, you didn't ask your boss for a day off, especially when you'd only been at your place of employment two years.

"I don't care," Dad said to me. "That boy wants to go to a game, and it's your responsibility to take him."

What had happened during the past year is that Phillip had started school, and the children who had already been exposed to baseball were constantly talking about the game, and he had grown curious. All of a sudden he was coming home and asking, "Daddy, who's Joe DiMaggio?"

Baseball had that effect on people, even the little ones. Baseball dominated America's sporting consciousness back then. Football was interesting and chaotic, but there was no stability in the National Football League and the games were sometimes hard to follow because of all the various rules that no one quite understood. Hockey was a game played by Canadians, for the entertainment of Canadians. Pro basketball was brand new, and like football, the fan base was rooted at the college level. Golf and tennis were for the rich and famous. Baseball was the game for the masses. Some Americans played it, and almost all followed it. And nowhere was baseball bigger than in New York City.

The Yankees. The Giants. The Dodgers. So many choices. Many of Phillip's little kindergarten friends had already experienced a trip to Yankee Stadium or the Polo Grounds or Ebbets Field. Yet here was Phillip, the son of a man who was intimately close to the game and to the world-famous Yankees, and he'd never eaten a ballpark frank, chomped on freshly roasted peanuts, or watched DiMaggio smash one out of the park or gracefully chase down a long fly.

To be honest, it was a sin—one that I decided had to be absolved.

I walked into my boss' office and asked for a day off. He said, "What for?" and when I explained my plight he said to me, "Joe, take your son to the ballgame."

When I asked Phillip if he'd like to go see the Yankees play, his gap-toothed smile lit up the room. I pulled from my wallet two tickets to the Yankees-Indians game for the next day, and he fondled them as if they were covered by velvet.

The morning dawned gloomy and I feared there might be a rainout, but soon the sun broke through the clouds and it was a beautiful June day in the Bronx. Hand in hand we walked the six blocks from our home on the Grand Concourse to Yankee Stadium, and just as Dad and I had done on our first visit to the arena back in 1923, we entered at Gate Six, still almost directly across the street from Dad's shop. As we walked through the turnstiles the memories of my inaugural entrance into the stadium washed over me. I looked down at my fair-haired son and when he gazed skyward at me, squinting into the bright sun, I could see he was bursting with anticipation, just as I had been.

I took Phillip's half-torn ticket stub and inserted it into my wallet for safe-keeping, and then we made our way through the concourse until we came upon the ramp that would lead us to our box seats. "Are you ready to go in?" I asked. "Yes," came the eager reply. Down the shaded narrow corridor we walked, Phillip squeezing my hand tighter with each step we took. As we neared the end of the tunnel, there came that burst of light that I so distinctly remembered, and suddenly it was all right in front of my little boy—the lush green grass, the rich brown dirt on the infield, the huge grandstands that seemed to rise to the clouds, the pinstriped players milling about playing catch or pepper in their usual pre-game manner.

On this day the ballpark looked different to me. It was beautiful again, just as it had been when it first opened in 1923. On this day, Yankee Stadium wasn't my office, it was my oasis, a place for a father and his son to share an experience so rich in Americana. This is what fathers and sons did in the middle of the twentieth century. It was about time Phillip and I did it.

– Chapter 13 –

1950

ONE DAY MIDWAY THROUGH THE 1950 season the legendary Ty Cobb was at Yankee Stadium and he was holding court in the press lounge before the game. We writers crowded around him, pencils and notebooks at the ready, and Cobb addressed a number of topics including the play of the Yankees' veteran shortstop, Phil Rizzuto.

"One of the few scientific hitters left in baseball today is Phil Rizzuto," Cobb began. "He's small, he's frail, and there are a hundred players in the big leagues who can hit a longer ball. But he can lay down a perfect bunt and poke his hits in any direction, and he gets results. Pound for pound he's the best baseball player alive today. I like to watch him field as well as bat. He picks off grounders like he's picking cherries, and he has the opposition jittery every time he comes to bat. They don't know what to expect. If it were not for Honus Wagner, who was a superman in every respect, I would make Phil Rizzuto my all-time all-star shortstop."

Playing in the shadow of Yankee greats such as Joe DiMaggio, Bill Dickey, Joe Gordon, Yogi Berra, Tommy Henrich, Mickey Mantle, and Charlie Keller for so many years, Rizzuto was perhaps the most under-rated player in team history. Because of his diminutive size—5-foot-6, barely 155 pounds—Rizzuto was never looked upon as one of the pillars of the Yankees, but he was.

He played a flawless shortstop, hit for average, was a demon on the basepaths, and there were some in the Yankee organization who dared to say that at times early in his career, he was just as important to the Yankee machine as the great DiMaggio. Never was that more apparent than in 1950. Rizzuto played in every game that season, collected 200 hits to bat a career-high .324, and he led all American League shortstops with a dazzling .982 fielding percentage, at one point handling a league record 288 chances without an error. I cast my MVP ballot as a member of the Baseball Writers Association of America with Rizzuto at the top as did many of my fellow ink-stained wretches and the Scooter won the award. Not bad for a kid Casey Stengel once said would "never be a big league ballplayer."

The first time Stengel saw Rizzuto was at a Dodgers tryout camp when Stengel was managing the Bums in 1936. Rizzuto's speed was obvious, but he was plunked in the small of his back in batting practice that day and thereafter couldn't hit the ball out of the infield. Stengel said, "Kid, you're too small, you ought to go out and shine shoes."

Years later, Rizzuto was still bitter toward Stengel, even while he was playing for Stengel. "It's not that I was rejected; rejection is part of living. It was that I was made to look like a fool for showing up," Rizzuto once said of that Dodger tryout. Rizzuto never let that issue die. He repeatedly brought it up whenever a new writer joined the Yankees beat, and Stengel hated it.

After Stengel shucked him aside, Rizzuto sorrowfully packed his belongings and headed to the next tryout camp, this one being held by the Giants, and he found manager Bill Terry to be equally uninterested. Finally, he turned to the Yankees where perceptions were a bit different. Head scout Paul Krichell looked past Rizzuto's lack of size and focused on his strengths, which were plentiful. Krichell could see the little guy had quick reflexes, peerless glove skills, running speed and—with full of range of motion in his swing because he hadn't been hit by a pitch—an ability to hit with surprising authority. After a couple of days the Yankees offered the 18-year-old Brooklynite a contract and he signed immediately, for $75 a month.

Rizzuto worked his way through the minors in four years, and following the 1940 season with Kansas City when he hit .347 and was named Minor League Player of the Year, he earned his promotion to the big club, tagged as the replacement for the eminently popular Frank Crosetti.

That made it tough for Rizzuto that first year, 1941. The players didn't respect him, mainly because he looked like a little munchkin, but also because this snot-nosed punk was being hailed as the heir apparent to Crosetti, the Yankee shortstop since 1932. Led by Bill Dickey and Red Ruffing, who lockered on either side of Rizzuto, Phil was given the silent treatment by all the veterans. He couldn't even get into the batting cage during the first couple weeks of spring training because players would jump in front of him in line, and the passive Rizzuto—who was afraid of insects, mice, and his own shadow—never fought for himself. Finally, it was DiMaggio who stepped in on his behalf. DiMaggio always took batting practice first, that's just the way it was, so he was never part of the ridicule. Besides, he was much too big for that sophomoric nonsense. DiMaggio knew that management was intent on playing Rizzuto—Crosetti had hit a weak .194 the year before and was slowing down in the field—so he explained to his teammates that "if this kid is going to play short for us this year, we'd better give him a chance."

Once the god had spoken the cold shoulder treatment ended, but perhaps just as important to Rizzuto as gaining acceptance was the stand that Crosetti took. A true professional and team player, Crosetti took Rizzuto under his wing and coached him on how to play shortstop in the major leagues. Here was the man who was losing his job tutoring the kid who was taking said job.

Because Rizzuto was involved with the Yankee broadcasts for nearly 40 years after his retirement, he has always been around the ballpark and he and I became good friends. Marie and I would go to Phil's house in Hillside, New Jersey, for dinner, and we would occasionally reciprocate and entertain him and his wife, Cora, at our place. I remember Phil telling me one time, "Without Crosetti, I would never have made it as soon as I did. You've got to remember that when I came up, Crosetti was idolized by all the Yankees. He wasn't one of the sluggers, but Crosetti was the glue for that whole infield. And here I was, a fresh rookie coming up and trying to take his job. And they resented me. Crosetti took the time before each ballgame to position me on every pitch. He made me look good and here I am trying to take his job away."

Buoyed by Crosetti's knowledge and his own talent, Rizzuto broke into the lineup for good in May right around the time DiMaggio's historic hitting streak started. He went on to hit .307 as a rookie, which led Joe McCarthy to say, "For a little fellow to beat a big fellow he has to be terrific, he has to have everything, and Rizzuto's got it."

Rizzuto had another excellent year in 1942, but then he enlisted in the Navy and missed three seasons. Upon his return he regained his position and remained entrenched for nine years before age began to slow him down, and he was only a part-time player in 1955 and 1956 when he was unceremoniously released in one of the most classless acts I've ever witnessed.

That year, Billy Martin returned from a two-year military hitch and took back his second base position, so Stengel moved versatile Gil McDougald from second to shortstop, signaling the end for Rizzuto. However, rather than let Phil serve in a utility role and then ask him to retire at the end of the year, George Weiss called him into Stengel's office one day under the guise that he and the manager were seeking Rizzuto's advice about cutting a player. It turned out the player they wanted to cut was Rizzuto, and that's how his career ended.

Vic Raschi summed up Rizzuto's value when he said, "My best pitch is anything the batter grounds, lines, or pops up in the direction of Rizzuto."

*   *   *

When the 1949 season ended, DiMaggio was mentally and physically exhausted and he gave serious consideration to retirement. He couldn't stay free from injuries and, as he told me, he just didn't feel like he used to at the plate when he would step in and know that he could hit anything any pitcher in the world threw up there. Dan Topping talked him out of quitting, told him to go home to San Francisco and relax for a couple months. DiMaggio did that, and it worked wonders. When he arrived at St. Petersburg in late February he remarked that, "This is the best I've felt in years."

When the Yankees rallied from a 9-0 deficit at Fenway Park to win their opener against the Red Sox, 15-10, DiMaggio leading the way, it looked as if it would be a glorious year in the Bronx. DiMaggio was happy, healthy, and he was even talking to his teammates. His good nature didn't last, though, and the season-long drama that revolved around DiMaggio nearly cost the Yankees the pennant.

On the day I took Phillip to the stadium for the first time, DiMaggio collected the 2,000th hit of his career, but it was one of the few highlights of his season to date. He was barely hitting .250 in late June and the Yankees were struggling to stay in first place with Detroit, Boston, and Cleveland hot on their tail. DiMaggio wasn't hitting, he wasn't fielding up to par, and he wasn't talking. One day I sat down at his locker, taking advantage of one of the few times he didn't duck into the trainer's room to avoid dealing with the media. He confided to me that he was depressed, and it was affecting his play on the field. His ex-wife, Dorothy Arnold, had teased Joe about a possible reconciliation, something he had been hoping for almost from the time she filed for divorce in 1942. But just as DiMaggio's hopes were rising, she crushed them early in the season when she told him there was no chance of their getting back together. Further, she was leaving New York with their son, Joe Jr., and was moving to Los Angeles so she could try to resuscitate her sagging acting career. As was the understanding with DiMaggio and all of the writers, I was not allowed to write any of that. If I did, I would be cut off from DiMaggio's inner circle, which was shrinking rapidly.

DiMaggio wasn't helping the club, and Stengel sought a solution. Flanking DiMaggio in the outfield were Hank Bauer and Gene Woodling, both of whom were playing well. Languishing on the bench were young outfielders Cliff Mapes and Jackie Jensen. Meanwhile, first base was a mess as Tommy Henrich and Johnny Mize were both injured and young Joe Collins couldn't hit his weight. A light bulb went off over Casey's head: he would bench Collins, move DiMaggio to first, and send Mapes out to center. He ran the idea past Topping, and the owner thought it was wise. In fact, Topping, figuring it might save Stengel some aggravation, was the one who broke the news to DiMaggio.

"This is strictly my idea," Stengel said. "DiMaggio is going to give it a try because he is that type of player. When I asked him whether he'd try playing the bag, he said, 'Certainly, I'll play anywhere you want if you think it will help the club.'"

What a load of crap that was. DiMaggio was furious about the switch and was dead set against it, but what was he going to do? The owner himself had asked him, the same owner who was paying him $100,000 a year.

On July 3, DiMaggio started at first base in Griffith Stadium against the Senators. It was the first major league game he'd ever played as anything but an outfielder. It was also the last. DiMaggio handled 13 putouts without an error, but he was clearly uncomfortable in the infield. Fortunately for him, Bauer sprained an ankle that day and was forced to the sidelines, so the next day DiMaggio was back in center field where he remained until mid-August. That's when Stengel pulled another unthinkable act—he benched the game's most recognizable star.

DiMaggio, who was mired in a deep slump, said, "I know some people say I'm through, but those are the same people who said the same thing in 1946." All Stengel would say—at least what was discernible—is that "The way we're hitting, I should bench the entire team."

The Yankees were three games behind the Tigers, who were managed by ex-Yankee Red Rolfe and being helped by the resurgent Charlie

Keller, whom the Yankees had released at the end of 1949. With DiMaggio on the bench, the deficit grew to four, and DiMaggio brooded as he'd never brooded before. Not only had Dorothy broken his heart, Stengel had wounded his enormous pride and smashed his ego. Someone was going to pay, and thankfully for the Yankees, DiMaggio chose opposing pitchers to foot the bill.

He was reinserted into the lineup a week later and in his first game he hit a solo home run in the ninth inning to deliver a 3-2 victory over the Athletics. The Yankees won 10 of 11 games with DiMaggio clipping along at a .400 pace and New York moved back into first place.

Another nagging injury set DiMaggio back as August melted into September, but upon his return he went wild, hitting in 19 straight games to fuel the drive to the pennant. The Tigers remained competitive, and Briggs Stadium was electric in mid-September when the Yankees came to play a three-game set that figured to decide the race. DiMaggio helped win the first game with a two-run homer, and after Detroit took the middle contest, DiMaggio's two-run ninth-inning single broke up a 1-1 tie in the rubber match and the Yankees went on to score seven times for an 8-1 victory, a rookie pitcher named Whitey Ford winning his eighth decision without a loss. The Yankees left the Motor City with a 1 1/2-game lead and never relinquished their stronghold as Detroit, Boston, and Cleveland all fell away quietly.

It wasn't easy, but the Yankees were kings of the American League again. One bothersome occurrence dulled the excitement for players, writers, and fans, though: The end of the line for Henrich, one of the nicest, talented, loyal men to ever wear the pinstripes.

Late in the season Weiss acquired first baseman Johnny Hopp from the Pirates to give the Yankees an extra pinch-hitter and insurance at first base in case Mize broke down. In doing so, Weiss was admitting that he had given up on Henrich, who never was able to shake his nagging knee injury and played only 73 games. When Weiss announced the World Series roster, Henrich—a Yankee stalwart since 1937—was not included. It was just one of what became a lengthy list of cold-hearted personnel moves by Weiss.

The night before the Series opener against Philadelphia's amazing Whiz Kids, I was in Toots Shor's restaurant having a drink with DiMaggio, who expressed disgust over Weiss's decision to deactivate Henrich. DiMaggio said to Toots and me, "I'd rather lose with Tom than win without him."

DiMaggio did not get his wish.

– *1950 World Series* –

An hour after the Yankees had rallied in the final two innings to capture Game Three of the World Series and take a commanding 3-0 lead over the Phabulous Phillies of '50, Casey Stengel sat in his office conducting one of his long, drawn-out bull sessions with "my writers," as he used to call us.

Vic Raschi and Allie Reynolds had gone the victorious distance in the first two games at Shibe Park. Eddie Lopat had pitched just as well in the third game at Yankee Stadium, but by the time his teammates started scoring he had been lifted for a pinch-hitter, so when Jerry Coleman singled home the winning run in the bottom of the ninth, Lopat wasn't eligible for the winner's decision.

Stengel had gotten exactly what he had expected out of his three frontline starters. Now he had a decision to make. Based on the season-long rotation, Tommy Byrne was in line to be the Game Four starter, but there was that brash rookie, Eddie Ford, the kid they called Whitey, to consider. It was hard to ignore what Ford had done in the second half of the season, winning his first nine decisions before dropping a meaningless game after the pennant had been clinched. Byrne was a reliable veteran who'd won 30 games the past two years, so picking Byrne would have been easy. Stengel picked Ford.

"It'll be Ford tomorrow," Stengel said. "That kid's got moxie."

And then Stengel launched into a story that, in Casey's roundabout way, explained why he was asking Ford to close out the Series.

The previous year when the Yankees were battling the Red Sox down to the wire for the American League flag, Ford was dominating at Class A Binghamton. Stengel said Ford phoned him in September and told him, "You may think I'm cocky, but I can win for you. I've learned all I can in the minor leagues."

Stengel declined Ford's offer to come help the Yankees win the pennant, "But I'll bet he would have done just what he said he would do."

Never mind that Casey was making the whole thing up. I asked Ford about it one time and he looked at me like I was crazy. "I wouldn't have called Stengel, I didn't even know him," Ford said. "Even *I* wasn't ballsy enough to call Stengel directly."

He did dial up head scout Paul Krichell, though, and asked if the Yankees would consider bringing him up because Binghamton's championship season was over. "I called Krichell because I knew him," Ford

said. "All he said was if I behaved myself they'd take me to spring training the next year."

Ford was fairly impressive at St. Petersburg, but he started the year
at Triple-A Kansas City. Midway through the season Ford didn't need to
call anybody. The Yankees were coming off a poor month of June and
were in need of a spark, so they called him. "Maybe you can go out and
beat somebody and put some life back into our guys," Stengel told him.
That's what Ford did.

Ford was born to be a Yankee. A New York City native with Hollywood handsome good looks, he was a perfect fit for the fast life of his
hometown and the glare of the spotlight that accompanied playing for
the Yankees. Ford was great, on the field and off. He could baffle any
hitter in the American League with his varied assortment of pitches,
and then he could baffle you at the bar with his fondness for libations
and laughter. I spent many hours pounding beer, gin, scotch, vodka, or
whatever the flavor of the night was with Ford and his favorite running
mates, Mickey Mantle and Billy Martin. My God, could those three
drink.

Ford grew up in the Astoria section of Queens playing youth baseball in the Police Athlete League and the Kiwanis League, mostly as a
decent-hitting first baseman. When he tried out with the Yankees and
the Giants, that was his position of choice, and both teams liked him.
The Giants offered a $6,000 bonus, the Yankees $7,000, and that made
the decision easy for Ford.

There was one hitch, though. Krichell wanted Ford to try pitching
and when Ford displayed good velocity and excellent movement on his
curve, Krichell told him to forget first base. Ford spent his last year in
high school honing his pitching skills and Krichell signed him in October 1946. After a 3 1/2-year journey through the minor-league system,
during which time he won 51 of 71 decisions, he landed in New York
brimming with bravado.

I'll never forget the first time I saw Ford. I was having breakfast at
the Kenmore Hotel where the team was staying in Boston. I'm sipping
coffee and I look over at the entrance to the restaurant and there's Ford
and Martin standing there with two beautiful blondes. There were a few
other players in the place, Allie Reynolds and Hank Bauer come to mind.
Right away everyone thought the two rookies had spent the night with
these women and were coming down for breakfast, showing off their
prize catches. That's not how it was. Martin had met the two women

the night before, but he'd gone to bed alone and invited them for breakfast the next morning. Naturally, Martin never included those mundane
details in his recounting of the story. Regardless, it was a hell of an impression for Ford to make.

Later that day Whitey made his Yankee debut in relief of Byrne. He
wasn't very successful, but little did the Fenway faithful know that they
were witnessing the beginning of a Hall of Fame career. His first start
came a few days later, a no-decision against Washington, and then he
earned the first of his Yankee-record 236 victories on July 17, beating the
White Sox. Right away Ford was a hit and Yankees pitching coach Jim
Turner said Ford had "the guts of a cat burglar."

With the Yankees embroiled in another tight pennant race, Ford
played a vital role as he kept winning every time Stengel trotted him out
to the mound. After he won Game Four of the Series, it was clear Ford
was going to become a mainstay in the Yankee rotation, but his mete-
oric rise was stunted by the Korean War and during the next two years
he had to fulfill a military commitment. He returned in 1953 and his 18-
6 record helped propel the Yankees to their record fifth consecutive
championship.

Over the next 12 years he was one of baseball's greatest pitchers, and
by the time a circulation problem in his left arm forced him into retirement in early 1967, Ford had the highest winning percentage (.690) in
major league history of any pitcher with at least 200 victories.

"Ford was the best left-handed pitcher I ever played with or against,"
said Moose Skowron, Ford's teammate for nine years. "It's who wins,
who's on the pennant winners. The Yanks with Ford on the team won a
lot of championships."

Mantle agreed. "Whitey was the best clutch pitcher I ever saw, and
one of the smartest," Mantle said. "The tougher the opponent, the bigger the game, the better he was. Whitey's weakness was that he couldn't
start every day."

*   *   *

All year long it looked like Brooklyn was once again the class of the
National League. The Dodgers had another terrific team with the same
cast of characters—Duke Snider, Gil Hodges, Jackie Robinson, Pee Wee
Reese, Roy Campanella, Carl Furillo, Gene Hermanski, Don Newcombe,
and Preacher Roe. With players like that, it still baffles me that the
Dodgers perpetually lost to the Yankees because they were every bit as

good, and sometimes better. But in 1950 they didn't even get the chance to lose to the Yankees. They lost to the Phillies.

Entering 1950 the Phillies had finished above .500 twice in the past 32 years and on 16 occasions they closed in last place. They were one of the worst franchises in baseball, but then Eddie Sawyer took over the club late in 1948, and he began assembling a pretty sound unit. Players such as Richie Ashburn, Del Ennis, Granny Hamner, Dick Sisler, Andy Seminick, and Puddin' Head Jones began to jell, and aided by a pitching staff led by Robin Roberts, Curt Simmons, and Jim Konstanty, the Phillies finished third in 1949, then held off the fast-charging Dodgers by winning a thrilling down-to-the-last-day pennant race in 1950, and once again tears spilled in Brooklyn. The Phillies franchise had been around since 1883, but this would be just its second World Series appearance. It didn't last long.

Sawyer's mound staff had been depleted at the end of the year because of injuries and a military call-up of Simmons, so the manager gave the ball to Konstanty to start the opener at Shibe Park. The 33-year-old right-hander had set a major league record by appearing in 74 games, all in relief, and he won 16 while saving 22. He'd started one game in the last five years, so naturally Sawyer's choice set off shock waves in the press corps, and the Phillies themselves were rather stunned by the news.

You couldn't argue with Sawyer's strategy at the conclusion of Game One. Konstanty, the first recognized reliever to start a Series game since Wilcy Moore did it for the Yankees in Game Four of the 1927 Classic, was superb, limiting the Yankees to one run on four hits over eight innings. Unfortunately for him, Vic Raschi was even better as he blanked the Phillies on two hits, never allowing a runner to touch third base, and the Yankees escaped with a 1-0 victory.

In the very first inning Raschi twisted his left knee fielding a bunt by Ashburn, and though he said nothing, there were a few moments when he was apprehensive about whether he could continue. Upstairs in the press box it certainly didn't seem like anything was wrong. He had a no-hitter going into the fifth before Jones singled, and after Seminick singled to left with two outs, Raschi struck out Mike Goliat. Only one more batter reached base for the Phillies, Eddie Waitkus, who drew Raschi's only free pass of the game in the sixth.

The Yankees didn't have much luck with Konstanty, but in the fourth Bobby Brown doubled down the left-field line, took third on Hank Bauer's long fly to center and scored on Jerry Coleman's deep fly to left, and that's all they needed, thanks to Raschi's paralyzing performance.

"Raschi wins because he pitches here, here, and there," Casey Stengel said pointing to his arm, his heart and his head.

*   *   *

Raschi was one of those guys who would scare the hell out of you if you didn't know him. Gladly, I knew him, and on days when he wasn't pitching he was a swell guy. But when it was his turn in the rotation, he was as intense a competitor as I've ever encountered, his reputation enhanced by a menacing scowl and his unshaven scruff. On those days you learned to stay clear, and that included his catcher, Yogi Berra.

It was Raschi who pitched the pressure-packed 1949 season finale against Boston, and when he got into a spot of trouble in the ninth, Berra called time and trotted out to the mound to make sure he was okay. Raschi looked at him and barked, "Just give me the damn ball and get out of here."

Yet as gruff as he was, he was not immune to something as silly as superstition. Whenever the Yankees were throwing around the horn after an out, Raschi would stand on the mound with his right foot on the rubber waiting for the return of the ball. The third baseman—usually Bobby Brown or Billy Johnson—always got the ball last and it was their job to toss it back to Raschi. Once in a while if the Yankees were way ahead they'd purposely throw it off line to make Raschi remove his foot from the rubber, and after Raschi would shoot them his frightening glare, they'd have to turn their heads to hide the giggle. I never noticed the routine until Brown pointed it out to me one day during Raschi's last year with the club.

Raschi was scouted by the Yankees when he was a 14-year-old schoolboy in West Springfield, Massachusetts, the same town where Leo Durocher was raised. When he eventually signed with New York, he did so with the provision that the team pay for his college education. Every off-season of his playing career he attended William & Mary until he earned a degree, a feat that was as impressive as his lifetime record of 132-66.

Nicknamed the Springfield Rifle because the manufacturer of that particular shotgun was headquartered in his hometown, Raschi started in the Yankee farm system, then served in the Air Force as a physical fitness trainer during the war until his release in 1945. He spent most of 1946 at Newark, and he made his Yankee debut that September.

Raschi's bulldog mentality was cultivated by the Yankee pitching coach, Jim Turner. Turner had managed Raschi in the minors at Portland

and he knew right away the young man had a future. The physical skills were all there, but there were maddening lapses in his concentration. Turner taught Raschi to bear down on every hitter, and to not only study hitters, but find a way to master them and if that took being a mean-spirited son of a bitch, then so be it. Down in St. Petersburg before the 1950 season began, Raschi recalled a talk Turner had given him long ago. "Vic, those hitters are your enemy and if they get their way, you're out of baseball," Turner told him. "I've seen pitchers with talent who might have made the major leagues, but they didn't hate hitters enough."

Raschi grew to hate hitters and it showed every fourth day. He led the Yankees four straight years in victories (1948–1951) and during the five-year championship run (1949–1953), Raschi's record was 92-40.

"Raschi was the greatest pitcher I ever had to be sure to win," said Stengel. "It looked like we would never make any mistakes when he was pitching. And he never would give in any time that he pitched, even when his stuff was ordinary. He wasn't a graceful pitcher, he just put so much on it."

Prior to the 1954 season Raschi got into a contract squabble with George Weiss, which was nothing new because every player got into a contract squabble with Weiss. You would have thought Weiss was paying these guys with his own money. Well, Raschi refused to agree to a pay cut, citing his meritorious service to the club, and he told Weiss he'd talk about money at spring training. He never got the chance. Weiss sold him to the St. Louis Cardinals, infuriating the other players. Maybe it was coincidence, but for the next two years the Yankees did not win the World Series.

*　*　*

The Yankees were clearly expecting to win this Series, but they didn't think it would be as tough as it was. In Game Two, Roberts hooked up with Reynolds in a pitching duel just as intense as the Raschi-Konstanty encounter. This time the game wasn't decided until the top of the 10th when Joe DiMaggio uncorked a long home run into the upper left-field stands for a 2-1 victory.

"I never hit a better one in my life," DiMaggio said in the jubilant clubhouse, caught up in the excitement of the moment. "That was the greatest homer of my career. This one tops any that I can remember."

This was the happiest DiMaggio had been all season, and the writers crowded around him as if he were giving us all 50-dollar bills. But

DiMaggio, who hadn't hit the ball out of the infield in his previous four turns against Roberts and who was hitless in six official at-bats to that point in the Series, wasn't the lone hero. Reynolds pitched a great game, even though the Phillies were far more threatening than they had been the day before. They touched Allie for three doubles and a triple, but he yielded just one run, that in the fifth, which tied the game after Gene Woodling's RBI infield single in the second.

"Good pitching, that's what it was today, just as it was yesterday," Stengel said. "When you get top pitching you can't blame the hitters. Reynolds was great. So was that Roberts. But good old Joe came back and it was like old times, that's all there was to it."

Reynolds missed DiMaggio's home run. He was in the clubhouse smoking a cigarette and listening to the radio when DiMaggio launched the winner. "God bless Joe DiMaggio," Reynolds said afterward. "If he hadn't hit it I'd probably still be pitching."

Both teams took the train back to New York, and another close, tense struggle ensued in Game Three. The Phillies fought hard and made the Yankees sweat, but in the end, the result was the same, this one a 3-2 Yankee victory.

The Phillies were clinging to a 2-1 lead on the strength of Sisler's RBI single in the sixth and Goliat's RBI single in the seventh, but with two outs in the eighth, Philadelphia starter Ken Heintzelman walked Coleman, Berra, and DiMaggio in succession to load the bases. Sawyer turned to his ace reliever, Konstanty, and Stengel sent lefty-swinging Brown up to pinch-hit for Bauer. Sawyer should have won the battle because Brown slapped a hard grounder to Hamner at short, and all he had to do was field it and flip to second for a force. Instead, the ball handcuffed him, he bobbled it, and by the time he recovered everyone was safe and the game was tied.

"I've made a lot of errors in my life, but that one . . ." Hamner said, preferring not to finish the sentence. Hamner took dead aim at making amends when he doubled to left-center for his third hit of the game in the top of the ninth, but he only made it to third base because Yankee reliever Tom Ferrick—on in place of Eddie Lopat—wriggled out of the jam.

In the bottom of the ninth Russ Meyer came on to pitch for Sawyer, and the manager was forced to insert Jimmy Bloodworth at second base because he had pinch-run for Goliat in the previous half-inning. It was a move that came back to haunt the Phillies. Meyer recorded two quick outs before the Yankees put together the winning rally. It started when Gene Woodling hit a slow roller up the middle that Bloodworth reached but couldn't make a play on, and Woodling was awarded a hit. Rizzuto followed with a hard shot that caromed off Bloodworth's glove and bounced toward the bag at second, and Rizzuto and Woodling were both safe. With the crowd in an uproar, Coleman—who had driven in New York's first run back in the third—came through with another clutch hit, a single to left-center that chased Woodling home with the winning run.

Afterward Stengel said he was considering pinch-hitting Johnny Hopp for Coleman in that situation, "but the idea kept pounding in my head to leave him in there, the kid's hot, he's got two hits and he may deliver again. And bang, sure enough, he wins the ballgame for us."

It was left for Ford, the Yankees own Whiz Kid, to wrap it up now, and the youngster did not disappoint. Before the game began Stengel told Ford, "Let's get it over with. Remember, this is the last game." Ford answered, "Yes sir," and proceeded to choke the Phillies on five hits through eight innings and took a 5-0 lead into the ninth. When the Phillies scored twice in their last hurrah thanks to an error by Woodling, and had the tying run at the plate with two outs, Stengel's nerves could take no more. His heart told him to leave Ford in, his brain told him to get the veteran Reynolds in to close it out. The Yankee Stadium throng booed Stengel, but their mood changed quickly when Reynolds fanned pinch-hitter Stan Lopata to secure the Yankees' 13th championship.

After Ford worked out of a tight spot in the first, the Yankees jumped on Bob Miller for two runs in the bottom of the first as Berra and DiMaggio delivered RBI hits. In desperation Sawyer brought in Konstanty, who by now must have had a pitching arm three inches longer than his other arm. Incredibly, Konstanty pitched another seven-plus innings and he held the Yankees in check through five as the score remained 2-0. Then in the sixth his good fortune finally expired as Berra led off with a homer, DiMaggio was hit by a pitch and scored on Brown's triple, and Brown trotted home on Bauer's line drive to left for a 5-0 cushion.

With Ford in control, the game was over.

Following Raschi's Game One masterpiece, Ford spotted the great Dizzy Dean outside the Yankee clubhouse. He brazenly walked up to Dean and said, "Hey Diz, they're so easy, now I can understand how you won so many games in the National League." Dean was speechless, and after running into Ford and the Yankees, so were the Phillies.

Most of the time when Casey Stengel started waving his arms animatedly as he discussed a particular topic, that was the writers' signal to take whatever he was spewing with a grain of salt. Casey was the great embellisher. Nobody enjoyed taking a few liberties with the truth more than the 'ol perfesser.

When I arrived in St. Petersburg for the start of spring training in February of 1950, I went down to the bar in the Soreno Hotel the first night, knowing Stengel would be holding court as he always did. There were rarely any players at the hotel bar because that's where Stengel did his drinking and socializing and he didn't want them around. He didn't want to know what they were up to, and he didn't want them to know what he was up to.

On this particular night, Stengel was in a lather. He was raving about some 18-year-old kid from Oklahoma named Mickey Mantle whom he had just watched for a week during a special rookie camp the Yankees held out in Phoenix.

"There's never been anything like this kid," Stengel said of Mantle. "He has more speed than any slugger and more slug than any speedster—and nobody has ever had more of both 'em together."

It wasn't until a week later when I gave what Stengel said any formative thought. That's when Bill Dickey, leaning up against a chain-linked fence that surrounded one of the practice diamonds, said to me, "Wait till you see this kid from Oklahoma. Just wait till you see this kid."

Coming from Dickey, a mild-mannered man never prone to hyperbole, that was a profound statement.

Throughout every season, the writers would get periodic updates on the progress of the hot prospects in the farm system, and in 1950 Mantle's name kept leaping to the forefront. Stengel never missed an opportunity to remind us how great Mantle was, and his numbers at Joplin, Missouri, certainly backed up Stengel's exuberance. By the time Joplin's Class C schedule was complete, Mantle had walloped 27 homers, driven in 136 runs, and his 199 hits computed to a batting average of .383.

Mantle and a group of other youngsters from the farm clubs were invited up to the big-league club for the final two weeks of the season to give them a taste of what it was like to be a Yankee. They traveled with the team, sat in on the skull sessions, and took batting and infield practice.

It was at Sportsman's Park in St. Louis when I caught my first glimpse of this kid from Oklahoma, this kid named Mantle. What a sight it was. He wasn't physically inspiring, about 5-foot-11, 165 pounds, but you could tell he had a powerful upper body with forearms as thick as a blacksmith's.

Mantle stepped into the batter's box after all the veteran players had taken their cuts and he put on a show that left everyone present awestruck. First he swung right-handed, then left-handed. It didn't matter which side of the plate he was on, though. His bat cut a wicked swath and the ball seemed to catapult off the white ash as if it were made of rubber. He hit tremendous shots into the deepest reaches of the old ballpark, and while Joe DiMaggio largely ignored what was going on, most of the other Yankees could not. They stopped what they were doing, just as all the writers did, to watch this kid rip blasts that rivaled those of Babe Ruth and Lou Gehrig.

Dickey played with those great sluggers so he knew what mammoth home runs looked and sounded like. Dickey was the man pitching batting practice to Mantle that first day in St. Louis, and I pulled him aside after the exhibition was over and told him, "Gee Bill, it looks like you might be right about that kid." Dickey just nodded.

When I think back to that day, I am always reminded of a comment Joe Collins made one time about Mantle. "Mickey tried to hit every one like they don't count if they're under 400 feet."

– Chapter 14 –

1951

HOURS AFTER RALPH BRANCA OF THE Dodgers had thrown the most famous pitch in baseball history, on which the Giants' Bobby Thomson
had hit the most famous home run in baseball history to end the most
famous game in baseball history, Branca stood face-to-face with a priest
named Father Rowley.

"Father, why me, tell me, why me?" Branca asked. "I don't smoke, I
don't drink, I don't run around. Baseball is my whole life. Why me?"

Father Rowley, who happened to be the cousin of Branca's fiancée,
looked at Branca's long, sorrowful face, stared deeply into his glossy
brown eyes and answered, "God chose you because He knew you had
faith and strength to bear this cross."

If that was the case, God must not have been a Dodgers fan. Or he
was in a bad mood that overcast afternoon at the Polo Grounds when
Branca served up a high fastball that Thomson launched for a three-run
homer in the bottom of the ninth inning. Known forever as the Shot
Heard 'Round the World, it gave the Giants a 5-4 victory over their hated
rivals from Brooklyn, and the National League pennant.

I was there. Yep, I was fortunate enough to have been present that
day beneath Coogans Bluff and personally witnessed what I must con-
cede—despite the absence of the Yankees—was, and still is, the greatest moment in baseball history. With the Yankees inactive and waiting
for their World Series opponent to be decided, I was assigned to help
our Dodgers and Giants beat writers cover the three-game National
League play-off series for the *Post*. And while the Yankees have provided me with almost all of my great sports memories, for pure excitement and drama, there was nothing quite like Thomson's home run.

Former Giants great Carl Hubbell, then a scout with the team, told me that day in the jubilant Giants clubhouse, "We won't live long enough to see anything like it again."

An overstatement, you say? Sure, Hubbell was overcome by the moment as we all were, but half a century later, he looks quite sagacious. Hubbell's right, it's matchless. I was present when Bill Mazeroski of the Pirates beat the Yankees in the 1960 World Series with his home run in the bottom of the ninth inning of Game Seven at Forbes Field. I watched on television Joe Carter's bottom-of-the-ninth blast in Game Six which ended the 1993 Series at Toronto's Skydome and gave the Blue Jays the world championship over Philadelphia. And I also watched on television when Kirk Gibson limped up to home plate and cranked one out in the bottom of the ninth to give the Dodgers a victory over Oakland in the first game of the 1988 Series.

But Thomson's home run, even though it didn't come in a World Series, stands alone when you consider:

> —This was the Giants vs. the Dodgers, certainly the most bitter and emotional rivalry in baseball at that time (and left-coasters will vouch that it remains that way today with the teams stationed in San Francisco and Los Angeles);
>
> —It came at the end of one of the greatest pennant races ever, as the Giants made up 13 games over the final six weeks of the regular season to catch Brooklyn and force the play-off;
>
> —In this decisive game the Giants were trailing by two runs and were in a do-or-die situation, whereas Mazeroski was hitting with a tie score, Carter and the Blue Jays still had another game to play if he hadn't homered, and Gibson's came in Game One;
>
> —The game was played in the media capital of the world—New York City—and you can never underestimate that dynamic.

"I don't care what anybody says, that's the most famous home run of them all," said Branca.

He should know, because for 50 years he has had to live with the agony Thomson's clout inflicted upon him. Branca told me that anecdote about his talk with Father Rowley probably 30 years ago, and in recalling the priest's explanation, Branca said, "I accepted that, that it would be something that I would have to bear for the rest of my life."

However, in an interview that he gave to another writer probably 10 years after that, he admitted he was tired of bearing the burden. "It's time to bury it," Branca said.

The ever-modest Thomson agreed that the home run has taken on a long life of its own, a comment he made even before the controversial *Wall Street Journal* story came out in early 2001. In commemorating the golden anniversary of the Shot Heard 'Round the World, the paper insinuated that the Giants had concocted an elaborate sign-stealing system and were cheating throughout their chase of the Dodgers, and that Thomson himself may have known what was coming on the historic homer.

"This whole thing is still just a little bit crazy," said Thomson, who denied knowledge of what pitch Branca was throwing. "I had no idea that what happened back then would still be famous."

* * *

Before Thomson and Branca etched their names into baseball lore, there was the matter of the 1951 season which ranks in my mind as one of the most newsworthy of all baseball years.

There was the epic National League pennant race; Allie Reynolds pitched two no-hitters for the Yankees; Bill Veeck took over ownership of the moribund St. Louis Browns, then pulled the ultimate publicity stunt when he employed a midget named Eddie Gaedel to bat during a game in August; a kid named Willie Mays was called up by the Giants; Bob Feller of the Indians threw the third no-hitter of his career; Happy Chandler's contract was not renewed and Ford Frick became commissioner of baseball; and of course there was the swan song for Joe DiMaggio and the arrival of Mickey Mantle.

For me this momentous baseball journey began in early February when I made the first trip of my life west of St. Louis. Yankees co-owner Del Webb had long been pining to bring the Yankees out west, mainly to show the team off to his friends and business associates. Webb was a major developer in the Southwest and he conceived the idea of swapping spring training sites with the New York Giants for one year. Giants owner Horace Stoneham agreed, so the Yankees went to Phoenix, Arizona, while the Giants took over the Yankees' digs in St. Petersburg.

Just as they had done the previous year, the Yankees were holding a special rookie camp preceding the regular training camp, and Dorothy Schiff, the publisher of the *Post*, decided it would be a great opportunity for the writers on the beat to make connections with Mantle. There was no doubt he was the new phenom, the man who was going to take over for DiMaggio in center field, so the wheels started turning within the

Post's hierarchy. In the ultracompetitive New York City newspaper game, there was a never-ending struggle to outscoop each other. Schiff consulted Editor James Wechsler, Executive Editor Paul Sann, Managing Editor Henry Moscow, and Sports Editor Ike Gellis, and the funds were approved to send us out to Phoenix early and schmooze with Mantle, get to know him, develop a relationship, become his friend, make it known that if he ever had anything to say, the *Post* was the place to say it.

I was never a big fan of this strategy. I liked to do things naturally. I expected a player to earn my respect with his play on the field and behavior in the clubhouse, and I expected to earn the players' respect by treating them equally and honestly, in good times and in bad. Besides, just about every other paper sent writers out to Phoenix early to chronicle Mantle's exploits, so the *Post* had no right to expect to get preferential treatment from the budding star. That is, until I sat down with the young man at a bar around the corner from the team hotel one night.

Earlier in the day Mantle had been taunted by fans about his recent 4-F military classification due to his childhood case of osteomyelitis, meaning he didn't have to serve his country in the Korean War. In June of 1950 the Soviet-equipped North Korean People's Army invaded South Korea, so the United Nations invited its members to assist the South Koreans. President Truman immediately sent American air and naval forces into the fray, and a few days later ground troops moved in. Little did we know what we were getting into. The war ultimately lasted until the middle of 1953 at a cost of about four million lives including more than 54,000 Americans.

Our boys had been over in Korea for eight months when spring training began, and here was Mantle, a young, strapping lad who was sunning himself in the Arizona desert, learning how to play the outfield instead of learning how to handle a rifle. Many people began to wonder why Mantle was here and not in Korea and they called him a "draft dodger" and a "Communist" and a "coward."

They didn't know the story behind Mantle's osteomyelitis. I did, and having lived with the condition for nearly 12 years before the miracle drug penicillin was introduced, I knew exactly what Mantle had endured as a teenager, and the potential risks of reoccurrence he still faced.

I had heard the rude comments from the stands, and right then I decided I was going to share with him my story and let him know someone understood his dilemma. Later that evening I walked into that bar and by chance Mantle was there. He was alone, which was nothing out of the ordinary in those first few weeks. He was a painfully shy country boy, and it didn't seem like he had made many friends on the team. I knew he palled around a bit with Billy Martin, but Martin was not with him when I strolled in.

"Hey Mickey, I'm Joe Kimmerle," I said in introduction.

"Hello, sir," was his reply.

"Mickey, do you mind if I sit down and join you?"

"No, go right ahead, sir."

I planted myself, ordered a vodka on the rocks, lit a Chesterfield and told Mantle that I worked for the *New York Post* and that if he kept hitting the way he had been, we'd be seeing an awful lot of each other. He smiled, but really didn't offer a response. I made some more small talk about what had been going on in practice, and when I sensed he was wishing I would just leave him alone, I switched gears and told him to ignore all the loudmouths who were razzing him about his military status. That seemed to perk his interest in the conversation.

"Mr. Kimmerle, I'd gladly go over there and fight if they'd let me, but they turned me down," he said apologetically.

I told him I understood, because I'd gone through the same thing at the outset of World War II.

He took a sip of his gin, put the drink down on the bar, and pivoted on his stool so that he was looking directly at me, now earnestly paying attention to what I had to say. I told him about my osteomyelitis and all the things it prevented me from doing such as playing sports as a boy and later, fighting in World War II. I described the throbbing pain that would keep me awake at nights, and the relief I felt when I started taking doses of penicillin. I shared with him some of my tales as a Yankee batboy, and within that context I relived the time Babe Ruth, Lou Gehrig, and Waite Hoyt came to visit me in the hospital.

He was so enthralled that when Martin bounced into the bar looking for a partner to hit the town with, Mantle actually turned him down in order to continue our chat.

Mantle shared with me as well, and then I was enthralled.

He told me about his life in Commerce, Oklahoma, how he worked as a teenager in the lead and zinc mines with his father, a man they called Mutt Mantle. He told me that his mother made every baseball uniform he wore as a child, and how she never objected to his playing ball because she always reasoned it was a better way to make a living than working in the black holes where Mutt earned his $75 a week. Mickey said he played baseball from dawn to dusk on the dusty fields of Oklahoma, and Mutt pushed him with a vengeance.

Mutt had dreamed of being a pro ballplayer, but it had never worked out for him, so he was going to live his dream through his son, and Mickey was fine with that. Mickey loved the game so much, he said, that he never had an inkling to rebel against having baseball forced on him from the time he was old enough to walk. He wanted to play, wanted to practice, and he never objected to the endless teaching sessions with Mutt and his grandfather, Charles, a semipro player of renown in Oklahoma during his day.

Mickey recalled for me the greatest Christmas of his youth, when he was 14 years old and Mutt bought him a full-sized baseball glove, a $22 Marty Marion model. With money as tight as it was in the Mantle stead, it was a gift of enduring love and Mickey said he cherished that mitt.

Even though I knew most of the details, I inquired about how he joined the Yankees' organization, and he happily retold the story. Tom Greenwade was the scout who discovered him, but when he first saw Mickey playing for the Baxter Springs Whiz Kids in 1948, Mickey was only 16. Greenwade told him he'd come back the following year when he was graduated from high school, and Greenwade kept his promise. He signed Mantle to a $1,500 bonus, and years later, I recalled Greenwade saying, "That's when I knew what Paul Krichell must have felt like when he saw Lou Gehrig."

We talked for probably two hours, and that night I forged a bond with Mantle that only strengthened through the years, and it remained unbroken until the day he died in 1995. I was 15 years older than Mickey, but I felt like I could relate to him, and not only because of our common disability. I always enjoyed talking and drinking with the younger players. I was so young when I came on the beat and every one of my colleagues was older than I. Even at this point, going on 35 years old with 14 years in the business, I was still considered the young pup of the group. I knew how Mantle was feeling, and I think he realized that I knew how he was feeling. I guess this is what Mrs. Schiff had been hoping for when she sent me to Phoenix early. I was just glad I didn't have to be a phony about it.

The next day Mantle greeted me with a "Hi, Mr. Kimmerle" when he saw me in the clubhouse. I went over, exchanged a few words including giving him the edict that my name was Joe, then walked away, the eyes of many of my colleagues burning a hole through me.

Mantle enjoyed a prolific spring with the bat as his average soared near .400, and he was smashing balls Ruthian distances in the light, dry air of the desert. In the field, things weren't quite as commendatory. Tommy Henrich, who had retired in the off-season, was asked by Stengel to come to spring training to help teach Mantle how to play the outfield. Every day Henrich drilled Mantle on the finer points, hitting him fungoes, teaching him how to catch the ball in a ready position to throw, how to field grounders or play caroms off the fence. It was a slow go.

One day Mantle lost a battle with the sun and had a fly ball conk him right on the head. Another day he overthrew his cutoff man by a bit—the ball landed in the bleachers behind third base. But all the while, he was mashing the ball with his bat, and that alone was enough to convince Stengel to bring him back to New York for the start of the regular season even though he'd never played higher than Class C level minor league ball.

On Opening Day in Washington, Mantle was in right field, starting along with three other rookies—infielder Gil McDougald, outfielder Jackie Jensen, and pitcher Tom Morgan. "I wish I didn't have so many green peas," Stengel said, "but I can't win with my old men. We have to rebuild."

The Yankees didn't have to rebuild, but they were in a retooling process.

Mantle started well. Early in the season he was leading the American League in home runs, RBI, and average, and he was playing a passable right field, but pretty soon the wily pitchers began to catch on to Mantle. They saw they could feed him high fastballs and he'd chase after them and catch nothing but air. Mantle's average plummeted, and his slump at the plate began to affect him in the field. He was depressed, and he even broke down and cried one day in the dugout after striking out for the fourth time.

It was during this stretch when Mantle began to grow wary of many of my fellow writers, and it was an uneasiness he carried with him for most of the rest of his career. We had built him up in the press to be the heir apparent to DiMaggio, and many of the fans—hero worshippers of DiMaggio—resented Mantle. Even at home he was booed when he struck out or made an error, and he was confused by this. He told me he wished people would stop trying to reserve his spot in Cooperstown before he'd even played a month in the major leagues.

I told him that's just the way it was. Everything was bigger in New York City, especially one's fame, and he was going to have to learn to cope with his celebrity. Luckily, I was in his inner circle. He trusted me, and to honor that trust I tried not to write in such mythic tones about

Mantle. Quite honestly, it wasn't so difficult that first year. By mid-July he was struggling terribly, and Stengel had no choice but to send him down to Triple-A Kansas City. Mantle was crushed. He thought he'd failed, and he couldn't help wondering what his father would think. Before he left for Kansas City, I talked to him in the clubhouse as he was packing his bag.

"Mickey, I've seen a lot of young players come and go, and the ones that end up staying are the ones who want to," I told him. "If you want to come back, and I know they want you to come back, go down there and work your ass off."

"I will Joe," he said. "I want to come back up here."

So Mantle departed, and the Yankees went on with the pennant chase. Cleveland and Chicago were worthy suitors, and for the rest of the summer that triumvirate battled relentlessly for the top spot. When the White Sox began to fade around Labor Day, it was left for the Indians to challenge the Yankees, but DiMaggio keyed a critical two-game sweep of Cleveland in mid-September, and then on September 28 the Yankees swept a doubleheader from the Red Sox—Allie Reynolds throwing his second no-hitter of the year in the opener—to clinch the pennant.

It was the third straight for Stengel, and it was further testament to his managing skills. The Yankees did not have one player with more than 30 home runs or 90 RBI and only McDougald finished with an average above .300. DiMaggio had career lows with 12 homers, 71 RBI and a .263 average and it was obvious—though he didn't make it official until after the season—that the legend was through.

Still, there they were, champions of the American League, ready to play in another World Series against an opponent to be determined in three days.

*   *   *

The Giants had begun the season horribly, losing 12 of their first 13 games. Meanwhile, the Dodgers were tearing it up and when they swept a July 4 doubleheader from the Giants, their lead was 7 1/2 games and Brooklyn manager Charlie Dressen boasted, "The Giants is dead. Those two beatings we gave them knocked them out of it. They'll never bother us again."

After completing a three-game sweep of New York on August 9, the Dodgers were 15 games ahead in the loss column, and they celebrated by taunting the Giants from the side-by-side clubhouses at Ebbets Field, Jackie Robinson leading the way by pounding a bat against the Giants door. This infuriated Leo Durocher, the former Dodgers skipper who was now managing the Giants. But it also served to light a fire under the Giants.

The lead was 13 when Brooklyn split a doubleheader with the Boston Braves on August 11, but the next day the Giants began a 16-game winning streak, and when the schedule ran out, the teams had matching 96-58 records and a three-game play-off was necessary to decide the pennant.

The first two games were split, and the stage was set for the rubber match. Durocher sent Sal Maglie to the mound while Dressen went with his ace, Don Newcombe. The Dodgers snapped a 1-1 tie with three runs in the eighth as Thomson failed to come up with a pair of screaming grounders to third that scored two runs, and Thomson recalled the mood in the dugout at the start of the bottom of the ninth. "There was a feeling of total dejection. In the eighth inning Don Newcombe had blown us down so easily, it didn't look like we'd have a chance."

Alvin Dark's leadoff single failed to stir much emotion, and in fact, the Brooklyn fans began making their way down to the railings so that they could hop over and join their team in celebration when the formality of the ninth inning was complete. At the same time up in the press box an announcement was made informing the Dodgers writers that their credentials for the next day's World Series opener at Yankee Stadium could be picked up at the Biltmore Hotel.

The next batter, Don Mueller, noticed that Dodgers' first baseman Gil Hodges was holding Dark on the bag, a tactical mistake given the three-run lead. Newcombe delivered a belt-high fastball and Mueller punched it the opposite way through the hole for a clean single. Dark scampered to third and now the Polo Grounds jumped to attention, as did the Dodgers bullpen because Branca and Carl Erskine began to throw.

After Newcombe induced Monte Irvin to foul out meekly to Hodges at first, Dressen strolled to the mound to talk to his pitcher. After conferring with Newcombe and Robinson, Dressen decided to leave Newcombe in. It was an error in judgment because Whitey Lockman lined a shot into the left-field corner for a double that scored Dark and chased Mueller to third. Mueller sprained his ankle sliding into the bag, and after a 10-minute delay, he was carried off to the clubhouse out behind the center field fence and was replaced by Cliff Hartung.

While Mueller was being attended to, Dressen made the fateful call to the bullpen and summoned Branca on the advice of pitching coach Clyde Sukeforth.

Erskine was bouncing his curveball in front of the plate while Branca was humming pretty well and looked warm, so when Dressen asked "Who's ready?" Sukeforth replied, "Branca."

"I was bouncing it in the dirt," Erskine said of his curve. "Considering what happened next, that was a pretty good pitch to have."

Thomson had been standing near third watching the trainer work on Mueller. When he started walking toward the plate to resume the action, Durocher said, "If you've ever hit one, hit one now."

Branca started Thomson with a grooved fastball that home plate umpire Lou Jorda called a strike. "That first pitch was a blur, not because it was so fast but because I was so nervous my eyeballs were vibrating," Thomson said. "I had to step out for a second to get myself oriented. But to tell you the truth, I wasn't feeling very much better when I stepped back in."

That changed with one powerful swing of his bat.

Branca uncorked another fastball, this one just a touch higher, but still right in Thomson's power zone. Thomson swung and sent the ball soaring toward the fence in left field.

In the radio booth, broadcasting for WMCA in New York, Russ Hodges watched the ball jump off Thomson's bat and he screamed, "There's a long drive . . . "

"I thought I had a home run, I really laid into it, but then as I got away from the plate, I began to wonder," Thomson said. "It started out high and then looked like it was sinking, so I started to think at least I've got a base hit. I figured it would be off the wall, enough to get Whitey in with the tying run."

"It's gonna be . . . I believe . . . " bellowed Hodges.

"And then the ball disappeared into the lower stands," said Thomson. "I was more excited than I ever was in my life."

And so was Hodges, who finished perhaps the most memorable radio call ever by repeating over and over, "The Giants win the pennant, the Giants win the pennant, the Giants win the pennant, I don't believe it, the Giants win the pennant."

As pandemonium erupted all around them, as Thomson danced around the bases, as Eddie Stanky jumped on Durocher's back and rode him all the way to home plate, as the bashful rookie Mays—who was in the on-deck circle—felt utter relief that he wouldn't have to bat, the

Dodgers just watched with eyes wide open, paralyzed in disbelief. Brooklyn's Andy Pafko leaned against the wall in left. Robinson stood at second base making sure Thomson touched all the bases. Duke Snider dropped to his knees in center and slammed his glove into the grass. And Branca took his mitt off, hung his head down to his chest, and began the long walk to the clubhouse.

I just sat there with my mouth hanging open. It really was quite unbelievable.

One writer walked into the clubhouse, spotted the crestfallen Branca deep in sorrow and wrote: "One of the saddest sights I've ever seen. There was an upper level and a lower level joined by a broad set of steps. Ralph Branca lay on these steps face down, his feet on the floor, his head buried in his hands on the top step."

The next day, the Giants had to somehow come down to earth and play Game One of the World Series against the Yankees. I didn't think they could possibly do it.

– *1951 World Series* –

As I left the Yankee Stadium press box after having filed my story about Game One of the 1951 World Series, I distinctly remember feeling as if I hadn't cared what had happened. One day earlier I had witnessed an epic baseball drama unfold when Bobby Thomson hit his National League pennant-winning home run to lift the Giants over the Dodgers. Quite simply, Game One of the Fall Classic was anticlimactic.

Nothing the Giants and Yankees could have done that day would have impressed anyone, and that was too bad because on reflection, what the Giants accomplished was actually quite impressive. They managed to corral their emotions 24 hours after pulling off the greatest victory in baseball history, and they strafed Allie Reynolds for eight hits and five runs during a 5-1 victory.

Thomson had said in the moments after his triumphant home run that he hoped "this cloud I'm on never gets to find a landing field. I could keep riding it the rest of my baseball life."

In Game One, he grabbed young left-hander Dave Koslo and took him along for the excursion. Koslo, starting only because Durocher had used Sal Maglie, Jim Hearn, and Larry Jansen in the play-off series, stymied the Yankees on seven hits in a distance-going effort that moved Casey Stengel to say, "Control was the big thing in this game. The other fellow (Koslo) had it and my man didn't. Koslo pitched a good game, we couldn't hit him."

The Giants jumped to a 2-0 lead in the first, Monte Irvin's steal of home the highlight, then stretched their advantage to 5-1 in the sixth when Alvin Dark hit a two-out, three-run homer which ended Reynolds's day. The Yankees never really threatened to make it close and the Giants, who were starting to look more and more like destiny's darlings, were up one game.

The Yankees won Game Two, 3-1, behind junkballing Eddie Lopat's five-hitter, but victory came at a price. By the time his career was finished, Mickey Mantle rated as one of baseball's all-time greats. But who knows how much greater Mantle would have become if he hadn't torn his knee to shreds in the fifth inning of Game Two? I would have loved to have found out. Willie Mays lofted a fly ball into right-center and DiMaggio glided into the alley from center field while Mantle ran full speed from right. When the ball was hit, Mantle didn't think the aging DiMaggio had a chance of making the play, but what Mantle hadn't noticed was that DiMaggio had gotten a great break. DiMaggio always got a great break because he knew every hitter's tendencies, he knew what the pitch was and how the pitcher was throwing it, and he used this information like no outfielder ever had. When Mantle realized DiMaggio was going to make the catch, he tried to stop his momentum to avoid plowing into DiMaggio. He happened to pick the tiny spot in the outfield where a drainage cover was located, his spikes caught, and his knee buckled like someone had chopped it with an ax. Mantle went down just as DiMaggio was closing his mitt, and then he lay there in agony.

Years later Mantle revealed that he held a grudge against DiMaggio. He claimed that DiMaggio never called for the ball until he was absolutely certain he could make the catch look easy. DiMaggio prided himself on making every play look routine, and Mantle's assertion was that on this play, DiMaggio wasn't sure he'd get there so he waited to make the call. It was DiMaggio's late call, Mantle said, that caused his injury.

Mantle was never the same player after that. He would never again possess that legendary speed, and this injury seemed to lead to a series of later ailments which caused Mantle to play in constant pain. It was such a shame.

The last time anyone saw Mantle run freely was in the top of the first when he laid down a gorgeous drag bunt and beat it out for a single. Phil Rizzuto followed with his own bunt single, and Mantle eventually scored on Gil McDougald's blooper to right. A big inning was spoiled when DiMaggio grounded into a double play.

In the second inning Joe Collins poked a home run to right, and Lopat was on cruise control the rest of the way. "I'd say Lopat pitched excellently," said Durocher.

* * *

I remember in Whitey Ford's first spring with the club in 1950 he said he learned more about pitching in one month than he had in three minor league years. Why? Because pitching coach Jim Turner schooled him on mechanics, and Eddie Lopat taught him how to think on the mound. Thinking was the key to Lopat's success as a major leaguer, the main reason why he won 113 games and lost only 59 during his eight-year Yankee career.

Lopat was a scientist on the mound. He couldn't throw hard, so he relied on an assortment of curves, screwballs, sliders, and knucklers, all thrown at different speeds, to baffle American League hitters. Ben Epstein of the *New York Mirror* tabbed Lopat "The Junkman," and never was there a more appropriate sobriquet.

"Lopat looks like he's throwing wads of tissue paper," Stengel once said. "Every time he wins a game fans come down out of the stands asking for a contract."

He looked harmless, but batters couldn't hit him, especially the Indians, who he beat 40 times in 52 decisions. One of the great Lopat stories was the time he snuck into Municipal Stadium in Cleveland to watch the Indians take batting practice. It was four hours before game-time, but Lopat was bored at the hotel so he and Johnny Sain walked to the park. Normally teams don't take batting practice until about 90 minutes before a game, but there were the Indians taking whacks against a pitcher named Sam Zoldak.

I happened to be there early because I was working on a feature story about Bob Feller, and as I was walking from the field up to the press box, I noticed Lopat and Sain spying from one of the exit ramps. I went over and asked what they were doing, and before I could get a response, Lopat asked me what the Indians were up to. I guessed that they were just getting some extra work in, but he said, "Look at how Zoldak is pitching. He's pitching like me. They're trying to get used to my style of pitching. Oh, we're gonna have fun tonight."

Zoldak was feeding the Indians a variety of slow curves and the batters were patiently poking the ball into right field. That night, Lopat told Yogi Berra to call mostly fastballs the first time around the order. Berra did, and the surprised Indians couldn't touch Lopat, who could sneak a fastball by you when he needed to. The next time through he reverted to his junk and by game's end, the Indians didn't know what was coming. They were losers again, scoreless for the night.

The Indians became so desperate they held a special promotion in 1951—Beat Eddie Lopat Night. The organization handed out 15,000 rabbit's feet, and one fan even ran onto the field and threw a black cat at Eddie. It worked, because after losing 11 decisions in a row to Lopat, the Indians beat him that night.

The first trade George Weiss made as Yankees general manager was acquiring Lopat from the White Sox for three players. During the Yankees' run of five straight world championships Lopat put together a fabulous record of 80-36, topped by his 21-9 All-Star season in 1951.

"They'd put Lopat in between Raschi and Reynolds who could really throw smoke, and Eddie would fool 'em with his junk," said backup catcher Charlie Silvera. "He'd come at you with this jerky type of shoulder motion. People would be swinging at the ball before it got to the plate."

Lopat was a New York City kid, born and raised in the Bronx about 10 blocks from where I grew up, and he attended the same high school I did, Dewitt Clinton. He was two years younger than I so we were never in the same classes, and I couldn't recall ever noticing him on the school grounds. However, he knew who I was. He was an ardent Yankee fan during the Ruth and Gehrig Era and he told me that he remembered seeing me on the field serving as batboy and wishing that job were his.

He toiled in the minor leagues for seven years and nearly quit baseball as he grew tired of making almost no money and living the life of a bush leaguer. He finally earned a shot with the White Sox during the war in 1944, though had it not been for the weakened state of baseball, he may never have gotten that opportunity.

Reynolds once described Lopat this way: "Lopat rarely threw a strike and he won. I tried to throw a lot of them and I won. My delivery was smooth, Lopat was like a windup doll that needed WD-40 and new cogs. The hitters' mouths used to water while they waited to hit. When they came back they were foaming at the mouth. Lopat drove hitters nuts."

* * *

When the Series shifted over to the Polo Grounds the Giants regained the lead as they roughed up Vic Raschi inside of five innings and ran off with a 6-2 victory in Game Three. This loss was not all Raschi's fault, though, as two Yankee errors led to five unearned runs in the fifth inning.

Already leading 1-0 after Thomson doubled in the second and scored on Willie Mays's single, the resourceful Giants put this one away with a typically gritty flair. With one out in the fifth Stanky drew a walk, then attempted a steal to second base. Yogi Berra made a perfect throw to Rizzuto who put the tag on, but Stanky craftily kicked the ball out of Rizzuto's glove and was called safe by umpire Bill Summers. As the ball rolled into the outfield, Stanky sprang up and raced to third. Rizzuto immediately went after Summers, claiming Stanky never touched second base, but Summers disagreed. "Stanky hasn't touched second base yet," Rizzuto fumed in the clubhouse afterward.

An error by Berra and a three-run homer by Whitey Lockman made it 6-0, and though Lockman never should have batted in the inning, Raschi wasn't seeking excuses. "That Lockman homer was the crusher," he said. "They might be unearned, but they all count."

The Yankees were in an unfamiliar position, trailing in a World Series after three games, staring at a virtual must-win situation against the Giants ace, Maglie, with their leader, DiMaggio, mired in an 0-for-11 slump. Stengel announced he was going to pitch Johnny Sain in the fourth game, but he caught a huge break when heavy rain forced postponement of the game. This allowed Stengel to come back with his Game One starter, Reynolds, and this is where the Series turned in favor of the Yankees.

Reynolds shook off his first-game routing and, with the help of four double plays, pitched a complete-game eight-hitter as the Yankees chalked up a 6-2 victory. Reynolds wasn't the only Yankee making amends. DiMaggio snapped out of his funk with a two-run homer in the fifth that broke open a 2-1 game, his last home run as a big-leaguer. "It was a great feeling to see it go out," the Yankee Clipper said.

Lopat had gotten the Yankees back on track in Game Two, and it was the crafty lefty who got the call in the pivotal fifth game. As it turned out I could have pitched that game, so supportive were the Yankee bats. McDougald hit a grand slam in the third inning to chase Larry Jansen to the showers, Rizzuto hit a two-run shot in the fourth, and DiMaggio drove in three runs as the Yankees rolled to a 13-1 victory. Meanwhile, Lopat allowed just five hits and the only run was unearned, thanks to an error by Woodling in the first inning. So in 18 innings Lopat had yielded just 10 hits and one earned run.

Chub Feeney, the vice-president of the Giants, facetiously chided Durocher afterward when he said, "Look here, I've got news for you. I'm getting damned tired of you doing things the hard way. Seven games we've got to go to win, what the heck."

It never made it that far. The next day back at Yankee Stadium the Yankees jumped on Game One hero Koslo to take a 4-1 lead through six innings, then held off another improbable Giants rally. Durocher's stout-hearted team put eight men on base in the final three innings against Raschi, Sain, and Bob Kuzava, but the Yankees wiggled out of each jam and the closest the Giants could get was the 4-3 final. "They're all champions in my book," Durocher said of his players. "They played all the way, right up to the ninth inning."

Raschi and Koslo dueled through five innings with the score knotted at 1-1 before the Yankees produced what proved to be the winning rally in the sixth, capped by Hank Bauer's bases-clearing three-run triple which sent the crowd into a frenzy.

And Bauer wasn't through impacting this game.

Sain, who pitched out of trouble in the seventh and eighth innings after relieving Raschi, was right back in a pickle in the ninth. Stanky led off with a single, Dark beat out a bunt for a single, and Lockman singled to load the bases with none out. Stengel hobbled out to the mound and made a pitching change that had everyone questioning his sanity. With two right-handed power hitters due up, Monte Irvin and Thomson, Stengel called for Kuzava, a left-hander of little renown who hadn't even pitched in the Series.

Five minutes later, Stengel looked like a genius.

Irvin drove a deep fly to left that Woodling caught, but all three runners advanced with Stanky scoring to make it 4-2. Thomson did the same thing and Dark trotted home to inch the Giants even closer, but now the Giants were down to their final breath. With Lockman perched at second, Durocher sent up pinch-hitter Sal Yvars who, like Kuzava, had yet to play in the Series. Kuzava laid his first pitch down the middle, figuring Yvars would take a strike, but Yvars was hacking immediately and he lined a shot into right field that for a moment looked as if it were going to drop in for a game-tying hit. Instead, Bauer raced over and made a fine catch, tumbling to the ground just as the ball nestled into his mitt. Just like that, one of the greatest baseball seasons in history was over, and the Yankees were champions again.

Stengel was joyously relieved. He knew the Giants were going to be tough to beat, but as he said, "The Yankees are still the Yankees."

It was probably a week after I had my talk with Mickey Mantle in the spring of 1951 that I had the occasion to participate in another meaningful conversation with a ballplayer—this one not as exclusive, but pretty close. Joe DiMaggio invited me, Jim Dawson from the Times, *Ben Epstein from the* Mirror, *and a fellow named Jack Orr who worked for a tiny paper called* The Compass *up to his room to announce that 1951 would be his final season in the big leagues.*

DiMaggio was pissed at most of the writers from the other papers for their incessantly pestering him concerning his ex-wife, Dorothy Arnold, who had been on the scene in Phoenix, heightening rumors that she and DiMaggio were going to reconcile, though it never happened. DiMaggio was also tired of answering questions about the wonder kid, Mantle, and his own subpar 1950 performance. To DiMaggio it was all a bunch of crap, none of it worth talking about, so he decided it was time to give to the few scribes that he trusted who were on hand in Phoenix something really interesting to report.

The four of us who were given the scoop ran with the story in our next day editions, and it quickly became a raging issue as the other writers scrambled to catch up. But even after I wrote my story, I didn't quite believe DiMaggio would retire.

DiMaggio was clearly not the player he once was. At 36 years old how could he be? Yet, in my opinion, even though his decline continued during the 1951 regular season, he was still better than the majority of major leaguers, and he was the heart and soul of the Yankees, the undisputed leader of the team.

As I would find out, this was not an opinion shared by baseball insiders, most notably Brooklyn Dodgers advance scout Andy High, a man who had played third base in the National League from 1922 to 1931 for the Dodgers, Braves, and Cardinals, a man who knew the game.

With the Dodgers seemingly in control of the National League pennant chase, the 70-year-old High had spent the final month of the 1951 season scouting the Yankees for what seemed to be the inevitable World Series meeting between the teams. When the Dodgers choked away the pennant, High's scouting report never should have seen the light of day. Instead, it wound up publicly humiliating DiMaggio, and if DiMaggio was harboring any second thoughts about retiring, the release of that report stamped his retirement as official.

This is what happened. When the Dodgers were eliminated by Bobby Thomson's dramatic home run, High gave his report to the Giants' Leo Durocher. After all, if the Dodgers couldn't win the World Series, the next best thing was for a National League team to win, especially when the American League opponent was the Yankees.

After the Giants took the first game Durocher praised the report, said it was a piece of art, one of the best scouting jobs he'd ever encountered, and that it certainly helped the Giants win the game. "I never saw a report like it," he said, though as good as High's work was, it still couldn't prevent the Giants from losing the Series. When the Series was complete, a Giants statistician named Clay Felker shadily used High's report to benefit his own career. Felker was trying to land a position with Life *magazine, and when he told the editors he could get his hands on the High report, they reportedly offered him a job in exchange.*

Following the final game of the Series, DiMaggio backed off on his preseason retirement announcement and played coy regarding his future. "With this victory, I don't know how I feel," he said. "Right now I haven't a thing to say on the subject. If I told you yes or no and changed my mind we'd both look bad—you for writing it and me for saying it. The truth is, I don't know what I'm going to do."

I began to think that my original diagnosis was true, that DiMaggio wasn't going to hang up his cleats. Then the High report was published, and it was shocking in its cruelty to DiMaggio. "His reflexes are very slow and he can't pull a good fastball at all," High wrote. "He cannot stop quickly and throw hard, and you can take the extra base on him. He can't run."

When DiMaggio saw the magazine, he was livid, but he also recognized that much of what High had said was true, and his good friend and my colleague at the Post, *Jimmy Cannon, wrote, "Despair seized him about his vanishing gifts."*

DiMaggio was off on a playing tour with the Yankees in Japan so he didn't have to comment on the publication. When he returned stateside, he phoned Dan Topping and told him to call a farewell press conference. Topping tried to talk DiMaggio out of quitting and he even dangled another $100,000 contract under his nose. It didn't persuade DiMaggio.

The press was summoned to the Yankee offices in the Squibb Tower on Fifth Avenue in midtown Manhattan on the afternoon of December 11 where DiMaggio read from a prepared statement, part of which included this telling phrase: "I only wish I could have had a better year. But even if I hit .350, this would have been the last year for me. You all know I've had more than my share of physical injuries and setbacks during my career. In recent years these have been too frequent to laugh off. When baseball is no longer fun, it's no longer a game. And so, I've played my last game."

He answered a few questions after he had finished reading, and the one I posed to him was, "What was the final factor in your decision?" He replied, "I just don't have it anymore."

DiMaggio was one of the most perplexing men I ever knew. He could be so classy, so kind, and then be so petulant, so nasty. If you were his friend—which I was from the first time I saw him in the Yankee clubhouse in 1936—he would do just about anything for you. Of course, that also meant you had to do just about anything for him. If you weren't his friend, no man could shiver you with such a cold shoulder, no man could hold a grudge like DiMaggio.

On the ball field, he was simply beautiful, as elegant a ballplayer as there ever was. I just wish he could have enjoyed himself a little more. Sure, he had his pals at Toots Shor's place, and there was always drinking and dining and womanizing. But when DiMaggio was at the park, he was never one of the guys, especially after his old buddies like Lefty Gomez, George Selkirk, Red Ruffing, and Charlie Keller left the team. Naturally, he was the star and the elder statesman in his final years and that made him a little different. But while the rest of the players socialized with each other, joked around with each other, celebrated the victories and commiserated the losses together, DiMaggio always separated himself. The most famous man in America was a lonely man.

As the years passed after his retirement, I didn't stay particularly close to DiMaggio. I would call him to get a quote about some baseball topic or player, and I would also use that time to catch up with his personal life. He would call me occasionally, and I would meet him out for drinks when he was in New York, a few times while he was in the company of Marilyn Monroe. Funny, though. After I retired from the Post in 1981, he never called me again. Once I didn't have a voice in the New York papers I sort of felt like I no longer mattered to him, and I wondered if I ever mattered to him. During the last 15 or so years of his life, the only time I would see DiMaggio was at Old-Timers Day at the stadium. I always made sure I attended because it was a great way to keep in touch with the fellas from the past. DiMaggio and I would converse, but it was mostly idle chitchat without meaning.

His dismissal of me did not leave a bitter taste in my mouth, though. For more than 40 years I counted myself among a very select group of people— DiMaggio's inner circle—and it paid huge dividends throughout my journalistic career. And whenever an ill thought about DiMaggio creeps into my head, I harken back to his days as a player and I smile at the memories he provided for me. Of him tracking down a fly ball in the deepest recesses of Yankee Stadium, of his towering home runs and pulsating line drives, of the way he effortlessly moved from first to third on a base hit. Those are the things I remember most about DiMaggio, and in announcing his retirement, those were the things he wanted to remember most about himself.

"I once made a solemn promise to myself that I wouldn't try to hang on once the end is in sight," he told us that night. "I've seen too many beat-up players struggle to stay up there and it was always a sad spectacle."

The day after the news hit the streets, a reporter contacted DiMaggio's brother, Tom, out in San Francisco to get a comment, and Tom put it more succinctly. "He quit because he wasn't Joe DiMaggio anymore."

– Chapter 15 –

1952

A GROUP OF US WRITERS were standing around down in St. Petersburg
one morning in 1947—standing around became habitual when you were
covering spring training—and Rud Rennie of the *Herald Tribune* asked
new Yankees manager Bucky Harris, "You're not really thinking of keeping him, are you? He doesn't even look like a Yankee."

Rennie was referring to Yogi Berra.

Harris laughed at the question, then said, "He's not ugly. He could
become the most beautiful hitter in baseball."

That may have been the first and only time the word beautiful was
used during a conversation that centered on Berra. "Yogi's the only
catcher whose looks improved with his mask on," Lefty Gomez once
said.

No, Yogi wasn't beautiful. But Yogi was a great player, one of the all-
time Yankees, a Hall of Famer, and as he once said, "All you have to do in
this racket is hit the ball, and I never saw anyone hit with his face."

Berra grew up in a section of St. Louis known as "The Hill" which
was heavily populated by Italian immigrants, one of whom was his lifelong friend and fellow major league catcher, Joe Garagiola. His given
name was Lawrence Peter Berra, but his friends started calling him Yogi
after attending a short subject travelogue film about India. In the movie
there was a character referred to as a yogi, and it occurred to one of the
boys that the yogi looked an awful lot like Larry. A nickname, and a legend, was born.

Berra was the best athlete on The Hill, better than Garagiola, yet
Garagiola was signed by the hometown Cardinals to a contract that included a $500 bonus. Branch Rickey was then in charge of the St. Louis

club, and he had a chance to sign Berra as well, but after watching him play, Rickey concluded that Berra would never be good enough to make it to the major leagues. He did offer a $250 bonus, but Berra rejected it, saying he wanted what his buddy, Garagiola, got.

A few months later, the Yankees bullpen coach, Johnny Schulte, who lived in St. Louis during the off-season, was asked by George Weiss—then in charge of the Yankee farm system—to check out Berra and if he looked good, to sign him. Berra agreed to join the Yankees, just as long as he got that Garagiola treatment—a $500 bonus.

Berra played 1943 at Class-B Norfolk, Virginia, then enlisted in the Navy and was part of the D-Day invasion of Normandy. When his military hitch expired in 1946, he was sent to Newark to play for the Triple-A Bears, and by the end of the season he earned a promotion to the Yankees, where he hit a home run in his first at-bat at Yankee Stadium. During his brief trial he batted .346 and that was enough to convince President Larry MacPhail to invite Berra to spring training in 1947.

As Rennie said, Berra didn't have the distinguished look of a Yankee, but it was obvious the pudgy kid with the scatter arm could hit the cover off the ball and therefore, room on the roster needed to be cleared. During his first two seasons, Berra split time at catcher and in right field, then starting in 1949 when Casey Stengel arrived, receiving became his primary duty. That year the Yankees brought in the great Bill Dickey to teach Berra how to catch like a big-leaguer, and he molded Berra into a clone of himself, to which Berra said, "Bill is learning me his experiences."

One day I wrote a story about the tutoring process, and Dickey told me how he was going to turn Berra into an all-star. It began with the very basic skill of catching the ball. Berra had a tendency to stab the ball and Allie Reynolds would fume at him because Berra would carry the ball out of the strike zone with his stabbing motion. Dickey taught him to catch the ball and frame it in the strike zone, thus enabling him to steal strikes.

Base stealers had a field day with Berra during his first two years, and Dickey quickly discovered why. Berra was sitting too far behind the plate and that extra sliver of length on his throws often made the difference between safe and out; that is, when the throws were on target, of which few were. So Dickey moved him two feet closer to the plate to cut down the distance, then taught him a more economical and accurate way to throw the ball.

Dickey worked hard on teaching Berra how to block low pitches with his body, and Berra paid the price with a body full of bruises, but he was a willing and able student and he never complained. He listened to everything Dickey said, adapted to the new style of play, and pretty soon, Berra became the best all-around catcher in baseball. Starting in 1948 Berra made the American League all-star team 15 straight years, and interspersed throughout the 1950s were three league MVP awards. In 1958 he played the entire season without making an error.

One thing never needed work: Berra's batting stroke. He could hit anything thrown in the strike zone, and for that matter, just about anything outside the strike zone. Berra used to drive pitchers crazy because they'd try to waste a pitch and Berra would still make enough contact to get a hit. His philosophy was, "If I can see it, I can hit it" and he usually did.

For all his greatness as a player, there is no question what Berra is remembered most for: his malapropisms. Here is a man who is in the Hall of Fame and a member of the all-century team that was picked in 1999, but his everlasting legacy is his repetitive fracturing of the English language.

I have been acquainted with Berra for more than 50 years, and he has told me on numerous occasions that half the stuff that was attributed to him he never said. In fact, that pronouncement led to one of his great Yogi-isms: "I really didn't say everything I said." But Berra always rolled with the punches because he enjoyed the attention. Gene Woodling once told me, "Yogi got a lot of mileage out of all that."

It didn't take long for this side of Berra to shine through. In his rookie year, the people of St. Louis arranged for a special night for their returning hero when the Yankees were in town to play the Browns. Before the game at Sportsman's Park he told the audience, "I want to thank those who made this night necessary." We roared in the press box, and pretty soon all of the writers started going to Berra for quotes in the hope that he would say something profoundly dumb.

Admittedly I fell into this practice early in Berra's career, but after awhile I began to realize that he wasn't as doltish as we portrayed him to be. For evidence, there was the improvement in his catching. If he was so dumb, how was he able to relearn his position so adeptly? And in conversations I would have on plane or train rides with Berra, he intimated that he knew what to do with the money he was making. As I sit in my modest home, I can look around and say I did all right for myself.

But Berra is a millionaire a couple times over thanks to prudent investments and an uncanny business sense that belied his comical appearance. He did all right for himself, too.

I was playing golf with Berra one time near his home in New Jersey, and he said to me, "You know Joe, it really bothered me for a lot of years that everyone thought I was stupid. But I just took it all in stride and bit my lip because I knew I was going to be fine. It was fun being the character."

*   *   *

It was not fun being Mickey Mantle at the start of the 1952 season.

There was the matter of his damaged right knee that prevented him from taking over for Joe DiMaggio in center field right away, but of far greater significance, there was the death of his father, Mutt.

The day Mickey suffered his injury in Game Two of the 1951 World Series, he was transferred to Lenox Hill Hospital in a taxi, his father riding by his side. When Mickey got out of the cab he leaned on Mutt for support, and Mutt collapsed under his son's weight. Both men were admitted, and they wound up sharing a room where they watched the rest of the Series on television.

Within a couple of days, the doctors revealed that Mickey would heal up just fine after his successful surgery. The prognosis for Mutt wasn't as encouraging. He was suffering from an irreversible and advanced case of Hodgkin's disease.

Mickey and his wife, Merlyn, spent the off-season in Mickey's Oklahoma hometown seeking treatment options for Mutt, but it became obvious his condition was grave and nothing could be done. With his mind preoccupied, Mickey did not properly rehabilitate his injury, and when he reported for spring training, his knee was not ready for action.

With Mantle playing himself into condition in right field—where there was less ground to cover—the Yankees stumbled out of the gate as a spate of other injuries hampered their effort and it appeared a fourth consecutive pennant and World Series title were remote possibilities.

Just when it looked like Mantle was ready to move to center and things might turn for the better, news came that Mutt Mantle died. Mickey went home to grieve for five days, and it wasn't until two weeks after that before he started in center.

The Yankees ended May with a mundane 18-17 record and were wallowing in fifth place. But after winning 13 of their first 15 games in June—

during which time Berra went on a rampage, hitting 10 home runs—the Yankees moved into first place and by mid-July were 5 1/2 games clear of the Indians, the preseason pennant favorite. New York held a slim lead into August, but a three-game sweep at the hands of the White Sox and a fourth straight loss inflicted by the Indians late that month enabled Cleveland to pull even. By Labor Day the Yankees fell 2 1/2 games in arrears, and it took all their legendary resolve to battle back, but they did it.

The Yankees won a big game in mid-September at Cleveland as Eddie Lopat beat Mike Garcia in front of more than 73,000 fans at Municipal Stadium to give the Yankees the lead, and when Cleveland responded by winning 10 of its next 11, the Yankees were equal to the test as they won nine of their next 10, including a doubleheader sweep of the Red Sox at Fenway Park on September 24. That day Sain won the opener and saved the nightcap, Mantle hit a home run, two doubles, a triple and a single, and drove in six runs combined, and Martin accepted 24 chances in the field, a major league record for a doubleheader. The sweep gave New York a two-game lead with four to play, and two days later, Martin's two-run single in the 11th keyed a 5-2 victory over the Philadelphia Athletics at Shibe Park that ended the chase.

Nothing came easy during the achieving of Stengel's fourth straight American League pennant. Appropriately, winning his fourth consecutive World Series was not easy, either.

– *1952 World Series* –

It was a sound you grew accustomed to hearing at Ebbets Field, especially at World Series time. It was the sound of exasperation, and it would blow across the ball field, out over the right-field fence and right on down Bedford Avenue like a Nor'easter marching up the Atlantic coast.

There would be the usual packed house at the tiny bandbox, Brooklynites rabid with excitement as their Dodgers would tease them with the remnants of a winning rally. And then one of those Bums would do something inexplicable and inexcusable, and just like that the rally was dead, the game was over, and the Dodgers were losers again. And again. And again.

On the afternoon of Game Seven of the 1952 World Series, I heard that sound twice within a matter of seconds, and what a sound it was.

It was the bottom of the seventh inning, the Dodgers were trailing the Yankees 4-2, but they had the bases loaded with only one out and sluggers Duke Snider and Jackie Robinson scheduled to bat.

Ebbets Field was in an uproar as Casey Stengel wobbled out to the mound and took the ball from an exhausted Vic Raschi and a few moments later handed it to Bob Kuzava. That's right, *the* Bob Kuzava, *the left-handed* Bob Kuzava, in a ballpark where left-handed pitchers began swearing the moment they put their uniforms on. The great Warren Spahn, the all-time winningest left-handed pitcher in Major League Baseball, was rarely allowed to pitch at Ebbets Field. It was suicide, no matter how good you were. Yet here was Stengel asking Kuzava to save the World Series.

I turned to my colleague at the *Post*, Milton Gross, who covered the Dodgers, and said, "Has the old man lost his mind?" Then I remembered. These were the Yankees. These were the Dodgers. Stengel himself could have pitched and the Yankees would have escaped the jam.

Naturally, the Yankees did escape, but it took one of the great plays in World Series history to do it.

Kuzava at least had the percentages on his side when he faced the lefty-swinging Snider, and he induced the Duke of Flatbush to pop out meekly to Gil McDougald at third for the second out. He did not have that advantage when the right-handed Robinson stepped into the batter's box. With all 33,195 top-coated fans living and dying with every pitch, Kuzava carefully worked the count to 3-and-2 and now the tension was unbearable.

The payoff pitch was a curveball and Robinson's swing was just a fraction of an inch off, which is often the difference between being a hero and a goat in baseball. He raised a towering pop fly to the right side of the mound, and there came that sound of exasperation emanating from deep in the lungs of those frustrated Brooklynites.

I just shook my head and grinned, but as I did, I realized something was amiss. As the ball soared to the heavens, none of the Yankee infielders moved. Yogi Berra had come out from behind the plate to make the call and he yelled for first baseman Joe Collins to take it. What Berra didn't know was that as the ball reached its apex, Collins was blinded by the sun and had no idea where it was. Now the ball was in descent, careening toward the field like a meteor, and in the gusty breeze it started to drift away from the infielders and back toward the plate.

As the hearts of Yankee fans watching on television or listening on radio stopped beating, Ebbets Field suddenly jumped to life in anticipation of a long-overdue miracle. Carl Furillo, who had walked to start the inning, was across home plate and Billy Cox, who had singled, was just about there with the tying run. On the 3-2 pitch Pee Wee Reese was off with the crack of the bat from first base and he was already around second and on his way to third. As all this was happening, my grin disappeared and the only thing that came out of my mouth was "Holy Shit!"

Fortunately for the Yankees, Billy Martin did not panic. He had been playing on the edge of the outfield grass at second base, but when he saw that Collins couldn't find the ball, McDougald had gone back to cover third, shortstop Phil Rizzuto was too far away to have a chance, and Berra and Kuzava were clearly under the assumption that Collins was going to catch it, Martin began a mad dash toward the mound. At the last instant Martin reached out in front of him and snared the ball at about knee level, squeezing his glove as he tumbled to the ground with the prize still nestled safely inside.

The Dodgers had been foiled once more, and there came that sound again, whistling through the saddened borough. The game wasn't over, but it was. When Kuzava waltzed through the eighth and ninth innings, the Yankees were winners, and the Dodgers were losers. Again.

* * *

Billy Martin was always Casey Stengel's favorite player. He was never my favorite. In all honesty, Martin could be a real prick. Not so much when he was playing, but certainly when he became the on-again, off-again manager of the Yankees during the soap opera era of the mid-to-late 1970s and early 1980s when I was winding down my career as a journalist.

I found him to be rude, arrogant, conniving, and often uncooperative, and it didn't matter if he was dealing with me—someone who had covered or been associated with the Yankees since before he was born— or a new writer or broadcaster on the beat.

Martin grew up dirt poor on the hard streets of West Berkeley, California, where you used your fists to survive, and he survived just fine. His father had run out on his mother when he was an infant, and though his mother remarried, there was very little money coming in to the household.

Martin was always a runt, and his oversized nose caused him to be the butt of many jokes. The other kids called him Pinocchio and banana nose, but what they didn't know was that this "little bugger," as Stengel used to call him, was usually the toughest guy in the bunch and his prowess as a fighter was legendary. As Martin would walk home from school through Jenxton Park there was always someone challenging him to a fight. To back down would only provoke the antagonists, so Martin would fight, and he'd win. Pretty soon they stopped picking fights with him.

Who knows what kind of life Martin would have led had it not been for his proficiency in athletics. He was never a good student, so he had no chance of going to college, but he starred for the baseball, football, and basketball teams in high school. Sports kept him out of serious trouble, and ultimately it was baseball that gave him a life.

When he was 18 years old he played semipro baseball for a team in Oakland that was sponsored by the Triple-A Oakland Oaks of the Pacific Coast League. The Oaks signed him to a contract and after playing in the Arizona-Texas League for Phoenix in 1947 and winning the MVP award Martin was promoted to Oakland where Stengel was the manager. Stengel took Martin under his wing and virtually became Martin's surrogate father. He loved Martin's combativeness and the way he could spark his teammates with his feisty attitude. "He's got it in here," Stengel would often say, pointing to his heart.

The year after Stengel became the Yankees manager he convinced general manager George Weiss to purchase Martin's contract, which Weiss did.

Martin played behind Jerry Coleman his first two years, then took over at second base when Coleman was drafted into the military in 1952 and Martin helped lead the Yankees to the fourth and fifth straight championships of the early Stengel dynasty.

During that time he was buddies with Mickey Mantle and Whitey Ford when Ford rejoined the team in 1953 after a two-year service hitch. They became the Three Musketeers, inseparable off the field, and their antics spiced things up around the often staid Yankees. I had become friendly with Mantle, and Ford was a nice enough guy, but Martin I found to be barely tolerable. Mantle used to tell me, "Joe, Billy rubs a lot of people the wrong way, you just have to let him grow on you."

I'll say this: He did grow on me as a player. Martin was a good fielder who used intelligence and hustle to make up for his lack of size, and with the bat he always had a knack for coming through in the clutch. "I never had the average, but my 1-for-4 would kill you," he once said. Never was he better than in the World Series as he batted .333 in 28 career games, scoring 15 runs and driving in 19.

None of this mattered to Weiss. Weiss never liked Martin, even though he was a vitally important player in both the 1952 and 1953 World Series. Weiss often decried his contributions, and of his great catch that saved the '52 Series, Weiss was convinced Martin was just showing off, that he made an easy play look tough.

Weiss knew Martin and Mantle were tight and he feared that Martin's rambunctious nature would rub off on Mantle. Mantle was the meal ticket that Weiss felt needed to be protected. The way to do that, or so Weiss thought, was to find a way to get rid of Martin. That was laughable because if Weiss only knew half the trouble Mantle used to get into on his own when Martin was nowhere to be found, he might have been looking for ways to get rid of his slugger. Regardless, like a gift from above, the incident at the Copacabana in 1957 provided Weiss all the ammunition he needed to jettison Martin, even though it was completely bogus.

Mantle and Ford arranged a birthday celebration for Martin on the evening of May 15 because the Yankees had a scheduled day off on the 16th, Martin's actual birthday. Though the day off was eliminated when a rainout made it necessary to use the 16th as a makeup date, plans had been made so the players still went out. It was Mantle, Ford, Hank Bauer, Yogi Berra, and Johnny Kucks and their wives, and Martin who went stag.

They started the evening with dinner at Danny's Hideaway, advanced to the Waldorf where Lena Horne was performing, and finally, after midnight, they went to the Copacabana on East 60th Street to catch Sammy Davis Jr. The Yankees were seated at a table near the back of the room, next to a group of drunken bowlers. One of the men directed a racial slur at Davis, and Bauer—the ex-Marine—told him to shut up. It didn't take long before a fight was proposed. Bauer and the bowler went to a private room with Martin and another bowler in tow. What happened is that while Bauer was priming himself for battle and Martin was trying to defuse the situation verbally, a Copacabana bouncer was summoned and he punched the drunk bowler's lights out.

Bauer and Martin never threw a punch, but they and the rest of the Yankee party were ushered out a back door before any explanations were given. It just so happened that a *Daily News* police reporter got wind of the story when the bloodied bowler told the cops that Bauer had punched him and that he wanted to press charges. The reporter called Bauer at 4:30 in the morning to get a comment, Bauer said he didn't do anything, yet the headline in the paper screamed "Yankees in Brawl at Copa." Weiss flipped when he saw the story, and the moment he read Martin's name in the account, he immediately blamed the whole incident on his peppery second baseman.

"Billy wasn't guilty that time," Ford said, "but the Copa thing gave Weiss a chance to trade him." Which he did, to the Kansas City Athletics. Martin's playing career slumped from that moment on and he admitted years later, "It was like a nightmare. It took a lot out of me. I wasn't the same ballplayer that I'd been."

Martin bounced around from Kansas City to Cleveland to Cincinnati to Minnesota, making a mark with none of those clubs. He finally quit playing in 1961, then began a scouting, coaching, and managing career that eventually made him one of the most popular and controversial figures in baseball history.

*   *   *

Joe Black started more games during one week's time (three) in the 1952 World Series than he had started his entire rookie season with the Dodgers (two). There were many of us in the press who thought Dodgers manager Charley Dressen was making a mistake relying so heavily on the youngster when he had other seasoned pros such as Preacher Roe, Billy Loes, Carl Erskine, and Ben Wade at his disposal, men who combined to start 96 games that year. But Dressen's managerial style was often unconventional, and at least for Game One, pitching Black proved to be the right move.

The day before the game Black said he wasn't the least bit nervous about facing the mighty Yankees because, in his view, "These aren't the same Yankees that I used to pay to see when they had DiMaggio, Henrich, and Keller. They're wearing the same letters on their shirts, but I don't believe they frighten anybody."

The Yankees wouldn't have frightened anybody that first game. Black looked like an African-American version of Bob Feller as he limited the Yankees to six meek hits to become the first pitcher of color to win a Series game. "This is no club of jittery rookies," Dressen said of his supremely confident Dodgers after the 4-2 victory at Ebbets Field. "They're all experienced players in top form, well-rested and ready to go."

Black had appeared in 56 games during the year, only two as a starter, but he went the distance and Stengel conceded, "Black pitched a good game. He held us to two runs; he must be pretty good to do that, to keep us from getting started."

The Dodgers gave Black plenty of support as Jackie Robinson, Duke Snider, and Pee Wee Reese all hit homers to account for the Brooks' four runs.

The Dodgers had never won the opening game of a World Series, and Vic Raschi made sure they didn't take a commanding two-game lead. He put on a clinic in Game Two, striking out nine and allowing just three hits during a 7-1 Yankee romp. It was Martin who wielded the knockout punch during a five-run Yankee sixth against Erskine and Loes, hitting a three-run home run. Roy Campanella's RBI single gave the Brooks a 1-0 lead in the third, but Mantle doubled and scored on Berra's sacrifice fly in the fourth, and Martin's RBI single in the fifth made it 2-1 before New York blew it open.

The third game pitted two junkball artists, Eddie Lopat and Preacher Roe, and Roe's junk was a bit more effective than Lopat's during Brooklyn's 5-3 victory at Yankee Stadium. "I gave them everything I had, but it wasn't good enough," said Lopat following the only World Series loss of his career. "I wasn't as sharp as usual, and they had the advantage of a couple bloopers that paid off."

The Dodgers snapped a 1-1 tie in the fifth when Cox led off with a single, went to second on a sacrifice by Roe, and scored with two outs as Reese blooped one off his wrists that landed softly in right field. Clinging to a 3-2 lead in the ninth, the Dodgers pulled off a double steal as Reese stole third and Robinson second off reliever Tom Gorman. That maneuver proved critical when both men scored on a passed ball by Berra which was more than enough to offset Johnny Mize's pinch-hit homer in the ninth for New York.

Stengel had planned to use Ewell Blackwell in Game Four if his team had the advantage, but now that he desperately needed to win, he turned instead to Reynolds even though the Chief would be working on one day less rest. Then again, Dressen's plan all along was to come back with Black in Game Four, so that evened out the physicality of the pitching matchup. What Black couldn't match was Reynolds's experience. In a game he knew he had to win, Reynolds threw a four-hit shutout, striking out 10, and Mize's second home run in two days started the Yankees on their way to a 2-0 victory.

"I'm getting too old for this," the 39-year-old Mize said after his home run to left provided Reynolds the only run he would need.

In the spring of 1949, Stengel's first year with the Yankees, he had sidled up to Mize before an exhibition game in Florida and asked, "How do you feel?" Mize replied, "All right, but I'm not playing much." Stengel said, "If you were over here you'd play." Mize answered, "Well, make a deal."

That August Giants owner Horace Stoneham had drinks with the Yankee owners, Dan Topping and Del Webb, and they convinced him to sell Mize to the Yankees. The price was $50,000, and for that investment, Mize—who National League followers felt was over the hill—became the American League's most feared pinch-hitter and he went on to earn five World Series rings with the Yankees.

In his last season with the Yankees I remember talking to Mize about hitting, and he revealed to me just how astute a student of the game he was. "Every night before I went to bed I looked in the paper to see who was pitching the next day, then I'd lie awake half an hour or so just imagining I was standing at the plate," he said. "I tried to visualize how I might be thrown to, what to look for."

Stengel knew what he was looking for from Mize in the fourth game, and Mize delivered. Joe Collins had gone 0-for-11 in the first three games and Stengel needed production at first base, so he decided to start Mize even though he wasn't nearly the fielder Collins was. As usual, Stengel's move paid off because Mize also contributed a double and handled six chances in the field without incident.

Mantle provided Reynolds an insurance run in the eighth when he ripped a 450-foot triple over Snider's head and came all the way around to score when Reese's relay throw to third wound up in the stands, but Reynolds didn't need the help. To gauge how good the Chief was, I went over to the Brooklyn clubhouse and sought out Robinson, who whiffed in three consecutive at-bats on nine total pitches. "How could I argue when I couldn't even see the ball," Robinson said. "I didn't strike out, I looked out."

The next day was October 5, and pitching the fifth game of the Series for Brooklyn on the day of his fifth wedding anniversary was Erskine. You want more? In the fifth inning Erskine allowed five runs, and by the time the game was over, he had allowed only those five runs as well as five hits. Five was certainly his lucky number, especially given that his teammates produced six runs, the last coming in the top of the 11th inning when Snider doubled home Cox to give the Dodgers a thrilling victory which left the Bums tantalizingly close to their first championship.

Erskine pitched perhaps the game of his life. He went all the way, 11 innings, and after the Yankees raked him in the fifth to take a 5-4 lead, he retired the last 19 batters he faced. In nine innings, the Yankees failed to register a hit, their only safety outside the fifth inning being a bunt single by Mantle in the fourth.

Author Peter Golenbock interviewed Erskine at length for his marvelous oral history about the Dodgers entitled *Bums*, and Erskine shared a wonderful anecdote regarding Dressen's visit to the mound that afternoon during the fifth-inning mayhem.

"He comes out to the mound, takes the ball from me, glances around a little bit, and he says, 'Are you all right?'" Erskine recalled. "I said, 'I feel lousy, but I'm all right.' Then he says, 'Is this your wedding anniversary?' which darned near floored me. Then he says, 'Is your wife at the game.' I said, 'Yeah, she's here.' Finally he asks me, 'Are you going to celebrate your anniversary tonight?' This was real strange. I said, 'Well, I suppose we will, Charley.' With that he takes my glove and turns it up and slams the ball back in it and here's what he said: 'Well, see if you can get the side out before it gets dark.'"

He retired Berra on a fly to Furillo in right, and then set the Yankees down 1-2-3 over the final six innings.

Stengel started Blackwell, and the old Cincinnati Red, a late-season acquisition brought in to beef up the rotation, simply didn't have his best stuff. Already leading 1-0 on Pafko's RBI single in the second, the Dodgers increased their margin to 4-0 in the fifth, the big blow a two-run homer by Snider. After the Yankees put together their lone offensive flurry of the game, capped by Mize's three-run homer that made it 5-4, Johnny Sain took the mound in the sixth and he ended up going the rest of the way, so it was his game to lose when Snider came through with a tying RBI single in the seventh, then hit his winning double in the 11th. For the day, Snider had three hits and four RBI.

"I always had pretty good luck batting against Johnny Sain, but this time I hit the jackpot," said the Duke. "It's like somebody made me king for a day."

What Snider really wanted to be was king for the entire off-season. In other words, a world champion.

The Dodgers were now one win away from realizing their dreams, and Game Six was played before a deranged mob at Ebbets Field. For six innings, young Billy Loes blanked the Yankees, stretching to 12 innings their futility against Dodger pitching. Meanwhile, the red-hot Snider slammed his third homer of the Series in the sixth to give Loes a 1-0 lead. But then the Bronx Bombers swung into action with a pair of runs in the seventh—one on Berra's home run that bounded down Bedford Avenue—and another in the eighth on the first of Mantle's career Series-record 18 home runs. Snider's second bomb of the day cut the Brooklyn deficit to 3-2, but with Reynolds saving Raschi's strong outing, the Yankees held on and the Series was even at three games apiece. As Snider said, "How much of this can one guy take?"

For just the fourth time in the team's illustrious World Series history, the Yankees were pushed to a seventh game. For three decades they had built their dynasty on team play. They always had a superstar or two in their midst, but by and large, they won championships because every man on the roster contributed in some way, especially during Stengel's era when platooning became vogue. And that's how they won this championship.

Lopat started on the mound, but he was helped by the tireless Reynolds and Raschi, and finally, by the obscure Kuzava. The runs came from Mize on a RBI single, a Woodling home run, a Mantle home run, and a RBI single by Mantle. In the field, there was Berra handling the four pitchers flawlessly and Martin's dazzling catch that averted a disaster in the seventh. And of course there was Stengel—matching Joe McCarthy's record of four straight World Series victories—making all the right moves.

"There's the greatest manager in baseball, make no mistake about it," said Bill Dickey after the Yankees came away with a 4-2 victory. "There's nobody around who can approach him. The way he has handled this club, not only in the Series, but from the start of the season, stamps him among the greatest of all time."

Mantle broke a 2-2 tie when he launched an epic home run off Black, and his RBI single in the seventh came off Roe and gave the Yankees a 4-2 cushion, setting the stage for Martin's dramatic catch.

"I could see that (Collins) didn't know where the ball was and I knew if he didn't get it the ball would drop and two, probably three runs would score, so I took off," Martin explained amidst the din of the uproarious clubhouse celebration. "I could tell the wind was taking it toward home plate and I was thinking about Yogi. I was afraid he'd be coming out for the ball and sometimes when he did he kept his mask on. I heard nothing, no one calling me off the ball, but I knew I might knock into somebody. I didn't realize how long a run I had to make. I didn't think the play was so much until I got to the dugout and they were all slapping me on the back and saying what a great play it was."

When Kuzava finished off the Dodgers there was utter silence in that little stadium. You had to feel bad for the Brooks. So close, yet such heartbreak.

But at least one Dodger was prepared for the inevitable. Loes had made a comment to a group of us writers before the Series began that, "When you figure all the angles, it looks like the Yankees in seven." When Dressen read that comment, he confronted his pitcher and asked "What's wrong with you?" Loes's reply: "I was misquoted, Skip. I picked them in six games."

In 1994 when Mickey Mantle collaborated with sportswriter and author Mickey Herskowitz on the book All My Octobers, he finally revealed the truth about his supposed 565-foot home run that flew out of Washington's Griffith Stadium on the night of April 17, 1953. Because there are times when the facts get in the way of a good story, only a handful of people—including yours truly—knew the real story of Mantle's epic home run, until he spilled the beans in his book.

For those who may not have read Mickey's explanation, here's a summation:

It was a windy night in the nation's capital, and Mantle came to the plate in the fifth inning with two outs and Yogi Berra on first base. The Washington pitcher was Chuck Stobbs, and after missing low for a ball, the left-hander made a big mistake on his second offering. He fired a fastball right down the middle about letter high, and Mantle, swinging right-handed, absolutely creamed it. I mean if President Eisenhower had been at his White House residence a couple miles away instead of in Georgia playing golf with newly crowned Masters champion Ben Hogan at Augusta National Golf Club, he probably would have heard the explosion.

Left field at Griffith Stadium was about as tough and cavernous as left field in Yankee Stadium, but there wasn't a ballpark in the world that would have kept this missile within its boundaries. When it soared over the fence at the 391-foot marker the ball seemed to be laughing. Beyond the fence there were 32 rows of bleachers, the football scoreboard, and a 60-foot high beer sign in its path, and it cleared everything, ricocheting off the top of the sign on its way out of the stadium.

This much I know is true, because I saw it happen. But where the ball wound up and how far it really traveled remains a mystery. Who could have known? Well, like everyone else covering the game that night, we thought Red Patterson, the Yankees' publicity director, knew.

As soon as the ball was hit we became mesmerized by its flight pattern, and when it disappeared from sight, Patterson leaped from his seat and yelled, "That one's got to be measured." He then exited the press box and we didn't see him again for another half-hour. When he returned, he claimed to have all the details. He said when he got outside he spotted the ball in the hands of a 10-year-old boy and when he asked the kid to show him where he found it, he was led to the *backyard of a home at 434 Oakdale Street across from the stadium. The little boy, whose name was Donald Dunaway, reportedly showed him the exact spot where the ball came to rest, and from that location Patterson did the requisite pacing and concluded that the ball had traveled 565 feet. His calculation included 391 feet to the fence, 69 feet to the rear wall of the bleachers, and then another 105 feet to the backyard.*

Without all of us trooping out there to verify it, we bought the story. It seemed well researched and on the level, so that's what we wrote, and it became part of the Mantle legend.

However, a few years later after Patterson had left the Yankees to go to work for the Dodgers when they moved to Los Angeles, Patterson confessed to Mantle that he had never actually gone out to pace the home run. Patterson was a large man, and he admitted that by the time he got down to field level, he was tired and decided to abort his mission. It turned out that he chugged a couple beers at a concession stand, then went back upstairs and fibbed to us. Apparently the little boy showed up in the clubhouse with the ball, and he traded it for a couple other balls, some cash and a Mantle autograph.

When Mantle found out about Patterson's ruse, he decided not to spoil the myth. He told a few of the Yankees and he told a couple of us writers, but that was it.

So how far did that ball travel that night in Washington? No one knows, but take it from someone who saw Babe Ruth play on a regular basis—that home run by Mantle was majestic, no matter the distance.

Incredibly, it may not have been the longest one Mantle ever hit. I know in the spring of his rookie season when the Yankees were barnstorming through California he hit a shot during an exhibition against the University of Southern California that traveled an estimated 645 feet. And Gene Woodling swears the drive he hit in St. Louis' newly renamed Busch Stadium, two weeks after the tour de force in Washington, was even longer. Again, there was really no way to know for sure.

"No one, including Babe Ruth, hit them consistently as far as Mantle did," Woodling once said. "Mantle was unbelievable. I don't think he ever realized the talent he had. He was just a small-town boy who came to New York to swing a bat."

The ball from Washington, which was grossly lopsided, and the bat—which Mantle had borrowed from teammate Loren Babe—were requested for enshrinement by Baseball Hall of Fame curator Sid Keener. Before they went to Cooperstown, though, the equipment was placed on display at Yankee Stadium for the remainder of the 1953 season.

One place the ball wasn't going was back to Mantle's native Commerce, Oklahoma.

"If I send the ball home, I know what will happen to it," he said. "My twin brothers will take it out on the lot like any 20-cent rocket. I got the ball I hit for my first major league home run and sent it home all autographed and dolled up. The kids belted it out of shape."

– Chapter 16 –

1953

IT WAS CASEY STENGEL'S OPINION that four championships in a row were not enough. "We're out to win a fifth straight pennant, something no club has yet been able to do in the major leagues," Stengel said before the 1953 season began.

And there was no reason to believe the Yankees couldn't do it. For the first time in Stengel's tenure the team was set in spring training and was free of distractions and injuries. The lineup would be Joe Collins at first, Billy Martin at second, Phil Rizzuto at shortstop and Gil McDougald at third, Yogi Berra behind the plate, and Mickey Mantle, Gene Woodling, and Hank Bauer in the outfield. Off the bench there was Johnny Mize, Irv Noren, and Don Bollweg. On the mound, Whitey Ford was returning from the military to join Eddie Lopat and Vic Raschi as regular starters, while Allie Reynolds, Jim McDonald, and Johnny Sain would share the fourth slot in the rotation. Those latter three plus Bob Kuzava and Tom Gorman would combine to form a reliable and experienced bullpen.

This team was so good on paper that my brethren in the national media actually thought the Yankees were worthy enough to be considered favorites in the American League. It's hard to believe, but in each of the first four years of Stengel's championship run the Yankees were never the consensus pick to win the pennant, let alone the World Series.

"The reason this club hasn't made a deal is, why should we?" Stengel said when someone asked him if it had been wise of George Weiss to stand pat in the off-season. "If the players are good enough to win four years in a row, they should be good enough to win five."

They were. New York won 11 of its 14 games in April, and on May 11 it moved into first place for good. Yet this season, more than any other, Stengel rode his players like a drill sergeant. In fact there were times when he was downright vicious, and the more the Yankees won, the more of an edge Stengel seemed to have. "If we're going to win the pennant, we've got to start thinking we're not as good as we think we are," he said. That was tough, especially during the team's 18-game winning streak which ran from May 27 to June 14.

Oh, Stengel was mad the day the St. Louis Browns snapped the streak and in the process ended their own 14-game losing skein. The Yankees were two wins away from breaking the American League record of 19 straight set by the 1906 Chicago White Sox and the 1947 Yankees. But Stengel had his eye on an even loftier target, the 26 consecutive wins achieved by his old mentor with the New York Giants, John McGraw, in 1916.

Stengel revered McGraw. He played three seasons for McGraw (1921–1923), the Giants won the National League pennant all three years, and twice they beat the Yankees in the World Series. "I learned more from McGraw than anybody," Stengel once said. "My platoon thinking started with the way McGraw handled me in my last years on the Giants. He had me in and out of the lineup, and he used me all around the outfield. He put me in when and where he thought I could do the most good. And after I got into managing I platooned whenever I had the chance, long before I came to the Yankees."

In 1923 Stengel started apprenticing for his managerial career during spring training when McGraw had him coach the Giants' B squad. During the season he made frequent visits to McGraw's home in Westchester County and the two men would talk baseball and strategy for hours.

Stengel owed much of his success to the schooling from McGraw, yet that did not deter him in his zealousness to better the old master. "You know," Stengel said after he won his fourth straight World Series in 1952, "John McGraw was a great man in New York and he won a lot of pennants, but Stengel is in town now, and he's won a lot of pennants, too."

Stengel never did break McGraw's winning streak record, but he did tie him with 10 league pennants, and his seven World Series triumphs were more than double McGraw's three.

The 18-game streak was not all Stengel's doing. Most of the games were lopsided, as evidenced by the cumulative score during the streak:

Yankees 129, Opponents 44. His players were on top of their games. In mid-June Mantle was hitting the cover off the ball and at one point he compiled a 17-game hitting streak and was a contender for the triple crown. Berra was mashing long balls, Bauer and Woodling were hitting well above .300, the pitching was superb with Ford and Lopat each winning their first seven decisions, and going about his business quietly, but ever so efficiently, was McDougald.

*   *   *

By the end of the 1953 season, McDougald would lead the team in hits (154), doubles (27), and triples (7), he would be second in runs scored (82), third in RBI (83), and as usual he played the field with grace and skill. Yet no one ever seemed to pay attention. It was always that way with him.

McDougald had the misfortune of breaking into the major leagues with the Yankees the same year Mantle joined the team. Never mind that McDougald outperformed Mantle in that 1951 season and was named the American League's Rookie of the Year. Mantle was a headliner, McDougald an underling. But it was because the Yankees always had players like McDougald that they won so consistently.

McDougald began his Yankee career as a second baseman, but Stengel recognized right away in that first spring training that he was versatile. Stengel was not enamored with Billy Johnson at third base, and Bobby Brown—an excellent hitter but an inadequate fielder in Stengel's eyes—was due to leave for Korea. Stengel looked to McDougald for help and asked if he'd give third base a try. McDougald's response was, "I've never played there before, but I'll try. They can't do no more than knock my teeth out."

Through the years McDougald jockeyed between third, second, and shortstop and he is the only Yankee player in history to start regularly at three infield positions and start an All-Star Game at all three stations.

McDougald was one of those young players who benefited greatly from Stengel's tutorial managing style. Casey loved to work with "green peas" as he called the youngsters, especially in spring training when he demanded that every player, regardless of his experience, go back to the basics.

"Casey felt that everyone should go through fundamentals each spring because it was easy to forget things over the winter," McDougald once said.

McDougald usually listened to his manager, but only about fielding matters. When it came to hitting, McDougald was stubborn as a mule and he insisted on using his quirky right-handed batting stance during the first four years of his career. He would stand at the plate with his legs spread wide apart, his left foot pointed at the pitcher, his right foot at a right angle, and his body would be turned inward so that his belt buckle was staring at the pitcher. It was a stance he had started using in the minor leagues and he maintained it was the reason why he was always above .300. That first year Stengel said, "He's the lousiest looking ballplayer in the world, but he gets things done."

However, he didn't get things done as well in the next few years as he couldn't top .300 and by early in the 1955 season Stengel had had enough. McDougald was really in a lull, down around .240, and Stengel told him to either conform to a more conventional style or get used to life back in the minor leagues. This time McDougald made the change and it worked wonders. His average soared as he began spraying line drives all over, and in 1956 he batted .311 and finished second to Mantle in American League MVP voting.

There was also strategy involved in Stengel's request. McDougald was a dead pull hitter, and when he did get a base hit, most went to left field and it was tougher for runners on first to make it to third. When McDougald changed his stance, he was able to hit the ball to all fields and that helped the Yankees manufacture more runs.

I remember McDougald describing his workmanlike attitude this way: "It's easy to have a good day when you feel good, and it's easy to have a horseshit day when you feel horseshit. The question is when you feel horseshit, can you still have a good day?" McDougald could, until a dark day in 1957 when he was involved in the most disturbing on-field accident I have ever witnessed.

Herb Score was a rising star pitcher for the Indians who led the American League in strikeouts in 1955 and was named Rookie of the Year, and in 1956 had won 20 games and started in the All-Star Game. Boston owner Tom Yawkey was so impressed with the young fireballer that he offered the Indians $1 million cash for Score, and Cleveland turned it down. Early in 1957 Score was on the mound at Municipal Stadium against the Yankees when his career was effectively ruined. McDougald, still reaping the benefits of his new batting stance, lashed a line drive back toward the mound that struck Score flush on the right eye. I'll never forget the sound when that ball hit Score's head, like a melon smashing on the ground. Blood poured from Score's eye socket and broken nose and we all feared that Score would lose his vision.

Thankfully, Score regained his eyesight, but while he returned to pitch in 1958, he was never the same hurler. Score retired in 1962 and went into broadcasting and he worked the Indians games for more than 30 years so I saw him frequently and came to know him well. He never had a harsh word for McDougald, and he refused to blame that incident for the deterioration of his career, but McDougald never forgot it.

I remember that night talking to McDougald through a towel that was draped over his head as tears rolled down his cheeks. He swore that if Score was blind, he was going to quit baseball. It didn't come to that, but despite Score's return to health, McDougald continued to be devastated by the accident and like Score, was never the same player. He couldn't wash away the gruesome memory, and while he kept playing, baseball just didn't mean as much to him as it had. It was almost as if McDougald was afraid to hit a ball back through the middle, fearing he might hurt another pitcher, and his average hovered in the .250s thereafter. He retired following the Yankees' loss to Pittsburgh in the 1960 World Series, even though the expansion Los Angeles Angels tried to lure him back with a big-money contract.

"I could have played again, but my heart wasn't in it and I didn't want to start all over again with a new team," he said to me a few years later when he was coaching the baseball team at Fordham University.

His was a career filled with success and personal glory, yet I have always thought McDougald was one of the most overlooked of those 1950s Yankees and there was an incident in 1956 that I offer as evidence. President Eisenhower threw out the first ball on Opening Day at Griffith Stadium and for some reason, McDougald was selected to catch it, a job usually reserved for the catcher. Anyway, McDougald took the ball back to the box seats and asked the president to autograph it, which he did: "To Joe McDougald, Best Wishes."

*   *   *

When the 18-game winning streak came to an end the Yankees were 10 1/2 games ahead of second-place Cleveland, easily the largest lead Stengel had ever enjoyed to that point in his managerial career. It eventually ballooned to 12 and Stengel's record-breaking fifth straight pennant appeared to be a lock, though there were some anxious moments in late June when the team went into an inexplicable nine-game losing streak that whittled the margin back down to five. Every loss came at home, and Stengel took out some of his frustration on the press as he barred us from the clubhouse after the eighth loss. But all was well two days later when Vic Raschi's complete game victory over Boston ended the skid. Stengel lashed into the team after the victory, a 40-minute diatribe that basically laid down the edict that winning was what was expected, and the Yankees better keep doing it.

Stengel got off a good crack against "his writers" when the slump ended. Angered by the predictable negative publicity his closing of the clubhouse generated, Stengel told Arthur Daley of the *Times,* "When we lost nine straight, everything fell apart at once. Our batting was bad, our fielding was bad, our pitching was bad, and our managing was bad. And judging by what I read in the newspapers, the Yankee writers was in a slump, too. They didn't do so good, either." Touché.

Despite their star pitching staff, the Indians couldn't make any headway on the Yankees throughout July and the White Sox moved into second place and were within five games when they came to New York for a four-game set in early August. Chicago manager Paul Richards claimed he had discovered a weakness in the Yankees and he was going to exploit it in this series. Richards never told the press what it was. We asked Stengel what he thought of Richards's proclamation and he replied, "If he's so smart, how come he can't beat the Philadelphia A's?"

Turned out the Yankees didn't have a weakness in this series. They won three of the four games and Chicago was never heard from again.

This Yankee team won 99 games, led the American League in runs scored, fewest runs allowed, batting average, and ERA. Yet over in Brooklyn, the Dodgers—perennial bridesmaids to the Yankees—were being hailed as one of the best teams ever and were considered favorites in the World Series based on their 105 wins in the National League.

The boys over at the *Daily News,* namely my good friend Dick Young and his editor Jimmy Powers, had always been arch enemies of Branch Rickey and they constantly derided the Dodgers in print until Walter O'Malley fired Rickey after the 1950 season. O'Malley hired Buzzie Bavasi to be his general manager with explicit instructions to "get these fellows Powers and Young off our backs. Buy them dinner, buy them suits, buy them a whole wardrobe if you have to. Spend what it takes, just get them off our backs." Nattily attired, the two powerful writers suddenly became mouthpieces for the Dodgers, and it was their opinion that the 1953 Dodgers were finally going to end their frustration in the World Series.

Decades later, Roger Kahn, who covered the Dodgers in 1952 and 1953 for the *Herald Tribune*, wrote a book about this Dodger team called *The Boys of Summer*. I always felt it was an awful lot of hype about a team that, as usual, failed in the clutch. When it came time to play the World Series, the Boys of Summer played like the same old Dodgers of Fall.

– *1953 World Series* –

On a sultry July evening the Yankees were cruising through the streets of Philadelphia on a bus en route from Connie Mack Stadium to the train station following a victory over the Athletics. I was on board, as were the rest of the writers and broadcasters who traveled with the team. We were within a few hundred yards of the station when the driver made what could have been a drastic mistake, pulling into a lane marked "Taxis only." Why was it for cabs only? Because the clearance underneath the trestle wasn't high enough to accommodate a bus. The bus smashed into the overhang, shearing off almost the entire roof and throwing around us occupants like we were pinballs.

Thankfully, no one was seriously hurt. I suffered a bloody gash on my left temple when I was hit by a piece of flying baggage. Yogi Berra and Gene Woodling, who had been standing in the back when the accident occurred, were thrust all the way to the front. Casey Stengel and pitching coach Jim Turner fell into the aisle. A couple of players were cut by glass. And the driver was knocked unconscious when his head slammed into the windshield.

It wasn't until the following day, when Allie Reynolds awoke with terrible pain in his back, that we realized not everyone had escaped unscathed. Reynolds was 38 years old at the time and he didn't have very many big-league seasons left in his powerful right arm. However, the back injury he suffered in this mishap affected his performance thereafter, and it hastened his retirement at the end of the 1954 season, ending one of the greatest careers of any Yankee pitcher.

Reynolds attended what is now Oklahoma State University on a track scholarship and he also was a star running back on the football team in the mid-1930s. Baseball held no interest for him until he began pitching in intramural games to kill time in the spring when a foot injury prevented him from running track. Hank Iba, the legendary basketball coach who also coached baseball at the time, persuaded him to pitch batting practice to his varsity team. Reynolds blew the ball past almost every hitter, and Iba asked him to join the team.

When he graduated in 1939 having won 25 of 27 collegiate decisions, the New York football Giants and baseball's Cleveland Indians inquired about his services, and on Iba's advice, he chose to play baseball and signed with the Indians. After four years in the minors Reynolds didn't exactly set the world on fire when he made it to the Indians, thanks to his propensity for wildness.

At the end of 1946, Yankee president Larry MacPhail was looking to unload Joe Gordon, and knowing Cleveland was in the market for a second baseman, he asked for a pitcher in return. He had his choice between Reynolds, Steve Gromek, or Red Embree, so MacPhail asked Joe DiMaggio for advice and the Jolter said, "Take Reynolds." Even though Reynolds struggled with his control, it was DiMaggio's opinion that you could teach control, but you couldn't teach speed, and Reynolds had plenty of speed. DiMaggio knew pitchers, and he was dead on in his assessment of Reynolds. The man we called Chief played eight years for the Yankees during which time the team won the World Series six times. His record as a Yankee: 131-60 with a 3.30 ERA and 41 saves.

"The Yankees were different," Reynolds once said. "I had been in the major leagues five seasons, but when I was traded to the Yankees it was like going from a church supper to the Stork Club. Playing in New York after playing in Cleveland, at least in those days, was like going from the minor leagues to the majors. I could throw a bad pitch to Bobby Doerr and think base hit, then turn around to see DiMaggio with that easy grace track the ball down as if it were a routine fly. All of the Yankees could make a good pitcher even better."

"Reynolds threw harder than anybody I ever saw," Eddie Lopat said to me one time at an Old-Timers get-together. "Some days he was impossible to hit and his record shows that. Feller had a good fastball, but on a given day for three or four innings Reynolds could throw harder than anyone."

But what ultimately made Reynolds a great pitcher was his acceptance of the theory—espoused first by Spud Chandler and later by Lopat—that pitching wasn't all about throwing smoke. Chandler told him, "Don't just throw the ball, think about what you're doing. Change speeds. Set hitters up. Think, think, think."

Becoming a complete pitcher is what enabled Reynolds to excel in his dual role as a starter and reliever in his last few years. Not only did he save wear and tear on his arm by not trying to throw every pitch through Berra's glove, he gained the confidence necessary to amble into a men-on-base relief situation and put out the fire. "That's the hell of it," Reynolds once said. "You get smart only when you begin getting old."

In the 1952 Series he made four appearances, two as a starter, two as a reliever, and he was credited with one win starting, one win relieving, and one save. Then in the 1953 Series he pitched in three games, saving the fifth game and getting credit for the victory in the clincher as the Yankees set the new standard for baseball excellence by winning their fifth straight championship.

"Reynolds is two ways great, which is starting and relieving, which no one can do like him," Stengel said.

* * *

It looked as if Reynolds was going to have almost no role in the 1953 Series. The bus accident back injury bothered him the rest of the year, and then he tweaked it during his Game One start and had to leave in the sixth inning with a 5-4 lead.

After allowing a solo home run to Gil Hodges and a two-run blast to pinch-hitter George Shuba, Reynolds was rescued by Stengel, and his chance to get the winning decision went by the wayside in the seventh when Johnny Sain yielded three straight singles that allowed Brooklyn to tie the game.

Not that it mattered to Reynolds because Joe Collins homered into the right-field stands to put New York back in front in the bottom of the seventh, and Sain's two-run double in the eighth provided some insurance as the Yankees went on to a 9-5 victory. Winning was all that mattered to Reynolds, not which pitcher was credited with the victory.

"I hurt my back in the third inning and again in the fifth," said Reynolds. "I thought that I had a big enough lead to start the sixth, but I was wrong. I just didn't have it. Pitching past the fifth inning was a mistake—my mistake."

At least he made it that far. Carl Erskine, the ace of the Dodgers staff who had carried the Dodgers to the brink of the 1952 championship with his transcendent 11-inning Game Five performance, was routed for four runs on two hits and three walks in the first inning, and didn't come out to pitch the second inning.

"I was wild, I couldn't get the ball over and some of those I did get over were bad pitches," Erskine said, singling out the two hanging curves he threw to Billy Martin and Hank Bauer that resulted in triples, Martin's a three-run shot that gave the Yankees a 4-0 lead.

Reynolds came back to the park the next day and reported that he had suffered from spasms the night before and that he was still feeling a little stiff, but that he thought he might be able to pitch in a day or two. That was certainly good news for Stengel, and the manager's day only improved when his crafty 35-year-old left-hander, Eddie Lopat, outdueled the Dodgers' crafty 35-year-old left-hander, Preacher Roe, to give the Yankees a two-game lead.

Roe had frustrated the Yankees for six innings, limiting them to two hits, and on the strength of Billy Cox's two-run double in the fourth he led 2-1. But Martin homered to left to tie the game and then Mantle followed a Bauer single with a two-run homer that brought a 4-2 victory.

Now the Dodgers were desperate as they headed back to Brooklyn for the next three games. Manager Chuck Dressen had told Erskine before the Series began that he was going to be his horse and that if need be, he would start him three times. Normally that would entail the first, fourth and, if necessary, seventh games, but having gone only one inning in the opener, the time to come back with Erskine was in Game Three, and Dressen did. It proved to be a smart decision.

Pitching much the way he did in the 1952 Series, Erskine set a new postseason record by striking out 14 Yankees, and the Dodgers won a thriller at Ebbets Field, 3-2.

"I wasn't shooting at any record, all I was aiming to do was get our backs away from the wall," Erskine said in the jubilant clubhouse. "We're still a long way from being home yet, but at least we're moving uphill. If nothing else, at least the Yankees know we're in the Series."

There were two funny things about the strikeout record. Erskine had no idea when he fanned Johnny Mize in the ninth that he had surpassed the old Series mark of 13 set in 1929 by Howard Ehmke of the Athletics. And the fact that Mize was the dubious record-breaker was a hoot because as Mantle told me off the record afterward, Mize had been sitting on the bench the whole game barking at his teammates to stop chasing the low ones. According to Mantle, Mize's refrain was, "How can you guys keep swinging at that pitch in the dirt?" So what did Mize do? He swung at a pitch in the dirt and missed it for strike three. "When he sat down, no one said a word," Mantle said to me, quietly. "But Mize wasn't the only one who couldn't hit the guy. He had good stuff. He put my bat in my back pocket all day."

Like Roe in Game Two, Vic Raschi was a hard-luck loser. The game was tied at 2-2 in the bottom of the eighth when Raschi threw a high fastball to Roy Campanella who crushed it for the game-winning home run. "It wasn't a strike, but I didn't get it high enough and Campy belted it," Raschi said.

The Yankees had just pulled even in the top of the eighth on Woodling's clutch two-out RBI single, only to see Campanella, playing with a sore thumb that made it hard to swing the bat, homer a few minutes later.

The Yankees had made a habit of playing in pressure-packed World Series games. Whitey Ford had not. When he took the mound to start Game Four, he hadn't pitched in the Fall Classic since 1950 when he won the clincher against the Philadelphia Phillies. Further, he had never pitched at Ebbets Field, a notorious horror house for most left-handers.

Just like Erskine in the opener, Ford didn't make it past the first inning. He gave up three runs on three hits and a walk, Stengel sent him to the showers, and two hours later, the rest of the Yankees joined Ford in a somber clubhouse pondering another drag-it-out brawl with the Dodgers. Brooklyn cruised to a 7-3 Series-tying victory as Duke Snider led the way with a two-run double off Ford in the first, a solo homer off Sain in the sixth and a RBI double off Art Schallock in the seventh.

"Whitey was just bad, he didn't have it," Stengel said of his precocious lefty. Ford wasn't apt to agree as he said, "I thought I had good stuff, but I guess not. What else is there to say?"

Nothing, unless you were a Dodger. "Somebody asked me what I thought of our chances in the Series and I said I couldn't answer then," Dressen said, referring to a question that had been posed to him two days earlier when his team was down two games to none. "Now I'd say it's going to be a pretty interesting Series."

This game started badly for the Yankees and never improved. Bauer misjudged Jim Gilliam's leadoff warning track fly to right in the first inning and the ball landed safely and then bounced into the seats for a ground-rule double, touching off a three-run outburst.

Gil McDougald's two-run homer off Billy Loes in the fourth brought the Yankees within 4-2, but the Dodgers put it away with two runs in the sixth when Snider homered and Cox, who had doubled, scored on Gilliam's liner to right.

It had been Stengel's plan to go with Reynolds in Game Five, but the Chief's back condition forced Stengel to reach into the bullpen and use a second-line starter, Jim McDonald, in the pivotal game of the Series. Erskine's flameout in the opener had Dressen's rotation off-kilter, too, and he had a decision to make. Go with young Johnny Podres, a 21-year-old rookie left-hander who had won nine games during the regular season, to combat the Yankees left-hand power hitters, or veteran righty Russ Meyer. Meyer had come over from Philadelphia in the off-season and played a major role, winning 15 of 20 decisions. Meyer fully expected to be starting, and was admittedly aggravated when he received word that Podres was getting the nod. "You trade for a guy, I start for him all year and win 15 ballgames, and I can't start in the Series because he's a big believer in percentages," Meyer said. Who knows what would have happened had Meyer started, but he didn't, and the Yankees jumped on young Podres for five runs inside three innings and rolled to an 11-7 victory.

It was 1-1 in the third when the roof caved in on Podres. With Phil Rizzuto on third and two out, Collins hit a grounder to Hodges at first that should have ended the inning, but Gil Hodges booted the ball and Rizzuto scored. Podres then hit Bauer with a pitch and walked Berra to load the bases, so Dressen decided now was the time to bring in the veteran, Meyer, to face Mantle. His last piece of advice before trotting back to the dugout was, "Make him hit your curveball," because Erskine had struck out Mantle four times in Game Three, all with his curve. Meyer's first pitch was a curve on the outer half of the plate. Mantle, batting left-handed, took a mighty swing and launched the ball on a majestic flight out toward left-center for a grand slam.

My friend, Roger Kahn, recalled in *The Boys of Summer* that the ball "sailed and sailed, carried and carried, high into the upper deck, landing with such force some claimed to have heard the sound of furniture splintering. That sort of thing just didn't happen, a left-handed batter reaching the upper deck in left-center at Ebbets Field. Not many right-handed batters could clout a ball that far. I remember sitting in the press box in disbelief."

I remember feeling the same way.

Meyer was heartsick after the game. "When you throw your best pitch and a guy hits it like that Mantle did, then there's just nothing you can do about it," he said.

I saw Meyer down in Florida during spring training a few years after he had retired and I asked him about that home run and he said, "I believe it was the hardest and longest ball ever hit off me."

The score ballooned to 10-2 as Martin hit a two-run homer in the seventh, and when McDonald encountered difficulty in the eighth, Bob

Kuzava and Reynolds closed it out for him. "Before the game I promised myself I'd win this one if I never did anything else in my life," McDonald said. "Winning was the biggest kick I've ever gotten out of baseball. It wasn't so long ago I was pitching for the St. Louis Browns and I never dreamed of working in a World Series."

Down on the field before the start of the sixth game at Yankee Stadium, I was chatting with Martin while he waited his turn at the batting cage. Brash as ever, Martin said, "The Dodgers are the Dodgers. If they had eight Babe Ruths they couldn't beat us."

Hours later, after Martin had delivered a Series-winning RBI single in the bottom of the ninth to give New York a 4-3 victory, Martin remembered what he had told me and repeated it for the masses crowded around his locker. Oh well, it would have been a nice quote to have all to myself.

It was a ninth inning that was not soon forgotten by anyone who was there. Before Martin stepped into the hero's role, Carl Furillo had lifted the spirits of Brooklyn with a dramatic game-tying two-run homer off Reynolds. But as Martin said, the Dodgers were the Dodgers. Clem Labine, the third Brooklyn pitcher, walked Bauer to start the bottom of the ninth. Berra lined to right, but Mantle legged out an infield hit with Bauer advancing to second. Martin then stepped up and slapped a 1-1 pitch over second base, his 12th hit of the Series which tied an all-time record, and Bauer rumbled home with the clinching run as the crowd went berserk and the Yankee dugout emptied onto the field in celebration.

"When I crossed first base and realized that we had won, a thousand sensations seemed to pass through my body all at once," said Martin. "I just couldn't believe it. Now I know how Bobby Thomson felt when he hit that pennant-winning home run against Brooklyn. He said he didn't run around the bases that day, he rode around them on a cloud. Believe me, the cloud I was on after that hit was higher than Thomson's."

In the gloom of the Brooklyn clubhouse, Dressen was heard to mutter, "We was beaten by a .257 hitter." That was Martin's batting average during the regular season, but he had drummed the Dodgers to the tune of .500. Stengel said with a chuckle, "That's the worst thing that coulda happened to Martin. I ain't going to be able to live with that little son of a bitch next year."

Rather than pitch Lopat, who was ready to go, Stengel played a hunch that Ford would rebound from his disastrous outing in Game Four and he gave the youngster a mulligan. Ford went seven innings, allowed just six hits and one run and left the game with a 3-1 lead. As sound a choice as starting Ford was, his removal of Ford in favor of Reynolds was terrible, and Stengel was lucky it didn't cost him the game.

"I was not tired and when Casey removed me I was on the angry side," said Ford. "Anyway, we won and that's the most important thing."

"I figured Reynolds with a two-run lead would hold it for two innings," said Stengel. He didn't, but Martin took the manager off the hook.

It was supposed to be the Dodgers' year. That's what we had all been led to believe. And while their time would eventually come, this was still the Yankees' time. "I'm afraid nobody can sell me on their being lucky," Erskine said that day. "A team that wins as often as they do has to have something more than luck. They're a good ball club."

When he was interviewed by Peter Golenbock for *Bums,* Erskine reflected sadly on the Dodgers' frustrations. "Those suckers were tough," he said. "I don't know if psychologically there was a difference, or whether Yankee tradition played a part, I don't know what it was, but there was a fine line there somehow."

On the 20th anniversary of Brooklyn's first and only World Series champi-onship, I tracked down Sandy Amoros to get his recollections of the historic Game Seven victory he had helped deliver to the Dodgers at the expense of the Yankees in 1955. Amoros didn't know what all the fuss was about.

"When I see my catch, I feel good," Amoros said of the spectacular running grab he made near the foul line in left field in the sixth inning at Yankee Sta-dium. "Everybody talks about my catch, but for me, that was not the thrill. It all was. I never dreamed that I would play in the major leagues. It still makes me feel good. That was just one play that other people made a big deal out of."

Well, for the hearty souls of Brooklyn, there was plenty to make a big deal out of.

With the Dodgers clinging to a precarious 2-0 lead, Yogi Berra threatened to erase that deficit when he lifted a fly ball into the left-field corner with nobody out and two runners aboard. The lefty-swinging Berra was a dead pull hitter and Amoros was playing him toward the alley in left-center, so naturally he and everyone else was surprised when Berra's fly ball angled down the line. But Amoros got a great jump, raced into the corner at full speed, and with the entire borough of Brooklyn holding its collective breath, he made a spearing catch just before it landed about five feet inside the foul line.

Billy Martin, who was playing it safe on second base, retreated easily, but Gil McDougald wasn't so fortunate. He had run all the way to second before realizing he had to turn around and go back to first. Amoros fired a perfect relay to shortstop Pee Wee Reese, and the 36-year-old Dodger shortstop and captain turned and threw a rope back to first baseman Gil Hodges, doubling up McDougald.

"I didn't think Amoros would catch that ball," McDougald said. "I thought he might shy away from the left-field fence. I know this much, if Amoros hadn't caught the ball, I would have scored from first."

Said Berra: "I don't see how Amoros caught the ball. If he misses, we have two runs and I'm on third with none out."

Hank Bauer grounded out to end the inning with the Dodgers still two runs ahead. Brooklyn starter Johnny Podres was never in trouble again and when Elston Howard grounded out to Reese with two outs in the bottom of the ninth, the Brooklyn curse—winless in seven previous World Series appearances *including the last five at the hands of the hated Yankees—had been broken. That fine line Carl Erskine had talked about had finally been crossed.*

Amoros told me that many people had stopped him through the years and told him they remembered his catch, and he always found himself mildly surprised that people still recalled the play. But he had no trouble recounting it.

"I ran as fast as I could and stretched as far as my arm would go and made the catch with the tip of my glove," he said. "Another two inches and that ball was gone."

And given their history, gone, too, may have been Brooklyn's dream of finally winning the Series. The Dodgers had dropped the first two games at Yankee Stadium, and history told us that no team had ever rallied to win a Series after falling in a 2-0 hole.

But the Dodgers returned to Ebbets Field, swept three in a row, and rode the subway back to the Bronx needing just one victory to end their misery. In Game Six, a five-run first-inning mauling of Brooklyn pitcher Karl Spooner gave Whitey Ford more support than he needed in the Yankees' 5-1 victory, setting up the deciding seventh game at Yankee Stadium.

Tommy Byrne started for New York and he held the Dodgers hitless through three innings, but in the fourth, Roy Campanella doubled into the left-field corner, and eventually scored on Hodges's single, and in the sixth the count rose to 2-0 when Reese opened with a single and eventually scored on Hodges's sacrifice fly. Pinch-hitter George Shuba grounded out with the bases loaded so the Dodgers failed to blow the game open, but Brooklyn manager Walter Alston's decision to bat Shuba for second baseman Don Zimmer paid huge dividends a few minutes later.

With Zimmer out of the game, Alston brought Jim Gilliam in from left field to play second base in place of Zimmer, and he sent Amoros out to left field to start the sixth inning.

Of Berra's fly into the corner Gilliam admitted, "I never would have caught it." For once, the gods were smiling on Brooklyn.

– Chapter 17 –

1956

IT MUST HAVE BEEN A MONTH OR SO after the Yankees lost to the Dodgers when I encountered a man named Harold. My association with Harold lasted approximately 30 seconds, but I have never forgotten him. I know his name only because he approached me one day when I was in a grocery store a few blocks from my home and introduced himself. I have never forgotten him because of what he said to me. Somehow he knew that I covered the Yankees for the *Post*, and as a self-proclaimed "huge" fan of the team, I guess he felt an obligation to share with me the reason he thought the Dodgers had finally broken their World Series curse against the Yankees in 1955.

"Ya know," Harold began, "the Yankees never lost to them Bums before they got that nigger on their team. As soon as they get the nigger, they lose." I wanted to punch that racist prick right in the face, but I thought better of it and just walked away shaking my head without telling him that Elston Howard, the first man black man to wear the Yankee pinstripes, was one of the finest men I knew.

Sadly, Harold probably wasn't alone in his thinking. Racial tension in this country was a serious problem in the 1950s, especially when African-Americans began standing up for their rights, reasoning that if they were worthy enough to fight and die for our country, they should be allowed to attend the same schools, eat at the same restaurants, and drink from the same water fountains as white people. In 1954 when the Supreme Court declared segregation in public schools unconstitutional, and later in 1955 when Rosa Parks refused to give up her seat on a Montgomery, Alabama, city bus to a white man, many irrational white people rebelled, and the resulting race riots tore our nation apart.

In baseball, Jackie Robinson had broken the color barrier in 1947, and most teams had black players on their rosters by the early 1950s. The Yankees did not, so the organization was perceived as racist, and, truth be told, it was an accurate charge. It was widely known that general manager George Weiss did not want black players on the Yankees, so there weren't. It was only when the pressure became too great, or in Weiss's view when a black player was good enough to play for the Yankees, that Weiss relented and brought Howard up to the club in 1955.

That year I saw first-hand what racism really was. Howard was not allowed to stay with the rest of the team at the Soreno Hotel, so he boarded with a family in the black section of St. Petersburg. At the end of the spring the team barnstormed through Alabama on its way north and because an Alabama ordinance prevented white players from competing against black players, Weiss opted against canceling the game and instead told Howard he couldn't play. And on the team's first western road trip, Howard was banned from the team hotels in Chicago and Kansas City.

When James Wechsler, the editor of the *Post*, heard about that last transgression, he assigned my colleague, Ted Poston, a black civil-rights reporter, to travel with the team on the second trip out west with instructions to room with Howard and report on every injustice the player faced. Weiss rebutted immediately and denied Poston permission to travel with the team because he wasn't an accredited baseball writer, so Poston quickly gained his accreditation. Then Weiss said reporters weren't allowed to room with players, so Poston said he wouldn't room with him, but he was still coming. Fearing the negative publicity, Weiss realized he had to make things right. He grudgingly called the hotels in Chicago and Kansas City and demanded Howard be accepted or the team would stay elsewhere. The hotels agreed, and the *Post* backed down and did not send Poston on the trip.

I never had much of a working relationship with Weiss, but whatever cooperation I and the other *Post* baseball writers received from Weiss ceased from that point on, and I'm sure he took his anger over this incident to his grave.

Born in St. Louis, Howard was a four-sport high school star who turned down college scholarship offers to pursue a professional baseball career, thinking Robinson's entrance into the major leagues would open the floodgates for other black players. The Yankees purchased his contract from the Kansas City Monarchs of the Negro Leagues, but Weiss had done so merely to show that the team had black prospects in the minor leagues. He never wanted to bring Howard or Vic Power or Artie Wilson to New York. Howard's stellar performance forced the issue.

He starred for one year at the Class-A level, and after a two-year military hitch he returned to baseball in 1953 with Triple-A Kansas City. In the spring of 1954 Stengel saw that Howard was too slow to play the outfield full-time so he asked Bill Dickey to perform the same miracle he had on Yogi Berra. By switching Howard to catcher, Stengel was bashed in the press because it was thought the Yankees—knowing Berra was in his prime—were purposely trying to bury Howard in the system. Stengel was furious over the accusation and said, "His best chance to make the major leagues is as a catcher, and I've got news for you, he's going to be a great catcher. With the proper amount of experience he can be tremendous."

There was plenty of teeth gnashing, but none of it was coming from Howard. I interviewed Howard that spring to gauge his interest in becoming a catcher and he said, "I'll try anything, I just want to play in the big leagues. I don't see why there has to be all this fuss about me being changed to a catcher. If Casey Stengel thinks I've got a better chance to make the big leagues as a catcher, then I'm willing to stick with that job."

I then asked Dickey what he thought of his new student, and Dickey agreed with Stengel: The kid had a chance to be very good. "It's going to take him a little while to master the knack of handling low pitches, but he's going to get it," Dickey said. "Aside from that, there isn't anything else he can't do pretty well right now."

When Howard tore up the International league playing for Toronto in 1954, winning the league MVP award, Weiss could no longer keep him in the minors. Howard made the Yankees in 1955 and as a reserve catcher, outfielder, and pinch-hitter he batted .290 and started all seven games in left field against the Dodgers in the World Series.

Fortunately for Howard, the Yankee players did not follow Weiss's lead. None of them had a problem with a black player joining the team and they treated Howard with respect just as they would any other player. I wondered about the team's moral compass that first spring in 1955 when no one made a stink over the fact that Howard couldn't stay at the team hotel. But I also recognized that the players were merely mimicking our segregated society.

One of the more heartwarming scenes I witnessed occurred early in Howard's rookie season after he'd hit a game-winning triple in the bottom of the ninth. He entered the clubhouse and found a row of towels leading from the door to his locker. "It was like the red carpet treatment,"

Howard recalled. "When they did that, I figured I was accepted just like anyone else. No one in the Yankee organization made me conscious of my color."

Howard was a perfect fit for Stengel's platoon system because he provided the manager with options. He could catch, play left or right field and first base, and that was his role until Berra finally began to slow down in 1960 and Howard became the primary catcher. Howard was such a fine player he was chosen to play in the All-Star game nine straight years (1957–1965), even though the first half of that stint he wasn't even a regular starter for the Yankees.

"You can substitute, but you can rarely replace, and with Howard I have a replacement, not a substitute," said Stengel.

When the Yankees beat the Braves in the 1958 World Series, Howard was the key player and though Bob Turley won the official MVP award, we in the Baseball Writers Association of America chose Howard. In 1963 he became the first black player to win the American League MVP award.

Though it wasn't his intention, nor the team's, Howard became the perfect man to at long last integrate the Yankees. "The Yankees claimed they were waiting for the right man," outfielder Norm Siebern said. "In retrospect, you'd have to say they couldn't have done better. He had great morals, personality, and character. He was just an outstanding individual."

Instead of walking away, that's what I should have said to Harold that day in the grocery store.

*   *   *

There was a noticeable edge to spring training when the Yankees convened in St. Petersburg in 1956. It had now been two years without World Series bonus checks, an unthinkable drought for a team that had previously achieved five championships in a row. In 1954 the Yankees had won 103 games, the most ever for a Casey Stengel team, yet they didn't even win the pennant as Cleveland set what was then the all-time American League record for victories with 111 before tanking to the Giants in the World Series.

And then there was 1955, and the horror of losing the Series to the — gasp! — Dodgers.

It was one thing to lose the World Series to the Cardinals, which they had done in 1926 and 1942. It was an entirely different matter losing to the Dodgers. The atmosphere in the locker room following the Game

Seven loss to Brooklyn was funereal, and teary-eyed Billy Martin pointed at Stengel and told the press, "It's a shame for a great manager like that to have to lose," defining the anguish the Yankees were dealing with.

The Yankees were always on a mission to win the Series, but what made the 1956 quest so distinct was that for the first time, they would be chasing the hated Dodgers for supremacy. The Dodgers had done what for so long had been undoable and unthinkable: They had won the championship, and now it was the Yankees who would have to "Wait 'til next year."

The Yankees didn't like the sound of that.

I sat down with Mickey Mantle one night at a restaurant in St. Petersburg and we talked at length about what had happened the year before. Mantle had been a spare part in that Series due to a leg injury, and he admitted that it bothered him the whole off-season knowing that if he had been healthy, he might have been the difference between winning and losing. He also told me that he was unhappy in New York City and asked me, "Why can't these fucking fans get off my back, Joe?" Even though he had won his first home run crown in 1955 by hitting 37, he was being booed on a regular basis in Yankee Stadium, and he didn't understand why.

I told him why I thought that was. With all the hype surrounding his arrival in New York, the fans had expected much more than Mantle had delivered. Mantle—due in large part to Stengel's constant raving about him—was looked upon as the heir to Joe DiMaggio's throne, and in the fans' eyes, he hadn't lived up to that enormous responsibility.

"What more do they want, we've won the World Series three times in the five years I've been here," Mantle said. I replied, "Mickey, that's not good enough. I know it's not fair, but they're always going to compare you to DiMaggio. Last year was the first time you hit more than 30 home runs in a season. DiMaggio did it seven times. You've only had one year when you topped 100 RBI. DiMaggio did that his first seven years and nine times overall. You struck out more in your first four years than DiMaggio did his whole career."

He rolled his eyes and said, "Joe, I'm never going to be able to do the things DiMaggio did, we're different ballplayers."

"Mickey, I know that and you know that, but the guy in the stands sees you hit the ball 500 feet and he thinks you should do that every time you come up to the plate. And the other thing that bothers the fans is that you don't acknowledge them. You run around the bases with your head down, you don't smile very often, you don't tip your cap, and you don't like talking to most of the writers so the fans don't ever see you quoted in the paper. They feel like they don't know you."

As I spoke he sat there listening intently, nodding his head, but I knew nothing was going to change. He was still a shy country kid who was embarrassed by all the attention he received and he wasn't ready to open up and let Gotham see who he really was. But he was ready to have his breakout season.

This was not good news for the rest of the American League. The Yankees were already very good, and now with this Dodger-induced incentive to win, plus the emergence of Mantle as a true superstar, they were nearly untouchable. Stengel's men won seven of their first eight games and by May 16 they were on top for good. They ultimately outdistanced Cleveland by nine comfortable games to capture their seventh pennant in Stengel's eight years.

Washington was the first team to feel the wrath of the Yankees, dropping a 10-4 Opening Day decision as Mantle hit two prodigious home runs over the distant center-field fence at Griffith Stadium, the first player to clear that barrier twice in one game.

"I only saw one ball hit over that fence before," Yankee coach Bill Dickey said, "and that was by the Babe. Mantle's got more power than any hitter I ever saw, including the Babe."

So began one of the most productive individual seasons in major league history. This is what the fans expected, and though Mantle remained reclusive, the fans stopped booing as all his otherworldly talents meshed in a harmonic symphony of brilliance during 1956. Mantle led the American League in average (.353), home runs (52), and RBI (130) to win the triple crown, a feat that has been accomplished only 13 times in major league history, never by DiMaggio. Even more impressive, Mantle led the majors in all three categories, something only Rogers Hornsby (1925), Lou Gehrig (1934), and Ted Williams (1942) have done.

"He can hit better than anyone else, he can field better than anyone else, he can throw better than anyone else. What else is there?" Baltimore manager Paul Richards said.

By Memorial Day Mantle was hitting .425 and his 20 homers put him 11 games ahead of Babe Ruth's 60-home run pace in 1927. Despite Mantle's heroics, the Yankees couldn't shake Chicago and at the end of June, the White Sox—thanks to a four-game sweep over the Yankees at Comiskey Park—were within two games of the lead.

Mantle missed about a week of action just before the All-Star break with a knee injury, but he played in the annual classic, hit a home run, then resumed his mauling of the American League. The White Sox wilted under the barrage of an 11-game Yankee winning streak, by August the pennant race was pretty much decided, and the focus shone brightly on Mantle's pursuit of Ruth and the triple crown. On August 1 he led in all three requisite categories with a .368 average, 34 homers and 89 RBI, and nothing changed as the calendar advanced into September.

However, his home run pace slowed in the final weeks of the season and he hit only five round-trippers to finish with 52, eight behind Ruth. More worrisome to Stengel wasn't that Mantle had lost his home run stroke, he had lost his hitting stroke, and with the World Series on the horizon, Stengel needed his star to get back into form. Stengel and coach Bill Dickey pulled him aside, told him to calm down and stop putting so much pressure on himself, and they worked on his swing.

The Yankees clinched the pennant on September 18 with Mantle hitting his 50th home run of the season in the 11th inning to beat Chicago. At that moment he led the league in homers and RBI, but trailed Ted Williams of the Red Sox in average by five points. He went on a binge in Boston to surpass Williams, and then he appeared only as a pinch-hitter in five of the last six games as Stengel insisted he rest his sore legs for the Series. Williams nearly caught him in the batting race, and Detroit's Al Kaline inched close in the RBI race, but neither player could overtake him.

"I was very conscious of it the last week," Mantle said of his quest for the triple crown. "To be honest I even dreamed about it at night. It was certainly nerve-wracking."

In his book *All My Octobers,* Mantle wrote, "Winning the triple crown was the highlight (of my career). But perhaps more important, 1956 was the first time I accomplished the things that had been predicted for me, and I finally established myself in the major leagues."

And he got the fans off his back.

The Yankees were itching for a rematch with the Dodgers, and when Brooklyn beat the Pirates on the last day of the season to secure the National League pennant by a scant one game over Milwaukee, the rematch was on. Little did we know this would be the last Subway Series of the century, and the last, period, for the folks in Brooklyn.

– *1956 World Series* –

Casey Stengel stood in the visitors' clubhouse at Ebbets Field, steam billowing from his floppy ears as he talked to the press following the

Yankees' embarrassing 13-8 loss to Brooklyn in Game Two of the 1956 World Series.

"I'll tell you what's really wrong with our pitchers," Stengel said. "They're making the wrong pitches. They're throwing exactly what they shouldn't be throwing."

After dropping Game One, 6-3, the Yankees had ripped Dodger ace Don Newcombe for six runs in the first two innings and seemed well on their way to evening the Series before heading back to the Bronx for the next three games. But Brooklyn responded with six runs in the bottom of the second to tie the score, and none of the Series-record seven pitchers Stengel ultimately used were able to derail the Dodgers' potent offense thereafter.

"If they could have got out the right men in the right spots, it might have been different today," Stengel said of his beleaguered mound staff.

One man Stengel was particularly angry with was starter Don Larsen. He walked four, gave up one single, a long sacrifice fly, and was hurt by first baseman Joe Collins's error which meant the four runs he allowed were unearned. Although all the damage wasn't Larsen's fault, the Indiana native wasn't sharp, Stengel knew it, and he had yanked him in the second inning.

The Yankees' pitching woes dissipated over the next two days as Whitey Ford and Tom Sturdivant turned in back-to-back complete game victories at Yankee Stadium to deadlock the Series at two games apiece. But in the critical fifth game, rather than use Johnny Kucks, who had won 18 games in the regular season, Stengel turned to the unpredictable Larsen, and the defending champion Dodgers couldn't think of anyone they would rather be facing.

"He was no problem for us in Game Two and I really figured that while the Yankees were tough hitters, I would probably win the game because we could score all day against Larsen," Sal Maglie, the Dodgers' Game Five starter, told me a year later after he had been sold to the Yankees.

The Dodgers couldn't score against Larsen. They couldn't hit against Larsen. They couldn't even draw a walk off Larsen. Twenty-seven men faced the tall right-hander, and 27 men trooped back to the dugout with their heads down as Larsen pitched the first and only perfect game in World Series history.

* * *

"I still find it hard to believe I really pitched the perfect game," Larsen has said for more than four decades. "It's almost like a dream, like something that happened to somebody else."

The day it happened, Larsen wasn't the only one who couldn't believe it. Joe Trimble, with an assist from his comrade at the *Herald Tribune,* the great Red Smith, summed up the occasion succinctly when he wrote, "The imperfect man just threw a perfect game."

This was one of those performances that simply defied all logic. Larsen was the last guy in the world you would have expected to make history, unless the competition was carousing.

Two years before Larsen had fashioned one of the worst pitching records ever (3-21) for a bad Baltimore team, which prompted this remark on the back of his 1955 bubble gum card: "It is safe to say that Big Don would have won more games with a better hitting team behind him."

Then again, maybe not. He'd won his final four decisions of the 1956 regular season to finish 11-5, yet he still brought a deficient 30-40 lifetime mark into his surprise Game Five assignment. And beyond the perfect game, Larsen went on to win 51 games and lose 51 games before retiring in 1967. He was never more than an average pitcher no matter what team he played on. But for two hours on the sunny afternoon of October 8, 1956, he was the best pitcher who ever lived.

Larsen began his career in 1947 and after four years in the minors and two years in the military, he finally made it to the majors in 1953 with the St. Louis Browns, where he went 7-12 for the worst team in the American League. The Browns moved to Baltimore in 1954 and became the Orioles, but a change of scenery did them no good. They lost 100 games and Larsen was tagged with just over one-fifth of those defeats. Incredibly, two of his three wins came against the Yankees, and when the Yankees and Orioles concocted a blockbuster 18-player trade, Larsen was included in the package that was shipped off to New York.

"I figure maybe if I hadn't gone 3-21, I wouldn't have been a Yankee at all," he said.

In 1955 he spent half the season in Triple-A Kansas City, but he returned to the Yankees when the team released longtime star Eddie Lopat in late July. He went 9-2 and drew the start in Game Four of the Series where he pitched poorly and was beaten by the Dodgers.

At the start of 1956 Larsen's reputation as a party animal had become well-known. His former manager with the Orioles, Jimmy Dykes, once said, "The only thing Larsen fears is sleep." Larsen didn't help matters when, in a celebrated incident during spring training, he wrapped his brand new Oldsmobile around a telephone pole in St. Petersburg and quipped, "The pole was speeding." Upon hearing the news, Stengel said, "Where he was going and what he was doing remains a mystery, but he couldn't have done it in a museum."

On a number of occasions Mantle, a man as proficient a drinker as he was a home run hitter, told me, "That Larsen can throw 'em back. I've never seen a guy drink the way he can."

Stengel was convinced that if Larsen would have stopped drinking and started dedicating himself to baseball, he could have been a star. One day when Stengel was holding court in the dugout before a game he pointed in Larsen's direction and said, "See that big feller out there. He can throw, he can hit, he can field and he can run. He can be one of baseball's great pitchers anytime he puts his mind to it."

During the regular season Larsen was his usual erratic self. He'd pitch good one game, lousy the next, and he was growing so frustrated he said to a group of writers, "The hell with it, if things don't get better for me soon I'm going to join the Navy."

Shortly thereafter Larsen began experimenting with a no-windup pitching motion and his fortunes—at least for 1956—changed. He went on his mini-winning streak and that was enough to earn the start in Game Two against Brooklyn. After his flameout, though, it was hard to imagine Stengel would come back with him in Game Five, and Larsen knew it.

Legend has it that Larsen, thinking he was done for the Series, went out the night before his perfect game, drank heavily, and didn't stumble back home until the wee hours of the morning. He then went to the ballpark and looking through fogged-over eyes, found the practice ball in his shoe placed there by coach Frank Crosetti indicating he was that day's starting pitcher.

I've heard about five different versions of what really happened, and I was glad that Don wrote a book a couple years ago—*The Perfect Yankee*—where he came clean about his whereabouts that night. He swears he ate dinner and had a couple of beers with his friend, Arthur Richman, at a bar owned by former Giants outfielder Bill Taylor, and he was back at the Concourse Plaza Hotel—where he lived that year—before midnight.

I've never talked to him about it, so I don't really know the truth. But I do know the part about finding the ball in his shoe was true, because that was the routine. Stengel had made up his mind the night before the game to go with Larsen, but he decided not to tell him, perhaps sparing him a nervous night.

As they say, Larsen took that ball and ran with it.

Jim Gilliam struck out to start the game, and Pee Wee Reese, Brooklyn's second batter, did the same. Reese's appearance would be the longest any Dodger would stand in the batter's box all day as he worked Larsen to a full count before looking at strike three. That was the only three-ball count Larsen would be faced with.

In the bottom of the first, Maglie, a ferocious competitor who, even at the age of 39, could still bring it and had gone 13-5 in the regular season, let it be known that he had his best stuff as he zipped through the Yankee order.

Two weeks before the Series Maglie had thrown a no-hitter against Philadelphia in a pressure-packed pennant race game. And in Game One five days earlier, he had handcuffed the Yankees during a complete game victory.

Maglie and Larsen matched perfection through 3 1/2 innings before Maglie made a mistake, and it was all Larsen would need. He hung a two-out curveball to Mantle, and as Maglie said, "Mantle just blasted it for a home run. It was a curve that broke, I'd say, right over the middle of the plate."

The large crowd stirred in the fifth when Gil Hodges lifted a deep fly to left-center which Mantle ran down with a backhanded catch. "I caught up with it at the last instant and made the grab over my shoulder—as good a catch as I ever made," Mantle said. The next hitter, Sandy Amoros, roped a certain home run down the right-field line, but the ball hooked foul just before it reached the seats. Amoros eventually grounded meekly to second.

After a much more comfortable sixth, Larsen was given an added cushion in the bottom half of the inning. Andy Carey led off with a single and Larsen sacrificed him to second. Hank Bauer then singled to left to chase Carey home and it was 2-0 New York. Maglie allowed Collins to single, but he snuffed out the uprising when Bauer's base-running blunder resulted in a double play.

Gilliam hit a hard one-hopper to short to open the seventh, but Gil McDougald made the play flawlessly, and Reese and Duke Snider flied out to end the inning.

"Some time during the sixth or seventh inning I realized I had not allowed a man to reach first base," Larsen remembered. "The guys on the bench wouldn't even look at me when we were batting. Everyone was nervous, afraid of breaking the no-hitter or jinxing it."

Said Maglie: "By the seventh, I was still pitching a great game and we were down 2-0 and it dawned on us that Larsen was pitching a smooth game and we didn't have a hit. Then we realized he hadn't given up a walk. It kind of snuck up on us."

It hadn't snuck up on the 64,519 fans. Everyone knew what was happening and the stadium rocked with every out Larsen chalked up. As Arthur Daley wrote in the *New York Times,* "The crowd seemed to get a mass realization of the wonders that were being unfolded. Tension kept mounting until it was as brittle as an electric light bulb."

In the eighth Jackie Robinson grounded back to Larsen, third baseman Carey caught Hodges's low liner, and Amoros struck out, leaving Larsen three outs away from eminence.

Carl Furillo worked Larsen hard to start the ninth, fouling off four pitches, but he finally succumbed on a fly to right. Roy Campanella followed with a grounder to Billy Martin at second, and that brought Dale Mitchell, pinch-hitting for Maglie, to the plate as the last Dodger hope.

"He really scared me," Larsen said of Mitchell. "I knew how much pressure he was under. He must have been paralyzed. That made two of us. I'm not what you'd really call a praying man, but once I was out there in the ninth inning I said to myself 'Help me out, somebody.'"

Plate umpire Babe Pinelli, calling the final game of his 24-year-career, provided that help. After looking at a ball, Mitchell took a strike, swung at a fastball and missed, then fouled the next offering into the stands leaving the count 1-2. Mitchell considered swinging at Larsen's 97th and final pitch of the game, but he deemed it to be a bit outside and checked his swing. Pinelli thought otherwise and called Mitchell out on strikes to end the game.

"Pinelli seemed to take an extra split second, then raised his arm for strike three and the final out," Mantle recalled. "I had a clear view from center field, and if I was under oath, I'd have to say the pitch looked like it was outside."

It didn't matter what Mantle thought. Pinelli punched out Mitchell, Berra jumped into Larsen's arms, and baseball had another landmark moment courtesy of the Yankees.

"When Dale Mitchell checked his swing for a called strike three to end the game and Yogi jumped into Larsen's arms and the perfect game was history, we didn't have a sense of how important it was," Maglie said. "It didn't seem like he threw a no-hitter or a perfect game. The fact that no one else has done it in nearly 100 World Series makes me proud that I was a part of it. I just wish I had thrown it and not Larsen."

The clubhouse scene was a zoo. I had never seen more reporters congregated in one area in my life. With all the bulbs flashing from the still cameras, the lights from the TV cameras, and the writers screaming over each other to ask questions, it was complete chaos. But wow, was it ever fun, especially when one rookie reporter, who shall remain nameless, was so caught up in the excitement he actually asked Larsen: "Is that the best game you ever pitched?"

*   *   *

The Series opened at Ebbets Field under glorious sunshine with Mantle belting a two-run homer off Maglie in the first inning and all of Brooklyn feared painful retribution from 1955. However, by the end of the third inning the Dodgers had tagged Ford for five runs on the strength of a solo homer by Robinson and a two-run blast by Hodges. With Maglie baffling the Yankees the rest of the way, Game One turned into a frustrating 6-3 defeat for New York.

After a day of rain, Larsen took the mound for Game Two and it looked like he'd be in for an easy day. Berra's grand slam highlighted a five-run second inning which put the Yankees ahead 6-0, but then came Brooklyn's six-run response, followed by seven more runs courtesy of 12 hits and 11 walks from Yankee pitchers.

Brooklyn's first six runs were unearned, a point that Stengel recognized, but he added, "Sure the error by Collins hurt. That put the second man on. But who put the first man on? And who didn't get out the others they should have gotten out? The pitching was to blame, not Collins."

For only the second time in their history, and not since 1922, the Yankees had lost the first two games of a World Series. Game Three was a must-win, Stengel knew it, and even though he was unhappy with the way Ford had pitched in the opener, Stengel turned to Ford.

It was games such as this that built Ford's legend. When the Yankees had to win, Ford almost always delivered, and he did so here with a complete-game eight-hitter, the 5-3 victory secured when the ageless Enos Slaughter—a longtime National League star who had been acquired in a roster-bolstering move late in the season—whacked a three-run homer in the sixth.

Joe DiMaggio was in the press box because he was writing an "expert" column for one of the wire services, and he made an interesting observation to me after the game was over. "In my column I'm going to point out the difference in Ford's pitching there and here," DiMaggio said, referring to the two vastly different ballparks. "He didn't seem to be worrying about the fences today like he seemed to be in Brooklyn."

Down in the clubhouse I asked Whitey if Joe's inference was correct, and he said it was. "The difference between the two ballparks is this," Ford said. "When spectators come to Ebbets Field they're all equipped with fielder's gloves. When they come to the Stadium, they bring binoculars."

The sense of urgency for the Yankees didn't change much the next day. They still couldn't afford to lose and fall into a 3-1 hole, so the pressure was on young Sturdivant to beat Carl Erskine, and he did. Like Ford, Sturdivant went all the way, giving up six hits and six walks. He wasn't always pretty, but with Mantle hitting a solo homer in the sixth and Bauer ripping a two-run homer in the seventh, Sturdivant had more than enough support to gain the 6-2 victory.

Stengel, as only Stengel could, summed up the day when he said, "This Series is more even now than it was."

Larsen's gem put the Yankees up three games to two, and as Mantle said, "The celebration for Larsen rivaled any seventh-game victory party." But now they had to somehow come back down to earth and win the clincher, and they had to do it back at Ebbets Field. "It's hard to believe," Bauer said of Larsen's perfect game. "And it's hard to realize we have another game tomorrow."

Though neither Bob Turley for the Yankees nor Clem Labine for the Dodgers pitched a no-hitter or perfect game, both pitched magnificently during a tense, scoreless struggle that wasn't decided until Robinson's single to right in the bottom of the 10th plated Gilliam with the only run. In tying the Series and forcing a seventh game, the Dodgers broke Turley's heart. He allowed only four hits and set a new Yankee postseason record with 11 strikeouts.

"I pitched the best game of my major league career, but we didn't score any runs off Labine," said Turley. "I did everything right, keeping the ball in the park at Ebbets Field."

Stengel was spellbound by the randomness by which baseball chose its heroes. "I can't figger that fella (Turley) out," Stengel began. "He don't smoke, he don't drink, he don't chase around none. But he can't win as good as that misbehavin' feller you know about who was perfect."

During the game Gilliam was the only runner to touch third base. In only two innings did the Yankees have two runners aboard at the same time. Brooklyn did it in the eighth when Labine led off with a ground-rule double to left, and Snider was intentionally walked with two out. Turley then got Robinson to pop to third to end the threat.

In the 10th, he wasn't as fortunate. With one out Gilliam walked and Reese followed with a sacrifice. Snider was again given an intentional pass, and this time Robinson made Turley pay. Playing the second-to-last game of his career, Robinson had already left five runners on base in his previous at-bats, but he lined a 1-1 pitch into left field. Slaughter thought the ball was going to land in front of him so he took a couple steps in before the horror of his mistake struck him. The ball was much higher than he thought, and despite a valiant effort to scramble back, it went sailing over his 42-year-old head and Gilliam trotted home with the winning run.

"That was heartbreaking," said Turley.

Martin wasn't heartbroken. He was mad that the Yankees had blown the game and he shared his feelings with Stengel. "If you're going to keep playing that National League bobo (Slaughter) out there, we're going to blow the Series," Martin said to Stengel on the bus ride back to the Bronx. "You better put Elston out there, and you better get [Moose] Skowron's ass back on first base [in place of Collins]."

Only Martin could get away with talking to Stengel like that. Stengel paid heed, and in the decisive seventh game, Howard—who had been unavailable the first six games due to a hospital stint brought on by strep throat—started in left field and Skowron was at first. Howard hit a home run and a double while Skowron crashed a grand slam as the Yankees cruised to a 9-0 victory and regained their baseball supremacy.

It was all set up for the Dodgers to win their second straight championship. They had Newcombe, their 27-game winner, working on four days' rest, pitching against Kucks, who had never started a Series game. Newcombe was shelled for five runs within four innings and was bombarded with boos, while Kucks tossed a three-hit shutout.

"I don't think I ever saw Newk have more stuff when he was getting them out," Dodgers manager Walter Alston said. "But it seemed like he either struck them out or they hit it out of the ballpark."

Berra opened the onslaught with a two-run homer in the first, and he continued it with a two-run homer in the third. That gave him 10 RBI for the Series, a new Yankee record. When Howard led off the fourth with a home run to make it 5-0, Alston yanked Newcombe and Ebbets Field directed all its anger at the downtrodden pitcher. "I felt bad for Newcombe, he deserved better treatment from the fans," Ford said. "Those who booed him should be ashamed."

Roger Craig was on the mound for Brooklyn in the seventh when the Yankees added the exclamation point. Martin singled, Mantle and Berra walked, and Skowron—who was miffed by his lack of use in the Series after spending most of the season as the regular first baseman—pulled his home run into the left-field seats.

"It was a great Series," Stengel said. "New Yorkers ought to be proud that they have the two best teams in Major League Baseball."

New York wouldn't be able to make that claim too much longer. As I packed my belongings that day, it never occurred to me that this would be the last time I would watch a game from the press box at Ebbets Field. But it was.

My passion for baseball and the Yankees never gripped my son Phillip the way it did me. He liked baseball, he always enjoyed going to games with his grandfather, and he followed the Yankees through my prose in the Post, *but he didn't find baseball to be particularly exciting. Football was his favorite sport. We attended the 1958 NFL championship game together at Yankee Stadium, the so-called "Greatest Game Ever Played" between the New York Giants and Baltimore Colts, and even though our Giants lost in overtime, Phillip cherished the experience and became enthralled with the gridiron.*

While I had worshipped men such as Babe Ruth and Lou Gehrig as a child, Phillip's idols were Frank Gifford and Sam Huff. The autumn after the Giants-Colts game when Phillip was 15, he tried out for his high school football team and it turned out that he had a real talent for the game. He played running back and safety and was chosen the team's most valuable player his senior year. Always an excellent student, he was accepted at Boston College, and he played four years of football for the Eagles, one on the freshman team and three on the varsity. By the time he graduated in 1966, he had earned two varsity letters as the starting safety, and more importantly, the first Kimmerle man to attend college came away with a degree in business.

My nephew Sammy, now he was a different story. That kid was a baseball fanatic and no other sport registered on his radar screen. He was the oldest of my sister Carmela's three boys, and I'm proud to say that I was one of Sammy's heroes. My job fascinated him. He couldn't believe that I actually was paid to go to baseball games, talk to the players, and write stories about what I saw and heard. "Uncle Joe," he used to tell me, "when I get old, if I can't play baseball I want to have the same job as you."

Sammy and my brother-in-law, Ed, were frequent visitors to Ebbets Field and Yankee Stadium. Ed was a native of Brooklyn and therefore was a rabid Dodgers fan. I am still at a loss to explain this, but somehow, even though he lived in Brooklyn, Sammy wound up a Yankees fan. I think I had something to do with that, but I also think Sammy just didn't like being associated with a team that always played second fiddle. You can imagine the pain his father, a man who bled Dodger blue, endured.

Sammy started playing ball when he was a little tyke and he grew to become a line-drive-hitting outfielder with good speed and an average arm. In 1954 he was attending St. Francis Prep, an all-boys parochial school in downtown Brooklyn, when he met a chubby kid named Joe Torre, whose older brother Frank was, at that time, in the minor league system of the Milwaukee Braves. Sammy and Joe became good friends, and they both tried out and made the roster of the Brooklyn Cadets, a storied sandlot team that sent a number of players to the major leagues including Waite Hoyt, Sandy Koufax, Marius Russo, Joe Pepitone, Rusty Torres, Bob Aspromonte, Matt Galante, Frank Tepedino, Don McMahon, and more recently, Manny Ramirez. Later, they also played together for the high school team at St. Francis.

After he sold the shoe store and retired, my father never missed one of Sammy's games, and whenever I could—usually on a day when the Yankees were playing at night—I'd go over to the Parade Grounds in Brooklyn and watch Sammy and the Cadets play. Sometimes Phillip would come to cheer his cousin, but usually I'd go alone because I would drive right to the Stadium from the sandlot without stopping home. When I'd show up Sammy's eyes would illuminate. He'd tell his friends, "That's my uncle Joe, you know, the guy who writes about the Yankees for the newspaper." Invariably I'd have five or six boys huddled around me after their game, asking questions about Mickey Mantle or Whitey Ford or Yogi Berra. Torre was always among that group.

Of course, Joe had a little inside knowledge about the major leagues because by the time he and Sammy became mainstays for the Cadets, Frank Torre had made it to the major leagues with the Braves. When Milwaukee beat the Yankees in the 1957 World Series, Frank came home to Brooklyn a conquering hero after hitting two home runs. This pleased Joe to no end because he hated the Yankees, first as a Giants fan, and then as a converted Braves fan.

When Joe was 16 he was 6-foot-1 and weighed a robust 240 pounds, three inches taller and 50 pounds heavier than me. He played mostly at third base and first base, but because of his size, he wasn't very agile and the scouts didn't think he was a big-league prospect, good genes be damned. I knew some of the bird dogs, and I would always talk Joe up whenever I could. Usually I'd focus on his hitting, and the scouts nodded in agreement that the kid could "sure swing the stick" but that was almost always followed by the negative refrain "he's too fat, he can't play the field."

It was Frank—a man who had been watching out for his little brother ever since their abusive father left their home when Joe was 11—who came up with a solution. He asked the Cadets' coach, Jim McElroy, to switch Joe to catcher. Frank reasoned that speed and agility weren't as important behind the plate, and if Joe could hide his physical deficiencies long enough to get himself in better shape, he'd have a chance to impress the scouts.

The move to catcher was a stroke of genius. Joe learned quickly the intricacies of receiving, he maintained his potent batting stroke, and thankfully, with Frank riding him hard, he shed weight. Milwaukee signed Joe to a bonus in 1959 which he used to pay off the mortgage on the family house at Avenue T and 34th Street in Brooklyn, and at the tail end of the 1960 season he joined the Braves and was a teammate of his brother's for a couple of weeks.

The Torres were quickly separated, though. Frank was farmed out in 1961, then was sold to the Phillies where he played two more years before retiring in 1963. Meanwhile Joe became a fixture for the Braves. He filled in for injured catcher Del Crandall much of 1961, then assumed Milwaukee's starting backstop role in 1962. Fifteen years later, his resume showed 2,209 games played, 2,342 hits, 252 home runs, 1,185 RBI, a .297 average, nine All-Star appearances, one Gold Glove, and the 1971 National League MVP award.

Joe played his entire career in the National League for the Braves in both Milwaukee and Atlanta, for the Cardinals, and finally for the Mets. Thus, when I was covering the Yankees full-time, the only chance I got to see him play was at the All-Star game. When I was elevated to a columnist position and got off the day-to-day grind of the Yankees beat in the late 1960s, it freed me up to attend other events. I usually spent the summers at Yankee Stadium, but whenever I could, I'd go watch Joe play at Shea Stadium when his team came to town.

My relationship with Joe is one that I have always treasured. He had taken a shine to me when he was a teenager, and I often felt that in some small way I helped to fill the father figure gap in Joe's life. Joe rarely saw his own father after his parents split up, and in fact, when I first met Joe he was in the midst of a six-year period when he did not speak to his dad. Although Joe is 24 years my junior, we formed a bond that remains strong to this day. I would guess that in the 40 years since he broke into the major leagues not a week has gone by when I haven't either talked to Joe on the phone, corresponded via a letter, or in these computer-crazed times, communicated by e-mail. And I can honestly say that it was Joe who revitalized an aging old man in 1996 when, after being hired as the Yankees manager, he asked permission from team owner George Steinbrenner to employ me as a sort of personal confidant.

Unlike Joe, Sammy wasn't good enough to make it to the major leagues, and he never did take up sportswriting. He tried Brooklyn College for a semester, hated it, and ended up enlisting in the Marines and was part of the initial wave of troops sent to Vietnam for combat duty. During one of the first engagements with North Vietnamese regulars at Ia Drang in 1965 Sammy was killed by mortar fire. I still have a letter that Sammy sent to me two weeks before he died, and in it, he asked if the Yankees were responding positively to new manager Johnny

Keane, and he asked how Joe and the Braves were doing. Even from a jungle on the other side of the world, Sammy's love of baseball was undeterred.

I wrote Sammy a response, telling him that the Yankees were playing terribly under Keane, and that Joe was batting in the .290s, but the Braves weren't really challenging the Dodgers in the pennant race. I know there's no way he could have received my letter before he was killed.

I called Joe to pass along the news of Sammy's death, and I'll never forget when Joe flew into New York from Milwaukee on a rare day off to attend Sammy's funeral. Sammy had been his friend, and he wanted to pay his respects. That's the kind of guy Joe is.

It is almost impossible for me not to think of my nephew when I am with Joe. And it tears at my heart that Sammy didn't live to see this most recent run of glory his beloved Yankees have enjoyed, winning the World Series four times in five years with his good friend, Joe Torre, managing the team.

– Chapter 18 –

1958

AS FAR BACK AS 1955 my colleague at the *Post,* Milton Gross, had been waving a cautionary flag regarding the possibility of Dodgers owner Walter O'Malley moving his team out of Brooklyn. I never thought it would happen. How could O'Malley even consider such a travesty? The Dodgers played in an antiquated ballpark, yet they annually drew more than one million fans to Ebbets Field, and it was no secret the Dodgers were one of the most profitable teams in Major League Baseball. The Dodgers were Brooklyn. No fan base was more passionate about its team. Brooklyn without the Dodgers would be like a human without lungs.

About a year later I started hearing rumblings that Giants owner Horace Stoneham was growing tired of the ancient Polo Grounds where attendance had dipped into the 600,000 range, and he, too, was thinking of moving his team out of New York City. I never thought that would happen, either. The Giants had been playing baseball in New York City since 1883. They were an institution, and some would argue that despite all the Yankees' success, the Giants were still New York's most followed team.

But as Stoneham would say on that dreary August afternoon in 1957 when he announced what had once been unthinkable, that he was relocating his team to San Francisco, "I feel bad for the kids. I've seen a lot of them at the Polo Grounds. But I haven't seen many of their fathers lately." A couple months later when O'Malley told us the Dodgers were joining their arch rivals on the West Coast, leaving Brooklyn for the sun and fun of Los Angeles, baseball in New York City as we knew it ceased to exist.

Both O'Malley and Stoneham had looked on with envy the previous few years as the Braves transferred their operation from Boston to Milwaukee, the Browns moved from St. Louis to Baltimore and became the Orioles, and the Athletics bolted Philadelphia for Kansas City. All three franchise shifts had proved highly profitable for the team owners, but in our New York arrogance, we scoffed at those situations. That couldn't possibly happen in New York, the greatest city in the world. You didn't leave New York City to get rich, you came here to get rich.

Obviously, I stand corrected. Both the Dodgers and Giants found unbound wealth in California where they remain today two of the most successful teams in baseball. But to old-timers of my generation, the hurt caused by their fleeing has never healed.

Though I was in Boston covering the season opener for the Yankees on April 15, 1958, I know that back home, Dodger and Giant fans—fierce enemies for more than half a century—united in sorrow as their respective ballparks stood empty and quiet that afternoon. As San Francisco's Seals Stadium rocked with excitement when the Dodgers of Los Angeles played the Giants of San Francisco in the first regular season major league game west of St. Louis, rivers of tears were spilled in New York.

Do not for one moment think that Yankee fans were unaffected by this event. The departure of the Dodgers and Giants meant that the Yankees had New York all to themselves—at least until the arrival of the expansion New York Mets in 1962. But Yankee fans were still saddened by the gutting of baseball in New York City. For Yankee fans, half the fun derived from winning championships was beating the Dodgers or the Giants in the World Series. Sure, it was great when they beat a team from Cincinnati or Chicago or St. Louis, but there was nothing better than owning bragging rights over the Dodgers or Giants.

At the time of the exodus, baseball ruled the sporting world, and New York was baseball's capital. The game's soul resided in New York. Hell, the World Series trophy resided in New York every year between 1949 and 1956. Now all that resided in New York were the Yankees.

On a personal and selfish level, my despondency was quelled by the fact that I still had a job. With two fewer baseball teams to cover, a number of writers now had eight-month holes in their calendars. Rather than taking a professional step backward, many of these men opted to seek work at other papers around the country, and I counted my blessings that I survived the upheaval. Given my 21 years covering the Yankees, the hierarchy at the *Post* deemed me an asset worth keeping, so I remained locked into my position as the primary Yankees beat man, and I headed down to St. Petersburg to chronicle a team that was coming off a bitter seven-game loss to the Braves in the 1957 World Series.

In 1957 the Yankees had rolled through the American League, winning by eight games over the White Sox as Mickey Mantle won his second straight MVP award on the basis of a .365 average and 34 home runs. The Braves won their first pennant since 1914 when the team was stationed in Boston thanks to Warren Spahn's 21 victories and Hank Aaron's league-leading totals of 44 homers and 132 RBI.

In the Series, New York was undressed by Lew Burdette, who was once Yankee property. He pitched three complete game victories including a seven-hit shutout in the seventh game at Yankee Stadium. Spahn was supposed to pitch that game, but he came down with a debilitating case of the flu. "Fred Haney asked if I could pitch on two days' rest," said Burdette, who also hurled a seven-hit shutout in Game Five and was unscored on over the final 24 innings he pitched. "I said, 'Sure, I'd go as long as I could.' The hitters cooperated well. You always need that."

The Yankees won two of the first three games including a 12-3 blowout in Game Three at County Stadium when Rookie of the Year shortstop Tony Kubek—playing in front of his hometown fans—hit two home runs for the Yankees. Milwaukee rebounded to win the fourth game on Eddie Mathews's two-run homer off Bob Grim in the 10th inning, and then the Braves took Game Five, 1-0, as Joe Adcock drove in the only run Burdette needed with a sixth-inning single.

Facing elimination, Casey Stengel trotted out Bob Turley at Yankee Stadium, and he came up with a clutch four-hitter as New York won, 3-2, though Turley's effort was forgotten when Milwaukee won the Series the next day.

* * *

One of Stengel's favorite pitching expressions was, "Throw the ball as far from the bat and close to the plate as possible." This was a philosophy that Turley didn't always adhere to. The lanky right-hander was blessed with an often overpowering fastball, and he knew he could throw it past any hitter he faced. However, there were days when he didn't have the hop on the fastball nor the control he needed to get away with deficient speed, and batters could light him up like a Christmas tree.

Inconsistency plagued him throughout his eight years with the Yankees and it was the reason why he really only had one great season, 1958, when he went 21-7 and became the first Yankee and first American Leaguer to win the Cy Young Award at a time when the honor was given to just one pitcher covering both leagues.

Turley had been part of the landmark 18-player swap between New York and Baltimore in 1954, the same deal that brought Don Larsen to the Yankees. In his first season in pinstripes Turley went 17-13 as the No. 2 starter behind Whitey Ford, but with a chance to give New York a 3-0 lead in the 1955 World Series against Brooklyn, Turley was bombed, the Dodgers went on to win, and it turned the momentum of the Series in Brooklyn's favor.

He won nine fewer games the following season, but if the Yankees could have scored one run for him in the sixth game of the 1956 Series, his disappointing 8-4 record would have been forgotten. Instead, with a chance to close out the Series on the heels of Larsen's perfect game, Turley pitched one of the finest games of his life only to lose, 1-0, to Brooklyn's Clem Labine in 10 innings.

A couple nights after the Yankees had won that Series I was standing with Turley at the team's victory party in the ballroom of the Waldorf-Astoria when Stengel sidled up to him and said, "You pitched the best ball game I ever witnessed in my life. It was better than Larsen's."

After a solid 1957 season Turley was quite simply the best pitcher in baseball in 1958. His willingness to at least try mixing up his pitches was an integral part of his success. Eddie Lopat was managing the Yankees' farm club in Richmond at the time and during spring training he worked with Turley. I wrote a story prior to the start of the 1958 Series about Turley's magnificent transformation, and he told me what Lopat had preached.

"I used to stand out there and throw it 90 miles per hour, and then I'd throw the next one even harder," he explained. "Eddie said the key was to make batters hit the ball before it reached the plate or after it passed the plate. To do this I had to learn to change speeds, keep them off balance. I had Elston and Yogi call more curves, changes, and sliders in out situations."

For some reason, Stengel lost faith in Turley in 1959. He pitched him nearly 100 innings less, and like the rest of the team, Turley went into a funk, prompting Dick Young of the *Daily News* to write, "Last year he pitched like Cy Young, this year he pitches like Dick Young."

Turley never regained his 1958 form. Bone chips in his elbow limited his effectiveness in 1960, and after winning Game Two of the World Series against Pittsburgh, he was knocked out in the second inning of the decisive seventh game, a game the Yankees went on to lose. He was dis-

abled much of the next two years and was finally sold to the Los Angeles Angels after the 1962 season, retiring in 1963.

His career may not have been spectacular, but Turley was a solid citizen and reliable player for most of his time in New York. It's funny, but what I remember most about Turley had nothing to do with pitching. First, he was one of the straight-arrow guys who rarely went out drinking or carousing. He was married, a "milk drinker" as Stengel would say, and he would spend his time on the plane or at the team hotel playing cards with the guys—he and Larsen were always pinochle partners—or reading books that dealt with business, finance, or real estate. Second, I remember his uncanny ability to steal signs from opposing teams. Mantle told me that Turley would routinely call pitches for him when he was at the plate, and the two had a little whistling signal system worked out. Mantle would look back into the dugout, get the sign from Turley, and more times than not, the pitch Turley predicted is the pitch Mantle saw. "I called a tremendous amount of home runs for Mickey," Turley said.

* * *

"Congratulations to the Braves for now, but I only hope we can have another chance at them next October," Mantle said at the conclusion of the 1957 Series. To which Burdette replied, "We'd like to play them again next year. I'm sure we're going to win the pennant, but I'm not sure about them." When Spahn added, "The Yankees couldn't finish fifth in the National League" you could hear every other team in the American League gasping and saying "Thanks, Spahnie" as soon as the words filtered out of his mouth.

Four days into the 1958 season the Yankees moved into first place, and they never left, winning their fourth pennant in a row and ninth in Stengel's 10 years at the helm.

Before 1958 there were only two teams Yankee fans pined to see opposite their club in the World Series—the Giants or the Dodgers. That changed in 1958 because those teams barely existed to New Yorkers now that they were relocated to California. And to be honest, even if the Dodgers and Giants hadn't moved, the Braves—thanks to the scathing comments made by Spahn and Burdette—would still have been the preferred opponent. When Milwaukee won the National League rather easily over Pittsburgh, the Yankees and their fans had the matchup they were thirsting for.

– 1958 World Series –

As anxious as the Yankees were to avenge their 1957 loss to Milwaukee, on the eve of the Series opener at County Stadium they certainly resembled a team ill-prepared to put up a fight. They had played below .500 ball the last six weeks of the season and they looked like an easy mark for the Braves.

The pitching staff was in disarray, third baseman Gil McDougald was in a deep batting slump due to back spasms, shortstop Tony Kubek lost 20 pounds and noticeable strength after having an impacted wisdom tooth removed, first baseman Moose Skowron was slowed by a bad back, Mickey Mantle was playing with a sore shoulder, and Hank Bauer, now 36 years old, barely hit above .200 the last two months.

Off the field, things were equally unnerving. Rookie Ryne Duren's reputation as a heavy drinker was proven true during a train ride from Kansas City to Detroit following the team's pennant-clinching party. Duren, drunk out of his mind, picked a fight with coach Ralph Houk, and during the brief melee Don Larsen was kicked in the mouth. That incident prompted George Weiss to hire private detectives to follow some of the players around once they arrived in Detroit. The first night in the Motor City I was in the lobby of the Statler-Hilton Hotel shooting the breeze with Mantle and Ford when Ford spotted two shady-looking characters across the way. I thought nothing of it, but right away Ford said, "I'll bet that fuckin' Weiss hired those guys to follow us." Ford decided to test his theory. He, Mantle, and Darrell Johnson walked out the front door to see if the two men would react, and they did. Once outside, the three players jumped into a cab, and the two detectives hurriedly got into their own car and commenced a chase. All the players did was take a ride around the block, and when they returned to the hotel, they waved to the detectives and laughed out loud. And they weren't done. An hour later they played hopscotch on the sidewalk in front of the hotel. I could just imagine Weiss's reaction when he read that report. I wasn't the only writer who witnessed the incident, and the next day the readers of three New York City newspapers were entertained by the story, and Weiss was so embarrassed he called off his spies.

So to review. The Yankees were beat up, they were pissed at their general manager, and Casey Stengel was wondering how this ensemble was going to compete against Warren Spahn, Lew Burdette, Hank Aaron, and Eddie Mathews.

Two days into the Series, Stengel was still wondering.

Near the team hotel in downtown Milwaukee there was a movie theater and the week of the Series the main attraction was *Damn Yankees* starring Tab Hunter, Gwen Verdon, and Ray Walston. On the marquee, some industrious wiseguy added a preface to the movie title. It read: "Beat the," and that's what the Braves did in the first two games.

The two men who had laid down the gauntlet following the 1957 Series, Spahn and Burdette, frustrated the Yankees with complete game victories, limiting New York to a combined 15 hits in beating Stengel's best two pitchers, Ford and Turley. "We're not in what I would call a rosy position, but the thing is not over by a long shot," Stengel said before the team boarded its plane for the gloomy flight back to New York. "Why, only two years ago we lost the first two to Brooklyn. I seem to remember we won it at the end, didn't we? There's no law that says we can't do it again."

There was also no quantifiable proof that these Yankees were capable of pulling off such a comeback.

In the opener, Spahn and Ford dueled into the eighth with the Yankees—on the strength of home runs by Skowron and Bauer—clinging to a 3-2 lead. When Mathews walked and Aaron doubled to right-center to start the bottom of the inning, Stengel relieved Ford with Duren. The rookie fireballer struck out Joe Adcock, but Wes Covington lifted a fly ball to center that enabled Mathews to score the tying run.

Duren worked out of a two-on, one-out jam in the bottom of the ninth, but in the 10th the Braves strung together three singles by Adcock, Del Crandall, and Billy Bruton to win the game.

Duren was the losing pitcher, but he was not disconsolate afterward. "I'm not overjoyed by what happened, but I can't fault my job too much," he said. "Anytime I throw the percentage of strikes I did in my three innings, I feel I've pitched pretty well."

Duren was right. He hadn't pitched poorly in allowing four hits and a walk while striking out five. Later in the Series he would pitch even better. It's just too bad Duren's reckless nature ruined what could have been a very promising career.

*   *   *

In the spring of 1957, Duren was pitching for Kansas City in an exhibition game against the Yankees and he was his usual self—incredibly fast, and frighteningly wild. Bauer told Stengel to tell Weiss to either buy the guy, or get him banned from the league. Weiss acquired him along with Harry Simpson in the trade that sent Billy Martin to the Athletics.

"He takes a drink or 10, comes in with those coke bottles, throws one on the screen and scares the shit out of 'em," Stengel said in describing Duren. Stengel was making a joke, but it was no joke. "I would not admire hitting against Duren because if he ever hit you in the head you might be in the past tense," Stengel said.

It was that fear he instilled in hitters that was Duren's greatest asset as a pitcher. No one dug in against him because, as Stengel said, if he ever hit a batter, he could kill him. And the thing was, the batter never knew where the ball was going once it left Duren's hand, and neither did Duren.

Exacerbating Duren's aura was the fact that his eyesight was terrible. A case of rheumatic fever when he was 20 years old affected the muscular balance in his eyes, and it wasn't until just before he joined the Yankees that he saw an eye specialist who corrected his problem with prescription glasses. He wore the thick specs on the mound, and when he took them off he literally couldn't see because his uncorrected vision was 20/200. Mantle used to laugh when he'd see Duren in the shower with his glasses on and all fogged up. Imagine hitting against a wild blind man who could throw 100 miles per hour. Never mind a wild blind man who was an alcoholic.

"I had been drinking from the time I was about 13," Duren once told me. "I had a macho concept about drinking, believing that the more you could drink, the better man you were. I also believed that saying 'Never trust a man who won't have a drink with you.' I was proud that I could drink. No one ever told me I was an alcoholic. I didn't realize it myself until I was pitching in the majors."

Duren spent nine long years in the minors as his erratic pitching and behavior hindered his chance to break into the big leagues. But once he began wearing the proper glasses, he improved dramatically and gave the Yankees a couple solid years in 1958 and 1959 before his drinking problems ruined his career.

The Yankees gave up on Duren early in 1961 and traded him to the Los Angeles Angels for Bob Cerv and Tex Clevenger, two players who helped the Yankees return to glory that year. Duren bounced around the majors until 1965, fighting his demons every step of the way. On numerous occasions he contemplated suicide including one instance when he climbed up on a bridge in Washington only to be talked down by his manager, Gil Hodges.

Duren had sought help for his problems, but he invariably would fall off the bandwagon and go back to the bottle. Finally, in May of 1968 a rehab stint straightened him out and he went on to become a counselor and he ran the alcoholics' rehabilitation program at a hospital in Stoughton, Wisconsin.

I spent a few nights drinking with Duren at places like Frankie and Johnny's and at Harold's Club which were both on 48th Street. He was a fun guy to be around, until that sixth or seventh scotch started to set in. Then he could become unruly, and once he was drunk, he always seemed to be picking a fight with somebody. Most of the time we'd get out of those haunts without anything happening because Mantle or Johnny Blanchard or Skowron would step in and smooth the rough edges. I know Marie always frowned when I would tell her Duren was part of the crowd I had been with on a particular evening. She always felt like he was the kind of guy who could really get his friends in trouble just for being associated with him. Marie never objected to my going out with the players or the other writers after a game, but Duren worried her. When he was traded away, my wife was one happy lady.

* * *

Game Two was over inside half an hour. Turley retired one batter in the first inning, Duke Maas got one man out, and Johnny Kucks recorded the third out. In between, the Braves scored seven runs and coasted to a 13-5 blowout as Burdette beat the Yankees for the fourth straight time. Mantle hit a pair of home runs and Bauer hit his second in two days, but it mattered little.

"Desperate? Desperate? Who says we're desperate?" said Stengel. "We're going home now and someone might get them out. We gotta get more hitting, and we gotta get more pitching, and I think maybe we'll get more of both now."

The Yankees flew back to New York and on the off day held a workout at the Stadium after which an incident occurred that served as a harbinger of things to come in the media world. It has long been my viewpoint, shared by almost all of us who ever slaved over a typewriter, that television "journalists" were, and are more than ever today, a bunch of starch-haired idiots. There have been some TV men I have respected, who all of us on the print side have respected, but the vast majority of these stumblebums couldn't string two tangible sentences together, let alone report news with any intelligence. Here I offer proof that this was the case even in television's infancy in the late 1950s.

One of the talking heads asked Stengel, "Do you think your team is choking?" You didn't ask Stengel a question like that, not after nine pennants and six World Series titles in 10 years. Stengel was infuriated and he replied, "Do you choke on that fuckin' microphone?" With that, knowing the camera was still running, he turned around and mimicked like he was scratching his rear end. As "his writers" stood there biting our lips to keep from laughing, Stengel walked past Mantle with a sly grin and a wink and said, "When I cursed I knocked out their audio, and when I scratched my ass I ruined their picture."

At the time of that episode, I thought that particular television reporter was a pompous fool. Turns out I was only half-right. He was pompous, but he was no fool. His tactics improved with time and he was the rare TV man who asked the same probing and thoughtful questions most of the good writers asked. Over the next two decades he became one of the most famous members of the sporting press, and I admired him more than any other television reporter who ever came down the pike. His name was Howard Cosell.

When the Series resumed, the Yankees were in need of one of those standout performances by one player that they always seemed to get. They got it, this time from Bauer. The aging veteran, slumping at the plate at the end of the season, continued his torrid streak in the Series with three hits including a two-run single in the fifth and a two-run homer in the seventh, his third round-tripper in three games. Bauer's four RBI produced a 4-0 Yankee victory as Larsen pitched seven innings and allowed six harmless singles, and Duren picked up the save despite three walks over the final two innings.

Stengel wrapped Bauer in a hug after the game and said, "You had a pretty good day, you did a big job." A few minutes later in his office Stengel told the assembled press, "Bauer did all the work. I don't know where we'd be without him."

Of the home run, Bauer said, "It was supposed to be a slider, I guess, but he got it inside and I hit it. Funny thing, just before I homered I heard Warren Spahn ribbing me from the bench, something about me looking out for a close pitch."

*   *   *

The last thing Bauer would be afraid of would have been a brushback pitch. After all, this was a man who fought in the heavy action of World War II, a man who stormed beachheads, a man who had taken a piece of flying shrapnel in the left thigh, a man who came home with two Purple Heart citations for bravery. At Okinawa, "We went in with 64 and six of us came out," he said. "The only thing they ever told us was to keep your head and your ass down." This is a man who feared nothing.

Bauer was always an excellent player, and while he never achieved the star status of men like Joe DiMaggio, Berra, Ford, or Mantle, there wasn't a more respected man in the clubhouse than Bauer. "The only guy I ever saw who hustled more than Bauer was Enos Slaughter," DiMaggio once said, which led to someone in *Time* magazine writing that "Bauer never led the league in anything except hustle, and that made him a Yankee great." It was a perfect summation of Bauer's 12 years in New York.

Usually, leaders fit neatly into two categories: those who lead with their words, or with their actions. Bauer did it both ways. He was the first guy who would cuss out a teammate if he didn't think that player was giving his all, and then he would go out and show that player how it was done.

One of my favorite Bauer stories comes from Skowron, who upon joining the Yankees in 1954 felt Bauer's wrath. Bauer and the other veteran Yankees had come to expect that World Series bonus check every year, and they made sure the newcomers knew how important that extra cash was. "I'm nervous and all that," Skowron recounted, "and Hank comes up to me right off and says, 'Don't mess with my money, Skowron. I'm used to winning. I'm used to driving a new car every year, my wife likes a mink coat, you understand? I want you to remember that. We play as a team here. When Joe Collins is at first base I want you to cheer for him. When you're at first base, I want Joe Collins to cheer for you.' I did what Hank told me to do. I didn't mess up his money."

Bauer signed with the Yankees in 1941 and after playing one year in the minors he enlisted in the Marines and spent 32 harrowing months fighting for his country. When he was discharged in 1946, he resumed his playing career in the Yankees farm system and was promoted to the big club in September of 1948. In one of his first games Bauer was playing right field and he ranged deep into right-center to haul in a fly ball. He looked over to center field and noticed DiMaggio glaring at him, so he asked what was wrong. "Nothing, but you're the first son of a bitch who ever invaded my territory," DiMaggio said.

When Stengel took over the team in 1949, Bauer made the roster and became part of Stengel's platoon system as he and Gene Woodling shared playing time. Neither man liked platooning and they often expressed their displeasure to Stengel, but they never won the argument. All they ever won were World Series titles, and after five in a row, Bauer conceded that maybe Stengel knew what he was doing. "The old man knew baseball, he knew how to handle men," he said.

I know Mantle loved Bauer. When Mantle came up to the team, Bauer took the youngster under his wing that first year in 1951 and Mantle learned about baseball by watching and listening to Bauer. To him, Bauer was the consummate professional.

The Yankees traded Bauer to Kansas City at the end of the 1959 season in the deal that brought Roger Maris to New York. In 1961 Bauer served as player-manager of the Athletics, and in 1964 he began a 4 1/2-year stint as manager of the Baltimore Orioles, where he won the 1966 World Series.

Bauer came back to the Yankees as a part-time scout in the early 1980s, but he didn't last too long. He couldn't stand the lackadaisical attitude so many players possessed and he told me, "What drove me out of baseball were those guys who wouldn't run 90 feet to first base."

Bauer ran to first base when he drew a walk. He ran back and forth from the dugout to his outfield position. He ran hard every time he hit the ball, and of the 164 home runs he hit in the major leagues, there isn't one instance where he didn't run full speed until he knew the ball was safely over the fence. Pete Rose played the game the way Bauer played it. Today, very few players could live up to Bauer's standard.

*　　*　　*

Bauer began the fourth game riding a World Series record 17-game hitting streak. He hadn't taken a collar since Game Seven of the 1955 Series against Brooklyn, but Spahn had all his magic working and his two-hitter stopped Bauer and the rest of the Yankees cold. Milwaukee walked away with a 3-0 victory and pushed the Yankees to the brink of extinction.

The Braves pitching coach, Whit Wyatt, the old Dodger, said that day, "I don't think I've ever seen him sharper than he was today. Del Crandall didn't have to move his mitt. Once he set it as a target Spahnie hit it."

After the game I had dinner with my father, and I expressed the opinion that the Braves just seemed to have the Yankees' number and a Yankee comeback seemed improbable. After all, only one team in history—the 1925 Pirates—had rallied from a 3-1 deficit to win the Series. Dad said maybe that was so, but he really thought Burdette's mastery over the Yankees was going to come to an end. "Sooner or later they're going to start hitting him," Dad said.

It happened sooner, and later. In Game Five, Gil McDougald hit a solo homer in the third to give New York a 1-0 lead, and with Turley looking like the pitcher he had been for most of the regular season, the Yankees played confidently. With one out and one on in the sixth, Howard, back in the lineup, made a dazzling catch of a sinking line drive to short left by Red Schoendienst. Knowing Bill Bruton was moving on a hit and run, Howard scrambled to his feet and fired the ball back to Skowron at first to complete a double play. With the huge crowd still buzzing, the energized Yankees went to work in their half of the inning, shattering Burdette's hex on them. They erupted for six hits and six runs off Burdette and Juan Pizarro to win by a 7-0 count.

"That was the turning point," Mantle said of Howard's catch when the game was still in doubt. "It was the greatest catch I've ever seen. I never dreamed Ellie had half a chance to get to that ball."

When we returned to Milwaukee I noticed right away that the town seemed subdued and that the Braves fans, so assured of triumph after the first two games, were now wary. The Yankees had shown tremendous resolve in staving off elimination, and it appeared to me that the citizenry of Milwaukee feared the momentum had shifted to the Bronx Bombers. Braves manager Fred Haney must have felt this, too, because he announced that Spahn was going to pitch Game Six on just two days' rest. It was a risky proposition. Most observers felt the prudent move would be to trot out Bob Rush, and if a seventh game was necessary, Haney could use both Spahn and Burdette if need be. Stengel felt he had no choice. Even though Ford had rested only two days, he had to come back with his best because the Yankees were still in a win-or-else situation.

Based on the way the starters performed, this should have been a Braves victory. Ford was showering before the second inning was over, while Spahn was toiling gamely into the 10th inning. However, the Yankee trio of Art Ditmar, Duren, and Turley held things together long enough for the Bombers to pull out a thrilling 4-3 overtime victory.

Bauer hit his fourth home run of the series in the first inning, but the Braves took a 2-1 lead in the second. The Yankees tied it in the sixth when Mantle and Howard singled and Berra's sacrifice fly brought home Mantle, then Duren took the mound to start the Milwaukee sixth. Over the next four innings the Braves had only two base runners and they struck out seven times as the game moved into extra innings.

McDougald led off the 10th with a home run to left, and after Spahn got two outs, Howard and Berra both singled and Haney had to remove his warrior. "That was the hardest thing I've had to do the whole Series was to go out there and take Spahn out," Haney said. Don McMahon entered and gave up Skowron's RBI single that made it 4-2, setting up high drama in the bottom of the inning.

Hank Aaron's RBI single cut the Braves' deficit to 4-3, but with runners on the corners, Turley—even though he had pitched a complete game two days earlier—was summoned to save the game, and on his third pitch he got Frank Torre to pop out to McDougald at second base. "What a feeling of relief when I saw Torre lift that easy shot to me," McDougald said. "There are no bad hops up there."

So for the fourth straight year, and second in a row with Milwaukee, the Yankees would be involved in a World Series Game Seven. Everyone knew Burdette was pitching for Milwaukee. An hour before the first pitch would be thrown Stengel told Larsen that he was starting. It didn't go well for Larsen early, but it could have been worse. The Braves scored in the first, but they also left the bases loaded when Larsen struck out Crandall.

In the second the Yankees extracted two runs without the benefit of a hit as first baseman Torre made a pair of throwing errors. "I don't think I deserved the errors," Torre said after the game, "but if you want to have a goat, it might as well be me as somebody else." Regardless of who was at fault, the Braves trailed, 2-1.

When Larsen got into a jam in the third, Stengel lifted him and brought in Turley, and there were many of us in the press box who expected doom. Turley had gone the distance in Game Five, had thrown briefly in Game Six, and now he was being expected to stymie the Braves again. As he would say later, "I was not a bit tired. In fact, I felt better out there today than I had felt at any time this season."

It showed. He cleaned up Larsen's mess without allowing a run, and the only mistake he made the rest of the day was a gopher ball served up to Crandall in the sixth that tied the game at 2-2.

Burdette had recovered from the turbulence of the second inning and was frustrating the Yankees again as he had given up just three hits when the eighth inning began. The tension in the ballpark was noticeable, and there was a sense that whichever team scored the next run was going to win the championship. That team was the Yankees.

After McDougald flied out and Mantle struck out, Berra lashed a double off the wall in right-center and Howard followed with a bouncer up the middle that shortstop Johnny Logan just barely missed. Berra raced home with what proved to be the winning run, but the Yankees were leaving nothing to chance. Andy Carey ripped a single off Eddie Mathews's glove at third, and then Skowron launched a three-run homer into the left-field stands providing Turley a comfortable 6-2 lead, and the Milwaukee faithful began streaming for the exits in disappointment.

"I guess we can play in the National League now," Stengel said in reference to Spahn's caustic remark from a year earlier.

It was a wild victory celebration in the clubhouse, the Yankees fully aware that they had accomplished something special in beating Spahn and Burdette back-to-back on the road. "Sure I'm excited," Stengel said. "And why not? My men proved they're a great team. They had to be to make that wonderful comeback. This was the greatest Series we ever won."

During the 1958 season Yankee owners Dan Topping and Del Webb concluded that Casey Stengel was finished as manager of the Yankees. At the end of the year when Stengel's contract was up, Topping and Webb were going to thank Stengel for a glorious run, then send the 68-year-old out to the glue factory and install young Ralph Houk as the new skipper.

Stengel screwed up the plan. The Yankees weren't supposed to win the World Series that year, but they did. And because Stengel had guided them to the championship for the seventh time in his 10 years with the club, Topping and Webb knew there would be a fan and media mutiny if they let the wildly popular Stengel go on the heels of what happened in Milwaukee. So they signed him to a new two-year contract and told Houk, who from 1955 to 1957 had proved to be a fine manager with the Yankees' top farm team in Denver, to be patient.

After a disastrous 1959 season when the Yankees slumped to a 79-75 record and a third-place finish, the worst of Stengel's tenure, the old man guided the club back to the top of the American League in 1960, winning his 10th pennant. As we later found out, nothing Stengel could have done in 1960—not even winning the World Series—would have prolonged his Yankee career, but it would have been interesting to see what would have happened had the Yankees defeated the Pittsburgh Pirates. Bill Mazeroski saved Topping and Webb some grief, capping what may have been the most unusual Series ever by hitting the first, and still only, Game Seven World Series walk-off home run to give the Pirates the championship.

The Yankees outscored the Pirates 55-27, outhit them 91-60, outhomered them 10-4, and set a new Series record for team batting average at .338 which was 82 points better than Pittsburgh's mark. And they lost.

While the Yankees were winning the second, third, and sixth games by scores of 16-3, 10-0, and 12-0, the Pirates won the first, fourth, and fifth games by 6-4, 3-2, and 5-2. On paper the Series had been a mismatch, but there the Pirates were, face-to-face with the mighty Yankees in a deciding seventh game where anything could happen, and pretty much did. Of all the World Series conflicts that I've seen, there was never a game that contained more emotional swings and dramatic moments as this one.

The Pirates bombed Bob Turley inside two innings and opened a 4-0 lead. Moose Skowron homered in the fifth off Pirate starter Vern Law, and then the

Yankees went on another of their run-scoring binges in the sixth and drove Law off the mound while taking a 5-4 lead. During this uprising Pittsburgh manager Danny Murtaugh brought in Elroy Face, a pitcher who throughout the Series had been bad-mouthing the Yankees in print. The Yankees took great joy in making him pay for his loose lips, and when Yogi Berra crashed a three-run homer into the upper deck in right field, he silenced Face and the rabid Pittsburgh crowd.

When the Yankees tacked on two more runs in the eighth for a 7-4 advantage, they appeared to be strolling down Easy Street. Thankfully I didn't start typing my lead at that point because that would have been a waste of paper and typewriter ribbon.

Gino Cimoli, pinch-hitting for Face, opened the bottom of the eighth with a single, but when Virdon hit a grounder to shortstop Tony Kubek, it looked like a tailor-made double play. Instead the ball took a bad hop and struck Kubek in the throat. Both runners were safe, Kubek had to be helped off the field, and as he was being transported to the hospital, the Pirates put together a dizzying rally that turned Forbes Field into New Orleans at Mardi Gras time. Dick Groat singled home one run, Roberto Clemente another, and then Hal Smith hit a three-run homer off Jim Coates to put the Pirates ahead 9-7. "Maybe God can do something about such a play," Stengel said of the Virdon bad-hop grounder, "but man cannot."

I thought about writing then, giving some private thought as to how I was going to make Hal Smith—a backup catcher of little renown—a hero. Something told me to hold off. Another wise decision. In the top of the ninth Bobby Richardson and Dale Long singled off Bob Friend, and when Murtaugh brought in Harvey Haddix, Mantle came through with a RBI single and Berra tied the game with a fielder's choice grounder.

During the break between half innings I agreed with my pal, Dick Young of the Daily News, *that we were witnessing one of the greatest games in World Series history, and we hadn't even turned our attention back to the field when Mazeroski cemented that notion by hitting Ralph Terry's second pitch of the bottom of the ninth far over the ivy-covered left-field wall to bring sudden death to the Yankees.*

The picture of Berra standing with his back to the diamond watching the ball disappear burned into the memory of countless Yankee fans watching on television. I would guess that's how Dodgers fans must have felt when they watched Bobby Thomson's homer sail over the fence at the Polo Grounds in 1951. Though I maintain Thomson's homer was still the most dramatic in baseball history, this one ranked a very close second.

The Yankees were stunned, and they were bitter. "What do you think?" Stengel snapped when he was asked if he thought the better team had won. "I can't believe it," Berra said. And Long, a former Pirate, chimed in "I'll never believe it." But it was true, the Pirates had beaten the Yankees and Face crystallized the moment for the Yankees when he opened the door to the visiting clubhouse, peeked his mug inside and said, "Fuck you guys."

Topping and Webb weren't quite as crude, but five days later they basically told Stengel the same thing. New York Mayor Robert Wagner sent a telegram to Stengel pleading for him to return as manager in 1961. Our New York chapter of the Baseball Writers Association of America took the unprecedented action of formulating a petition which 35 writers signed begging Stengel to return. You see, we all assumed Stengel's future was in his own hands. It wasn't. Topping and Webb had decided, probably when they gave him his contract after 1958, that 1960 was going to be the Ol' Perfesser's last year regardless of what happened.

A massive entourage of journalists gathered at the Savoy-Hilton Hotel for the announcement of Stengel's departure as manager. With Webb out in California tending to his construction business, Topping ran the press conference. Or at least he tried.

Topping began the proceeding by reading from a prepared statement as Stengel stood off to the side. Topping said Stengel had signed a two-year contract after 1958 with the option to retire after 1959 if he chose to. "Keeping in mind his possible retirement, the Yankees set out to develop a program for the eventual replacement of Casey," read Topping, which in other words meant they were grooming Houk to be his successor. Topping went on to say that Stengel "has been, and deservedly so, the highest-paid manager in baseball history. Casey has been—and is—a great manager. He is being well-rewarded with $160,000 to do with as he pleases."

Stengel, more serious than I could ever remember, then stepped to the microphone and read from a prepared statement that shed no light on whether he was being fired or he was quitting. Joe Reichler, the baseball writer for the Associated Press, finally blurted out the question we all should have been asking. "Casey, tell us the truth, were you fired?" And Stengel replied, "You're goddamn right I was fired." And with that, Topping and Webb were unmasked. The only reason Stengel was being let go was because of his age. Today, there probably would have been a lawsuit.

"I commenced winning pennants when I got here, but I didn't commence getting any younger," Stengel said as Topping fidgeted uncomfortably, dragging on a cigarette. "They told me my services were no longer desired because they wanted to put in a youth program as an advance way of keeping the club going. When a club gets to discharging a man on account of age, they can if they want to. The trick is growing up without growing old. Most guys are dead at my age anyway. You could look it up."

Later, Stengel went to the hotel bar with most of "his writers" in tow, looking for other juicy nuggets that he might offer. After a couple of bourbon and sodas, he said, "I'll never make the mistake of being 70 years old again."

– Chapter 19 –

1961

JUST BEFORE I RETIRED FROM THE *Post* in 1981 I was asked to write a series of nostalgic articles looking back on what was then my six-decade association with the Yankees. It was heavily promoted as "revered *Post* columnist Joe Kimmerle's farewell gift to his legion of readers."

I was never comfortable with that type of spotlight shining on me. I always considered myself a nuts-and-bolts kind of guy and my goal was always to do my job to the best of my ability in the least intrusive manner possible. Had a television show such as my late friend Dick Schaap's *The Sports Reporters* been around in my heyday, I wouldn't have been inclined to appear if asked. That just wasn't my style. But I understood this was a special situation, and as my editor told me, "Joe, we just want to celebrate your career."

I appreciated that praise, and it sure gave Marie some material to work with—"Here he comes, the revered one," she would say with her brightest smile when I would enter a room. Marie's good-natured teasing notwithstanding, the assignment excited me because it gave me an opportunity to reflect on my career and relive the greatest moments in Yankees' history. I also looked on it as a chance to enlighten a new generation of Yankee fans, most of who had never seen the greatest Yankees like Babe Ruth, Lou Gehrig, Joe DiMaggio, and Mickey Mantle play.

One of the articles dealt with the unforgettable 1961 season when Roger Maris broke Ruth's home run record.

There was no Yankee season during the time when I was a full-time beat reporter that compared to 1961. Later on when I was a columnist, the mid-1970s Bronx Zoo era went unsurpassed in terms of soap operatic drama and controversy, but for its time, 1961 was quite remarkable.

It began with the upheaval at the top as Ralph Houk took over for the deposed Casey Stengel, and Roy Hamey became the general manager when George Weiss stepped down two weeks after Stengel's dismissal. The team won 109 games, the second-most in its history to that point, yet it spent much of the time trailing the Tigers in the standings. Those standings now included 10 teams as expansion came to the American League. Los Angeles was granted a team, and when the Washington Senators moved to Minnesota and became the Twins, a new team was placed in the nation's capital. Whitey Ford won 25 games and lost only four while reliever Luis Arroyo saved 29 games, exceptional achievements that were rendered nearly meaningless by their teammates who combined for 240 home runs, a major league record that stood for more than 35 years. There was Mantle, who hit a career-high 54 home runs that season and was in the hunt for Ruth's record right up until the final few weeks when physical problems derailed him. For the first time in his career he was playing in front of adoring crowds who had finally stopped booing him, their recognition of his greatness at long last complete. But above all else, there was Maris, marching inexorably and joylessly into history.

Maris's dogged pursuit of Ruth's record provided even more compelling prolonged drama than DiMaggio's hitting streak 20 years earlier. DiMaggio's streak remains the ultimate baseball performance, and it is a standard that I don't think will ever be surpassed. Maris's mark was obliterated when Mark McGwire hit 70 home runs in 1998, and then Barry Bonds extended the record to 73 in 2001. Still, the circumstances surrounding Maris's achievement made him the better story when you consider:

DiMaggio wasn't chasing the game's most beloved character, nor was he taking aim at what, at that time, was the most hallowed record in sport. DiMaggio was a hero to everyone and the masses rooted for him. Maris was perceived as public enemy number one even by ardent Yankee supporters, a man deemed unworthy of bumping the beloved Babe down a notch. DiMaggio's streak spanned roughly two months and ended long before the 1941 pennant race kicked into gear. Maris's quest was a season-long odyssey during which the Yankees were embroiled in a tight struggle to win the American League. The pressure of having to hit home runs as well as win games was so overwhelming that he lost clumps of hair, suffered from stress headaches and ulcers, and his docile demeanor was darkly altered. DiMaggio dealt primarily with the coterie of New York writers. For the last couple months of 1961 Maris dealt with us in the insatiable New York press as well as writers and broadcasters from all over the country, some of whom couldn't tell the difference between a baseball and a basketball. It was a mass media bombardment that we used to only see during World Series week, and one day, an exasperated Maris said, "The only time I'm by myself is when I'm taking a crap."

One night in August of that year, after the latest media horde had vacated the space in front of his locker, I happened to be hanging around in that vicinity, having just finished a conversation with Tony Kubek. Maris came over and asked me, "Why the hell can't you guys leave me alone?" I told him, "Because, Roger, you might break one of the most sacred records in all of sport. It's pretty big news." He just didn't understand what all the fuss was about.

I felt bad for him because he didn't ask for the treatment he received, nor did he deserve it. I must also admit this: While I liked Roger very much and felt that after all he had gone through he deserved to get the record, I wasn't exactly pulling for him to do it. I was like a lot of people who wished the Babe's legacy would last forever, and I had a more vested interest because the Babe had been my friend.

So, on the afternoon of October 1 when Maris sent No. 61 sailing into the right-field bleachers at Yankee Stadium, I cursed aloud at Boston pitcher Tracy Stallard who served up the record-breaking homer. As a writer you always root for the best story and Maris breaking the record was the best story. But I didn't have to be excited about having to write the best story.

Twenty years later, my feelings changed, and I felt embarrassed to have been part of the group of writers who were hoping Maris didn't succeed. I telephoned or interviewed in person a number of the principal characters from that season, and from that game—including Maris— and this is the retrospective I pieced together as it appeared in the *Post:*

By Joe Kimmerle
New York Post

Whitey Ford had some work to do, but the work could wait. After all, the most exalted record in baseball history was on the brink of being broken, and if it was going to happen, Ford was making damn well sure he wouldn't miss it.

It was the 1961 regular-season finale at Yankee Stadium and Roger Maris stood tied with the legendary Babe Ruth for most home runs in a season. Forget Baseball Commissioner Ford Frick's ruling that because Maris was playing in a season that contained 162 games, any record he might set would have to carry "a distinguishing mark" in the record book because Ruth hit his 60 home runs in the 154-game 1927 season. As far as Whitey and the Yankees were concerned, a season was a season regardless of length, Maris was gunning for immortality, and this game against the hated Boston Red Sox was his last chance.

Maris had flied out to Carl Yastrzemski in left field in the first inning, and now he was stepping in to face Boston rookie right-hander Tracy Stallard for the second time, in the fourth.

"When the inning started I jogged down to the bullpen," Ford recalled 20 years after the fact. "I was starting the World Series opener (three days later), but I wanted to throw for about 15 minutes. I got out there just as Roger came up. (Bullpen catcher) Jim Hegan had a ball and his big glove and he wanted to get going. I said, 'Not yet. After Roger.'"

Ford had been a part of so many memorable occurrences since making his Yankee debut in 1950, but one that he mostly missed was Don Larsen's perfect game against Brooklyn in the 1956 World Series.

"Larsen didn't have a lot of stamina and Casey [Stengel] was afraid he would lose it," Ford recalled. "Sometimes he could lose it quick, and the score was only 2-0. I was in the bullpen and I threw every inning from the sixth inning on, so I missed most of the perfect game. When he struck out Dale Mitchell for the last out I was probably busting off a curve in the bullpen. I missed that. I didn't want to miss this."

Neither did Ford's fellow Yankee pitcher, Bob Turley.

"I moved to the left side of the bullpen (closest to the right-field seats), because if it went in there I wanted to see it," Turley said. "And if it came into the bullpen I wanted to catch it. I wanted to be the guy to give it to Roger."

So with Ford and Turley in position, Maris dug his cleats into the batter's box. Elsewhere, every Yankee crept to the edge of the bench in anticipation. Manager Ralph Houk fiddled nervously with pebbles in front of the dugout. The fans in the right-field bleachers, knowing Maris hit almost all of his home runs there, shifted anxiously in their seats, wondering if the lefty-swinging slugger would deposit the historic home run in their lap. And in Manhattan's Lenox Hill Hospital, fallen Yankees Bob Cerv (knee surgery) and Mickey Mantle (infected abscess on his hip) sat together in Mantle's room watching on television.

Stallard's first delivery was high and outside, his next, low and inside, and the crowd of 23,104 began to boo, thinking Stallard was pitching around Maris in an effort to avoid being linked ignominiously to history.

"I heard it, but I didn't get concerned over it," Stallard said. "I wasn't trying to walk anybody in a o-o game. Heck, Yogi was the next hitter and he could hit one out as easily as Roger could. I don't know what Maris was feeling, but I didn't feel any particular tension. I didn't think much about his home run record. I wanted to win because it was the last day of the season and I wanted to go back home to Virginia leaving a good impression with the club."

So with that thought, Stallard reared back and delivered a waist-high fastball over the heart of the plate. As the ball sped toward him Maris's eyes lit up. He knew the pitch was to his liking, he knew that if he was going to break this damn record—the chase which had turned his life upside down the past few months—this was a pitch he had to swing at.

Maris lifted his right foot and stepped toward Stallard, who at the same time was finishing his follow-through and thinking he might have made a mistake with this offering. As he strode, Maris uncoiled his 35-inch, 33-ounce Louisville Slugger in a rhythmic yet violent motion, striking the ball flush on the fat part of the lumber. At that moment of sweet impact, as the ball began its flight into baseball annals, Maris knew he had done it. As he set off on his 61st trot around the bases, he did so effortlessly, carrying with him only his natural 200 pounds, now devoid of the backbreaking, ulcer-inducing, personality-changing weight of his tortuous pursuit of Ruth.

Throughout the summer of 1961 this quiet, unassuming man from Fargo, North Dakota by way of Hibbing, Minnesota, had been cast in the role of villain by so many old-timers who revered Ruth and refused to believe—or accept—that his record could be broken. What should have been one of the greatest times of Maris's life had become an ongoing nightmare. The relentless pressure had cost him clumps of hair, not to mention the pure joy playing baseball once provided him. But now it was over, and "distinguishing mark" or not, no man had ever hit more home runs in one season than he.

"As soon as I hit it I knew it was No. 61," Maris said. "It was the only time that the number of the homer ever flashed into my mind as I hit it. Then I heard the tremendous roar from the crowd. I could see them all standing, then my mind went blank again. I couldn't even think as I went around the bases. I couldn't tell you what crossed my mind, I don't think anything did. I was in a daze, I was all fogged out from a very, very hectic season and an extremely difficult month."

When he reached the dugout, his teammates refused to let him enter. Always a modest man, Maris uncomfortably doffed his cap and waved to the cheering crowd.

"I was afraid I was being corny and tried to get into the dugout, but my teammates held me up and wouldn't let me get down," Maris said. "It began to feel as if they would never let me down. I felt very proud, but also humble. I felt that I was a very fortunate man. I had done something that no one else had ever done. I couldn't believe it. Sometimes I still find it hard to believe. I didn't care about it being in 162 games, it was the biggest home run of my life."

Yankees shortstop Tony Kubek remembered the feeling in the moments after the cheering had finally receded and Maris was allowed entrance back into the dugout.

"After everyone settled down, I sat there on the bench and let out a big sigh of relief," Kubek said. "We had all gone through it with Roger and Mickey and in a way it was as much a relief for us to have it over as it was for Roger. I looked over at him and for an instant his eyes were closed and I could see him breathing deeply. So much pressure had built up, so much tension over those past weeks, it was incredible. I think that Roger's feeling wasn't as much excitement over doing what nobody in baseball had ever done. It was just relief, plain, old-fashioned relief."

Maris had been voted the American League's MVP after the 1960 season in which he hit 39 home runs—one less than league-leader Mantle—and drove in a league-high 112 runs. It was his first year as a Yankee after coming to the Bronx in a trade from Kansas City, and although he wasn't initially thrilled about leaving his beloved Midwest, being part of the fearsome Yankee lineup jump-started his career.

As the 1961 season got underway, Maris found himself mired in a slump and unable to generate the numbers he had produced the year before. On the way to spring training, Maris's car—carrying his two-month pregnant wife Pat and the couple's three children—broke down in Georgia. When the family finally arrived in St. Petersburg, site of the Yankees' spring base, Pat was hospitalized due to complications with her pregnancy. A doctor told the Marises that Pat would inevitably lose the baby, so throughout the exhibition season, Maris was saddled with that sad news.

He hit miserably, and he continued to flail away unsuccessfully when the Yankees moved north to start the season. During the first month, Pat's condition was reevaluated and it was determined that she and the baby were safe, yet still, Maris struggled at the plate. It wasn't until the 11th game that he hit his first home run of the year, a drive off Detroit's Paul Foytack at Tiger Stadium on April 26.

Five more games passed without a big fly, but on May 3 in Minneapolis, he connected off Pedro Ramos of the Twins, and from then on, it was clear Maris had regained his stroke from 1960. From May 17 to June 22 Maris hit 24 home runs in 38 games, a period unmatched in baseball history. During Ruth's 60-homer season, his best stretch was 24 homers in 41 games from August 16 to September 30.

On July 18, with Maris and Mantle each well ahead of Ruth's record pace, Frick announced that any record would count only if it was accomplished in 154 games, the duration of the 1927 season when Ruth set the standard.

"Commissioner Frick makes the rules," Maris said a couple years later. "If all I'm entitled to will be an asterisk, it will be all right with me. However, I never made up any schedules. Do you know any other record that's been broken since they started playing 162 games that's got an asterisk? I don't. Commissioner Frick should have said that all records made during the new schedule should have an asterisk."

Entering September Maris stood at 51. Every move Maris made was chronicled and he began to react adversely. He was surly with reporters, and he had grown tired of the constant berating from fans at home and on the road. He made the mistake of insulting Yankee fans when he said, "They are a lousy bunch of frontrunners. Hit a home run and they love you, but make an out and they start booing you. Give me the fans in Kansas City anytime."

"One of the hardest things for Roger was the recognition he started getting," said Mantle. "Everywhere we'd go, people would want his autograph. I'd been through all that for 10 years, so it wasn't new to me, but it got to where we couldn't go out to eat, couldn't go downstairs in the hotel. Roger didn't like that. He'd always been kind of private, away from things, and now he couldn't be."

Interestingly, it was Mantle who helped to keep Maris sane. Throughout the chase there was a perception that Mantle and Maris were at odds with each other, but nothing could have been further from the truth. In actuality, they were good friends who shared an apartment with Cerv over near Forest Hills. When Maris needed someone to talk to, it was Mantle who provided an attentive ear.

Through it all, the quest continued. Mantle reached 53 homers on September 10 to trail Maris by three, but Mantle's regular season was about to come to an end. He had been suffering from a heavy cold, and, on the advice of Yankees broadcaster Mel Allen, went to see a doctor that Allen knew. The doctor gave Mantle a shot in his hip, and a few days later the area became infected and Mantle landed in the hospital with a painful abscess.

When the Yankees took the field at Baltimore's Memorial Stadium on September 20 to play the Orioles, it was their 154th game, the last chance for Maris to break Ruth's record within Frick's time frame. He stood at 58, and in the third inning, he tagged Milt Pappas for No. 59. But on the night the Yankees wrapped up the American League pennant with a 4-2 victory, Maris was unable to hit another homer.

"At the ballpark the situation was unbelievable," Maris said. "People all looked at me in a funny way. It was as if they were studying me to see how I was reacting, to see if I was cracking up. I had given it my best. I felt very relieved when the 154th game was over. It had been the toughest game I had ever played, there had been more pressure than I had ever known before."

Maris hit his 60th homer off Baltimore's Jack Fisher at Yankee Stadium on September 26, then went homerless for three more games leading to the finale against Boston and Stallard.

"I appreciate the fact that he was man enough to pitch to me and to get me out," Maris said of Stallard. "When he got behind me he came in with the pitch to try to get me out."

Maris finished with 142 RBIs, winning the RBI title by one over Baltimore's Jim Gentile. He hit .269, scored 132 runs, and was an easy American League MVP winner for the second year in a row.

He played five more years in New York, hitting another 103 home runs. After the 1966 season, he was traded to St. Louis, and in 1967 he helped the Cardinals win a World Series. Maris retired after an injury-plagued 1968 season with 275 career homers, 851 RBIs, a .260 batting average, and baseball's most storied record.

Twenty years later, the wounds that were inflicted that season have still not healed. He continues to hold the record, and a grudge.

"My going after the record started off as such a dream," said Maris. "I was living a fairy tale for a while. I never thought I'd ever get a chance to break such a record. But every day and every night people wanted to talk to me and they all asked the same damn question: 'Do you think you can break Babe Ruth's record?' How the hell should I know?

"It was no fun to hear all those boos. The pressure from all sides was just tremendous. I was a disliked player and there's a difference when you played as a liked player and a disliked player. I understand why it happened. A lot of people, especially older people, did not want me to break Ruth's record."

Like Maris, the Yankees started the 1961 season quite unremarkably and despite Maris's three-run homer, they lost on June 3 to the White Sox and their record dipped to 24-19. At that point they were 3 1/2 games behind Detroit, Maris had 14 home runs, and nothing special seemed in the works.

Soon thereafter things got interesting.

By winning 11 of their next 12 they pulled alongside the Tigers, and when the teams split a July 4 doubleheader in front of 74,246 fans, the largest crowd at Yankee Stadium since 1947, Detroit was just one length ahead.

By the end of July the Yankees had gone in front, but only by 1 1/2 games even though Maris now had 40 homers and Mantle 39, and Ford was 19-2. A stretch where they won 10 of 11 games in early August extended their advantage to four games, but the Tigers kept growling and when they arrived at Yankee Stadium for a series to be played on the first three days of September, they were within 1 1/2 games.

"If someone had told me early this spring that Maris would have 50 home runs, Mantle would have close to 50, and Ford would have 20 wins, I would have bet you the Yankees would be leading the league by 25 games," said Detroit manager Bob Scheffing a couple of hours before the first game.

Well, they were leading by 4 1/2 by the time the series concluded as the Yankees swept all three and finally, the Tigers had been tamed. They gradually fell off the rest of the way and New York—thanks largely to a 65-16 home record—finished eight games in front.

Weeks before Maris hit his 61st home run, a Sacramento, California, restaurant owner named Sam Gordon said he would pay $5,000 to the person who caught the record-breaking ball. That person turned out to be 19-year-old Brooklyn truck driver Sal Durante, who was sitting in Box 163D of Section 33. As soon as he caught it, Durante was jostled about by other fans who tried to get the ball, but Durante hung on and was escorted away by stadium security for a meeting with Maris in the clubhouse while the Yankees were batting in the bottom of the fifth. Durante offered to give the ball to Maris, but Maris told him to collect the money. He had enough memories of the previous few months to last a lifetime. It was time to move on. It was time to validate the season by winning the World Series.

– *1961 World Series* –

Roger Maris's record-breaking performance served as camouflage for Ralph Houk. With so much focus on Maris and Mickey Mantle and finally just Maris, no one seemed to pay attention to the Yankees' new manager. It was extraordinarily good fortune because with the flap over Casey Stengel's dismissal eclipsed by the home run derby, Houk, after an early spat of trouble, was able to remain contently in the background, going about his daily business in the most routine manner. Never has anyone replaced a legend as seamlessly and quietly as Houk did that year.

Houk was an entirely different personality to work with. He wasn't as energetic in his dealings with the press as Stengel, and in a way he was suspicious of the media. He was not nearly as willing to tell us things the way Stengel did, so it made our jobs a little more difficult, and naturally, some of us used our dissatisfaction with Houk against him.

Early in spring training when the Yankees were playing terribly and losing almost every day, there were frequent references made about Houk's apparent inability to live up to Stengel's high standard. My *Post* colleague, Jimmy Cannon, even wondered in print if Houk was calling Stengel for advice. Houk was angered and after denying that, he said, "I'm not another Casey. I worked for him most of my baseball life and no man ever had a better teacher, but I'm not Casey. I won't talk like him and I won't act like him."

Pretty soon what he did do like Stengel was win, and, not that it mattered to him, he began to earn the respect of the writers and Stengel became a distant memory.

Houk started with the Yankees as a catcher in the farm system in 1939, but after three decent years his pursuit of a major league career was put on hold by the Japanese bombing of Pearl Harbor. He received his draft notice in January 1942 and by the end of 1943 he was overseas in the thick of the war. Houk fought heroically at Normandy, and then was assigned the hazardous duty of riding in the point jeep as his reconnaissance company advanced across Northern France. He was wounded during one mission, but later returned to become his company's commander. In the Battle of the Bulge he earned a Silver Star, and before the war ended, he rose to the rank of major.

When Houk came home he resumed his baseball career and after one year in the minors he made Bucky Harris's Yankees in 1947 and even got a pinch hit in that year's World Series. After spending 1948 in the minors at Kansas City he returned to the Yankees late in 1949 where he remained until 1954 when he retired as a player.

Houk's playing days were few and far between. He wasn't going anywhere on the Yankees with Yogi Berra and Charlie Silvera in front of him and his career consisted of only 91 games at 158 at-bats with no home runs. But as he sat interminably on the bench he observed Stengel's managerial style, he learned the game, and when he decided to retire, it was clear that his future was in managing.

In 1955 he was assigned to the organization's top farm team in Denver and for three years at the Triple-A level Houk excelled, winning the 1957 American Association pennant and the Little World Series. During that time he helped mold future Yankees such as Tony Kubek, Bobby Richardson, Johnny Blanchard, Ralph Terry, and Ryne Duren.

When other major league teams began inquiring about his availability, Yankee co-owner Dan Topping grew nervous. He wanted Houk to eventually replace Stengel, so as a way of stashing Houk, he promoted him to the Yankees to serve as one of Stengel's coaches in 1958 with the intention of installing him as manager in 1959. He didn't take over until 1961, but the wait was worth it.

He won three consecutive pennants and two World Series, then was transferred upstairs to the general manager position when Roy Hamey retired following 1963. This, however, was a move that did not pan out. The team started coming unglued in 1964 though it won a pennant under new manager Yogi Berra, and then it crashed with Johnny Keane at the helm in 1965.

Houk fired Keane early in 1966 and returned to the field where he remained through the 1973 season, but his second tour of duty wasn't nearly as productive as his first because the Yankees never finished better than fourth. He left New York after George Steinbrenner bought the team, and later managed the Tigers and Red Sox before retiring for good after the 1984 season. In all those years nothing ever topped his first year—1961. "That was my best year in baseball," he said. "It was just a great, great year. It was a pleasure managing that team. They played so good all season. What a season that was."

* * *

When the 1961 campaign began, a wide-open race was expected in the National League. Five teams were considered pennant contenders—the defending champion Pirates, Dodgers, Cardinals, Giants, and Braves. Three teams figured to bring up the rear—the Reds, Cubs, and Phillies. The Reds disagreed with this prognosis and then went out and stated their case.

Cincinnati was a team that finished 20 games below .500 in 1960, but under manager Fred Hutchinson the Reds came back to win 93 games and the National League pennant. Led by Frank Robinson and Vada Pinson they were a solid, competitive team. They also had no chance against the Yankees.

Hutchinson tried to downplay predictions of gloom on the eve of the opener by saying, "Why should odds scare us? Last April they were 60-to-1 we wouldn't win the pennant. I read that we're not supposed to win, but I haven't told my players yet." It was a brave front, and for a couple of days Hutchinson's longshots looked as if they were cooking up an upset on par with Pittsburgh's the year before. After losing the first game, the Reds took Game Two, and owned the lead late in Game Three before Maris nailed a decisive ninth-inning home run, and Cincinnati crumbled thereafter, losing the last two games in embarrassing fashion.

In the opener Whitey Ford was simply dominant, just as he had been all season. He dazzled the Reds with a two-hit shutout as the Yankees won, 2-0. Ford received the backing of Elston Howard and Moose Skowron who hit solo homers in the fourth and sixth innings, respectively.

"Whitey was just great, he was the chairman of the board out there," said Howard, who caught the gem while Berra played left field.

"It was one of those happy days when I had both good stuff and good control," said Ford. "I felt strong all the way and never had any real doubts about being able to finish. The way things went today, I'm sure I can make three starts in the Series if there's any need for it."

There wouldn't be.

The only negative to the day was the fact that Mantle's grotesque hip abscess was too painful to allow him to play, and that was also the case in Game Two. The Yankees could have used him as Cincinnati rebounded for a 6-2 triumph behind Joey Jay who threw a four-hit complete game. "Where is the expert who picked the Yankees to win in four games?" Hutchinson crowed afterward.

The Yankees were unusually sloppy as they committed three errors and Howard allowed a passed ball that sent Cincinnati's eventual winning run across the plate in the fifth inning.

In the first two games Maris had gone 0-for-7 with three strikeouts and he'd hit just one ball out of the infield. When questioned about his lack of production, he became annoyed and answered, "What's 0-for-7 for me? I've gone much longer without a hit several times during the season. I wouldn't say the Reds have shown any special pattern in pitching to me. I'll keep swinging and see what happens."

Maris did indeed keep swinging, and one of those swings turned the Series irreversibly in New York's favor.

When the Yankees arrived in Cincinnati, they conducted a workout and Mantle took a few swings to test his injury. He sent six balls over the Crosley Field fences, but on each one he grimaced in pain as his weight shifted to his right side where the abscess was. I tried to talk to Mantle after the practice, but in a rare display of noncooperation toward me, he said, "I don't want to say anything about it, Joe." I left him alone, understanding his frustration over not being able to play in the Series.

Houk, who spent part of the day standing in the outfield alongside Mantle, spoke for his superstar. "Personally I don't think Mickey will play tomorrow. After all, he still has that big hole in him and you can't expect miracles. He said he felt better than he thought he would, but we'll have to wait and see about tomorrow."

Houk was a bit on edge as he discussed Mantle's condition. He didn't like the way Game Two went, and now with three in a row in Cincinnati I could sense he was a little apprehensive about the status of the Series. I think he fully expected to be up two games when the teams headed west, but now it was tied at one game each and he was pitching young Bill Stafford in Game Three, a 21-year-old kid with limited postseason experience.

When Stafford took the mound, he did so with Mantle behind him in center field. Having watched Mantle his whole career, this did not surprise me. The guy was a gamer, that's all there was to it. The team doctor, Sid Gaynor, wrapped thick gauze bandages around his waist in the hopes of preventing the blood from draining and it worked, but Mantle never really tested the leg. He went 0-for-4 with two fly outs and two strikeouts and only had to make one catch in the field so his running was minimal.

While Mantle was only able to provide an emotional lift to his team in the tense third game, it was Maris who delivered the victory. Johnny Blanchard had tied the game at 2-2 with a two-out solo homer off Bob Purkey, and then in the top of the ninth inning Maris led off against Purkey with a long home run to right field that brought a 3-2 triumph.

Maris had done nothing in his first three at-bats and you could hear the buzz in the press box about how the heir to Ruth's throne was 0-for-10 and choking on the grand stage. But then Maris connected with a 2-1 slider and all of his past misdeeds were forgotten.

Houk's demeanor changed dramatically. Now he had the lead, and he had Ford ready to go in Game Four. The Yankees were back in control, and soon, they would be back in their familiar position as world champions of baseball.

The fourth game saw Mantle limp off the field in the fourth inning with blood oozing through his uniform, and Ford exit in the sixth with a foot injury, but the two stars were hardly missed as the Yankees bludgeoned Cincinnati, 7-0, opening a commanding three games to one lead.

I really felt for Mantle. For the fourth time in a World Series he had been unable to perform at his peak because of an injury, and his emotions bubbled over when he hobbled to the dugout amidst a rousing ovation from the partisan Cincinnati fans. His wound had torn open as he lashed a drive off the scoreboard in left-center and he could only make it to first base, unable to put any weight on his right leg. Houk sent Hector Lopez out to run for him, and Mantle tearfully departed, his season over. "As it turned out, my body couldn't afford the price my mind was willing to pay," Mantle wrote years later.

After the game Mantle's teammates were bowled over by his courage. "The bandages were so thick I couldn't believe how the blood could come through," said Ford. Blanchard described the hole in Mantle's hip "as deep as a golf ball with blood oozing out of it." Bobby Richardson was spiked at second base turning a double play later in the game and, inspired by Mantle, he went the distance despite a bloody gash that soaked through his sock. "I'd be ashamed to come out of the game after Mickey's been playing with what he's got," Richardson said.

Ford worked his way through five uneventful innings and had a 4-0 lead when he foul tipped a ball off his foot in the top of the sixth. He tried to pitch, but after Chacon singled to start the bottom of the sixth, Ford signaled to Houk that the pain was too great and he couldn't continue. He left with another record in his hip pocket, his streak of scoreless World Series innings having been stretched to 32, breaking Babe Ruth's record of 29 straight between 1916 and 1918 when he pitched for the Red Sox. "It sure wasn't a very good year for the Babe," Ford quipped afterward.

"Don't forget, we still have to take another game," the always cautious Houk said. "Somehow that last one is always the toughest."

It wasn't. The next day New York routed Jay for five runs in the first inning and seven other Cincinnati pitchers had little luck slowing down the Bronx Bombers during a 13-5 wipeout that ended the Series.

"That was some explosion out there today," said Houk after watching his troops pound out 15 hits, seven for extra bases.

Mantle had played sparingly. Maris finished with just two hits. Ford was curtailed by an injury, as was Berra who missed Game Five. Yet it was still a cakewalk for this powerhouse Yankee team.

"This is the best all-around team I've ever seen," Houk said. "This team has much more power down through the lineup and the finest defensive infield I've ever seen. With Raschi, Reynolds, and Lopat those other Yankee teams had more experienced pitching, but our young staff did mighty well."

For Houk, it was sweet vindication. In becoming only the third rookie manager in baseball history to win a World Series, he laid to rest any doubts about his abilities as a skipper and made people forget all about Stengel.

And for Maris, it was the end of an extraordinary yet trying season. The Yankees threw a victory party at the Savoy Hotel the next night, but Maris made up his mind in the clubhouse after the game that he wasn't going. "It's been a long season," he said. "I'm anxious to go home. No party is good enough to keep me from my family."

Mickey Mantle called me in the winter of 1962 to gauge my interest in ghost-writing a book about his life in baseball. Naturally I was intrigued, and we set a dinner date at Gallagher's Steakhouse on West 52nd Street for January 13 to discuss the details.

I hadn't seen Mantle since the World Series the previous October, and when he walked into the restaurant I was glad to see that his abscessed hip had healed and he was no longer grimacing with every step he took. It wasn't fair for a man who had just turned 30 years old, but Mantle usually had a gimp in his gait because of his old knee surgeries and the other ailments that had plagued him throughout his career. Baseball had taken its toll on his body, and Mantle didn't do himself any favors with his hard drinking and disdain for exercise.

We sat down at the bar for a predinner cocktail, exchanged pleasantries, then got down to the brass tacks of what he had in mind. Just as he began to explain the project, we were called to our table, so we grabbed our drinks and walked into the dining room where, naturally, all eyes were fixated on Mantle. He was a superstar, and you didn't have to be a baseball fan to know who he was. He shook a few hands and offered a few waves, but once we sat down, the patrons left him alone except for one little boy, probably eight or nine years old, who tiptoed over for an autograph.

We ordered our entrees and were into our second round of scotch when the maitre d' approached our table to inform me that I had a phone call at the reception desk. Only Marie knew where I was, and as I walked to the front entrance, I knew whatever Marie had to tell me couldn't have been good news because she wouldn't call me otherwise. I hesitantly picked up the receiver, said hello, and I could hear Marie crying on the other end.

"Calm down, calm down, tell me what happened," I said, fearing a problem with one of my kids.

"Joe, I just got off the phone with your sister Carm," Marie said between sobs. "Dad had a heart attack tonight and he died."

I had no response as the words hung in the air, numbing my entire body. They were words I knew I would eventually hear in my lifetime, but they were words you are never prepared to comprehend. Ten or 15 seconds must have lapsed before I heard Marie's voice again. "Joe, are you all right? Did you hear what I said?"

"Yeah, yeah. What, what happened?" I stammered.

As Marie relayed what she knew, which wasn't much, the anguish in my face alerted Mantle that something was wrong. He could see me from our table about 40 feet away, and as Marie continued to talk I noticed him coming toward me, his rugged face shrouded in concern.

After I blindly handed the phone back to the young lady at the desk, Mantle put his hands on my shoulders and asked me, "Is everything all right?"

"Mick," I replied, my eyes beginning to moisten, "that was my wife. My dad had a heart attack and he passed away about an hour ago."

Mantle, of course, knew this pain. He had lost his father 10 years earlier and he had never gotten over Mutt Mantle's death. He had confided to me on several occasions that he still missed his father deeply, that time had not healed the wound. He knew he would have to carry that sorrow with him for the rest of his life. Now I would truly know what that was like.

Dad had been the picture of health. He was 72 years old, the same age as Casey Stengel, and if you would have stood the two of them side by side, my dad would have looked 40 compared to ol' Casey. Death was not an option for my father. I thought he was going to live forever, but the Lord had other plans for Dad.

Mantle went back to our table, left some money for the waiter, then led me outside where he hailed a cab and accompanied me back to my home which was now in Mount Vernon, just north of the Bronx. Through the years Mantle and I had our disagreements over things I had written like any player and writer would, but as I've said, my relationship with him on a personal level was uncommon, even during an era when ballplayers and writers generally coexisted quite comfortably. I respected him enormously as a player and a man, and he reciprocated that respect for my work, and, I think, for the person I was. No matter what I may have written, we were friends at the end of the day. It meant a great deal to me that on one of the saddest nights of my life, my good friend, Mickey Mantle, shared in my family's grief.

Mantle knew my father. Just as he had constructed shoes for Babe Ruth and Lou Gehrig and Joe DiMaggio, Dad made Mantle a couple of pairs when he first came to the Big Apple in 1951. Mantle was painfully shy, but Dad would always loosen him up when he happened to be in the store and I know Mantle felt comfortable in Dad's presence. When Dad retired in 1956 he lost contact with most of the players, but Mantle would regularly ask me how he was doing and it made Dad smile when I would tell him that.

Mantle was only supposed to be in New York overnight before flying back to Dallas to enjoy his last month of vacation before the start of spring training. But he stayed an extra three days so that he could attend Dad's funeral, and that gave me an opportunity to ask him for a huge favor. I told Mantle that my dad had served as a pallbearer for Ruth, so I asked Mantle if he would help carry Dad's casket and he gladly agreed. There were probably 20 current or so ex-Yankees in attendance at Dad's funeral, paying their respects to a man who happened to be a fan of them all. Young Joe Torre, by now the starting catcher for the Milwaukee Braves who was home in Brooklyn for the off-season, also came to the service and sat with his buddy, my nephew Sammy.

Before I said my final good-bye to my father, I affixed a Yankee pin to the lapel of his blazer, and in his breast pocket I tucked away a poem that I had written in tribute to him, thanking him for my life, for the sacrifices he made, for the wisdom he imparted, and for the good times that we shared. It was one piece of prose that did not carry my byline and was not for publication. No one, not even my mother or Marie, read that poem, and that's the way it will always be.

The 1962 season obviously wasn't one of my favorites. The death of my father—the man who had introduced me to baseball and to the Yankees—hit me very hard and for the first time in my 46-year life I found it difficult to summon the enthusiasm to watch the Yankees. A piece of me was gone, and even though Dad and I never sat together during games, I knew when he was coming and I'd always try to spend a few minutes before the first pitch chatting with him and his friends in the stands.

Being at the ballpark just wasn't the same that year, and what I missed most were the phone conversations I'd have with Dad after the games when he'd second-guess the moves made by Joe McCarthy or Bucky Harris or Stengel or Ralph Houk. There were times when something would happen on the field, and my first thought was "Dad's going to have a mouthful to say about that." But then I'd remember Dad wouldn't be calling that night.

The Yankees won another World Series in 1962. I'm sure Dad was cheering from his new perch in the uppermost deck. I was glad the Yankees beat the Giants, now of San Francisco, but in all honesty, that year's championship meant very little to me.

– Chapter 20 –

1962

I WASN'T THE ONLY PERSON who had a lousy 1962.

On the day that the expansion New York Mets were to play the Yankees for the first time in what had to be the most anticipated spring training game in history, Roger Maris set himself up for what would become a miserable year for him, too.

Before the game—which was played in St. Petersburg, now the home of the Mets because the Yankees had moved their operation to Fort Lauderdale—a photographer asked Hall of Famer Rogers Hornsby if he would pose for a picture with Maris. Hornsby was serving as a Met coach under manager Casey Stengel, and the photographer thought it might be swell to get the record-breaking home run hitter Maris together for a shot with Hornsby, who possessed the highest career batting average in National League history. Hornsby agreed. Maris did not.

Hornsby, a truly ornery man throughout his playing, managing, and coaching career, had been highly critical of Maris the previous year when Maris broke Babe Ruth's home run record. Like so many other people, Hornsby didn't think Maris was worthy of such a record and he stated so publicly. Maris remembered the acid-tongued Hornsby's comments, and when the photographer asked him to come over and smile with Hornsby, he refused and walked away. I can't say that I blamed him. Hornsby's reply was, "He's a busher. He couldn't carry my bat. He's a punk little ballplayer."

Hey, Maris had every right to refuse that request. Hornsby was a prick to everybody, and given all that Hornsby had said the previous season, if I were Maris, I'd have told him to go screw himself, too. However, Maris picked the wrong day to take his stand. With so much attention focused on this silly exhibition game, there was an overflow of newsmen milling about and a number of writers witnessed Maris's blow off of Hornsby. The first to ask him what happened was Oscar Fraley of the United Press International wire service. When Maris told him, "No comment," the angered Fraley stalked up to the press box and wrote a vicious column attacking Maris's character as well as his ability as a ballplayer. He called Maris an "ingrate" and went on to say, "guys like Maris bat a round zero with me." I have to say it was one of the most classless acts I've witnessed in journalism, and when you consider I worked my entire career in New York City, that's saying an awful lot. Fraley, who went on to gain fame as the writer of "The Untouchables" television show, let his emotions cloud his judgment and that's something writers, and especially columnists, can never let happen. It's one thing to have an opinion, but another to besmirch a man without just cause.

Fraley's column was picked up nationwide and caused unnecessary and irreparable harm to Maris's reputation. A few days later when Maris failed to show up for an interview with Jimmy Cannon, my former colleague at the *Post* who now was working for the *Journal American*, Cannon laid into him just as fiercely as Fraley. Cannon's column was also syndicated and therefore readers around the country absorbed another negative portrayal of Maris. The man did not deserve it, and I honestly took no umbrage in his standoffishness with the press the rest of that year. We gave him no reason to trust us, so he decided to ignore most of us. It didn't help his image, but at least it gave him some peace when the majority of writers stopped pestering him. Because I had earned a measure of respect in the clubhouse after a quarter century on the job, Maris did not shut me off completely, but his quotes were mostly bland clichés that lent nothing to my stories.

It was a season of discontent for Maris. He hit 33 home runs, a fine year for most players, but it wasn't good enough for a man who'd hit 61 the year before. The booing of Maris reached outlandish proportions, and what was so disturbing is that the fans at Yankee Stadium were among the worst. I could never understand it. Here was a man who was in the midst of helping the Yankees win their third pennant in a row, and later, their second consecutive World Series. He had won the American League's MVP award two years running, and he wasn't a bad guy. His only sin was that he wasn't Mickey Mantle, and that cracked me up because most of the same people who were booing Maris did the same to Mantle up until 1960. That was the year Maris came to New York, so I guess he became the new whipping boy. I love my fellow New Yorkers, but we are a puzzling lot sometimes.

As for the rest of the team, 1962 started off just fine, but trouble arose when Mantle, Whitey Ford, and Luis Arroyo went down with injuries within a four-day span, and without three of their best players, all of a sudden the Yankees descended to mortal status, and if not for the play of second baseman Bobby Richardson, the Yankees might have sunk further.

*   *   *

Mantle won the MVP award in 1962, but many people—including Mantle and me—thought the runner-up in the voting, Richardson, deserved the honor. In fact, Mantle sent a Christmas card to Richardson that December and addressed it to the "MVP." In 1962, Richardson had the season of his life and he played a key role in New York's defense of the World Series title.

Casey Stengel once said of Richardson, "Look at him. He don't drink, he don't smoke, he don't chew, he don't stay out late and he still can't hit .250." None of that changed in 1962. Richardson, a devout Christian who had been raised in the Bible Belt of South Carolina, still didn't drink, smoke, chew, or carouse, and he didn't hit .250. Instead he hit .302, set an American League record with 692 at-bats, and produced a league-high 209 hits. He also earned the second of his five straight Gold Glove awards, the second of his six straight nominations to *The Sporting News* All-Star team, and played in the first of five straight All-Star Games.

It all came together in 1962 for Richardson, and Ralph Houk was a primary reason for his success. Houk had managed Richardson in the minors and loved the way he played. When he took over the Yankees in 1961, he moved Richardson from eighth in the batting order to leadoff or second, and he wrote his name on the lineup card every day that season. "Ralph had confidence in me and kept me in there even when my batting wasn't as sharp as it could have been," Richardson said. "He stayed with me through the slumps, didn't pull me out for pinch-hitters, and it gave me a great desire to reward his confidence with a good performance."

Those rewards were plentiful.

On the strength of his 11 hits and record 12 RBI he won the 1960 World Series MVP award even though the Yankees lost to the Pirates. In 1961 he played in every regular-season game, turned an astounding

136 double plays to win his first Gold Glove, and in the Series he pounded out nine hits to help the Yankees defeat the Reds. In the 1962 Series, he made the game-saving and Series-ending catch of Willie McCovey's screaming line drive.

"Bobby was the best second baseman in the league," Joe DeMaestri, who was a Yankee utility infielder for a brief period, once said. "He was so quick. As a hitter Bobby could handle a bat as good as anybody I ever saw. Depending on where the ball was pitched he'd either flip his wrist or just reach out with the bat and he'd have a hit. He was a threat because he could always hit the ball somewhere, often with extra-base power. He made a great leadoff man, batting in front of Tony Kubek."

He also made a great double-play partner for Kubek. Those two were artistic around the keystone sack, and with Mantle in center and Howard behind the plate, the Yankees were probably the strongest team in baseball up the middle in the late 1950s and early 1960s.

"I came up as a shortstop and Casey said, 'I have a good man (Phil Rizzuto and later Gil McDougald) at that position so you better learn to play second base,'" Richardson recalled. "Frank Crosetti was the infield coach and he did the coaching. He taught me to position myself closer to the bag in double-play situations, that way you can be in position until the last possible second if a man is stealing and the batter is swinging."

Richardson's religious virtues were well-known, but what was nice is that he never pushed his beliefs on anyone else. All the players knew Richardson wasn't ever going to swear or lose his temper and they respected him for it. But there were times when his presence was a little unnerving. Clubhouse language is often vile, and the players tried to curb their behavior when Richardson was around. However, occasionally someone would be telling a dirty joke or sharing a story about a particular sexual conquest, and Richardson would come in unexpectedly and spoil the fun. Not that he meant to, but the players knew he frowned upon such things and rather than subject his ears to the story, they would cut it off and leave everyone else hanging.

Mantle told me the story of the day in the dugout when Moose Skowron made an out and came back to the bench swearing up a blue streak. He walked past Richardson and stopped cussing long enough to say, "Excuse me, Bobby," and then continued down the line swearing again. Even Richardson laughed at that one.

* * *

Just as Stengel had told Richardson to learn a different position if he wanted to stick with the Yankees, he advised Moose Skowron to do the same. Skowron began his baseball career as a shortstop, which seems hard to believe given his bulky physical stature. He also played some at third base and in the outfield, but as a fielder, he was competent at none of those stations. "Moose, the only way to the big leagues for you is first base," Stengel said. So Skowron listened and began to train as a first baseman.

Part of that training one year was attending the Arthur Murray dance studio in St. Petersburg three nights a week during the spring, which Stengel thought would help Moose's dexterity around the bag.

"Casey kept after me," Skowron said.

It worked. He wasn't a Gold Glove candidate, but Skowron made himself into an above-average first baseman. Though he wasn't prone to making spectacular plays, he made all the ones he was supposed to make. He knew how to play the hitters and was rarely out of position, and when he wasn't sure of something, he wasn't afraid to yell into the dugout for instruction. A lot of players would not expose their egos like that, but ego was a foreign term to Skowron. He didn't have one, and that's why he was so popular among his teammates and us in the press.

There was never a question about his ability as a hitter. He swung a potent stick and hit over .300 the first four years he was with the Yankees.

"Moose was one of those guys who when he hit a grounder the ball seemed to pick up speed as it went through the infield because of all the top spin he put on it," Houk said. "He was a good all-around ballplayer."

Funny thing about Skowron. His nickname was Moose and for a long time I assumed it was because of his big-boned body. It turned out that when he was about eight years old his grandfather had given him a terrible haircut, actually shaved him bald. The older kids in his Chicago neighborhood started calling him Mussolini after the dictator of Italy. Later it was shortened to Moose and Skowron told me one time, "My grandfather never saw me play a game in the major leagues, but I always wanted to thank him because whenever I would strike out or hit into a double play I couldn't separate the 'Moooose!' from the 'Booooos!'"

Skowron was a fun-loving guy in the clubhouse. His teammates used to pick on him and he'd always take it in stride, never got mad. Mantle used to say he was one of the ugliest guys he'd ever met and he'd say it looked like Moose "got run over by a train." He was the butt of many a practical joke, and he'd pretend to get angry and chase the jokester around, but he'd never do anything about it. In fact, he enjoyed the attention.

One time I was interviewing Skowron after a game. He'd had a good day, was in a good mood, and wasn't paying attention to his clothes as he put them on. He had a new pair of green-checkered pants that he was particularly fond of and as I was looking down at my notebook while scribbling his comments, I noticed that one of the legs of his pants had been cut off at the knee. I looked up at him and because he wasn't aware of it; he just kept talking. Then our eyes met and that's when he realized something was wrong. He looked down and just said, "Aw, fellas, c'mon."

* * *

Houk's mantra throughout the dark days when Mantle, Ford, and Arroyo were sidelined was, "When we get healthy, we will win." Houk was right. Cleveland was leading the American League in June, but the Indians faded badly and with its stars back in the galaxy New York won 10 in a row in the middle of July and moved into first place for good. The Yankees could never get a comfortable lead, though, as the surprising Los Angeles Angels and Minnesota Twins stayed within shouting distance throughout the summer. Minnesota pulled as close as 2 1/2 games, but on September 10 Mantle hit his 400th career home run in Detroit and Ralph Terry pitched beautifully to win his 21st game, and the next day Yogi Berra hit his 350th career home run to key another win over the Tigers. The Twins lost both days to fall 4 1/2 behind and the Yankees ended up winning the flag by five games.

– *1962 World Series* –

I can't even fathom the pressure Ralph Terry must have been feeling as he stared down from the Candlestick Park pitchers' mound at Willie McCovey who was standing menacingly 60 feet and 6 inches away. Game Seven of the World Series, bottom of the ninth inning, two outs, San Francisco runners on second and third, the Yankees clinging to a 1-0 lead, and Terry's checkered World Series past weighing on his broad shoulders like a block of concrete.

It was Terry who threw the pitch that Bill Mazeroski hit over the fence at Pittsburgh's Forbes Field in the bottom of the ninth inning in Game Seven of the 1960 World Series. With that pitch, Terry gift-wrapped the championship for the Pirates and forever joined Ralph

Branca, Mickey Owen, and Fred Merkle in the Baseball Hall of Shame. And now here was Terry again, two years later, bidding to become class valedictorian.

All the massive McCovey had to do was bloop a little single over the infield and speedy runners Willie Mays and Matty Alou both would have scored to give the Giants their first title since the move to San Francisco. Mazeroski should have been the extent of Terry's torture. No man deserved to be twice thrown into an inferno armed only with a can of gasoline. Yet rather than look negatively on this cruel twist of fate, Terry chose to spin positively.

"I was thankful to have the opportunity to pitch a seventh game, to have a real shot at redemption," he said. "A lot of people in life never get a second chance. And a lot of players never even got into a World Series."

Thankfully, Terry's spin wasn't the only positive to come out of this sticky situation.

"This was a lot different than 1960," a gleeful Terry said moments after McCovey hit a line drive safely into the glove of Bobby Richardson, securing the Yankees' 20th world championship.

Terry had an adventurous tenure in New York. As an 18-year-old in 1954, he signed a contract to play with the Yankees, but he also signed to play with the Cardinals and commissioner Ford Frick had to resolve the matter, ruling in favor of the Yankees. He spent two years in the minors, then pitched sparingly in New York in 1956. Considered a flop, Terry was traded to Kansas City along with Billy Martin. "He always does two or three things that boggle him up, and he don't win," Casey Stengel said.

Terry didn't win for the Athletics, but for some reason George Weiss decided to reacquire him. Terry was no great shakes in 1959, he made progress in 1960 with a 10-8 record, then suffered two defeats in the Series. The Mazeroski home run was traumatic enough to end the careers of some men, but Terry became one of baseball's best pitchers the next two years as he went 16-3 in 1961 and 23-12 in 1962. One reason for the transformation was Ralph Houk's hiring of Johnny Sain as pitching coach before the 1961 season. Terry had always been too finicky. He had an overpowering fastball when he was sharp, but he was fond of throwing off-speed and breaking pitches, and those were the ones opposing hitters feasted on. Sain taught Terry how to throw a hard-breaking slider, and that pitch replaced the meaty curveball in his repertoire and became the one he relied on in clutch situations.

While Terry's pitch selection used to cause Stengel to pull his hair out, he drove Houk crazy with his obsession for golf. After the 1957 season Terry was involved in an auto accident, and he spent that winter in traction recovering from a fractured hip. When he went to spring training the following February he couldn't do any running, so a couple of friends suggested he take up golf as a form of exercise. Golf became his passion, and after he retired from baseball, it became his livelihood.

Terry began to play golf every chance he got and within three years he was a scratch player and routinely won celebrity tournaments. I had numerous opportunities to play with him, but golf wasn't a game most kids from the Bronx grew up playing. I began dabbling a little in my late 30s and early 40s and I could hit the ball pretty well, but I had no skill around the greens and breaking 100 was a major event for me. Terry would give me a stroke per hole, sometimes two on the really challenging holes, and I still couldn't beat him. Neither could his teammates, though Mickey Mantle and Whitey Ford gave him a much better fight than I.

"He got to thinking so much about golf at the end that I think it bothered his pitching a little, he couldn't concentrate on it enough, and he was the kind of guy who had to concentrate," Houk once said.

After winding up his baseball career playing for Cleveland, Kansas City, and the Mets, Terry became a golf pro, bought part of Roxiticus Country Club in New Jersey, and served as the head pro. He spent a couple of winters playing on the South African pro tour, and when the PGA Senior Tour was conceived, he tried on a couple of occasions to obtain playing privileges, but fell just short. He wound up in Kansas as a head club pro, won a bunch of regional events, and today he's still striping it down the middle at retirement age.

I don't know what Terry considered his best sport, but it would not be hard to argue that his performance throughout the 1962 baseball season was the highlight of his athletic career when he carried the Yankees to the pennant.

Houk's plan for the World Series was to pitch Ford three times if necessary, but due to the rainy weather that turned this Classic into a two-week marathon, he was able to get three starts each out of Ford and Terry. And the way things fell, Terry was the chosen one to pitch Game Seven. As Joe DiMaggio told him when it was over, "This was the best-pitched World Series game I've ever seen. You can forget about that Pittsburgh thing now, Ralph."

* * *

The Yankees and Giants hadn't played each other in a World Series since 1951. That year the Giants needed to defeat the Dodgers in a special three-game play-off to capture the National League flag, and they did it by scoring four runs in the ninth inning of Game Three. In 1962, the Giants and Dodgers finished tied for first again, and another three-game play-off was needed. Instead of playing it in New York City at Ebbets Field and the Polo Grounds, this one took place in California at Los Angeles' Dodger Stadium and San Francisco's Candlestick Park. The locales were different, but the result was amazingly similar. After splitting the first two games, the Giants won the rubber match by scoring four runs in the ninth inning, and it was on to the World Series to meet the Yankees. It really was déjà vu all over again.

New York was rested and ready for the opener; the Giants were spent. They had made up four games in the standings in the final week to catch Los Angeles, the three-game play-off sapped their remaining energy, and the Yankees cruised to a 6-2 victory.

The noise from San Francisco's riotous celebration of the National League title—a first for this city—had barely subsided when Roger Maris stepped up to bat in the top of the first inning of Game One. With Bobby Richardson and Tom Tresh already aboard via singles, Maris silenced the frenzied mob with a double to right that would have been a home run had Felipe Alou not leaped over the chain-link fence to swat the ball back into play. Richardson and Tresh scored easily for a 2-0 lead.

Ford's World Series record consecutive innings streak came to an end at 33 in the second inning, and after the Giants tied the game at 2-2 in the third, they were never heard from again. Ford settled down and earned what proved to be the 10th and final Series victory of his career as Clete Boyer hit a solo homer in the seventh to give the Yankees the lead for good.

The Giants were far from distraught after the game and they weren't making any excuses for the loss. "We weren't tired," manager Alvin Dark claimed. "We'll be back tomorrow. It was just Ford. He pitched a great game. They can't throw two guys in a row as good as he is."

In 1962 the Yankees could, and they did. Terry was the Game Two starter and he was even more effective than Ford. However, Dark's starter, 24-game winner Jack Sanford, was even better. Sanford tossed a three-hit shutout at the Yankees and Terry lost despite giving up just two runs on five hits, his career Series record slipping to 0-4.

"I hope I get another shot at them," said Terry, not knowing at that moment how sweet his retribution would be.

Terry made only two mistakes all day, and both cost him runs. Chuck Hiller led off the bottom of the first with a shot into right field that Maris nearly made a great catch on, but the ball bounced out of his glove as he hit the ground and Hiller sprinted into second with a double, scoring later on a ground ball. Then in the seventh Terry left a fat pitch out over the plate to Willie McCovey and he launched it way over the right-field fence for the only other run of the game.

The teams flew across the country to New York for the next three games, and excitement pulsated throughout the city when the Giants arrived. It was as if a long lost son had come home. There were thousands of Giants fans in New York, still ardent followers of the team even though it now resided 3,000 miles away. They were angry with Horace Stoneham for moving the club five years earlier, but not with the players whom they continued to root for. Upon arriving at Yankee Stadium on the off-day Mays walked onto the field, stared up at the rows of empty seats and raised his hands as if to say, "I'm back." The photographers loved it.

Before the game I was standing around the batting cage chatting with Maris as he watched that day's starting pitcher, Bill Stafford, taking fruitless swings. "You really hit that ball, young fellow," Maris chided. Stafford turned around and said, "OK, then, I'll let you drive in the runs for me."

For 6 1/2 innings no one drove in any runs. Stafford limited the Giants to one hit and Billy Pierce stymied the Yankees on two hits. When the bottom of the seventh inning started, the three scheduled hitters were Tresh, Mantle, and Maris and there was a sense throughout the ballpark that something had to happen right here if the Yankees were going to win. Something happened, and Maris—just as Stafford had implored him to do—played the starring role.

With runners on second and third Maris lined a shot into right field. Tresh trotted home from third, and when McCovey misplayed the ball for an error Mantle steamed around to make it 2-0 as the stadium thundered its approval.

Here, Maris showed why he was such an underrated player. Not only did he take second base on McCovey's error, he alertly tagged up and moved to third when Elston Howard hit a fly ball into relatively deep center field. From there he was able to score New York's third run on Boyer's grounder to short. When Ed Bailey hit a two-run homer off Stafford in the ninth, Maris's run was the winner.

I talked to Mantle about what Maris did in the seventh inning. How he drove in two runs, then scored the third run by his own astute manufacturing. "This is what people miss about Roger, but not his teammates," Mantle said. "He can do it all. That was the ballgame."

"I can't remember a Series where there's been such great pitching for the first three games," Houk said.

There would be plenty more, but not much of it came from the Yankees in Game Four. Ford hooked up with young Juan Marichal who had won 18 games in his third big-league season, but their much-anticipated battle was short-lived. Marichal hurt his hand while batting in the fifth inning and had to leave the game. And after the Yankees scored twice in the bottom of the sixth to tie the score at 2-2, Houk lifted Ford for a pinch-hitter. Yogi Berra came through by drawing a walk to load the bases, but Tony Kubek grounded out to spike the rally.

Exhilarated by that narrow escape, the Giants lit up Jim Coates and Marshall Bridges and Hiller's grand slam in the seventh sent the Giants on to a 7-3 victory, tying the Series at two apiece. Ironically, on the sixth anniversary of his perfect World Series game, ex-Yankee Don Larsen was the winning pitcher. He'd faced only two batters—Berra and Kubek in the sixth—and then was pulled for a pinch-hitter in the seventh, but his timing was perfect to get the win.

In what would become commonplace for this Series, rain interrupted play the next day, though it really had no bearing on the pitching matchup for Game Five. It was going to be a rematch of Game Two with Terry opposing Sanford. We just had to wait an extra 24 hours.

I talked to Terry about the delay and he said, "It makes no difference to me." I was impressed by his calmness, especially for a man who was fast becoming an October disaster. I would have thought someone who was 0-4 lifetime in the World Series would be anxious to get his next outing underway, but he was unperturbed by the postponement.

When Game Five started Terry looked sharp, but Sanford looked better. Again. The Yankees were having a devil of a time hitting Sanford, and their confidence was wobbling. Terry, however, gritted his teeth and kept plugging away in the hope that his teammates would shake their offensive doldrums. His hard work was rewarded when Tresh followed singles by Kubek and Richardson with a game-winning three-run homer in the bottom of the eighth.

Visiting the Yankee clubhouse afterward was Casey Stengel, and he walked over to Terry and said, "I'm glad you finally did it." Terry replied, "I'm only sorry I couldn't have done it for you."

Because I was flying on the team charter I wasn't going to have time to go home after the game. Marie packed my suitcase in the morning, I brought it to the ballpark, and a couple hours after the game, I was on the way to San Francisco. Cautioning for the chance the Giants might force a seventh game, Marie packed enough clothes for three days.

It's a good thing the hotel had laundry service.

Typhoon Frieda arrived in the Bay Area just around the time our plane was touching down, and she drenched the region for four straight days, creating the longest World Series delay since 1911 when rain forced a week's worth of postponements between the Athletics and Giants.

Considering this storm killed about 50 people in Washington, Oregon, and British Columbia, Canada, our plight seemed rather inconsequential. The way I looked at it, if I had my choice of cities where this had to happen, San Francisco would be high on my list. The town was famous for its restaurants, and the writers sampled a few of them on these off-days. It sure beat press box food, though the accountants back at the *Post* probably weren't thrilled with the expense reports I filed.

During the evening most of the writers hung out together playing cards or drinking at the bar where we were staying, the posh Town House. Ford cracked me up one night when he started grumbling about the newspaper column he was writing for a suburban New York paper. "When I took the job I thought I made a whale of a deal," he said. "But the way this thing has strung out I figure I'll wind up getting about eight bucks a column. Even you newspapermen make more than that."

I passed some of the time on Saturday afternoon watching the Texas-Oklahoma college football game on television in Mantle's room, and that wasn't a lot of fun because Mantle's beloved Sooners lost, 9-6.

The rain relented on Sunday, but with the field an unplayable quagmire, Game Six was called off for the third straight day. A promising weather report gave every indication that we'd be back in business on Monday, so both teams trekked 80 miles south to Modesto, California to conduct workouts at the tiny ballpark that was home to the minor-league Modesto Colts. Happily, the players found they could still swing, catch, and throw, and just as happily, about 5,000 people watched the practices. Who would have ever thought the World Series would come to Modesto?

The sun did indeed blaze down from a cloudless San Francisco sky on Monday, but it still took extraordinary measures to get the sixth game in. The maintenance crew at Candlestick Park requested the use of helicopters to help speed the drying process and at baseball's expense, three were brought in to hover over the soaked grass. The tactic worked, and never were the players more enthused to hear umpire Charley Berry bellow, "Play ball."

With a well-rested Ford on their side, the Yankees were confident this was going to be their last game of the season. Billy Pierce had other ideas. It wasn't a Candlestick gust blowing Ford off the mound inside five innings. Rather, it was his suddenly scattershot arm. He allowed nine hits and five runs, committed an error on a vain pickoff attempt, and with Pierce stifling the Yankees on three hits, the Giants won easily, 5-2.

"I didn't think Billy was nearly as sharp as he had been in New York," Howard said, referring to Pierce's hard-luck Game Three performance when he lost to Stafford. "He seemed to be just laying the ball in there and daring us to hit it. But we couldn't."

The game was scoreless when the Giants came to bat in the fourth, but with two men on, Ford's wild pickoff throw to second sailed into the outfield and Felipe Alou raced home with the first run. Orlando Cepeda then doubled home a second run, and he scored on Jim Davenport's single to give the Giants a 3-0 lead. The Yankees never caught up.

Over in the Giants clubhouse, Dark's troops were ecstatic. With the home-field advantage and Ford out of the way, they were the confident team now, and for the third time in this Series, Sanford would square off with Terry. The Giants liked their chances.

"I've been saying all along that we're going to win this Series in seven games," Dark said. "We've got the club to do it."

The Giants gave it all they had. In fact, if McCovey had hit his ninth-inning line drive one foot in either direction, they would have won. But he didn't.

Terry was flat-out brilliant. He retired the first 17 Giants he faced, his bid for a perfect game broken up with two outs in the sixth by, of all people, the opposing pitcher, as Sanford lined a clean single into right-center. By that time Terry was working with a 1-0 lead as Moose Skowron had singled, taken third on Boyer's single, and scored on Kubek's double-play grounder.

Terry avoided trouble in the seventh when he struck out Cepeda after McCovey had tripled, and then the Giants escaped a real jam in the eighth when the Yankees loaded the bases with none out, chasing Sanford in the process. However, Billy O'Dell strolled into this beehive and came out with nary a sting. Maris's grounder forced Richardson at the plate, and Howard grounded into a double play to end the inning.

Despite being stoked with enthusiasm the Giants were quickly dispatched in the bottom of the eighth, and after the Yankees went just as quietly in the ninth, Terry trotted out to the mound three outs away from completing the pinnacle performance of his career.

It started badly when pinch-hitter Matty Alou beat out a bunt for a single, it improved when Terry whiffed Felipe Alou and Hiller, and then terror set in as Mays dug himself into the batter's box. "I wanted to get them in order so I wouldn't have to face Mays and McCovey with anybody on," Terry recalled. With that plan scuttled, Terry was forced to confront Mays.

"I threw two fastballs inside trying to keep the ball in on him because the wind was blowing in real strong from left field so if he hit the ball I wanted him to drive it into that gale," Terry said. "And after two pitches inside I figured I better not stay in there because he's strong enough where he can still knock it out of anywhere."

Terry threw a very good pitch, low and away about knee-high with good velocity, but Mays punched it down the line in right and for a moment it looked as if Matty Alou was going to be able to score the tying run. With the crowd screaming in excitement, Maris showed why he was so much more than just a home run hitter. He tracked the ball down and made a perfect throw to Richardson just in time to prevent Alou from trying to score. It was a stellar defensive play, the kind that doesn't show up in the box score, but every Yankee agreed it was the play that saved the game.

Now Houk and Howard strolled out to the mound, and they asked Terry if he wanted to walk McCovey and pitch to Cepeda, a right-handed hitter. It was the obvious move, but Terry reasoned that if the bases were loaded, his room for error dwindled because a walk would force in a run. He decided to battle McCovey, and Houk let him. Two pitches later, the game was over as McCovey ripped a liner right into Richardson's mitt.

Someone asked Terry if he had flashbacks to 1960 and Pittsburgh when McCovey hit the ball. "I saw it go by me and right at Richardson," said Terry. "I didn't have time to worry about anything. I knew I had a man over there somewhere. He hit my best pitch very hard and it went right to Bobby."

Somewhere up above, my father breathed a sigh of relief and raised a glass of whiskey in celebration. It was the last time he would do so for quite a while.

When you get to be an octogenarian, individual 14-year time periods seem Lilliputian in nature. Hell, 14 years ago I was an old man, and all I am now is an older old man.

But when you are the New York Yankees, 14 years without winning a World Series is a long time. A very long time. It seems almost generational.

Remember that from 1923 through 1962, the Yankees never went more than four years without winning a championship as they constructed one of the most enduring dynasties in the history of sport. And for the Yankees, it wasn't just about winning. It was about winning it all. During that 40-year stretch of dominance they averaged one championship every two seasons. No matter how many games they won during the regular schedule, no matter how many American League pennants they raised over Yankee Stadium, no year was considered successful unless they won the World Series. That's just the way it was.

Having lived almost all my life connected in some way to the team, one simple fact had always been a constant for me: The Yankees won. They were the standard by which all other baseball teams measured themselves. So it is hard for me to describe the morbidity that engulfed this proud franchise during the epoch from 1963 to 1976 when it did not win a World Series, and at one juncture became a baseball laughingstock, stripped naked of its noble heritage.

Fourteen years. It doesn't seem that long to me now, but when I reflect on this extended session of Yankee infirmity, I am jarred by the consequential nature of those times. A lot happened in those 14 years.

One of our most beloved presidents, John F. Kennedy, was assassinated while motorcading through the streets of Dallas, Texas. Another of our presidents, Richard Nixon, resigned in disgrace before being impeached, his term undone by revelations of corruption and abuse of power stemming from the Watergate scandal.

Within two months in 1968 two other shocking assassinations occurred. With the civil rights movement gaining momentum and bringing racial tensions to a boiling point, the man who spearheaded the drive for equality, Dr. Martin Luther King Jr., was gunned down in Memphis, Tennessee. And President Kennedy's senatorial brother, Robert, in the midst of his own campaign for the presidency, was murdered in a Los Angeles hotel ballroom shortly after winning the California primary.

America became embroiled in the unwinnable Vietnam War, and during more than 10 years of fighting 57,000 of our men and women—including my nephew Sammy—lost their lives in the Asian jungles. The never-ending wars between the Catholics and Protestants in Northern Ireland and the Jews and Arabs in the Middle East continued in bloody earnest, and violence on a smaller scale erupted worldwide in the form of civil protests, none more tragic than the Kent State University incident where four students were killed by National Guard troops. Even the sports world was not spared because Palestinian terrorists killed 11 Jewish athletes at the 1972 Munich Olympics.

We said good-bye to former presidents Truman and Eisenhower; entertainers Spencer Tracy, Louis Armstrong, Jack Benny, Betty Grable, and Walter Winchell; athletic icons Jackie Robinson, Vince Lombardi, Bobby Jones, Roberto Clemente, Rocky Marciano, and Casey Stengel; nearly 100 daily newspapers around the country, the Saturday Evening Post, *and, almost, New York City before a $2 billion federal bailout saved the city from bankruptcy.*

All the news wasn't bad, though.

In what I still consider the greatest human achievement, certainly in my lifetime, the United States figured out how to send men into space, allow them to walk on the moon, and then bring them back to earth safely. Unless you lived through it, there is no way you can appreciate the depth of that accomplishment. Modern technology also provided us with calculators to add numbers, VCRs to record TV shows, and computers to help us do our work, and you could play a game called Pong on your television screen while eating a frozen dinner and drinking a "light" beer containing half the calories.

On the medical front, a surgeon in South Africa successfully transplanted the heart of a dead woman into the body of a living man, an American biochemist synthesized biologically active DNA in a test tube, and the CAT scan was introduced.

Television was every family's friend and we didn't need ratings to warn us of the content each show contained. We watched The Big Valley (I loved Barbara Stanwick), Mission: Impossible (the weekly series, not the 1990s Tom Cruise movie), variety shows hosted by Johnny Carson, Ed Sullivan, Carol Burnett, and Dick Cavett, Monday Night Football (Howard Cosell finally became the star he always envisioned himself becoming), The Mary Tyler Moore Show, All in the Family, Laugh-In, The Brady Bunch, M*A*S*H, Happy Days, and Saturday Night Live. When only the big screen would suffice we paid a buck or two to watch movies such as Dr. Strangelove, The Sound of Music, Dr. Zhivago, True Grit, Patton, The Sting, Dirty Harry, The Godfather, One Flew Over the Cuckoo's Nest, Jaws, and Rocky.

When the Beatles crawled across the ocean from Great Britain, rock and roll, much to my chagrin, became the prevalent form of musical expression. Elvis Presley had started this noisy revolution, but it was fostered by those four mopheads, John, Paul, George, and Ringo, as well as other artists such as the Rolling Stones, Bob Dylan, and Jimi Hendrix. Soon they were joined by a grungy-looking kid from across the river in New Jersey named Bruce Springsteen, who actually graced the covers of Time and Newsweek during the same week in 1975.

In the world of sports, the brash and beautiful Cassius Clay won the heavyweight boxing championship, changed his name to Muhammad Ali, relinquished his title, and was banned from fighting for 40 months when he refused induction into the Army based on his religious Muslim beliefs, then regained his crown seven years after he'd lost it and became the most popular athlete on the planet. The ultimate underdogs, the New York Mets and New York Jets, won the World Series and the Super Bowl within 10 months of each other in 1969. The New York Knicks won a pair of NBA titles, something they haven't done since. Jack Nicklaus stole the spotlight from Arnold Palmer and reinvented the game of golf. In 1972 the American basketball team lost for the first time in Olympic competition, but swimmer Mark Spitz eased some of the furor by winning a record seven gold medals. Teams such as the Boston Celtics, Green Bay Packers, Miami Dolphins, Toronto Maple Leafs, Montreal Canadiens, and UCLA Bruins enjoyed repetitive championship prosperity, and in addition to Ali, Nicklaus, and Spitz, the individual heroes of the day included O.J. Simpson, Joe Namath, Kareem Abdul-Jabbar, Bill Walton, Bobby Orr, Jean Beliveau, Billie Jean King, Olga Korbut, and Henry Aaron, who broke my friend Babe Ruth's career home run record.

Professionally and personally, it was a time of great reward for me. In 1966 I gave up the daily grind of the Yankees beat and was promoted to a columnist position at the Post which allowed me to spread my wings and cover a myriad of sporting events. Instead of being editorially bound to providing only the details, I was able to render opinions on what I saw. It was an invigorating time in my life and a welcome break from the doldrums in the Bronx where the glory days were a distant memory. Perhaps out of habit and loyalty, I still spent the majority of my time with the Yankees in the summer, but it was nice not to have to be there. If I wanted, I could go over to Shea and watch the Mets—which I did plenty of in 1969—or when the respective sports were in season, I could opine about pro and college football and basketball, hockey, and an occasional golf or tennis tournament.

On the homefront the Kimmerle clan endured some hardships. Sammy's death hit us all very hard and that was a wound that remained open for several years.

Marie and I lost our remaining parents as well. My mother lived until she was 81, and she was active right up until her last few months when finally, her lung disease was too much to overcome. It was her time to go, and seeping through my sadness was a tinge of relief. She had been in pain at the end, every breath a struggle, and she prayed to the Lord that He would reunite her with my father in heaven. Unlike my father's death, which had come so suddenly 11 years earlier, I was prepared for Mom's passing, but that didn't soothe the grief.

What did help to soften our sorrow and replenish our familial void was the birth of our first two grandchildren later in 1973. Phillip's son, Phillip Jr., was born in August and Katherine's son, Robert, came along in December. Eventually Marie and I would become the proud grandparents of four boys and three girls, one of which followed in his grandpa's footsteps and served as a Yankee batboy for a couple of summers.

During his two-year stint with the team, my grandson Kevin saw some of the worst Yankee baseball ever as the team played a combined 48 games under .500 in 1990 and 1991. I felt bad for Kevin because he didn't get to experience the thrills I had, working for a dominant team made up of legendary figures who routinely won championships. Those years Kevin worked reminded me of the drought the Yankees suffered through in the 1960s and 1970s.

The first warning signs of the team's imminent demise came in the 1963 World Series when the Los Angeles Dodgers embarrassed New York with a four-game sweep as Sandy Koufax made the Yankees look like bush-leaguers. Even with Mickey Mantle sidelined two-thirds of that season with a broken foot the Yankees won 104 games against a weaker-than-normal American League and breezed to the pennant, but they batted .171 against the Dodgers and suffered their first Series sweep since 1922.

In a plan that had been devised a year earlier but never made public, general manager Roy Hamey retired after the Dodger wipeout, Ralph Houk moved upstairs, and the managerial reins were turned over to Yogi Berra. That the Yankees won their fifth straight pennant in 1964 and extended the St. Louis Cardinals to seven games in the World Series before losing was miraculous. The team did not play well for Berra, who made numerous mistakes in his first year as a manager, and only a late-season surge carried New York past the White Sox.

Mantle played October baseball for the last time and he treated us with a glorious three-homer outburst against the Cardinals to surpass Ruth as the all-time leader in Series homers with 18, but it wasn't enough. When Bob Gibson mowed down the Yankees in Game Seven, the Cardinals were champions, and the Yankees, as we had known them, were no more.

Berra was fired a couple weeks later, Johnny Keane—the victorious Cardinals manager—was hired, and the team never responded to Keane's energetic and somewhat militant approach to the game. The veterans didn't respect him and constantly broke curfew in spring training. I personally allowed Mantle to sleep in the other bed in my hotel room in Fort Lauderdale when he was out past the bewitching hour. This drove Keane nuts, but there wasn't much he could do about it. He tried to gain control with heavy-handed treatment of the younger players, and all that did was turn the entire team against him. What transpired was the worst Yankee season in 40 years.

That wasn't the worst of it. Things bottomed out in 1966. Keane was fired two months into the season and Houk reassigned himself as the team's manager, but not even Houk—who won three pennants in his first three years—could right this sinking ship. The Yankees finished dead last in the American League for the first time since 1912. Houk stayed at the helm through 1973 and only once did the Yankees finish with a single-digit gap in the games behind column. "Fans in other cities started to cheer for us, as if they felt sorry for the Yankees," pitcher Steve Hamilton said. "That really used to make me mad."

It was a strange period for me because I had never had to cover a losing team before, and when I was driving to the stadium in August and September knowing the Yankees were hopelessly out of the pennant chase, I admit the job became just that—a job. That's why I was fortunate to have received my promotion to columnist after that dreadful 1966 season which enabled me to escape the tedium if I chose.

As the 1960s melted away, so did the Yankee roster as players such as Whitey Ford, Elston Howard, Bobby Richardson, Tony Kubek, Roger Maris, and Clete Boyer either retired or were traded. And with the farm system running dry as the new baseball draft rules prevented teams from signing and stockpiling talent, there were fewer viable replacements available. When once Yankee scouts unearthed talents such as Mantle, Ford, and Berra, now they found Horace Clarke, Steve Whitaker, and Jerry Kenney.

As bad as things were, at least Mantle was still there. That is until the spring of 1969 when Mantle came to Fort Lauderdale and announced his retirement, ending his brilliant and sometimes star-crossed career. Mantle knew at the end of 1968 that he was through. His legs were ravaged and he couldn't catch up to mundane fastballs. Once in a while he'd send one into outer space, but it happened much too infrequently, and because he wasn't adept at playing first base, he was a liability in the outfield.

"I can't hit when I need to, I can't go from first to third when I need to," Mantle said at his farewell press conference. "There's no use trying."

Like Babe Ruth and Joe DiMaggio before him, Mantle had grown to icon status and Yankee fans were left to wonder if they'd ever see the likes of a player of that caliber again. To date, we haven't. There have been scores of terrific players to wear the pinstripes since then, some who have gone on to the Hall of Fame, but none carried the same aura that Mantle did. I will say this, however. Derek Jeter, if he plays his entire career in New York, has an excellent chance to reach that level.

With Mantle gone, there really was nothing to pay attention to in Yankee land. Not that anyone cared in 1969. That was the year of the Amazin' Mets, when Gil Hodges's team defied the odds and won the World Series. They stole the headlines every day, for good reason, and for the first time since the glory days of John McGraw's Giants the Yankees were not kings of New York City baseball.

Tired of the mediocrity and the failure to make money, CBS, owners of the team since the mid-1960s, decided to get out of baseball. Network executive Mike Burke, who doubled as Yankees president, was told to find a buyer, and it was tougher than he thought. However, after being turned down by countless businessmen and corporations in the New York area, Burke received a call from Cleveland Indians president Gabe Paul informing him that a friend of his, a shipping magnate from Ohio who was now based in Tampa, Florida, might be interested in purchasing the club. A meeting was set up and negotiations were conducted. One day after Burke had taken the offer back to the CBS hierarchy, the sale was approved in 1973 for a price of $10 million. The new Yankee owner's name was George Steinbrenner who claimed on the day the deal was consummated, "I have no intentions in getting involved in the day-to-day operations of the club. I have a shipbuilding business to run." I was at that press conference. He said that. Really.

Houk quit as manager following Steinbrenner's first year, and Bill Virdon skippered the club for a year and a half before he was fired late in 1975 when former Yankee star Billy Martin—in the midst of establishing himself as a successful manager—became available after his firing in Texas. Virdon did not deserve to be axed, but Steinbrenner wanted Martin, so that was that.

Virdon did leave with one mark of distinction. Since the erection of Yankee Stadium in 1923, Virdon is the only Yankee manager to never have managed a home game there. During 1974 and 1975 the stadium was closed as it underwent a massive renovation that was supposed to cost about $36 million, but wound up spiraling into the $80 or $90 million range. The Yankees became tenants of the Mets over at Shea Stadium, much as they had been tenants of the Giants at the Polo Grounds six decades earlier.

It was a tough break for Virdon, but Martin was indeed the match who lit the Yankees ablaze, and pretty soon, the team was back in the business of winning championships.

– Chapter 21 –

1977

WHAT DO YOU GET WHEN YOU MIX George Steinbrenner, Billy Martin, Reggie Jackson, Thurman Munson, Mickey Rivers, Graig Nettles, Sparky Lyle, Ed Figueroa, Lou Piniella, the unrelenting fans of New York City, and the voracious New York City press together every day for eight long months? Trouble. Lots of it. And a World Series championship as well.

Covering the Yankees in 1977 was like covering a pinstriped version of Armageddon. *Days of Our Lives* had nothing on those conflicted Yankees. I have never encountered a more volatile, egotistical, antisocial, jealousy-driven clubhouse in all my days. Yet in the same breath I must add there are few teams that I've had more respect for because of the way that bunch rose above all the controversy and infighting to pull together the way great teams do when it counted the most. Based on their behavior, the 1977 Yankees deserved to finish last in the American League East. Based on their intestinal fortitude and their play, they deserved to win the World Series. And that's what they did.

When Steinbrenner bought the team and brought Gabe Paul in to run it, his instructions were simple: "Build me a winner, at any cost." Already in place were Munson, arguably the best catcher in the American League; Lyle, a terrific bullpen stopper; classy outfielder Roy White who played the field and handled the bat with equal acumen; and slugging third baseman Nettles who had just been acquired in a trade from Cleveland at the conclusion of the 1972 season.

Paul then methodically added to the assemblage. He stole outfielder Piniella in a trade with Kansas City in the winter of 1973. First baseman Chris Chambliss and pitcher Dick Tidrow came in a trade from Cleveland early in 1974. Paul traded away popular center fielder Bobby Murcer to San Francisco for Bobby Bonds, and while Bonds didn't do much in his one season (1975) with New York, he made a vital contribution in that he became the bait in a trade with the Angels prior to 1976 that brought Rivers and Figueroa to the Bronx. Finally, Steinbrenner set his money-spending precedent when he gave permission to Paul to sign free agent pitcher Catfish Hunter for a then-record $3.5 million prior to 1975.

When Martin began his first full season as manager in 1976, he had a team that after more than a decade of dormancy was on the verge of greatness. Augmented by other fine players such as Willie Randolph, Oscar Gamble, Dock Ellis, Doyle Alexander, and Ken Holtzman, Martin helped deliver to refurbished Yankee Stadium the American League pennant, the team's first since 1964. Chambliss's supersonic home run in the ninth inning of Game Five sent the Kansas City Royals to defeat in the American League Championship Series, but the Yankees were no match for Cincinnati's Big Red machine and suffered a four-game World Series sweep.

Steinbrenner had sipped champagne. In 1977, he wanted to gulp it.

Over the next six months he approved the signing of free agent pitcher Don Gullett, who had helped the Reds beat the Yankees in the Series, and the acquisitions of starting shortstop Bucky Dent, starting pitcher Mike Torrez and reserve outfielder Paul Blair. Oh, he also personally made sure a free agent outfielder named Reggie Jackson became a Yankee.

On paper, the Yankees were a powerhouse, far and away the best team in the American League and probably all of baseball. In reality, the Yankees were a powder keg and Jackson was cast in the role of the permanently lit fuse that threatened to blow them up at any moment, and on a few occasions, did. As Jackson would write years later in his autobiography written with Mike Lupica of the *Daily News*, "The year 1977 would turn out to be the worst of my life. I could've hit 300 home runs that year and I still would look back on the experience as being a sick one for me."

* * *

When my longtime colleague at the *Post*, Arch Murray, died in a hotel room fire he set when he fell asleep while smoking in 1962, Maury Allen took his place and we covered the Yankees together for a number of years. Maury has authored numerous books on the Yankees, all among the best ever penned about the team and its players. In fact, it was reading Maury's books through the years that ultimately convinced me to put together this tome.

Anyway, in his most recent compilation *All Roads Lead to October,* which deals with the reign of Steinbrenner, he shares a number of interesting tales including one that I think defines the tenor of the tumultuous 1977 season. Maury recalled Mickey Mantle, whom he had a sometimes frosty relationship with, telling him one day around the batting cage, "You piss me off just standing there." Maury analogized that in 1977, "Reggie Jackson also seemed to piss everybody off just standing there."

The only member of the Yankee organization who wanted Jackson was Steinbrenner, and he, of course, was the only one who mattered.

Jackson had played nine full seasons in the big leagues, the first eight with Oakland, during which time he won a MVP award, two home run titles, and three World Series rings. After playing in 1976 for the Baltimore Orioles, Jackson and his 281 career home runs became the hottest free agent commodity that fall on the newly-created open market, and Steinbrenner lusted after him.

In Steinbrenner's eyes Jackson was a true superstar, a box office draw who would not only have the fans flocking to Yankee Stadium in record numbers, but who would virtually guarantee the championship-starved Yankees the World Series crown. Jackson was the player who would enable Steinbrenner to gulp that champagne.

From the day the signing was announced, though, there was no chance for peace and harmony within the team because both of its leaders, Martin and Munson, were incensed by the acquisition. Martin wanted no part of Jackson. He had never managed him, but from afar he didn't like Jackson's style, his enormous ego, or his endless bantering with the media. Martin thought Jackson was the ultimate "me" guy. He also didn't like having someone in the locker room who was more of a presence than he was.

Maury Allen wrote of a conversation he had with Elston Howard, who was a Yankee coach under Martin, about Jackson. Howard intimated that Martin was "jealous" of Jackson and "hated the attention" Jackson received. "I think Billy wanted Reggie to fail more than he wanted the Yankees to win," Howard told Maury. As I look back on the events that shaped that stormy year, Howard may have been right on the money.

Then there was Munson. He was the reigning MVP of the American League. In 1976 he had been granted captaincy of the team, an honor no Yankee—not even Joe DiMaggio and Mantle—had held since Lou

Gehrig's retirement in 1939. Munson was Mr. Yankee, the most respected player on the team. If Jackson was worth $2.96 million for five years, so was he. Like Martin, Munson really didn't know Jackson personally. They had played against each other for about seven years, and they were teammates a few times at the All-Star Game, that was about it. But he had drawn his own conclusions about Jackson, fueled by some of the comments Jackson had made in the press. "I didn't come to New York to be a star; I brought my star with me," and "If I played there [New York], they'd name a candy bar after me." Munson wondered, "Who the hell does this guy think he is?" He decided he wasn't going to give Jackson the time of day.

We scoundrels in the press couldn't wait to get to Fort Lauderdale to watch this drama play out.

When spring training began it was clear all the suspicions we had about Jackson's presence causing disruption in the clubhouse were proving to be true. Martin's face turned red every time Jackson was referenced, and with Munson ignoring Jackson, most of the players followed their captain's lead and it made for a tension-filled room. Things only got worse when Munson got a taste of his own medicine. The reporters flocked to Jackson daily and virtually ignored Munson as well as the rest of the team. This really irritated Munson. He was an odd sort in that while he often derived pleasure from blowing off the media by hiding in the trainer's room—a common tactic practiced by this team—or by being uncooperative when he did decide to talk, he actually craved attention. In fact, he liked it almost as much as Jackson, but he wasn't nearly as proficient at obtaining it.

One afternoon, maybe a week into practice before the exhibition games had started, I was in the Banana Boat Lounge in Fort Lauderdale, a favorite watering hole of Mantle's. He and Whitey Ford were performing their usual honorary coaching duties at camp and most days when workouts were over they would go to the Banana Boat to drink, shoot the breeze, and play backgammon or cards. Mantle invited me along this day, and Jackson happened to be at the place. I went over to him and before I could introduce myself, he said, "I know who you are, Joe." Jackson was an avid reader, and his favorite topic was himself. He read every word penned about him in every paper. I had written about him periodically on his visits to New York when he played for Oakland and Baltimore, I'd already written about him since his signing with the Yankees, and with my picture attached to all my columns, I shouldn't have been surprised that he knew who I was.

Jackson asked me to join him and he bought me a beer. After some idle small talk I asked him how he was getting along with the team. Off the record he told me he didn't understand why they weren't accepting him. He had picked up on the negative attitude right away and it puzzled him. "It wasn't like this in Oakland. We all got along in Oakland," he said. "All I want to do is help these guys win."

Veteran Jimmy Wynn, who had quietly joined the team the day after Jackson had been signed, soaked in all the animosity and said, "If this club starts losing a lot early, the whole thing could blow up. If the guys' minds are right they can run away from the league. If these guys' minds are not right, then there's trouble."

The first game hadn't even been played and already there was enough material to fill a book.

Just like the old days I spent that entire spring with the Yankees. The Mets had fallen back on hard times and weren't worth paying much attention to—at least not until my young pal, Joe Torre, retired as a player and was named manager of the team in June. Actually, I had never really left the Yankees. Even in the worst of times I covered them frequently, and I'd spent most of the 1976 season chronicling their charge to the World Series. Though the times had changed, I was in the homestretch of my career, and I no longer spent nights on the road socializing with the players—well, maybe once in a while—I felt I had the pulse of this team. And what struck me about this team—and the one that defended the World Series title in 1978—was that it had personality. And it had some real personalities.

Rivers was a piece of work. We used to shake our heads watching him hobble to the plate slowly with the angled gait of an arthritic old man. Then he'd hit the ball, explode out of the batter's box like a gazelle and beat out an infield chopper, steal second, and score on a single. "If I didn't know who he was, I'd figure he walked on hot coals for a living," Lyle once quipped.

Make no mistake, Rivers was the sparkplug of the offense. In the leadoff spot he was so dangerous because of the scenario I just described, and he could have been more of a threat if Martin had turned him loose on the basepaths more often.

What I remember most about Rivers was the funny way he talked. He would ramble on about nothing, but somewhere amidst all the garble there was usually a message. One time I was present for one of his diatribes, and as I was going over my notes up in the press box, his common sense hit me right between the eyes. "Ain't no sense worrying about things you got control over because if you got control over them, ain't no sense worrying," he said. "And there ain't no sense worrying about things you got no control over because if you got no control over them, ain't no sense worrying." Brilliant when you think about it.

Chambliss was part of what might have been the best trade Gabe Paul ever made. At the time it was an unpopular move as Chambliss, Dick Tidrow, and Cecil Upshaw came to New York in exchange for Steve Kline, Fred Beene, Fritz Peterson, and Tom Buskey. All of the ex-Yankees in that deal were fan and team favorites, and throughout his first year with the Yankees Chambliss felt like an outsider. He won everyone over with his professional attitude and his fine play both in the field and at the plate. And the home run he hit to beat the Royals in the 1976 play-offs was the stuff of legend.

It was funny, but Chambliss never liked to talk about that home run. His reasoning was sound: If that's the last thing he was going to do that was worth talking about, then his career wouldn't be very successful. Chambliss did indeed add to his resume. He was an outstanding first baseman and a reliable hitter who didn't hit for great power, but using his grooved and relaxed swing he drove in at least 90 runs all three years the Yankees won the AL pennant in the 1970s.

The Yankees used to call Nettles "Puff." That's because after a game he would disappear like a puff of smoke. He used to aggravate us writers with the way he would avoid speaking to us, even when he played an integral part in a game, which was often. And woe if you were the official scorer—it was a job usually filled by one of the writers in those days—and you gave Nettles an error he felt he didn't deserve. He was notorious for questioning calls, and if he didn't like the way it went, he would freeze that writer out. Not that it mattered much because, as I said, he wasn't too talkative to begin with.

But while Nettles might have been a pain to deal with, he was a great player. His career included 390 home runs, and his glove was every bit as spectacular. "I'd say that without him at third base my years with the Yankees would not have been half as productive as they were," Lyle said. "He dives, he makes unbelievable plays, half in defense of his life, half just in defense."

Piniella was a lot like Munson in that he could be sort of gruff, sort of grumpy. Also like Munson, he was a fierce competitor, often an emotional tempest who wore his heart on his sleeve. Lyle once called Piniella "the best slow outfielder in baseball" and that was a pretty accurate assessment. Piniella wasn't nimble, but he made the plays he was supposed to because he had keen instincts and knew how to play.

I once asked Steinbrenner if he had a particular favorite player on the team, and I fully expected the owner to beg off on the question. Instead, he launched right into a description of Piniella. "He's my kind of ballplayer," said Steinbrenner, who in 1985 hired Piniella to manage the team. "He's a consummate competitor. I know people who knew him as a high school athlete [Piniella grew up in Tampa where Steinbrenner lives and operates his shipping company]. He wasn't a good loser. I'm not looking for a good loser on my team."

No, Sweet Lou didn't take kindly to losing. Everyone could see his tantrums on the field, and when he would come into the clubhouse after a loss he was just as entertaining. You were always on the lookout for him. He'd tear off his uniform, rip off a string of expletives, and then storm into the shower. Sometimes he came back, sometimes he didn't.

He's cooled off now that he's been a big-league manager for more than 15 years. But I know he still has his moments, and I have to laugh when I see him getting tossed out of a game. That's the Lou that I knew.

Lyle was the comedian on the team. Whenever the moment needed to be lightened—and Lord knows there were plenty of those in 1977—Lyle did the lightening. He was a funny guy, a practical joker, and everyone liked him.

Lyle's trademark was sitting on birthday cakes. It began when he was with Boston. Hawk Harrelson received a big cake for his birthday and Lyle thought it would be funny to strip naked and sit on the cake. He brought the gag to New York and the saying, "You can't have your cake and eat it, too" rang true for the Yankees.

When he came to the Yankees in 1972 Ralph Houk swore Lyle would be the key to restoring New York's lost glory. It just so happened that it took quite a few more ingredients before the Yankees' recipe for success was complete, but when the time came, just as Houk had predicted, Lyle played a pivotal role, and he won the Cy Young Award in 1977.

I once asked Munson what, outside of a nasty slider, was the key to Lyle's success and Munson replied, "Sparky is not afraid to fail." That is the character trait I most remember. He was fearless on the mound, and he seemed to enjoy pitching when the Yankees were in the tightest spot.

"Some people say you have to be nuts to be a relief pitcher," he said. "But the truth is I was nuts before I ever became one. I love it."

I'll never forget what Lyle said the day he accepted his Cy Young award. "I'm not the emotional type, and I've had so many ups and downs during my career that by next week this thing will be history to me. But I feel that on this one day, at least, I can be excited and proud and even fart in public if I want. I was on a team that won the pennant and the World Series despite enough crap to last an entire career."

*   *   *

The combination of "crap," lousy pitching, and lack of timely hitting affected the Yankees early in the season and they lost eight of their first 10 games. Jimmy Wynn had predicted a meltdown if the team started poorly, and here was the dreaded poor start. There were times when things got a little soupy, but somehow, the complete liquefying of the Yankees never occurred, partly because Munson made an effort to finally accept Jackson's presence.

The team won 14 of 16 games in one stretch so Steinbrenner stopped pestering Martin, Jackson began to feel some love, disgruntled Dock Ellis was shipped to Oakland for talented Mike Torrez, Hunter's arm was feeling better, Figueroa pitched five straight complete games, and Munson broke out of a batting slump.

Just when we began to think peace was perhaps possible, it all blew up.

That day back in March when I was in the Banana Boat Lounge in Fort Lauderdale with Jackson, a writer named Robert Ward who I had never heard of came into the bar and interrupted us. Ward worked for *Sport* magazine and had been trying to get Jackson to agree to an interview for a story he had been assigned to write. Jackson had declined, but on that day he let his guard down and decided to talk to the guy. I excused myself and rejoined Mantle and Ford who were yucking it up with some of the locals. Had I known what was about to happen, I would have dragged Jackson along with me.

He talked to Ward for more than an hour, and Jackson thought he had made it clear it was all off the record. According to Jackson, Ward didn't ask any leading questions, nor did he take any notes. I can't confirm the former, but I can the latter. Ward wasn't writing anything down.

Well, on May 23 the magazine hit the newsstands and the cover story was about Jackson. It was filled with outrageous quotes, all attributed to Jackson, most of them inflammatory.

In the story, Ward quoted Jackson as saying, "You know, this team . . . it all flows from me. I've got to keep it all going. I'm the straw that stirs the drink. It all comes back to me. I should say me and Munson, but really he doesn't enter into it. He's being so damned insecure about the whole thing. Munson thinks he can be the straw that stirs the drink, but he can only stir it bad."

Jackson claims to this day that he was misquoted, and he says it was the worst screwing he had ever received from the press. Fran Healy, who was Munson's backup and one of the few Yankees who befriended Jackson from the start, tried to soothe things over by telling Munson that perhaps Jackson had been misquoted. Munson's reply: "For three fucking pages?"

Obviously, Munson was furious. So were his teammates. Quite frankly, so were Yankee fans. How dare Jackson call out the captain!

Already branded an outcast by most of his teammates, now Jackson had really become an enemy in his own clubhouse. I felt bad for him because having seen him talking to Ward that day, I honestly felt he had gotten a raw deal. As a writer it was the rare occurrence when I ever sided with a player in a dispute with a writer. This was the rare case. I was highly skeptical of Ward, but there was no way the Yankees were going to buy Jackson's explanation.

When the Yankees arrived in Boston for a three-game weekend set a month later they were actually leading the Red Sox by half a game. They left Fenway trailing by 2 1/2 games. Boston inflicted a painful 9-4, 10-4, 11-1 sweep, and the middle debacle was the game that we all thought would send the season spiraling down the proverbial toilet once and for all.

That was the day Martin purposely humiliated Jackson on national television by sending Paul Blair out to right field to replace him in the middle of an inning after Martin felt Jackson hadn't hustled. When Jackson entered the dugout, he and Martin began screaming at each other, and then Martin tried three times to fight Jackson as coaches Elston Howard, Yogi Berra, and Dick Howser hung on for dear life trying to separate the two. This was NBC's *Game of the Week* so baseball fans around the country were introduced to the Bronx Zoo a year before Sparky Lyle's book came out.

I had seen a lot in my time, but I had never seen anything like that. Not a player being publicly embarrassed by his manager in the middle of an inning, and certainly not the ruckus that took place in the dugout. It was bizarre.

After the game Jackson was long gone, so when we got back to the Sheraton Hotel, a few of us—myself, Steve Jacobson of *Newsday,* Phil Pepe of the *Daily News,* and Paul Montgomery of the *Times*—all asked Jackson if he would talk and he told us to come to his room. Jackson and Torrez were sharing a bottle of wine, and when we were all in place, he gave us his side of the incident. Naturally, it was in direct contrast to what Martin had told us a few hours earlier. I sided with Jackson, and in a scathing column in the *Post* I called for Martin's firing.

I considered Martin a jerk and wanted him gone. When he would visit New York as manager of Minnesota, Detroit, or Texas, I always made it a point to speak to him, to say hello, reminisce a little about the old days, and more often than not he'd just blow me off. It was a puzzling reaction given that we'd known each other since the early '50s and one of my dear friends—Mickey Mantle—was one of his closest pals. When he returned to manage the team in 1976, I thought perhaps his attitude toward me would change, but it didn't. In fact, he was often caustic in his dealings with me, and that got my Italian blood boiling. Pretty soon we didn't even speak unless it was in a press conference or pack reporting session. He never told me what his beef was with me, but Mickey said it had something to do with a story I had written back when Martin was finishing out his playing career. I guess I told the truth when I wrote that he was a shell of his former self, and he didn't like it, nor did he ever forget it.

I remember when Billy turned 50 years old during the 1978 season, someone gave him a plaque that read: "Extraordinary achievement award to Billy Martin—For having reached the age of 50 without being murdered by someone—To the amazement of all who know him."

It was meant to be a gag gift. I think.

To my dismay, Martin wasn't fired following the Beantown Brawl, and when New York returned the favor and swept Boston the next weekend at Yankee Stadium, it started the Red Sox on a nine-game losing streak that thrust the Yankees back in the thick of the race. They stayed there the rest of the season.

The Yankees finally overtook the streaky Red Sox down the stretch, though it probably wouldn't have happened had Martin not swallowed his pride. Clearly out of spite Martin had used Jackson in the cleanup spot only 10 times until the evening of August 10. It was another way Martin could put the screws to Jackson. Yet even the stubborn manager realized he needed Jackson's power in that spot, so he finally relented and began batting Jackson fourth. The Yankees won 40 of their last 53 games and Jackson hit 13 homers and drove in 49 runs. I remember writing, "Martin finally locked his enormous ego in a cage and decided that perhaps one of the most feared sluggers in the game probably should bat fourth. If the Yankees go on to win the division, and maybe even win the World Series, will Martin admit his mistake? I doubt it."

Jackson hit a grand slam the night the Yankees clinched a tie for the division crown, and then while the Yankees were waiting out a rain delay a couple nights later, Baltimore's defeat of Boston officially ended the race.

In his office, with champagne drenching his clothes and tears filling his eyes, Martin said to Jackson, "You had a hell of a year, big guy. I love you." I had to wonder whether Billy had been spraying champagne, or guzzling it.

– *1977 World Series* –

It took less than a week for Billy Martin's supposed "love" of Reggie Jackson to wear off.

As Jackson wrote in his autobiography, "I won't say I carried the team because so many others played well, but if that September was a tug-of-war, I was the anchor man at the back of the line."

There was no denying this. Others had played well. Ron Guidry announced to the world that he was going to be the best pitcher in baseball very soon, winning 10 of his last 11 decisions to finish 16-7. Mike Torrez and Ed Figueroa were dominant at times and combined for 30 wins. Sparky Lyle overcame some rough outings and was back in stride just in time for the play-offs. Thurman Munson finished with 100 RBI and a .308 average, Chris Chambliss drove in 90 runs, Graig Nettles led the team with 37 homers, Mickey Rivers topped everyone with a .326 average, and Bucky Dent and Willie Randolph became a terrific defensive duo up the middle.

But Jackson stood above them all. Despite all the negativity he'd encountered, he hit 32 homers and led the team with 110 RBI, batted .286, and stole 17 bases. His 13 errors were second-worst among American League outfielders, but who besides Martin really cared? The Yankees wouldn't have won the division without him.

So what was his reward? Martin benched him at the start of the biggest game of the year.

During the first four games of the bitterly-fought American League Championship Series with the Kansas City Royals, Jackson made one hit in 14 at-bats. With the best-of-five series tied at two games apiece, Martin, in all his wisdom, started Paul Blair in right field in the winner-take-all fifth game.

I go back to what Elston Howard had told Maury Allen. "I think Billy wanted Reggie to fail more than he wanted the Yankees to win."

The Yankees and Royals had played a classic five-game championship series in 1976, and this was every bit its equal. Kansas City jumped on Don Gullett in the opener at Yankee Stadium and ran away with a 7-2 victory, but Guidry responded with a complete game three-hitter as New York won Game Two, 6-2.

Out to Kansas City we traveled for the final three games, and Royals' ace Dennis Leonard matched Guidry's excellence with a complete game four-hitter during a 6-2 victory over Torrez. On the brink of elimination the Yankees fought back to tie the series with a 6-4 triumph, necessitating a Game Five.

Kansas City manager Whitey Herzog pitched lefty Paul Splitorff, who had handcuffed the Yankees in the first game. Jackson was in a slump and he'd never hit Splitorff well, so Martin opted to sit him down. Percentage move? No, just a dumb, vindictive move. Jackson was a money player, he was a major threat, and even Splitorff couldn't believe his good fortune. "I had good luck against him, but my God, he was Reggie Jackson. He could hit it out on anybody. That was an edge for me. You know what else was important? Billy Martin was telling the world Reggie Jackson was afraid of me. Do you know what that did for my confidence?"

Martin was writing his own death certificate. If the Yankees lost with Jackson on the bench, Martin was gone and everyone knew it.

The Royals took a 3-1 lead into the eighth as the confident Splitorff had little trouble with the Yankee order. However, he began to tire and when Randolph singled, Herzog took him out in favor of right-hander Doug Bird. Bird struck out Munson, but Piniella singled, and to his credit Martin realized there was no way he could keep Jackson on the bench. "Get a bat" he barked. Jackson did, and he delivered a RBI single that cut the deficit to 3-2, then stayed in the game and played right field.

In the ninth, facing Leonard, Blair singled, Roy White walked, and after Larry Gura relieved for the Royals he yielded Rivers's RBI single that tied the game. Randolph's sacrifice fly put the Yankees ahead, and a throwing error by Royals third baseman George Brett gave New York a

5-3 cushion. Lyle closed it out, and the Yankees were headed back to the World Series.

*   *   *

Over in the National League, Tommy Lasorda's Dodgers won three of four against Philadelphia to claim the flag, the series turning when Los Angeles rallied from two runs down with two out in the ninth inning of Game Three to pull out a shocking 6-5 victory. Still in a fog the next day, the Phillies were no match for Tommy John, and the Dodgers made the short trip up to New York for the start of the World Series.

This was a different time. The Dodgers had been in Los Angeles 20 years and Brooklyn had long ago forgotten about its beloved Bums, but just the mere mention of those two nicknames in hyphenated form— Yankees-Dodgers—kindled a magical feeling. Flooding back into my conscience were memories of the glory days when the Yankees and Dodgers ruled their respective leagues and their reunions at World Series time defined passion and excitement and rivalry as they related to baseball.

The flashbacks were vivid. Mickey Owen's dropped third strike in 1941, Bill Bevens's near no-hitter in 1947, Tommy Henrich's Game One winning home run in 1949, Billy Martin's saving catch in 1952, Carl Erskine's 14-strikeout game in 1953, Sandy Amoros's brilliant catch in 1955, and Don Larsen's perfect game in 1956.

I tingled in anticipation of what new chapter these two storied teams would write, but the skeptic in me served as a mechanism against expecting too much. After all, how could these present-day Yankees and Dodgers with their big contracts and endorsement deals and their free agency and Marvin Miller-led union possibly live up to the standard set by their legendary forefathers? Especially now in an era when baseball and the World Series didn't hold the same grip on the nations sports fans the way it once did.

Shame on me for having doubted the game, my favorite game.

Game Six of the 1977 World Series was played at Yankee Stadium on a frosty but bearable mid-October night. The Yankees forged their way to a three games to two lead, but were coming off a 10-4 shellacking out in Los Angeles, and with his pitching staff dangerously close to being worn out, Martin needed for this Series to end.

One man made sure it did. And it was the man Martin had foolishly fought with all year, the man Martin wanted more than any other to disappear from the face of the earth, or, at the very least, from the Yankee clubhouse.

Jackson authored a performance that in my mind, in the annals of the World Series, is topped in virtuosity only by Larsen's perfect game. After taking a four-pitch, no swing walk in the second inning, Jackson went on to hit home runs on the next three pitches he saw, in the fourth, fifth, and eighth innings, carrying the Yankees to an 8-4 victory that secured the team's 21st world championship.

"That is the greatest performance I have ever seen," Lasorda said. "That is the greatest performance anyone will ever see."

It had been a season unlike any other in Yankee history, filled with so much hostility and melodrama, and Jackson was at the center of just about every controversial tornado that blew through the clubhouse. It only stood to reason that it should end the way it did, with this fabulous slugger doing the only thing he knew would get his critics off his back: hit home runs. Prodigious home runs. Home runs that would restore the Yankees to their long-vacated perch atop the baseball world.

There were only a few occasions in my career where I was truly spellbound by what I had witnessed, suffocated by the splendor of an athletic achievement, and this was one of them. It was a night when the words did not flow freely from my typewriter. The pressure was intense because this was the rare game that, as a writer, you knew you would always be associated with. What I wrote that night was going to follow me for the rest of my days, and days well beyond my own. History had been made, and I knew that my prose would forever be part of the documentation of this event. There was a higher standard to aim for, normalcy needed to be transcended. Jackson had made it that way, and I can only hope that I cleared the bar that he set. This is what I wrote:

By Joe Kimmerle
New York Post

Reggie Jackson sat on the bench in the Yankee dugout, his chest heaving as he struggled to get air in and out of his lungs. He had just hit his third home run in three pitches off a third different Los Angeles pitcher, a Ruthian shot—or was it a Jacksonian shot?—into Yankee Stadium's rarely reached black seats beyond center field, and hyperventilation was setting in.

Jackson sat there, his eyes ablaze, his head spinning like that young girl's in The Exorcist. *When he came to realize that a television camera was trained on him, he mouthed the words "Hi Mom," and then before he knew it, he was being pushed by his teammates up the dugout steps so he could bow to the 56,407 delirious worshipers who were creating a deafening din with their chanting of his name—"Reg-gie, Reg-gie, Reg-gie."*

His Yankee teammates had been pushing him all year. Pushing him away in their reluctance to accept him as a teammate. Pushing him to tears. Pushing him to frustration. Pushing him ever closer to insanity. The pushing never stopped, and now they were pushing him again. But it was this last push that provided a most ironic twist to this most extraordinary of Yankee seasons.

This was a push Jackson deserved. This was a push into the spotlight which he so craves, the same spotlight that had been the root of his troubles this year within the turbulent Yankee clubhouse.

The Yankees knew Jackson's reputation as a verbose egomaniac who spoke of "the magnitude of me" and how he was "the straw that stirs the drink" and how he "put the asses in the seats" and that "I didn't come to New York to be a star, I brought my star with me."

But when his star arrived with 2.96 million of George Steinbrenner's dollars bulging from his wallet and an edict from the owner of the Yankees to deliver a championship, the Yankees really didn't know Jackson. All they knew was what they had heard, and that was enough to convince them they weren't going to like him. They like him today because last night, with an electrifying performance that will forever stand the test of time, he brought all those asses out of all those seats, and in so doing, he put diamond championship rings on the fingers of those skeptical teammates.

Jackson's three home runs catapulted the Yankees to an 8-4 victory over the Los Angeles Dodgers that in turn brought the Yankees their first World Series championship since 1962.

"It was probably the greatest single-game performance I've ever seen," said third baseman Graig Nettles, one of Jackson's harshest critics. "It was amazing. It gave me chills when he hit that third one."

Steve Garvey, the classy first baseman of the Dodgers, was equally awed and he admitted, "When Reggie hit his third home run, and I was sure nobody was looking, I was applauding in my glove. Reggie rose to the occasion. I think he released a lot of emotional tension from the season in one game. I'm sure now he has peace of mind."

Right here, in the House That Ruth Built, Jackson did something only Ruth has ever done. In the 1926 and 1928 Series Ruth hit three home runs in one game. Something Ruth never did, though, was hit home runs in four consecutive at-bats—Jackson homered in his last plate appearance Sunday, and then walked in his first last night. And Ruth never hit five home runs in one World Series as Jackson did this past week.

This night did not begin well for the Yankees. Mike Torrez, pressed into starting duty when it was determined—controversially, of course— that Ed Figueroa was unfit to pitch, yielded two runs in the top of the first when Garvey lashed a two-run triple into the right-field corner.

New York pulled even when Jackson drew his walk in the second inning and then trotted home on Chris Chambliss's two-run homer off Burt Hooton.

Reggie Smith hit a solo home run in the third to put the Dodgers back on top, but then Jackson took center stage and never exited. Following a single by Thurman Munson in the fourth, Jackson creamed a flat Hooton fastball into the right-field stands to give the Yankees the lead for good.

"There's more where that came from," Jackson had told Willie Randolph following his pyrotechnic display during batting practice when he sent about 20 souvenirs into the stands. "I was still in batting practice, that's how I felt," Jackson said of the first home run.

Later in the fourth Chambliss wound up with a double when his blooper to left fell safely, and he scored on a sacrifice fly by Lou Piniella. Then in the fifth Jackson ripped an Elias Sosa fastball over the right-field fence for a two-run homer to make it 7-3.

"I stood there next to the plate watching (Sosa) warm up and I was thinking 'Please, God, let him hurry up and finish warming up so I don't lose this feeling I have,'" Jackson recalled. "He threw me a fastball right down Broadway. I call those mattress pitches because if you're feeling right you can lay over them. That was the hardest ball I hit all night."

Hard to believe when you consider that in the eighth Jackson sent a Charlie Hough floater on a 420-foot journey into the faraway black seats.

"I just wanted Charlie Hough to throw me one damn knuckleball," Jackson said. "I had nothing to lose. Even if I struck out, I had nothing to lose. Hough threw me a knuckler; it didn't knuckle."

The celebration raged all around him, champagne spraying like the mist that comes off Niagara Falls. Even Billy Martin, Jackson's year-long antagonist, could only say, "Reggie? He was sensational."

"Perhaps for one night I reached back and achieved that level of the overrated superstar," Jackson said. "I'm also happy for George Steinbrenner, whose neck was stuck out further than mine. There were times that this season was just too much for me."

It will be a long time before he forgets all the tumult that threatened to ruin this season. In fact, he may never forget it. Rest assured, he won't forget how this season ended, either.

Game One served as an omen of what was to come, a divinely rich contest that dripped with excitement and suspense before the Yankees came away with a 4-3 victory on Blair's RBI single off Rick Rhoden in the bottom of the 12th inning.

Gullett had pitched poorly in the opener of the ALCS against Kansas City, yet Martin had no choice but to lead off with him in the Series because Figueroa, Torrez, and Guidry had all pitched over the weekend. "After the last game there's no question that you give thought to what's gone wrong, why me, and so on and so forth," Gullett said. "But I felt good about this game. I had confidence I could throw the ball well."

It didn't look that way early when the Dodgers struck for two runs in the top of the first as Bill Russell tripled home a run and scored on a sacrifice fly by Ron Cey.

Rivers electrified the crowd when he threw out Garvey at the plate to end the sixth inning, and the crowd was still buzzing moments later when Randolph led off the bottom of the sixth with a solo homer to tie the game at 2-2.

New York took the lead in the eighth as Randolph led off with a walk and chugged home when Martin put the hit-and-run on and Munson lashed a double into the left-field corner. But the Dodgers pulled even in the ninth when pinch-hitter Lee Lacy hit a RBI single off Lyle.

Lyle blew the save, but he atoned by retiring the final 11 batters he faced. That put him in position for the victory when Blair—who had come in for Jackson as a defensive replacement in the ninth—followed a Randolph double and an intentional walk to Munson with a single between short and third.

The mood was vastly different in the Yankee clubhouse the next night. With Burt Hooton baffling them with his knuckle-curve, the Yankees managed five harmless hits and lost, 6-1. Still feeling that his rotation needed more rest, Martin gave the ball to Catfish Hunter who hadn't pitched in more than a month because of a hernia. Martin hoped for the best, feared the worst, and that's what he got. Hunter was not up to the assignment and he was shelled for three home runs inside three innings.

Jackson, still perturbed over his benching in Kansas City and by the fact that he was 3-for-22 in the postseason, had another reason to be mad. He thought Martin had done a disservice to a classy veteran like Hunter, throwing him to the wolves, so to speak. "How could the son of a bitch pitch him?" Jackson said. "How could he be expected to do anything? Cat did his best, but he hadn't pitched in so long. Ah, the hell with it."

Hunter, ever the professional, was fine with the move. "I knew it would be my start, they didn't have anybody else," Hunter said. "I've got to go out and pitch sometime. Billy didn't know what was going to happen."

This is what happened. Cey hammered a two-run homer to left in the first, Steve Yeager hit a solo shot in the second, and Reggie Smith crushed a tremendous home run to right-center in the third for a 5-0 advantage. Game over.

"It felt like spring training, I hadn't pitched for a month," Hunter said. "At least the people back home know I can still give up home runs. As the saying goes, the sun doesn't shine up the same dog's ass every year."

The sun was shining up everyone's ass once the Series shifted to beautiful southern California for the next three games. Everyone, that is, who wasn't wearing the classic gray Yankee road uniform. Team Turmoil was at it again and a dark cloud hovered ominously above its workout at Dodger Stadium as Martin reacted angrily to Jackson questioning his use of Hunter.

"Why do we have to have all this kind of talk now when we're trying to win a World Series?" Martin said. "It's not the Yankee kind of thing to do. A true Yankee wouldn't say that. Play your position, do your job and if you can't do your job, shut up. He's got enough trouble playing right field without second-guessing the manager."

"This is another chapter in the tumultuous life of the 1977 Yankees," said Gabe Paul. "Controversial ballplayers are many times better ballplayers because they are not afraid of the consequences." I don't know if Paul really believed that, but the controversial Yankees were the better club in Game Three. They jumped on Tommy John for three runs in the first inning with Jackson in the middle of the rally, and after Dusty Baker's three-run homer off Torrez tied it in the third, the Yankees scratched out two more runs and rode Torrez's complete game to a 5-3 triumph.

It is said that nobody forgets where he buried the hatchet. Ron Guidry buried his hatchet right in the collective skull of the Dodgers during Game Four. Providing a portent of what his future held, Guidry threw smoke for nine innings, the Dodgers touched him for just four hits, and the Yankees eased to a 4-2 victory that brought them to the verge of their first World Series championship since 1962.

"I wasn't nervous, I had confidence in myself and I just went out there and threw my game," Guidry said.

Another fast start keyed the Yankee win as they scored three runs in the second and chased Los Angeles starter Doug Rau out of the game. Jackson started the rally with a double and he scored the first run on Piniella's single.

Guidry had a momentary lapse in the third, his only one of the game, as he served up a two-run homer to Lopes, but for the rest of the game the Dodgers made only two hits. Jackson's solo home run closed the scoring in the sixth .

The Yankees lost the fifth game, but they had to lose the fifth game. It was almost as if it was preordained because if New York had wrapped up the Series in Los Angeles, imagine how history would have been altered. Jackson would have never gotten the opportunity to hit three home runs on three pitches and officially earn the nickname Mr. October. We didn't know it that sunny afternoon at Dodger Stadium, but the 10-4 Game Five loss was meant to be.

"We still have our backs to the wall, but we just can't let them close us out after the season we've had," Garvey said before he boarded the team plane bound for New York. "It would be like writing a story without a climax."

Garvey got his climax all right. Just not the one he was hoping for.

I started noticing a problem during the summer of 1977, but I really didn't think anything of it. I was 61 years old and in what my doctor called "splendid physical shape for a man who lives on press box food." Every night I was waking up two or three times to use the toilet, and when I would urinate, I felt like I wasn't emptying my bladder completely.

Marie grew concerned and she told me to visit Dr. Lombardo. I'm stubborn when it comes to doctors. I don't feel the need to see them on a regular basis. I put off making an appointment during the season because I was too busy, but as soon as the World Series ended, Marie literally dragged me in to see Dr. Lombardo, who had been our physician for probably 30 years.

Jerry gave me a thorough examination, and a couple days later when my test results came back, he summoned me to his office. He said my prostate specific antigen (PSA) test concerned him because my level was higher than normal, so he referred me to a urologist. This guy I wasn't too fond of, especially when he jammed his finger up my ass. Considering what he did for a living, I decided interviewing modern day athletes wasn't such a bad way to earn a wage.

After a couple more tests, the verdict came in: I had prostate cancer. You hear the word "cancer" and alarms start ringing in your ears, not to mention the sobbing of your wife. But before we got too far along in our gloom, Dr. VanDurren explained to me that prostate cancer was a very treatable form of cancer and that the odds of survival were in my favor. He warned me that it wasn't going to be a procedure I should take lightly, but he seemed quite confident that I'd be able to resume my life in a few months.

Luckily, he was right. I had my cancerous prostate gland removed right after Thanksgiving, and after a couple months of rest, I pronounced myself fit to attend spring training in Fort Lauderdale.

Marie had been making the trips to Fort Lauderdale with me for about seven or eight years. We had purchased a timeshare condominium down there and we used it for two months in the wintertime. We would drive down at the beginning of February and I'd take three weeks vacation, and then when the Yankees would start spring training, I used the condo as my home base. No more staying at the team hotel, though I didn't let the Post *off that easily. In exchange for not submitting a weekly hotel bill, I convinced the paper to pick up a portion of my condo charges. It was a nice arrangement.*

Marie and I cherished our time away from the cold winters of New York. My days were much shorter now that I was a columnist, and we had plenty of time on our hands. If we weren't socializing with other couples in the condo complex, we spent our evenings walking on the beach, going out to dinner, and attending concerts or movies. Once in a while I'd play golf and Marie would lounge around the pool. Ah, spring training. My favorite time of the year.

While recuperating from my surgery, I wasn't too involved in the off-season shenanigans of the Yankees. Surprisingly, I didn't miss too much.

There was change at the top as Gabe Paul, tired of putting up with George Steinbrenner, resigned his position and became part owner of the Cleveland Indians. In his place came the respected Al Rosen, a former star player with the Indians in the 1950s who'd been the American League MVP in 1953 and a friend of Steinbrenner's since the mid-1960s. That friendship was put to the test right away.

Steinbrenner continued his free spending ways as he lured star relief pitcher Goose Gossage away from the Pittsburgh Pirates for $2.75 million, creating an uncomfortable situation in the bullpen where the reigning American League Cy Young Award winner, Sparky Lyle, resided. The acquisition of Gossage relegated Lyle to second-rate status, he bitched about it all year, and it ultimately led to his being traded at the end of the year just before his entertaining tell-all book about the 1978 season, The Bronx Zoo, *was published.*

Gossage was the only major addition, and it was negated by the defection of Mike Torrez to the rival Red Sox for $2 million. The lineup was virtually the same, and so, too, were many of the problems that plagued the team in 1977. When spring training began, it was plainly obvious to me that these guys hadn't learned their lesson from the year before.

"Maybe the family that fights together, stays together," Bucky Dent quipped one day.

Reggie Jackson showed up in Fort Lauderdale a week later than the rest of the veterans, and predictably, Billy Martin jumped on him immediately, the heroic World Series performance of four months earlier a distant memory.

"I wish I could afford to quit," Lou Piniella told me one day after hearing of another spat between Martin and Jackson. "I'm sick of coming to the park every day and hearing all the garbage about Billy, Reggie, and George. It isn't baseball anymore. I hate to walk into the clubhouse. It's disgusting."

Meanwhile, the Red Sox were loaded for bear. They had bulked up their pitching staff by signing Torrez and Dennis Eckersley to join Luis Tiant and Bill Lee. And second baseman Jerry Remy came over from California to provide a table setter at the top of the order for all those sluggers such as Jim Rice,

Fred Lynn, Carlton Fisk, Dwight Evans, Butch Hobson, George Scott, and Carl Yastrzemski.

Don Zimmer's Red Sox were a fabulous team, and the Yankees, pretty good in their own right, nonetheless realized defending their World Series championship was the least of their worries. Defending their American League East division title was going to be a chore. They couldn't have known how tough it would actually be.

– Chapter 22 –

1978

THE SILENCE IS WHAT I remember most. Never before had 32,925 Bostonians made less noise. It was so quiet at Fenway Park in the moments after Bucky Dent's fly ball to left field landed in the screen atop the Green Monster, you could hear the manual scoreboard operator behind the bottom of the famed wall changing New York's run total from zero to three.

"It was like a funeral home," Reggie Jackson said in describing the eerie tranquility that hung sadly over the little Beantown bandbox.

Dent's three-run homer erased a 2-0 deficit and sent the Yankees on their way to a heart-stopping 5-4 victory that resulted in their third straight American League East division crown.

"We just blew it, that's all," a disconsolate Boston shortstop Rick Burleson said. "We should have never been in this game in the first place."

It may have been the only time in my life I truly felt sorry for the Red Sox and their fans.

When the sun set on the evening of July 19, the Red Sox were in first place with a gaudy record of 62-28. Milwaukee was nine games back, Baltimore 12 1/2, and the defending world champion Yankees were a mundane 48-42, mired in fourth place, 14 games in arrears. When the sun rose into a brilliant, cloudless Boston sky on the morning of October 2, the Red Sox had a record of 99-63. So did the Yankees. Over the previous 2 1/2 months New York had frenetically won 51 of 72 games, Boston just 37 of 72, leaving the teams in a dead heat and staring at a historic one-game sudden death play-off—the second of its kind in American League history—to decide the division championship.

"I have a tape of that game in my office," said George Steinbrenner. "I don't know how many times I've watched that game. Somebody wins the Series every year. There's only one game like that in a lifetime. I'd call it the greatest game in the history of American sports because baseball is the best and oldest game, and that's sure as hell the best baseball game I ever saw."

Steinbrenner is often given to hyperbole. It wasn't the greatest game in the history of mankind, but it was a great game.

I rode in a cab from the Sheraton to Fenway with my *Post* colleague Maury Allen, and Joe Durso of the *Times*. We got there around noon, 2 1/2 hours before the first pitch, and thousands of people had already congregated on Lansdowne and Ipswich streets. There was an undeniable electricity coursing through the pleasantly warm autumn air, and we knew this was no ordinary day at the ballpark.

"I felt nervous," Lou Piniella admitted, as did others.

Yet while butterflies stirred all the players' stomachs, the Yankees seemed confident that they would win. The Red Sox did not. The pressure was on the Red Sox. They had blown a 14-game lead to necessitate this theater. Further, by virtue of a coin toss, they were the home team and after winning 62 of 81 games at Fenway, a victory was expected. Never mind that the Yankees were throwing Ron Guidry at them.

* * *

A few of us writers were sitting in Billy Martin's little office at the spring training complex in March of 1977 and he was telling us a story about Steinbrenner and his insistence on trading Guidry.

"'I've got to get rid of him, he can't pitch,'" Martin said, paraphrasing what Steinbrenner had blurted a few days earlier. "'I've got to get rid of that skinny kid. I'm telling you he can't pitch.' Gabe and I knew he was wrong."

Martin and Gabe Paul talked Steinbrenner out of including Guidry in a couple of 1976 deals, and the 1977 trades that ultimately brought Mike Torrez from Oakland and Bucky Dent from the White Sox. Those might have been the most important personnel moves the Yankees didn't make.

Without Guidry, New York wouldn't have advanced to the play-offs in 1977 or 1978, let alone win the World Series. The kid they called Louisiana Lightning won 10 of his last 11 decisions in 1977 to help carry the

Yankees to the AL East crown, and he capped his season with a complete game victory in Game Four of the World Series.

In 1978 he was the best pitcher in the world. He won 25 games, lost only three, had an earned-run average of 1.74 which was the second lowest for a left-hander in American League history, and he pitched nine shutouts which were the most by an American League left-hander since Babe Ruth in 1916. Opponents batted just .193 against him, 15 of his wins followed Yankee losses, he struck out at least 10 batters eight times including 18 in one game against California, and his 248 strikeouts set a new team record. And in the postseason Guidry was the winning pitcher in the one-game play-off against Boston, and he won his only starts in both the American League Championship Series and the World Series.

"Nobody ever had a better year pitching in my time," said Piniella.

Guidry was a marvel. He stood just 5-foot-11 and weighed a scant 160 pounds, yet he could blow batters away with his 95 mph fastball. But for a spell there he gave Steinbrenner plenty of reasons to want to ship him out.

Because he couldn't master a breaking pitch in the minors, the Yankees converted Guidry to short relief and he saved 14 games for Triple-A Syracuse in 1975 which earned him a brief, unspectacular promotion to the big club.

Frustrated by his lack of use in 1976, Guidry nearly quit baseball. Upon learning he had been demoted back to Syracuse, he packed his car and started driving home to Louisiana, only to have his wife Bonnie talk him out of it. He did get another recall late in the year and finished out the season in New York as the Yankees rolled to the American League championship, and it was during this stint that he learned how to become a major league pitcher with the help of Sparky Lyle and Dick Tidrow. Tidrow taught him the mind games, the strategy of setting up hitters and working counts, while Lyle worked on his mechanics and introduced him to the slider.

"For six years I played in the Yankee farm system and not once did I get the kind of help and advice Tidrow and Lyle gave me," Guidry said. "In the minors they just give you the ball and say 'Here young man, go throw.' They emphasize that you should throw strikes. That's a great piece of advice."

Tidrow and Lyle could not alter Guidry's penchant for starting a season slowly, though, and when he struggled at the start of 1977 Steinbrenner was back on the trade bandwagon. "If you want to trade him, you send him out with the understanding that if he ever comes back to haunt you, you'll take the blame," Paul told Steinbrenner. The owner backed down, and Guidry turned his career around. By the time his career was ended by a sore arm in 1988, Guidry's record was 170-91 with a 3.29 ERA.

During the early difficulties of 1977, Martin chided Guidry by asking, "If there's anybody in this league you can get out, let me know and I'll let you pitch to him." In 1978, that list included just about every hitter in the American League.

Lyle recalled in his book *The Bronx Zoo* what it was like watching Guidry pitch. "Guidry's the most impressive pitcher I've ever seen. He's more impressive than Seaver, Palmer, or Ryan. You're sitting there watching the guy and he's just winding up, throwing the ball, and the catcher's throwing it back to him like they're playing catch. Before you know it, Jesus Christ, the ballgame is over, they've got three hits and he's won, 2-0."

* * *

Guidry was the Opening Day pitcher in Texas and he received a no-decision when Goose Gossage was tagged for a game-winning home run in the ninth in his Yankee debut. New York lost four of its first five games, then returned for its home opener against the White Sox. Before Guidry's complete game victory that day, the Yankees raised their 1977 championship banner, and doing the honors were Mickey Mantle and his home-run-hitting buddy, Roger Maris.

It was an emotional afternoon as Maris—his understandable bitterness finally receding—made his first appearance in the Bronx since the end of the 1966 season. The Yankees had been trying to get him to come back for years, but he always refused, figuring he would get booed just as he always had been. Steinbrenner predicted Maris would get a thunderous ovation, and Maris decided to test it out. The fans roared long and loud, the Maris ovation spilling into the introduction of Mantle. Maris had finally gotten his due. Too bad it took 17 years.

As advertised, the Red Sox were awesome as they won 34 of their first 50 games and it was obvious this was going to be a tough club to catch for a Yankee team that seemed to be getting along fairly well. What the Yankees needed was a good ol' controversy to light their fire. It came in July.

With his team unable to keep pace with the Red Sox, we all noticed the toll it was taking on Martin. He began to drink heavier than normal, he was arriving at the ballpark later and later, and his decisions seemed to be somewhat clouded. The Yankees lost 10 of their first 14 games in July, the last in that stretch a 9-7 defeat at home against Kansas City. That night Jackson deliberately disobeyed Martin and tried to bunt a runner into scoring position in the 10th inning with the score tied. Jackson struck out doing so, and after the Yankees lost, Martin went ballistic in the clubhouse, smashing a glass against a door and a clock radio against a wall. He was livid and he demanded Jackson be reprimanded. Steinbrenner agreed and Jackson was suspended for five games.

The Yankees won all five games in Jackson's absence and picked up four games on the Red Sox to pull within 10 of the lead. Then Jackson returned to the club, and Martin, angered just by the sight of the slugger, told Murray Chass of the *New York Times,* "The two of them (Steinbrenner and Jackson) deserve each other. One's a born liar, the other's convicted."

That was it. Steinbrenner hit the roof and the next day Martin resigned before the Boss could fire him. Bob Lemon, who had recently been fired by the White Sox, was brought in as the replacement, but five days later we found out Lemon was only a temporary solution. Prior to the Old-Timers Game at Yankee Stadium, public address man Bob Sheppard announced to the sellout crowd that Lemon would become general manager in 1980 and that Martin would return to manage the club. The fans went wild and gave Martin a lengthy ovation that brought tears to his eyes. It was a bizarre turn of events, and we in the media scoffed that it would never happen. I, for one, certainly hoped it didn't.

At the start of September the Yankees were 6 1/2 games behind and time was running out, but they knew that with seven games still to play against Boston, they were alive. New York began the final month by winning five of seven against Seattle and Detroit while Boston lost four of six to Oakland and Baltimore. The Red Sox lead was down to four games, and it was time for the Yankees to play four in a row at Fenway Park.

Winning three out of four was the Yankees' goal. Instead, they won all four and pulled into a tie for the division lead. They won the first two games with laughable ease, 15-3 and 13-2. Guidry threw a two-hit shutout to win the third game, 7-0, and the sweep was completed when Figueroa, with help from Gossage, earned a 7-4 triumph.

Boston won the next day to go back into the lead while the Yankees were idle, but then the Red Sox lost five in a row including the first two games of their final series of the season against New York. During that time, the Yankees built a 3 1/2-game cushion before the Red Sox salvaged the finale at Yankee Stadium behind Dennis Eckersley. During the final two weeks, Boston regained its composure and won 12 of 14 including its last eight. New York won six in a row in the last week, but on closing day, Cleveland beat the Yankees and Boston shut out Toronto. The teams were tied.

After arriving in Boston the night before the play-off game, I went to a joint called Daisy Buchanan's with a few other writers, and Munson, Piniella, and Hunter were already there. We talked, off the record, about what a wild ride it had been, and Piniella was saying that it was almost like this was meant to be. That these two excellent teams should wind up in this position after 162 games with nothing settled. He was right. And we couldn't wait for the settling to begin.

*　　*　　*

Guidry did not get off to a good start. Carl Yastrzemski lined a solo home run to right in the second inning and Boston center fielder Fred Lynn remembered thinking, "Guidry wasn't the same guy we saw earlier." In fact, Guidry didn't have his best stuff that day. Everyone was tired, and so was he.

The Gator persevered through some shaky moments, but with Torrez limiting the Yankees to two hits through six innings, it looked like New York was in trouble when the Red Sox extended their lead to 2-0 in the bottom of the sixth as Rick Burleson doubled, moved to third on Jerry Remy's bunt, and scored on Jim Rice's single. Boston could have padded its lead after Carlton Fisk walked with two outs, but Piniella peered through the blinding sun to make a dazzling catch of Lynn's drive to right, saving two runs.

"Guidry wasn't quick as usual," Piniella said. "Munson told me that his breaking ball was hanging so I played Lynn a few steps closer to the line than usual. I saw the ball leave the bat and then I lost it in the sun. I went to the place where I thought the ball would land."

Fenway screams were hushed as the Yankees trotted off the field still in the game. And then came the silence.

With one out in the seventh Chris Chambliss and Roy White hit back-to-back singles and Jim Spencer flied out, bringing Dent to the plate. He'd hit four home runs all season and was mired in a slump that had him batting .140 over his last 20 games. Dent fouled a 1-0 pitch off his shin and screeched in pain, and it took him a couple of minutes to hobble off the sting. During the delay, Mickey Rivers noticed a crack in Dent's bat and gave him his stick to swing. When Dent was ready, he stepped into the box and swung at Torrez's next pitch, a fastball. He hit it squarely and the ball arched its way into left field, but this was little Bucky Dent, so everyone assumed it would be a harmless fly ball for the third out.

"When Dent hit it, I thought we were out of the inning," said Torrez. "I started to walk off the mound."

Said Fisk: "After Dent hit it I let out a sigh of relief. I thought, 'We got away with that mistake pitch.' I almost screamed at Mike. Then I saw Yaz looking up and I said, 'Oh God.'"

Dent never saw the ball land in the netting. As soon as he connected he took off because he thought it would carom off the wall. "I didn't find out it was a home run until I passed first base and saw the umpire's signal," said Dent. "I didn't realize the magnitude of what I did until it was all over."

The Red Sox realized it right away. They were trailing 3-2.

Then it became 4-2. Torrez walked Rivers and was replaced by Bob Stanley, who promptly allowed Rivers to steal second before yielding Thurman Munson's RBI double.

Guidry departed after a George Scott single in the bottom of the seventh, and Gossage slammed the door by striking out pinch-hitter Bob Bailey.

In the eighth Jackson gave the Yankees more cushion as he plastered a Stanley fastball into the center field bleachers, and it became the winning run when Boston rallied in its half of the eighth. Remy doubled and scored on Yastrzemski's single. Then Fisk and Lynn singled to score Yaz and cut the New York lead to 5-4. But Gossage did what Steinbrenner was paying him millions to do: He put out the fire as Butch Hobson flied out and George Scott struck out.

On to the bottom of the ninth they went, and the Fenway faithful stirred again when Burleson drew a one-out walk and Remy slashed a line drive into right. Again, Piniella made a fabulous play to overcome the sun. He never saw the ball, but miraculously reached out his glove and knocked it down, preventing it from rolling to the wall. Burleson, thinking at first that Piniella was going to catch the ball in the air, held up and could not advance to third.

"I didn't want the ball hit to me, it was a nightmare out there in the sun," said Piniella. "When Remy hit it I saw it for a second and then lost it. I knew it would bounce, so I moved back three steps to prevent it from bouncing over me to the wall. I decoyed Burleson, I didn't want him to know I couldn't see it."

Runners at first and second, one out, and Rice and Yastrzemski due to bat. How good was this?

"I tried to calm myself down by thinking of the mountains of Colorado, the mountains that I love," said Gossage. "I thought the worst thing that could happen to me was that I'd be in those mountains tomorrow."

Rice just missed a fastball and sent Piniella back about 25 feet in front of the wall in right-center for the second out with Burleson moving along to third. Had he been able to make third on the previous play, the game would have been tied. "There's got to be fate involved," muttered Burleson.

Now came Yastrzemski, the longtime Red Sox hero, the sure-fire Hall of Famer, in the twilight of his career desperately trying to make it back to the World Series (he'd been there twice) and win it before he retired.

Gossage missed with the first pitch, but then threw a steamer that Yastrzemski swung at. At the last instant he'd wanted to pull the bat back, but it was too late. The ball popped up into foul territory wide of third base where Nettles made the catch to end the game. The Yankees poured out of their dugout and celebrated in front of the tear-filled fans of Fenway. The Red Sox stared in disbelief, wondering how this could have happened.

Yastrzemski was solemn in the Boston clubhouse. "It wasn't a good swing, but the guy made a hell of a pitch. The ball sailed in on me and at the speed he throws you don't have much time for correction. I'll always think about that swing."

Just as I, and anyone else who was fortunate enough to be there that day, will always think about that game.

– *1978 World Series* –

In the glow of the Yankee clubhouse following the triumph in Boston, Chris Chambliss repeated one of those oft-used clichés that we got used to hearing from the players: "We'll just try to sit back tonight and enjoy this a little bit." At least he got it right. The Yankees had only that night on the plane ride out to Kansas City to enjoy their victory because the next night they had to take the field at Royals Stadium to begin the American League Championship Series.

They had been challenged all season, and had passed every examination along the way. Now they were confronted with the ultimate test: trying to harness their emotions and remember that the long, arduous fight to win the division was merely the first step in the journey.

One of two things was going to happen in Game One. Either the Yankees were going to be emotionally and physically flat and they were going to lose, which is what Royals manager Whitey Herzog was hoping for—"I wish we were playing the first play-off game at 10 in the morning instead of at night. There might be a few hangovers that get off their plane." Or, the Yankees would ride their wave of momentum into Kansas City, rally behind young pitcher Jim Beattie who Bob Lemon was forced to start, and win.

They won. Beattie and Ken Clay combined on a two-hitter as New York romped, 7-1. Royals reliever Al Hrabowsy had said before the game that he would strike out Reggie Jackson every time he faced him. Jackson hit a three-run homer off Hrabosky in the eighth to punctuate the victory.

Game Two was a flop for New York as Ed Figueroa was knocked out during a four-run second inning and Kansas City went on to pound out 16 hits—matching New York's total in the first game—for a 10-4 blowout.

When the Series shifted to New York for its conclusion, the games improved. Game Three was an excellent affair during which the lead changed hands four times, the last in the bottom of the eighth. George Brett smashed three solo home runs off Catfish Hunter to lift the Royals into a 3-3 tie, and then Darrell Porter singled home one run and scored another in the top of the eighth for a 5-4 lead. However, Thurman Munson launched a 430-foot two-run homer—his first in 54 games—to left-center off reliever Doug Bird to win the game for New York.

It was Ron Guidry's turn in the rotation for Game Four, and as usual, he was splendid. Guidry said that he wasn't afraid of Brett and that "he's used up all his home runs." Brett replied, "Let's be honest, Guidry's not God. He's beatable." Not this time. Guidry and Goose Gossage combined on a seven-hitter and Graig Nettles and Roy White each hit solo home runs off Dennis Leonard to provide a 2-1 pennant-clinching victory.

Earlier in the day, the Dodgers polished off the Phillies for the second year in a row in the National League Championship Series, three games to one, so once again, it was a Yankees-Dodgers World Series.

*   *   *

On the flight out to Los Angeles I spent some time talking with Munson. He was very interested in what was going on with the New York newspaper strike that had crippled all of the city's dailies. The unionized press men had walked off the job and for more than two months each paper was only able to put out skeleton editions. The writers were allowed to cover the games home and away, just as we always did, but we couldn't provide the depth of coverage because there weren't enough people back in the office to do all the processing.

"Nice gig you got there, Joe," Munson said to me. "They still pay all your bills and you only have to do half the work."

After I shared what I knew about the strike, our conversation turned to aviation. During the 1977 season Munson had become interested in airplanes. Not riding in them, flying them. He began to take flying lessons which continued into the spring of 1978 when he was down in Fort Lauderdale. He visited numerous airports in Florida, began reading aviation magazines, and this new hobby became his passion. He told me he hoped to earn his pilot's license in the coming spring, and when he did he was going to buy a prop plane.

"Maybe someday I'll take you up with me, Joe," he said with a smile, and I said, "I'd like that."

Munson was such a paradoxical character. There were some days—in fact many days—when he could be a complete jerk, when he'd treat the press rudely, or ignore us altogether by hiding in the trainers' room, or he'd blow past the kids seeking autographs outside the stadium. "He's not moody," Sparky Lyle once said of him. "Moody means you're nice some of the time." It was a funny line, but not entirely true. Munson was nice some of the time. There were days when he could be a gem, a terrific conversationalist, a witty personality, a giver of his time who would sign autographs for everyone.

Among this era of Yankee players, I had known only Roy White longer, so I accepted Munson and recognized that his gruff public persona wasn't who he really was. Underneath the glacial façade, he was a warm, caring man who doted on his wife and three small children. "I like to kid around a lot, but I do it in kind of a grouchy way," he once said. "If you don't know me, you think I'm serious. It's just the way I am."

I was disappointed by Munson's stance when Reggie Jackson joined the team in 1977. I thought his treatment of Jackson was ill-mannered and unwarranted. Jackson certainly didn't help his own cause with his rapid-fire mouth, but still, it wasn't fair that the captain of the team refused to get along with a new teammate, knowing full well that the rest of the team would follow his lead.

On the field, Munson never disappointed. He was a great player who did whatever it took to win, the consummate gamer. When he came up to the Yankees for good in 1970 after having played just 99 minor league games, it was clear he had an abundance of talent which was borne out when he won the American League Rookie of the Year award. He had all the tools the great catchers have, and he swung a potent bat which vaulted him into a different class entirely. During his much-too-short 10 1/2-year career, the only catcher who could rival Munson in the American League was his bitter enemy, Boston's Carlton Fisk.

He was a great clutch hitter, and what made him so dangerous is that he could hit for power as well as control his bat and hit to all fields, but he was always prouder of his three Gold Glove awards that proved his defensive prowess. "I like hitting fourth and I like the good batting average," he told me one time. "But what I do behind the plate every day is a lot more important because it touches so many more people and so many more aspects of the game."

I found Munson to be an intelligent person. Jackson once claimed his IQ was 160 and Munson used to say, "My IQ might not be 160, but I'm no dummy." No, he wasn't. He had taken his baseball earnings, invested wisely, and he was comfortably wealthy. And because material possessions were important to this man who had grown up amid humble surroundings in Akron, Ohio, that prop plane was going to be the ultimate possession.

Coming off back-to-back World Series titles, Munson was already in a good mood when he came south for spring training in 1979, and when he received his pilot's license, his mood brightened further. He bought a Beechcraft Baron and flew it all over south Florida. He even took Lou Piniella on a flight out to the Bahamas one day.

But the little Beechcraft didn't suit Munson. He wanted something bigger, more powerful, and a few months later, he spent more than a million dollars on a sleek Cessna Citation jet. Piniella and a few of the other Yankees did not approve of the purchase. Though Munson was an excellent pilot, they didn't think he was ready to handle this class of plane. Billy Martin, who returned as the team's manager in mid-June of 1979, didn't like Munson flying. Neither did George Steinbrenner.

On the evening of August 1, 1979 the Yankees defeated the White Sox in Chicago, then boarded a commercial jet for the trip back to New York. With a scheduled off day, Munson passed on the team flight and instead flew his own jet from Chicago to Canton where the next day he was going to practice landings. Around three o'clock that following afternoon, Munson crashed the jet just short of the runway. Two copilot/instructors managed to escape the fiery heap. Munson did not. Even before the fire engulfed the plane, Munson's neck was broken and he died in that Cessna at the age of 32.

There has never been a night at Yankee Stadium quite like August 3, 1979 when the Yankees played the Baltimore Orioles. Grief gripped the grand venue, and tears spilled when eight Yankees took the field. The only position where a Yankee was not stationed was catcher, a tribute to the fallen captain. Forty years earlier Lou Gehrig had stood almost in the very spot where Munson should have been, and he tugged at our heartstrings with his famous speech. But Gehrig was still with us that day, we could see him and hear him and there was still hope that maybe by some miracle the disease that was ravaging his body would stop and he would go into remission. There was still a chance. Munson had no chance. Munson was gone.

Munson's face was displayed on the scoreboard in right-center field, and the fans stood and applauded for nearly eight minutes. To have not cried that night would not have been human.

The Yankees lost that game, and the next game, and the game after that, though no one really cared. The team was far out of the pennant race anyway. On the day of the funeral Steinbrenner chartered a flight to Canton so the team could attend the service and still return in time to play Baltimore later that evening. Bobby Murcer, one of Munson's closest friends who had just returned to the club barely a month earlier in a trade from the Chicago Cubs, delivered a moving eulogy at the funeral. He then went out and drove in all five runs as the Yankees defeated the first-place Orioles in a game they dedicated to Munson.

The Yankee captain was gone. But the Yankees had played a game that would have made Munson so proud. "We were playing in the spirit of Thurman," said Murcer. "I think that's what carried us through the game."

*   *   *

As the Dodgers were flying home to Los Angeles following their defeat of Philadelphia, they learned that their World Series opponent would once again be the Yankees. They were thrilled.

"I don't know how many players on this team would admit it, but we didn't like playing second fiddle to the Yankees last year," said outfielder Reggie Smith. "A lot of people said we were lucky just to be there. I think we dedicated ourselves to proving those people wrong this year."

Smith even went so far as to predict a Los Angeles sweep of the first two games at Dodger Stadium. "Last year we put a lot of pressure on ourselves to win at home in the Series, then we lost two out of three. We won't let that happen this year. We'll get the jump with the first two at home."

And so they did. They whipped the Yankees in the first two games by scores of 11-5 and 4-3. Not that it did them a lot of good in the end.

The opener was a farce for New York. The Dodgers jumped all over Figueroa and when he allowed home runs to Dusty Baker and Davey Lopes in the second inning that put Los Angeles up 3-0, Lemon lifted him. It didn't matter because the Dodgers kept right on hammering New York pitchers, ending the night with 15 hits. Lopes whacked a three-run homer in the fourth to make it 6-0 and Billy North lined a pinch-hit two-run double in the seventh to ice it for Los Angeles.

On paper it looked like a crushing defeat, but something good happened for the Yankees in this game that played a key role later in the week. On his second home run Lopes circled the bases with his forefinger raised in the air signifying he and the Dodgers were No. 1. The defending champion Yankees did not take kindly to that gesture.

"It kind of pissed us off, really, the way Lopes was acting," Guidry recalled. "Even when we were beating them the year before, we didn't say anything about it, we just beat them. We figured 'Hey, if you want to talk, let's do it out there, between the lines.'"

The Yankees did not respond immediately to Lopes's stirring of the embers. Bob Welch struck out Jackson to end Game Two in one of the great one-on-one World Series confrontations of all time.

Jackson's two-run double staked New York to an early lead, but Ron Cey's three-run homer in the sixth gave the Dodgers a 4-2 lead and it was 4-3 when the ninth inning began. The Yankees put two men on with one out, so Tommy Lasorda brought in Welch, a rookie flamethrower, to face Munson and Jackson. Munson lined out to right, bringing Mr. October to the plate with the game on the line. The sellout crowd, usually rather docile in Los Angeles, rose to its feet and roared in anticipation of what was about to take place.

"This is what I lived for as a baseball player," Jackson wrote in his autobiography. "This was the event. We were the event."

First there was a swinging strike, then a ball, then a blazing fastball that Jackson tried to cream and only ticked for a foul ball. The count was 1-2 and there was so much noise I'm sure the Hollywood sign up in the mountains overlooking the movie capital of the world was shaking. Two more fastballs, and each time Jackson managed to foul them off. Welch wasted a pitch hoping Jackson would chase it, but he didn't. Another foul ball, and then another pitch out of the strike zone that Jackson laid off. Now the count was 3-2 and indeed Jackson and Welch seemed all alone out there on the field.

Who was going to flinch? Finally, it was Jackson. Welch came with his best heater, his ninth offering in this sequence. Jackson took a mighty swing, and his bat touched nothing but air. Game over. Dodgers up two games to none. The stadium erupted, the Dodgers danced for joy, and Jackson cursed himself before trudging back to the dugout and slamming his bat against the wall in anger.

"Give him credit, he beat me fair and square," said Jackson.

The morning of that game the Dodgers had attended the funeral of Jim Gilliam, a longtime Dodger player and coach who had suffered a brain hemorrhage a few weeks earlier and then died the day before the start of the Series. They made it very clear they were playing in Gilliam's memory and that his spirit was carrying them to greatness. It made for a nice story, but it also served as inspiration for the Yankees to shut up the Dodgers.

Guidry recalled a bunch of Yankees standing around in the clubhouse the day of Game Three and Munson coming in and saying, "If it were any other team but the Dodgers, I might say let's forget it, but the way these guys have been carrying on, I would like nothing better than to beat them four straight."

The captain spoke. The team listened.

The Dodgers were thinking sweep when they arrived in New York. "We can do it, if we can beat Guidry Friday," Cey said. By getting eight hits and drawing seven walks off Guidry, Los Angeles should have beaten Guidry that night. They didn't because of Nettles.

Game Three will forever be remembered as the Nettles game. The Yankee third baseman put on possibly the greatest fielding performance in Series history, surpassing even Brooks Robinson's display back in 1970 against Cincinnati. Nettles made four eye-popping plays that by Guidry's calculations saved him at least six runs, and he was the difference in New York's 5-1 victory.

"Things were happening so fast I don't know how many runs I saved," Nettles said. "I just know I saved some. If you can save a few runs it's the same as driving them in. I know it picks the guys up and mentally helps the pitcher. I'd rather make a good defensive play than hit a home run."

Nettles had made a succession of plays to get the Yankees back into the Series. All it took the next day was one swivel of Jackson's hip to turn the Series in New York's favor. I don't remember who came up with the phrase "sacrifice thigh," but I wish I had. What a terrific description of what became the most controversial and meaningful play of the Series.

Los Angeles jumped out to a 3-0 lead in the fifth against Figueroa when Smith blasted a three-run homer, and with Tommy John mowing down the Yankees and shutting them out, Smith's home run looked very imposing. But in the sixth the Yankees scored twice, the second run touching off a rhubarb between the Dodgers and the umpires.

With one out White singled, Munson walked, and Jackson singled to chase White home. Piniella then lined to Russell at shortstop who purposely dropped the ball with the intent of turning a double play. He stepped on second to force Jackson, and then attempted to throw on to first to get the slow-footed Piniella. He would have had Piniella easily, but Jackson stopped halfway between first and second and when Russell threw, Jackson intentionally stuck his thigh out and the ball hit him. As it rolled on the infield, Munson chugged around third and scored.

Lasorda exploded out of the dugout screaming interference. "It had to be interference," said Lasorda. "He has to get out of the way. A guy should be allowed to throw to first base without someone standing in his way. It cost us the game." Jackson, of course, pleaded innocence. "No, I didn't throw my hip out," he said. I asked him if he would change his response under oath. He smiled and said, "That's a good question, but I can't answer that."

Regardless of whether he did it on purpose or not, the fact was Los Angeles still led, 3-2. It did not cost the Dodgers the game. While the Dodgers managed to make just one hit over the final four innings against Dick Tidrow and Goose Gossage, the Yankees kept plugging away and earned the victory.

In the eighth Paul Blair led off with a single and eventually scored the tying run on Munson's double down the line. And then in the 10th White drew a one-out walk, Jackson hit a two-out single, and Piniella drove a single into right-center off Welch to win the game.

The Dodgers were shaken, and the Yankees knew it. In the clubhouse I overheard Piniella telling Nettles, "The way the Dodgers walked off the field today, it won't take us more than two games to end this thing."

The Dodgers blamed Nettles's glove for their loss in Game Three and Jackson's thigh for their loss in Game Four. They had no one to blame but themselves for their loss in Game Five.

Three errors, a wild pitch, two passed balls and horrendous pitching added up to a 12-2 defeat, giving New York a clean sweep of the games at Yankee Stadium. And while the Dodgers should have been worrying about their abysmal play, they were more interested in lashing out at the New York fans. "I'm happy to get out of here," said Smith. "A couple of things were said to me that showed me how sick these people are. This city is filthy and their minds are filthy. They spend all their money trying to bring peace to the Middle East. They ought to spend the money to educate these idiots here."

Said Lopes: "They ought to drop a bomb on this place. These are the most vulgar fans I've ever seen. The whole atmosphere is bad, but that's not a rationalization for us losing here. The Yankees just beat the devil out of us."

Lemon gave the ball to Jim Beattie, the winner in the first game of the ALCS, and once again Beattie turned in a nifty effort, his first complete game of the year. After allowing Los Angeles to grab a 2-0 lead in the third, Beattie limited the Dodgers to four hits over the final six innings, while his teammates torched the Dodgers for 12 runs on 18 hits including a Series-record 16 singles.

"I think we've got it," said Dent. "We beat Boston in Boston and we can beat Los Angeles in Los Angeles."

There had been heroes galore in this Series for the Yankees. Nettles, Piniella, Munson, Jackson, all familiar names, had taken their turns. Now it was time for Dent and Brian Doyle.

Dent? Hadn't he already enjoyed his moment in the sun with his home run in Boston? He wasn't even a career .250 hitter. And Doyle? He was a backup second baseman playing only because Willie Randolph had pulled a hamstring in the last week of the regular season, knocking him out of postseason play. He was a guy who batted .192 in brief action during 1978. His only claim to fame was being the little brother of recently retired major leaguer Denny Doyle.

Yet in Game Six, with Catfish Hunter enjoying his final glory during a 7-2 Series-clinching victory, Dent and Doyle combined to bat 6-for-8 and were involved in all seven runs as they scored two and drove in five.

"They were throwing me 'Here, hit this, kid' pitches," Dent said, noting the Dodgers' lack of respect for him. So you can imagine what the Dodger pitchers were throwing at Doyle, and their utter shock when he—like Dent—knocked the ball all over the yard. "With a lineup like ours, they don't try to pitch around us," Doyle reasoned. "I would say we see more good pitches because we are at the bottom of the batting order."

The final numbers showed Dent with a .417 batting average with 10 hits and seven RBI which secured the Series MVP award, while Doyle registered at .438. Meanwhile, Dodger studs Garvey and Smith batted .208 and .200, respectively.

Lopes tagged Hunter for a solo homer in the first inning and Yankee fans must have sensed trouble, but Dent keyed a three-run second inning when he punched a two-run single up the middle for a 3-1 Yankee lead.

Joe Ferguson doubled and scored on Lopes's single in the third, but over the next four innings, Hunter allowed no runs on two hits before giving way to Goose Gossage. During that stretch, the Yankees increased their lead to 5-2, leaving only one last piece of unfinished business. In the seventh White led off with a walk and after Munson struck out, Jackson stepped in to take another shot at Welch, his Game Two tormentor. No contest. Jackson sent Welch's first pitch soaring over the wall in right-center, his seventh home run in the last two World Series. "I felt like it was just a continuation of the last at-bat in Game Two," Jackson said. "Didn't matter that the Series was nearly over. Welch knew it. I knew it. This was between me and him." This time, Jackson won.

And the Yankees had won. Again. For the 22nd time in their history they were World Series champions.

It had been a mind-boggling year that included more feuding, a managerial change, and an epic comeback from 14 games down in the middle of July. But here they were, swigging champagne at Dodger Stadium, undoubtedly recognized as the best team in baseball.

"Maybe now they'll stop questioning us," Munson said, probably referring to the media. "Maybe now all the talk will stop and people will just realize what we are—a great ball club."

It was two hours before Game One of the 1996 World Series was to begin and I was standing in front of the Yankees dugout talking to the team's manager, my friend of 45 years, Joe Torre.

Torre is a man who hides his emotions well. Look at him in the dugout and you can't tell whether the Yankees are winning or losing. In victory and in defeat he always conducts himself in an even-tempered manner when he deals with the abrasive New York press, his high-salaried players, his demanding boss, or even New York city traffic.

But on this glorious October night—before the Yankees would take the field in a World Series game for the first time in 15 years, before he would be introduced in a World Series game for the first time in his life—I could see Torre was on edge. His insides were churning, a bubbling cauldron cooking up a witches' brew consisting of excitement, uncertainty, and nervousness.

There was no concealing it, and I understood why. Back in 1957 and 1958 he had watched his brother, Frank, play in the World Series as a member of the Milwaukee Braves. Ever since, Joe had dreamed of doing the same thing. He played for the Braves, Cardinals, and Mets during a distinguished career, and in an odd bit of symmetry he later managed all three of those clubs in a mostly undistinguished manner. Every one of the 32 years Torre wore a major league uniform ended the same way—with him watching two teams play in the World Series, neither of which was his. Until this night when, as manager of the Yankees, his tortuous climb to baseball's summit was completed. After 4,272 major league games, Torre had made it.

"Look at that, Joe," he said to me, pointing to the scoreboard in left-center field. I glanced out there and knew immediately what he was going to say next. There was only one game on the major league schedule that night, and he was involved in it. "I'm so happy for you, Joe," I told him. "Now try and enjoy yourself."

He nodded to me, and wearing that warm-hearted smile under those dark, sunken eyes and prominent Italian nose, he put his right arm around me and said, "I know you're gonna enjoy it."

Fifteen autumns earlier I brought the curtain down on my 45-year sportswriting career. I retired from the New York Post following the Yankees' Game Six loss to the Los Angeles Dodgers in the 1981 World Series. That night, when I walked out of the Yankee Stadium press box, I packed away forever my typewriter—yes, I was still using one—and my unbiased opinions regarding the team. At 65 years of age, my life came full circle. I became biased again. I became a Yankee fan again.

In 1923 my father and I sat in brand-new Yankee Stadium rooting for the likes of Babe Ruth and Bob Meusel and Waite Hoyt. In 1982, unburdened by the professional journalistic code of objectivity, I spent many a summer day in refurbished Yankee Stadium with Marie or our grandchildren rooting for the likes of Dave Winfield and Ron Guidry and Dave Righetti.

But the Yankees went nowhere that year, and they went nowhere for many years. In the hollow seasons that followed, somewhere along the way I resigned myself to the fact that I wasn't going to see the Yankees play in another World Series in my lifetime. Then again, I didn't expect the Lord to keep me on this earth so long. I didn't expect to be sitting in Yankee Stadium nearly 20 years after my retirement, bouncing my great-grandson on my lap.

The Yankees did indeed return to glory, and some people, including me, say their run of four World Series triumphs in five years between 1996 and 2000 is their ultimate achievement, given the difficulty now associated with winning the championship.

So yes, Torre was right. I did enjoy that 1996 World Series, especially when the Yankees won it. I enjoyed it more than the championship in 1998, or the one in 1999, or the one in 2000. Beating the Atlanta Braves in 1996 was special not only because of Torre's involvement, but because it ended 18 years of desultory aggravation for Yankee fans.

Not since it took the franchise 21 years to win its first title after its birth as the Highlanders in 1903 had this team waited so long for a championship. The Yankees hadn't ruled the baseball world since 1978. They hadn't played in the World Series since 1981. For a franchise so steeped in tradition and excellence, that was just too long.

Between the time Goose Gossage recorded the last out and raised his arms in victory at Dodger Stadium in 1978 to John Wetteland doing the same at Yankee Stadium in 1996, George Steinbrenner made 17 managerial changes including four more separate hirings and firings of Billy Martin.

The period from 1965 to 1975 had been terrible, but this was worse, the nadir coming in 1990 when New York's 67-95 record was the worst in the American League. It was so bad, Andy Hawkins pitched a no-hitter against the White Sox, and lost. The Yankees became a national joke, the kings of the castle reduced to serfs.

Fortunes began to change when Buck Showalter took the managerial reins in 1992 and began rebuilding Yankee pride. The 1994 players' strike interrupted the progress, but in 1995, when the two leagues were split into three divisions and the play-off structure was expanded to include wild-card teams, Showalter guided the Yankees into the postseason. A heartbreaking three games to two loss to Lou Piniella's Seattle Mariners ended the Yankees' brief appearance, and once again the revolving door in the manager's office turned as Showalter quit in hopes of landing the skipper's job with the expansion Arizona Diamondbacks, which he ultimately did get. That left Steinbrenner sifting through resumes, trying to find someone who could take a team that was clearly on the rise and bring it back to the promised land. On the advice of longtime consultant Arthur Richman, Steinbrenner chose Torre.

The Daily News *called Torre "Clueless Joe" because he had never made it to the World Series. It was mean-spirited, and the* News *wasn't alone in its doubt. Torre had a record of 894 wins and 1,003 losses. He'd only made it to the postseason once in 14 years—that with Atlanta in 1982 and the Braves hadn't even won a play-off game as they were swept three straight in the National League Championship Series by St. Louis.*

Torre oozed class and humility, he was a born-and-bred New York guy, but his field boss pedigree was not promising. No one believed Torre was the right man for the job. Today, Joe and I laugh about it.

During the first nine years of my retirement, laughter was part of my daily routine. I had saved my money assiduously and Marie and I were able to live quite comfortably on our investments, my pension, and social security. Free to do whatever I pleased, I worked more frequently on my golf game, though I found out that just as your birthday number keeps getting larger, so, too, does your handicap. Marie and I traveled, we spent time with our children and their children, my sister and her family, and Marie's five siblings and their families. And using my special-issue lifetime press pass that the Yankees presented to me during a quaint retirement ceremony held in my honor, I spent much time at Yankee Stadium. Some days I would sit in the press box and mingle with my friends, other days I would take Marie or the grandkids and sit in the stands.

I had worked hard to get into a position where I could sit back with my wife and happily grow old together, and that's what we were doing. But then in the summer of 1991, I took Marie for her annual medical checkup, and during a routine examination her doctor noticed a potential problem with Marie's liver. Further tests revealed she had developed cancer, and within six months, the love of my life was dead at the age of 75.

Studies have shown that the majority of men die before their wives, and to be honest, I had always assumed—I guess based on the fact that my father had died long before my mother—that this was going to be the case with me. Once my cancerous prostate gland had been removed, that insidious disease never resur-

faced anywhere else in my body. I had the typical aches and pains associated with old age, but all in all, I was a pretty healthy man. But Marie could run laps around me. She was in astonishing condition for a woman her age and I just thought she would live forever. Before her diagnosis in August she was a strong and vibrant woman. By Christmas she was frail and failing. By Valentine's Day 1992, she was gone, and so, too, was a part of me.

I was not prepared to cope with life without Marie, and I found out exactly how my own mother felt when she lost my father. My mother had lived 11 years after Dad's death, but her spirit was never quite as vigorous once he was gone, and the same malady struck me. My children, Phillip and Katherine, and my seven grandchildren were supportive and for months they checked in on me every day to make sure I was all right. I pretended that I was, but the void in my life was canyonesque and I found myself breaking into tears regularly.

I needed something to do on a consistent basis to occupy my mind and body, and as if directed from the Lord above, the Yankees rescued me. Writers usually serve as official scorers at baseball games, but there had been some problems early in 1992 at the stadium. A couple of players had reacted angrily to decisions made by the official scorer, and when the scorer went into the locker room to perform his reporting duties, he was childishly frozen out in protest by all of the players. It's pretty tough to do your job when the whole team decides not to talk to you.

That summer I received a phone call from Gene Michael who was the team's general manager at the time. He told me the Yankees had decided to eliminate the conflict of interest by hiring an official scorer who was not connected to the team or the media. I had known Gene since he'd joined the Yankees as a player in 1968 and considered him a friend. The Yankee organization sent me a sympathy card when it learned of Marie's death, but Gene took the time to personally write his own letter of condolence. When this scoring situation arose, Gene thought of me, first because he respected my knowledge of the game and knew I could do the job, and second, he thought it would be a great diversion for me. No doctor could have prescribed a more effective cure for what was ailing me. I was going back to the stadium, going home in a sense.

The Yankees were out on a West Coast trip when I was hired, so it was a week or so later when I made my debut in late June with the Orioles in town.

That day I had the same invigorating feeling going to the ballpark that I used to have when I was covering the great championship teams of the Stengel era.

It was a thrill to be back, even though only a few of my old comrades were still covering the team by then. But that was okay because I was able to meet the new generation of writers and broadcasters and they took to me quickly. I guess they liked having this old fossil around because I was armed with so much infor-

mation about the Yankees' past, and because I'm blessed with such a fertile mind, I remember most of it. These kids like Mike Lupica of the Daily News *and Steve Serby of the* Post *were always asking me to tell a story about Babe Ruth or Joe DiMaggio or Yogi Berra or Mickey Mantle, and I obliged. I enjoyed the trips down memory lane, and I found it very rewarding when I'd pick up a paper and read facts that I had provided for that particular writer.*

I continued as the official scorer through the 1995 season, and that year, on the afternoon of August 13 my storytelling put me on center stage. Before the Yankees' game with Cleveland at the stadium, word came from Dallas that Mantle had succumbed to cancer at the age of 63. He had been ill for quite a while, but I thought the liver transplant he received just two months earlier was going to stabilize him and prolong his life. Instead, doctors found that the new liver mattered little because his cancer had spread to other major organs and his body virtually disintegrated.

I found myself surrounded by members of the media, most of whom knew Mantle and I had been close friends for more than 40 years. I dabbed an occasional tear from my eyes, but there was catharsis in the reminiscing. As I spoke of Mantle's antics during his playing career, it brought me back to a happier time and gave the illusion that he was still alive, smiling that wide country smile.

The last time I saw Mantle alive had been in January 1995 when he flew to Gotham to attend the annual New York chapter of the Baseball Writers Association of America dinner. I was still a member of the organization and went to the dinner every year. Because the 1994 season had been canceled by the players' strike, the organizers decided against inviting current players to be guests at the dinner and instead asked three former New York legends—Mantle, Willie Mays, and Duke Snider—to sit at the head table. That night more than 1,500 people filled the ballroom of the New York Sheraton and cheered loudly for these heroic figures. Mantle looked fairly well as he had just completed a stint at the Betty Ford Rehabilitation Center, curing him of his evil alcohol addiction. Sadly, he didn't get to enjoy sobriety very long. We talked deep into the night after the dinner had ended, and we made vague plans to catch up with each other later in the year when Mantle was back in New York. I never saw him again until I knelt in front of his casket and said a prayer at his wake.

I gave up official scoring after that year when I was offered another position within the organization. When Torre was hired in November to manage the team, he asked Steinbrenner if I could act as his personal consultant. Steinbrenner had known me for nearly 25 years and our relationship was sound, but he asked Torre why he needed someone other than Don Zimmer, his personally-selected bench coach, to consult with. Torre replied, "Joe has known me since I was a kid. He's one of my dearest friends, and sometimes you need someone

*other than a coach to talk to." Steinbrenner was fine with it, and he told me I
had access to the Yankee clubhouse any time, and I was welcome to go on the road
at his expense whenever Torre wanted to bring me along.*

I took him up on that offer, starting with spring training in 1996.

– Chapter 23 –

1996

THE WAY I LOOKED AT IT, George Steinbrenner paying for my six-week stay at the team's spring training hotel in Tampa was the least the Yankee owner could do for me.

After more than 30 years of training in Fort Lauderdale, Steinbrenner moved the Yankees to his hometown of Tampa in 1996 when he convinced city officials to build him a new stadium and player development complex.

This created quite a dilemma for me. When I was still working I would spend two months of every year living in a timeshare condominium in Fort Lauderdale, half the time vacationing, the other half covering the Yankees. When I retired, Marie and I continued to migrate to Fort Lauderdale for February and March, and when the Yankees hit town, Marie would sit next to the pool with her girlfriends and I'd go over to the ball fields and watch the team work out, play exhibition games, and catch up with old acquaintances. The only part of the routine that changed when Marie passed away is that I went to Florida by myself.

But once Steinbrenner announced his plan to move, it didn't make much sense for me to go to Fort Lauderdale anymore. I had to sell my interest in the timeshare and make Tampa my new winter haven. Before I researched buying into a timeshare there, I phoned Steinbrenner, explained my situation, and he told me if I wanted to come down to Tampa, he'd cover my expenses. Nice guy, ol' George. And to think, I used to beat George like a punching bag two or three times a season in my column.

The day Torre gathered the team for his first official meeting, I was invited into the clubhouse, and from my vantage point in the back of the room, I listened to him tell the club, "Every single one of my coaches has been to the World Series. I haven't. I plan to rectify that this year."

He had their attention immediately. What he didn't have was a grasp on the team. Because he had spent his entire career in the National League, Torre wasn't familiar with most of his players and he endured a difficult spring going through that learning process.

There was something else he didn't have. Don Mattingly.

*　　*　　*

Early in the exhibition season I was sitting in the first base stands at Legends Field enjoying the warm Tampa sun while watching the team play against a Montreal Expos split squad. The serene nature of the day was interrupted by a couple of young fellas behind me who were getting on the Yankees' new first baseman, Tino Martinez.

"Hey, are you the guy replacing Mattingly?" one of them yelled. Another said, "Hey, Captain Tino!"

Martinez glanced over a couple times and smiled, but he didn't say anything. I was going to turn around and tell those guys to give Martinez a break, but I decided not to. Glad I didn't because it turned out they were friends of Martinez's, just giving him some good-natured ribbing.

That incident turned out to be harmless, but as I sat there that day, I started thinking about what Martinez was likely to face this season once he got up to New York. I didn't know the kid yet, but I could only hope that he had the mental makeup to survive the unenviable task of replacing a Yankee legend.

It's safe to say that Mattingly is the greatest player in Yankee history with whom I did not have some type of relationship. He made his debut with the team late in the 1982 season, and he left baseball at the end of 1995 due to recurring back problems before Torre came aboard and brought me with him.

I watched Mattingly from afar, and when I took up official scoring for those few years, I would see him occasionally and we'd engage in brief, usually trivial conversation. For the most part he was a stranger to me, but that didn't prevent me from realizing that in his prime, before his debilitating back injury in 1990, he was a great player, so respected by his teammates that he was named Yankee captain, the first since Thurman Munson.

Mattingly was originally an outfielder, but he had worked a little at first base backing up Ken Griffey Sr. as a rookie in 1983 and had shown some punch with the bat. When Yogi Berra took over as manager in 1984 he knew he had to find a way to get Mattingly into the lineup regularly, and first base was the place.

Mattingly learned the position quickly, kept up his impressive hitting, and soon his star was born. In his first full year he became the first Yankee since Mickey Mantle in 1956 to win the American League batting crown with a .343 average, edging teammate Dave Winfield. Between 1984 and 1989 he was the best player in baseball, but the Yankees never made the postseason, robbing Mattingly of the chance to display his skills on the grandest stage—the World Series. Then, at the peak of his greatness, his career was sabotaged by a back injury that sapped much of his power.

Mattingly finally made it to the play-offs in 1995 when the Yankees earned the wild-card berth, and in the only five postseason games he would play, the man they called "Donnie Baseball" was terrific. Yet while he batted .417 with 10 hits and six RBI, it wasn't enough to prevent a series loss to the Mariners.

Mattingly never played again. He sat out the 1996 season hoping that a year off would heal his back, a decision that cost him that elusive World Series ring, and in January of 1997 he realized he could no longer play and officially called it quits. When the Yankees retired his number 23 that summer, the ever-modest Mattingly said, "I don't know what I did to deserve this."

With Mattingly out for 1996 the Yankees needed to find a first baseman. Ironically, one of the players who had ruined Mattingly's bid to reach the World Series in 1995—Seattle's Tino Martinez—was the man they went after.

His left-handed power stroke was perfectly suited for Yankee Stadium and one of the first moves new general manager Bob Watson made was acquiring Martinez and relief pitchers Jeff Nelson and Jim Mecir in exchange for third baseman Russ Davis and pitcher Sterling Hitchcock. Watson should have been thrown in jail for robbery.

Martinez had grown up in Tampa and was a Yankee fan. Mattingly was his favorite player, but his roots with the team dated back to the late 1970s. As a kid he followed the Bronx Zoo crew of Reggie Jackson, Thurman Munson, and Billy Martin, and he had a personal connection to Lou Piniella. Tino's father, Rene Martinez, grew up in the same Tampa neighborhood as Piniella and the two played sandlot ball together as kids. When Piniella became the Mariners' manager in 1993, his new first baseman was young Tino, and because Rene Martinez died of a brain tumor a few years earlier, Tino often sought Piniella's advice on various matters and the two men became close.

However, baseball is a business and the Mariners' pre-Paul Allen financial woes prevented them from retaining Tino's services. "When we knew we were going to trade Tino, I asked him where he would like to go," Piniella said. "He said New York. That's a positive in itself. It takes a special person to be able to play in New York. We knew we were giving the Yankees a heckuva player."

Just before the Yankees broke camp that spring, I happened to talk to Rick Cerone, the former Yankee catcher who knew what it was like to replace a legend. The winter after Thurman Munson's death, the Yankees acquired Cerone in a trade and gave him the tall order of taking over for Munson behind the plate.

"It's going to be tough because Mattingly is such a presence in the modern-day Yankee fan's mind," Cerone said. "It's going to be a little difficult for Tino, but I think he's going to be fine. He's a good, young player. As far as handling it, you go out and do the best you're capable of. He's coming off a great year and Yankee Stadium is made for him."

To his credit, Martinez knew what he was up against. "I think it will be tough at first for the fans because Mattingly's not here anymore, but as long as I go out and play hard, hit the ball and the team starts winning, I can win them over," he said.

It took some doing, but after a painfully slow start, he found his groove and his 25 homers and 117 RBI helped lead the Yankees to the AL East title.

*　　*　　*

Mattingly's absence was only one problem Torre was confronted with when he brought the team north to start the season. The only returning starting infielder was third baseman Wade Boggs. Martinez was going to be fine at first, but up the middle Torre had journeyman Mariano Duncan playing second, and he turned the vital shortstop position over to unproven rookie Derek Jeter. With Bernie Williams in center and Paul O'Neill in right, two of the outfield positions were set but left field was another matter, and Torre had to find an answer among Tim Raines, Gerald Williams, Ruben Sierra, and Ruben Rivera. At catcher, Joe Girardi was brought in to replace departed Mike Stanley, and while Girardi was strong defensively, his bat was much lighter than Stanley's.

As for the pitching staff, there were all kinds of questions. Fifteen-game winner Jack McDowell bolted for Cleveland, 11-game winner Hitchcock went to Seattle in the Martinez deal, Melido Perez was out for the year with an injury, Scott Kamieniecki and Bob Wickman were throwing cream puffs, David Cone and Jimmy Key were suffering from control problems, and rookie Mariano Rivera was throwing hard but too straight, and Torre feared major league hitters would catch up to him quickly. Torre was hoping left-handed free agent pickup Kenny Rogers could fill the Hitchcock void, and he banked on second-year man Andy Pettitte improving his 12-9 rookie record. As for Key and Cone, they were wily veterans and Torre was confident they'd come around. One area Torre wasn't concerned about was the bullpen where John Wetteland was a top-notch closer, Nelson could be a right-handed setup man, and Mariano Rivera and Ramiro Mendoza had great potential.

"It was to the point where I was saying, 'Oh my God, they dismantled the whole team and we'll be lucky to finish fifth,'" Boggs said after the season, recalling the early trepidation. "Then boom, everything started to fall into place."

Not right away.

The Yankees started slowly while Baltimore—the preseason division favorite—ran out to an 11-2 record. Torre did not panic, and his troops saw this. Right away they gained respect for their leader because he was calm, understanding, and patient. While there were new players in the lineup, most were veterans and they understood that it was going to take a little time for the team to jell.

Just when that started to occur the team was dealt what was thought to be a serious setback when it was discovered Cone had a career-threatening aneurysm in his right shoulder. He underwent surgery in early May and the assumption was his season was over. This would have been a devastating blow if not for the surprising emergence of Dwight Gooden. Gooden hadn't won a major league game since the middle of 1994 as he'd finished that strike-shortened season on the suspended list due to his continuing battle with substance abuse, and then he'd sat out all of 1995. It looked as if his career—once on track for the Hall of Fame—was over, but Steinbrenner threw him a lifeline and Gooden grabbed hold.

Cone's disabling opened a spot in the rotation, and with Gooden just starting to round into form, the timing was perfect. Torre gave him an opportunity to take Cone's place and on May 14 he provided one of the highlights of the season when he no-hit the Seattle Mariners at the stadium. Gooden pitched effectively into late August, winning 11 games before his aging arm wore out. And then just as Gooden started to descend, Cone shocked everyone by returning to the team in early September and he remained a key component through the World Series run.

This was a season-long trend. Whenever someone got hurt, someone else was able to step in. Whenever Torre needed something in a key moment, someone did it. The proof is in the roster usage. He utilized 25 position players and 24 pitchers during the regular season.

The Yankees hit their stride in June and moved into first place, but while Torre was pleased with the team, he wasn't in much of a mood to enjoy it. Between games of a June doubleheader in Cleveland he learned that his brother Rocco died of a heart attack. And word from Florida was that his oldest brother, Frank, was failing physically and the doctors couldn't pinpoint the problem.

This is when I earned my stripes as Joe's confidant. Joe and I had always shared a special relationship and we could talk to each other about anything. He had put up a brave front for his players when Rocco died, but privately, he wept on my shoulder. Once we buried Rocco, he put me in charge of trying to convince Frank to come up to New York where he could receive better medical care. That proved to be a tough assignment because Frank stubbornly refused, so I asked Joe's wife, Alice, for help, and she obliged. Frank was constantly on Joe's mind, but with Alice and me dealing with the problem, he could at least focus his energies on the ball club.

Right after the All-Star Game the Yankees went into Baltimore and swept four from the Birds, and by late July their lead ballooned to 12 games. When Cecil Fielder was acquired in a trade from Detroit for malcontent Ruben Sierra, Torre had a right-handed slugger to balance his lineup, and it looked as if the division race was a foregone conclusion.

No such luck, because August was a gruesome month, on the field and off. New York's lead shrank to four games, and worse than the Yankees' performance was the sight of Frank Torre after Alice and I finally convinced him to come up to New York. I went with Joe to gather Frank at the airport, and he looked like death warmed over. It shocked Joe to see his brother in such poor condition. We checked Frank into Columbia-Presbyterian Hospital and doctors told Joe if Frank didn't receive a heart transplant, he was going to die. All we could do was wait for a matching heart.

Just before the waiver deadline Watson picked up infielders Luis Sojo and Charlie Hayes, and then Cone made his valiant return and pitched seven no-hit innings in Oakland before Torre removed him. Rivera finished the one-hitter and the Yankees were primed for the stretch run. The season came down to a key series against Baltimore at the stadium in mid-September, and by taking two of three from the Orioles, their lead was four games with 10 to play, and Torre knew it was over.

At long last October had arrived for Torre. "We set out in the spring on a mission, and this is just a part of it," said Torre. "It was a team project right from the get-go. At this stage of my career to have this kind of ball club, this could be the start of the greatest experience of my career."

– *1996 World Series* –

The details of the 28-year-old man's death were never made public. All we knew is that before he died from a brain disease, the anonymous Bronx resident had signed an organ donor card, and in the early morning hours of October 25, 1996 when his heart was harvested, it was found to be a suitable match for the body of Frank Torre.

For more than two months Joe Torre's older brother had been lying in a bed at Manhattan's Columbia-Presbyterian Hospital waiting for a miracle. His own heart was failing, and if he didn't receive a new one very soon, he was going to die. Here came that miracle.

Hours earlier, Frank had watched a miracle of another type unfold on television. His brother's Yankees—who just a few days ago had flown to Atlanta trailing two games to none, looking hopelessly overmatched by the powerful Braves in the World Series—won their third straight game at Atlanta-Fulton County Stadium and now were on their way back to New York with a chance to win the championship.

Frank went to sleep with a smile on his face following the Yankees' pulsating 1-0 victory in Game Five, and he was looking forward to speaking to his brother in the morning. The conversation would have to wait. As the Yankees' plane—which I was on—was touching down at LaGuardia Airport, doctors woke Frank and informed him that a heart had been located, and that he would be the recipient.

Joe had been in bed at his New Rochelle home barely a half-hour when the phone rang with news that Frank was being prepped for the transplant. Given the complexity of the surgery and the fact that Frank was 64 years old, Joe was terrified at first, but then he realized this is what Frank and the Torre family had been waiting for. This was Frank's only chance.

Joe never did get back to sleep that morning. He and his wife Alice and Joe's sisters, Rae and Sister Marguerite, waited anxiously, praying that Frank would pull through. For those six hours, the World Series didn't seem all that important.

Just before noon a doctor friend of Joe's called. The operation was successful, and the surgeon who performed the procedure, Dr. Mehmet Oz—I'm not kidding, a doctor named Oz gave Frank his new heart—said all indications were that Frank's body was accepting the new organ.

After Joe phoned me to deliver the news, I sat down and thought to myself, "Who the hell is writing this script?"

*   *   *

The second postseason of Joe Torre's career began as ominously as the first. The only other time he'd participated in the play-offs, as manager of the Braves in 1982, Torre's team was trounced, 7-1, in the opener of what was then the best-of-five National League Championship Series. The Braves went on to lose the next two games for a clean sweep.

The Texas Rangers won the American League West and were making the first postseason appearance in the franchise's 25-year history. Since baseball had broken into divisions in 1969, the Rangers had been the only team to never play a postseason game, but their debut was a sparkler as John Burkett pitched a complete game, scattering 10 hits to beat David Cone, 6-2.

Torre admitted to me he was worried about the Rangers even before the series started. He knew they were a powerful team, and if the Yankee pitchers were not sharp—which Cone wasn't in the opener—Texas would take advantage. What Torre feared most, though, is that losing in the first round would ruin all that the team accomplished during the season. "If we lose this series, very few people will remember the 1996 Yankees," he said.

Texas hasn't beaten New York in a postseason game since. Torre's first play-off victory came the next night, a 5-4 thriller in 12 innings during which the Yankees rallied from a 4-1 deficit to win when Derek Jeter singled and later scored on a Charlie Hayes bunt that was misplayed by Texas third baseman Dean Palmer.

Game Three was another nail-biter as New York trailed 2-1 entering the ninth inning at The Ballpark in Arlington before Jeter and Tim Raines singled and eventually scored on Bernie Williams's sacrifice fly and Mariano Duncan's decisive two-out RBI single. And then with Williams hitting a solo home run from each side of the plate and Cecil Fielder contributing a pair of RBI singles, the Yankees eliminated Texas with a 6-4 victory punctuated by Torre's joyfully tearful press conference.

Baltimore became New York's surprising opponent in the American League Championship Series when it disposed of a Cleveland team that had won 99 games during the regular season. New York trailed the opener at the stadium until the eighth inning when one of the key moments of the season occurred. With one out Jeter hit a fly to right field that drove Tony Tarasco back to the wall. Just as the ball was about to either hit the wall or settle into Tarasco's glove, a 12-year-old boy named Jeffrey Maier reached out with his own glove and snatched it. Umpire Rich Garcia did not see the obvious fan interference, and he awarded Jeter a home run that tied the game. The Orioles went beserk, and I think everyone in the stadium was surprised that Garcia's call was not overturned by any of the other umpires. "It was like a magic trick because the ball just disappeared in midair," said Tarasco.

If justice had prevailed, Baltimore would have won the game when it put runners aboard in the ninth, 10th, and 11th innings, but John Wetteland and Mariano Rivera escaped each time, setting up the dramatic conclusion. Leading off the bottom of the 11th, Williams crashed a long solo home run to left off Randy Myers for a 5-4 victory. Jeffrey Maier became a hero, though the media deluge was rather ridiculous, which prompted Torre to say, "Anybody see the replay of Bernie's home run? That wasn't bad, either."

Rafael Palmeiro's two-run homer and a strong outing from David Wells led Baltimore to a 5-3 victory in Game Two, but when the Series shifted to Camden Yards, the Yankees returned to their rallying ways as Cecil Fielder's two-run homer during a four-run eighth helped deliver a 5-2 Game Three victory. Jeter pondered New York's fifth come-from-behind win in the past week and a half and he said, "It would be nice to just have one blowout, one easy game."

It wasn't exactly easy, but for the first time in eight games, the Yankees never trailed in winning Game Four, 8-4, and the next day when New York closed it out with a 6-4 victory on a lovely Sunday afternoon, Torre broke down emotionally again. At long last, he was going to the World Series.

"I hope Joe got the game ball," said Wetteland. "Knowing what he's been through, this is a special moment in his life. He gave me a hug and there were tears in his eyes. The man doesn't have to say a lot."

I stood in the back of the room during Joe's postgame press conference, and I smiled when he said, "When I got fired in St. Louis I figured I'd go back to broadcasting, but my wife said I couldn't give up on my dream. I thought the window for reaching the World Series was gone. It has been tough watching the Series through the years. Mostly, I turned it off. It's like watching someone else eat a hot fudge sundae. And that's not fun."

Darryl Strawberry knew what was fun.

"A World Series in New York? It's one of the best experiences you can go through," he said, speaking from the experience of having done so as a Met in 1986.

Having gone through a lifetime of Yankee Octobers, I couldn't agree with him more.

*   *   *

Atlanta was the defending World Series champion. After losing to Minnesota in 1991 and Toronto in 1992, the Braves had broken through in 1995 by defeating Cleveland in six games, and based on what happened in the last three games of the National League Championship Series, they had to be considered the favorites against the Yankees.

The Braves trailed St. Louis three games to one in the NLCS before winning three straight by a cumulative score of 32-1. It was a frightening display of skillful baseball as the storied Atlanta pitching staff held the Cardinals to 17 hits and all three of its aces—John Smoltz, Greg Maddux, and Tom Glavine—earned victories. Everyone knew the Braves could pitch, but, to borrow a phrase from my pal Phil Rizzuto, holy cow! If the Braves could keep hitting like that, the Yankees had no chance.

Torre had waited his whole life to get to the World Series, so one more day wasn't going to make a difference. Torrential rains washed out the first game and pushed the start back to Sunday night. By the time the opener was complete, he probably wished it hadn't stopped raining. The Braves picked up where they left off against St. Louis and pummeled Andy Pettitte and four other Yankee pitchers during a 12-1 rout.

Torre had been antsy before the game, and I had picked up on that as we chatted in front of the dugout during batting practice. He knew the Braves were on a roll, and he was concerned that his team hadn't played in a week. I told him to enjoy himself, and he did, right up until the first pitch was thrown and a magnificent light show of flashbulbs flickered throughout the stadium. Torre told me afterward that he was the happiest man in the world at that moment. The feeling dissipated quickly.

In the top of the second Atlanta's Javy Lopez singled up the middle, and 19-year-old center fielder Andruw Jones—who had played all of 31 major league games before the postseason—hit a monstrous home run into Monument Park beyond the distant left-field wall.

Then in the third inning the Braves scored six times for an insurmountable 8-0 lead as Jones hit another homer and the stadium—rocking with excitement less than an hour earlier—was eerily quiet. The game was over, and everyone knew it. "We were just overwhelmed tonight," Torre said. "They were tremendous."

As the team prepared to take the field for infield practice before Game Two, George Steinbrenner came blowing into Torre's office and proclaimed that this was a "must-win game." I was thinking to myself "Gee, George, no kidding. Did you really have to come in here and remind him?" But Torre's approach was totally opposite. He said, "George, you should be prepared for us to lose again tonight. But then we're going to Atlanta. Atlanta's my town. We'll take three games there and come back and win it here Saturday." Steinbrenner was flabbergasted. He didn't know how to respond to that. After George walked out I looked at Torre and said, "You're a beauty."

It's doubtful Steinbrenner took Torre's advice. He thinks his team is going to win every game, all year long. But Torre called it. Maddux pitched eight fabulous innings of six-hit shutout ball and the Braves eased their way to a 4-0 victory and a commanding two-game lead. Unlike the first game, the Yankees died a slow death in this one as Atlanta put up single tallies in the first, third, fifth, and sixth innings with Fred McGriff driving in the first three runs.

"They're getting frustrated," Torre said of his players. "You don't see pitching like that every day. Unfortunately we've seen it both days. You see guys like that occasionally in the American League like Roger Clemens and Kevin Appier. The problem is they're not all on the same team."

On the flight down to Atlanta I stayed away from Torre. He was in conference with his coaching staff at the front of the plane, so I tried to get some sleep. These late nights were starting to catch up to my 80-year-old body, but I wouldn't have missed this opportunity. Traveling with the team, attending World Series games, and being closer to the action now than I had been as a writer was a thrill for me. I almost felt like by allowing me to do this, Torre was giving me a mulligan. He was providing me the chance to relive my past, and nothing I could do for him could properly return the favor. He kept telling me I was, that my being around was a calming presence for him and he loved the outlet that I gave him, but someday when he's 80 years old, he'll know how much this meant to me.

Because of the rainout, there was no off day for travel between the second and third games, so after arriving in Atlanta at about four in the morning, both teams were right back at it later that day.

Prior to Game Three, Torre made three moves that tested his mettle, but as everything else in this magical season, they were moves that worked. With Atlanta throwing the left-handed Glavine, Torre sat down struggling Paul O'Neill, Tino Martinez, and Wade Boggs and replaced them with Darryl Strawberry in right, Fielder at first, and Hayes at third. Benching O'Neill was a particularly vexing decision for Torre, but he had been hobbled by a pulled leg muscle and just wasn't swinging the bat well. Martinez would have played first if the game were at Yankee Stadium, but without the use of the designated hitter in the National League park, Torre had to choose between Martinez and Fielder and he went with Fielder. Hayes for Boggs was a simple righty vs. lefty percentage play.

The less obvious move was one he had made before the Series even started, but was now going to pay dividends. In setting up his rotation, he went with Pettitte and Key in the first two games, mainly because both were left-handers, always the best stratagem at Yankee Stadium. But also, just in case the Yankees lost the first two games, Torre wanted the gritty Cone for the desperate third game. Torre knew Cone had spent the off-season fretting over his failure to put away the deciding game in the 1995 divisional series against Seattle. The Yankees took a 4-2 lead into the eighth inning, but Cone gave up two runs, the tying marker coming when he threw a 3-2 forkball in the dirt with the bases loaded. The Yankees went on to lose in 11 innings, but Cone blamed himself for not protecting the lead. Now Cone would get a golden opportunity to make amends.

The Yankees were a different team on this night, and following their clutch 5-2 victory, they were a confident team.

Williams's RBI single in the first gave New York its first lead of the Series and it was the first time Atlanta had trailed since the end of Game Four of the NLCS. Cone took the mound with that slim advantage and made it hold up. He was dynamite for six innings and he left with a 2-1 lead, having allowed just four hits, and his triumph was secured when Williams's two-run homer—his sixth of this postseason, tying a major league record—keyed a three-run eighth against reliever Greg McMichael.

"It's as important a game as I've ever pitched," Cone said. "This wasn't do-or-die, but without a doubt it was important. I think we were a little embarrassed in New York. We had nothing to lose so we came down to Atlanta and let it all hang out."

It was Torre's first World Series win, and though he still trailed two games to one, Torre sensed the momentum had been switched and there was going to be no stopping his team.

Game Four will live in infamy as one of the greatest in World Series history. I had seen in person every World Series game the Yankees had participated in since 1927, a Gehrig-like streak of about 175 straight games, and to my recollection only a handful could match the bloodcurdling drama of this one. It was four hours and 17 minutes of edge-of-your-seat tension, and when it was over, the Yankees had claimed an 8-6 victory in 10 innings. The Series was tied at two games apiece, and now there was no doubt in Torre's mind that his team was going to win the championship.

Torre said it was his finest performance as a manager. Every move he made worked, including leaving O'Neill, Martinez, and Boggs on the bench at the start again. He used every player on the 25-man roster except Pettitte, Cone, and Key, and they all made a valuable contribution. It was a victory that defined who the Yankees were in 1996: a team with talent, a team with depth, and a team with heart.

The night started disastrously. This was the game that was affected by the Saturday rainout. Torre had wanted to use a three-man rotation, but when Pettitte didn't pitch until Sunday and the off-day was lost, Torre had no choice but to use shaky Kenny Rogers in this Wednesday night fourth game. Rogers had been an average pitcher during the regular season and a lousy pitcher in his two postseason starts, knocked out twice inside of three innings. Nothing changed here. He was strafed for five hits and five runs in the first three innings before Torre sent him to the showers.

The Braves made it 6-0 in the fifth and history told us only two teams had ever rallied to win a World Series game when trailing by six runs or more, the 1929 Athletics against the Cubs (eight), and the 1956 Dodgers against the Yankees (six). History was about to be altered.

Atlanta's Denny Neagle was cruising into the sixth inning having allowed just two hits. But then Jeter singled, Williams walked, and both scored when Fielder's single to right caromed past Jermaine Dye and went to the wall. Fielder ended up at second and the big guy chugged in to score on Hayes's single. The Yankees were halfway back, and Neagle was out of the game.

Things were quiet until the top of the eighth, and then the excitement never ceased. With feared Atlanta closer Mark Wohlers on the mound, Jim Leyritz whacked an unbelievable game-tying three-run homer just over the left-field wall. Up in the visiting owners' private box, my aging legs catapulted me out of my seat and I exchanged an exuberant high-five with general manager Bob Watson. "Easily the biggest hit of my career," said Leyritz, who the year before had won Game Two of the series against Seattle with a dramatic 15th-inning solo homer at Yankee Stadium. "My wife is happy because I played that one so many times during the off-season, now I've got another one to play."

Mariano Rivera made it through the eighth without incident, and then the Yankees attacked Wohlers in the ninth. With two outs Fielder, Hayes, and Strawberry—those three guys playing for Martinez, Boggs, and O'Neill—all singled, but Duncan lined out to right field to end the inning as the sellout crowd breathed a huge sigh of relief. Rivera found trouble in the bottom of the ninth, so Torre brought in Graeme Lloyd to face McGriff and the result was an inning-ending double play started by Jeter.

On to the 10th and Wohlers was gone, replaced by Steve Avery who got two quick outs before Raines walked on four pitches, Jeter singled through shortstop, and Williams was intentionally walked to load the bases. Boggs was the only position player Torre had left, and this was a perfect spot for him. He pinch-hit for Andy Fox, and the eagle-eyed veteran drew what he called, "Probably the biggest walk I've ever had in my 15-year career."

Now trailing 7-6, Braves manager Bobby Cox ordered a double switch. He brought Brad Clontz in to pitch and slotted him into the fourth spot in the batting order, McGriff's spot, which was already passed. Then he brought in Klesko to play first base so Klesko would lead off the bottom of the 10th. This move backfired, too, when Hayes hit a little pop to first that Klesko lost in the lights. The ball fell to the ground, everyone was safe and Jeter scored an insurance run to make it 8-6.

Lloyd struck out Klesko to open the 10th, then Wetteland came in and after giving up a single to Andruw Jones, he got Dye and Terry Pendleton on a pair of fly balls to left, both of which Raines caught at the warning track to end the game.

I've never seen a team that was still two wins away from winning the World Series in a happier state. The reigning mood was elation, the only thing missing was champagne. What a victory.

"We're shocking the world," Jeff Nelson said.

They weren't shocking Torre. He knew this team had it in them, and they were proving him right.

"We've been going over the destiny kind of thing, and so far, it's getting kind of eerie," said Boggs. "The twilight zone is starting to evolve."

There was a different kind of tension in Game Five. Where Game Four had been wild and crazy, Game Five was a classic pitchers' duel between Smoltz and Pettitte, the two men who had started in Game One.

Although Smoltz was a righty, Torre couldn't take Fielder and Hayes out of the lineup so Martinez and Boggs sat again, but he did come back with O'Neill in place of Strawberry. Fielder wound up with three of New York's four hits including a RBI double in the fourth that drove in the only run in the Yankees' 1-0 victory, and O'Neill saved the game with a running catch in the bottom of the ninth.

Smoltz was marvelous, but Pettitte was even better. The kid pitched into the ninth without allowing a run and he was touched for just five hits and three walks, and then Wetteland earned the save when he stranded the tying run on third base.

"We've just got a lot of special things going on," Pettitte said. "I think we're destined to win this thing now. A lot of little things have happened, a lot of little breaks have gone our way and we've taken advantage."

For instance, the fourth inning when Hayes hit a fly ball into right-center that Marquis Grissom dropped for a two-base error, putting Hayes into position to score on Fielder's double.

Then there was the bottom of the ninth. Chipper Jones led off with a double and after Pettitte got McGriff to ground out to second with Jones moving to third, Wetteland entered. With the infield in, Wetteland induced Lopez to hit a sharp grounder right to Hayes at third and Jones was unable to score. Torre ordered Wetteland to intentionally walk the dangerous Klesko which would also set up a force at second, even though Klesko represented the winning run. Cox called on Luis Polonia, and after fouling off six straight fastballs, he slashed a drive into right field that at first looked like a routine out. Instead the ball kept carrying and O'Neill had to make a super lunging catch at the warning track to end the game. Strawberry most likely wouldn't have made the play.

The team didn't need the airplane to fly back to New York.

Torre arrived at the stadium on Saturday morning eight hours before Game Six was scheduled to start. He had visited Frank the night before and was thrilled that his brother was OK. Frank even asked Joe to procure tickets to the game for some of the hospital personnel. Joe called me after lunch and said, "If you're not busy, I'm at the stadium, come on down and keep me company." So I did.

As we sat in his office talking, mostly about Frank, he admitted to me that he was nervous about the game. Confident, but nervous. I guess the reality hit him that by the end of the night his team could be the world champion. The Braves were throwing Maddux who had been nearly unhittable in Game Two, so I asked Torre what he was going to do with the lineup. He said he was giving the start at third base to Boggs, Fielder would DH so Martinez would play first, O'Neill would be in right, and Strawberry was going to play left field in place of Raines.

"Sounds like a winner," I said, trying to pump Torre up.

Just then bench coach Don Zimmer came in, sat down and said, "You know, when we won our division title with the Cubs (in 1989 when Zimmer was manager), we took a victory lap around the field. You might want to think about it." That drew a relaxing smile and chuckle from Torre. He was ready.

Maddux was perfect for two innings before cracking ever so slightly in the third, and that was all the Yankees needed. O'Neill lined a double into the right-field corner and one out later Girardi swatted a letter-high fastball over Grissom's head in center field for a RBI triple. I thought the stadium was going to collapse from the noise. Jeter followed with a RBI single through the left side, and after he stole second and Boggs flied out, Williams came through with a RBI single to give the Yankees a 3-0 lead.

Atlanta got one back in the fourth as Jimmy Key walked Dye with the bases loaded to force in a run, and Torre was set to remove Key if he couldn't get the next batter, Pendleton, out. Pendleton grounded into an inning-ending double play.

Key did not survive the sixth inning, but the Yankees did as David Weathers and Lloyd worked out of a first-and-third, one-out jam to preserve the 3-1 lead. Rivera pitched two innings of no-hit relief, and then Wetteland trotted in from the bullpen in the ninth with a chance to win the World Series. He whiffed Andruw Jones, but Klesko beat out an infield single up the middle and Pendleton lashed a 1-2 pitch into right for a single, sending Klesko to third.

Polonia had battled Wetteland to death in Game Five, but this time Wetteland blew him away for the second out. Now the stadium rose to its collective feet and the noise was deafening, but Grissom induced silence with a first-pitch single to right that scored Klesko, cutting the lead to 3-2.

The tension was unbearable. Lemke was up, and as I stood in Steinbrenner's private box, I was chilled by the thought that Lemke was the Braves' last hope. He was a pesky hitter, just the kind of guy you didn't expect much from, but then he'd punch a single somewhere and kill you. All he needed was a single in this spot, and as he worked the count full I don't recall my heart beating. When he lifted a foul pop behind third base, I thought it was destined for the lower stands, but Hayes—who had replaced Boggs in the seventh inning—drifted over near the railing and when the ball barely stayed in play Hayes caught it for the final out.

Joe Torre was a world champion. The Yankees, for the first time since 1978, were world champions. And my heart started beating again.

"This has been a dreamland for me," Torre said. "The last 48 hours have just been incredible."

The Yankees took their victory lap, and the fans loved it. The most enduring scene was Boggs, riding shotgun on a police horse, waving to the crowd. He'd been one out away from winning the 1986 World Series as a member of the Boston Red Sox. Then Bill Buckner booted Mookie Wilson's ground ball, and the Red Sox curse lived on. Like Torre, Boggs had waited his whole life for this.

"It's like a Frank Merriwell story that us old guys used to read," Steinbrenner told me as we stood in the clubhouse watching player after player take a champagne shower. "What a story."

There wasn't a whole lot Joe Torre could do about the Baltimore Orioles in 1997. Torre's defending world champions made a four-game improvement in the standings over 1996, but the Orioles were better, plain and simple. Baltimore became just the third team in major league history (the 1927 Yankees and the 1984 Detroit Tigers were the others) to reside in first place wire-to-wire. Yet at 96-66, the Yankees were only two games off the pace when the schedule ran out.

It had been a good year, and the Yankees qualified for the play-offs, earning the wild-card berth without the slightest bit of a struggle. Where Torre went wrong was losing in the divisional round to the Cleveland Indians. To George Steinbrenner, that was unacceptable.

Never mind that Cleveland proved to be a very competent club when it went on to beat Baltimore in the American League Championship Series. Steinbrenner's appetite had been whetted by the World Series success of 1996 and anything less wasn't good enough.

So when spring training commenced in 1998, there were whispers that Torre's job was on the line. He'd won 188 regular-season games in his first two years, made the play-offs twice, and won a World Series. He had nothing to apologize for, and job security should not have been an issue. But there he was, acknowledging those who said he was under the gun to win it all.

"At least when you get fired here, you had a chance to win," he said. "When I got fired in St. Louis, I was told I needed to do more of this and that. Of course, it came down to the fact that we didn't have the team. Here you're going to get a better than honest chance because George isn't playing for second place."

Steinbrenner denied that Torre was on a short leash when he said, "I hope Joe doesn't feel pressure because nothing has changed. My relationship with Joe might be the best I've ever had with a manager. Joe will do his best and I'll go to the bank with him. If his best isn't enough I'll understand because a lot of things happen in a season. We're in the toughest division in baseball. We're just another team right now."

But he also added, "We've given Joe the horses," which was another way of saying, "Joe, I'm paying out about $75 million to these players this year. Now go win."

I wasn't with the team as much in 1997 as I had been in 1996. I went to spring training—I always went to spring training, especially now that Steinbrenner was paying—but that was the only road trip I made that year.

I had a few health problems, mostly a cranky hip that I eventually had to have replaced which knocked me out of commission for about three months. I had been a little too active in my first year as Torre's confidant, and even before I received my new hip I had decided to slow down. Joe agreed and he laughingly said, "I guess I'm a big boy, I don't need you to hold my hand every day."

In 1997 Steinbrenner signed free agent left-handed pitcher David Wells away from Baltimore, almost a tit-for-tat move as Jimmy Key had signed with the Orioles a week earlier. A much more ballyhooed signing during the year was that of Japanese star pitcher Hideki Irabu, but his contributions didn't come close to matching those of Wells. Mariano Rivera transferred into the closer's role with the free agent departure of John Wetteland and he became a star, and tough left-hander Mike Stanton was brought in to bolster the bullpen.

Those moves weren't enough to retain the championship, so after the elimination by the Indians, Steinbrenner's baseball people—now headed by young Brian Cashman, who took over the general manager position when Bob Watson resigned due to health concerns—formulated another wish list. Making like a genie in a bottle, Steinbrenner opened up his wallet and granted three of the wishes. He acquired second baseman Chuck Knoblauch from Minnesota in a trade for prospects and cash. Third baseman Scott Brosius came from Oakland in a deal that also rid the Yankees of inconsistent pitcher Kenny Rogers. And Steinbrenner outbid about 20 other teams for the services of right-handed pitcher Orlando Hernandez, a defector from Cuba seeking asylum in the United States so that he could display his vast talents in the major leagues.

With Knoblauch and Brosius joining shortstop Derek Jeter and first baseman Tino Martinez, the infield was set. So was two-thirds of the outfield with Bernie Williams in center and Paul O'Neill in right, and while left field would be a question mark, many teams were doing worse at this position than the combination of Chad Curtis, Daryl Strawberry, Tim Raines, and Ricky Ledee. Young Jorge Posada was rounding into a fine catcher and a productive hitter, and Joe Girardi was there to back him up as one of the best defensive receivers in the game. And with Cecil Fielder gone, Chili Davis was acquired to serve as the designated hitter, a role that Strawberry and Raines could also fill. Top to bottom, it was an outstanding lineup offensively and defensively.

As for the pitching staff, with Wells, Andy Pettitte, and David Cone soon to be joined by Hernandez in June, the starting rotation was excellent. Rivera was the best closer in the game, Stanton and Jeff Nelson were first-rate setup men, and Irabu and Ramiro Mendoza provided long relief and spot starts.

As Steinbrenner said, Joe had the horses. On paper, this team was awesome, and greatness was predicted. Now it was a matter of just how great.

– Chapter 24 –

1998

ON THE MORNING OF MAY 18, 1998, I participated in a charity golf tournament at Rolling Hills Country Club in Wilton, Connecticut hosted by Yankees pitching coach Mel Stottlemyre. Because of my new hip I didn't exactly play, but I stroked a few putts and chip shots and mostly just rode around in a golf cart enjoying the lovely spring day with Stottlemyre, Joe Torre, and Don Zimmer.

When we reached the ninth green, one of the tournament volunteers said, "Would you believe Wells chipped in for an eagle here a few minutes ago?"

Yes, I could believe it. David Wells was on a roll. The day before, he had thrown a perfect game against the Minnesota Twins at Yankee Stadium. At that moment I was tempted to go buy a New York Lotto ticket and have Wells choose my numbers.

Wells was a Yankee for only two seasons, but he was one of my favorite players. We hit it off right away after Torre told him that Babe Ruth had been a personal friend of mine. Wells worshiped Ruth. He was fascinated by the Babe's persona, and in many ways, they were kindred spirits.

When he asked me about Ruth, I proceeded to tell him my history with the Bambino. I happily recounted how Babe lobbied for me to become an assistant batboy; how I used to help him cheat at cards; how he visited me in the hospital after I broke my leg; how he became a family friend and that my father had served as a pallbearer at his funeral. Wells was enraptured by my tales. He couldn't get enough and he peppered me with question after question.

He then told me that when he was a kid he had written a couple of papers on how Ruth had helped save baseball after the Black Sox scandal of 1919. He laughed when he recalled playfully asking for Ruth's retired No. 3 uniform after he signed with the Yankees. Knowing he couldn't have it, he chose No. 33. Wells also told me he had purchased for $30,000 a Ruth cap that Babe had worn during the 1934 season and that he was planning to wear it in a game. The day he was going to do it, I happened to be in the clubhouse and he came over to show it to me. He said he was almost 100% sure it was the real thing, but he asked me if there was any way I could officially authenticate it. I gave it a thorough going over and surmised that it was the real thing. It also occurred to me that I had handled the hat on many occasions because Ruth would sometimes toss his caps to me after games so I could clean them up if need be. Wells was thrilled. He wore the cap for one inning before Torre ordered him to remove it because it didn't conform to the official uniform. I gave Torre hell for that one.

Wells reminded me of Ruth. Ruth had endured a hard-bitten youth, born into poverty in Baltimore and then placed into a home for poor or orphaned children at age seven. Wells's childhood wasn't nearly as bleak, but it was a bit unconventional. He grew up without his father, whom he did not meet until he was 22 years old. His mother Eugenia raised him, and during part of his adolescence the father figure in his life was a Hells Angels chapter president named Crazy Charlie. Wells told me Hells Angels bikers used to show up at his Little League games and they would pay him money for wins and strikeouts.

As they grew up, Ruth and Wells turned to baseball and the game ultimately brought them uncommon riches. Their commonality is quite obvious in terms of physical stature—though Wells is a little softer around the middle than Ruth had been during his prime playing years— and their nonconformity. Ruth wouldn't have approved of Wells's taste in head-banging heavy metal music, but he would have appreciated Wells's maverick personality, his willingness to throw down drinks, throw punches, or throw caution to the wind. I told Wells that Ruth would have loved him had he known him, and it made my day to see the smile that flashed across his face. I could see Wells was deeply touched by that thought.

I was sitting up in George Steinbrenner's private box with a few Yankee executives the day Wells threw his perfect game. It was a Sunday afternoon and nearly 50,000 fans were present thanks in part to a Beanie Baby promotion. The sun was shining, and though the season was barely six weeks old the Yankees were playing at a remarkable .700 clip and were already starting to run away with the division race. In other words, it was a great day. Then it became historic.

Stottlemyre had a feeling Wells was on after watching him warm up. "Mel came out of the bullpen and I asked him how it went. All he said was 'Wow,'" Torre said afterward. "That doesn't normally mean a perfect game or even a win. But it did today. The Boomer was outstanding. That's something he can take with him wherever he goes."

Wells breezed through the first six innings and as he walked off the mound the crowd was fully aware of what was happening. The fans stood as one to cheer him as he lumbered to the dugout, his teammates superstitiously ignoring him when he arrived. "They were killing me, man," he recalled with a laugh.

With two outs in the seventh there was a nervous moment when Paul Molitor worked the count to 3-1, but Wells threw a called strike and then whiffed Molitor swinging. Now Wells was starting to get anxious, and that's when David Cone—who one year later would match Wells's perfect game—sidled up to him and muttered out of the side of his mouth, "I think it's about time you break out the knuckleball." Wells cracked up and later said, "I can't tell you how much that helped me."

With the Yankees comfortably ahead, 4-0, all eyes were focused on the perfect game. In the eighth Derek Jeter bobbled a grounder at short but recovered in time to make the play, and then Ron Coomer roped a shot to second that Chuck Knoblauch knocked down, picked up and threw to first, the toughest out of the game. Alex Ochoa popped out to end the inning.

In the ninth, there was a World Series-like atmosphere and the fans never sat down. It took seven pitches to retire Jon Shave on a fly to Paul O'Neill in right. Javier Valentin struck out on four pitches, and that brought Pat Meares to the plate. With his shirt sloppily unbuttoned at the top you could almost see Wells's heart beating in his burly chest. After Meares fouled off a first-pitch fastball he punched Wells's 120th delivery into right, a routine fly that O'Neill had no trouble with. The stadium erupted, the Yankees mobbed Wells, and Bernie Williams and Daryl Strawberry performed the difficult chore of hoisting the 240-pounder onto their shoulders for a ride into the Yankee dugout.

"This is a dream come true for me," Wells said after becoming only the 13th pitcher in modern baseball history to throw a perfect game.

Wells's perfecto was only the second in Yankee history. The first had come in the 1956 World Series, authored by Don Larsen whose off-the-field antics would have made him an ideal Three Musketeers companion for Ruth and Wells. It was Joe Trimble of the *Herald Tribune* who wrote of Larsen, "The imperfect man just pitched a perfect game." Now Wells, the least perfect of the current Yankees, had joined him in illustriousness.

After the game George Steinbrenner's assistant, Arthur Richman, called Larsen on the phone from the Yankee clubhouse and Larsen and Wells spoke for the first time. Come to find out, the two perfect game Yankees had graduated 35 years apart from the same high school, Point Loma in San Diego, California.

"Talking to Don Larsen, that was a great phone call," Wells said. "And that we went to the same high school, it's unbelievable. The Lord works in mysterious ways."

George Vecsey of the *New York Times* also talked to Larsen after the game and Larsen told him of Wells, "We've never met. I'm sure we will—probably at some bar."

*   *   *

Like me, Torre had witnessed Larsen's perfect game because he was a spectator in the stands that day using tickets that had been given to him by his brother, Frank. He found the games to be quite similar. "I saw Don Larsen's perfect game and I did about as much managing in that game as I did in this one," Torre said with a smile.

The day of Wells's perfect game wasn't exactly an aberration for Torre during the 1998 season. There were many days and nights when he sat in the dugout with Don Zimmer at his side barely managing as he watched his ball club tear up the competition. I never thought I'd live to see the day when I would say there was a better baseball team than the 1927 Yankees. It was more than 70 years in the making, but that day arrived in late October 1998. I had been tempted to cast my vote in favor of the Mickey Mantle and Roger Maris 1961 Yankees, but didn't. I could not, however, deny the 1998 Yankees their proper due. With sincere apologies to my friend, Babe Ruth, the 1927 Yankees have been, at least in this crusty old man's opinion, surpassed as the greatest baseball ensemble in history.

"I don't think we can stack up with Hall of Famers," said David Cone. "And it's tough to compare with the ghosts of the past. But as a team, as a whole, it's an incredible unit."

The 1998 Yankees won 114 regular-season games, a team record and American League mark until Seattle won 116 in 2001. But by adding 11 more wins in the play-offs on the way to the World Series title, their total of 125 victories became the new one-season standard.

Because they played a 154-game schedule, the 1927 Yankees and their 110 wins computed to a .714 winning percentage, while the 1998 Yankees won at a .704 clip over 162 games. However, both teams finished 66 games over .500. And as for the theory that the 1998 Yankees played against watered down competition, consider this nugget: The 1927 team had the pleasure of playing the woeful St. Louis Browns and Boston Red Sox a combined 44 times, and they won 39 of those games. The 1998 Yankees played the two worst teams in the league, Tampa Bay and Detroit, only a combined 23 times. They won 20.

What impressed me most about the 1998 Yankees was the way they won games. The 1927 team simply clubbed its way into history with Ruth and Lou Gehrig hitting more home runs combined than all but one of the other 15 major league teams.

The 1998 Yankees had power as their 207 homers were the second-most in team history behind the 240 hit by the 1961 squad. But in a year when St. Louis' Mark McGwire shattered Maris's home run record by swatting 70, and Sammy Sosa of the Cubs also soared past Maris with 66, the Yankees did not have one player who topped 30. Instead, they tied a major league record by having 10 players hit at least 10.

Another pertinent fact is that the 1998 Yankees didn't have one positional player start in the 1998 All-Star Game. Yet when the midsummer classic was played, New York had a record of 61-20—the best ever at the midway point of a 162-game schedule—and an 11-game lead on Boston.

"You go back to the old Celtics," said Torre. "You thought about all those guys averaging 16, 18, 19 points a game, and they'd always win as a team. Nobody really cared if anybody scored 30 points. They worked together as a unit, and it was fun watching them. They only cared about the end result, which was winning. It's a great feeling for a manager to know when these guys come to the field, the only thing they're interested in is winning the game. They don't care who gets the winning hit. They all want to get the game-winning hit, but they don't want to talk about it. It's a very unusual club. The one thing I would love to have people think about this team is that there is no one name that comes to mind, but the team itself. It's a terrific ball club when it comes to self-motivation and determination."

Those two qualities were absent during the first week as the Yankees got off to a lousy start, losing four of their first five games on a

season-opening West Coast trip. Torre called a team meeting out in Seattle, Cone and O'Neill were among the speakers, and pretty soon the
Yankees were on a roll. They won their next eight games and 22 of 24.
When Wells pitched his masterpiece he improved New York's record to
28-9, and by the end of May the Yankees were 7 1/2 games in front. That
was as close as Boston would be the rest of the year.

It was about this time that Orlando Hernandez joined the team. It
was the only major personnel move the team made all season, and it was
a dandy.

*　　*　　*

Just seven months before Hernandez strolled to the mound at Yankee Stadium to pitch against the Tampa Bay Devil Rays, he was founder-
ing in the Atlantic Ocean on a 20-foot fishing boat trying to defect from
his homeland.

Hernandez had been a star pitcher on the Cuban national team, but
when his younger half-brother, Livan, defected to the United States in
1995, Orlando suffered the consequences. Fearing that Orlando would
follow his sibling's lead and possibly bring other talented Cuban players
with him, Fidel Castro banned him for life from playing baseball in Cuba,
and Orlando began working as a $10-a-month rehabilitation therapist in
a psychiatric hospital. The ban took effect in October of 1996, and for
the next year the only ball he played was softball in Havana's Lenin Park.

Livan became the MVP of the 1997 World Series, pitching the
Florida Marlins to the championship. That's when Orlando knew he had
to get to America, and a defection plan was conceived and executed the
day after Christmas, 1997.

The details of his voyage have been inconsistent. Original reports
were that Hernandez and a group of seven others including his com-
mon-law wife, Noris Bosch, set sail on what barely passed as a raft. In
the 10 hours it took to reach the deserted Bahamian island of Anguilla
Cay, death was imminent as the boat took on water and nearly sank as it
was tossed about the shark-infested sea. In interviews with three of the
passengers, *Sports Illustrated* revealed that this account was a grand
exaggeration, and that the trip to Anguilla Cay was perfectly calm. No
waves, no leaks, no sharks.

Once they reached the island the story becomes a little clearer. A
boat from Miami captained by a friend of one of the defectors was supposed to meet the party and take them to freedom in Miami, but that

boat encountered rough weather and was rescued five miles from Anguilla Cay the next day.

Thus the group was marooned on the island for three days, subsisting on stale bread, a couple of cans of Spam, sugar, water, and sea conchs before a U.S. Coast Guard cutter picked them up. Ironically, the Coast Guard boat was on its way to Cuba to deliver three repatriated Cubans, so Hernandez's group went along for that ride, fearing they would be discovered by Cuban authorities.

They were not. They were transferred to another Coast Guard boat bound for Bimini, just off the eastern shore of Miami. Bad weather prevented docking in Bimini, so the boat sailed on to Freeport, and from there, the group was flown to an immigration detention center in Nassau. Hernandez, Bosch, and another defecting ballplayer were offered humanitarian U.S. visas, but only Bosch accepted. That's because Joe Cubas, the Miami-based sports agent who specializes in representing Cuban-born baseball players, arrived on the scene after receiving a tip that Hernandez was part of the defecting group.

Cubas, who had represented Livan Hernandez when he came to America, explained to Orlando that accepting a visa would force him to enter the Major League Baseball amateur draft and there would be no control over where he ended up. By accepting a visa from Costa Rica, Hernandez would be a free agent and could choose which team he wanted to pitch for. Hernandez liked that idea, so he and the others went to Costa Rica while Bosch flew to Miami.

Cubas established residency for all of them, but he had grander plans for Hernandez. Baseball scouts were informed that Hernandez would perform for them in Costa Rica, and about 20 teams including the Yankees came to watch him in February of 1998. When the Yankees won the bidding war with a four-year $6.6 million offer that included a $1 million bonus, Cubas and his new client skipped off to Tampa and spring training.

During the spring sessions the Yankees took it slowly with Hernandez. They had been sky-high on Hideki Irabu the year before, but they rushed him up to the big club and he flopped. They didn't want to make the same mistake with Hernandez, so they sent him to triple-A Columbus to start the season.

In early June David Cone had to miss a start, and the man now universally known as El Duque was the choice to make it. Hernandez had gone 6-0 for Columbus, there was nothing more he could learn there, and the scouts told Torre when the call up was made, "He's as ready as he's ever going to be."

The Yankees still considered sending him back for more seasoning, but after he baffled the Tampa Bay Devil Rays for seven innings to earn the victory, he was told to stay put. Given another start a week later against Montreal, he pitched a complete game four-hitter. El Duque was never going back to Columbus.

When Hernandez came up to the Yankees he spoke no English. To this day he doesn't speak the language very well so it is hard to communicate with him. We mostly wave and smile at each other when our paths cross. I remember talking about him with outfield coach Jose Cardenal, a Cuban who was allowed to come to America to play baseball in the early 1960s by Castro, but was not able to return to his country for 24 years. "I feel he is a brave man," Cardenal said of El Duque. "If I'm in his shoes, I don't think I can jump in a little boat to do something like this. But when you're desperate, you do anything."

And because he had gone through that experience, Cardenal felt Hernandez would be unaffected by the pressure of pitching in the big leagues. I asked him if he thought Hernandez was talented enough to succeed at this level, something Irabu hadn't been, and Cardenal predicted Hernandez would be a smash hit on Broadway. He said his fastball was lively, and because he threw breaking balls from such a vast array of arm angles, he would be tough to figure out. Cardenal was right.

*　　*　　*

With Hernandez bumping the erratic Irabu out of the rotation, the Yankees were untouchable over the second half of the season. All the Red Sox could do was battle for the wild-card berth as the Yankees coldly marched on. New York earned its 100th victory in its 138th game, the earliest point in major league history in terms of schedule and calendar date. The division was clinched on September 9, second earliest clinching of a title in team history, and when the season was over, the 22-game spread over Boston was the largest in Yankee annals.

The final couple months of the season had been mostly meaningless, and as great as this team was, there was a concern in some quarters that it might have trouble turning the switch back on come play-off time. Torre was not among the worriers.

"We're ready," he said. "The players have been looking forward to this for a long time. To win 114 games is above and beyond, but now everybody is 0-0 and we start over. We're definitely ready."

– *1998 World Series* –

On the day the Yankees made the trade that brought third baseman Scott Brosius from the Oakland Athletics, Joe Torre said, "If he can give us good defense and hit .250, I'll be satisfied."

On the night that Brosius was caressing the World Series MVP trophy which he had been awarded in the visiting clubhouse at San Diego's Qualcomm Stadium, general manager Brian Cashman, the man who engineered the trade, said, "We knew he had ability, but we couldn't have expected this."

No one could have.

When Brosius was acquired, I had to admit I raised an eyebrow. In fact I mockingly asked Torre, "Is that Brosius as in atrocious?" This was a guy who had batted .203 in 1997 for the Athletics, and in four full seasons with Oakland had only one really productive year to his credit. But I also knew that the Yankees didn't want Wade Boggs or Charlie Hayes to be their third baseman in 1998. Neither was going to be re-signed, so someone had to play the hot corner, and Brosius did do one thing undeniably well: he could pick it with the glove.

"No other team wanted to trade for him," Gene Michael, now a Yankee scout, said. "We saw that his defense never went into a slump."

So Cashman pulled the trigger, got rid of Kenny Rogers in the process, and Brosius became one of the key cogs in this Yankees machine.

"The game can humble you and turn around, and this has certainly been a great turnaround for me," Brosius said at the conclusion of the Series, during which he decimated the Padres by going 8-for-17 with two home runs and six RBI.

"This is the type of thing that as a kid you dream about. It's something I've done in my backyard a hundred times. But you never know if you're going to get the opportunity to really do it, and then to come out and do something to help the team win feels real good."

That backyard was in a little place in Oregon called Milwaukie. I asked him about his hometown one time and he said, "Yes, the people there know how to spell. I guess they just wanted to be different than Wisconsin."

Brosius was a three-sport star in high school, and baseball was his favorite game. Oregon was a basketball-crazy place because the NBA's Portland Trail Blazers were the only major professional sports franchise in the state. Oddly enough when it came to baseball, Oregonians were partial not to the nearby Seattle Mariners, but to the Yankees, and Brosius couldn't explain why that was. All he knew is that he loved the Yankees, mainly because his father, Maury, did. Mickey Mantle was Maury's favorite player, and Scott wore Mantle's No. 7 when he made it to the big leagues with Oakland.

Despite his small town upbringing Brosius welcomed the opportunity to come to New York. Unlike the man he was traded for, Rogers, Brosius embraced the city and respected the passion that the fans at Yankee Stadium brought to the park each night. There had been no passion in Oakland.

"When the trade happened, I thought, 'Oh boy, I get to spend six months in New York,'" he said. "It's not a very comfortable place as a visiting player. But everything you hate about New York as a visitor you love as a home player."

Brosius never batted higher than seventh in the lineup all season, yet he drove in 98 runs, and while his bat was a tremendous bonus, his defense was every bit as good as Michael knew it would be. He solidified the infield with his sharp glove work, and no one in baseball made the charging barehanded scoop-and-fire like Brosius.

"I don't think they were expecting great things from me," he said. "I think they just wanted me to be solid. With this team it was easy to fit in and just be solid."

Torre, for one, said he would never forget the season Brosius had. "When I think of this team, you know what's going to come to mind," Torre said. "Scotty Brosius. I saw a picture of him in the paper after that home run (his second long ball in Game Three) and he had his mouth open, roaring like the MGM lion. His personality was a big part of this club."

*   *   *

The Texas Rangers served as the first-round sacrificial lambs. Three games, three wins for New York, and while all of them were close, I never got the sense that Texas was going to win any of them.

The opener turned out to be a tense pitchers' duel between David Wells and Todd Stottlemyre, Mel's son. "Tonight's game probably ended the best way," said Mel following the Yankees' 2-0 victory. "My son pitched well, and we won."

Next up was Andy Pettitte. He wasn't as good as Wells. He gave up one run. Didn't matter because the Yankees scored three on Shane

Spencer's solo homer and Brosius's two-run shot. The Rangers entered the series as the American League's top hitting team, and against left-handers they had batted .316. Against Wells and Pettitte they managed eight hits total.

Pettitte won 16 games during the regular season, but he had been erratic down the stretch. He was also rocked hard twice in the 1997 play-offs by Cleveland, his confidence was sagging, and the prevalent theory in the media was that Torre should relegate him to the bullpen and go with a three-man rotation of Wells, David Cone, and Orlando Hernandez. Pettitte quieted his critics and rewarded Torre's confidence. "This was a big game for me," Pettitte said. "Obviously there was a lot of doubt and people were questioning Joe for starting me. With Joe and Mel showing that much faith in me, it was nice to be able to do it for myself and the team."

The Yankees flew to Texas with no intention of staying very long. They needed one win to eliminate the Rangers, and they didn't want to spend the whole weekend trying to get it. Emotionally stoked by a video pep talk from Daryl Strawberry—who was back in New York awaiting surgery to remove a cancerous tumor from his colon—the Yankees completed the sweep. A three-hour rain delay only prolonged the inevitable for Texas. Just before the storm, O'Neill hit a solo homer and Spencer ripped a three-run shot off Aaron Sele to give Cone a 4-0 lead. When play resumed, Cone was out, but Graeme Lloyd, Jeff Nelson, and Mariano Rivera finished the shutout.

After flying home and hearing that Strawberry's surgery was successful and that his doctors expected a full recovery, life was good for the Yankees. It got better when Cleveland beat Boston in the other American League divisional series, giving the Yankees a chance to avenge their loss to the Indians in 1997.

* * *

I heard the booing of Mickey Mantle early in his career. I heard the booing of Roger Maris during his quest to break Babe Ruth's home run record. I've heard Yankee fans boo—at one time or another—just about every player who has donned the pinstripes over the past eight decades. But I never heard Yankee Stadium boo as vehemently for one of its own than the night Chuck Knoblauch stepped into the batter's box in the bottom of the 12th inning in Game Two of the 1998 American League Championship Series against Cleveland.

It was ugly, it was mean, and at that particular moment, it was warranted.

If that was an indication of what Knoblauch's baseball life was going to be like thereafter, all I can say is that for Chuck's sake, thank God the Yankees ended up rallying to win that series and advance to the World Series.

Had they lost to the Indians, Knoblauch would have never lived down his Little League-like tantrum that, at least for a couple days, appeared to turn the momentum in Cleveland's favor and put New York's momentous season in peril. That scene—Knoblauch standing on first base blowing a bubble like the child he seemed to be portraying, hands on hips, yelling at umpire Ted Hendry and ignoring the baseball that was behind him and still in play as Cleveland's Enrique Wilson was rounding the bases and scoring the go-ahead run—would have permanently lodged into the memories of Yankee fans, memories that are longer than infinity.

The Yankees had smoked the Indians in Game One, 7-2, as Wells pitched a shutout into the ninth inning, and his teammates blew Cleveland starter Jaret Wright—who had beaten them twice in the division series the year before—off the mound with a five-run first inning.

In Game Two Cone and Charles Nagy engaged in a terrific duel, though they were long gone when the game entered the 12th inning tied at 1-1. Jim Thome led off with a single and was replaced by pinch runner Wilson. Travis Fryman then laid a bunt down the first-base line and the fireworks began. Tino Martinez fielded the ball and tried to throw to Knoblauch covering first, but Fryman was slightly out of the base path and the throw hit him in the back and bounded out behind the bag. It was interference and everyone knew it except Hendry. Fryman reached first safely, and then Knoblauch reached brain lock. He stood on the bag yelling at Hendry for an interference call while the alert Indians kept running the bases. Wilson rounded second and headed for third, and then he rounded third and headed for home and still Knoblauch stood there.

"We were all saying 'Get the ball! Get the ball!'" Martinez said. "I don't think Knoblauch argues like that if he doesn't think he's right. Chuck was 100% sure. It was just the decision he made there."

Finally Knoblauch came to his senses and he scrambled back, picked up the ball and fired it home, but his throw was late and Wilson scored while Fryman went all the way to third. Fryman would eventually score on Kenny Lofton's two-run single that clinched Cleveland's 4-1 victory.

"I don't feel like I didn't play the ball out," Knoblauch said, ridiculously trying to defend himself. "I'm pretty shocked. I was kind of dumbfounded. I had no idea where the ball was, to begin with. And the runner was running straight at me so I expected him to be called out."

Clearly Knoblauch was missing the point. The umpire blew the call. That wasn't the first time that's ever happened, right? Knoblauch let his anger cloud his judgment, and it cost the Yankees the game.

"It was a terrible call," Torre said, agreeing with Knoblauch before admonishing him. "But I saw the replay and he was yelling at the umpire and you can't do that. You have got to make the play and then go back and argue. I think he was just shocked that they didn't make the call."

This play seemed such a departure for Knoblauch, a player who had always displayed grit, hustle, intelligence, and supreme skill playing in Minnesota.

He broke into the majors with a bang in 1991 when he captured American League Rookie of the Year honors and helped the Twins win the World Series. During his seven years in the Twin Cities he averaged .304, made the All-Star team four times, won the 1997 Gold Glove, and earned immense respect in the Yankee clubhouse. "Whenever we played the Twins our entire focus was on how to get him out," George Steinbrenner said shortly after he brought Knoblauch to New York. "As Knoblauch went, so went our chances."

Indeed, Knoblauch was considered one of the best players in the league, and when the Yankees acquired him before the 1998 season it was another case of the rich getting richer. Knoblauch was seen as the perfect table setter for Derek Jeter, Paul O'Neill, Bernie Williams, and Tino Martinez, and he would pair with Jeter to give the Yankees a dynamic double-play combination.

Knoblauch had a decent 1998, but not what the Yankee hierarchy expected, and when the postseason rolled around, he was in a slump both offensively and defensively. There were problems off the field, too. His father Ray, a former high school baseball coach, was diagnosed with Alzheimer's, and Knoblauch was known to be devastated by how the disease was eating away his once-vibrant father. Further, living and playing in the scrutinizing spotlight of New York was much tougher than Knoblauch realized.

"It wasn't a normal year for him," O'Neill said. And it all came to a head in the 12th inning of Game Two against Cleveland.

"It was a very horrible, horrible thing that I wouldn't wish on anybody," Knoblauch said the following spring, reliving the nightmare. "Really, when you walk up to bat after that and you have 50,000 people booing you, all you have are your teammates, the people closest to you, and yourself on your side. So to be in a situation like that, you can do one of two things. You can go down or bounce back. All you can do is go out and play as hard and as best as you can."

To his credit, Knoblauch put the incident behind him. He hit .375 in the World Series against San Diego and made only one error on 15 chances, and because the Yankees won the championship, it seemed like all would be forgotten.

He was better offensively in 1999, but his defensive woes heightened and by October Torre was deeply concerned. During the year his erratic throwing led to 26 errors, the most by a Yankee second baseman since Snuffy Stirnweiss in 1945, so Torre began using Luis Sojo as a defensive replacement in the late innings.

The worst was yet to come. In 2000, his father's condition worsened, his marriage dissolved into divorce, and his continuing throwing yips had Knoblauch contemplating retirement. He made three errors in one game against Chicago, walked off the field with a chorus of insults ringing in his ears, and drove home during the seventh inning. Limited to 102 games due to injuries, Knoblauch was used primarily as a designated hitter in the play-offs because Torre couldn't risk playing him in the field.

Torre solved the fielding problem in 2001 when he shifted Knoblauch to left field, but another poor offensive season removed him from New York's future plans. After the World Series loss to Arizona, Knoblauch signed a free agent contract with the Kansas City Royals.

During his four years in New York Knoblauch never lived up to the standard he had set in Minnesota, but as he left for Kansas City, he did so with three World Series rings, championships he helped the Yankees win.

*   *   *

The Cleveland fans were ready for Knoblauch with an array of merciless taunts when the ALCS resumed at Jacobs Field. More importantly, the Indian batters were ready for Pettitte. As good as Pettitte had been against Texas, he was that bad against Cleveland as he allowed four home runs—three of them in a decisive fifth inning—during a humbling 6-1 defeat.

The Yankees, winners of 114 games during the regular season, the preordained World Series champions, were officially in trouble. After

Game Three Torre, Don Zimmer, and I were sitting in the manager's office off the clubhouse when Steinbrenner came in and said, "If we don't win this thing, everybody will forget what we did all season." Torre looked up and said, "Don't worry Boss, we've got El Duque."

Who better to have pitching in the biggest game of the season than this crafty Cuban? This was a man who understood what pressure was all about. Defecting from your homeland is a little more nerve-wracking than pitching against the Cleveland Indians.

"I saw him at brunch and he asked me how I felt," Torre said following a 4-0 victory that evened the series at two games apiece. "I knew that was an indication that he was fine. He was very relaxed, very determined."

This was his first postseason start, and Hernandez made the Indians look like amateurs in what many people—including me—considered a season-saving triumph. "I had pressure, but no fear," Hernandez said. "I've been through so many different things on and off the field in my life."

Wiped away was the memory of Knoblauch's gaffe and Pettitte's gopher balls. The Yankees had their swagger back, and they came out and scored three times in the first inning of Game Five against overmatched Chad Ogea and went on to a 5-3 victory behind Wells. "I'm very proud of this team," Torre said. "Every time they've been faced with a challenge, they've responded."

The end came quickly back in New York. Nagy could not duplicate his strong outing in Game Two and was rocked for six runs on eight hits in the first three innings—the big blows a three-run homer by Brosius and a two-run triple by Jeter—and the Yankees cruised to a 9-5 pennant-clinching triumph.

"We were definite underdogs in 1996," Torre said, referring to his first trip to the World Series. "This year we were expected to win. There was a lot more pressure, and it makes it a lot more gratifying."

Thirty-one years and he never made it to one World Series. Now Torre was going back for the second time in three years.

* * *

Perhaps it was the depression of another October gone sour for the Braves, but Atlanta manager Bobby Cox could not have been thinking clearly when he said following his Braves' six-game loss to San Diego in the National League Championship Series, "I think the Padres have a really good chance of beating the Yankees. I like San Diego's chances."

The Padres were a nice story. They had won the National West rather easily, then whipped Houston and Atlanta—teams that combined to win 208 games during the regular season—in the divisional and championship series rounds. But they had no chance of beating the Yankees. Nasty right-hander Kevin Brown was a player to be feared, old warrior Tony Gwynn was a dangerous hitter and great leader, and Greg Vaughn was a big-time power hitter. But come on, Bobby. The Padres were overmatched, and that point was driven home in the seventh inning of Game One at Yankee Stadium.

Trailing the upstarts by a count of 5-2, the Yankees tore into Brown, Donnie Wall, and Mark Langston for seven runs to claim a 9-6 victory. If the Padres had any chance, that was it, and with two swings by Knoblauch and Martinez, it was gone in the space of 10 minutes.

Knoblauch and Martinez. Imagine that. The same Knoblauch who had been booed to near tears only a week earlier whacked a game-tying three-run homer. And Martinez, who entered this game batting .187 in three Yankee postseasons, won it with an upper-deck full-count grand slam. Both men were asked to take bows, and both did.

"I had a little smile on my face because Tino and I had been trying to pump each other up," said Knoblauch. "You try to lift each other up. I was probably more excited when he hit his home run than when I hit mine. It was just a great feeling. If you play baseball, it's a roller-coaster ride. There are a lot of ups and downs and you have to let it go."

Wells, born and raised in San Diego and a Padre fan growing up, struggled for the first time in the play-offs. He gave up five runs in his seven innings of work, but he received credit for the victory when the Yankees made their comeback. "They kicked my ass tonight," he said of the Padres.

Brown, Gwynn, and Vaughn—the three players who worried the Yankees the most—proved why, as Vaughn and Gwynn hit two-run homers and Brown bottled up the Yankees for six innings, but it wasn't enough. "We knew it was going to be a climb," Torre said of the 5-2 deficit. "It was incredible to come back like that."

Game Two wasn't nearly as dramatic. The Yankees tortured Padre starter Andy Ashby with 10 hits and took a 7-0 lead within three innings while Hernandez limited San Diego to six hits in seven innings as New York rolled to a 9-3 victory. Every Yankee starter had at least one hit, with Martinez and Brosius getting three, Knoblauch, Jeter, and Ricky Ledee getting two, and Jorge Posada and Williams each hitting two-run homers. "We still have to win two games," said Knoblauch.

I had considered not making the long trip to the West Coast. As usual I attended all the home games, but I hadn't gone to Texas or Cleveland. It was only when Torre reminded me that I hadn't missed seeing a Yankee World Series game in person since 1926 that I packed my bags and boarded the charter flight. I was glad I went.

"I don't think I've ever been in a louder ballpark," Torre remarked following Game Three. "I could feel the vibrations." But while the fans at Qualcomm Stadium, nearly 65,000 strong, put up quite a brave front, they couldn't will their team to victory.

Their Padres took a 3-0 lead in the sixth inning, but Brosius hit a pair of home runs and the Yankees pulled it out, 5-4, leaving them one win away from their 24th world title and another record: most championships won by a pro sports franchise, one ahead of the 23-time Stanley Cup champion Montreal Canadiens.

This was a victory that defined the 1998 team's legacy. Brosius's second home run, a three-run blast to straightaway center field in the eighth inning, came off Padres closer Trevor Hoffman. All Hoffman had done to that point was convert 53 of his last 54 save opportunities and he'd given up just three home runs all season.

Through five innings Cone had a no-hitter, but in the sixth, the opposing pitcher, Sterling Hitchcock, broke it up with a single, Quilvio Veras walked, and both scored when Gwynn singled to right and O'Neill threw the ball into the Yankee dugout for an error. Gwynn later scored on Ken Caminiti's sacrifice fly.

The stadium was still trembling when Brosius calmed things down with a solo homer to lead off the seventh, and another run scored when Shane Spencer doubled and came home on Caminiti's error. Then in the eighth came Brosius's bomb which was enough to offset Vaughn's sacrifice fly in the bottom half.

"There's nothing more fun than this," said Brosius.

He was wrong. Their post-Series celebration was more fun. The chants went up throughout the locker room for Brosius, for Pettitte who pitched a gem of a clincher all the while worrying about his father, Tom, who had just undergone a triple bypass heart operation. And then there was the chant for Strawberry, the fallen teammate, home in New York recovering from colon cancer surgery. "Straw man, Straw man" they yelled, and then Wells stood in the middle of the clubhouse and announced, "This one was for the Straw Man."

With a three games to none lead, the Yankees wanted this to be over, so they ended it. The doubters were knocking on Pettitte's door again after his flameout 11 days earlier in Cleveland, but he ignored them, pitched 7 1/3 innings of five-hit shutout ball, then watched anxiously as Jeff Nelson and Rivera put the finishing touches on the Yankees' 3-0 victory, their 125th and last of this magical season.

Brown was again tough for San Diego, pitching on just three days' rest. He matched Pettitte zero for zero through five, but in the sixth Jeter beat out an infield hit, raced to third on O'Neill's double to right, and scored on Williams's ground out. It was all Pettitte needed, though some insurance was provided in the eighth when Brosius drove a RBI single and Ledee hit a sacrifice fly.

"We were 125-50 this year," Jeter said. "That's ridiculous."

Immediately, the debate began as to whether this was the greatest team in the history of baseball.

"I think it will probably be talked about forever," said Brosius. "The comparisons will go on and on, and maybe nobody will have a definite answer. But you can look at this year and say we've had the single best season of any other team."

It was one of those perfect Florida nights that make springtime so wonderful. The temperature was mild and a slight breeze was blowing, just enough to stir the air, but not enough for me to slip a sweater over my golf shirt. The exhibition games hadn't started yet so Joe Torre and Don Zimmer had the evening to themselves and they asked me if I'd like to go with them to the St. Petersburg Kennel Club for the dog races. It is one of Zimmer's favorite activities, and Torre enjoys it, too. I could care less about the damn dogs. Whenever I go along, I place a few wagers, but I'm mostly there for the conversation and the laughs.

As we watched the greyhounds run around Derby Lane Torre made a joke about Zimmer's bum knee which in about a week's time would have to be operated on, and Torre said something like, "I might have to tell Doc Boyer to cut that leg off tomorrow."

Tomorrow was the day the players and coaches were required to take their medical examinations. Dr. Andy Boyer would poke and prod to make sure everything was where it was supposed to be, and for the older men, the coaches, he performed the standard tests that any other family physician would during a routine physical.

Torre never worried about his physical. He was approaching 59 years of age, but he was in fine shape. He was a little soft around the middle, but most men his age are. Outside of baseball injuries, he'd never had any health concerns.

Until now.

It was two days after the legendary Joe DiMaggio lost his battle with lung cancer when Torre phoned me in my room at the Holiday Inn Express to deliver another piece of chilling news. Dr. Boyer had diagnosed him with prostate cancer.

My initial reaction was one of vexation, but Torre didn't need that. He needed reassurance from someone who 22 years earlier had gone through the same ordeal. I made him aware that since my surgery in 1977 medical technology in this area had improved dramatically. Although the statistics showed that only lung cancer killed more men in America than prostate cancer, they also revealed that nearly 95% of those afflicted survive if the disease is detected early enough, provided it hasn't spread to the lymph system. Torre's had been caught in the beginning stage, and it had not spread.

"Look at Marv Levy," I said, speaking of the former coach of the Buffalo Bills who had been diagnosed in 1995. "He was around 70 years old when he was

operated on, and he was back coaching his team within a month. Arnold Palmer just had the surgery. General Schwarzkopf had it. And look at me. Twenty-two years later and I'm still here."

Torre knew all this. The statistics and the names of recent high-profile survivors had been recited to him, and as we talked I noticed his voice was unwavering. He did not seem frightened by what he was facing and I could tell he was confident he would be able to clear this formidable obstacle.

Frank Torre knew his brother would be fine. Frank was down in Tampa when the news broke. Now the tables were turned for the Torre brothers and Frank had to play the supporting role for his ailing brother. The reporters flocked to Frank for a comment and he told them, "Joe doesn't feel sorry for himself. He doesn't feel like, 'Why me?' He actually feels like one of the luckiest people in the world with as many wonderful things as have happened to him. He's certainly not going to lay down and die, because a lot more wonderful things are going to happen."

"The first thing that went through my head was, 'What's next?'" said catcher Joe Girardi when he heard the news. "You see one guy come back [Daryl Strawberry, who that same day was playing in his first game since his colon cancer surgery the previous October] and then another guy is struck with cancer. It takes something out of you. Once again we see how fragile life is."

Indeed. DiMaggio was dead, Torre was sick, and another Yankee legend, Catfish Hunter, offered further proof of the fragility of life that Girardi spoke of. Hunter was seen struggling to sign autographs during his annual trip to spring training, the effects of Lou Gehrig's disease—diagnosed in him three months before—already diminishing his motor skills. Reflecting on the gloom that hovered over his team, George Steinbrenner said, "This has been a tough week for the Yankees."

But the Boss also reminded everyone of the unyielding resiliency of the Yankee family when he added "Everybody is saying, 'What's next?' But we will handle it because that's what the Yankees are all about. We are a pillar of strength. We have a great capacity of being able to deal with adversity. Time after time after time, we've done it throughout this franchise's history. It's built into being a Yankee."

By the end of 1999, the Yankees needed every ounce of that toughness, that ability to deal with adversity, because sadness and personal heartache became a constant companion on the journey to another world championship.

Torre returned to work in mid-May with a clean bill of health, but it was all downhill from there. Strawberry was left behind in Tampa to do additional conditioning work, and he grew depressed, began drinking and using cocaine— the vices that had derailed his once-great career—and he hit rock bottom when

*he was arrested for soliciting a female Tampa police officer posing as a prosti-
tute. Hunter eventually died, and so did the fathers of Scott Brosius, Luis Sojo,
and Paul O'Neill.*

*The Team of the Century closed the millennium in grand style by claiming
its 25th World Series title, but this was a championship drenched not in champagne, but in tears.*

– Chapter 25 –

1999

BY NATURE, BERNIE WILLIAMS IS A QUIET, reserved, and respectful man, the Yankees' "silent leader," as Joe Torre likes to say. So it was not out of character for Williams to be sitting in front of his locker cubicle, content to watch rather than participate in the revelry exploding all around him. But I could tell this was different for Williams. As the Yankees celebrated their 1998 World Series victory in the visiting clubhouse at San Diego's Qualcomm Stadium, there was a measure of sadness, of closure, in Williams's deep brown eyes.

"This might be it for me, Mr. Kimmerle," he said to me after the media crush had dissipated and the merrymaking had wound down.

There had been talk for months that 1998 was going to be Williams's last year as a Yankee. The one-year contract extension he signed at the start of the season had now expired and he was officially free to swim in the lucrative waters of free agency. Every indication—both from his agent Scott Boras and the team—pointed to him signing with another club for the type of superstar money the Yankee organization wasn't sure he deserved.

When the team returned to New York for its ticker-tape parade through the Canyon of Heroes, Williams waved to his adoring fans as they chanted his name and pleaded for him to re-sign with the team. "You've gotta talk to this guy here," Williams said, pointing to owner George Steinbrenner, the man who held all the cards.

To my way of thinking, Williams's situation was a perplexing one. Steinbrenner was never averse to spending lavishly on big-name free agents. Yet he had battled Williams—a truly gifted player who had been a mainstay on the team since 1992 and a Yankee through and through—

at every turn. Williams's arbitration hearings following the 1995 and 1997 seasons had been strangely contentious, and then in 1998 Williams became the only player in baseball history to win a batting championship, a Gold Glove, and a World Series title in the same year, yet still there was an absence of respect for Williams. What more could the Yankees want?

It seemed to me that a comment made by former general manager Bob Watson in 1996 had stigmatized Williams in the eyes of the front office executives. "He's a good player, but not a great player," said Watson, who had almost traded the center fielder to Detroit for a couple of pitching prospects. That may have been true in the mid-1990s, but not anymore. Williams was a superstar, and though he cherished being a Yankee he wondered if it was time to move on.

"Paul O'Neill and Tino Martinez probably assumed they were going to stay with the teams they started with their whole careers, but probably the best thing that happened to them was coming here," Williams said. "Who's to say the same thing couldn't happen to me [somewhere else]."

Deep down, Williams did not believe that. He knew the best place for him was Yankee Stadium's vast center field where he was building his own legacy, gracefully following in the footsteps of Joe DiMaggio and Mickey Mantle.

A month after the World Series the Boston Red Sox made Williams a seven-year, $91 million offer that would be tough to refuse. With the Yankees already expressing an interest in surly slugger Albert Belle and productive Brian Jordan, it looked as if Williams's days were done in New York. Thankfully, both sides came to their senses. Williams ordered Boras to meet with Steinbrenner one more time, Steinbrenner agreed, and within two days Williams signed the richest Yankee contract to that point, a seven-year, $87.5 million blockbuster.

Williams never wanted to leave. Steinbrenner didn't want him to leave. All it took was both men admitting that to each other.

"We paid a hell of a price, but this is the way you build a team," Steinbrenner said when the deal was finalized the day before Thanksgiving. "It comes down to what the player is worth to you. He was going, but he didn't want to go. I needed to hear that."

Williams's reply was, "All I am looking forward to is to having a great second career with the organization."

If it's anything like his first career with the team, Williams may wind up with a monument out beyond the left-center field wall as well as a bust in Cooperstown. And that would sure be something when you consider his was a career that almost never came to be.

Growing up in Puerto Rico, Williams's first love—at his father's urging—was music. He began taking guitar lessons at the age of 8, and he made a two-hour round trip to San Juan every day so that he could attend a high school that specialized in music education. When he wasn't playing guitar, though, he was playing baseball, and his talent was undeniable.

When Williams was 17 years old and strumming a mean six-string, Doug Melvin, then the Yankees' scouting director, visited his home and helped convince Bernie's father to let his son play baseball. Melvin's rationale was sound. If baseball didn't work out Bernie could always go back to the guitar, but it couldn't be the other way around. Williams's father agreed, and before the scouts from other teams could find him Melvin signed Williams to a $15,000 bonus. Years later Melvin said the signing was one of the highlights of his career. Williams's progress was frustratingly slow, though, and it took nearly six years for him to reach the big leagues in 1991. Even then he started 1992 in Columbus before returning to the Yankees midway through the season. This time it was for good.

A decade later, with four World Series rings in his collection, his resume is among the most gaudy in baseball. But he'll never tell you that, and he prefers that you don't tell him that.

Outside of his baseball talent, what impresses me most about Williams is his reverence for Yankee history. He understands the tradition and what it means to wear the uniform. "I never take this job for granted," he told Mike Lupica of the *Daily News*. "I never lose sight of the ones who have come before me out there. It's not just Mr. DiMaggio you think about, and Mickey Mantle. You think about Bobby Murcer, and Mickey Rivers. You think about the kind of center field Paul Blair played when he was a Yankee."

His teammates respect his quiet nature, but many admit that they don't really know Williams. I am in the same boat. Whenever I talk to Williams it is usually in generalities, and always about baseball. It's not that Williams is aloof or conceited. Quite simply, he's a man who guards his privacy with the same intensity that he brings to each at-bat. "I don't try to be mysterious, I just don't let these guys know a whole lot," Williams said. "I'm very closed when it comes to personal things. That's just the way I am."

Ex-Yankee Tim Raines once said, "There's really nothing bad to say about Bernie because he doesn't do anything wrong. He's probably the best player nobody knows. And that's just the way he wants it."

* * *

Avoiding the spotlight became quite easy for Williams in the wake of Joe Torre's prostate cancer, but even before that announcement, Williams was pushed to the background when the Yankees traded the ever-popular David Wells to Toronto along with Graeme Lloyd and Homer Bush for superstar pitcher Roger Clemens.

Clemens, the longtime ace for the rival Red Sox, had left Boston following 1996 and signed a free agent deal with Toronto. After two years with the Blue Jays, during which he won 41 games and increased his Cy Young Award collection by two to a record total of five, Clemens announced that he wanted out of Toronto. He didn't think the team was committed to winning a championship, and going on 36 years old, he wanted a World Series ring to complete his trophy case.

A number of teams negotiated with the Blue Jays, but as usual, the Yankees came armed with the best package and the deal was hatched. Wells cried, and so did Yankee fans, not to mention bartenders all around the city. Wells loved being a Yankee, and he couldn't understand why the team would unload him after he'd won 34 regular-season games in two years, pitched a perfect game, and gone 5-0 in the play-offs.

Steinbrenner coldly explained that David Wells was David Wells. Roger Clemens was a Hall of Famer.

Clemens came to New York fully understanding that nothing less than brilliance was going to be enough to satisfy Yankee fans. "The expectations are always great, but in this situation, they are a little more serious," said Clemens. "But I'm going to have help. I don't see that I'm going to have to stop a lot of four-game losing streaks anymore."

He was right. The rotation included Orlando Hernandez, Andy Pettitte, David Cone, and Hideki Irabu, while Ramiro Mendoza was also available for spot starting duty. And when Clemens pitched, he wouldn't have to go the distance every outing to assure victory because the Yankee bullpen was solid with Jeff Nelson, Mike Stanton, and Mariano Rivera.

However, Clemens was not the same Rocket that Steinbrenner had been drooling over. He struggled to find his form all year and wound up with a mundane 14-10 record and a 4.60 earned-run average, the worst of his career.

Clemens pitched well on Opening Day in Oakland with eight strikeouts, but he received a no-decision and the Yankees lost Don Zimmer's first game as interim manager, 5-3. After winning the last two in Oakland, the Yankees flew home for their opener at Yankee Stadium, and that was a day filled with emotion. Fans grieved the death of the great DiMaggio. They vocalized get-well wishes to Torre who was absent, recovering from his prostate surgery. And they cheered wildly for the long-lost legend, Yogi Berra, who made his return to the Stadium after a self-imposed 14-year truancy.

DiMaggio had been scheduled to throw out the first ball at the opener, but his death prompted Steinbrenner to reach out to Berra. Since his firing as manager in 1985, Berra had vowed never to come back to the stadium as long as Steinbrenner was still in charge, and he'd held firm. But when the Boss made an impassioned plea and finally apologized for his actions, Berra relented. The sellout crowd roared long and loud for Yogi and he and Steinbrenner shared a touching embrace on the field. I sat with Berra up in Steinbrenner's private box that day, and I could see the radiance in Berra's craggy face. He had come home, and he couldn't have been happier.

Zimmer had the club in first place throughout his entire six-week stint, and after a brief slump when he handed the reins backs to Torre, the Yankees pulled it together in June and they were four games ahead of Boston at the All-Star break. Torre managed the American League squad in the midsummer classic at Fenway Park and Derek Jeter, Williams, and Cone represented the Yankees during a 4-1 American League victory. Cone pitched two innings and was knocked around for four hits and one earned run by the National League's finest. A week later, he met up with the National League again, this time in the form of the Montreal Expos at Yankee Stadium. That day, Cone fared a little better.

*   *   *

Sometimes the Lord works in mysterious ways, and on July 18, 1999, He was working overtime. How else can you explain what transpired that afternoon?

Before the Yankees hosted Montreal, on Joe Torre's 59th birthday by the way, they celebrated Yogi Berra Day. One of the invitees brought back to honor Yogi was Don Larsen, the man who threw the first perfect game in Yankee history, the only perfect game in World Series history. The 69-year-old Larsen tottered out to the mound and threw a ball as best he could toward Berra, a reenactment of the final pitch of the perfect game. Thankfully the 73-year-old Berra did not try to recreate his leap into Larsen's arms.

The two men simply shared a handshake as the crowd of 41,930, sweating in 95-degree heat and humidity, stood and cheered for the two old Yankees. From the bullpen Cone had paused his warmup to watch the show and applaud, and when the festivities concluded Cone came down to the dugout and shook hands with Larsen. Larsen patted him on the shoulder, said, "Good luck today" and then headed up to Steinbrenner's private box along with, among others, Berra, Whitey Ford, Phil Rizzuto, Bobby Richardson, Don Mattingly, and Gil McDougald.

I was also sitting in the box, and in the fifth inning, with the Yankees comfortably ahead by 5-0, Larsen got up and said he was going back to his hotel. I looked at him incredulously and said, "Are you kidding? He's throwing a perfect game!"

Larsen smiled sheepishly, sat down, watched the rest of the game, and when it was over and Cone had thrown the third perfect game in Yankee history Larsen said to me, "Jesus Christ, I'm glad I stayed."

The only way this cosmic confluence of Larsen and Cone could have been any more eerie was if the opponent had been Toronto, and Wells—the author of the only other Yankee perfect game—had been the opposing pitcher. As New York Mayor and unabashed Yankee fan Rudy Giuliani said, "Today was just one of those incredible Yankee days."

Cone was born and raised in Kansas City and was in dreamland back in 1981 when his hometown Royals selected him in the third round of the draft. It took until 1986 before he made it to the Royals and pitched in the stadium that was just a 15-minute ride from the home he grew up in. However, after appearing in only 11 games as a reliever, he was traded to the Mets before the 1987 season.

In New York Cone became a star on the field, and a knucklehead off the field. His record with the Mets during his 5 1/2 years was 76-48, but away from the ballpark Cone did some really stupid things, showed notorious immaturity—George King of the *New York Post* referred to Cone as the ringleader of baseball's version of *Animal House*—and the Mets gave up on him in 1992. When Toronto general manager Pat Gillick came looking for a pitcher who could put his team over the top in its quest for the World Series title, the Mets offered Cone.

Cone helped bring the championship to the Blue Jays, and that seemed to be a turning point for him. He grew up. He came home to Kansas City for two years and won the 1994 Cy Young Award, moved back to Toronto in 1995, then became a mercenary again later that year when Steinbrenner brought him in for the stretch run as the Yankees battled for the first-ever wild-card play-off berth. Cone went 9-2 for the Yankees, beat Seattle in the first game of the divisional series, and was leading 4-2 in the eighth inning of the decisive fifth game before allowing the tying runs to score. The Yankees went on to lose the game and the series, and Cone is still bothered by that letdown even today.

Cone re-signed with the Yankees and after surviving a scary bout with an aneurysm in his throwing shoulder in early 1996, he became the heart and soul of Torre's pitching staff. When he won 20 games in 1998, he set a major league record for longest interval between 20-win seasons (10 years), and in 1999, he won nine of his first 13 decisions, setting the stage for the perfect game.

"It is amazing," Cone said. "I didn't know if I would ever get the chance to do something special like this. You probably have a better chance of winning the lottery than this happening."

The game was decided quickly when the Yankees scored five runs in the second inning. Before Cone could start the third inning rain caused a 33-minute delay, yet he was undeterred. When play resumed he struck out the side, then used only 24 pitches to retire the Expos in the three middle innings. He struck out two batters in the seventh, and the eighth was an eight-pitch breeze, but then Cone had to sit through a lengthy bottom half as his teammates produced three hits and another run. Of Chili Davis's inning-ending double play, Cone said, "I was never happier to see a double-play ball, though I won't say that to Chili's face."

In the ninth Cone struck out Chris Widger on three pitches, and Ryan McGuire hit a 2-2 pitch into left field where Ricky Ledee stopped everyone's heart by stumbling before recovering to make the catch. Orlando Cabrera was Montreal's last hope, and he lifted a 1-1 pitch into foul ground wide of third where Scott Brosius squeezed the ball for the final out.

"You couldn't have written a greater script for today," said Derek Jeter, who in just four major league seasons had become an authority on scripts. He had already been part of two perfect games, a no-hitter by Dwight Gooden, and two World Series championships. "Larsen throwing out the first pitch on Yogi Berra Day. It just seems like it keeps getting better and better."

It could never get any better for Cone. You can't improve on perfection. But no one expected that it would rarely be good for Cone after that day. He was a mediocre pitcher the rest of the 1999 regular season, and after winning his only starts in the American League Championship Series and the World Series, Cone suddenly sank to the depths of despair in 2000. It was as if he had expended everything he had in 1999 and there was nothing left. He endured the worst season of his career with a dreadful 4-14 record and he pitched just 1 1/3 innings in the postseason. A month after the 2000 World Series Cone was informed that the Yankees were giving up on him.

"It was definitely emotional," said Yankees general manager Brian Cashman. "He has been very good for the Yankees. Ultimately we concluded it was time to turn the page. I thanked him for a major contribution. It wasn't easy, he is one of my favorites and one of the main reasons I have been considered successful. Because of his contributions, it's not easy to say good-bye."

Cone ended up signing with the rival Red Sox for two reasons. They wanted him, and as Boston general manager Dan Duquette said, "He wants to beat the Yankees. Why else would he sign with the Red Sox?"

*   *   *

The Yankees never relinquished their hold on first place, though Boston made a run in September and when the Red Sox came into Yankee Stadium and swept three in a row, they were within 3 1/2 games. New York then won 9 of 10 later in the month to clinch the pennant for the third time in four years.

The Yankees lost, 6-3, to Tampa Bay on the last day, dropping their all-time regular-season record in the twentieth century to 8,492 wins, 6,490 losses, and 83 ties. That was 2,002 games over .500. It had been a pretty good century.

– *1999 World Series* –

I had done it with my father in the Bronx, just as Scott Brosius had done it with his father in Milwaukie, Oregon, and Luis Sojo had done it with his father in Venezuela, and Paul O'Neill had done it with his father in Columbus, Ohio.

Baseball has always been a game for fathers and sons. A game you learn to play by having a catch with your dad, or standing in the batter's box at the neighborhood sandlot, flailing away as your dad tosses the ball over the plate and then fetches anything you might have hit. It's a game that you come to love by accompanying your father to watch the team in your town, whether it's the Yankees or the local high school nine. It's what fathers and their sons do.

"From the time I was five years old my father taught me how to play baseball," O'Neill said on the day his father died of heart failure and the Yankees won the 1999 World Series. "He taught me how to hit. He taught me how to throw. He taught me the most important part of the game, which is how to win. I haven't done all the things he wanted me to do . . . but I've always played to make him proud of me."

Charlie O'Neill would have been proud of his son on this night. Ambrosio Sojo, who died a week earlier of a heart attack, would have been proud of his son. And Maury Brosius, who died in mid-September of colon cancer, would have been proud of his son.

These boys played the game their fathers taught them, even though their hearts weren't in it and their minds were a million miles away. They played because that's what they were taught to do.

There was no other way this baseball season, this baseball century, could have ended. The Yankees had to win the World Series. Not only because they were the Team of the Century, but because after enduring so much personal trauma in 1999, they deserved to be world champions.

From the time the Yankees convened during the spring in Tampa to the time Chad Curtis caught the final out at Yankee Stadium against the Atlanta Braves to complete a four-game Series sweep, Charlie O'Neill, Maury Brosius, and Ambrosio Sojo died. Yankee legends Joe DiMaggio and Catfish Hunter died. Joe Torre battled prostate cancer. Chuck Knoblauch's father, Ray, continued to deteriorate due to Alzheimer's disease. Andy Pettitte's father, Tom, struggled with a damaged heart. Daryl Strawberry survived colon cancer surgery, but then slipped into drug and alcohol dependency and missed most of the season.

"This is a special group," Torre said. "I think we've gotten into a real good habit of dealing with whatever lowlights there are. Tragedy is a part of life. Just because you're an athlete doesn't mean you're exempt. This is just unusual to have all of these things happen at one time to one club."

If there was one scene that encapsulated the macabre reality of the Yankees' 1999 season, it was Paul O'Neill separating himself from the on-field celebration at the end of Game Four and collapsing into Torre's arms, tears streaming down his face, the gnashing of emotions he had fought all day finally breaking him down.

"I just told Paulie, 'Your dad was here to watch this one.'" And O'Neill, recalling that moment with a little-boy smile, said, "It's all his fault. I was doing fine until I got to Joe. That's when I lost it. All the stuff that had been bottled up inside me, it just came out."

When Charlie O'Neill passed away earlier that day Paul grieved the way any loving son would. And then he drove to Yankee Stadium and Torre knew he didn't have to ask Paul if he was up to playing.

"I did not have a conversation with him about that because I just assumed that when he showed up, that's what he was here for," Torre said.

Charlie O'Neill had been a minor league pitcher in the Brooklyn Dodgers organization, but he was injured in World War II and never played baseball again. Paul was the youngest of the six O'Neill children, and between Charlie and Paul's four brothers, Paul learned early on that he would have to fight for everything he got. That's where his passion and his intensity were manufactured, and both attributes continue to burn today.

I remember reading a story in *Newsday* about Paul, and Charlie was asked about his son's legendary competitiveness. "He'd cry if he didn't get a hit," Charlie said. "But then his older brothers would get all over him about crying, and he'd come back trying to prove something. He's always had that competitiveness, whether it was tennis, basketball, or math. He was so intense he probably could have done anything he wanted to do in life."

What he wanted to do was play major league baseball and he got that chance with Cincinnati. Drafted in 1981 out of high school, he made it to the Reds for good in 1987. Though he won a World Series in 1990 and made the National League All-Star team in 1991, O'Neill never hit higher than .276 and never drove in 100 runs with the Reds. In six full years, his average was .259.

When the Yankees offered center fielder Roberto Kelly in an even-up swap after the 1992 season the Reds jumped and O'Neill came to New York and turned his career around. He stopped trying to hit home runs and worked on driving the ball to all fields. His first six years in pinstripes he batted above .300 including an American League-best .359 mark in the strike-ruined 1994 season, and throughout his Yankee tenure—which ended following the 2001 World Series loss to Arizona when he announced his retirement—he was one of the inspirational leaders of the team.

No one cared more about winning, or more about the Yankees, than O'Neill. That's why he would get so furious when he made an out. He demanded perfection from himself, and in a game where even the best players fail seven out of 10 times, O'Neill's temperament was always questioned by outsiders, but never by his teammates.

"You hear people talk about Yankee pride," Dwight Gooden once said. "He is Yankee pride. He's like our Lou Gehrig, Pride of the Yankees."

* * *

Those poor Texas Rangers. They won the American League West in 1996 and qualified for the play-offs for the first time in their 25-year history, but their reward was a four-game spanking administered by the Yankees. They made the play-offs for the second time in 1998, met up with the Yankees again, scored one run in three play-off games and went home. Isn't the third time supposed to be the charm?

Not for the Rangers. They won their third AL West crown in 1999, drew the Yankees as their divisional round opponent, again scored one run in three games, and another season came to a sudden and frustrating end. "Does this seem like it's getting old?" Derek Jeter asked rhetorically. "No way."

Winning never gets old and no team knows that more than the Yankees.

Texas had won its very first postseason game back in 1996 against New York. By the time this latest series was over, the Rangers had lost nine in a row to the Yankees. "Mind-boggling," is how Texas manager Johnny Oates described it.

The Rangers led the American League in team hitting in 1998 at .289, then batted .141 in getting swept by the Yankees. They topped the American League in hitting in 1999 with a stellar .293 mark, then batted .152 during this sweep. Hey, at least there was some progress.

Orlando Hernandez took the ball in Game One at Yankee Stadium and gave up two hits in eight innings before Jeff Nelson finished off an 8-0 victory, Bernie Williams supplying the offense by driving in six runs.

It was Pettitte's turn the next night and he outdueled Rick Helling in a tough match that ended 3-1 as Brosius and Ricky Ledee had RBI doubles.

"I'm not usually real emotional, but it was a big game," Pettitte said. "I had another tough year mentally. A lot of people doubting me, and sometimes you start to doubt yourself."

After the game George Steinbrenner walked over to Pettitte's locker, patted his left-handed pitcher on the back and said, "That was a courageous performance. That was a typical big-game Andy Pettitte performance."

This from the man who wanted to ship Andy's ass out of New York on at least a couple of occasions, most recently a few months earlier.

*   *   *

Pettitte is a lot like Bernie Williams in that he has a quiet, unassuming personality. He doesn't say a whole lot, and he's a devout Christian man who prefers to spend time with his wife and children rather than hit the town with his teammates. But his laid-back nature should never be misconstrued. The kid's a bulldog on the mound. He always seems to be dead smack in the middle of the frying pan, and the hotter it gets, the better he pitches.

It was never hotter than Game Five of the 1996 World Series, and not surprisingly, Pettitte came up with what I consider the most important pitching performance of this current run of Yankee superiority. If Pettitte had not beat John Smoltz that night in Atlanta, the Yankees probably wouldn't have won that World Series. And by not winning that one, who knows what would have happened thereafter?

Pettitte was rocked by the Braves in the 1996 opener and that poor outing threatened to overshadow all he and the team had accomplished. So Pettitte looked to the heavens and asked for a chance to redeem himself, and his prayers were answered. "I was so happy when we won Game Three because that meant I'd get a chance to pitch again," he said. "My season didn't have to end with the way I pitched in Game One." Pettitte threw 8 1/3 innings of shutout ball, the Yankees won the game, 1-0, and they wrapped up the Series two nights later back in New York.

Fast forward three years to the summer of 1999. I was having dinner one night with Torre following a day-game loss and he expressed concern regarding his most recent conversation with Steinbrenner earlier that afternoon. "Boss wants to get rid of Andy," Torre said. "I know he's not pitching well, he's not hitting his spots, but we can't trade him. The kid's got guts. I know he'll get it together."

Steinbrenner had wanted to trade Pettitte in 1998, was talked out of it by Torre, and Pettitte went on to win 16 games plus two more in the postseason including the World Series clincher at San Diego. Frustrated by another slow Pettitte start in 1999, Steinbrenner was looking to deal him again, and Torre put up another argument in defense of his pitcher. In acquiescing this time to Torre, Steinbrenner made it clear that if Pettitte continued to flounder, Torre was going to take the heat for nixing the trade. "It's going to be your decision," Steinbrenner said.

If Torre has taught Steinbrenner anything during their six-plus years together, it is patience. Pettitte came around after a sluggish first half and he won a game in each of the first two rounds of the play-offs. Sometimes the best deals are the ones teams don't make. Pettitte was living proof.

*   *   *

Pettitte knew he needed to show the Boss he was worthy of his trust and he did it. Now it was Roger Clemens's turn. Clemens had not been overly reliable during the regular season, and while he defiantly denied anything was wrong physically, the truth is he was very much bothered by a sore hamstring that was sapping some of his power.

On top of that was his checkered postseason past, hanging around his neck like an anchor. He hadn't won a play-off game since 1986 and he carried an unseemly 1-8 record to the mound at The Ballpark in Arlington for Game Three.

Strawberry cracked a three-run homer before Clemens threw his first pitch, and then Clemens made that 3-0 lead hold up all night.

Goodbye Texas. Hello Boston.

Yankees and Red Sox. They sounded so good together. Peanut butter and jelly. Ginger Rogers and Fred Astaire. Yankees and Red Sox.

Only once before had these storied rivals met in the postseason, that in 1978 when the man forever known in Boston as Bucky "Fucking" Dent broke Beantown's collective heart in the American League East do-or-die play-off game. But with baseball's expanded play-offs in effect since 1995, it was now possible for the Yankees and Red Sox to play in October, and both cities were licking their chops in anticipation.

Boston had finished four games behind New York, but had easily outdistanced Oakland for the American League wild-card berth. While the Yankees were breezing past Texas, the Red Sox fell into an 0-2 hole against Central Division champion Cleveland before winning the final three games by a combined score of 44-18 including a 23-7 shellacking in Game Three.

The Red Sox were red hot. They figured to give New York all it could handle, and they did. For three games. The Yankees squeezed out a pair of one-run victories in New York, then were embarrassed 13-1 in the third game as Clemens was rocked in his return to Fenway Park. New York then settled down and pounded out two easy wins to take the series four games to one to claim its 36th American League pennant of the twentieth century.

Hernandez brought a microscopic 0.41 earned-run average into Game One, then was promptly knocked around for three runs on four hits in the first two innings, but the Yankees fought back and Jeter's RBI single in the eighth tied it, and Williams's solo homer off Rod Beck won it in the 10th.

Game Two was another tight, tense affair that New York won, 3-2. Cone and Ramon Martinez both pitched well and entering the bottom of the seventh Boston was clinging to a 2-1 lead, Nomar Garciaparra's two-run homer besting Tino Martinez's solo shot. Here, Knoblauch hit a RBI double and later scored the winning run when Williams drew a bases-loaded walk. It took five Yankee pitchers to seal the victory, but they did it, Rivera striking out Damon Buford with two runners aboard to end the game.

The victory was New York's 12th in a row in the postseason, tying the record set by the Yankees when they swept three straight World Series in 1927, 1928, and 1932, but the streak thudded to a halt when New York walked into the buzzsaw that was Fenway Park two days later. Stoked beyond imagination for the Game Three matchup between indomitable Pedro Martinez and Clemens, viewed by Bostonians as the ultimate traitor, the Red Sox exploded for a 13-1 victory.

Clemens never had a chance. With vitriol worse than what we're used to hearing at Yankee Stadium raining down on him, he was blown off the mound inside three innings while Martinez struck out 12 despite claiming that he had, "Nothing. I was hurting on every pitch."

Torre was impressed by the emotion of the Boston crowd which no doubt played a role in the game, but he added, "What we need to do is come out here and pitch the way we're capable of pitching. That normally quiets things down."

The Fenway faithful were in an uproar the next day, but doing just as Torre asked, Pettitte muzzled them. He pitched 7 1/3 innings and gave up eight hits but only two runs, none after the third inning, and New

York broke open a tight game with a six-run ninth inning to win 9-2. "To be able to keep them from 2-2 with us was huge," Pettitte said.

The Red Sox were mentally whipped now, and the final physical beating came in the form of a 6-1 defeat as El Duque pitched seven innings of five-hit, nine-strikeout ball and was backed by Jeter's two-run homer in the first and Jorge Posada's two-run shot in the ninth.

"To repeat after the incredible year we had last year is a great accomplishment," said Torre. "I tried to warn the club in spring training that we cannot compete against ourselves because it was a once-in-a-lifetime thing. We had to earn it this year. It's probably more satisfying this year."

New York City was on fire this week because while the Yankees were winning the American League pennant, the Mets were trying to beat Atlanta in the National League and set up a Subway Series. The Mets dropped the first three games, but then won two memorable affairs at Shea Stadium and seemed to have momentum on their side as they traveled to Georgia for Game Six. New York fell behind 5-0 in the first inning, rallied to tie, went ahead in the 10th inning, saw Atlanta pull even, and then the Braves finally knocked out the Mets with a run in the 11th. Pretty good stuff, and while everyone was disappointed the World Series wouldn't be sequestered completely in New York, there was excitement over a Yankees-Braves rematch of 1996. Besides, it seemed appropriate that the two best teams in baseball in the 1990s should duke it out for the last championship of the decade, and the century.

The day before the opener at Turner Field, Atlanta's three-year-old ballpark which I was visiting for the first time, Hernandez was asked which Braves' hitter worried him the most. "All the ones that have bats in their hands," he said through an interpreter. There was good reason for El Duque to be concerned. In two starts against the Braves during the interleague portion of the previous two regular seasons he had been smoked by Atlanta, lasting less than five innings in both losses. He needn't have worried in Game One.

El Duque allowed one hit—Chipper Jones's solo home run in the fourth—in seven innings of work, and he gained credit for New York's 4-1 victory when his teammates struck for all their runs in the top of the eighth against Greg Maddux and John Rocker.

Maddux had been a last-minute replacement for Tom Glavine who came down with the flu, and he was terrific for seven innings as he yielded three hits. However, the Yankees pecked away in the eighth to knock him out of the game. Brosius singled to left, Strawberry pinch-hit for Hernandez and drew a walk, Knoblauch loaded the bases by reaching safely when first baseman Brian Hunter fumbled his bunt, and when Jeter singled to left to tie the game, Maddux was replaced by Rocker.

Rocker fell behind O'Neill 3-1 and served up a meatball that O'Neill roped into right for a two-run single, and when Hunter botched the relay for his second error of the inning, Jeter and O'Neill moved to second and third. Williams was intentionally walked, and after Rocker struck out Tino Martinez and Posada, pinch-hitter Jim Leyritz drew a walk to force in the fourth run.

"We're used to playing close games, and when you win enough of them, you feel like you're going to win," said O'Neill. "We got a break on the bunt and that set up the whole inning for us. It was a game of pitching tonight, and our pitchers, I guess, were a little bit better."

That was also the case in Game Two.

For the second night in succession the Yankee starter—Cone this time—allowed just one hit through seven innings, and unlike the opener, the Braves starter—Kevin Millwood—was not able to match that excellence. New York knocked Millwood out of the box by jumping to a 5-0 lead by the third inning, and the Yankees cruised to a 7-2 victory, their 10th straight in World Series competition.

The evening had begun spectacularly when the All-Century baseball team, a 30-man ensemble voted on by fans throughout the 1999 season, was honored before the start of the game. All 18 living members were in attendance including Yankees Roger Clemens and Yogi Berra. The other Yankees voted to the team were Babe Ruth, Lou Gehrig, Joe DiMaggio, and Mickey Mantle. It was a fabulous remembrance for the greats of baseball, and it was too bad the game that followed did not come close to matching the pregame theater.

The clubhouse was calm after the game. Although they were up 2-0 and going back to Yankee Stadium, this veteran club wasn't taking anything for granted. "We are aware of what happened in '96 and we came back against them," Torre said. "I don't have to say anything to my team in regard to '96."

Said Cone: "They can get hot in a hurry. This Series is far from over."

Cone was right about one thing. The Braves were capable of getting hot, and they did so at the start of Game Three. However, when the Yankees rallied from a 5-1 deficit to win on Chad Curtis's home run in the 10th inning, the Series was no longer far from over.

442 A Lifetime of Yankee Octobers

"It's always someone you don't expect," Atlanta manager Bobby Cox said of New York's latest hero, Curtis, who also hit a solo homer in the fifth inning. "You never know where it's coming from."

"I'm amazed, and yet I'm not amazed," Torre said of this remarkable club of his.

Pettitte didn't have it and he was routed for 10 hits and five runs inside four innings. But for all their batting success, the Braves still left eight runners on base through five innings, and that would come back to haunt them. They committed a cardinal sin by not putting the Yankees away when they had the chance. Curtis, playing left field in place of Ricky Ledee because lefty Tom Glavine was pitching for Atlanta, took Glavine deep in the bottom of the fifth, a solo shot that cut New York's deficit to 5-2. In the seventh Martinez whacked a solo homer, and it looked as if Glavine—still recovering from the flu—was starting to wilt. Cox asked if he was OK to start the eighth and Glavine said he was. He wasn't. Joe Girardi hit his first pitch for a single, and Knoblauch lifted his fourth pitch out to right field. Brian Jordan went back, leaped, and the ball ticked off the top of his glove and fell over the wall for a tying two-run homer.

"We got beat by a pop to right field," Cox lamented.

No, the Braves got beat by Curtis's drive off Mike Remlinger in the 10th.

Clemens got the call for the clincher and as usual, the Yankees had a flare for the moment. Who better to win the last game than Clemens, the man who hauled his sure-fire Hall of Fame credentials to New York for one reason: to win a World Series.

Clemens was great. The Boston massacre was behind him, and soon, so were the Braves. He blew through the helpless Atlanta batting order, giving up just four hits and one run before stepping aside so Nelson and Rivera could tie the ribbon around New York's 25th world championship.

"I finally know what it feels like to be a Yankee," said Clemens, who left the clubhouse a half-hour after the game ended and returned to the field to acknowledge the cheering fans still lingering in the ballpark.

Early in the season when the Yankees received their World Series rings from 1998, Clemens skipped the ceremony as he sat in the clubhouse. He hadn't been a part of that team and didn't feel he belonged in the dugout. "I was standing in the clubhouse watching it on TV," Clemens recalled. "The guys came back in and every one of them told me they were going to get me one. This is what they've said it's all about."

Torre remembered that day, too. "I saw how he looked at the rings. It wasn't envy, it was hunger. This was the perfect way to end the Series. The man came here because he wanted a World Series ring."

Like his start in Texas, Clemens was given an early 3-0 lead and he did not flinch. He was tagged for a run in the eighth when the Braves cobbled together three singles, the last off Nelson, before Rivera put out the fire by inducing Chipper Jones to ground out to Luis Sojo at second. It was Sojo's first action of the Series after he'd missed the first three games while burying his father in Venezuela.

Clemens was unimpressed by his own performance. All he wanted to talk about was the bravery O'Neill had shown playing on such a terrible day.

"I don't know if I could have done what Paul O'Neill did today," the Rocket said. "Same thing with Luis Sojo coming back to his teammates. If it was my mother in that situation, I just don't know. You're talking about heavy hearts and guys that are warriors. I just feel very blessed to be part of this."

O'Neill sat in front of his locker long after the game ended, alternately answering questions and accepting condolences, wiping away a tear every now and then.

"This team cares about things more than any other," he said. "We care more about each other, and we care more about baseball. That's why we're sitting here as world champions right now."

When the first spring training of the new millennium dawned I was reminded of Joe Torre's words the previous October when he closed the book on the 1999 championship season by saying, "We finished the century out right. Hopefully we can start the next century out on the right foot."

Torre was talking in terms of winning another championship, but he was also expressing the profound hope that in the 2000 season the Yankees would be granted the luxury of concentrating on baseball and be spared the off-field heartaches that had plagued them throughout 1999.

"This team's been through an awful lot," Torre said to me one day during the off-season. "How much more do we have to take?"

This is how much.

Barely one week into the regular season pitching coach Mel Stottlemyre told Torre that he had been diagnosed with multiple myeloma, a form of bone marrow cancer, and would begin undergoing treatment immediately. So began another character-testing ordeal for the emotionally weary Yankees.

But as tough as it was going to be for the Yankees to cope with seeing another member of their family fight cancer, it paled in comparison to what lay ahead for the Stottlemyre family. It wasn't enough that Mel would have to endure several rounds of nauseating chemotherapy leading up to a stem-cell transplant that doctors could only hope would chase the cancer into remission. Now Stottlemyre, his wife Jean, and their two sons, Mel Jr. and Todd, would have to relive the painful memories from nearly 20 years earlier when Jason Stottlemyre, the youngest of Mel and Jean's three boys, died of leukemia.

Jason was 11 years old when he died in 1981. He had been in and out of hospitals for five years, and during that time he taught lessons to his family that have never been forgotten.

There was a beautiful story written about the Stottlemyres by Bob Nightengale in Baseball Weekly, and Todd Stottlemyre was quoted as saying, "I think we can all look back and say to this day that an 11-year-old boy provided us with the greatest lesson in life. He taught us how to live. He taught us how to die. And he did both so gracefully."

Can there be anything worse in this world than watching your child die? Mel watched his son die. Watched how he died with uncommon dignity and bravery for such a little boy, and there was strength to be found in that experience.

Mel had been using it ever since, and as he said shortly before he began his chemo-therapy treatments, "I will continue to draw from Jason, more so as things go on."

Outside of Torre, Mel was the person on this Yankee team I had known the longest. I wrote about him when he came up to the Yankees in August 1964 and won nine games, helping the team reach the World Series. He started three games against the Cardinals in that fall classic, all against Hall of Famer Bob Gibson, and won one and lost one, the loss coming in Game Seven. I floated a theory that day that with Whitey Ford closing in on retirement, Stottlemyre could ascend to the role of staff ace and become the next great Yankee pitcher.

It turned out that I was right, but Stottlemyre's excellence did not translate into success for the Yankees and his achievements were forever overshadowed. During the final 10 years of his career, all spent with the Yankees, Stottlemyre pitched for bad or mediocre clubs and the Yankees rarely competed for league or division titles. Yet Stottlemyre rose above his team's ineptness and managed to win 25 more games than he lost. Relying on a quick-dropping sinker and rugged determination and durability, he had three 20-win seasons, appeared in five All-Star games, his career earned-run average was 2.97, and he still ranks second in Yankee history in shutouts (40), and third in games started (356) and innings pitched (2,661).

When a torn rotator cuff forced him to retire during the spring of 1975, Stottlemyre turned to coaching. He has worked for Seattle, the Mets, Houston, and now the Yankees, and the championship void he felt as a player has been replenished with five World Series rings (one with the Mets and four with the Yankees) during his tenure as one of baseball's most respected pitching tutors.

Mel never wanted his personal life to interfere with his work, so he left baseball for a couple years after Jason died to care for his wife and Mel Jr. and Todd. Now Mel would need to be cared for, and I know Mel was more concerned about his family than he was about his own well-being. That's just how Mel is.

He knew about his cancer a year before he went public with the news. He underwent extensive tests throughout 1999 as his doctors studied the progress of the cancer and determined what the best course of action would be. As the Yankees were enduring a seemingly endless string of personal tragedies, Mel priva-tized his own situation and selflessly lent his support to Torre, Paul O'Neill, Scott Brosius, Luis Sojo, Chuck Knoblauch, Daryl Strawberry, and Andy Pettitte.

Jean Stottlemyre received the phone call she and Mel had been dreading in late March 2000. The doctor told her that Mel's condition had become life-threat-ening and that the cancer needed to be treated. During the season Mel was with the club for brief periods, then he would have to take time off for his chemo treatments. He left the team for good in August, underwent the stem-cell trans-plant in mid-September, and cheered for his wife from his in-season home in

New Jersey when she threw out the first pitch prior to Game Two of the World Series against the Mets.

That night Jean gave us an update on how Mel was doing, and the news was encouraging. A visit to the doctor shortly thereafter confirmed her exuberance. The transplant had worked, and there were no cancer cells left in Mel's body.

When it was time for the Yankees to gather in Tampa in February 2001, Mel was there looking fit and trim, most of his hair grown back, wearing that rugged smile and extolling the virtues of second chances. He remembered what his son had gone through, he remembered the lessons Jason taught him. "I never have said 'Why me?'" Stottlemyre said. "Because it's really easy to say 'Why not me?'"

– Chapter 26 –

2000

I REMEMBER SQUIRMING UNCOMFORTABLY on my sofa and wondering what the hell Buck Showalter was doing. It was Game Five of the 1995 American League Divisional Series between the Yankees and Mariners. Seattle had just tied the game against David Cone by scoring two runs in the bottom of the eighth inning, and the world seemed to be crumbling all around the Yankees. The bases were still loaded, there were two outs, the season was on the line, and the Yankee manager replaced Cone with 25-year-old rookie right-hander Mariano Rivera.

I couldn't believe my eyes, and as I threw up my arms in amazement, I began to think aloud to my son Phillip, who was at my house watching the game with me.

I asked Phillip, "Why not Wetteland?" I know Showalter only liked to use his closer, John Wetteland, to protect leads in the ninth inning, but if the Yankees didn't stop Seattle right now, Wetteland wouldn't have to pitch in anger for another five months. "What about McDowell?" was my next inquiry, eliciting the same shrugged shoulder response from my son. Jack McDowell had started Game Three two days earlier, but he'd only pitched into the sixth inning. Surely he had enough gas left in his tank to get through this crisis. When I blurted out, "What about Bob Wickman?" I'm sure I saw Phillip's eyes roll. Finally I said, "My God, he can't pitch Rivera in this situation," to which Phillip replied, "Dad, Rivera's a hell of a pitcher."

This time, Father didn't know best.

"I know what people were probably thinking then," Rivera said a few years later, long after we had all come to understand why Showalter used him that night. "I guess if I were a fan I would have felt the same way. Who is this guy?"

That night we found out who Mariano Rivera was. He strode confidently to the middle of the Kingdome diamond, the noise probably as loud as it was the day they imploded that deplorable building in 1999, and the young Panamanian threw three straight fastballs that blew away Mike Blowers to end the inning.

Wow!

In the end, Rivera's effort was wasted when McDowell—one of the guys I had called for from my armchair manager's perch 3,000 miles away—gave up two runs in the bottom of the 11th inning to lose the game and the series.

If ever there was a silver lining encased in bitter defeat, it was the Yankees' discovering exactly what they had in Rivera. Not the starter that he was projected to be, but a dominant reliever who could put out a fire faster than a flood.

"You knew he had stuff," Cone recalled during the playing of the 2000 World Series. "He had great stuff. But what was amazing was how calm he was, how coming into that situation didn't get to him at all. When a rookie is that unflappable, you have to figure he's got something special inside him."

Over the past six years, we have come to learn just how special Rivera is.

"I think my background, my family, everything I come from helped to shape the way I am, the way I think in a game," Rivera said. "But it was God who gave me the ability to pitch the way I do."

God was certainly in a generous mood the day he created this lithe dart thrower.

Rivera was born in Puerto Caimito, Panama, into a loving, hardworking, religious family. Like the great Joe DiMaggio, Rivera was the son of a fisherman. His father, Mariano Sr., captained his own commercial fishing boat and was a good provider, but the Riveras were not wealthy. When he was 16 Mariano was a superb athlete who excelled in baseball and soccer, but he needed to help support his family so he went to work for his father on the boat. He figured his dream of playing professional soccer—his true sporting passion—was dead. And it was. But when Yankee scout Herb Raybourn happened to catch a glimpse of Rivera throwing rockets past overmatched hitters in a sandlot game one day in Puerto Caimito, Rivera's professional fishing career died, too.

Raybourn eventually signed Rivera and with his father's blessing, Rivera was allowed to leave his job and his homeland to go to America to try to make a life for himself in baseball.

In his first year of rookie ball with Tampa in 1990 Rivera pitched 52 innings and allowed one earned run. Injuries slowed his progress, but after five years in the minors, his ERA was 2.04, his fastball had gained 5 mph into the mid-90 range, and the Yankees had to bring him up.

At first Showalter used Rivera as a starter and long reliever with middling results. After his success against the Mariners in that play-off game, Joe Torre became manager in 1996 and converted Rivera to setup man, a role he adapted to nicely as he set a Yankee relief pitcher record with 130 strikeouts. "He should be banned from baseball, he should be at a higher level," an impressed Minnesota Twins manager Tom Kelly said.

When Wetteland left via free agency before 1997, Rivera was handed the closer role, and he became one of the most dominant forces in the game, his mastery never more evident than in the postseason when he put together an all-time record scoreless streak of 34 innings.

"There's no decision-making, the managing stops once we get to the ninth inning with a lead," Torre said, expressing awe over Rivera's reliability. "It's an incredible thing to have on your side. He bores me with his consistency, but I love it."

*   *   *

That was about all that bored Torre during the 2000 regular season. Coming off back-to-back World Series victories, the Yankees were again the team to beat, and a good many teams took great pleasure in doing so. After breaking from the gate with a record of 22-9, the Yankees played .500 baseball the last 4 1/2 months and limped across the finish line just barely ahead of the Boston Red Sox.

The Yankees went into a mysterious tailspin in September and lost 15 of their last 18 games including their final seven. When the season mercifully came to an end their 87-74 record was only the fifth-best in the American League, and the worst the franchise had ever brought into a postseason. If not for the mediocrity of the rest of the division, the Yankees wouldn't have made the play-offs.

"Nothing came easy for us this year," Bernie Williams said. "Nothing."

That's because this was a good team, but a flawed team. Paul O'Neill and David Cone were aging, Chuck Knoblauch still couldn't throw to first base, Scott Brosius was coming off a horrible offensive year, Roger

Clemens still had to prove to many Yankee fans that he was worth David Wells plus all the money George Steinbrenner was paying him, and there was no reliable fifth starter, left fielder, or designated hitter.

Steinbrenner knew there were problems, so in June he instructed general manager Brian Cashman to start fixing them, and Cashman embarked on a roster retooling that ultimately helped deliver another championship to the Bronx.

Jose Vizcaino, Jose Canseco, Glenallen Hill, Denny Neagle, and Luis Sojo joined the club, but those moves paled in comparison to Cashman's fleecing of Cleveland as he sent two prospects to the Indians in exchange for outfielder David Justice. That became the most important trade of the 2000 major league season because Justice hit 21 homers for the Yankees.

By mid-September New York had built a nine-game cushion on Boston, and as it turned out, the Yankees needed every bit of that lead as the late-season skid turned clinching the division into a laborious exercise.

The slump hadn't been Jeter's fault. While the losses piled up, Jeter went on a tear that allowed him to become just the third Yankee in history to surpass 200 hits three years in a row, joining Lou Gehrig and Don Mattingly. Over the past 60 years only three men have held the title of Yankee captain—Gehrig, Mattingly, and Thurman Munson. It's my belief that it's only a matter of time before Jeter is given that honor because, as Don Zimmer says, "He's something very special."

* * *

Back in Torre's first spring as manager of the team in 1996, Jeter was a precocious 21-year-old rookie who seemed to possess loads of potential, but didn't quite appear ready for the major leagues. One day Gene Michael, then the team's director of scouting, told Torre, "You're going to have to be patient with Jeter. He's made some errors in the past, he'll get better, but he may not be ready from day one."

As the exhibition games played out, Torre concluded that there wouldn't be time to wait for Jeter. Jeter was the best he had, and for the first time since Tom Tresh in 1962, the Yankees started a rookie at shortstop on Opening Day.

It took all of one day to convince Torre he made the right call. In his first major league game Jeter homered against the Indians at Jacobs Field, made a dazzling catch of a pop fly, handled his other chances flawlessly, and the Yankees won the game. By the end of the season Jeter was named American League Rookie of the Year, he helped lead the Yankees to their first world championship since 1978, and it was obvious this wiser-than-his-years kid would be patrolling the vital real estate between second and third base at Yankee Stadium for a very long time.

Jeter was born in Pequannock, New Jersey, and though he grew up in Kalamazoo, Michigan, he often spent summers with his grandparents back in northern New Jersey and he became a Yankee fan. It was his grandmother who turned him on to the Yankees. A lifelong fan, Dot Connors grew up cheering for Joe DiMaggio and Mickey Mantle, and, like me, she viewed Babe Ruth's casket the day it was on display at Yankee Stadium in 1948.

In his eighth-grade yearbook there were predictions for what each student would be doing in 10 years and next to Jeter's name it said that he would be playing for the Yankees. As fate would have it, the Yankees selected Jeter in the first round of the 1992 amateur draft and this is the only organization he has ever known.

The lineage of Yankee greatness starts with Ruth and is connected through the eras by Lou Gehrig, DiMaggio, Yogi Berra, Mantle, Thurman Munson, Reggie Jackson, Don Mattingly, and now, Jeter. Jeter is this generation's chosen one, the next Yankee superstar destined to have his number retired and a plaque erected out in Monument Park in his honor. To earn that distinction he must continue to play as he has during the first six years of his career, but there is no reason to believe he won't do that.

He is a multitalented player who can hit for average, hit for power, drive in runs, steal bases, field his position, and provide leadership despite his youth. He is like a matinee idol to the throngs who flock to Yankee Stadium. He is a well-mannered young man who has never called me anything except Mr. Kimmerle. He respects the game, the position he plays, the stadium he calls home, and the team whose famous uniform he wears. But above all else, he is a winner. Nothing less than a championship is good enough for him. For so many of today's players this game is all about money and statistics and fame and ego. Jeter is the richest Yankee ever, thanks to the 10-year, $189 million contract he signed before the 2001 season, but it's not about the money for Jeter—it's all about the ring, and while four World Series rings in six years is nice, he wants more. It his belief that the World Series is the Yankees' domain. The Yankees belong at the top of the heap, and like the great Yankees of the past, he has taken it upon himself to make sure they have a chance to be there every year.

"This is something I've been waiting for my whole life," he said. "To me, Yankee Stadium is still the best. There's something about it. Maybe it's the pride and tradition. The Yankees are the most recognized team in all of sports, and all of the tradition makes Yankee Stadium that much more special. One of the best things about being a Yankee is that you have guys like Whitey Ford, Phil Rizzuto, Ron Guidry, and Reggie Jackson wandering around the locker room offering you advice."

I sat down in the clubhouse one day next to David Cone sometime during 1999 and we were talking about Jeter, and Cone expressed genuine veneration regarding this kid who was nine years his junior. "It is really remarkable to see how he has handled everything at such a young age," Cone said. "It's hard to fathom the type of mass appeal that Derek has. It's hard to compare to anyone. It's enormous popularity. More than any I've seen of any young player. There's a long list of young players in similar situations who have made mistakes. It's tough for me to identify because I make those mistakes or have made them. Jeter came in very grounded from day one and has remained level-headed. He has watched and learned from other people's mistakes."

Paul O'Neill, long considered the heart and soul of this latest Yankee dynasty, joined Cone and me that day and added, "I don't know that he knows how good he is going to become. I hate to put that on people because it puts a lot of pressure on what they're supposed to become. But he's a great player right now, and he's getting better."

And better, and better, and better.

*   *   *

With the play-offs on the horizon, Torre knew what he would get from Jeter, but he really didn't know what to expect from the rest of the team on the heels of its putrid finish. However, Torre clung to the fact that this was a veteran group hardened by the experience of winning three championships in the previous four years, and if any team in baseball was capable of flipping on the switch, it was this team.

"We're going to find out," Torre said. "We still have to show up, with or without our confidence, and play. The answers will come. I'm not predicting anything, but I don't think this streak was indicative of how we'll show up. I don't think it's going to affect the play-offs. I'm confident it's all new."

As usual, he was right.

– *2000 World Series* –

The phone calls started coming the day after the Yankees won the American League pennant and joined the National League champion Mets in the World Series. For the first time in 44 years the World Series was going to be conducted exclusively in New York and newspaper writers, radio talk show hosts, and television reporters all took turns trying to set up interviews with me, desperately seeking any anecdotal information this octogenarian and survivor of every Subway Series contested could provide.

For a while there I felt about as popular as Derek Jeter.

I was only too happy to oblige the requests, eager to reminisce about the days of Mickey, Willie, Duke, Pee Wee, Scooter, Yogi, Whitey, and Jackie.

The Yankees and the Mets in the World Series at the same time. Imagine that. Many New York City baseball fans had been waiting their whole lives for this. More than half of my own life had passed since the last borough battle to decide baseball's championship.

"Everybody wants to witness it," said Joe Torre, who like me was sitting in Yankee Stadium watching Don Larsen throw a perfect game against the Brooklyn Dodgers in 1956, the last time the Yankees hosted another team from New York in the World Series. "It's an event; it's not just a baseball game. When I was a kid, I was spoiled. Any kid growing up in New York, you got to see the World Series every year in your town. I thought that's the way it always was."

So often it seemed that way.

Thirteen times between 1921 and 1956 the Yankees played either the Dodgers or Giants in the World Series. In nine of the 10 years between 1947 and 1956, at least one New York team was in the fall classic, and on seven of those occasions, the Series was an all-New York affair.

Baseball in October meant baseball in New York and there was nothing better than baseball in New York in October.

But then the Dodgers and Giants bolted for the West Coast, the Yankees suffered through two lengthy championship droughts, and from 1965 to 1995, the Yankees and Mets played in only three World Series each, not once coming close to playing each other.

It wasn't until 1999 that the chance for a Subway Series even existed, though the Mets failed to live up to their end of the bargain. Both teams made it back to the postseason in 2000, and the rumblings of a possible encounter grew louder than the No. 4 and No. 7 trains clacketing along on the elevated tracks next to Yankee and Shea stadiums, respectively. When the Yankees drove through Oakland and Seattle to claim their spot, and the wild-card Mets did likewise by upsetting San Francisco and St. Louis, the Subway Series finally came to pass. There was an eruption of excitement in the city and the days leading up to the Saturday night opener brought memories of yesteryear flooding back into my consciousness.

Back in the 1940s and 1950s when these city skirmishes took place on a regular basis, everyone talked baseball. On every street corner, in every school, office, restaurant, pub, barber shop, or soda shop, baseball was the topic of conversation. Yankees, Dodgers, Giants. Everyone had a team, everyone had a passion, everyone had an opinion. It was a magical time.

And now, 44 years later, it was happening again. When I wasn't doing interviews or attending the Yankees' practices at Yankee Stadium, I made it a point to go into the city, walk the streets and bathe myself in the electricity that was coursing through the crisp autumn air. The city is always vibrant, always alive, but there was an extra hop in everyone's step, more of a willingness to talk to the person next to you in line at the delicatessen or the bank or the grocery store. Nobody was talking about the Jets or the Giants or the Knicks or the Rangers. Never mind the decline of the blue chips, the tumbling of tech stocks, and the other problems on Wall Street. Forget the presidential campaigning of George W. Bush and Al Gore. Right now, and for the next week or so, baseball was king again.

Our world had certainly changed since the last Subway Series.

In 1956 Yankees manager Casey Stengel earned $80,000, Mickey Mantle topped the Yankee player payroll at $32,500, tickets to the World Series were priced between $4 and $10.50, and a subway token cost 15 cents. The New York football Giants defeated the Chicago Bears to win the NFL Championship. Elvis Presley sang "Heartbreak Hotel," which was his first No. 1 pop hit. On television, we watched the debuts of the soap operas *Edge of Night* and *As The World Turns,* and Chet Huntley and David Brinkley revolutionized TV news with the nightly Huntley-Brinkley Report. Yul Brynner won the Oscar for his performance in *The King and I.* Dwight D. Eisenhower won reelection to the White House in a romp over Adlai Stevenson. Soviet Premier Nikita Khrushchev told a group of Western ambassadors, "History is on our side. We will bury you." And in New York, plans were made to begin construction of a beltway around the city to be called the Middlesex Freeway.

In 2000, Yankees manager Joe Torre earned $3 million, Bernie Williams banked $12.3 million, World Series tickets went for $160 with some scalpers getting $1,500, and it cost $1.50 to ride the subway. The New York football Giants posted the best record in the National conference and went on to play in the Super Bowl where they lost to Baltimore—not the Colts, but the Ravens. The teenage heartthrobs were Backstreet Boys and Britney Spears. Reality television became all the rage with shows such as "Survivor," and you didn't even need a TV to watch that program because it was available on your computer via the internet. Kids were still playing baseball, but they were doing it on PlayStation 2 instead of on a sandlot. Bush won the White House over Gore in the closest election in history, one that took more than a month to decide thanks to voting discrepancies in Florida. The Soviet Union only buried itself as it dissolved and lost its superpower world status. And the Middlesex Freeway, now known as Interstate 287, is one of the busiest highways in America.

But one segment of our world has stayed very much the same. At its core, the game of baseball is unchanged. They are still using white balls with red stitching, wooden bats, and leather gloves. Three strikes and you're still out, three up and three down still means the end of an inning, and nine innings still constitutes a game. The pitchers' rubber is still 60 feet, 6 inches from home plate, the bases are still 90 feet apart, and the players still scratch their crotches and spit tobacco juice everywhere. And in New York City the disdain Yankee and Met fans have for each other is similar to what Yankee, Dodger, and Giant fans once had for each other.

"I've been on record for years saying I'd love to see this," Yankee pitcher and ex-Met hurler David Cone said of the Subway Series.

He and seven million other New Yorkers.

*　　*　　*

When the postseason began it didn't look like a Subway Series would be possible. While the Yankees were stumbling badly, their first opponent, the American League West champion Oakland Athletics, played superbly down the stretch, winning 22 of their last 29 games to capture their division crown. These were two teams heading in opposite directions, and most baseball experts predicted Oakland would upend the two-time defending world champions. Meanwhile, the Mets were going against San Francisco, winners of a major-league-high 97 games in 2000.

Well, so much for bad karma. The Mets eliminated the Giants in four games while the Yankees came up with a gritty Game Five victory at Oakland to break the Athletics' young hearts. "We're older, but I don't think we're too old," Torre said. "I like to look at it as experience. And when the postseason comes, we're going to make somebody beat us."

The next team to get that chance was Lou Piniella's Seattle Mariners who had wiped out the Chicago White Sox, owners of the best record in the American League in 2000, in their divisional series. The Mariners continued their roll and won the opener, 2-0, at Yankee Stadium behind the pitching of young Freddy Garcia and a solo home run by Alex Rodriquez.

Faced with the daunting prospect of playing the middle three games in Seattle, the Yankees knew Game Two was a must-win. Seven innings went into the books, they still hadn't scored against the Mariners, and as Luis Sojo said, "There was a little tension." But in the eighth inning David Justice led off with a double, Bernie Williams singled him home to tie the game at 1-1, and the Yankees were alive. "When Bernie got that base hit everybody jumped like we had won the Little League World Series or something," said Sojo. After Seattle left-fielder Al Martin dropped Tino Martinez's line drive, Jorge Posada drove in Williams with the go-ahead run, and when Derek Jeter stroked a three-run homer to right, the Yankees had seven runs in the inning and a 7-1 victory. "I just sense that we relieved a lot of pressure today," Torre said.

By the time the Yankees and Mariners were in Seattle for Game Three, the Mets had defeated the Cardinals twice in St. Louis, and Subway Series fever began to heat up. Of course, there was the matter of the Yankees beating the Mariners, which Torre warned was not going to be easy. "This is something that's going to go on for awhile," Torre said. "I think it's going to be a hell of a series."

In Game Three Andy Pettitte fought through a tough start and the Yankees broke open a tight game in the ninth and rolled to an 8-2 victory. Then Roger Clemens took the mound in Seattle and put on the type of show everyone in the Yankee organization had been waiting two years for. Clemens tossed a one-hit shutout and struck out an ALCS-record 15 batters as the Yankees moved within one game of their third straight pennant with a 5-0 victory.

The following afternoon the Yankees failed to put the Mariners away as Seattle rebounded for a 6-2 victory, scoring five runs in the fifth off Denny Neagle and Jeff Nelson, but as they came home, they needed only one win in two tries to claim the flag. That was one more than the

Mets needed. After losing Game Three at Shea, Bobby Valentine's team twice pounded the Cardinals into submission by scores of 10-6 and 7-0 to win the National League pennant and fill half the Subway Series' dance card.

Now it was left for the Yankees to flip the switch on the city's madness with a Game Six victory in the Bronx. The Mariners did their best to spoil the party as they jumped out to a 4-0 lead against Orlando Hernandez. Posada's two-run double and Paul O'Neill's RBI single cut the deficit to 4-3 in the fourth, but reliever Brett Tomko silenced the Yankees for the next two innings as the score remained unchanged. When the Yankees came to bat in the seventh, you could sense throughout the ballpark that time was running out. Yes, there was a seventh game if necessary, but no one wanted to prolong this anticipation another night. The Yankees needed to end this series. Someone needed to do something, someone needed to produce one of those Yankee moments that have defined this team's greatness throughout the century. Justice, in his third month as a Yankee, volunteered.

With two men on and Justice due up, Piniella handed the ball to left-hander Arthur Rhodes who the Yankees had battered during the seven-run explosion that decided Game Two. When Rhodes served up a juicy 3-1 fastball Justice sent it soaring into the night, deep into the upper deck, and the noise that three-run homer generated could be heard all the way over in Queens where Mets fans were salivating over playing the Yankees in the World Series.

In all my years at Yankee Stadium, I've never heard a roar like that. And for a man who was 84 at the time and whose hearing was in a state of disrepair, that's quite a statement. I had goose bumps all over my body as Justice rounded the bases, pumping his fists. What a moment. A truly Yankee moment.

New York tacked on three more runs which became important when the Mariners rallied for three runs in the eighth, snapping Mariano Rivera's postseason record scoreless streak. But Rivera settled down in the ninth to complete the pennant-clinching 9-7 victory, and the city that never sleeps didn't that night.

I saw Phil Rizzuto in the hallway outside the locker room after the game and the Scooter was revved up. "This one is going to be a dandy," said the man who played in seven Subway Series. "I think it's going to be great—if the city can handle it. It's going to be rocking and rolling."

* * *

The day the World Series began was a busy one for me. That afternoon my daughter Katherine and her husband David and I drove over to Columbia University to watch their son, my youngest grandson, Jason, play football against Ivy League rival Dartmouth. Jason was Katherine and David's little guy, although at 6-foot-1, 220 pounds he wasn't so little anymore. He was a starting outside linebacker for Columbia and I tried my best to never miss one of his home games. Fortunately the Lions were home the day of Game One, and a good day it was for the blue. A kid named Johnathan Reese rushed for a school-record 236 yards and four touchdowns, Jason made seven tackles, and Columbia rolled past the Big Green by 49-21.

After spending a few minutes after the game congratulating Jason, Katherine and David took me home where I waited for my Yankee driver to pick me up and bring me to the stadium. Over the last couple years my driving skills had deteriorated and I really didn't like to travel very far in the car, maybe to the grocery store or movie theater, but that was about it. So Torre set up a transportation service for me. Whenever I wanted to come to the ballpark, the team either sent one of its young interns out to my home in Mount Vernon to pick me up, or arranged for a taxi to ferry me back and forth. I felt sorry for the poor kid who was assigned to me the night of Game One.

At 1:04 in the morning, a World Series record 4 hours and 51 minutes after it began, the first game of New York's decades-in-waiting civil baseball war ended when Jose Vizcaino punched a two-out, bases-loaded single to left field to score Tino Martinez with the winning run, giving the Yankees a breathtaking 4-3 victory. I got home at 3:30 in the morning. I had been up 20 straight hours. Tired as I was, I couldn't fall asleep because the excitement of the game was still buzzing in my head.

"We came in with very little World Series experience and got a lot of it in one night," Mets manager Bobby Valentine said.

"It was heart-stopping at times, it was kind of ugly at times, but it was a great Game One," said Cone. "If they're all like this, buckle your seat belts. This should be some kind of Series."

If they were going to be all like this, I wasn't sure my old ticker would survive.

Two left-handers, Pettitte and Al Leiter, were given the initial starting assignments, and they were up to the task. They zipped through five innings allowing a combined five hits and no runs as the stadium crowd waited patiently for the first indelible moment. It came in the sixth.

Mets rookie sensation Timo Perez led off with a single, stayed put for two outs, and then became the third out when he made a rookie mistake. Todd Zeile lashed a drive into left field and after running hard to second base, Perez downshifted to jogging mode thinking the ball had cleared the wall for a home run. Instead, it hit the top padding, came back into play, and as Perez got to third he realized what was going on and tried to pick up his pace and scoot home. Justice hit Jeter with the relay, and then Jeter fired a strike to the plate where Posada slapped the inning-ending tag on Perez as the stadium erupted in glee.

"We needed Jeffrey Maier," Zeile cracked afterward. "Where was he when we needed him?"

Seizing that momentum, the Yankees took the lead in the bottom of the sixth when Justice ripped a two-run double to left-center, but it was short-lived as the Mets manufactured three runs in the top of the seventh. Pinch-hitter Bubba Trammell's two-run single to left tied it, and then with two outs and runners on second and third, Edgardo Alfonzo legged out a tapper to third as Todd Pratt charged across the plate with the go-ahead run.

Leiter left after seven, John Franco worked a scoreless eighth, and then in the ninth Valentine handed the ball to his closer, Armando Benitez, only to watch Benitez cough up the lead. With one out O'Neill worked a classic nine-pitch walk after falling in a 0-2 hole. Luis Polonia pinch-hit for Scott Brosius and singled, Vizcaino also singled to load the bases, and Chuck Knoblauch's sacrifice fly to left tied the game.

After the Yankees blew glorious scoring chances in the 10th and 11th innings, they finally brought down the curtain in the 12th. With one out Met reliever Turk Wendell was tagged for a single by Martinez and a double by Posada. O'Neill was walked intentionally, and after Luis Sojo fouled out to the catcher, Vizcaino—who Torre had started at second base on a hunch which paid off in four hits—stepped into the hero's role with his first-pitch single to left, giving the Yankees their record 13th straight World Series win.

"I kissed him on the cheek after the game and said, 'Thanks for making me look good,'" Torre said.

As if Game Two needed any hype after that epic, Clemens was the starter for the Yankees, and he would be pitching against Mike Piazza for the first time since he had beaned him back in an interleague game in July. The New York press did all it could to stir the pot, and then Clemens tossed a blowtorch into the gasoline tanker that this game already was.

In the top of the first Clemens struck out Perez and Alfonzo with the same untouchable heat he'd had in Seattle. Up stepped Piazza who looked at two strikes, took a ball, then fouled Clemens's fourth offering off to the right side, his bat shattering in his hands with the barrel bounding out to the mound at Clemens's feet. Piazza wasn't sure where the ball was so he sort of half-trotted down the line. At the same time Clemens scooped the shard of lumber and threw it dangerously close to where Piazza was. The bat skipped past Piazza, who quickly glared in disbelief at Clemens and took a few steps toward the Yankee pitcher. Posada and home plate umpire Charlie Reliford immediately stepped between the two players, but the Met bench was incensed, and to be honest, the partisan Yankee crowd seemed almost a little embarrassed by Clemens's display.

More than three hours later when the Yankees' 6-5 victory was complete, nobody was talking about the fact that the Yankees were two games up on the Mets. All anybody wanted to discuss was the Clemens-Piazza incident.

"There was no intent," Clemens said. "I was fired up and emotional and flung the bat toward the on-deck circle where the batboy was. I had no idea that Mike was running. When I came back into the dugout I said, 'I've got to get control of my emotions and calm down.'"

The Mets weren't buying Clemens's explanation. "It was just so bizarre," said Piazza, clearly annoyed that he had been involved in another tenuous situation with Clemens. "When he threw the bat I basically walked out and kept asking him what his problem was. He really had no response. I was more shocked and confused than anything else."

Torre was irritated that the media wouldn't stop asking questions about it, and he was unusually caustic in his response. "Let's try to analyze it. Why would he throw it at him? So he could get thrown out of the game in the second game of the World Series? Does that make sense to anybody? Somebody answer me. You guys ask me questions, somebody answer mine. Why would he do it, because he's angry at him?"

When someone answered "yes," Torre said, "That's the reason? Because he's angry at Mike, so he screws 24 other people on his team?"

Torre was still steaming when he got back to his office and slammed the door shut. I was in there, so was George Steinbrenner and Don Zimmer. "God damned media," Torre said, to which the old sportswriter replied, "Yeah, they're all assholes." About a second passed and then Torre laughed a hearty laugh.

The highlight of the game was the bat toss. Clemens gained control of himself and overpowered the Mets while the Yankees methodically built a 6-0 lead, scoring three runs in the first two innings off Mike Hampton, and then held on when the Mets put together a five-run rally in the ninth before Rivera struck out Kurt Abbott to end it.

The off-day couldn't have come at a worst time because now, rather than getting right back into another game, there was more time to re-gurgitate the Clemens-Piazza affair. I have to admit, had I still been a writer I would have loved it. Now, as a fan, it drove me crazy. The press was unrelenting, and it seemed the only people who realized the Mets were down two games and desperate for a victory were the Mets. Kudos to Valentine for getting his players to put the distractions behind them and play a near flawless third game, which is what it took to snap Orlando Hernandez's eight-game postseason winning streak and the Yankees' 14-game World Series winning streak.

"I think guys were so exhausted about talking about the incident that baseball was actually a relief," Zeile said following the Mets' 4-2 victory that, at least for the moment, saved the Series.

There had been games during his 8-0 postseason run when Hernandez was lucky to come out on top. In an odd twist, this was a game he really deserved to win, but didn't. When Robin Ventura went down swinging to start the bottom of the eighth it was El Duque's 12th strikeout of the night. But in a flash all his hard work went to waste as Zeile singled and raced around to score on Benny Agbayani's double to left center to break a 2-2 tie. After Mike Stanton relieved, Trammell lofted a sacrifice fly that plated an insurance run. Benitez shook off his Game One meltdown and picked up the save for Franco, who had pitched the eighth.

"Everybody was saying El Duque was unbeatable in the postseason," said Trammell. "I suppose we know there's a first time for everything."

And for the first time since Game Two in 1996, the Yankees were losers in a Series game. It was quiet in the clubhouse, not so much because the streak was over, but because the Mets were back in the Series. "Those wins are special, that streak is special," said Posada. "But that streak didn't matter tonight."

"We're not concerned about the streak, we're concerned about to-morrow," said Jeter.

The flashbulbs that greet every opening pitch to a World Series game hadn't even stopped flickering when Jeter emphasized his concern about Game Four. He hammered that first pitch, thrown by Bobby J. Jones, over the fence in left field, silencing an already energetic crowd and starting the Yankees on their way to a critical 3-2 victory.

"I've been known to swing at the first pitch," said Jeter. "When you play games like this you want to score early, you want to take the crowd out of the game. I got a good pitch to hit and I hit it well."

Torre decided to sit Vizcaino and he opted to play Sojo at second instead of the still fragile-in-the-field Knoblauch. Rather than have Sojo bat leadoff, Torre shifted Jeter into that spot, and once again Torre came out smelling like a rose.

"We feel like we're playing great," Mets pitcher Glendon Rusch said. "It's just that they're playing a little better."

How many ballplayers over the past eight decades have said that?

In the second inning O'Neill, suffering from a sore hip and clearly off his game, laced a triple to right and scored on Brosius's sacrifice fly. Then in the third Jeter tripled to right-center, and with Valentine curiously playing his infield at normal depth, Jeter was able to scamper home on Sojo's groundout for a 3-0 lead. "You never give up a run, not in a Series game," Sojo said of the run that ultimately proved to be the difference.

Neagle, whom Torre was nervous about starting, circumvented the first two innings with ease before hanging a change-up in the third which Piazza mashed for a two-run homer, but that would be it for the scoring. The Yankee bullpen of Cone, Nelson, Stanton, and Rivera blanked the Mets on two hits, leaving the Yankees on the brink of becoming the first team to three-peat since the Oakland Athletics of 1972–74.

The night of Game Five marked the 14th anniversary of the Mets' last world championship, their seven-game triumph over the Red Sox, with the clincher coming at Shea. The gleaming World Series trophy made another appearance at Shea, only this time it wasn't the Mets parading it around their misty clubhouse.

The smell of sewer water was in the air following Game Four when a water pipe burst and flooded the visiting clubhouse at Shea. But if your senses were keen enough, you could also pick up the scent of blood. The Mets were hemorrhaging. The Yankees were sniffing and circling. There was no need to prolong this any further. It was time for the kill. Ruthless, heartless, cold-blooded killers. That's who the Yankees always were in these situations.

And the end came in such a uniquely Yankee way.

Two outs, top of the ninth, tie score and Leiter—who up to that point had pitched a brilliant game—delivered a 3-2 pitch to Posada that barely missed being an inning-ending strike. Posada trotted to first, then ran to second when Brosius followed with a single. Next came Sojo, in the game only because Torre couldn't trust Knoblauch in the field. Leiter's first pitch, his 142nd and final one of the night, was hit up the middle by Sojo. Leiter just missed flagging it down, and the middle infielders, Abbott and Alfonzo, converged out behind second base seemingly in position to at least knock it down and hold Posada at third, but somehow the ball found a gap between them and dribbled on into center field. With the fans screaming in horror Posada motored around third and scored the go-ahead run, and when center fielder Jay Payton's throw ended up in the Mets' dugout, Brosius was awarded home plate and just like that, the Yankees had a 4-2 lead.

Ten minutes later, after Piazza's fly ball to left-center—which when it was hit appeared destined to wind up in the bleachers as a dramatic two-run game-tying homer—was corralled at the warning track by Williams, the 2000 Subway Series was over, and the Yankees were world champions for the 26th time.

"Whether you like us or not, we're winners," said O'Neill.

Pettitte and Leiter pitched wonderfully in a rematch of Game One. Williams, hitless in the World Series, broke out with a solo home run in the second inning, the Mets answered with two runs in their half, and then Jeter hammered another home run in the sixth to create a 2-2 tie. After a scoreless seventh Torre went to his bullpen. Valentine did not. "I told Bobby I have four months to rest before February 21st," Leiter said. "Let me keep pitching. And he did."

And he lost. Undeservedly so, but he lost.

"It's the happiest day of my life," said Sojo. "Today they gave me a chance to come through and I did. It was unbelievable. I don't want to retire. I want to play until I'm 50. It's something about this team, man. You walk in here, and you can feel it. These guys, they know what to do. They know how to win, and they know nothing else matters. I love the Yankees."

*   *   *

It was three o'clock in the morning and the bedlam inside the visiting clubhouse at Shea had finally ceased. Every ounce of Dom Perignon had been spilled and sprayed and swallowed, every victory cigar had been smoked, and now, every member of the Yankees organization had gone on their merry way, primed to party deep into the wee hours of a fantastic Friday. Everyone, that is, but Torre and me.

At three o'clock in the morning, three hours after the end of Game Five, Torre was still sitting in the cramped manager's office, still wearing his champagne-stained uniform, his eyes still red from crying, perfectly content to bask in the blissful peace that comes from supreme achievement.

Outside those walls New York City was aglow in celebration of another baseball championship, and the strains of Yankee fans tormenting Met fans could be heard from the top of the Bronx all the way down to the lower tips of Manhattan and Brooklyn. But here was Torre, looking physically exhausted and emotionally drained, still trying to comprehend what he and his Yankees had achieved. Three straight World Series championships and four in the previous five years, bringing the number of all-time Yankee titles to an unfathomable and unprecedented 26.

A couple of hours earlier the mass media was tossing around the word "dynasty" just the way I and a previous generation of sportswriters had when the Yankees won four straight championships under Joe McCarthy from 1936 to 1939, and five in a row from 1949 to 1953 with Casey Stengel at the helm.

Torre had said, "I think we can hold up to any one of those great teams because of what we have accomplished. In this day and age, when you have to come through layer after layer of postseason play, we can put our record, our dedication, our resolve up against any team that has ever played the game of baseball in my mind."

As someone who had now personally witnessed all 26 of the Yankees' World Series championships, I felt uniquely qualified, at three o'clock in the morning sitting across the desk from Torre in that little office, to tell my good friend that he was right. His team does measure up to the all-time great Yankee clubs.

"Joe," I said to him just as a couple of workers entered the clubhouse to begin the task of cleaning up the celebration, "this might be the greatest Yankee team of them all. Ruth and DiMaggio and Mantle never had to do what these young fellas have done."

I deplore so much about baseball in this Generation X era. To name just a few of my pet peeves, in no particular order: the ridiculously high salaries, the love affair with the long ball, the lack of quality pitching, specialization, the inconsistent strike zone, the interminable length of the games, and the loud rock music that blares over the loudspeakers at the stadiums.

But while I'm old-fashioned, and downright old, I'm not senile. I can still recognize achievement when I see it, and as much as I long for the "good ol' days" there is no denying that the modern-day Yankees have leaped to the forefront of Yankee dynasties. Of sports dynasties.

McCarthy won four in a row, Stengel won five in a row, but never did those two great old sages have to guide a team through the land mines that are the divisional play-offs and the League Championship Series. To capture four championships in five years, Torre's Yankees won 12 of 13 play-off series. During that time, the team was 46-15, including one record-breaking stretch where it won 14 World Series games in a row.

Simply astounding. End of discussion. These are the good ol' days.

When Torre and I were all talked out and our champagne glasses were dry, he stripped off his uniform and headed into the shower. As I waited for him, I noticed a game program on the desk, so to pass the time I began leafing through its slick and colorful pages. In it there was a promotional slogan the team had come up with at the beginning of the 2000 season, promising its fans that while 25 World Series champion-ships in the twentieth century was nice, "We'll try to do better in the next century."

Well, they're certainly off to a good start.

Epilogue

. . . To quote my good friend, and as of today my former colleague, Red Smith, "Sportswriting is the most pleasant way of making a living that man has yet devised."

Imagine being paid to watch sporting events for the past 45 years, to do so from the comfort of a press box, and then have the opportunity to talk to the participants afterward. If you can't imagine it, don't feel bad because there have been times during this epoch when I have had to pinch myself to prove I wasn't dreaming.

What an honor. What a privilege. What a blast.

And to think the bulk of that time was spent chronicling the exploits of the greatest sports franchise known to mankind—the New York Yankees.

I have watched some of the greatest athletes in history perform, and then discussed those performances with them afterward. To name just a few, Joe Louis, Sugar Ray Robinson, and Muhammad Ali; Ben Hogan, Arnold Palmer, and Jack Nicklaus; Sid Luckman, Johnny Unitas, and Jim Brown; Wilt Chamberlain, Kareem Abdul-Jabbar, and Bill Russell; Gordie Howe, Rocket Richard, and Bobby Orr; Rod Laver, Billie Jean King, and Bjorn Borg, and of course, Secretariat (didn't talk to him).

But baseball has always been my passion, my specialty, my beat. It is a game beset with problems today, I know this, but it remains our greatest game, and it is the game that gave me the wonderful life I have led.

I grew up on River Avenue in the Bronx, right across the street from Yankee Stadium, where as a young boy I watched the grand arena rise before me, a scrubby plot of land transformed into a baseball shrine that, nearly 60 years later, continues to exude an unequaled dignity.

The day the stadium opened its glorious doors in 1923 I was there with my father to cheer our friend, Babe Ruth, who rose to the occasion the way only he could, christening the park with a titanic home run. Later I cleaned the Babe's shoes and laundered his uniform during my tenure as a

Yankee batboy and clubhouse assistant, broke bread with him in the apartment where I was born and raised, and long after I had fulfilled my dream of becoming a Yankee beat writer I wrote his obituary for this newspaper the day after he died in 1948.

I watched Lou Gehrig play most of the 2,130 consecutive games he participated in, and I cried like a child the day the dying slugger told us he was the "luckiest man on the face of the earth" . . . I saw Joe DiMaggio hit in 56 straight games, but I can't remember him diving to catch a fly ball because he rarely had to . . . I saw Mickey Mantle hit baseballs farther than any man was supposed to hit them . . . I saw Yogi Berra jump into Don Larsen's arms the day Larsen pitched the only perfect game in World Series history . . . I watched Roger Maris hit 61 home runs to break Ruth's record of 60 . . . I watched the Yankees win seven World Series championships under Joe McCarthy and another seven under Casey Stengel . . . I watched Reggie Jackson hit three home runs on three consecutive pitches . . . I watched Bucky Dent break Boston's heart . . . and I cried again the day when the captain, Thurman Munson, perished in a plane crash.

For the past 45 years I watched, I wrote, I laughed, I cried, I praised, I criticized. What I did most, though, was have fun. As Casey Stengel once said "There comes a time in every man's life, and I've had plenty of them." . . .

By Joe Kimmerle, New York Post
November 4, 1981

THAT WAS AN EXCERPT FROM the farewell column my dad wrote for the *New York Post* upon his retirement in 1981. I thought it summed up pretty well what he thought about his life, his career, baseball, and his beloved New York Yankees. I felt it needed to be included in this tome. I hope Dad doesn't mind.

We buried my dad the other day. He died of a heart attack at the age of 85. We buried him in his blue pinstriped suit with an old Yankees cap at his side. We thought he'd appreciate that.

He had been in good spirits, keeping busy the way no man his age could or should keep busy. In fact with the holidays come and gone he was planning his annual February trip to Florida which served the dual purpose of enabling him to escape the New York winter and hang out with his good friend, Joe Torre, and the other members of his Yankee family at spring training in Tampa.

The night before his heart stopped beating I had talked to him on the phone to remind him I'd be over in the early afternoon to pick him up at his house in Mount Vernon and bring him to mine in Dobbs Ferry for Sunday dinner. He countered with a late-morning pickup request so we could get back to my home in time to watch the first game of that day's National Football League play-off doubleheader. Baseball was always Dad's game, but he liked all sports, and I gladly agreed to attend an earlier morning mass to accommodate him.

When I arrived, I knocked on the door as a courtesy, then let myself in. I found him sitting peacefully in his favorite recliner, the *Post* sports section on his lap, the television tuned to ESPN.

While I waited for the paramedics to arrive I called my wife Charlotte, then my sister Katherine, and knowing neither would be able to pass on the news, I contacted as many family members as I could. It wasn't until I returned home later that afternoon that I called Torre at his New Rochelle stead. Next to telling Katherine, that was the toughest conversation of all. Joe had known my dad more than 40 years dating back to when Joe and I were teenagers and he and my cousin Sammy played sandlot baseball together in Brooklyn. Joe was like a second son to my dad, and he loved my dad almost as dearly as I. To that point I had held my emotions in check, but when I heard the Yankee manager sobbing at the other end of the line, my own tear ducts burst open as the reality of the day finally hit me.

Dad had once told me that it was his wish to have his funeral mass celebrated at St. Patrick's Cathedral in Manhattan because that's where his friend and hero Babe Ruth's funeral had been held. Torre helped make that happen for Dad, and he also enlisted Yogi Berra, Phil Rizzuto, and Whitey Ford to serve along with himself as pallbearers, joining my two sons, Phillip Jr. and Kevin, and Katherine's two boys, Robert and Jason. As I looked around the famous church, I spotted numerous other former Yankee players and executives including team owner George Steinbrenner, who made a special trip up from Tampa. I can't describe the gratitude I felt seeing so many of these great men paying their respects to their friend, my father.

Dad had been working on this book for about two years, and he had only recently put the finishing touches on it after the Yankees lost the 2001 World Series last November to Arizona. The manuscript was all printed out, and the gentleman he had hired to proofread it was about halfway through when I informed him that Dad had passed away.

I told him to keep going, and then I phoned Dad's editor and assured him the text would be delivered on time. He passed along his condolences, thanked me for my diligence, and predicted that Dad's book would become a bestseller.

At first I was sad that Dad was never going to see his painstaking work come to fruition. But in retrospect I realized there was nothing to be sad about because he hadn't written this book for himself. He had written it for all of us.

Dad had already lived his thrilling life, already experienced eight fascinating decades of Yankee baseball in a way no other man had and no other man ever will. He had already counted as his friends Babe Ruth, Lou Gehrig, Joe DiMaggio, Joe McCarthy, Tommy Henrich, Mickey Mantle, Casey Stengel, Phil Rizzuto, Yogi Berra, Whitey Ford, Roger Maris, Ron Guidry, Reggie Jackson, Paul O'Neill, Derek Jeter, and Joe Torre. He had already witnessed in person close to 10,000 Yankee games including all but 18 of the team's 212 World Series games. He had traveled all over the country, met thousands of people, and had his newspaper stories and columns read by millions upon millions of people through the years.

And now, as his last gift to us, he was leaving behind his recollections of Yankees history, which were essentially the recollections of his life, for all of us to revel in. As he said in that farewell column, "What a blast."

I thought about that when I did the one thing Dad hadn't been able to do: mail the final manuscript to the publishing house.

In loving memory of my father,
Phillip S. Kimmerle.

Bibliography

The following magazines, newspapers, wire services, and online services were referenced: *Sporting News, Sports Illustrated, Baseball Weekly, New York Times, New York Mirror, New York Herald–Tribune, New York Post, New York Daily News, Newsday, Newark Star-Ledger, Cleveland Plain–Dealer, Washington Post, Philadelphia Inquirer, Los Angeles Times, Dallas Morning News, Seattle Times, Rocky Mountain News, St. Louis Post–Dispatch, Kansas City Star, Fort Lauderdale Sun–Sentinel, San Francisco Chronicle, Rochester (NY) Democrat and Chronicle,* Associated Press, United Press International, Gannett News Service, CBS Sportsline.com, and ESPN.com.

The following books were referenced:

Allen, Maury. *Where Have You Gone Joe DiMaggio?* New York: New American Library, 1975.

———. *Roger Maris—A Man for All Seasons.* New York: Donald I. Fine, 1986.

———. *Jackie Robinson—A Life Remembered.* New York: Franklin Watts, 1987.

———. *All Roads Lead to October—Boss Steinbrenner's 25-Year Reign Over the New York Yankees.* New York: St. Martin's Press, 2000.

Anderson, Dave, Murray Chass, Robert Creamer, and Harold Rosenthal. *The Yankees—The Four Fabulous Eras of Baseball's Most Fabulous Team.* New York: Random House, 1979.

Bak, Richard. *Lou Gehrig—An American Classic.* Dallas, TX: Taylor Publishing Company, 1995.

———. *Casey Stengel—A Splendid Baseball Life.* Dallas, TX: Taylor Publishing Company, 1997.

Baseball: The Biographical Encyclopedia. New York: Total/Sports Illustrated, 2000.

Berkow, Ira, and Jim Kaplan. *The Gospel According to Casey.* New York: St. Martin's Press, 1992.

Blake, Mike. *Baseball Chronicles—An Oral History of Baseball Through the Decades.* Cincinnati, OH: Betterway Books, 1994.

Cramer, Richard Ben. *Joe DiMaggio—The Hero's Life.* New York: Simon & Schuster, 2000.

Creamer, Robert. *Baseball in '41.* New York: Viking Penguin, 1991.

Danzig, Allison, and Joe Reichler. *The History of Baseball.* Upper Saddle River, NJ: Prentice Hall, 1959.

Dickey, Glenn. *The History of American League Baseball.* New York: Stein and Day, 1980.

Dickson, Paul. *Baseball's Greatest Quotations.* New York: HarperCollins, 1991.

DiMaggio, Joe. *Lucky To Be A Yankee.* New York: Putnam, 1946.

Durocher, Leo, and Ed Linn. *Nice Guys Finish Last.* New York: Simon & Schuster, 1975.

Durso, Joseph. *Yankee Stadium—Fifty Years of Drama.* Boston: Houghton Mifflin, 1972.

———. *DiMaggio—The Last American Knight.* New York: Little, Brown and Company, 1995.

Felker, Clay. *Casey Stengel's Secret.* New York: Walker & Company, 1961.

Ford, Whitey, and Phil Pepe. *Slick.* New York: William Morrow and Company, 1987.

Ford, Whitey, Mickey Mantle, and Joseph Durso. *Whitey and Mickey—An Autobiography of the Yankee Years.* New York: Viking Press, 1977.

Frommer, Harvey. *New York City Baseball: The Last Golden Age: 1947–1957.* Atheneum, 1985.

———. *The New York Yankee Encyclopedia.* New York: Macmillan, 1997.

Gallagher, Mark. *Day By Day in New York Yankees History.* New York: Leisure Press, 1983.

———. *Explosion—Mickey Mantle's Legendary Home Runs.* New York: Arbor House, 1987.

———. *The Yankee Encyclopedia.* Champaign, IL: Sports Publishing, 2000.

Golenbock, Peter. *Dynasty—The New York Yankees 1949–64.* Upper Saddle River, NJ: Prentice Hall, 1975.

———. *Bums.* New York: G.P. Putnam's Sons, 1984.

Guidry, Ron, and Peter Golenbock. *Guidry.* Upper Saddle River, NJ: Prentice Hall, 1980.

Hageman, William, and Warren Wilbert. *New York Yankees Seasons of Glory.* Middle Village, NY: Jonathan David Publishers, 1999.

Halberstam, David. *Summer of '49.* New York: Avon Books, 1989.

Henrich, Tommy, and Bill Gilbert. *Five O'Clock Lightning.* New York: Carol Publishing Group, 1992.

Honig, Donald. *Baseball when the Grass was Real.* New York: Coward, McCann & Geoghegan, 1975.

———. *Baseball Between the Lines.* New York: Coward, McCann and Geoghegan, 1976.

———. *The October Heroes.* New York: Simon & Schuster, 1979.

———. *Baseball in the 50s—A Decade of Transition.* New York: Crown Publishers, 1987.

Houk, Ralph, and Robert Creamer. *Season of Glory—The Amazing Saga of the 1961 New York Yankees.* New York: G.P. Putnam's Sons, 1988.

Hunter, Jim, and Armen Keteyian. *Catfish—My Life in Baseball.* New York: McGraw-Hill, 1988.

Jacobson, Steve. *The Best Team Money Could Buy.* New York: New American Library, 1978.

Kahn, Roger. *Joe & Marilyn—A Memory of Life.* New York: William Morrow and Company, 1986.

———. *The Era—1947–1957—When the Yankees, the Giants and the Dodgers Ruled the World.* Boston: Ticknor and Fields, 1993.

Lally, Dick. *Pinstriped Summers.* New York: Arbor House, 1985.

Larsen, Don, and Mark Shaw. *The Perfect Yankee.* Champaign, IL: Sagamore Publishing, 1996.

Lupica, Mike. *Reggie—The Autobiography of Reggie Jackson.* New York: Villard Books, 1984.

Lyle, Sparky, and Peter Golenbock. *The Bronx Zoo.* New York: Crown Publishers, 1979.

Mantle, Mickey. *The Education of a Baseball Player.* New York: Simon & Schuster, 1967.

Mantle, Mickey, and Mickey Herskowitz. *All My Octobers.* New York: Harper, 1994.

Maris, Roger, and Jim Ogle. *Roger Maris at Bat.* New York: Duell, Sloan and Pearce, 1962.

Mazer, Bill. *Bill Mazer's Amazing Baseball Book.* New York: Kensington Publishing, 1990.

Mosedale, John. *The Greatest of All: The 1927 Yankees.* New York: Dial Press, 1975.

Oakley, J. Ronald. *Baseball's Last Golden Age, 1946–1960.* Jefferson, NC: McFarland and Company, 1994.

Okrent, Daniel, and Steve Wulf. *Baseball Anecdotes.* New York: Harper and Row, 1989.

Peary, Danny. *We Played the Game.* New York: Hyperion, 1994.

Pepe, Phil. *The Wit and Wisdom of Yogi Berra.* New York: St. Martin's Press, 1974.

———. *The Yankees—An Authorized History of the New York Yankees.* Dallas, TX: Taylor Publishing Company, 1995.

Richardson, Bobby. *The Bobby Richardson Story.* Old Tappan, NJ: Fleming H. Revell Company, 1965.

Ritter, Lawrence S. *The Glory of Their Times.* New York: Collier Books, 1966.

Robinson, Jackie, and Alfred Duckett. *I Never Had It Made.* New York: G.P. Putnam's Sons, 1972.

Robinson, Ray. *Iron Horse—Lou Gehrig in His Time.* New York: W.W. Norton, 1990.

Robinson, Ray, and Christopher Jennison. *Yankee Stadium — 75 Years of Drama, Glamor and Glory.* New York: Penguin, 1998.

Rosenfeld, Harry. *Roger Maris — A Title to Fame.* New York: Prairie House, 1991.

Ruth, Mrs. Babe, and Bill Slocum. *The Babe and I.* Upper Saddle River, NJ: Prentice Hall, 1959.

Salant, Nathan. *Superstars, Stars and Just Plain Heroes.* New York: Stein and Day, 1982.

Schoor, Gene. *Casey Stengel — Baseball's Greatest Manager.* New York: Julian Messner, 1953.

———. *The Scooter.* New York: Scribners, 1982.

Siner, Howard. *Sweet Seasons.* New York: Pharos Books, 1988.

Smelser, Marshall. *The Life That Ruth Built.* New York: Quadrangle/New York Times Book. Co., 1975.

Solomon, Burt. *The Baseball Timeline.* New York: Avon Books, 1997.

Sullivan, George, and John Powers. *Yankees: An Illustrated History.* Upper Saddle River, NJ: Prentice Hall, 1997.

Torre, Joe, and Tom Verducci. *Chasing The Dream — My Lifelong Journey to the World Series.* New York: Bantam Books, 1997.

Tullius, John. *I'd Rather Be A Yankee.* New York: Macmillan, 1986.

Zanger, Jack. *Great Catchers of the Major Leagues.* New York: Random House, 1970.